Madonna Mary by Mrs. Oliphant

Margaret Oliphant Wilson was born on April 4th, 1828 to Francis W. Wilson, a clerk, and Margaret Oliphant, at Wallyford, near Musselburgh, East Lothian.

Her youth was spent in establishing a writing style and by 1849 she had her first novel published: Passages in the Life of Mrs. Margaret Maitland.

Two years later, in 1851 Caleb Field was published and also an invitation to contribute to Blackwood's Magazine; the beginning of a life time business relationship.

In May 1852, Margaret married her cousin, Frank Wilson Oliphant. Their marriage produced six children but, tragically, three died in infancy. When her husband developed signs of the dreaded consumption (tuberculosis) they moved to Florence, and then to Rome where, sadly, he died.

Margaret was naturally devastated but was also now left without support and only her income from writing to support the family. She returned to England and took up the burden of supporting her three remaining children by her literary activity.

Her incredible and prolific work rate increased both her commercial reputation and the size of her reading audience. Tragedy struck again in January 1864 when her only remaining daughter Maggie died.

In 1866 she settled at Windsor to be closer to her sons, who were being educated at near-by Eton School.

For more than thirty years she pursued a varied literary career but family life continued to bring problems. Cyril Francis, her eldest son, died in 1890. The younger son, Francis, who she nicknamed 'Cecco', died in 1894.

With the last of her children now lost to her, she had little further interest in life. Her health steadily and inexorably declined.

Margaret Oliphant Wilson Oliphant died at the age of 69 in Wimbledon on 20th June 1897. She is buried in Eton beside her sons.

Index of Contents

CHAPTER I

Major Ochterlony had been very fidgety after the coming in of the mail. He was very often so, as all his friends were aware, and nobody so much as Mary, his wife, who was herself, on ordinary occasions, of an admirable composure. But the arrival of the mail, which is so welcome an event at an Indian station, and which generally affected the Major very mildly, had produced a singular impression upon him on this special occasion. He was not a man who possessed a large correspondence in his own person; he had reached middle life, and had nobody particular belonging to him, except his wife and his little children, who were as yet too young to have been sent "home;" and consequently there was nobody to receive letters from, except a few married brothers and sisters, who don't count, as everybody knows. That kind of formally affectionate correspondence is not generally exciting, and even Major Ochterlony supported it with composure. But as for the mail which arrived on the 15th of April, 1838, its effect was different. He went out and in so often, that Mary got very little good of her letters, which were from her young sister and her old aunt, and were naturally overflowing with all kinds of pleasant gossip and domestic information. The present writer has so imperfect an idea of what an Indian bungalow is like, that it would be impossible for her to convey a clear idea to the reader, who probably knows much better about it. But yet it was in an Indian bungalow that Mrs. Ochterlony was seated—in the dim hot atmosphere, out of which the sun was carefully excluded, but in which, nevertheless, the inmates simmered softly with the patience of people who cannot help it, and who are used to their martyrdom. She sat still, and did her best to make out the pleasant babble in the letters, which seemed to take sound to itself as she read, and to break into a sweet confusion of kind voices, and rustling leaves, and running water, such as, she knew, had filled the little rustic drawing-room in which the letters were written. The sister was very young, and the aunt was old, and all the experience of the world possessed by the two together, might have gone into Mary's thimble, which she kept playing with upon her finger as she read. But though she knew twenty times better than they did, the soft old lady's gentle counsel, and the audacious girl's advice and censure, were sweet to Mary, who smiled many a time at their simplicity, and yet took the good of it in a way that was peculiar to her. She read, and she smiled in her reading, and felt the fresh English air blow about her, and the leaves rustling—if it had not been for the Major, who went and came like a ghost, and let everything fall that he touched, and hunted every innocent beetle or lizard that had come in to see how things were going on; for he was one of those men who have a great, almost womanish objection to reptiles and insects, which is a sentiment much misplaced in India. He fidgeted so much, indeed, as to disturb even his wife's accustomed nerves at last.

"Is there anything wrong—has anything happened?" she asked, folding up her letter, and laying it down in her open work-basket. Her anxiety was not profound, for she was accustomed to the Major's "ways," but still she saw it was necessary for his comfort to utter what was on his mind.

"When you have read your letters I want to speak to you," he said. "What do your people mean by sending you such heaps of letters? I thought you would never be done. Well, Mary, this is what it is—there's nothing wrong with the children, or anybody belonging to us, thank God; but it's very nearly as bad, and, I am at my wit's end. Old Sommerville's dead."

"Old Sommerville!" said Mrs. Ochterlony. This time she was utterly perplexed and at a loss. She could read easily enough the anxiety which filled her husband's handsome, restless face; but, then, so small a matter put him out of his ordinary! And she could not for her life remember who old Sommerville was.

"I daresay you don't recollect him," said the Major, in an aggrieved tone. "It is very odd how everything has gone wrong with us since that false start. It is an awful shame, when a set of old fogies put young people in such a position—all for nothing, too," Major Ochterlony added: "for after we were actually married, everybody came round. It is an awful shame!"

"If I was a suspicious woman," said Mary, with a smile, "I should think it was our marriage that you called a false start and an awful shame."

"And so it is, my love: so it is," said the innocent soldier, his face growing more and more cloudy. As for his wife being a suspicious woman, or the possible existence of any delicacy on her part about his words, the Major knew better than that. The truth was that he might have given utterance to sentiments of the most atrocious description on that point, sentiments which would have broken the heart and blighted the existence, so to speak, of any sensitive young woman, without producing the slightest effect upon Mary, or upon himself, to whom Mary was so utterly and absolutely necessary, that the idea of existing without her never once entered his restless but honest brain. "That is just what it is," he said; "it is a horrid business for me, and I don't know what to do about it. They must have been out of their senses to drive us to marry as we did; and we were a couple of awful fools," said the Major, with the gravest and most care-worn countenance. Mrs. Ochterlony was still a young woman, handsome and admired, and she might very well have taken offence at such words; but, oddly enough, there was something in his gravely-disturbed face and pathetic tone which touched another chord in Mary's breast. She laughed, which was unkind, considering all the circumstances, and took up her work, and fixed a pair of smiling eyes upon her perplexed husband's face.

"I daresay it is not so bad as you think," she said, with the manner of a woman who was used to this kind of thing. "Come, and tell me all about it." She drew her chair a trifle nearer his, and looked at him with a face in which a touch of suppressed amusement was visible, under a good deal of gravity and sympathy. She was used to lend a sympathetic ear to all his difficulties, and to give all her efforts to their elucidation, but still she could not help feeling it somewhat droll to be complained to in this strain about her own marriage. "We were a couple of fools," she said, with a little laugh, "but it has not turned out so badly as it might have done." Upon which rash statement the Major shook his head.

"It is easy for you to say so," he said, "and if I were to go no deeper, and look no further—It is all on your account, Mary. If it were not on your account—"

"Yes, I know," said Mrs. Ochterlony, still struggling with a perverse inclination to laugh; "but now tell me what old Sommerville has to do with it; and who old Sommerville is; and what put it into his head just at this moment to die."

The Major sighed, and gave her a half-irritated, half-melancholy look. To think she should laugh, when, as he said to himself, the gulf was yawning under her very feet. "My dear Mary," he said, "I wish you would learn that this is not anything to laugh at. Old Sommerville was the old gardener at Earlston, who went with us, you recollect, when we went to—to Scotland. My brother would never have him back again, and he went among his own friends. He was a stupid old fellow. I don't know what he was good for, for my part;—but," said Major Ochterlony, with solemnity, "he was the only surviving witness of our unfortunate marriage—that is the only thing that made him interesting to me."

"Poor old man!" said Mary, "I am very sorry. I had forgotten his name; but really,—if you speak like this of our unfortunate marriage, you will hurt my feelings," Mrs. Ochterlony added. She had cast down her eyes on her work, but still there was a gleam of fun out of one of the corners. This was all the effect made upon her mind by words which would have naturally produced a scene between half the married people in the world.

As for the Major, he sighed: he was in a sighing mood, and at such moments his wife's obtusity and thoughtlessness always made him sad. "It is easy talking," he said, "and if it were not on your account, Mary—The fact is that everything has gone wrong that had any connection with it. The blacksmith's house, you know, was burned down, and his kind of a register—if it was any good, and I am sure I don't know if it was any good; and then that woman died, though she was as young as you are, and as healthy, and nobody had any right to expect that she would die," Major Ochterlony added with an injured tone, "and now old Sommerville; and we have nothing in the world to vouch for its being a good marriage, except what that blacksmith fellow called the 'lines.' Of course you have taken care of the lines," said the Major, with a little start. It was the first time that this new subject of doubt had occurred to his mind.

"To vouch for its being a good marriage!" said Mrs. Ochterlony: "really, Hugh, you go too far. Our marriage is not a thing to make jokes about, you know—nor to get up alarms about either. Everybody knows all about it, both among your people and mine. It is very vexatious and disagreeable of you to talk so." As she spoke the colour rose to Mary's matron cheek. She had learned to make great allowances for her husband's anxious temper and perpetual panics; but this suggestion was too much for her patience just at the moment. She calmed down, however, almost immediately, and came to herself with a smile. "To think you should almost have made me angry!" she said, taking up her work again. This did not mean to imply that to make Mrs. Ochterlony angry was at all an impossible process. She had her gleams of wrath like other people, and sometimes it was not at all difficult to call them forth; but, so far as the Major's "temperament" was concerned, she had got, by much exercise, to be the most indulgent of women—perhaps by finding that no other way of meeting it was of any use.

"It is not my fault, my love," said the Major, with a meekness which was not habitual to him. "But I hope you are quite sure you have the lines. Any mistake about them would be fatal. They are the only proof that remains to us. I wish you would go and find them, Mary, and let me make sure."

"The lines!" said Mrs. Ochterlony, and, notwithstanding her self-command, she faltered a little. "Of course I must have them somewhere—I don't quite recollect at this moment. What do you want them for, Hugh? Are we coming into a fortune, or what are the statistics good for? When I can lay my hand upon them, I will give them to you," she added, with that culpable carelessness which her husband had already so often remarked in her. If it had been a trumpery picture or book that had been mislaid, she could not have been less concerned.

"When you can lay your hands upon them!" cried the exasperated man. "Are you out of your senses, Mary? Don't you know that they are your sheet-anchor, your charter—the only document you have—"

"Hugh," said Mrs. Ochterlony, "tell me what this means. There must be something in it more than I can see. What need have I for documents? What does it matter to us this old man being dead, more than it matters to any one the death of somebody who has been at their wedding? It is sad, but I don't see how it can be a personal misfortune. If you really mean anything, tell me what it is."

The Major for his part grew angry, as was not unnatural. "If you choose to give me the attention you ought to give to your husband when he speaks seriously to you, you will soon perceive what I mean," he said; and then he repented, and came up to her and kissed her. "My poor Mary, my bonnie Mary," he said. "If that wretched irregular marriage of ours should bring harm to you! It is you only I am thinking of, my darling—that you should have something to rest upon;" and his feelings were so genuine that with that the water stood in his eyes.

As for Mrs. Ochterlony, she was very near losing patience altogether; but she made an effort and restrained herself. It was not the first time that she had heard compunctions expressed for the irregular marriage, which certainly was not her fault. But this time she was undeniably a little alarmed, for the Major's gravity was extreme. "Our marriage is no more irregular than it always was," she said. "I wish you would give up this subject, Hugh; I have you to rest upon, and everything that a woman can have. We never did anything in a corner," she continued, with a little vehemence. "Our marriage was just as well known, and well published, as if it had been in St. George's, Hanover Square. I cannot imagine what you are aiming at. And besides, it is done, and we cannot mend it," she added, abruptly. On the whole, the runaway match had been a pleasant frolic enough; there was no earthly reason, except some people's stupid notions, why they should not have been married; and everybody came to their senses rapidly, and very little harm had come of it. But the least idea of doubt on such a subject is an offence to a woman, and her colour rose and her breath came quick, without any will of hers. As for the Major, he abandoned the broader general question, and went back to the detail, as was natural to the man.

"If you only have the lines all safe," he said, "if you would but make sure of that. I confess old Sommerville's death was a great shock to me, Mary,—the last surviving witness; but Kirkman tells me the marriage lines in Scotland are a woman's safeguard, and Kirkman is a Scotchman and ought to know."

"Have you been consulting him?" said Mary, with a certain despair; "have you been talking of such a subject to—"

"I don't know where I could have a better confidant," said the Major. "Mary, my darling, they are both attached to you; and they are good people, though they talk; and then he is Scotch, and understands. If anything were to happen to me, and you had any difficulty in proving—"

"Hugh, for Heaven's sake have done with this. I cannot bear any more," cried Mrs. Ochterlony, who was at the end of her powers.

It was time for the great coup for which his restless soul had been preparing. He approached the moment of fate with a certain skill, such as weak people occasionally display, and mad people almost always,—as if the feeble intellect had a certain right by reason of its weakness to the same kind of defence which is possessed by the mind diseased. "Hush, Mary, you are excited," he said, "and it is only you I am thinking of. If anything should happen to me—I am quite well, but no man can answer for his own life:—my dear, I am afraid you will be vexed with what I am going to say. But for my own satisfaction, for my peace of mind—if we were to go through the ceremony again—"

Mary Ochterlony rose up with sudden passion. It was altogether out of proportion to her husband's intentions or errors, and perhaps to the occasion. That was but a vexatious complication of ordinary life; and he a fidgety, uneasy, perhaps over-conscientious, well-meaning man. She rose, tragic without knowing it, with a swell in her heart of the unutterable and supreme—feeling herself for the moment an outraged wife, an insulted woman, and a mother wounded to the heart. "I will hear no more," she said, with lips that had suddenly grown parched and dry. "Don't say another word. If it has come to this, I will take my chance with my boys. Hugh, no more, no more." As she lifted her hands with an impatient gesture of horror, and towered over him as he sat by, having thus interrupted and cut short his speech, a certain fear went through Major Ochterlony's mind. Could her mind be going? Had the shock been too much for her? He could not understand otherwise how the suggestion which he thought a wise one, and of advantage to his own peace of mind, should have stung her into such an incomprehensible passion. But he was afraid and silenced, and could not go on.

"My dear Mary," he said mildly, "I had no intention of vexing you. We can speak of this another time. Sit down, and I'll get you a glass of water," he added, with anxious affection; and hurried off to seek it: for he was a good husband, and very fond of his wife, and was terrified to see her turn suddenly pale and faint, notwithstanding that he was quite capable of wounding her in the most exquisite and delicate point. But then he did not mean it. He was a matter-of-fact man, and the idea of marrying his wife over again in case there might be any doubtfulness about the first marriage, seemed to him only a rational suggestion, which no sensible woman ought to be disturbed by; though no doubt it was annoying to be compelled to have recourse to such an expedient. So he went and fetched her the water, and gave up the subject, and stayed with her all the afternoon and read the papers to her, and made himself agreeable. It was a puzzling sort of demonstration on Mary's part, but that did not make her the less Mary, and the dearest and best of earthly creatures. So Major Ochterlony put his proposal aside for a more favourable moment, and did all he could to make his wife forget it, and behaved himself as a man naturally would behave who was recognised as the best husband and most domestic man in the regiment. Mary took her seat again and her work, and the afternoon went on as if nothing had happened. They were a most united couple, and very happy together, as everybody knew; or if one of them at any chance moment was perhaps less than perfectly blessed, it was not, at any rate, because the love-match, irregular as it might be, had ended in any lack of love.

CHAPTER II

Mrs. Ochterlony sat and worked and listened, and her husband read the papers to her, picking out by instinct all those little bits of news that are grateful to people who are so far away from their own country. And he went through the births and marriages, to see "if there is anybody we know,"—notwithstanding that he was aware that corner of the paper is one which a woman does not leave to any reader, but makes it a principle to examine herself. And Mary sat still and went on with her work, and not another syllable was said about old Sommerville, or the marriage lines, or anything that had to do with the previous conversation. This tranquillity was all in perfect good faith on Major Ochterlony's side, who had given up the subject with the intention of waiting until a more convenient season, and who had relieved his mind by talking of it, and could put off his anxiety. But as for Mary, it was not in good faith that she put on this expression of outward calm. She knew her husband, and she knew that he was pertinacious and insisting, and that a question which he had once started was not to be made an end of, and finally settled, in so short a time. She sat with her head a little bent, hearing the bits of news run on like an accompaniment to the quick-flowing current of her own thoughts. Her heart was beating quick, and her blood coursing through her veins as if it had been a sudden access of fever which had come upon her. She was a tall, fair, serene woman, with no paltry passion about her; but at the same time, when the occasion required it, Mary was capable of a vast suppressed fire of feeling which it gave her infinite trouble to keep down. This was a side of her character which was not suspected by the world in general—meaning of course the regiment, and the ladies at the station, who were all, more or less, military. Mrs. Ochterlony was the kind of woman to whom by instinct any stranger would have appropriated the name of Mary; and naturally all her intimates (and the regiment was very "nice," and lived in great harmony, and they were all intimate) called her by her Christian—most Christian name. And there were people who put the word Madonna before it,—"as if the two did not mean the same thing!" said little Mrs. Askell, the ensign's baby-wife, whose education had been neglected, but whom Mrs. Ochterlony had been very kind to. It was difficult to know how the title had originated, though people did say it was young Stafford who had been brought up in Italy, and who had such a strange adoration for Mrs. Ochterlony, and who died, poor fellow—which was perhaps the best thing he could have done under the circumstances. "It was a special providence," Mrs. Kirkman said, who was the Colonel's wife: for, to be sure, to be romantically adored by a foolish young subaltern, was embarrassing for a woman, however perfect her mind and temper and fairest fame might be. It was he who originated the name, perhaps with some faint foolish thought of Petrarch and his Madonna Laura: and then he died and did no more harm; and a great many people adopted it, and Mary herself did not object to be addressed by that sweetest of titles.

And yet she was not meek enough for the name. Her complexion was very fair, but she had only a very faint rose-tint on her cheeks, so faint that people called her pale—which with her fairness, was a drawback to her. Her hair was light-brown, with a golden reflection that went and came, as if it somehow depended upon the state of her mind and spirits; and her eyes were dark, large, and lambent,—not sparkling, but concentrating within themselves a soft, full depth of light. It was a question whether they were grey or brown; but at all events they were dark and deep. And she was, perhaps, a little too large and full and matronly in her proportions to please a youthful critic. Naturally such a woman had a mass of hair which she scarcely knew what to do with, and which at this moment seemed to betray the disturbed state of her mind by unusual gleams of the golden reflection which sometimes lay quite tranquil and hidden among the great silky coils. She was very happily married, and Major Ochterlony was the model husband of the regiment. They had married very young, and made a runaway love-match which was one of the few which everybody allowed had succeeded to perfection. But yet—There are so few things in this world which succeed quite to perfection. It was Mrs. Kirkman's opinion that nobody else in the regiment could have supported the Major's fidgety temper. "It would be a great trial for the most experienced Christian," she said; "and dear Mary is still among the babes who have to be fed with milk; but Providence is kind, and I don't think she feels it as you or I would." This was the opinion of the Colonel's wife; but as for Mary, as she sat and worked and listened to her husband reading the papers, perhaps she could have given a different version of her own composure and calm.

They had been married about ten years, and it was the first time he had taken this idea into his head. It is true that Mrs. Ochterlony looked at it solely as one of his ideas, and gave no weight whatever to the death of old Sommerville, or the loss of the marriage lines. She had been very young at the time of her marriage, and she was motherless, and had not those pangs of wounded delicacy to encounter, which a young woman ought to have who abandons her home in such a way. This perhaps arose from a defect in Mary's girlish undeveloped character; but the truth was, that she too belonged to an Indian family, and had no home to speak of, nor any of the sweeter ties to break. And after that, she had thought nothing more about it. She was married, and there was an end of it; and the young people had gone to India immediately, and had been very poor, and very happy, and very miserable, like other young people who begin the world in an inconsiderate way. But in spite of a hundred drawbacks, the happiness had always been pertinacious, lasted longest, and held out most stedfastly, and lived everything down. For one thing, Mrs. Ochterlony had a great deal to do, not being rich, and that happily quite preserved her from the danger of brooding over the Major's fidgets, and making something serious out of them. And then they had married so young that neither of them could ever identify himself or herself, or make the distinction that more reasonable couples can between "me" and "you." This time, however, the Major's restlessness had taken an uncomfortable form. Mary felt herself offended and insulted without knowing why. She, a matron of ten years' standing, the mother of children! She could not believe that she had really heard true, that a repetition of her marriage could have been suggested to her—and at the same time she knew that it was perfectly true. It never occurred to her as a thing that possibly might have to be done, but still the suggestion itself was a wound. Major Ochterlony, for his part, thought of it as a precaution, and good for his peace of mind, as he had said; but to Mary it was scarcely less offensive than if somebody else had ventured to make love to her, or offer her his allegiance. It seemed to her an insult of the same description, an outrage which surely could not have occurred without some unwitting folly on her part to make such a proposal possible. She went away, searching back into the far, far distant years, as she sat at work and he read the papers. Had she anyhow failed in womanly restraint or delicacy at that moment when she was eighteen, and knew of nothing but honour, and love, and purity in the world? To be sure, she had not occupied herself very much about the matter—she had taken no pains for her own safety, and had not an idea what registrars meant, nor marriage laws, nor "lines." All that she knew was that a great many people were married at Gretna Green, and that she was married, and that there was an end of it. All these things came up and passed before her mind in a somewhat hurrying crowd; but Mary's mature judgment did not disapprove of the young bride who believed what was said to her, and was content, and had unbounded faith in the blacksmith and in her bridegroom. If that young woman had been occupying herself about the register, Mrs. Ochterlony probably, looking back, would have entertained but a mean opinion of her. It was not anything she had done. It was not anything special, so far as she could see, in the circumstances: for hosts of people before and after had been married on the Scottish border. The only conclusion, accordingly, that she could come to, was the natural conclusion, that it was one of the Major's notions. But there was little comfort in that, for Mrs. Ochterlony was aware that his notions were persistent, that they lived and lasted and took new developments, and were sometimes very hard to get rid of. And she sighed in the midst of the newspaper reading, and betrayed that she had not been listening. Not that she expected her husband's new whim to come to anything; but because she foresaw in it endless repetitions of the scene which had just ended, and endless exasperation and weariness to herself.

Major Ochterlony stopped short when he heard his wife sigh—for he was not a man to leave anything alone, or to practise a discreet neglect—and laid down his paper and looked with anxiety in her face. "You have a headache," he said, tenderly; "I saw it the moment I entered the room. Go and lie down, my dear, and take care of yourself. You take care of everybody else," said the Major. "Why did you let me go on reading the paper like an ass, when your head aches?"

"My head does not ache. I was only thinking," said Mrs. Ochterlony: for she thought on the whole it would be best to resume the subject and endeavour to make an end of it. But this was not the Major's way. He had in the meantime emptied his reservoir, and it had to be filled again before he would find himself in the vein for speech.

"But I don't want you to think," said Major Ochterlony with tender patronage: "that ought to be my part of the business. Have you got a novel?—if not, I'll go over and ask Miss Sorbette for one of hers. Lie down and rest, Mary; I can see that is all you are good for to-day."

Whether such a speech was aggravating or not to a woman who knew that it was her brain which had all the real weight of the family affairs to bear, may be conjectured by wives in general who know the sort of thing. But as for Mary, she was so used to it, that she took very little notice. She said, "Thank you, Hugh; I have got my letters here, which I have not read, and Aunt Agatha is as good as a novel." If this was not a very clear indication to the Major that his best policy was to take himself off for a little, and leave her in peace, it would be hard to say what could have taught him. But then Major Ochterlony was a man of a lively mind, and above being taught.

"Ah, Aunt Agatha," he said. "My dear, I know it is a painful subject, but we must, you know, begin to think where we are to send Hugh."

Mary shuddered; her nerves—for she had nerves, though she was so fair and serene—began to get excited. She said, "For pity's sake, not any more to-day. I am worn out. I cannot bear it. He is only six, and he is quite well."

The Major shook his head. "He is very well, but I have seen when a few hours changed all that," he said. "We cannot keep him much longer. At his age, you know; all the little Heskeths go at four—I think—"

"Ah," said Mary, "the Heskeths have nothing to do with it; they have floods and floods of children,—they don't know what it is; they can do without their little things; but I—Hugh, I am tired—I am not able for any more. Let me off for to-day."

Major Ochterlony regarded his wife with calm indulgence, and smoothed her hair off her hot forehead as he stooped to kiss her. "If you only would call things by the same names as other people, and say you have a headache, my dear," he said, in his caressing way. And then he was so good as to leave her, saying to himself as he went away that his Mary too had a little temper, though nobody gave her credit for it. Instead of annoying him, this little temper on Mary's part rather pleased her husband. When it came on he could be indulgent to her and pet her, which he liked to do; and then he could feel the advantage on his own side, which was not always the case. His heart quite swelled over her as he went away; so good, and so wise, and so fair, and yet not without that womanly weakness which it was sweet for a man to protect and pardon and put up with. Perhaps all men are not of the same way of thinking; but then Major Ochterlony reasoned only in his own way.

Mary stayed behind, and found it very difficult to occupy herself with anything. It was not temper, according to the ordinary meaning of the word. She was vexed, disturbed, disquieted, rather than angry. When she took up the pleasant letter in which the English breezes were blowing, and the leaves rustling, she could no longer keep her attention from wandering. She began it a dozen times, and as often gave it up again, driven by the importunate thoughts which took her mind by storm, and thrust everything else away. As if it were not enough to have one great annoyance suddenly overwhelming her, she had the standing terror of her life, the certainty that she would have to send her children away, thrown in to make up. She could have cried, had that been of any use; but Mrs. Ochterlony had had good occasion to cry many times in her life, which takes away the inclination at less important moments. The worst of all was that her husband's oft-repeated suggestion struck at the very roots of her existence, and seemed to throw everything of which she had been most sure into sudden ruin. She would put no faith in it—pay no attention to it, she said to herself; and then, in spite of herself, she found that she paid great attention, and could not get it out of her mind. The only character in which she knew herself—in which she had ever been known—was that of a wife. There are some women—nay, many women—who have felt their own independent standing before they made the first great step in a woman's life, and who are able to realize their own identity without associating it for ever with that of any other. But as for Mary, she had married, as it were, out of the nursery, and except as Hugh Ochterlony's wife, and his son's mother, she did not know herself. In such circumstances, it may be imagined what a bewildering effect any doubt about her marriage would have upon her. For the first time she began to think of herself, and to see that she had been hardly dealt with. She began to resent her guardian's carelessness, and to blame even kind Aunt Agatha, who in those days was taken up with some faint love-affairs of her own, which never came to anything. Why did they not see that everything was right? Why did not Hugh make sure, whose duty it was? After she had vexed herself with such thoughts, she returned with natural inconsistency to the conclusion that it was all one of the Major's notions. This was the easiest way of getting rid of it, and yet it was aggravating enough that the Major should permit his restless fancy to enter such sacred grounds, and to play with the very foundations of their life and honour. And as if that was not enough, to talk at the end of it all of sending Hugh away!

Perhaps it would have been good for Mary if she had taken her husband's advice and lain down, and sent over to Miss Sorbette for a novel. But she was rebellious and excited, and would not do it. It was true that they were engaged out to dinner that night, and that when the hour came Mrs. Ochterlony entered Mrs. Hesketh's drawing-room with her usual composure, and without any betrayal of the agitation that was still smouldering within. But that did not make it any easier for her. There was nobody more respected, as people say, in the station than she was—and to think that it was possible that such a thing might be, as that she should be humiliated and pulled down from her fair elevation among all those women! Neither the Major nor any man had a right to have notions upon a matter of such importance. Mary tried hard to calm herself down to her ordinary tranquillity, and to represent to herself how good he was, and how small a drawback after all were those fidgets of his, in comparison with the faults of most other men. Just as he represented to himself, with more success, how trifling a disadvantage was the "little temper" which gave him the privilege, now and then, of feeling tenderly superior to his wife. But the attempt was not successful that day in Mrs. Ochterlony's mind; for after all there are some things too sacred for discussion, and with which the most fidgety man in the world cannot be permitted to play. Such was the result of the first conversation upon this startling subject. The Major found himself very tolerably at his ease, having relieved his mind for the moment, and enjoyed his dinner and spent a very pleasant evening; but as for Madonna Mary, she might have prejudiced her serene character in the eyes of the regiment had the veil been drawn aside only for a moment, and could anybody have seen or guessed the whirl of thoughts that was passing through her uneasy mind.

CHAPTER III

The present writer has already lamented her inability to convey to the readers of this history any clear account of an Indian bungalow, or the manner in which life goes on in that curious kind of English home: so that it would be vain to attempt any detailed description of Mary Ochterlony's life at this period of her career. She lived very much as all the others lived, and gave a great deal of attention to her two little boys, and wrote regularly by every mail to her friends in England, and longed for the day when the mail came in, though the interest of her correspondence was not absorbing. All this she did like everybody else, though the other ladies at the station had perhaps more people belonging to them, and a larger number of letters, and got more good of the eagerly looked-for mail. And she read all the books she could come by, even Miss Sorbette's novels, which were indeed the chief literary nourishment of the station; and took her due share in society, and was generally very popular, though not so superior as Miss Sorbette for example, nor of remarkable piety like Mrs. Kirkman, nor nearly so well off as Mrs. Hesketh. Perhaps these three ladies, who were the natural leaders of society, liked Mary all the better because she did not come in direct contact with their claims; though if it had ever entered into Mrs. Ochterlony's head to set up a distinct standard, no doubt the masses would have flocked to it, and the peace of the station might have been put in jeopardy. But as no such ambitious project was in her mind, Mary kept her popularity with everybody, and gained besides that character of "She could an if she would," which goes a great deal farther than the limited reputation of any actual achievement. She was very good to the new people, the young people, the recent arrivals, and managed to make them feel at home sooner than anybody else could, which was a very useful gift in such society; and then a wife who bore her husband's fidgets so serenely was naturally a model and example for all the new wives.

"I am sure nobody else in the station could do so well," Mrs. Kirkman said. "The most experienced Christian would find it a trying task. But then some people are so mercifully fitted for their position in life. I don't think she feels it as you or I should." This was said, not as implying that little Mrs. Askell—to whom the words were ostensibly addressed—had peculiarly sensitive feelings, or was in any way to be associated with the Colonel's wife, but only because it was a favourite way Mrs. Kirkman had of bringing herself down to her audience, and uniting herself, as it were, to ordinary humanity; for if there was one thing more than another for which she was distinguished, it was her beautiful Christian humanity; and this was the sense in which she now spoke.

"Please don't say so," cried the ensign's wife, who was an unmanageable, eighteen-year-old, half-Irish creature. "I am sure she has twenty thousand times more feeling than you and—than both of us put together. It's because she is real good; and the Major is an old dear. He is a fidget and he's awfully aggravating, and he puts one in a passion; but he's an old dear, and so you would say if you knew him as well as I."

Mrs. Kirkman regarded the creature by her side, as may be supposed, with the calm contempt which her utterance merited. She looked at her, out of those "down-dropt," half-veiled eyes, with that look which everybody in the station knew so well, as if she were looking down from an infinite distance with a serene surprise which was too far off and elevated to partake of the nature of disgust. If she knew him as well as this baby did! But the Colonel's wife did not take any notice of the audacious suggestion. It was her duty, instead of resenting the impertinence to herself, to improve the occasion for the offender's own sake.

"My dear, there is nobody really good," said Mrs. Kirkman. "We have the highest authority for that. I wish I could think dear Mary was possessed of the true secret of a higher life; but she has so much of that natural amiability, you know, which is, of all things, the most dangerous for the soul. I would rather, for my part, she was not so 'good' as you say. It is all filthy rags," said Mrs. Kirkman, with a sigh. "It might be for the good of her soul to be brought low, and forced to abandon these refuges of lies—"

Upon which the little Irish wild-Indian blazed up with natural fury.

"I don't believe she ever told a lie in her life. I'll swear to all the lies she tells," cried the foolish little woman; "and as for rags—it's horrible to talk so. If you only knew—if you only could think—how kind she was to me!"

For this absurd little hapless child had had a baby, as might have been expected, and would have been in rags indeed, and everything that is miserable, but for Mary, who had taken her in hand; and being not much more than a baby herself, and not strong yet, and having her heart in her mouth, so to speak, she burst out crying, as might have been expected too.

This was a result which her companion had not in the least calculated upon, for Mrs. Kirkman, notwithstanding her belief in Mary's insensibility, had not very lively feelings, and was not quick at divining other people. But she was a good woman notwithstanding all her talk. She came down off her mountain top, and soothed her little visitor, and gave her a glass of wine, and even kissed her, to make matters up.

"I know she has a way, when people are sick," said the Colonel's wife; and then, after that confession, she sighed again. "If only she does not put her trust in her own works," Mrs. Kirkman added.

For, to tell the truth, the Chaplain of the regiment was not (as she thought) a spiritual-minded man, and the Colonel's wife was troubled by an abiding consciousness that it was into her hands Providence had committed the souls of the station. "Which was an awful responsibility for a sinful creature," she said, in her letters home; "and one that required constant watch over herself."

Perhaps, in a slightly different way, Mrs. Ochterlony would have been similarly put down and defended in the other two centres of society at the station. "She is intelligent," Miss Sorbette said; "I don't deny that she is intelligent; but I would not say she was superior. She is fond of reading, but then most people are fond of reading, when it's amusing, you know. She is a little too like Amelia in 'Vanity Fair.' She is one of the sweet women. In a general way, I can't bear sweet women; but I must confess she is the very best specimen I ever saw."

As for Mrs. Hesketh, her opinion was not much worth stating in words. If she had any fault to find with Mrs. Ochterlony, it was because Mary had sometimes a good deal of trouble in making the two ends meet. "I cannot endure people that are always having anxieties," said the rich woman of the station, who had an idea that everybody could be comfortable if they liked, and that it was an offence to all his neighbours when a man insisted on being poor; but at the same time everybody knew that she was very fond of Mary. This had been the general opinion of her for all these years, and naturally Mrs. Ochterlony was used to it, and, without being at all vain on the subject, had that sense of the atmosphere of general esteem and regard which surrounded her, which has a favourable influence upon every character, and which did a great deal to give her the sweet composure and serenity for which she was famed.

But from the time of that first conversation with her husband, a change came upon the Madonna of the station. It was not perceptible to the general vision, yet there were individual eyes which found out that something was the matter, though nobody could tell what. Mrs. Hesketh thought it was an attack of fever coming on, and Mrs. Kirkman hoped that Mrs. Ochterlony was beginning to occupy herself about her spiritual state; and the one recommended quinine to Mary, and the other sent her sermons, which, to tell the truth, were not much more suitable to her case. But Mary did not take any of the charitable friends about her into her confidence. She went about among them as a prince might have gone about in his court, or a chief among his vassals, after hearing in secret that it was possible that one day he may be discovered to be an impostor. Or, if not that,—for Mary knew that she never could be found out an impostor,—at least, that such a charge was hanging over her head, and that somebody might believe it; and that her history would be discussed and her name get into people's mouths and her claims to their regard be questioned. It was very hard upon her to think that such a thing was possible with composure, or to contemplate her husband's restless ways, and to recollect the indiscreet confidences which he was in the habit of making. He had spoken to Colonel Kirkman about it, and even quoted his advice about the marriage lines; and Mary could not but think (though in this point she did the Colonel injustice) that Mrs. Kirkman too must know; and then, with a man of Major Ochterlony's temperament, nobody could make sure that he would not take young Askell, the ensign, or any other boy in the station, into his confidence, if he should happen to be in the way. All this was very galling to Mary, who had so high an appreciation of the credit and honour which, up to this moment, she had enjoyed; and who felt that she would rather die than come down to be discussed and pitied and talked about among all these people. She thought in her disturbed and uneasy mind, that she could already hear all the different tones in which they would say, "Poor Mary!" and all the wonders, and doubts, and inquiries that would rise up round her. Mrs. Kirkman would have said that all these were signs that her pride wanted humbling, and that the thing her friends should pray for, should be some startling blow to lead her back to a better state of mind. But naturally this was a kind of discipline which for herself, or indeed for anybody else, Mary was not far enough advanced to desire.

Perhaps, however, it was partly true about the pride. Mrs. Ochterlony did not say anything about it, but she locked the door of her own room the next morning after that talk with the Major, and searched through all her repositories for those "marriage lines," which no doubt she had put away somewhere, and which she had naturally forgotten all about for years. It was equally natural, and to be expected, that she should not find them. She looked through all her papers, and letters, and little sacred corners, and found many things that filled her heart with sadness and her eyes with tears—for she had not come through those ten years without leaving traces behind her where her heart had been wounded and had bled by the way—but she did not find what she was in search of. She tried hard to look back and think, and to go over in her mind the contents of her little school-girl desk, which she had left at Aunt Agatha's cottage, and the little work-table, and the secretary with all its drawers. But she could not recollect anything about it, nor where she had put it, nor what could have become of it; and the effect of her examination was to give her, this time in reality, a headache, and to make her eyes heavy and her heart sore. But she did not say a syllable about her search to the Major, who was (as, indeed, he always was) as anxiously affectionate as a man could be, and became (as he always did) when he found his wife suffering, so elaborately noiseless and still, that Mary ended by a good fit of laughing, which was of the greatest possible service to her.

"When you are so quiet, you worry me, Hugh," she said. "I am used to hear you moving about."

"My dear, I hope I am not such a brute as to move about when you are suffering," her husband replied. And though his mind had again begun to fill with the dark thoughts that had been the occasion of all Mary's annoyance, he restrained himself with a heroic effort, and did not say a syllable about it all that night.

But this was a height of virtue which was quite impossible any merely mortal powers could keep up to. He began to make mysterious little broken speeches next day, and to stop short and say, "My darling, I mustn't worry you," and to sigh like a furnace, and to worry Mary to such an extremity that her difficulty in keeping her temper and patience grew indescribable. And then, when he had afflicted her in this way till it was impossible to go any further—when he had betrayed it to her in every look, in every step, in every breath he drew—which was half a sigh—and in every restless movement he made; and when Mrs. Ochterlony, who could not sleep for it, nor rest, nor get any relief from the torture, had two red lines round her eyes, and was all but out of her senses—the stream burst forth at last, and the Major spoke:

"You remember, perhaps, Mary, what we were talking of the other day," he said, in an insidiously gentle way, one morning, early—when they had still the long, long day before them to be miserable in. "I thought it very important, but perhaps you may have forgot—about old Sommerville who died?"

"Forgot!" said Mary. She felt it was coming now, and was rather glad to have it over. "I don't know how I could forget, Hugh. What you said would have made one recollect anything; but you cannot make old Sommerville come alive again, whatever you do."

"My dear, I spoke to you about some—about a—paper," said the Major. "Lines—that is what the Scotch call them—though, I daresay, they're very far from being poetry. Perhaps you have found them, Mary?"

said Major Ochterlony, looking into her face in a pleading way, as if he prayed her to answer yes. And it was with difficulty that she kept as calm as she wished to do, and answered without letting him see the agitation and excitement in her mind.

"I don't know where I have put them, Hugh," she said, with a natural evasion, and in a low voice. She did not acknowledge having looked for them, and having failed to find them; but in spite of herself, she answered with a certain humility, as of a woman culpable. For, after all, it was her fault.

"You don't know where you put them?" said the Major, with rising horror. "Have you the least idea how important they are? They may be the saving of you and of your children, and you don't know where you have put them! Then it is all as I feared," Major Ochterlony added, with a groan, "and everything is lost."

"What is lost?" said Mary. "You speak to me in riddles, Hugh. I know I put them somewhere—I must have put them somewhere safe. They are, most likely, in my old desk at home, or in one of the drawers of the secretary," said Mary calmly, giving those local specifications with a certainty which she was far from feeling. As for the Major, he was arrested by the circumstance which made her faint hope and supposition look somehow like truth.

"If I could hope that that was the case," he said; "but it can't be the case, Mary. You never were at home after we were married—you forget that. We went to Earlston for a day, and we went to your guardian's; but never to Aunt Agatha. You are making a mistake, my dear; and God bless me, to think of it, what would become of you if anything were to happen to me?"

"I hope there is nothing going to happen to you; but I don't think in that case it would matter what became of me," said Mary in utter depression; for by this time she was worn out.

"You think so now, my love; but you would be obliged to think otherwise," said Major Ochterlony. "I hope I'm all right for many a year; but a man can never tell. And the insurance, and pension, and everything—and Earlston, if my brother should leave it to us—all our future, my darling. I think it will drive me distracted," said the Major, "not a witness nor a proof left!"

Mary could make no answer. She was quite overwhelmed by the images thus called before her; for her part, the pension and the insurance money had no meaning to her ears; but it is difficult not to put a certain faith in it when a man speaks in such a circumstantial way of things that can only happen after his death.

"You have been talking to the doctor, and he has been putting things into your head," she said faintly. "It is cruel to torture me so. We know very well how we were married, and all about it, and so do our friends, and it is cruel to try to make me think of anything happening. There is nobody in the regiment so strong and well as you are," she continued, taking courage a little. She thought to herself he looked, as people say, the picture of health, as he sat beside her, and she began to recover out of her prostration. As for spleen or liver, or any of those uncomfortable attributes, Major Ochterlony, up to this moment, had not known whether he possessed them—which was a most re-assuring thought, naturally, for his anxious wife.

"Thank God," said the Major, with a little solemnity. It was not that he had any presentiment, or thought himself likely to die early; but simply that he was in a pathetic way, and had a naïf and innocent pleasure in deepening his effects; and then he took to walking about the room in his nervous manner. After a while he came to a dead stop before his wife, and took both her hands into his.

"Mary," he said, "I know it's an idea you don't like; but, for my peace of mind; suppose—just suppose for the sake of supposing—that I was to die now, and leave you without a word to prove your claims. It would be ten times worse than death, Mary; but I could die at peace if you would only make one little sacrifice to my peace of mind."

"Oh, Hugh, don't kill me—you are not going to die," was all Mary could say.

"No, my darling, not if I can help it; but if it were only for my peace of mind. There's no harm in it that I can see. It's ridiculous, you know; but that's all, Mary," said the Major, looking anxiously into her face. "Why, it is what hosts of people do every day. It is the easiest thing to do—a mere joke, for that matter. They will say, you know, that it is like Ochterlony, and a piece of his nonsense. I know how they talk; but never mind. I know very well there is nothing else you would not do for my peace of mind. It will set your future above all casualties, and it will be all over in half an hour. For instance, Churchill says—"

"You have spoken to Mr. Churchill, too?" said Mary, with a thrill of despair.

"A man can never do any harm speaking to his clergyman, I hope," the Major said, peevishly. "What do you mean by too? I've only mentioned it to Kirkman besides—I wanted his advice—and to Sorbette, to explain that bad headache of yours. And they all think I am perfectly right."

Mary put her hands up to her face, and gave a low but bitter cry. She said nothing more—not a syllable. She had already been dragged down without knowing it, and set low among all these people. She who deserved nothing but honour, who had done nothing to be ashamed of, who was the same Madonna Mary whom they had all regarded as the "wisest, virtuousest, discreetest, best." By this time they had all begun to discuss her story, and to wonder if all had been quite right at the beginning, and to say, "Poor Mary!" She knew it as well as if she had heard the buzz of talk in those three houses to which her husband had confided his difficulty. It was a horrible torture, if you will but think of it, for an innocent woman to bear.

"It is not like you to make such a fuss about so simple a thing," said Major Ochterlony. "You know very well it is not myself but you I am thinking of; that you may have everything in order, and your future provided for, whatever may happen. It may be absurd, you know; but a woman mustn't mind being absurd to please her husband. We'll ask our friends to step over with us to church in the morning, and in half an hour it will be all over. Don't cover your face, Mary. It worries me not to see your face. God bless me, it is nothing to make such a fuss about," said the Major, getting excited. "I would do a great deal more, any day, to please you."

"I would cut off my hand to please you," said Mary, with perhaps a momentary extravagance in the height of her passion. "You know there is no sacrifice I would not make for you; but oh, Hugh, not this, not this," she said, with a sob that startled him—one of those sobs that tear and rend the breast they come from, and have no accompaniment of tears.

His answer was to come up to her side, and take the face which she had been covering, between his hands, and kiss it as if it had been a child's. "My darling, it is only this that will do me any good. It is for my peace of mind," he said, with all that tenderness and effusion which made him the best of husbands.

He was so loving to her that, even in the bitterness of the injury, it was hard for Mary to refuse to be soothed and softened. He had got his way, and his unbounded love and fondness surrounded her with a kind of atmosphere of tender enthusiasm. He knew so well there was none like her, nobody fit to be put for a moment in comparison with his Mary; and this was how her fate was fixed for her, and the crisis came to an end.

CHAPTER IV

"I am going with you, Mary," said Mrs. Kirkman, coming suddenly in upon the morning of the day which was to give peace to Major Ochterlony's mind, and cloud over with something like a shadow of shame (or at least she thought so) his wife's fair matron fame. The Colonel's wife had put on her last white bonnet, which was not so fresh as it had been at the beginning of the season, and white gloves which were also a little the worse for wear. To be sure the marriage was not like a real marriage, and nobody knew how the unwilling bride would think proper to dress. Mrs. Kirkman came in at a quicker pace than ordinary, with her hair hanging half out of curl on either side of her face, as was always the case. She was fair, but of a greyish complexion, with light blue eyes à fleur de la tête, which generally she kept half veiled within their lids—a habit which was particularly aggravating to some of the livelier spirits. She came in hastily (for her), and found Mary seated disconsolate, and doing nothing, which is, in such a woman, one of the saddest signs of a mind disturbed. Mrs. Ochterlony sat, dropped down upon a chair, with her hands listlessly clasped in her lap, and a hot flush upon her cheek. She was lost in a dreary contemplation of the sacrifice which was about to be exacted from her, and of the possible harm it might do. She was thinking of her children, what effect it might have on them—and she was thinking bitterly, that for good or evil she could not help it; that again, as on many a previous occasion, her husband's restless mind had carried the day over her calmer judgment, and that there was no way of changing it. To say that she consented with personal pain of the most acute kind, would not be to say all. She gave in, at the same time, with a foreboding utterly indistinct, and which she would not have given utterance to, yet which was strong enough to heighten into actual misery the pain and shame of her position. When Mrs. Kirkman came in, with her eyes full of observation, and making the keenest scrutiny from beneath the downcast lids, Mrs. Ochterlony was not in a position to hide her emotions. She was not crying, it is true, for the circumstances were too serious for crying; but it was not difficult to form an idea of her state of mind from her strangely listless attitude, and the expression of her face.

"I have come to go with you," said Mrs. Kirkman. "I thought you would like to have somebody to countenance you. It will make no difference to me, I assure you, Mary; and both the Colonel and I think if there is any doubt, you know, that it is by far the wisest thing you could do. And I only hope—"

"Doubt!" said Mary, lighting up for the moment. "There is no more doubt than there is of all the marriages made in Scotland. The people who go there to be married are not married again afterwards that I ever heard of. There is no doubt whatever—none in the world. I beg your pardon. I am terribly vexed and annoyed, and I don't know what I am saying. To hear any one talk of doubt!"

"My dear Mary, we know nothing but what the Major has told us," said Mrs. Kirkman. "You may depend upon it he has reason for what he is doing; and I do hope you will see a higher hand in it all, and feel that you are being humbled for your good."

"I wish you would tell me how it can be for my good," said Mrs. Ochterlony, "when even you, who ought to know better, talk of doubt—you who have known us all along from the very first. Hugh has taken it into his head—that is the whole matter; and you, all of you know, when he takes a thing into his head—"

She had been hurried on to say this by the rush of her disturbed thoughts; but Mary was not a woman to complain of her husband. She came to a sudden standstill, and rose up, and looked at her watch.

"It is about time to go," she said, "and I am sorry to give you the trouble of going with me. It is not worth while for so short a distance; but, at least, don't say anything more about it, please."

Mrs. Kirkman had already made the remark that Mary was not at all "dressed." She had on her brown muslin, which was the plainest morning dress in her possession, as everybody knew; and instead of going to her room, to make herself a little nice, she took up her bonnet, which was on the table, and tied it on without even so much as looking in the glass. "I am quite ready," she said, when she had made this simple addition to her dress, and stood there, looking everything that was most unlike the Madonna of former days—flushed and clouded over, with lines in her forehead, and the corners of her mouth dropped, and her fair large serene beauty hidden beneath the thunder-cloud. And the Colonel's wife was very sorry to see her friend in such a state of mind, as may be supposed.

"My dear Mary," Mrs. Kirkman said, taking her arm as they went out, and holding it fast. "I should much wish to see you in a better frame of mind. Man is only the instrument in our troubles. It must have been that Providence saw you stood in need of it, my dear. He knows best. It would not have been sent if it had not been for your good."

"In that way, if I were to stand in the sun till I got a sunstroke, it would be for my good," said Mary, in anger. "You would say, it was God's fault, and not mine. But I know it is my fault; I ought to have stood out and resisted, and I have not had the strength; and it is not for good, but evil. It is not God's fault, but ours. It can be for nobody's good."

But after this, she would not say any more. Not though Mrs. Kirkman was shocked at her way of speaking, and took great pains to impress upon her that she must have been doing or thinking something God punished by this means. "Your pride must have wanted bringing down, my dear; as we all do, Mary, both you and I," said the Colonel's wife; but then Mrs. Kirkman's humility was well known.

Thus they walked together to the chapel, whither various wondering people, who could not understand what it meant, were straying. Major Ochterlony had meant to come for his wife, but he was late, as he so often was, and met them only near the chapel-door; and then he did something which sent the last pang of which it was capable to Mary's heart, though it was only at a later period that she found it out. He found his boy with the Hindoo nurse, and brought little Hugh in, 'wildered and wondering. Mr. Churchill by this time had put his surplice on, and all was ready. Colonel Kirkman had joined his wife, and stood by her side behind the "couple," furtively grasping his grey moustache, and looking out of a corner of his eyes at the strange scene. Mrs. Kirkman, for her part, dropt her eyelids as usual, and looked down upon Mary kneeling at her feet, with a certain compassionate uncertainty, sorry that Mrs. Ochterlony did not see this trial to be for her good, and at the same time wondering within herself whether it had all been perfectly right, or was not more than a notion of the Major's. Farther back Miss Sorbette, who was with Annie Hesketh, was giving vent in a whisper to the same sentiments.

"I am very sorry for poor Mary: but could it be all quite right before?" Miss Sorbette was saying. "A man does not take fright like that for nothing. We women are silly, and take fancies; but when a man does it, you know—"

And it was with such an accompaniment that Mary knelt down, not looking like a Madonna, at her husband's side. As for the Major, an air of serenity had diffused itself over his handsome features. He knelt in quite an easy attitude, pleased with himself, and not displeased to be the centre of so interesting a group. Mary's face was slightly averted from him, and was burning with the same flush of indignation as when Mrs. Kirkman found her in her own house. She had taken off her bonnet and thrown it down by her side; and her hair was shining as if in anger and resistance to this fate, which, with closed mouth, and clasped hands, and steady front, she was submitting to, though it was almost as terrible as death. Such was the curious scene upon which various subaltern members of society at the station looked on with wondering eyes. And little Hugh Ochterlony stood near his mother with childish astonishment, and laid up the singular group in his memory, without knowing very well what it meant; but that was a sentiment shared by many persons much more enlightened than the poor little boy, who did not know how much influence this mysterious transaction might have upon his own fate.

The only other special feature was that Mary, with the corners of her mouth turned down, and her whole soul wound up to obstinacy, would not call herself by any name but Mary Ochterlony. They persuaded her, painfully, to put her long disused maiden name upon the register, and kind Mr. Churchill shut his ears to it in the service; but yet it was a thing that everybody remarked. When all was over, nobody knew how they were expected to behave, whether to congratulate the pair, or whether to disappear and hold their tongues, which seemed in fact the wisest way. But no popular assembly ever takes the wisest way of working. Mr. Churchill was the first to decide the action of the party. He descended the altar steps, and shook hands with Mary, who stood tying her bonnet, with still the corners of her mouth turned down, and that feverish flush on her cheeks. He was a good man, though not spiritually-minded in Mrs. Kirkman's opinion; and he felt the duty of softening and soothing his flock as much as of teaching them, which is sometimes a great deal less difficult. He came and shook hands with her, gravely and kindly.

"I don't see that I need congratulate you, Mrs. Ochterlony," he said, "I don't suppose it makes much difference; but you know you always have all our best wishes." And he cast a glance over his audience, and reproved by that glance the question that was circulating among them. But to tell the truth, Mrs. Kirkman and Miss Sorbette paid very little attention to Mr. Churchill's looks.

"My dear Mary, you have kept up very well, though I am sure it must have been trying," Mrs. Kirkman said. "Once is bad enough; but I am sure you will see a good end in it at the last."

And while she spoke she allowed a kind of silent interrogation, from her half-veiled eyes, to steal over Mary, and investigate her from head to foot. Had it been all right before? Might not this perhaps be in reality the first time, the once which was bad enough? The question crept over Mrs. Ochterlony, from the roots of her hair down to her feet, and examined her curiously to find a response. The answer was plain enough, and yet it was not plain to the Colonel's wife; for she knew that the heart is deceitful above all things, and that where human nature is considered it is always safest to believe the worst.

Miss Sorbette came forward too in her turn, with a grave face. "I am sure you must feel more comfortable after it, and I am so glad you have had the moral courage," the doctor's sister said, with a certain solemnity. But perhaps it was Annie Hesketh, in her innocence, who was the worst of all. She advanced timidly, with her face in a blaze, like Mary's own, not knowing where to look, and lost in ingenuous embarrassment.

"Oh, dear Mrs. Ochterlony, I don't know what to say," said Annie. "I am so sorry, and I hope you will always be very, very happy; and mamma couldn't come—" Here she stopped short, and looked up with candid eyes, that asked a hundred questions. And Mary's reply was addressed to her alone.

"Tell your mamma, Annie, that I am glad she could not come," said the injured wife. "It was very kind of her." When she had said so much, Mrs. Ochterlony turned round, and saw her boy standing by, looking at her. It was only then that she turned to the husband to whom she had just renewed her troth. She looked full at him, with a look of indignation and dismay. It was the last drop that made the cup run over; but then, what was the good of saying anything? That final prick however, brought her to herself. She shook hands with all the people afterwards, as if they were dispersing after an ordinary service, and took little Hugh's hand and went home as if nothing had happened. She left the Major behind her, and took no notice of him, and did not even, as young Askell remarked, offer a glass of wine to the assistants at the ceremony, but went home with her little boy, talking to him, as she did on Sundays going home from church; and everybody stood and looked after her, as might have been expected. She knew they were looking after her, and saying "Poor Mary!" and wondering after all if there must not have been a very serious cause for this re-marriage. Mary thought to herself that she knew as well what they were saying as if she had been among them, and yet she was not entirely so correct in her ideas of what was going on as she thought.

In the first place, she could not have imagined how a moment could undo all the fair years of unblemished life which she had passed among them. She did not really believe that they would doubt her honour, although she herself felt it clouded; and at the same time she did not know the curious compromise between cruelty and kindness, which is all that their Christian feelings can effect in many commonplace minds, yet which is a great deal when one comes to think of it. Mrs. Kirkman, arguing from the foundation of the desperate wickedness of the human heart, had gradually reasoned herself into the belief that Mary had deceived her, and had never been truly an honourable wife; but notwithstanding this conclusion, which in the abstract would have made her cast off the culprit with utter disdain, the Colonel's wife paused, and was moved, almost in spite of herself, by the spirit of that faith which she so often wrapped up and smothered in disguising talk. She did not believe in Mary; but she did, in a wordy, defective way, in Him who was the son of a woman, and who came not to condemn; and she could not find it in her heart to cast off the sinner. Perhaps if Mrs. Ochterlony had known this divine reason for her friend's charity, it would have struck a deeper blow than any other indignity to which she had been subjected. In all her bitter thoughts, it never occurred to her that her neighbour stood by her as thinking of those Marys who once wept at the Saviour's feet. Heaven help the poor Madonna, whom all the world had heretofore honoured! In all her thoughts she never went so far as that.

The ladies waited a little, and sent away Annie Hesketh, who was too young for scenes of this sort, though her mamma was so imprudent, and themselves laid hold of Mr. Churchill, when the other gentlemen had dispersed. Mr. Churchill was one of those mild missionaries who turn one's thoughts involuntarily to that much-abused, yet not altogether despicable institution of a celibate clergy. He was far from being celibate, poor man! He, or at least his wife, had such a succession of babies as no man could number. They had children at "home" in genteel asylums for the sons and daughters of the clergy, and they had children in the airiest costume at the station, whom people were kind to, and who were waiting their chance of being sent "home" too; and withal, there were always more arriving, whom their poor papa received with mild despair. For his part, he was not one of the happy men who held appointments under the beneficent rule of the Company, nor was he a regimental chaplain. He was one of that hapless band who are always "doing duty" for other and better-off people. He was almost too old now (though he was not old), and too much hampered and overlaid by children, to have much hope of anything better than "doing duty" all the rest of his life; and the condition of Mrs. Churchill, who had generally need of neighbourly help, and of the children, who were chiefly clothed—such clothing as it was—by the bounty of the Colonel's and Major's and Captain's wives, somehow seemed to give these ladies the upper hand of their temporary pastor. He managed well enough among the men, who respected his goodness, and recognised him to be a gentleman, notwithstanding his poverty; but he stood in terror of the women, who were more disposed to interfere, and who were kind to his family and patronised himself. He tried hard on this occasion, as on many others, to escape, but he was hemmed in, and no outlet was left him. If he had been a celibate brother, there can be little doubt it would have been he who would have had the upper hand; but with all his family burdens and social obligations, the despotism of the ladies of his flock came hard upon the poor clergyman; all the more that, poor though he was, and accustomed to humiliations, he had not learned yet to dispense with the luxury of feelings and delicacies of his own.

"Mr. Churchill, do give us your advice," said Miss Sorbette, who was first. "Do tell us what all this means? They surely must have told you at least the rights of it. Do you think they have really never been married all this time? Goodness gracious me! to think of us all receiving her, and calling her Madonna, and all that, if this be true! Do you think—"

"I don't think anything but what Major Ochterlony told me," said Mr. Churchill, with a little emphasis. "I have not the least doubt he told me the truth. The witnesses of their marriage are dead, and that wretched place at Gretna was burnt down, and he is afraid that his wife would have no means of proving her marriage in case of anything happening to him. I don't know what reason there can be to suppose that Major Ochterlony, who is a Christian and a gentleman, said anything that was not true."

"My dear Mr. Churchill," said Mrs. Kirkman, with a sigh, "you are so charitable. If one could but hope that the poor dear Major was a true Christian, as you say. But one has no evidence of any vital change in his case. And, dear Mary!—I have made up my mind for one thing, that it shall make no difference to me. Other people can do as they like, but so far as I am concerned, I can but think of our Divine Example," said the Colonel's wife. It was a real sentiment, and she meant well, and was actually thinking as well as talking of that Divine Example; but still somehow the words made the blood run cold in the poor priest's veins.

"What can you mean, Mrs. Kirkman?" he said. "Mrs. Ochterlony is as she always was, a person whom we all may be proud to know."

"Yes, yes," said Miss Sorbette, who interrupted them both without any ceremony; "but that is not what I am asking. As for his speaking the truth as a Christian and a gentleman, I don't give much weight to that. If he has been deceiving us for all these years, you may be sure he would not stick at a fib to end off with. What is one to do? I don't believe it could ever have been a good marriage, for my part!"

This was the issue to which she had come by dint of thinking it over and discussing it; although the doctor's sister, like the Colonel's wife, had got up that morning with the impression that Major Ochterlony's fidgets had finally driven him out of his senses, and that Mary was the most ill-used woman in the world.

"And I believe exactly the contrary," said the clergyman, with some heat. "I believe in an honourable man and a pure-minded woman. I had rather give up work altogether than reject such an obvious truth."

"Ah, Mr. Churchill," Mrs. Kirkman said again, "we must not rest in these vain appearances. We are all vile creatures, and the heart is deceitful above all things. I do fear that you are taking too charitable a view."

"Yes," said Mr. Churchill, but perhaps he made a different application of the words; "I believe that about the heart; but then it shows its wickedness generally in a sort of appropriate, individual way. I daresay they have their thorns in the flesh, like the rest; but it is not falsehood and wantonness that are their besetting sins," said the poor man, with a plainness of speech which put his hearers to the blush.

"Goodness gracious! remember that you are talking to ladies, Mr. Churchill," Miss Sorbette said, and put down her veil. It was not a fact he was very likely to forget; and then he put on his hat as they left the chapel, and hoped he was now free to go upon his way.

"Stop a minute, please," said Miss Sorbette. "I should like to know what course of action is going to be decided on. I am very sorry for Mary, but so long as her character remains under this doubt—"

"It shall make no difference to me," said Mrs. Kirkman. "I don't pretend to regulate anybody's actions, Sabina; but when one thinks of Mary of Bethany! She may have done wrong, but I hope this occurrence will be blessed to her soul. I felt sure she wanted something to bring her low, and make her feel her need," the Colonel's wife added, with solemnity; "and it is such a lesson for us all. In other circumstances, the same thing might have happened to you or me."

"It could never have happened to me," said Miss Sorbette, with sudden wrath; which was a fortunate diversion for Mr. Churchill. This was how her friends discussed her after Mary had gone away from her second wedding; and perhaps they were harder upon her than she had supposed even in her secret thoughts.

CHAPTER V

But the worst of all to Mrs. Ochterlony was that little Hugh had been there—Hugh, who was six years old, and so intelligent for his age. The child was very anxious to know what it meant, and why she knelt by his father's side while all the other people were standing. Was it something particular they were praying for, which Mrs. Kirkman, and the rest did not want? Mary satisfied him as she best could, and by-and-by he forgot, and began to play with his little brother as usual; but his mother knew that so strange a scene could not fail to leave some impression. She sat by herself that long day, avoiding her husband for perhaps the first time in her life, and imagining a hundred possibilities to herself. It seemed to her as if everybody who ever heard of her henceforth must hear of this, and as if she must go through the world with a continual doubt upon her; and Mary's weakness was to prize fair reputation and spotless honour above everything in the world. Perhaps Mrs. Kirkman was not so far wrong after all, and there was a higher meaning in the unlooked-for blow that thus struck her at her tenderest point; but that was an idea she could not receive. She could not think that God had anything to do with her husband's foolish restlessness, and her own impatient submission. It was a great deal more like a malicious devil's work, than anything a beneficent providence could have arranged. This way of thinking was far from bringing Mary any consolation or solace, but still there was a certain reasonableness in her thoughts. And then an indistinct foreboding of harm to her children, she did not know what, or how to be brought about, weighed upon Mary's mind. She kept looking at them as they played beside her, and thinking how, in the far future, the meaning of that scene he had been a witness to might flash into Hugh's mind when he was a man, and throw a bewildering doubt upon his mother's name, which perhaps she might not be living to clear up; and these ideas stung her like a nest of serpents, each waking up and darting its venom to her heart at a separate moment. She had been very sad and very sorry many a time before in her life,—she had tasted all the usual sufferings of humanity; and yet she had never been what may be called unhappy, tortured from within and without, dissatisfied with herself and everything about her. Major Ochterlony was in every sense of the word a good husband, and he had been Mary's support and true companion in all her previous troubles. He might be absurd now and then, but he never was anything but kind and tender and sympathetic, as was the nature of the man. But the special feature of this misfortune was that it irritated and set her in arms against him, that it separated her from her closest friend and all her friends, and that it made even the sight and thought of her children, a pain to her among all her other pains.

This was the wretched way in which Mary spent the day of her second wedding. Naturally, Major Ochterlony brought people in with him to lunch (probably it should be written tiffin, but our readers will accept the generic word), and was himself in the gayest spirits, and insisted upon champagne, though he knew they could not afford it. "We ate our real wedding breakfast all by ourselves in that villanous little place at Gretna," he said, with a boy's enthusiasm, "and had trout out of the Solway: don't you recollect, Mary? Such trout! What a couple of happy young fools we were; and if every Gretna Green marriage turned out like mine!" the Major added, looking at his wife with beaming eyes. She had been terribly wounded by his hand, and was suffering secret torture, and was full of the irritation of pain; and yet she could not so steel her heart as not to feel a momentary softening at sight of the love and content in his eyes. But though he loved her he had sacrificed all her scruples, and thrown a shadow upon her honour, and filled her heart with bitterness, to satisfy an unreasonable fancy of his own, and give peace, as he said, to his mind. All this was very natural, but in the pain of the moment it seemed almost inconceivable to Mary, who was obliged to conceal her mortification and suffering, and minister to her guests as she was wont to do, without making any show of the shadow that she felt to have fallen upon her life.

It was, however, tacitly agreed by the ladies of the station to make no difference, according to the example of the Colonel's wife. Mrs. Kirkman had resolved upon that charitable course from the highest motives, but the others were perhaps less elevated in their principles of conduct. Mrs. Hesketh, who was quite a worldly-minded woman, concluded it would be absurd for one to take any step unless they all did, and that on the whole, whatever were the rights of it, Mary could be no worse than she had been for all the long time they had known her. As for Miss Sorbette, who was strong-minded, she was disposed to consider that the moral courage the Ochterlonys had displayed in putting an end to an unsatisfactory state of affairs merited public appreciation. Little Mrs. Askell, for her part, rushed headlong as soon as she heard of it, which fortunately was not till it was all over, to see her suffering protectress. Perhaps it was at that moment, for the first time, that the ensign's wife felt the full benefit of being a married lady, able to stand up for her friend and stretch a small wing of championship over her. She rushed into Mrs. Ochterlony's presence and arms like a little tempest, and cried and sobbed and uttered inarticulate exclamations on her friend's shoulder, to Mary's great surprise, who thought something had happened to her. Fortunately the little eighteen-year-old matron, after the first incoherence was over, began to find out that Mrs. Ochterlony looked the same as ever, and that nothing tragical could have happened, and so restrained the offer of her own countenance and support, which would have been more humbling to Mary than all the desertion in the world.

"What is the matter, my dear?" said Mrs. Ochterlony, who had regained her serene looks, though not her composed mind; and little Irish Emma, looking at her, was struck with such a sense of her own absurdity and temerity and ridiculous pretensions, that she very nearly broke down again.

"I've been quarrelling with Charlie," the quick-witted girl said, with the best grace she could, and added in her mind a secret clause to soften down the fiction,—"he is so aggravating; and when I saw my Madonna looking so sweet and so still—"

"Hush!" said Mary "there was no need for crying about that—nor for telling fibs either," she added, with a smile that went to the heart of the ensign's wife. "You see there is nothing the matter with me," Mrs. Ochterlony added; but notwithstanding her perfect composure it was in a harder tone.

"I never expected anything else," said the impetuous little woman; "as if any nonsense could do any harm to you! And I love the Major, and I always have stood up for him; but oh, I should just like for once to box his ears."

"Hush!" said Mary again; and then the need she had of sympathy prompted her for one moment to descend to the level of the little girl beside her, who was all sympathy and no criticism, which Mary knew to be a kind of friendship wonderfully uncommon in this world. "It did me no harm," she said, feeling a certain relief in dropping her reserve, and making visible the one thing of which they were both thinking, and which had no need of being identified by name. "It did me no harm, and it pleased him. I don't deny that it hurt at the time," Mary added after a little pause, with a smile; "but that is all over now. You need not cry over me, my dear."

"I—cry over you," cried the prevaricating Emma, "as if such a thing had ever come into my head; but I did feel glad I was a married lady," the little thing added; and then saw her mistake, and blushed and faltered and did not know what to say next. Mrs. Ochterlony knew very well what her young visitor meant, but she took no notice, as was the wisest way. She had steeled herself to all the consequences by this time, and knew she must accustom herself to such allusions and to take no notice of them. But it was hard upon her, who had been so good to the child, to think that little Emma was glad she was a married lady, and could in her turn give a certain countenance. All these sharp, secret, unseen arrows went direct to Mary's heart.

But on the whole the regiment kept its word and made no difference. Mrs. Kirkman called every Wednesday and took Mary with her to the prayer-meeting which she held among the soldiers' wives, and where she said she was having much precious fruit; and was never weary of representing to her companion that she had need of being brought down and humbled, and that for her part she would rejoice in anything that would bring her dear Mary to a more serious way of thinking; which was an expression of feeling perfectly genuine on Mrs. Kirkman's part, though at the same time she felt more and more convinced that Mrs. Ochterlony had been deceiving her, and was not by any means an innocent sufferer. The Colonel's wife was quite sincere in both these beliefs, though it would be hard to say how she reconciled them to each other; but then a woman is not bound to be logical, whether she belongs to High or Low Church. At the same time she brought Mary sermons to read, with passages marked, which were adapted for both these states of feeling,—some consoling the righteous who were chastened because they were beloved, and some exhorting the sinners who had been long callous and now were beginning to awaken to a sense of their sins. Perhaps Mary, who was not very discriminating in point of sermon-books, read both with equal innocence, not seeing their special application: but she could scarcely be so blind when her friend discoursed at the Mothers' Meeting upon the Scripture Marys, and upon her who wept at the Saviour's feet. Mrs. Ochterlony understood then, and never forgot afterwards, that it was that Mary with whom, in the mind of one of her most intimate associates, she had come to be identified. Not the Mary blessed among women, the type of motherhood and purity, but the other Mary, who was forgiven much because she had much loved. That night she went home with a swelling heart, wondering over the great injustice of human ways and dealings, and crying within herself to the Great Spectator who knew all against the evil thoughts of her neighbours. Was that what they all believed of her, all these women? and yet she had done nothing to deserve it, not so much as by a light look, or thought, or word; and it was not as if she could defend herself, or convince them of their cruelty: for nobody accused her, nobody reproached her—her friends, as they all said, made no difference. This was the sudden cloud that came over Mary in the very fairest and best moment of her life.

But as for the Major, he knew nothing about all that. It had been done for his peace of mind, and until the next thing occurred to worry him he was radiant with good-humour and satisfaction. If he saw at any time a cloud on his wife's face, he thought it was because of that approaching necessity which took the pleasure out of everything even to himself, for the moment, when he thought of it—the necessity of sending Hugh "home." "We shall still have Islay for a few years at least, my darling," he would say, in his affectionate way; "and then the baby,"—for there was a baby, which had come some time after the event which we have just narrated. That too must have had something to do, no doubt, with Mary's low spirits. "He'll get along famously with Aunt Agatha, and get spoiled, that fellow will," the Major said; "and as for Islay, we'll make a man of him." And except at those moments, when, as we have just said, the thoughts of his little Hugh's approaching departure struck him, Major Ochterlony was as happy and light-hearted as a man who is very well off in all his domestic concerns, and getting on in his profession, and who has a pleasant consciousness of doing his duty to all men and a grateful sense of the mercies of God, should be, and naturally is. When two people are yoked for life together, there is generally one of the two who bears the burden, while the other takes things easy. Sometimes it is the husband, as is fit and right, who has the heavy weight on his shoulders; but sometimes, and oftener than people think, it is the wife. And perhaps this was why Major Ochterlony was so frisky in his harness, and Madonna Mary felt her serenity fall into sadness, and was conscious of going on very slowly and heavily upon the way of life. Not that he was to blame, who was now, as always, the best husband in the regiment, or even in the world. Mary would not for all his fidgets, not for any reward, have changed him against Colonel Kirkman with his fishy eye, nor against Captain Hesketh's jolly countenance, nor for anybody else within her range of vision. He was very far from perfect, and in utter innocence had given her a wound which throbbed and bled daily whichever way she turned herself, and which she would never cease to feel all her life; but still at the same time he stood alone in the world, so far as Mary's heart was concerned: for true love is, of all things on earth, the most pertinacious and unreasonable, let the philosophers say what they will.

And then the baby, for his part, was not like what the other babies had been; he was not a great fellow, like Hugh and Islay; but puny and pitiful and weakly,—a little selfish soul that would leave his mother no rest. She had been content to leave the other boys to Providence and Nature, tending them tenderly, wholesomely, and not too much, and hoping to make men of them some day; but with this baby Mary fell to dreaming, wondering often as he lay in her lap what his future would be. She used to ask herself unconsciously, without knowing why, what his influence might be on the lives of his brothers, who were like and yet so unlike him: though when she roused up she rebuked herself, and thought how much more reasonable it would be to speculate upon Hugh's influence, who was the eldest, or even upon Islay, who had the longest head in the regiment, and looked as if he meant to make some use of it one day. To think of the influence of little weakly Wilfrid coming to be of any permanent importance in the lives of those two strong fellows seemed absurd enough; and yet it was an idea which would come back to her, when she thought without thinking, and escaped as it were into a spontaneous state of mind. The name even was a weak-minded sort of name, and did not please Mary; and all sorts of strange fancies came into her head as she sat with the pitiful little peevish baby, who insisted upon having all her attention, lying awake and fractious upon her wearied knee.

Thus it was that the first important scene of her history came to an end, with thorns which she never dreamed of planted in Mrs. Ochterlony's way, and a still greater and more unthought-of cloud rising slowly upon the broken serenity of her life.

CHAPTER VI

Everything however went on well enough at the station for some time after the great occurrence which counted for so much in Mrs. Ochterlony's history; and the Major was very peaceable, for him, and nothing but trifling matters being in his way to move him, had fewer fidgets than usual. To be sure he was put out now and then by something the Colonel said or did, or by Hesketh's well-off-ness, which had come to the length of a moral peculiarity, and was trying to a man; but these little disturbances fizzed themselves out, and got done with without troubling anybody much. There was a lull, and most people were surprised at it and disposed to think that something must be the matter with the Major; but there was nothing the matter. Probably it occurred to him now and then that his last great fidget had rather gone a step too far—but this is mere conjecture, for he certainly never said so. And then, after a while, he began to play, as it were, with the next grand object of uneasiness which was to distract his existence. This was the sending "home" of little Hugh. It was not that he did not feel to the utmost the blank this event would cause in the house, and the dreadful tug at his heart, and the difference it would make to Mary. But at the same time it was a thing that had to be done, and Major Ochterlony hoped his feelings would never make him fail in his duty. He used to feel Hugh's head if it was hot, and look at his tongue at all sorts of untimely moments, which Mary knew meant nothing, but yet which made her thrill and tremble to her heart; and then he would shake his own head and look sad. "I would give him a little quinine, my dear," he would say; and then Mary, out of her very alarm and pain, would turn upon him.

"Why should I give him quinine? It is time enough when he shows signs of wanting it. The child is quite well, Hugh." But there was a certain quiver in Mrs. Ochterlony's voice which the Major could not and did not mistake.

"Oh yes, he is quite well," he would reply; "come and let me feel if you have any flesh on your bones, old fellow. He is awfully thin, Mary. I don't think he would weigh half so much as he did a year ago if you were to try. I don't want to alarm you, my dear; but we must do it sooner or later, and in a thing that is so important for the child, we must not think of ourselves," said Major Ochterlony; and then again he laid his hand with that doubting, experimenting look upon the boy's brow, to feel "if there was any fever," as he said.

"He is quite well," said Mary, who felt as if she were going distracted while this pantomime went on. "You do frighten me, though you don't mean it; but I know he is quite well."

"Oh yes," said Major Ochterlony, with a sigh; and he kissed his little boy solemnly, and set him down as if things were in a very bad way; "he is quite well. But I have seen when five or six hours have changed all that," he added with a still more profound sigh, and got up as if he could not bear further consideration of the subject, and went out and strolled into somebody's quarters, where Mary did not see how light-hearted he was half-and-hour after, quite naturally, because he had poured out his uneasiness, and a little more, and got quite rid of it, leaving her with the arrow sticking in her heart. No wonder that Mrs. Kirkman, who came in as the Major went out, said that even a very experienced Christian would have found it trying. As for Mary, when she woke up in the middle of the night, which little peevish Wilfrid gave her plenty of occasion to do, she used to steal off as soon as she had quieted that baby-tyrant, and look at her eldest boy in his little bed, and put her soft hand on his head, and stoop over him to listen to his breathing. And sometimes she persuaded herself that his forehead was hot, which it was quite likely to be, and got no more sleep that night; though as for the Major, he was a capital sleeper. And then somehow it was not so easy as it had been to conclude that it was only his way; for after his way had once brought about such consequences as in that re-marriage which Mary felt a positive physical pain in remembering, it was no longer to be taken lightly. The consequence was, that Mrs. Ochterlony wound herself up, and summoned all her courage, and wrote to Aunt Agatha, though she thought it best, until she had an answer, to say nothing about it; and she began to look over all little Hugh's wardrobe, to make and mend, and consider within herself what warm things she could get him for the termination of that inevitable voyage, and to think what might happen before she had these little things of his in her care again—how they would wear out and be replenished, and his mother have no hand in it—and how he would get on without her. She used to make pictures of the little forlorn fellow on shipboard, and how he would cry himself to sleep, till the tears came dropping on her needle and rusted it; and then would try to think how good Aunt Agatha would be to him, but was not to say comforted by that—not so much as she ought to have been. There was nothing in the least remarkable in all this, but only what a great many people have to go through, and what Mrs. Ochterlony no doubt would go through with courage when the inevitable moment came. It was the looking forward to and rehearsing it, and the Major's awful suggestions, and the constant dread of feeling little Hugh's head hot, or his tongue white, and thinking it was her fault—this was what made it so hard on Mary; though Major Ochterlony never meant to alarm her, as anybody might see.

"I think he should certainly go home," Mrs. Kirkman said. "It is a trial, but it is one of the trials that will work for good. I don't like to blame you, Mary, but I have always thought your children were a temptation to you; oh, take care!—if you were to make idols of them—"

"I don't make idols of them," said Mrs. Ochterlony, hastily; and then she added, with an effort of self-control which stopped even the rising colour on her cheek, "You know I don't agree with you about these things." She did not agree with Mrs. Kirkman; and yet to tell the truth, where so much is concerned, it is a little hard for a woman, however convinced she may be of God's goodness, not to fail in her faith and learn to think that, after all, the opinion which would make an end of her best hopes and her surest confidence may be true.

"I know you don't agree with me," said the Colonel's wife, sitting down with a sigh. "Oh, Mary, if you only knew how much I would give to see you taking these things to heart—to see you not almost, but altogether such as I am," she added, with sudden pathos. "If you would but remember that these blessings are only lent us—that we don't know what day or hour they may be taken back again—"

All this Mary listened to with a rising of nature in her heart against it, and yet with that wavering behind,—What if it might be true?

"Don't speak to me so," she said. "You always make me think that something is going to happen. As if God grudged us our little happiness. Don't talk of lending and taking back again. If He is not a cheerful giver, who can be?" For she was carried away by her feelings, and was not quite sure what she was saying—and at the same time, it comes so much easier to human nature to think that God grudges and takes back again, and is not a cheerful giver. As for Mrs. Kirkman, she thought it sinful so much as to imagine anything of the kind.

"It grieves me to hear you speak in that loose sort of latitudinarian way," she said; "oh, my dear Mary, if you could only see how much need you have to be brought low. When one cross is not enough, another comes—and I feel that you are not going to be let alone. This trial, if you take it in a right spirit, may have the most blessed consequences. It must be to keep you from making an idol of him, my dear—for if he takes up your heart from better things—"

What could Mary say? She stopped in her work to give her hands an impatient wring together, by way of expressing somehow in secret to herself the impatience with which she listened. Yet perhaps, after all, it might be true. Perhaps God was not such a Father as He, the supreme and all-loving, whom her own motherhood shadowed forth in Mary's heart, but such a one as those old pedant fathers, who took away pleasures and reclaimed gifts, for discipline's sake. Perhaps—for when a heart has everything most dear to it at stake, it has such a miserable inclination to believe the worst of Him who leaves his explanation to the end,—Mary thought perhaps it might be true, and that God her Father might be lying in wait for her somewhere to crush her to the ground for having too much pleasure in his gift,—which was the state of mind which her friend, who was at the bottom of her heart a good woman, would have liked to bring about.

"I think it is simply because we are in India," said Mrs. Ochterlony, recovering herself; "it is one of the conditions of our lot. It is a very hard condition, but of course we have to bear it. I think, for my part, that God, instead of doing it to punish me, is sorry for me, and that He would mend it and spare us if something else did not make it necessary. But perhaps it is you who are right," she added, faltering again, and wondering if it was wrong to believe that God, in a wonderful supreme way, must be acting, somehow as in a blind ineffective way, she, a mother, would do to her children. But happily her companion was not aware of that profane thought. And then, Mrs. Hesketh had come in, who looked at the question from entirely a different point of view.

"We have all got to do it, you know," said that comfortable woman, "whether we idolize them or not. I don't see what that has to do with it; but then I never do understand you. The great thing is, if you have somebody nice to send them to. One's mother is a great comfort for that; but then, there is one's husband's friends to think about. I am not sure, for my own part, that a good school is not the best. That can't offend anybody, you know; neither your own people, nor his; and then they can go all round in the holidays. Mine have all got on famously," said Mrs Hesketh; and nobody who looked at her could have thought anything else. Though, indeed, Mrs. Hesketh's well-off-ness was not nearly so disagreeable or offensive to other people as her husband's, who had his balance at his banker's written on his face; whereas in her case it was only evident that she was on the best of terms with her milliner and her jeweller, and all her tradespeople, and never had any trouble with her bills. Mary sat between the woman who had no children, and who thought she made idols of her boys—and the woman who had quantities of children, and saw no reason why anybody should be much put out of their way about them; and neither the one nor the other knew what she meant, any more than she perhaps knew exactly what they meant, though, as was natural, the latter idea did not much strike her. And the sole strengthening which Mrs. Ochterlony drew from this talk was a resolution never to say anything more about it; to keep what she was thinking of to herself, and shut another door in her heart, which, after all, is a process which has to be pretty often repeated as one goes through the world.

"But Mary has no friends—no female friends, poor thing. It is so sad for a girl when that happens, and accounts for so many things," the Colonel's wife said, dropping the lids over her eyes, and with an imperceptible shake of her head, which brought the little chapel and the scene of her second marriage in a moment before Mary's indignant eyes; "but there is one good even in that, for it gives greater ground for faith; when we have nothing and nobody to cling to—"

"We were talking of the children," Mrs. Hesketh broke in calmly. "If I were you I should keep Hugh until Islay was old enough to go with him. They are such companions to each other, you know, and two children don't cost much more than one. If I were you, Mary, I would send the two together. I always did it with mine. And I am sure you have somebody that will take care of them; one always has somebody in one's eye; and as for female friends—"

Mary stopped short the profanity which doubtless her comfortable visitor was about to utter on the subject. "I have nothing but female friends," she said, with a natural touch of sharpness in her voice. "I have an aunt and a sister who are my nearest relatives—and it is there Hugh is going," for the prick of offence had been good for her nerves, and strung them up.

"Then I can't see what you have to be anxious about," said Mrs. Hesketh; "some people always make a fuss about things happening to children; why should anything happen to them? mine have had everything, I think, that children can have, and never been a bit the worse; and though it makes one uncomfortable at the time to think of their being ill, and so far away if anything should happen, still, if you know they are in good hands, and that everything is done that can be done—And then, one never hears till the worst is over," said the well-off woman, drawing her lace shawl round her. "Good-by, Mary, and don't fret; there is nothing that is not made worse by fretting about it; I never do, for my part."

Mrs. Kirkman threw a glance of pathetic import out of the corners of her down-dropped eyes at the large departing skirts of Mary's other visitor. The Colonel's wife was one of the people who always stay last, and her friends generally cut their visits short when they encountered her, with a knowledge of this peculiarity, and at the same time an awful sense of something that would be said when they had withdrawn. "Not that I care for what she says," Mrs. Hesketh murmured to herself as she went out, "and Mary ought to know better at least;" but at the same time, society at the station, though it was quite used to it, did not like to think of the sigh, and the tender, bitter lamentations which would be made over them when they took their leave. Mrs. Hesketh was not sensitive, but she could not help feeling a little aggrieved, and wondering what special view of her evil ways her regimental superior would take this time—for in so limited a community, everybody knew about everybody, and any little faults one might have were not likely to be hid.

Mrs. Kirkman had risen too, and when Mary came back from the door the Colonel's wife came and sat down beside her on the sofa, and took Mrs. Ochterlony's hand. "She would be very nice, if she only took a little thought about the one thing needful," said Mrs. Kirkman, with the usual sigh. "What does it matter about all the rest? Oh, Mary, if we could only choose the good part which cannot be taken away from us!"

"But surely, we all try a little after that," said Mary. "She is a kind woman, and very good to the poor. And how can we tell what her thoughts are? I don't think we ever understand each other's thoughts."

"I never pretend to understand. I judge according to the Scripture rule," said Mrs. Kirkman; "you are too charitable, Mary; and too often, you know, charity only means laxness. Oh, I cannot tell you how those people are all laid upon my soul! Colonel Kirkman being the principal officer, you know, and so little real Christian work to be expected from Mr. Churchill, the responsibility is terrible. I feel sometimes as if I must die under it. If their blood should be demanded at my hands!"

"But surely God must care a little about them Himself," said Mrs. Ochterlony. "Don't you think so? I cannot think that He has left it all upon you—"

"Dear Mary, if you but give me the comfort of thinking I had been of use to you," said Mrs. Kirkman, pressing Mary's hand. And when she went away she believed that she had done her duty by Mrs. Ochterlony at least; and felt that perhaps, as a brand snatched from the burning, this woman, who was so wrapped up in regard for the world and idolatry of her children, might still be brought into a better state. From this it will be seen that the painful impression made by the marriage had a little faded out of the mind of the station. It was there, waiting any chance moment or circumstance that might bring the name of Madonna Mary into question; but in the meantime, for the convenience of ordinary life, it had been dropped. It was a nuisance to keep up a sort of shadowy censure which never came to anything, and by tacit consent the thing had dropped. For it was a very small community, and if any one had to be tabooed, the taboo must have been complete and crushing, and nobody had the courage for that. And so gradually the cloudiness passed away like a breath on a mirror, and Mary to all appearance was among them as she had been before. Only no sort of compromise could really obliterate the fact from anybody's recollection, or above all from her own mind.

And Mary went back to little Hugh's wardrobe when her visitors were gone, with that sense of having shut another door in her heart which has already been mentioned. It is so natural to open all the doors and leave all the chambers open to the day; but when people walk up to the threshold and look in and turn blank looks of surprise or sad looks of disapproval upon you, what is to be done but to shut the door? Mrs. Ochterlony thought as most people do, that it was almost incredible that her neighbours did not understand what she meant; and she thought too, like an inexperienced woman, that this was an accident of the station, and that elsewhere other people knew better, which was a very fortunate thought, and did her good. And so she continued to put her boy's things in order, and felt half angry when she saw the Major come in, and knew beforehand that he was going to resume his pantomime with little Hugh, and to try if his head was hot and look at his tongue. If his tongue turned out to be white and his head feverish, then Mary knew that he would think it was her fault, and began to long for Aunt Agatha's letter, which she had been fearing, and which might be looked for by the next mail.

As for the Major, he came home with the air of a man who has hit upon a new trouble. His wife saw it before he had been five minutes in the house. She saw it in his eyes, which sought her and retired from her in their significant restless way, as if studying how to begin. In former days Mrs. Ochterlony, when she saw this, used to help her husband out; but recently she had had no heart for that, and he was left unaided to make a beginning for himself. She took no notice of his fidgeting, nor of the researches he made all about the room, and all the things he put out of their places. She could wait until he informed her what it was. But Mary felt a little nervous until such time as her husband had seated himself opposite her, and began to pull her working things about, and to take up little Hugh's linen blouses which she had been setting in order. Then the Major heaved a demonstrative sigh. He meant to be asked what it meant, and even gave a glance up at her from the corner of his eye to see if she remarked it, but Mary was hard-hearted and would take no notice. He had to take all the trouble himself.

"He will want warmer things when he goes home," said the Major. "You must write to Aunt Agatha about that, Mary. I have been thinking a great deal about his going home. I don't know how I shall get on without him, nor you either, my darling; but it is for his good. How old is Islay?" Major Ochterlony added with a little abruptness: and then his wife knew what it was.

"Islay is not quite three," said Mary, quietly, as if the question was of no importance; but for all that her heart began to jump and beat against her breast.

"Three! and so big for his age," said the guilty Major, labouring with his secret meaning. "I don't want to vex you, Mary, my love, but I was thinking perhaps when Hugh went; it comes to about the same thing, you see—the little beggar would be dreadfully solitary by himself, and I don't see it would make any difference to Aunt Agatha—"

"It would make a difference to me," said Mary. "Oh, Hugh, don't be so cruel to me. I cannot let him go so young. If Hugh must go, it may be for his good—but not for Islay's, who is only a baby. He would not know us or have any recollection of us. Don't make me send both of my boys away."

"You would still have the baby," said the Major. "My darling, I am not going to do anything without your consent. Islay looked dreadfully feverish the other day, you know. I told you so; and as I was coming home I met Mrs. Hesketh—"

"You took her advice about it," said Mary, with a little bitterness. As for the Major, he set his Mary a whole heaven above such a woman as Mrs. Hesketh, and yet he had taken her advice about it, and it irritated him a little to perceive his wife's tone of reproach.

"If I listened to her advice it is because she is a very sensible woman," said Major Ochterlony. "You are so heedless, my dear. When your children's health is ruined, you know, that is not the time to send them home. We ought to do it now, while they are quite well; though indeed I thought Islay very feverish the other night," he added, getting up again in his restless way. And then the Major was struck with compunction when he saw Mary bending down over her work, and remembered how constantly she was there, working for them, and how much more trouble those children cost her than they ever could cost him. "My love," he said, coming up to her and laying his hand caressingly upon her bent head, "my bonnie Mary! you did not think I meant that you cared less for them, or what was for their good, than I do? It will be a terrible trial; but then, if it is for their good and our own peace of mind—"

"God help me," said Mary, who was a little beside herself. "I don't think you will leave me any peace of mind. You will drive me to do what I think wrong, or, if I don't do it, you will make me think that everything that happens is my fault. You don't mean it, but you are cruel, Hugh."

"I am sure I don't mean it," said the Major, who, as usual, had had his say out; "and when you come to think—but we will say no more about it to-night. Give me your book, and I will read to you for an hour or two. It is a comfort to come in to you and get a little peace. And after all, my love, Mrs. Hesketh means well, and she's a very sensible woman. I don't like Hesketh, but there's not a word to say against her. They are all very kind and friendly. We are in great luck in our regiment. Is this your mark where you left off? Don't let us say anything more about it, Mary, for to-night."

"No," said Mrs. Ochterlony, with a sigh; but she knew in her heart that the Major would begin to feel Islay's head, if it was hot, and look at his tongue, as he had done to Hugh's, and drive her out of her senses; and that, most likely, when she had come to an end of her powers, she would be beaten and give in at last. But they said no more about it that night; and the Major got so interested in the book that he sat all the evening reading, and Mary got very well on with her work. Major Ochterlony was so interested that he even forgot to look as if he thought the children feverish when they came to say good-night, which was the most wonderful relief to his wife. If thoughts came into her head while she trimmed little Hugh's blouses, of another little three-year-old traveller tottering by his brother's side, and going away on the stormy dangerous sea, she kept them to herself. It did not seem to her as if she could outlive the separation, nor how she could permit a ship so richly freighted to sail away into the dark distance and the terrible storms; and yet she knew that she must outlive it, and that it must happen, if not now, yet at least some time. It is the condition of existence for the English sojourners in India. And what was she more than another, that any one should think there was any special hardship in her case?

CHAPTER VII

The next mail was an important one in many ways. It was to bring Aunt Agatha's letter about little Hugh, and it did bring something which had still more effect upon the Ochterlony peace of mind. The Major, as has been already said, was not a man to be greatly excited by the arrival of the mail. All his close and pressing interests were at present concentrated in the station. His married sisters wrote to him now and then, and he was very glad to get their letters, and to hear when a new niece or nephew arrived, which was the general burden of these epistles. Sometimes it was a death, and Major Ochterlony was sorry; but neither the joy nor the sorrow disturbed him much. For he was far away, and he was tolerably happy himself, and could bear with equanimity the vicissitudes in the lot of his friends. But this time the letter which arrived was of a different description. It was from his brother, the head of the house—who was a little of an invalid and a good deal of a dilettante, and gave the Major no nephews or nieces, being indeed a confirmed bachelor of the most hopeless kind. He was a man who never wrote letters, so that the communication was a little startling. And yet there was nothing very particular in it. Something had occurred to make Mr. Ochterlony think of his brother, and the consequence was that he had drawn his writing things to his hand and written a few kind words, with a sense of having done something meritorious to himself and deeply gratifying to Hugh. He sent his love to Mary, and hoped the little fellow was all right who was, he supposed, to carry on the family honours—"if there are any family honours," the Squire had said, not without an agreeable sense that there was something in his last paper on the "Coins of Agrippa," that the Numismatic Society would not willingly let die. This was the innocent morsel of correspondence which had come to the Major's hand. Mary was sitting by with the baby on her lap while he read it, and busy with a very different kind of communication. She was reading Aunt Agatha's letter which she had been dreading and wishing for, and her heart was growing sick over the innocent flutter of expectation and kindness and delight which was in it. Every assurance of the joy she would feel in seeing little Hugh, and the care she would take of him, which the simple-minded writer sent to be a comfort to Mary, came upon the mother's unreasonable mind like a kind of injury. To think that anybody could be happy about an occurrence that would be so terrible to her; to think that anybody could have the bad taste to say that they looked with impatience for the moment that to Mary would be like dying! She was unhinged, and for the first time, perhaps, in her life, her nerves were thoroughly out of order, and she was unreasonable to the bottom of her heart; and when she came to her young sister's gay announcement of what for her part she would do for her little nephew's education, and how she had been studying the subject ever since Mary's letter arrived, Mrs. Ochterlony felt as if she could have beaten the girl, and was ready to cry with wretchedness and irritation and despair. All these details served somehow to fix it, though she knew it had been fixed before. They told her the little room Hugh should have, and the old maid who would take care of him; and how he should play in the garden, and learn his lessons in Aunt Agatha's parlour, and all those details which would be sweet to Mary when her boy was actually there. But at present they made his going away so real, that they were very bitter to her, and she had to draw the astonished child away from his play, and take hold of him and keep him by her, to feel quite sure that he was still here, and not in the little North-country cottage which she knew so well. But this was an arrangement which did not please the baby, who liked to have his mother all to himself, and pushed Hugh away, and kicked and screamed at him lustily. Thus it was an agitated little group upon which the Major looked down as he turned from his brother's pleasant letter. He was in a very pleasant frame of mind himself, and was excessively entertained by the self-assertion of little Wilfrid on his mother's knee.

"He is a plucky little soul, though he is so small," said Major Ochterlony; "but Willie, my boy, there's precious little for you of the grandeurs of the family. It is from Francis, my dear. It's very surprising, you know, but still it's true. And he sends you his love. You know I always said that there was a great deal of good in Francis; he is not a demonstrative man—but still, when you get at it, he has a warm heart. I am sure he would be a good friend to you, Mary, if ever—"

"I hope I shall never need him to be a good friend to me," said Mrs. Ochterlony. "He is your brother, Hugh, but you know we never got on." It was a perfectly correct statement of fact, but yet, perhaps, Mary would not have made it, had she not been so much disturbed by Aunt Agatha's letter. She was almost disposed to persuade herself for that moment that she had not got on with Aunt Agatha, which was a moral impossibility. As for the Major, he took no notice of his wife's little ill-tempered un-enthusiastic speech.

"You will be pleased when you read it," he said. "He talks of Hugh quite plainly as the heir of Earlston. I can't help being pleased. I wonder what kind of Squire the little beggar will make: but we shall not live to see that—or, at least, I shan't," the Major went on, and he looked at his boy with a wistful look which Mary used to think of afterwards. As for little Hugh, he was very indifferent, and not much more conscious of the affection near home than of the inheritance far off. Major Ochterlony stood by the side of Mary's chair, and he had it in his heart to give her a little lesson upon her unbelief and want of confidence in him, who was always acting for the best, and who thought much more of her interests than of his own.

"My darling," he said, in that coaxing tone which Mary knew so well, "I don't mean to blame you. It was a hard thing to make you do; and you might have thought me cruel and too precise. But only see now how important it was to be exact about our marriage—too exact even. If Hugh should come into the estate—"

Here Major Ochterlony stopped short all at once, without any apparent reason. He had still his brother's letter in his hand, and was standing by Mary's side; and nobody had come in, and nothing had happened. But all at once, like a flash of lightning, something of which he had never thought before had entered his mind. He stopped short, and said, "Good God!" low to himself, though he was not a man who used profane expressions. His face changed as a summer day changes when the wind seizes it like a ghost, and covers its heavens with clouds. So great was the shock he had received, that he made no attempt to hide it, but stood gazing at Mary, appealing to her out of the midst of his sudden trouble. "Good God!" he said. His eyes went in a piteous way from little Hugh, who knew nothing about it, to his mother, who was at present the chief sufferer. Was it possible that instead of helping he had done his best to dishonour Hugh? It was so new an idea to him, that he looked helplessly into Mary's eyes to see if it was true. And she, for her part, had nothing to say to him. She gave a little tremulous cry which did but echo his own exclamation, and pitifully held out her hand to her husband. Yes; it was true. Between them they had sown thorns in their boy's path, and thrown doubt on his name, and brought humiliation and uncertainty into his future life. Major Ochterlony dropped into a chair by his wife's side, and covered his face with her hand. He was struck dumb by his discovery. It was only she who had seen it all long ago—to whom no sudden revelation could come—who had been suffering, even angrily and bitterly, but who was now altogether subdued and conscious only of a common calamity; who was the only one capable of speech or thought.

"Hugh, it is done now," said Mary; "perhaps it may never do him any harm. We are in India, a long way from all our friends. They know what took place in Scotland, but they can't know what happened here."

The Major only replied once more, "Good God!" Perhaps he was not thinking so much of Hugh as of the failure he had himself made. To think he should have landed in the most apparent folly by way of being wise—that perhaps was the immediate sting. But as for Mrs. Ochterlony, her heart was full of her little boy who was going away from her, and her husband's horror and dismay seemed only natural. She had to withdraw her hand from him, for the tyrant baby did not approve of any other claim upon her attention, but she caressed his stooping head as she did so. "Oh, Hugh, let us hope things will turn out better than we think," she said, with her heart overflowing in her eyes; and the soft tears fell on Wilfrid's little frock as she soothed and consoled him. Little Hugh for his part had been startled in the midst of his play, and had come forward to see what was going on. He was not particularly interested, it is true, but still he rather wanted to know what it was all about. And when the pugnacious baby saw his brother he returned to the conflict. It was his baby efforts with hands and feet to thrust Hugh away which roused the Major. He got up and took a walk about the room, sighing heavily. "When you saw what was involved, why did you let me do it, Mary?" he said, amid his sighs. That was all the advantage his wife had from his discovery. He was still walking about the room and sighing, when the baby went to sleep, and Hugh was taken away; and then to be sure the father and mother were alone.

"That never came into my head," Major Ochterlony said, drawing a chair again to Mary's side. "When you saw the danger why did you not tell me? I thought it was only because you did not like it. And then, on the other side, if anything happened to me—. Why did you let me do it when you saw that?" said the Major, almost angrily. And he drew another long impatient sigh.

"Perhaps it will do no harm, after all," said Mary, who felt herself suddenly put upon her defence.

"Harm! it is sure to do harm," said the Major. "It is as good as saying we were never married till now. Good heavens! to think you should have seen all that, and yet let me do it. We may have ruined him, for all we know. And the question is, what's to be done? Perhaps I should write to Francis, and tell him that I thought it best for your sake, in case anything happened to me—and as it was merely a matter of form, I don't see that Churchill could have any hesitation in striking it out of the register—"

"Oh, Hugh, let it alone now," said Mrs. Ochterlony. "It is done, and we cannot undo it. Let us only be quiet and make no more commotion. People may forget it, perhaps, if we forget it."

"Forget it!" the Major said, and sighed. He shook his head, and at the same time he looked with a certain tender patronage on Mary. "You may forget it, my dear, and I hope you will," he said, with a magnanimous pathos; "but it is too much to expect that I should forget what may have such important results. I feel sure I ought to let Francis know. I daresay he could advise us what would be best. It is a very kind letter," said the Major; and he sighed, and gave Mary Mr. Ochterlony's brief and unimportant note with an air of resigned yet hopeless affliction, which half irritated her, and half awoke those possibilities of laughter which come "when there is little laughing in one's head," as we say in Scotland. She could have laughed, and she could have stormed at him; and yet in the midst of all she felt a poignant sense of contrast, and knew that it was she and not he who would really suffer—as it was he and not she who was in fault.

While Mary read Mr. Ochterlony's letter, lulling now and then with a soft movement the baby on her knee, the Major at the other side got attracted after a while by the pretty picture of the sleeping child, and began at length to forego his sighing, and to smooth out the long white drapery that lay over Mary's dress. He was thinking no harm, the tender-hearted man. He looked at little Wilfrid's small waxen face pillowed on his mother's arm—so much smaller and feebler than Hugh and Islay had been, the great, gallant fellows—and his heart was touched by his little child. "My little man! you are all right, at least," said the inconsiderate father. He said it to himself, and thought, if he thought at all on the subject, that Mary, who was reading his brother's letter, did not hear him. And when Mrs. Ochterlony gave that cry which roused all the house and brought everybody trooping to the door, in the full idea that it must be a cobra at least, the Major jumped up to his feet as much startled as any of them, and looked down to the floor and cried, "Where—what is it?" with as little an idea of what was the matter as the ayah who grinned and gazed in the distance. When he saw that instead of indicating somewhere a reptile intruder, Mary had dropped the letter and fallen into a weak outburst of tears, the Major was confounded. He sent the servants away, and took his wife into his arms and held her fast. "What is it, my love?" said the Major. "Are you ill? For Heaven's sake tell me what it is; my poor darling, my bonnie Mary?" This was how he soothed her, without the most distant idea what was the matter, or what had made her cry out. And when Mary came to herself, she did not explain very clearly. She said to herself that it was no use making him unhappy by the fantastical horror which had come into her mind with his words, or indeed had been already lurking there. And, poor soul, she was better when she had had her cry out, and had given over little Wilfrid, woke up by the sound, to his nurse's hands. She said, "Never mind me, Hugh; I am nervous, I suppose;" and cried on his shoulder as he never remembered her to have cried, except for very serious griefs. And when at last he had made her lie down, which was the Major's favourite panacea for all female ills of body or mind, and had covered her over, and patted and caressed and kissed her, Major Ochterlony went out with a troubled mind. It could not be anything in Francis's letter, which was a model of brotherly correctness, that had vexed or excited her: and then he began to think that for some time past her health had not been what it used to be. The idea disturbed him greatly, as may be supposed; for the thought of Mary ailing and weakly, or perhaps ill and in danger, was one which had never yet entered his mind. The first thing he thought of was to go and have a talk with Sorbette, who ought to know, if he was good for anything, what it was.

"I am sure I don't know in the least what is the matter," the Major said. "She is not ill, you know. This morning she looked as well as ever she did, and then all at once gave a cry and burst into tears. It is so unlike Mary."

"It is very unlike her," said the doctor. "Perhaps you were saying something that upset her nerves."

"Nerves!" said the Major, with calm pride. "My dear fellow, you know that Mary has no nerves; she never was one of that sort of women. To tell the truth, I don't think she has ever been quite herself since that stupid business, you know."

"What stupid business?" said Mr. Sorbette.

"Oh, you know—the marriage, to be sure. A man looks very silly afterwards," said the Major with candour, "when he lets himself be carried away by his feelings. She ought not to have consented when that was her idea. I would give a hundred pounds I had not been so foolish. I don't think she has ever been quite herself since."

The doctor had opened de grands yeux. He looked at his companion as if he could not believe his ears. "Of course you would never have taken such an unusual step if there had not been good reason for it," he ventured to say, which was rather a hazardous speech; for the Major might have divined its actual meaning, and then things would have gone badly with Mr. Sorbette. But, as it happened, Major Ochterlony was far too much occupied to pay attention to anybody's meaning except his own.

"Yes, there was good reason," he said. "She lost her marriage 'lines,' you know; and all our witnesses are dead. I thought she might perhaps find herself in a disagreeable position if anything happened to me."

As he spoke, the doctor regarded him with surprise so profound as to be half sublime—surprise and a perplexity and doubt wonderful to behold. Was this a story the Major had made up, or was it perhaps after all the certain truth? It was just what he had said at first; but the first time it was stated with more warmth, and did not produce the same effect. Mr. Sorbette respected Mrs. Ochterlony to the bottom of his heart; but still he had shaken his head, and said, "There was no accounting for those things." And now he did not know what to make of it: whether to believe in the innocence of the couple, or to think the Major had made up a story—which, to be sure, would be by much the greatest miracle of all.

"If that was the case, I think it would have been better to let well alone," said the doctor. "That is what I would have done had it been me."

"Then why did not you tell me so?" said Major Ochterlony. "I asked you before; and what you all said to me was, 'If that's the case, best to repeat it at once.' Good Lord! to think how little one can rely upon one's friends when one asks their advice. But in the meantime the question is about Mary. I wish you'd go and see her and give her something—a tonic, you know, or something strengthening. I think I'll step over and see Churchill, and get him to strike that unfortunate piece of nonsense out of the register. As it was only a piece of form, I should think he would do it; and if it is that that ails her, it would do her good."

"If I were you, I'd let well alone," said the doctor; but he said it low, and he was putting on his hat as he spoke, and went off immediately to see his patient. Even if curiosity and surprise had not been in operation, he would still probably have hastened to Madonna Mary. For the regiment loved her in its heart, and the loss of her fair serene presence would have made a terrible gap at the station. "We must not let her be ill if we can help it," Mr. Sorbette said to himself; and then he made a private reflection about that ass Ochterlony and his fidgets. But yet, notwithstanding all his faults, the Major was not an ass. On thinking it over again, he decided not to go to Churchill with that little request about the register; and he felt more and more, the more he reflected upon it, how hard it was that in a moment of real emergency a man should be able to put so little dependence upon his friends. Even Mary had let him do it, though she had seen how dangerous and impolitic it was; and all the others had let him do it; for certainly it was not without asking advice that he had taken what the doctor called so unusual a step. Major Ochterlony felt as he took this into consideration that he was an injured man. What was the good of being on intimate terms with so many people if not one of them could give him the real counsel of a friend when he wanted it? And even Mary had let him do it! The thought of such a strange dereliction of duty on the part of everybody connected with him, went to the Major's heart.

As for Mary, it would be a little difficult to express her feelings. She got up as soon as her husband was gone, and threw off the light covering he had put over her so carefully, and went back to her work; for to lie still in a darkened room was not a remedy in which she put any faith. And to tell the truth, poor Mary's heart was eased a little, perhaps physically, by her tears, which had done her good, and by the other incidents of the evening, which had thrown down as it were the separation between her and her husband, and taken away the one rankling and aching wound she had. Now that he saw that he had done wrong—now that he was aware that it was a wrong step he had taken—a certain remnant of bitterness which had been lurking in a corner of Mary's heart came all to nothing and died down in a moment. As soon as he was himself awakened to it, Mary forgot her own wound and every evil thought she had ever had, in her sorrow for him. She remembered his look of dismay, his dead silence, his unusual exclamation; and she said, "poor Hugh!" in her heart, and was ready to condone his worst faults. Otherwise, as Mrs. Ochterlony said to herself, he had scarcely a fault that anybody could point out. He was the kindest, the most true and tender! Everybody acknowledged that he was the best husband in the regiment, and which of them could stand beside him, even in an inferior place? Not Colonel Kirkman, who might have been a petrified Colonel out of the Drift (if there were Colonels in those days), for any particular internal evidence to the contrary; nor Captain Hesketh, who was so well off; nor any half dozen of the other officers. This was the state of mind in which Mrs. Ochterlony was when the doctor called. And he found her quite well, and thought her an unaccountable woman, and shrugged his shoulders, and wondered what the Major would take into his head next. "He said it was on the nerves, as the poor women call it," said the doctor, transferring his own suggestion to Major Ochterlony. "I should like to know what he means by making game of people—as if I had as much time to talk nonsense as he has: but I thought, to be sure, when he said that, that it was a cock-and-bull story. I ought to know something about your nerves."

"He was quite right," said Mrs. Ochterlony; and she smiled and took hold of the great trouble that was approaching her and made a buckler of it for her husband. "My nerves were very much upset. You know we have to make up our minds to send Hugh home."

And as she spoke she looked up at Mr. Sorbette with eyes brimming over with two great tears—real tears, Heaven knows, which came but too readily to back up her sacred plea. The doctor recoiled before them as if somebody had levelled a pistol at him; for he was a man that could not bear to see women crying, as he said, or to see anybody in distress, which was the true statement of the case.

"There—there," he said, "don't excite yourself. What is the good of thinking about it? Everybody has to do it, and the monkeys get on as well as possible. Look here, pack up all this work and trash, and amuse yourself. Why don't you go out more, and take a little relaxation? You had better send over to my sister for a novel; or if there's nothing else for it, get the baby. Don't sit working and driving yourself crazy here."

So that was all Mr. Sorbette could do in the case; and a wonderfully puzzled doctor he was as he went back to his quarters, and took the first opportunity of telling his sister that she was all wrong about the Ochterlonys, and he always knew she was. "As if a man could know anything about it," Miss Sorbette said. And in the meantime the Major went home, and was very tender of Mary, and petted and watched over her as if she had had a real illness. Though, after all, the question why she had let him do so, was often nearly on his lips, as it was always in his heart.

CHAPTER VIII

What Mrs. Ochterlony had to do after this was to write to Aunt Agatha, settling everything about little Hugh, which was by no means an easy thing to do, especially since the matter had been complicated by that most unnecessary suggestion about Islay, which Mrs. Hesketh had thought proper to make; as if she, who had a grown-up daughter to be her companion, and swarms of children, so many as almost to pass the bounds of possible recollection, could know anything about how it felt to send off one's entire family, leaving only a baby behind; but then that is so often the way with those well-off people, who have never had anything happen to them. Mary had to write that if all was well, and they could find "an opportunity," probably Hugh would be sent by the next mail but one; for she succeeded in persuading herself and the Major that sooner than that it would be impossible to have his things ready. "You do not say anything about Islay, my dear," said the Major, when he read the letter, "and you must see that for the child's sake—"

"Oh, Hugh, what difference can it make?" said Mrs. Ochterlony, with conscious sophistry. "If she can take one child, she can take two. It is not like a man—" But whether it was Islay or Aunt Agatha who was not like a man, Mary did not explain; and she went on with her preparations with a desperate trust in circumstances, such as women are often driven to. Something might happen to preserve to her yet for a little while longer her three-year-old boy. Hugh was past hoping for, but it seemed to her now that she would accept with gratitude, as a mitigated calamity, the separation from one which had seemed so terrible to her at first. As for the Major, he adhered to the idea with a tenacity unusual to him. He even came, and superintended her at the work-table, and asked continually, How about Islay? if all these things were for Hugh?—which was a question that called forth all the power of sophistry and equivocation which Mrs. Ochterlony possessed to answer. But still she put a certain trust in circumstances that something might still happen to save Islay—and indeed something did happen, though far, very far, from being as Mary wished.

The Major in the meantime had done his best to shake himself free from the alarm and dismay indirectly produced in his mind by his brother's letter. He had gone to Mr. Churchill after all, but found it impracticable to get the entry blotted out of the register, notwithstanding his assurance that it was simply a matter of form. Mr. Churchill had no doubt on that point, but he could not alter the record, though he condoled with the sufferer. "I cannot think how you all could let me do it," the Major said. "A man may be excused for taking the alarm, if he is persuaded that his wife will get into trouble when he is gone, for want of a formality; but how all of you, with cool heads and no excitement to take away your judgment—"

"Who persuaded you?" said the clergyman, with a little dismay.

"Well, you know Kirkman said things looked very bad in Scotland when the marriage lines were lost. How could I tell? he is Scotch, and he ought to know. And then to think of Mary in trouble, and perhaps losing her little provision if anything happened to me. It was enough to make a man do anything foolish; but how all of you who know better should have let me do it—"

"My dear Major," said Mr. Churchill mildly, "I don't think you are a man to be kept from doing anything when your heart is set upon it;—and then you were in such a hurry—"

"Ah, yes," said Major Ochterlony with a deep sigh; "and nobody, that I can remember, ever suggested to me to wait a little. That's what it is, Churchill; to have so many friends, and not one among them who would take the trouble to tell a man he was wrong."

"Major Ochterlony," said the clergyman, a little stiffly, "you forget that I said everything I could say to convince you. Of course I did not know all the circumstances—but I hope I shall always have courage enough, when I think so, to tell any man he is in the wrong."

"My dear fellow, I did not mean you," said the Major, with another sigh; and perhaps it was with a similar statement that the conversation always concluded when Major Ochterlony confided to any special individual of his daily associates, this general condemnation of his friends, of which he made as little a secret as he had made of his re-marriage. The station knew as well after that, that Major Ochterlony was greatly disturbed about the "unusual step" he had taken, and was afraid it might be bad for little Hugh's future prospects, as it had been aware beforehand of the wonderful event itself. And naturally there was a great deal of discussion on the subject. There were some people who contented themselves with thinking, like the doctor, that Ochterlony was an ass with his fidgets; while there were others who thought he was "deep," and was trying, as they said, to do away with the bad impression. The former class were men, and the latter were women; but it was by no means all the women who thought so. Not to speak of the younger class, like poor little Mrs. Askell, there were at least two of the most important voices at the station which did not declare themselves. Mrs. Kirkman shook her head, and hoped that however it turned out it might be for all their good, and above all might convince Mary of the error of her ways; and Mrs. Hesketh thought everybody made a great deal too much fuss about it, and begged the public in general to let the Ochterlonys alone. But the fact was, that so far as the ordinary members of society were concerned, the Major's new agitation revived the gossip that had nearly died out, and set it all afloat again. It had been dying away under the mingled influences of time, and the non-action of the leading ladies, and Mrs. Ochterlony's serene demeanour, which forbade the idea of evil. But when it was thus started again the second time, it was less likely to be made an end of. Mary, however, was as unconscious of the renewed commotion as if she had been a thousand miles away. The bitterness had gone out of her heart, and she had half begun to think as the Major did, that he was an injured man, and that it was her fault and his friends' fault; and then she was occupied with something still more important, and could not go back to the old pain, from which she had suffered enough. Thus it was with her in those troubled, but yet, as she afterwards thought, happy days; when she was very miserable sometimes and very glad—when she had a great deal, as people said, to put up with, a great deal to forgive, and many a thing of which she did not herself approve, to excuse and justify to others. This was her condition, and she had at the same time before her the dreadful probability of separation from both of her children, the certainty of a separation, and a long, dangerous voyage for one of them, and sat and worked to this end day after day, with a sense of what at the moment seemed exquisite wretchedness. But yet, thinking over it afterwards, and looking back upon it, it seemed to Mary as if those were happy days.

The time was coming very near when Hugh (as Mrs. Ochterlony said), or the children (as the Major was accustomed to say) were going home; when all at once, without any preparation, very startling news came to the station. One of the little local rebellions that are always taking place in India had broken out somewhere, and a strong detachment of the regiment was to be sent immediately to quell it. Major Ochterlony came home that day a little excited by the news, and still more by the certainty that it was he who must take the command. He was excited because he was a soldier at heart, and liked, kind man as he was, to see something doing; and because active service was more hopeful, and exhilarating, and profitable, than reposing at the station, where there was no danger, and very little to do. "I don't venture to hope that the rogues will show fight," he said cheerfully; "so there is no need to be anxious, Mary; and you can keep the boys with you till I come back—that is only fair," he said, in his exultation. As for Mary, the announcement took all the colour out of her cheeks, and drove both Hugh and Islay out of her mind. He had seen service enough, it is true, since they were married, to habituate her to that sort of thing; and she had made, on the whole, a very good soldier's wife, bearing her anxiety in silence, and keeping a brave front to the world. But perhaps Mr. Sorbette was right when he thought her nerves were upset. So many things all coming together may have been too much for her. When she heard of this she broke down altogether, and felt a cold thrill of terror go through her from her head to her heart, or from her heart to her head, which perhaps would be the most just expression; but she dared not say a word to her husband to deter or discourage him. When he saw the two tears that sprang into her eyes, and the sudden paleness that came over her face, he kissed her, all flushed and smiling as he was, and said: "Now, don't be silly, Mary. Don't forget you are a soldier's wife." There was not a touch of despondency or foreboding about him; and what could she say who knew, had there been ever so much foreboding, that his duty was the thing to be thought of, and not anybody's feelings? Her cheek did not regain its colour all that day, but she kept it to herself, and forgot even about little Hugh's reprieve. The children were dear, but their father was dearer, or at least so it seemed at that moment. Perhaps if the lives of the little ones had been threatened, the Major's expedition might have bulked smaller—for the heart can hold only one overwhelming emotion at a time. But the affair was urgent, and Mary did not have very much time left to her to think of it. Almost before she had realized what it was, the drums had beat, and the brisk music of the band—that music that people called exhilarating—had roused all the station, and the measured march of the men had sounded past, as if they were all treading upon her heart. The Major kissed his little boys in their beds, for it was, to be sure, unnaturally early, as everything is in India; and he had made his wife promise to go and lie down, and take care of herself, when he was gone. "Have the baby, and don't think any more of me than you can help, and take care of my boys. We shall be back sooner than you want us," the Major had said, as he took tender leave of his "bonnie Mary." And for her part, she stood as long as she could see them, with her two white lips pressed tight together, waving her hand to her soldier till he was gone out of sight. And then she obeyed him, and lay down and covered her head, and sobbed to herself in the growing light, as the big blazing sun began to touch the horizon. She was sick with pain and terror, and she could not tell why. She had watched him go away before, and had hailed him coming back again, and had known him in hotter conflict than this could be, and wounded, and yet he had taken no great harm. But all that did her little good now; perhaps because her nerves were weaker than usual, from the repeated shocks she had had to bear.

And it was to be expected that Mrs. Kirkman would come to see her, to console her that morning, and put the worst thoughts into her head, But before even Mrs. Kirkman, little Emma Askell came rushing in, with her baby and a bundle, and threw herself at Mary's feet. The Ensign had gone to the wars, and it was the first experience of such a kind that had fallen to the lot of his little baby-wife; and naturally her anxiety told more distinctly upon her than it did upon Mary's ripe soul and frame. The poor little thing was white and cold and shivering, notwithstanding the blazing Indian day that began to lift itself over their heads. She fell down at Mary's feet, forgetting all about the beetles and scorpions which were the horror of her ordinary existence, and clasped her knees, and held Mrs. Ochterlony fast, grasping the bundle and the little waxen baby at the same time in the other arm.

"Do you think they will ever come back?" said poor little Emma. "Oh, Mrs. Ochterlony, tell me. I can bear it if you will tell me the worst. If anything were to happen to Charlie, and me not with him! I never, never, never can live until the news comes. Oh, tell me, do you think they will ever come back?"

"If I did not think they would come back, do you think I could take it so quietly?" said Mary, and she smiled as best she could, and lifted up the poor little girl, and took from her the baby and the bundle, which seemed all one, so closely were they held. Mrs. Ochterlony had deep eyes, which did not show when she had been crying; and she was not young enough to cry in thunder showers, as Emma Askell at eighteen might still be permitted to do; and the very sight of her soothed the young creature's heart. "You know you are a soldier's wife," Mary said; "I think I was as bad as you are the first time the Major left me—but we all get used to it after a few years."

"And he came back?" said Emma, doing all she could to choke a sob.

"He must have come back, or I should not have parted with him this morning," said Mrs. Ochterlony, who had need of all her own strength just at that moment. "Let us see in the meantime what this bundle is, and why you have brought poor baby out in her night-gown. And what a jewel she is to sleep! When my little Willy gets disturbed," said Mary, with a sigh, "he gives none of us any rest. I will make up a bed for her here on the sofa; and now tell me what this bundle is for, and why you have rushed out half dressed. We'll talk about them presently. Tell me first about yourself."

Upon which Emma hung down her pretty little head, and began to fold a hem upon her damp handkerchief, and did not know how to explain herself. "Don't be angry with me," she said. "Oh, my Madonna, let me come and stay with you!—that was what I meant; I can't stay there by myself—and I will nurse Willy, and do your hair and help sewing. I don't mind what I do. Oh, Mrs. Ochterlony, don't send me away! I should die if I were alone. And as for baby, she never troubles anybody. She is so good. I will be your little servant, and wait upon you like a slave, if you will only let me stay."

It would be vain to say that Mrs. Ochterlony was pleased by this appeal, for she was herself in a very critical state of mind, full of fears that she could give no reason for, and a hundred fantastic pains which she would fain have hidden from human sight. She had been taking a little comfort in the thought of the solitude, the freedom from visitors and disturbance, that she might safely reckon on, and in which she thought her mind might perhaps recover a little; and this young creature's society was not specially agreeable to her. But she was touched by the looks of the forlorn girl, and could no more have sent her away than she could repress the little movement of impatience and half disgust that rose in her heart. She was not capable of giving her an effusive welcome; but she kissed poor little Emma, and put the bundle beside the baby on the sofa, and accepted her visitor without saying anything about it. Perhaps it did her no harm: though she felt by moments as if her impatient longing to be alone and silent, free to think her own thoughts, would break out in spite of all her self-control. But little Mrs. Askell never suspected the existence of any such emotions. She thought, on the contrary, that it was because Mary was used to it that she took it so quietly, and wondered whether she would ever get used to it. Perhaps, on the whole, Emma hoped not. She thought to herself that Mrs. Ochterlony, who was so little disturbed by the parting, would not feel the joy of the return half so much as she should; and on these terms she preferred to take the despair along with the joy. But under the shadow of Mary's matronly presence the little thing cheered up, and got back her courage. After she had been comforted with tea, and had fully realized her position as Mrs. Ochterlony's visitor, Emma's spirits rose. She was half or quarter Irish, as has been already mentioned, and behaved herself accordingly. She recollected her despair, it is true, in the midst of a game with Hugh and Islay, and cried a little, but soon comforted herself with the thought that at that moment her Charlie could be in no danger. "They'll be stopping somewhere for breakfast by a well, and camping all about, and they can't get any harm there," said Emma; and thus she kept chattering all day. If she had chattered only, and been content with chattering, it would have been comparatively easy work; but then she was one of those people who require answers, and will be spoken to. And Mary had to listen and reply, and give her opinion where they would be now, and when, at the very earliest, they might be expected back. With such a discipline to undergo, it may be thought a supererogation to bring Mrs. Kirkman in upon her that same morning with her handkerchief in her hand, prepared, if it were necessary, to weep with Mary. But still it is the case that Mrs. Kirkman did come, as might have been expected; and to pass over conversation so edifying as hers, would, under such circumstances, be almost a crime.

"My dear Mary," Mrs. Kirkman said when she came in, "I am so glad to see you up and making an effort; it is so much better than giving way. We must accept these trials as something sent for our good. I am sure the Major has all our prayers for his safe return. Oh, Mary, do you not remember what I said to you—that God, I was sure, was not going to let you alone?"

"I never thought He would leave me alone," said Mrs. Ochterlony; but certainly, though it was a right enough sentiment, it was not uttered in a right tone of voice.

"He will not rest till you see your duty more clearly," said her visitor; "if it were not for that, why should He have sent you so many things one after another? It is far better and more blessed than if He had made you happy and comfortable as the carnal heart desires. But I did not see you had any one with you," said Mrs. Kirkman, stopping short at the sight of Emma, who had just come into the room.

"Poor child, she was frightened and unhappy, and came to me this morning," said Mary. "She will stay with me—till—they come home."

"Let us say if they come home," said Mrs. Kirkman, solemnly. "I never like to be too certain. We know when they go forth, but who can tell when they will come back. That is in God's hands."

At this speech Emma fell trembling and shivering again, and begged Mrs. Kirkman to tell her the worst, and cried out that she could bear it. She thought of nothing but her Charlie, as was natural, and that the Colonel's wife had already heard some bad news. And Mrs. Kirkman thought of nothing but improving the occasion; and both of them were equally indifferent, and indeed unaware of the cold shudder which went through Mary, and the awful foreboding that closed down upon her, putting out the sunshine. It was a little safeguard to her to support the shivering girl who already half believed herself a widow, and to take up the challenge of the spiritual teacher who felt herself responsible for their souls.

"Do not make Emma think something is wrong," she said. "It is so easy to make a young creature wretched with a word. If the Colonel had been with them, it might have been different. But it is easy just now for you to frighten us. I am sure you do not mean it." And then Mary had to whisper in the young wife's ear, "She knows nothing about them—it is only her way," which was a thing very easily said to Emma, but very difficult to establish herself upon in her own heart.

And then Mrs. Hesketh came in to join the party.

"So they are gone," the new-comer said. "What a way little Emma is in, to be sure. Is it the first time he has ever left you, my dear? and I daresay they have been saying something dreadful to frighten you. It is a great shame to let girls marry so young. I have been reckoning," said the easy-minded woman, whose husband was also of the party, "how long they are likely to be. If they get to Amberabad, say to-morrow, and if there is nothing very serious, and all goes well, you know, they might be back here on Saturday—and we had an engagement for Saturday," Mrs. Hesketh said. Her voice was quite easy and pleasant, as it always was; but nevertheless, Mary knew that if she had not felt excited, she would not have paid such an early morning visit, and that even her confident calculation about the return proved she was in a little anxiety about it. The fact was, that none of them were quite at their ease, except Mrs. Kirkman, who, having no personal interest in the matter, was quite equal to taking a very gloomy view of affairs.

"How can any one think of such vanities at such a moment?" Mrs. Kirkman said. "Oh, if I could only convince you, my dear friends. None of us can tell what sort of engagement they may have before next Saturday—perhaps the most solemn engagement ever given to man. Don't let misfortune find you in this unprepared state of mind. There is nothing on earth so solemn as seeing soldiers go away. You may think of the band and all that, but for me, I always seem to hear a voice saying, 'Prepare to meet your God.'"

To be sure the Colonel was in command of the station and was safe at home, and his wife could speculate calmly upon the probable fate of the detachment. But as for the three women who were listening to her, it was not so easy for them. There was a dreadful pause, for nobody could contradict such a speech; and poor little Emma dropped down sobbing on the floor; and the colour forsook even Mrs. Hesketh's comely cheek; and as for Mary, though she could not well be paler, her heart seemed to contract and shrink within her; and none of them had the courage to say anything. Naturally Mrs. Hesketh, with whom it was a principle not to fret, was the first to recover her voice.

"After all, though it's always an anxious time, I don't see any particular reason we have to be uneasy," she said. "Hesketh told me he felt sure they would give in at once. It may be very true all you say, but at the same time we may be reasonable, you know, and not take fright when there is no cause for it. Don't cry, Emma, you little goose; you'll have him back again in two or three days, all right."

And after awhile the anxious little assembly broke up, and Mrs. Hesketh, who though she was very liberal in her way, was not much given to personal charities, went to see some of the soldiers' wives, who, poor souls, would have been just as anxious if they had had the time for it, and gave them the best advice about their children, and promised tea and sugar if they would come to fetch it, and old frocks, in which she was always rich; and these women were so ungrateful as to like her visit better than that of the Colonel's wife, who carried them always on her heart and did them a great deal of good, and never confined herself to kindness of impulse. And little Emma Askell cried herself to sleep sitting on the floor, notwithstanding the beetles, reposing her pretty face flushed with weeping and her swollen eyes upon the sofa, where Mary sat and watched over her. Mrs. Hesketh got a little ease out of her visit to the soldiers' wives, and Emma forgot her troubles in sleep; but no sort of relief came to Mary, who reasoned with herself all day long without being able to deliver herself from the pressure of the deadly cold hand that seemed to have been laid upon her heart.

CHAPTER IX

And Mary's forebodings came true. Though it was so unlikely, and indeed seemed so unreasonable to everybody who knew about such expeditions, instead of bringing back his men victorious, it was the men, all drooping and discouraged, who carried back the brave and tender Major, covered over with the flag he had died for. The whole station was overcast with mourning when that melancholy procession came back. Mr. Churchill, who met them coming in, hurried back with his heart swelling up into his throat to prepare Mrs. Ochterlony for what was coming; but Mary was the only creature at the station who did not need to be prepared. She knew it was going to be so when she saw him go away. She felt in her heart that this was to be the end of it from the moment when he first told her of the expedition on which he was ordered. And when she saw poor Mr. Churchill's face, from which he had vainly tried to banish the traces of the horrible shock he had just received, she saw that the blow had fallen. She came up to him and took hold of his hands, and said, "I know what it is;" and almost felt, in the strange and terrible excitement of the moment, as if she were sorry for him who felt it so much.

This was how it was, and all the station was struck with mourning. A chance bullet, which most likely had been fired without any purpose at all, had done its appointed office in Major Ochterlony's brave, tender, honest bosom. Though he had been foolish enough by times, nobody now thought of that to his disadvantage. Rather, if anything, it surrounded him with a more affectionate regret. A dozen wise men might have perished and not left such a gap behind them as the Major did, who had been good to everybody in his restless way, and given a great deal of trouble, and made up for it, as only a man with a good heart and natural gift of friendliness could do. He had worried his men many a time as the Colonel never did, for example; but then, to Major Ochterlony they were men and fine fellows, while they were only machines, like himself, to Colonel Kirkman; and more than one critic in regimentals was known to say with a sigh, "If it had only been the Colonel." But it was only the fated man who had been so over-careful about his wife's fate in case anything happened to him. Young Askell came by stealth like a robber to take his little wife out of the house where Mary was not capable any longer of her society; and Captain Hesketh too had come back all safe—all of them except the one: and the women in their minds stood round Mary in a kind of hushed circle, looking with an awful fellow-feeling and almost self-reproach at the widowhood which might have, but had not, fallen upon themselves. It was no fault of theirs that she had to bear the cross for all of them as it were; and yet their hearts ached over her, as if somehow they had purchased their own exemption at her expense. When the first dark moment, during which nobody saw Madonna Mary—a sweet title which had come back to all their lips in the hour of trouble—was over, they took turns to be with her, those grieved and compunctious women—compunctious not so much because at one time in thought they had done her wrong, as because now they were happy and she was sorrowful. And thus passed over a time that cannot be described in a book, or at least in such a book as this. Mary had to separate herself, with still the bloom of her life unimpaired, from all the fair company of matrons round her; to put the widow's veil over the golden reflections in her hair, and the faint colour that came faintly back to her cheek by imprescriptible right of her health and comparative youth, and to go away out of the high-road of life where she had been wayfaring in trouble and in happiness, to one of those humble by-ways where the feeble and broken take shelter. Heaven knows she did not think of that. All that she thought of was her dead soldier who had gone away in the bloom of his days to the unknown darkness which God alone knows the secrets of, who had left all his comrades uninjured and at peace behind him, and had himself been the only one to answer for that enterprise with his life. It is strange to see this wonderful selection going on in the world, even when one has no immediate part in it; but stranger, far stranger, to wake up from one's musings and feel all at once that it is one's self whom God has laid his hand upon for this stern purpose. The wounded creature may writhe upon the sword, but it is of no use; and again as ever, those who are not wounded—those perhaps for whose instruction the spectacle is made—draw round in a hushed circle and look on. Mary Ochterlony was a dutiful woman, obedient and submissive to God's will; and she gave no occasion to that circle of spectators to break up the hush and awe of natural sympathy and criticise her how she bore it. But after a while she came to perceive, what everybody comes to perceive who has been in such a position, that the sympathy had changed its character. That was natural too. How a man bears death and suffering of body, has long been one of the favourite objects of primitive human curiosity; and to see how anguish and sorrow affect the mind is a study as exciting and still more interesting. It was this that roused Mrs. Ochterlony out of her first stupor, and made her decide so soon as she did upon her journey home.

All these events had passed in so short a time, that there were many people who on waking up in the morning, and recollecting that Mary and her children were going next day, could scarcely realize that the fact was possible, or that it could be true about the Major, who had so fully intended sending his little boys home by that same mail. But it is, on the whole, astonishing how soon and how calmly a death is accepted by the general community; and even the people who asked themselves could this change really have happened in so short a time, took pains an hour or two after to make up little parcels for friends at home, which Mary was to carry; bits of Oriental embroidery and filagree ornaments, and little portraits of the children, and other trifles that were not important enough to warrant an Overland parcel, or big enough to go by the Cape. Mary was very kind in that way, they all said. She accepted all kinds of commissions, perhaps without knowing very well what she was doing, and promised to go and see people whom she had no likelihood of ever going to see; the truth was, that she heard and saw and understood only partially, sometimes rousing up for a moment and catching one word or one little incident with the intensest distinctness, and then relapsing back again into herself. She did not quite make out what Emma Askell was saying the last time her little friend came to see her. Mary was packing her boys' things at the moment, and much occupied with a host of cares, and what she heard was only a stream of talk, broken with the occasional burden which came in like a chorus "when you see mamma."

"When I see mamma?" said Mary, with a little surprise.

"Dear Mrs. Ochterlony, you said you would perhaps go to see her—in St. John's Wood," said Emma, with tears of vexation in her eyes; "you know I told you all about it. The Laburnums, Acacia-road. And she will be so glad to see you. I explained it all, and you said you would go. I told her how kind you had been to me, and how you let me stay with you when I was so anxious about Charlie. Oh, dear Mrs. Ochterlony, forgive me! I did not mean to bring it back to your mind."

"No," said Mary, with a kind of forlorn amusement. It seemed so strange, almost droll, that they should think any of their poor little passing words would bring that back to her which was never once out of her mind, nor other than the centre of all her thoughts. "I must have been dreaming when I said so, Emma: but if I have promised, I will try to go—I have nothing to do in London, you know—I am going to the North-country, among my own people," which was an easier form of expression than to say, as they all did, that she was going home.

"But everybody goes to London," insisted Emma; and it was only when Mr. Churchill came in, also with a little packet, that the ensign's wife was silenced. Mr. Churchill's parcel was for his mother who lived in Yorkshire, naturally, as Mrs. Ochterlony was going to the North, quite in her way. But the clergyman, for his part, had something more important to say. When Mrs. Askell was gone, he stopped Mary in her packing to speak to her seriously as he said, "You will forgive me and feel for me, I know," he said. "It is about your second marriage, Mrs. Ochterlony."

"Don't speak of it—oh, don't speak of it," Mary said, with an imploring tone that went to his heart.

"But I ought to speak of it—if you can bear it," said Mr. Churchill, "and I know for the boys' sake that you can bear everything. I have brought an extract from the register, if you would like to have it; and I have added below—"

"Mr. Churchill, you are very kind, but I don't want ever to think of that," said Mrs. Ochterlony. "I don't want to recollect now that such a thing ever took place—I wish all record of it would disappear from the face of the earth. Afterwards he thought the same," she said, hurriedly. Meanwhile Mr. Churchill stood with the paper half drawn from his pocket-book, watching the changes of her face.

"It shall be as you like," he said, slowly, "but only as I have written below—If you change your mind, you have only to write to me, my dear Mrs. Ochterlony—if I stay here—and I am sure I don't know if I shall stay here; but in case I don't, you can always learn where I am, from my mother at that address."

"Do you think you will not stay here?" said Mary, whose heart was not so much absorbed in her own sorrows that she could not feel for the dismayed, desponding mind that made itself apparent in the poor clergyman's voice.

"I don't know," he said, in the dreary tones of a man who has little choice, "with our large family, and my wife's poor health. I shall miss you dreadfully—both of you: you can't think how cheery and hearty he always was—and that to a down-hearted man like me—"

And then Mary sat down and cried. It went to her heart and dispersed all her heaviness and stupor, and opened the great sealed fountains. And Mr. Churchill once more felt the climbing sorrow in his throat, and said in broken words, "Don't cry—God will take care of you. He knows why He has done it, though we don't; and He has given his own word to be a father to the boys."

That was all the poor priest could find it in his heart to say—but it was better than a sermon—and he went away with the extract from the register still in his pocket-book and tears in his eyes; while for her part Mary finished her packing with a heart relieved by her tears. Ah, how cheery and hearty he had been, how kind to the down-hearted man; how different the stagnant quietness now from that cheerful commotion he used to make, and all the restless life about him; and then his favourite words seemed to come up about and surround her, flitting in the air with a sensation between acute torture and a dull happiness. His bonnie Mary! It was not any vanity on Mary's part that made her think above all of that name. Thus she did her packing and got ready for her voyage, and took the good people's commissions without knowing very well to what it was that she pledged herself; and it was the same mail—"the mail after next"—by which she had written to Aunt Agatha that Hugh was to be sent home.

They would all have come to see her off if they could have ventured to do it that last morning; but the men prevented it, who are good for something now and then in such cases. As it was, however, Mrs. Kirkman and Mrs. Hesketh and Emma Askell were there, and poor sick Mrs. Churchill, who had stolen from her bed in her dressing-gown to kiss Mary for the last time.

"Oh, my dear, if it had been me—oh, if it had only been me!—and you would all have been so good to the poor children," sobbed the poor clergyman's ailing wife. Yet it was not her, but the strong, brave, cheery Major, the prop and pillar of a house. As for Mrs. Kirkman, there never was a better proof that she was, as we have so often said, in spite of her talk, a good woman, than the fact that she could only cry helplessly over Mary, and had not a word to say. She had thought and prayed that God would not leave her friend alone, but she had not meant Him to go so far as this; and her heart ached and fluttered at the terrible notion that perhaps she had something to do with the striking of this blow. Mrs. Hesketh for her part packed every sort of dainties for the children in a basket, and strapped on a bundle of portable toys to amuse them on the journey, to one of Mrs. Ochterlony's boxes. "You will be glad of them before you get there," said the experienced woman, who had once made the journey with half-a-dozen, as she said, and knew what it was. And then one or two of the men were walking about outside in an accidental sort of way, to have a last look of Mary. It was considered a very great thing among them all when the doctor, who hated to see people in trouble, and disapproved of crying on principle, made up his mind to go in and shake hands with Mrs. Ochterlony; but it was not that he went for, but to look at the baby, and give Mary a little case "with some sal volatile and so forth, and the quantities marked," he said, "not that you are one to want sal volatile. The little shaver there will be all right as soon as you get to England. Good-bye. Take care of yourself." And he wrung her hand and bolted out again like a flash of lightning. He said afterwards that the only sensible thing he knew of his sister, was that she did not go; and that the sight of all those women crying was enough to give a man a sunstroke, not to speak of the servants and the soldiers' wives who were howling at the back of the house.

Oh, what a change it was in so short a time, to go out of the Indian home, which had been a true home, with Mr. Churchill to take care of her and her poor babies, and set her face to the cold far-away world of her youth which she had forgotten, and which everybody called home by a kind of mockery; and where was Hugh, who had always taken such care of his own? Mary did not cry as people call crying, but now and then, two great big hot tears rolled out of the bitter fountain that was full to overflowing, and fell scalding on her hands, and gave her a momentary sense of physical relief. Almost all the ladies of the station were ill after it all the day; but Mary could not afford to be ill; and Mr. Churchill was very kind, and went with her through all the first part of her journey over the cross roads, until she had come into the trunk road, where there was no more difficulty. He was very, very kind, and she was very grateful; but yet perhaps when you have had some one of your very own to do everything for you, who was not kind but did it by nature, it is better to take to doing it yourself after, than have even the best of friends to do it for kindness' sake. This was what Mary felt when the good man had gone sadly back to his sick wife and his uncertain lot. It was a kind of relief to her to be all alone, entirely alone with her children, for the ayah, to be sure, did not count—and to have everything to do; and this was how they came down mournfully to the sea-board, and to the big town which filled Hugh and Islay with childish excitement, and Mary bade an everlasting farewell to her life, to all that she had actually known as life—and got to sea, to go, as they said, home.

It would be quite useless for our purpose to go over the details of the voyage, which was like other voyages, bad and good by turns. When she was at sea, Mrs. Ochterlony had a little leisure, and felt ill and weak and overworn, and was the better for it after. It took her mind for the moment off that unmeasured contemplation of her sorrow which is the soul of grief, and her spirit got a little strength in the interval of repose. She had been twelve years in India, and from eighteen to thirty is a wonderful leap in a life. She did not know how she was to find the things and the people of whom she had a girl's innocent recollection; nor how they, who had not changed, would appear to her changed eyes. Her own people were very kind, like everybody. Mary found a letter at Gibraltar from her brother-in-law, Francis, full of sympathy and friendly offers. He asked her to come to Earlston with her boys to see if they could not get on together. "Perhaps it might not do, but it would be worth a trial," Mr. Ochterlony sensibly said; and there was even a chance that Aunt Agatha, who was to have met with Hugh at Southampton, would come to meet her widowed niece, who might be supposed to stand still more in need of her good offices. Though indeed this was rather an addition to Mary's cares; for she thought the moment of landing would be bitter enough of itself, without the pain of meeting with some one who belonged to her, and yet did not belong to her, and who had doubtless grown as much out of the Aunt Agatha of old as she had grown out of the little Mary. When Mrs. Ochterlony left the North-country, Aunt Agatha had been a middle-aged maiden lady, still pretty, though a little faded, with light hair growing grey, which makes a woman's countenance, already on the decline, more faded still, and does not bring out the tints as dark hair in the same powdery condition sometimes does. And at that time she was still occupied by a thought of possibilities which people who knew Agatha Seton from the time she was sixteen, had decided at that early period to be impossible. No doubt twelve years had changed this—and it must have made a still greater change upon the little sister whom Mary had known only at six years old, and who was now eighteen, the age she had herself been when she married; a grown-up young woman, and of a character more decided than Mary's had ever been.

A little stir of reviving life awoke in her and moved her, when the weary journey was over, and the steam-boat at length had reached Southampton, to go up to the deck and look from beneath the heavy pent-house of her widow's veil at the strangers who were coming—to see, as she said to herself, with a throb at her heart, if there was anybody she knew. Aunt Agatha was not rich, and it was a long journey, and perhaps she had not come. Mary stood on the crowded deck, a little apart, with Hugh and Islay on each side of her, and the baby in his nurse's arms—a group such as is often seen on these decks—all clad with loss and mourning, coming "home" to a country in which perhaps they have no longer any home. Nobody came to claim Mrs. Ochterlony as she stood among her little children. She thought she would have been glad of that, but when it came to the moment—when she saw the cold unknown shore and the strange country, and not a Christian soul to say welcome, poor Mary's heart sank. She sat down, for her strength was failing her, and drew Hugh and Islay close to her, to keep her from breaking down altogether. And it was just at that moment that the brightest of young faces peered down under her veil and looked doubtfully, anxiously at her, and called out impatiently, "Aunt Agatha!" to some one at the other side, without speaking to Mary. Mrs. Ochterlony did not hear this new-comer's equally impatient demand: "Is it Mary? Are those the children?" for she had dropped her sick head upon a soft old breast, and had an old fresh sweet faded face bent down upon her, lovely with love and age, and a pure heart. "Cry, my dear love, cry, it will do you good," was all that Aunt Agatha said. And she cried, too, with good will, and yet did not know whether it was for sorrow or joy. This was how Mary, coming back to a fashion of existence which she knew not, was taken home.

CHAPTER X

Aunt Agatha had grown into a sweet old lady: not so old, perhaps, but that she might have made up still into that elderly aspirant after youth, for whose special use the name "old maid" must have been invented. And yet there is a sweetness in the name, and it was not inapplicable to the fair old woman, who received Mary Ochterlony into her kind arms. There was a sort of tender misty consciousness upon her age, just as there is a tender unconsciousness in youth, of so many things that cannot but come to the knowledge of people who have eaten of the tree in the middle of the garden. She was surrounded by the unknown as was seemly to such a maiden soul. And yet she was old, and gleams of experience, and dim knowledge at second hand, had come to her from those misty tracts. Though she had not, and never could have, half the vigour or force in her which Mary had even in her subdued and broken state, still she had strength of affection and goodness enough to take the management of all affairs into her hands for the moment, and to set herself at the head of the little party. She took Mary and the children from the ship, and brought them to the inn at which she had stayed the night before; and, what was a still greater achievement, she repressed Winnie, and kept her in a semi-subordinate and silent state—which was an effort which taxed all Aunt Agatha's powers. Though it may seem strange to say it, Mary and her young sister did not, as people say, take to each other at that first meeting. It was twelve years since they had met, and the eighteen-year-old young woman, accustomed to be a sovereign among her own people, and have all her whims attended to, did not, somehow, commend herself to Mary, who was broken, and joyless, and feeble, and little capable of glitter and motion. Aunt Agatha took the traveller to a cool room, where comparative quiet was to be had, and took off her heavy bonnet and cloak, and made her lie down, and came and sat by her. The children were in the next room, where the sound of their voices could reach their mother to keep her heart; and then Aunt Agatha took Mary's hand in both of hers, and said, "Tell me about it, my dear love." It was a way she had of speaking, but yet such words are sweet; especially to a forlorn creature who has supposed that there is nobody left in the world to address her so. And then Mary told her sad story with all the details that women love, and cried till the fountain of tears was for the time exhausted, and grief itself by its very vehemence had got calm; which was, as Aunt Agatha knew by instinct, the best way to receive a poor woman who was a widow, and had just set her solitary feet for the first time upon the shores which she left as a bride.

And so they rested and slept that first night on English soil. There are moments when sorrow feels sacramental, and as if it never could be disturbed again by the pettier emotions of life. Mrs. Ochterlony had gone to sleep in this calm, and it was with something of the same feeling that she awoke. As if life, as she thought, being over, its cares were in some sense over too, and that now nothing could move her further; unless, indeed, it might be any harm to the children, which, thank God, there was no appearance of. In this state of mind she rose up and said her prayers, mingling them with some of those great tears which gather one by one as the heart fills, and which seem to give a certain physical relief when they brim over; and then she went to join her aunt and sister at breakfast, where they had not expected to see her. "My love, I would have brought you your tea," said Aunt Agatha, with a certain reproach; and when Mary smiled and said there was no need, even Winnie's heart was touched,—wilful Winnie in her black muslin gown, who was a little piqued to feel herself in the company of one more interesting than even she was, and hated herself for it, and yet could not help feeling as if Mary had come in like the prodigal, to be feasted and tended, while they never even killed a kid for her who had always been at home.

Winnie was eighteen, and she was not like her sister. She was tall, but not like Mary's tallness—a long slight slip of a girl, still full of corners. She had corners at her elbows, and almost at her shoulders, and a great many corners in her mind. She was not so much a pretty girl as a girl who would, or might be, a beautiful woman. Her eyebrows were arched, and so were her delicate nostrils, and her upper lip—all curved and moveable, and ready to quiver and speak when it was needful. When you saw her face in profile, that outline seemed to cut itself out, as in some warm marble against the background. It was not the beauté du diable, the bewildering charm of youth, and freshness, and smiles, and rose tints. She had something of all this, and to boot she had features—beaux traits. But as for this part of her power, Winnie, to do her justice, thought nothing of it; perhaps, to have understood that people minded what she said, and noticed what she did because she was very handsome, would have conveyed something like an insult and affront to the young lady. She did not care much, nor mind much at the present moment, whether she was pretty or not. She had no rivals, and beauty was a weapon the importance of which had not occurred to her. But she did care a good deal for being Winifred Seton, and as such, mistress of all she surveyed; and though she could have beaten herself for it, it galled her involuntarily to find herself thus all at once in the presence of a person whom Providence seemed to have set, somehow, in a higher position, and who was more interesting than herself. It was a wicked thought, and she did it battle. If it had been left to her, how she could have petted and cared for Mary, how she would have borne her triumphantly over all the fatigues of the journey, and thought nothing to take the tickets, and mind the luggage, and struggle with the railway porters for Mary's sake! But to have Mary come in and absorb Aunt Agatha's and everybody's first look, their first appeal and principal regard, was trying to Winnie; and she had never learned yet to banish altogether from her eyes what she thought.

"It does not matter, aunt," said Mary; "I cannot make a recluse of myself—I must go among strangers—and it is well to be able to practise a little with Winnie and you."

"You must not mind Winnie and me, my darling," said Aunt Agatha, who had a way of missing the arrow, as it were, and catching some of the feathers of it as it flew past.

"What do you mean about going among strangers?" said the keener Winnie. "I hope you don't think we are strangers; and there is no need for you to go into society that I can see—not now at least; or at all events not unless you like," she continued with a suspicion of sharpness in her tone, not displeased, perhaps, on the whole that Mary was turning out delusive, and was thinking already of society—for which notwithstanding she scorned her sister, as was natural to a young woman at the experienced age of eighteen.

"Society is not what I was thinking of," said Mary, who in her turn did not like her young sister's criticism; and she took her seat and her cup of tea with an uncomfortable sense of opposition. She had thought that she could not be annoyed any more by petty matters, and was incapable of feeling the little cares and complications of life, and yet it was astonishing how Winnie's little, sharp, half-sarcastic tone brought back the faculty of being annoyed.

"The little we have at Kirtell will be a comfort to you, my love," said the soothing voice of Aunt Agatha; "all old friends. The vicar you know, Mary, and the doctor, and poor Sir Edward. There are some new people, but I do not make much account of them; and our little visiting would harm nobody," the old lady said, though with a slight tone of apology, not quite satisfied in herself that the widow should be even able to think of society so soon.

Upon which a little pucker of vexation came to Mary's brow. As if she cared or could care for their little visiting, and the vicar, and the doctor, and Sir Edward! she to whom going among strangers meant something so real and so hard to bear.

"Dear Aunt Agatha," she said, "I am afraid you will not be pleased; but I have not been looking forward to anything so pleasant as going to Kirtell. The first thing I have to think of is the boys and their interests. And Francis Ochterlony has asked us to go to Earlston." These words came all confused from Mary's lips. She broke down, seeing what was coming; for this was something that she never had calculated on, or thought of having to bear.

A dead pause ensued; Aunt Agatha started and flushed all over, and gave an agitated exclamation, and then a sudden blank came upon her sweet old face. Mary did not look at her, but she saw without looking how her aunt stiffened into resentment, and offence, and mortification. She changed in an instant, as if Mrs. Ochterlony's confused statement had been a spell, and drew herself up and sat motionless, a picture of surprised affection and wounded pride. Poor Mary saw it, and was grieved to the heart, and yet could not but resent such a want of understanding of her position and sympathy for herself. She lifted her cup to her lips with a trembling hand, and her tea did not refresh her. And it was the only near relative she had in the world, the tenderest-hearted creature in existence, a woman who could be cruel to nobody, who thus shut up her heart against her. Thus the three women sat together round their breakfast-table, and helped each other, and said nothing for one stern moment, which was a cruel moment for one of them at least.

"Earlston!" said Aunt Agatha at last, with a quiver in her voice. "Indeed it never occurred to me—I had not supposed that Francis Ochterlony had been so much to—But never mind; if that is what you think best for yourself, Mary—"

"There is nothing best for myself," said Mrs. Ochterlony, with the sharpness of despair. "I think it is my duty—and—and Hugh, I know, would have thought so. Our boy is his uncle's heir. They are the—the only Ochterlonys left now. It is what I must—what I ought to do."

And then there was another pause. Aunt Agatha for her part would have liked to cry, but then she had her side of the family to maintain, and though every pulse in her was beating with disappointment and mortified affection, she was not going to show that. "You must know best," she said, taking up her little air of dignity; "I am sure you must know best; I would never try to force my way of thinking on you, Mary. No doubt you have been more in the world than I have; but I did think when a woman was in trouble that to go among her own friends—"

"Yes," said Mary, who was overwhelmed, and did not feel able to bear it, "but her friends might understand her and have a little pity for her, aunt, when she had hard things to do that wrung her heart—"

"My dear," said Aunt Agatha, with, on her side, the bitterness of unappreciated exertion, "if you will think how far I have come, and what an unusual journey I have made, I think you will perceive that to accuse me of want of pity—"

"Don't worry her, Aunt Agatha," said Winnie, "she is not accusing you of want of pity. I think it a very strange sort of thing, myself; but let Mary have justice, that was not what she meant."

"I should like to know what she did mean," said Aunt Agatha, who was trembling with vexation, and with those tears which she wanted so much to shed: and then two or three of them dropped on the broad-brimmed cambric cuff which she was wearing solely on Mary's account. For, to be sure, Major Ochterlony was not to say a relation of hers that she should have worn such deep mourning for him. "I am sure I don't want to interfere, if she prefers Francis Ochterlony to her own friends," she added, with tremulous haste. She was the very same Aunt Agatha who had taken Mary to her arms the day before, and sat by her bed, listening to all the sad story of her widowhood. She had wept for Hugh, and she would have shared her cottage and her garden and all she had with Mary, with goodwill and bounty, eagerly—but Francis Ochterlony was a different matter; and it was not in human nature to bear the preference of a husband's brother to "her own friends." "They may be the last Ochterlonys," said Aunt Agatha, "but I never understood that a woman was to give up her own family entirely; and your sister was born a Seton like you and me, Winnie;—I don't understand it, for my part."

Aunt Agatha broke down when she had said this, and cried more bitterly, more effusively, so long as it lasted, than she had cried last night over Hugh Ochterlony's sudden ending: and Mary could not but feel that; and as for Winnie, she sat silent, and if she did not make things worse, at least she made no effort to make them better. On the whole, it was not much wonder. They had made great changes in the cottage for Mary's sake. Aunt Agatha had given up her parlour, her own pretty room that she loved, for a nursery, and they had made up their minds that the best chamber was to be Mary's, with a sort of sense that the fresh chintz and the pictures on the walls—it was the only bed-room that had any pictures—would make up to her if anything could. And now to find all the time that it was Francis Ochterlony, and not her own friends, that she was going to! Winnie sat quite still, with her fine profile cut out sternly against the dark green wall, looking immovable and unfeeling, as only a profile can under such circumstances. This was what came of Mary's placid morning, and the dear union of family support and love into which she thought she had come. It was harder upon Mrs. Ochterlony than if Aunt Agatha had not come to meet her. She had to sit blank and silent like a criminal, and see the old lady cry and the young lady lift up the stern delicacy of that profile against her. They were disappointed in Mary; and not only were they disappointed, but mortified—wounded in their best feelings and embarrassed in secondary matters as well; for naturally Aunt Agatha had told everybody that she was going to bring her niece, Mrs. Ochterlony, and the poor dear children home.

Thus it will be seen that the first breakfast in England was a very unsatisfactory meal for Mary. She took refuge with her children when it was over, and shut up, as she had been forced to do in other days, another door in her heart; and Aunt Agatha and Winnie, on the other hand, withdrew to their apartment and talked it over, and kindled each other's indignation. "If you knew the kind of man he was, Winnie!" Aunt Agatha said, with a severity which was not entirely on Mary's account; "not the sort of man I would trust those poor dear children with. I don't believe he has any religious principles. Dear, dear, to think how Mary should have changed! I never could have thought she would have preferred Francis Ochterlony, and turned against her own friends."

"I don't know anything about Francis Ochterlony," said Winnie, "but I know what a lot of bother we have had at home making all those changes; and your parlour that you had given up, Aunt Agatha—I must say when I think of that—"

"That is nothing, my love," said Aunt Agatha; "I was not thinking of what I have done, I hope—as if the sacrifice was anything." But nevertheless the tears came into her eyes at the thought. It is hard when one has made a sacrifice with a liberal heart, to have it thrown back, and to feel that it is useless. This is hard, and Aunt Agatha was only human. If she had been alone, probably after the first moment of annoyance she would have gone to Mary, and the two would have cried together, and after little Hugh's prospects had been discussed, Miss Seton would have consented that it was best for her niece to go to Earlston; but then Winnie was there to talk it over and keep up Aunt Agatha's indignation. And Mary was wounded, and had retired and shut herself up among her children. And it was thus that the most trifling and uncalled-for of cares came, with little pricks of vexation and disappointment, to disturb at its very outset the new chapter of life which Mrs. Ochterlony had imagined herself to be entering upon in such a calm of tranquillising grief.

They were to go to London that day, and to continue their journey to the North by the night train: but it was no longer a journey in which any of the party could take any pleasure. As for Mary, in the great revulsion of her disappointment, it seemed to her as if there was no comfort for her anywhere. She had to go to Earlston to accept a home from Francis Ochterlony, whom she had never "taken to," even in her young days. And it had occurred to her that her aunt and sister would understand why, and would be sorry for her, and console her under this painful effort. When, on the contrary, they proved to be affronted and indignant, Mary's heart shut close, and retreated within itself. She could take her children into her arms, and press them against her heart, as if that would do it some good; but she could not talk to the little things, nor consult them, nor share anything with them except such smiles as were practicable. To a woman who has been used to talk all her concerns over with some one, it is terrible to feel her yearnings for counsel and sympathy turned back upon her own soul, and to be struck dumb, and feel that no ear is open to her, and that in all the world there is no one living to whom her affairs are more than the affairs of a stranger. Some poor women there are who must have fellowship somehow, and who will be content with pity if sympathy is not to be had. But Mary was not of this kind of women. She shut her doors. She went in, into herself in the silence and solitude, and felt her instinctive yearning to be helped and understood come pouring back upon her like a bitter flood. And then she looked at her little boys in their play, who had need of all from her, and could give her back but their childish fondness, and no help, or stay, or counsel. It is hard upon a woman, but yet it is a thing which every woman must confront and make up her mind to, whom God places in such circumstances. I do not know if it is easier work for a man in the same position. Mary had felt the prop of expected sympathy and encouragement and affection rudely driven from under her, and when she came in among her innocent helpless children she faced her lot, and did not deceive herself any more. To judge for herself, and do the best in her lay, and take all the responsibilities upon her own head, whatever might follow; to know that nobody now in all the world was for her, or stood by her, except in a very secondary way, after his or her concerns and intentions and feelings had been carefully provided for in the first place. This was how her position appeared to her. And, indeed, such was her position, without any exaggeration. It was very kind of Francis Ochterlony to be willing to take her in, and very kind of Aunt Agatha to have made preparations for her; and kindness is sweet, and yet it is bitter, and hard, and cold, and killing to meet with. It made Mary sick to her heart, and filled her with a longing to take up her babes and rush away into some solitary corner, where nobody would ever see her again or hear of her. I do not say that she was right, or that it was a proper state of mind to be in. And Mary was too right-minded a woman to indulge in it long; but that was the feeling that momentarily took possession of her as she put the doors to in her heart, and realized that she really was alone there, and that her concerns were hers alone, and belonged to nobody else in the world.

And, on the other hand, it was very natural for Aunt Agatha and Winnie. They knew the exertions they had made, and the flutter of generous excitement in which they had been, and their readiness to give up their best for the solace of the widow. And naturally the feeling that all their sacrifices were unnecessary and their preparations made in vain, turned the honey into gall for the moment. It was not their part to take Mary's duty into consideration, in the first place; and they did not know beforehand of Francis Ochterlony's letter, nor the poor Major's confidence that his brother would be a friend to his widow. And then Aunt Agatha's parlour, which was all metamorphosed, and the changes that had been made through the whole house! The result was, that Aunt Agatha, offended, did not so much as offer to her niece the little breathing-time Mary had hoped for. When they got to London, she re-opened the subject, but it was in an unanswerable way.

"I suppose your brother-in-law expects you?" she said. "I think it will be better to wait till to-morrow before you start, that he may send the carriage to the station for you. I don't ask you to come to me for the night, for it would be a pity to derange the children for so short a time."

"Very well, aunt," said Mary, sadly. And she wrote to Mr. Ochterlony, and slept that night in town—her strength almost failing her at the thought that, in her feebleness and excitement, she had to throw herself immediately on Francis Ochterlony's tender mercies. She even paused for a moment to think, might she not really do as her heart suggested—find out some corner of refuge for herself with which nobody could intermeddle, and keep apart from them all? But Mary had come "home to her friends," as everybody said at the station; and she had a woman's prejudices, and it seemed unnatural to her to begin, without any interposition of the people belonging to her, that strange and solitary life of independence or self-dependence which was what she must decide upon some time. And then there was always Mr. Ochterlony's letter, which was so kind. Thus it was fixed by a few words, and could not be changed. Aunt Agatha had a terrible compunction afterwards, and could not get Mary's look out of her head, as she owned to Winnie, and would have got up out of her bed in the middle of the night, and gone to Mary and begged her to come to the cottage first, if it had not been that Winnie might have woke up, and that she would have to cross a passage to Mary's room; and in an hotel where "gentlemen" were continually about, and who could tell whom she might meet? So they all slept, or pretended to sleep, and said nothing about it; and the next day set off with no further explanations, on their way "home."

CHAPTER XI

Earlston is a house which lies in a little green valley among the grey folds of the Shap Fells. It is not an inviting country, though the people love it as people do love everything that belongs to them; and it has a very different aspect from the wooded dell a little farther north, where strays the romantic little Kirtell, and where Aunt Agatha's cottage smiled upon a tufted slope, with the music of the cheery river in its ears day and night. The rivers about Earlston were shallow, and ran dry in summer, though it was not because of any want of rain; and the greyness of the hills made a kind of mist in the air to unaccustomed eyes. Everybody, who has ever gone to the north that way, knows the deep cuttings about Shap, where the railway plunges through between two humid living limestone walls, where the cottages, and the fences, and the farm-houses all lead up in level tones of grey to the vast greyness of the piebald hills, and where the line of pale sky above is grey too in most cases. It was at one of the little stations in this monotonous district that Mrs. Ochterlony and her children and her ayah were deposited—Aunt Agatha, with an aspect of sternness, but a heart that smote her, and eyes that kept filling with tears she was too proud to shed, looking on the while. Winnie looked on too without the compunction, feeling very affronted and angry. They were going further on, and the thought of home was overcast to both these ladies by the fact that everybody would ask for Mary, and that the excitement of the past few weeks would collapse in the dreariest and suddenest way when they were seen to return alone. As for Mary, she looked grey like the landscape, under her heavy veil—grey, silent, in a kind of dull despair, persuading herself that the best thing of all was to say nothing about it, and shut only more closely the doors of that heart where nobody now had any desire to come in. She lifted her little boys out, and did not care even to look if the carriage was waiting for her—and then she came to the window to bid her aunt and sister good-bye. She was so disappointed and sick-hearted, and felt for the moment that the small amount of affection and comprehension which they were capable of giving her was so little worth the trouble of seeking for, that Mary did not even ask to be written to. She put up her pale face, and said good-bye in a dreary unexpectant tone that doubled the compunction in Aunt Agatha's bosom. "Oh, Mary, if you had but been coming with us!" cried that inconsistent woman, on the spur of the moment. "It is too late to speak of it now," said Mary, and kissed her and turned away; and the heartless train dashed off, and carried off Aunt Agatha with that picture in her eyes of the forlorn little group on the platform of the railway station—the two little boys clinging close to their mother, and she standing alone among strangers, with the widow's veil hanging over her colourless face. "Can you see the carriage, Winnie?—look out and tell me if you can see it," said Aunt Agatha. But the engine that carried them on was too quick for Winnie, and had already swept out of sight. And they pursued their journey, feeling guilty and wretched, as indeed, to a certain extent, they deserved to feel. A two months' widow, with a baby and two helpless little boys—and at the best it could only be a servant who had come to meet her, and she would have everything to do for herself, and to face her brother-in-law without any support or helper. When Aunt Agatha thought of this, she sank back in her corner and sobbed. To think that she should have been the one to take offence and be affronted at Mary's first word, and desert her thus: when she might have taken her home and comforted her, and then, if it must have ended so, conveyed her to Earlston: Aunt Agatha cried, and deserved to cry, and even Winnie felt a twinge at her heart; and they got rather angry with each other before they reached home, and felt disposed to accuse each other, and trembled both of them before the idea of meeting Peggy, Miss Seton's domestic tyrant, who would rush to the door with her heart in her mouth to receive "our Miss Mary and the puir dear fatherless bairns." Mary might be silent about it, and never complain of unkindness; but it was not to be expected that Peggy would have the same scruples; and these two guilty and miserable travellers trembled at the thought of her as they made their wretched way home.

When the train had disappeared, Mary tried to take a kind of cold comfort to herself. She stood all alone, a stranger, with the few rustic passengers and rustic railway officials staring at her as if she had dropped from the skies, and no apparent sign anywhere that her coming had been looked for, or that there was any resting-place for her in this grey country. And she said to herself that it was natural, and must always be so henceforth, and that it was best at once to accustom herself to her lot. The carriage had not come, nor any message from Earlston to say she was expected, and all that she could do was to go into the rude little waiting-room, and wait there with the tired children till some conveyance could be got to take her to her brother-in-law's house. Her thoughts would not be pleasant to put down on paper, could it be done; and yet they were not so painful as they had been the day before, when Aunt Agatha failed her, or seemed to fail. Now that disappointed craving for help and love and fellowship was over for the moment, and she had nothing but her own duty and Francis Ochterlony to encounter, who was not a man to give any occasion for vain hopes. Mary did not expect fellowship or love from her brother-in-law. If he was kind and tolerant of the children, and moderately considerate to herself, it was all she looked for from him. Perhaps, though he had invited her, he had not been prepared to have her thrown on his hands so soon; and it might be that the domestic arrangements of Earlston were not such as to admit of the unlooked-for invasion of a lady and a nursery on such very short notice. But the most prominent feeling in Mrs. Ochterlony's mind was weariness, and that longing to escape anywhere, which is the most universal of all sentiments when the spirit is worn out and sick to death. Oh, that she had wings like a dove!—though Mary had nowhere to flee to, nobody to seek consolation from; and instead of having a home anywhere on earth awaiting her, was herself the home, the only shelter they understood, of the little pale fatherless children who clustered round her. If she could but have taken possession of one of those small cottages, grey and homely as they looked, and put the little ones to bed in it, and drawn a wooden chair to the fire, and been where she had a right to be! It was July, but the weather was cold at Shap, and Mary had that instinct common to wounded creatures of creeping to the fire, as if there was a kind of comfort in its warmth. She could have borne her burden bravely, or at least she thought so, if this had been what awaited her. But it was Earlston and Francis Ochterlony that awaited her—a stranger and a stranger's house. All these thoughts, and many more, were passing through her mind, as she sat in the little waiting-room with her baby in her arms, and her two elder boys pressing close to her. The children clung and appealed to her, and the helpless Hindoo woman crouched at her mistress's side; but as for Mary, there was nobody to give her any support or countenance. It was a hard opening to the stern way which had henceforward to be trodden alone.

Francis Ochterlony, however, though he had a certain superb indifference to the going-out and coming-in of trains, and had forgotten the precise hour, was not a wretch nor a brute, and had not forgotten his visitors. While Mary sat and waited, and while the master of the little station made slow but persevering search after some possible means of conveyance for her, a heavy rumbling of wheels became audible, and the carriage from Earlston made its tardy appearance. It was an old-fashioned vehicle, drawn by two horses, which betrayed their ordinary avocations much in the same way as the coachman did, who, though dressed, as they were, for the occasion, carried a breath of the fields about him, which was more convincing than any conventionalism of garments. But such as it was, the Earlston carriage was not without consideration in the country-side. All the people about turned out in a leisurely way to lift the children into it, and shoulder the boxes into such corners as could be found for them—which was an affair that demanded many counsellors—and at length the vehicle got under way. Twilight began to come on as they mounted up into the grey country, by the winding grey roads fenced in with limestone walls. Everything grew greyer in the waning light. The very trees, of which there were so few, dropped into the gathering shadows, and deepened them without giving any livelier tint of colour to the scene. The children dropped asleep, and the ayah crooned and nodded over the baby; but Mary, who had no temptation to sleep, looked out with steady eyes, and, though she saw nothing distinctly, took in unawares all the comfortless chill and monotony of the landscape. It went to her heart, and made her shiver. Or perhaps it was only the idea of meeting Francis Ochterlony that made her shiver. If the children, any one of them, had only been old enough to understand it a little, to clasp her hand or her neck with the exuberance of childish sympathy! But they did not understand, and dropped asleep, or asked with timid, quivering little voices, how long it would be before they got home. Home! no wonder Mrs. Ochterlony was cold, and felt the chill go to her heart. Thus they went on for six or seven weary miles, taking as many hours, as Mary thought. Aunt Agatha had arrived at her cottage, though it was nearly thirty miles further on, while the comfortless party were still jogging along in the Earlston carriage; but Mary did not think particularly of that. She did not think at all, poor soul. She saw the grey hill-side gliding past her, and in a vague way, at the same moment, seemed to see herself, a bride, going gaily past on the same road, and rehearsed all the past over again with a dull pain, and shivered, and felt cold—cold to her heart. This was partly perhaps because it is chilly in Cumberland, when one has just come from India; and partly because there was something that affected a woman's fanciful imagination in the misty monotony of the limestone country, and the grey waste of the hills.

Earlston, too, was grey, as was to be expected; and the trees which surrounded it had lost colour in the night. The hall was but dimly lighted, when the door was opened—as is but too common in country houses of so retired a kind—and there was nobody ready at the instant to open the door or to receive the strangers. To be sure, people were called and came—the housekeeper first, in a silk gown, which rustled excessively, and with a certain air of patronizing affability; and then Mr. Ochterlony, who had been sitting, as he usually did, in his dressing-gown, and who had to get into his coat so hurriedly that he had not recovered from it when he shook hands with his sister-in-law; and then by degrees servants appeared, and lifted out the sleepy, startled children, who, between waking and sleeping, worn out, frightened, and excited, were precisely in the condition which it is most difficult to manage. And the ayah, who could hold no Christian communication with anybody around her, was worse than useless to her poor mistress. When Mr. Ochterlony led the way into the great, solemn, dark, dining-room—which was the nearest room at hand—the children, instead of consenting to be led upstairs, clung with one unanimous accord to their mother. Little Wilfrid got to her arms, notwithstanding all remonstrances, and Hugh and Islay each seized silently a handful of her black dress, crushing the crape beyond all remedy. It was thus she entered Earlston, which had been her husband's birthplace, and was to be her son's inheritance—or so at least Mary thought.

"I hope you have had a pleasant journey," Mr. Ochterlony said, shaking hands with her again. "I daresay they are tired, poor little things—but you have had good weather, I hope." This he said after he had indicated to Mary a large easy-chair in carved oak, which stood by the side of the fire-place, and into which, with little Wilfrid clinging to her, and Islay and Hugh holding fast by her dress, it was not so easy to get. The master of the house did not sit down himself, for it was dreary and dark, and he was a man of fine perceptions; but he walked to the window and looked out, and then came back again to his sister-in-law. "I am glad you have had such good weather—but I am sure you must all be tired," he said.

"Yes," said Mary, who would have liked to cry, "very tired; but I hope we did not come too soon. Your letter was so kind that I thought—"

"Oh don't speak of it," said Mr. Ochterlony; and then he stood before her on the dark hearth, and did not know what more to say. The twilight was still lingering, and there were no lights in the room, and it was fitted up with the strictest regard to propriety, and just as a dining-room ought to be. Weird gleams of dull reflection out of the depths of old mahogany lay low towards the floor, bewildering the visitor; and there was not even the light of a fire, which, for merely conventional motives, because it was July, did not occupy its usual place; though Mary, fresh from India, and shivering with the chill of excitement and nervous grief, would have given anything to be within reach of one. Neither did she know what to say to her almost unknown brother-in-law, whose face even she could see very imperfectly; and the children grasped her with that tight hold which is in itself a warning, and shows that everything is possible in the way of childish fright and passion. But still it was indispensable that she should find something to say.

"My poor little boys are so young," she said, faltering. "It was very good of you to ask us, and I hope they won't be troublesome. I think I will ask the housekeeper to show us where we are to be. The railway tires them more than the ship did. This is Hugh," said Mary, swallowing as best she could the gasp in her throat, and detaching poor little Hugh's hand from her crape. But she had tears in her voice, and Mr. Ochterlony had a wholesome dread of crying. He gave his nephew a hurried pat on the head without looking at him, and called for Mrs. Gilsland, who was at hand among the shadows rustling with her silk gown.

"Oh!" he said hurriedly. "A fine little fellow I am sure;—but you are quite right, and they must be tired, and I will not detain you. Dinner is at seven," said Mr. Ochterlony. What could he say? He could not even see the faces of the woman and children whom it was his dread but evident duty to receive. When they went away under Mrs. Gilsland's charge, he followed them to the foot of the stairs, and stood looking after them as the procession mounted, guided by the rustle of the housekeeper's gown. The poor man looked at them in a bewildered way, and then went off to his library, where his own shaded lamp was lit, and where everything was cosy and familiar. Arrived there, he threw himself into his own chair with a sigh. He was not a brute, nor a wretch, as we have said, and the least thing he could do when he heard of his poor brother's death was to offer a shelter—temporarily at least—to the widow and her children; but perhaps a lurking hope that something might turn up to prevent the invasion had been in his mind up to this day. Now she was here, and what was he to do with her? Now they were here, which was still more serious—three boys (even though one of them was a baby) in a house full of everything that was daintiest and rarest and most delicate! No wonder Mr. Ochterlony was momentarily stupefied by their arrival; and then he had not even seen their faces to know what they were like. He remembered Mary of old in her bride-days, but then she was too young, too fresh, too unsubdued to please him. If she were as full of vigour and energy now, what was to become of a quiet man who, above all things, loved tranquillity and leisure? This was what Francis Ochterlony was thinking as his visitors went upstairs.

Mrs. Ochterlony was inducted into the best rooms in the house. Her brother-in-law was not an effusive or sympathetic man by nature, but still he knew what was his duty under the circumstances. Two great rooms gleaming once more with ebon gleams out of big wardrobes and half-visible mirrors, with beds that looked a little like hearses, and heavy solemn hangings. Mrs. Gilsland's silk gown rustled about everywhere, pointing out a thousand conveniences unknown at the station; but all Mary was thinking about was one of those grey cottages on the road, with the fire burning brightly, and its little homely walls lighted up with the fitful, cheerful radiance. If she could but have had a fire, and crept up to it, and knelt on the hearth and held herself to the comforting warmth! There are times when a poor creature feels all body, just as there are times when she feels all soul. And then, to think that dinner was at seven! just as it had been when she came there with Hugh, a girl all confident of happiness and life. No doubt Mr. Ochterlony would have forgiven his sister-in-law, and probably indeed would have been as much relieved as she, if she had but sent an apology and stayed in her room all the evening. But Mary was not the kind of woman to do this. It did not occur to her to depart from the natural routine, or make so much talk about her own feelings or sentiments as would be necessary even to excuse her. What did it matter? If it had to be done, it had to be done, and there was nothing more to be said. This was the view her mind took of most matters; and she had always been well, and never had any pretext to get out of things she did not like, as women do who have headaches and handy little illnesses. She could always do what was needful, and did always do it without stopping to make any questions; which is a serviceable kind of temperament in life, and yet subjects people to many little martyrdoms which otherwise they might escape from. Though her heart was sick, she put on her best gown all covered with crape, and her widow's cap, and went down to dine with Francis Ochterlony in the great dining-room, leaving her children behind, and longing unspeakably for that cottage with the fire.

It was not such an unbecoming dress after all, notwithstanding what people say. Mary was worn and sad, but she was not faded; and the dead white of the cap that encircled her face, and the dead black of her dress, did not do so much harm as perhaps they ought to have done to that sweet and stedfast grace, which had made the regiment recognise and adopt young Stafford's fanciful title. She was still Madonna Mary under that disfigurement; and on the whole she was not disfigured by her dress. Francis Ochterlony lifted his eyes with equal surprise and satisfaction to take a second look at poor Hugh's widow. He felt by instinct that Phidias himself could not have filled a corner in his drawing-room, which was so full of fine things, with a figure more fair or half so appropriate as that of the serene woman who now took her seat there, abstracted a little into the separation and remoteness of sorrow, but with no discord in her face. He liked her better so than with the group of children, who made her look as if she was a Charity, and the heavy veil hanging half over her face, which had a conventual and uncomfortable effect; and he was very courteous and attentive to his sister-in-law. "I hope you had good weather," he said in his deferential way; "and I trust, when you have been a few days at Earlston, the fatigue will wear off. You will find everything quiet here."

"I hope so," said Mary; "but it is the children I am thinking of. I trust our rooms are a long distance off, and that we will not disturb you."

"That is quite a secondary matter," said Mr. Ochterlony. "The question is, are you comfortable? I hope you will let Mrs. Gilsland know if anything is wanted. We are not—not quite used to these sort of things, you know; but I am sure, if anything is wanted—"

"You are very kind," said Mary; "I am sure we shall be very comfortable." And yet as she said so her thoughts went off with a leap to that little cottage interior, and the cheerful light that shone out of the window, and the fire that crackled and blazed within. Ah, if she were but there! not dining with Mr. Ochterlony in solemn grandeur, but putting her little boys to bed, and preparing their supper for them, and cheating away heavy thoughts by that dear common work for the comfort and service of her own which a woman loves. But this was not a sort of longing to give expression to at Earlston, where in the evening Mr. Ochterlony was very kind to his sister-in-law, and showed her a great many priceless things which Mary regarded with trembling, thinking of two small barbarians about to be let loose among them, not to speak of little Wilfrid, who was old enough to dash an Etruscan vase to the earth, or upset the rarest piece of china, though he was still only a baby. She could not tell how they were so much as to walk through that drawing-room without doing some harm, and her heart sank within her as she listened to all those loving lingering descriptions which only a virtuoso can make. Mr. Ochterlony retired that evening with a sense always agreeable to a man, that in doing a kind thing he had not done a foolish one, and that the children of such a fair and gracious woman could not be the graceless imps who had been haunting his dreams ever since he knew they were coming home; but Mary for her part took no such flattering unction to her soul. She sighed as she went upstairs sad and weary to the great sombre room, in which a couple of candles burned like tiny stars in a world of darkness, and looked at her sleeping boys, and wondered what they were to do in this collection of curiosities and beauties. She was an ignorant woman, and did not, alas! care anything at all for the Venus Anadyomene. But she thought of little Hugh tilting that marble lady and her pedestal over, and shook and trembled at the idea. She trembled too with cold and nervous agitation, and the chill of sorrow in her heart. In the lack of other human sources of consolation, oh! to go to that cottage hearth, and kneel down and feel to one's very soul the comfort of the warm consoling fire.

CHAPTER XII

It had need to be a mind which has reached the last stage of human sentiment which can altogether resist the influence of a lovely summer morning, all made of warmth, and light, and softened sounds, and far-off odours. Mrs. Ochterlony had not reached this last stage; she was still young, and she was only at the beginning of her loneliness, and her heart had not sickened at life, as hearts do sometimes which have made a great many repeated efforts to live, and have to give in again and again. When she saw the sunshine lying in a supreme peacefulness upon those grey hills, and all the pale sky and blue depths of air beaming softly with that daylight which comes from God, her courage came back to her in spite of herself. She began the morning by the shedding of those silent tears which are all the apology one can make to one's dead, for having the heart to begin another day without them; and when that moment was over, and the children had lifted all their daylight faces in a flutter of curiosity and excitement about this new "home" they had come to, after so long talking of it and looking forward to it, things did not seem so dark to Mary as on the previous evening. For one thing, the sun was warm and shone in at her windows, which made a great difference; and with her children's voices in her ears, and their faces fresh in the morning light, what woman could be altogether without courage? "So long as they are well," she said to herself—and went down stairs a little consoled, to pour out Mr. Ochterlony's coffee for him, thanking heaven in her heart that her boys were to have a meal which had nothing calm nor classical about it, in the old nursery where their father had once eaten his breakfasts, and which had been hurriedly prepared for them. "The little dears must go down after dinner; but master, ma'am—well, he's an old bachelor, you know," said Mrs. Gilsland, while explaining this arrangement. "Oh, thank you; I hope you will help me to keep them from disturbing him," Mary had said; and thus it was with a lighter heart that she went down stairs.

Mr. Ochterlony came down too at the same time in an amiable frame of mind. Notwithstanding that he had to put himself into a morning coat, and abjured his dressing-gown, which was somewhat of a trial for a man of fixed habits, nothing could exceed the graciousness of his looks. A certain horrible notion common to his class, that children scream all night long, and hold an entire household liable to be called up at any moment, had taken possession of his mind. But his tired little guests had been swallowed up in the silence of the house, and had neither screamed, nor shouted, nor done anything to disturb its habitual quiet; and the wonderful satisfaction of having done his duty, and not having suffered for it, had entered Mr. Ochterlony's mind. It is in such circumstances that the sweet sense of well-doing, which is generally supposed the best reward of virtue, settles upon a good man's spirits. The Squire might be premature in his self-congratulations, but then his sense of relief was exquisite. If nothing worse was to come of it than the presence of a fair woman, whose figure was always in drawing, and who never put herself into an awkward attitude—whose voice was soft, and her movements tranquil, Mr. Ochterlony felt that self-sacrifice after all was practicable. The boys could be sent to school as all boys were, and at intervals might be endured when there was nothing else for it. Thus he came down in a benign condition, willing to be pleased. As for Mary, the first thing that disturbed her calm, was the fact that she was herself of no use at her brother-in-law's breakfast-table. He made his coffee himself, and then he went into general conversation in the kindest way, to put her at her ease.

"That is the Farnese Hercules," he said; "I saw it caught your eye last night. It is from a cast I had made for the purpose, and is considered very perfect; and that you know is the new Pallas, the Pallas that was found in the Sestina Villa; you recollect, perhaps?"

"I am afraid not," said Mary, faltering; and she looked at them, poor soul, with wistful eyes, and tried to feel a little interest. "I have been so long out of the way of everything—"

"To be sure," said the Squire, encouragingly, "and my poor brother Hugh, I remember, knew very little about it. He went early to India, and had few advantages, poor fellow." All this Mr. Ochterlony said while he was concocting his coffee; and Mary had nothing to do but to sit and listen to him with her face fully open to his inspection if he liked, and no kindly urn before her to hide the sudden rush of tears and indignation. A man who spent his life having casts made, and collecting what Mary in her heart with secret rage called "pretty things!"—that he should make a complacent contrast between himself and his brother! The suggestion filled Mrs. Ochterlony with a certain speechless fury which was born of her grief.

"He knew well how to do his duty," she said, as soon as she could speak; and she would not let her tears fall, but opened her burning eyes wide, and absorbed them somehow out of pride for Hugh.

"Poor fellow!" said his brother, daintily pouring out the fragrant coffee. "I don't know if he ever could have had much appreciation of Art; but I am sure he made a good soldier, as you say. I was very much moved and shocked when I heard—but do not let us talk of such painful subjects; another time, perhaps—"

And Mary sat still with her heart beating, and said no more—thinking through all the gentle flow of conversation that followed of the inconceivable conceit that could for a moment class Francis Ochterlony's dilettante life with that of her dead Hugh, who had played a man's part in the world, and had the heart to die for his duty's sake. And this useless Squire could speak of the few advantages he had! It was unreasonable, for, to tell the truth, the Squire was much more accomplished, much better instructed than the Major. The Numismatic Society and the Society of Antiquaries, and even, on certain subjects, the British Association, would have listened to Francis Ochterlony as if he had been a messenger from heaven. Whereas Hugh the soldier would never have got a hearing nor dared to open his lips in any learned presence. But then that did not matter to his wife, who, notwithstanding her many high qualities, was not a perfectly reasonable woman. Those "few advantages" stood terribly in Mary's way for that first morning. They irritated her far more than Mr. Ochterlony could have had the least conception or understanding of. If anybody had given him a glass to look into her heart with, the Squire would have been utterly confounded by what he saw there. What had he done? And indeed he had done nothing that anybody (in his senses) could have found fault with; he had but turned Mary's thoughts once more with a violent longing to the roadside cottage, where at least, if she and her children were but safely housed, her soldier's memory would be shrined, and his sword hung up upon the homely wall, and his name turned into a holy thing. Whereas he was only a younger brother who had gone away to India, and had few advantages, in the Earlston way of thinking. This was the uppermost thought in Mrs. Ochterlony's mind as her brother-in-law exhibited all his collections to her. The drawing-room, which she had but imperfectly seen in her weariness and preoccupation the previous night, was a perfect museum of things rich and rare. There were delicate marbles, tiny but priceless, standing out white and ethereal against the soft, carefully chosen, toned crimson of the curtains; and bronzes that were worth half a year's income of the lands of Earlston; and Etruscan vases and Pompeian relics; and hideous dishes with lizards on them, besides plaques of dainty porcelain with Raphael's designs; the very chairs were fantastic with inlaying and gilding—curious articles, some of them worth their weight in gold; and if you but innocently looked at an old cup and saucer on a dainty table wondering what it did there, it turned out to be the ware of Henri II., and priceless. To see Mary going over all this with her attention preoccupied and wandering, and yet a wistful interest in her eyes, was a strange sight. All that she had in the world was her children, and the tiny little income of a soldier's widow—and you may suppose perhaps that she was thinking what a help to her and the still more valuable little human souls she had to care for, would have been the money's-worth of some of these fragile beauties. But that was not what was in Mrs. Ochterlony's mind. What occupied her, on the contrary, was an indignant wonder within herself how a man who spent his existence upon such trifles (they looked trifles to her, from her point of view, and in this of course she was still unreasonable) could venture to look down with complacency upon the real life, so honestly lived and so bravely ended, of his brother Hugh—poor Hugh, as she ventured to call him. Mr. Ochterlony might die a dozen times over, and what would his marble Venus care, that he was so proud of? But it was Hugh who had died; and it was a kind of comfort to feel that he at least, though they said he had few advantages, had left one faithful woman behind him to keep his grave green for ever.

The morning passed, however, though it was a long morning; and Mary looked into all the cabinets of coins and precious engraved gems, and rare things of all sorts, with a most divided attention and wandering mind—thinking where were the children? were they out-of-doors? were they in any trouble? for the unearthly quietness in the house seemed to her experienced mother's ear to bode harm of some kind—either illness or mischief, and most likely the last. As for Mr. Ochterlony, it never occurred to him that his sister-in-law, while he was showing her his collections, should not be as indifferent as he was to any vulgar outside influence. "We shall not be disturbed," he said, with a calm reassuring smile, when he saw her glance at the door; "Mrs. Gilsland knows better," and he drew out another drawer of coins as he spoke. Poor Mary began to tremble, but the same sense of duty which made her husband stand to be shot at, kept her at her post. She went through with it like a martyr, without flinching, though longing, yearning, dying to get free. If she were but in that cottage, looking after her little boys' dinner, and hearing their voices as they played at the door—their servant and her own mistress, instead of the helpless slave of courtesy, and interest, and her position, looking at Francis Ochterlony's curiosities! When she escaped at last, Mary found that indeed her fears had not been without foundation. There had been some small breakages, and some small quarrels in the nursery, where Hugh and Islay had been engaged in single combat, and where baby Wilfrid had joined in with impartial kicks and scratches, to the confusion of both combatants: all which alarming events the frightened ayah had been too weak-minded and helpless to prevent. And, by way of keeping them quiet, that bewildered woman had taken down a beautiful Indian canoe, which stood on a bracket in the corridor, and the boys, as was natural, with true scientific inquisitiveness had made researches into its constitution, such as horrified their mother. Mary was so cowardly as to put the boat together again with her own hands, and put it back on its bracket, and say nothing about it, with devout hopes that nobody would find it out—which, to be sure, was a terrible example to set before children. She breathed freely for the first time when she got them out—out of Earlston—out of Earlston grounds—to the hill-side, where, though everything was grey, the turf had a certain greenness, and the sky a certain blueness, and the sun shone warm, and nameless little English wild flowers were to be found among the grass; nameless things, too insignificant for anything but a botanist to classify, and Mrs. Ochterlony was no botanist. She put down Wilfrid on the grass, and sat by him, and watched for a little the three joyful unthinking creatures, harmonized without knowing it by their mother's presence, rolling about in an unaccustomed ecstacy upon the English grass; and then Mary went back, without being quite aware of it, into the darker world of her own mind, and leant her head upon her hands and began to think.

She had a great deal to think about. She had come home obeying the first impulse, which suggested that a woman left alone in the world should put herself under the guidance and protection of "her friends:" and, in the first stupor of grief, it was a kind of consolation to think that she had still somebody belonging to her, and could put off those final arrangements for herself and by herself which one time or other must be made. When she decided upon this, Mary did not realize the idea of giving offence to Aunt Agatha by accepting Francis Ochterlony's invitation, nor of finding herself at Earlston in the strange nondescript position—something less than a member of the family, something more than a visitor—which she at present occupied. Her brother-in-law was very kind, but he did not know what to do with her; and her brother-in-law's household was very doubtful and uneasy, with a certain alarmed and suspicious sense that it might be a new and permanent mistress who had thus come in upon them—an idea which it was not to be expected that Mrs. Gilsland, who had been in authority so long, should take kindly to. And then it was hard for Mary to live in a house where her children were simply tolerated, and in constant danger of doing inestimable mischief. She sat upon the grey hill-side, and thought over it till her head ached. Oh, for that wayside cottage with the blazing fire! but Mrs. Ochterlony had no such refuge. She had come to Earlston of her own will, and she could not fly away again at once to affront and offend the only relation who might be of service to her boys—which was, no doubt, a sadly mercenary view to take of the subject. She stayed beside her children all day, feeling like a prisoner, afraid to move or to do anything, afraid to let the boys play or give scope to their limbs and voice. And then Hugh, though he was not old enough to sympathize with her, was old enough to put terrible questions. "Why shouldn't we make a noise?" the child said; "is my uncle a king, mamma, that we must not disturb him? Papa never used to mind." Mary sent her boy back to his play when he said this, with a sharp impatience which he could not understand. Ah, how different it was! and how stinging the pain that went to her heart at that suggestion. But then little Hugh, thank heaven, knew no better. Even the Hindoo woman, who had been a faithful woman in her way, but who was going back again with another family bound for India, began to make preparations for her departure; and, after that, Mrs. Ochterlony's position would be still more difficult. This was how the first day at Earlston—the first day at home as the children said—passed over Mary. It was, perhaps, of all other trials, the one most calculated to take from her any strength she might have left. And after all this she had to dress at seven o'clock, and leave her little boys in the big dark nursery, to go down to keep her brother-in-law company at dinner, to hear him talk of the Farnese Hercules, and of his collections, and travels, and, perhaps, of the "few advantages" his poor brother had had: which for a woman of high spirit and independent character, and profound loyal love for the dead, was a very hard ordeal to bear.

The dinner, however, went over very fairly. Mr. Ochterlony was the soul of politeness, and, besides, he was pleased with his sister-in-law. She knew nothing about Art; but then, she had been long in India, and was a woman, and it was not to be wondered at. He meant no harm when he spoke about poor Hugh's few advantages. He knew that he had a sensible woman to deal with, and of course grief and that sort of thing cannot last for ever; and, on the whole, Mr. Ochterlony saw no reason why he should not speak quite freely of his brother Hugh; and lament his want of proper training. She must have known that as well as he did. And, to tell the truth, he had forgotten about the children. He made himself very agreeable, and even went so far as to say that it was very pleasant to be able to talk over these matters with somebody who understood him. Mary sat waiting with a mixture of fright and expectation for the appearance of the children, who the housekeeper said were to come down to dessert; but they did not come, and nothing was said about them; and Mr. Ochterlony was fond of foreign habits, and took very little wine, and accompanied his sister-in-law upstairs when she left the table. He came with her in that troublesome French way with which Mary was not even acquainted, and made it impossible for her to hurry through the long passages to the nursery, and see what her forlorn little boys were about. What could they be doing all this time, lost at the other end of the great house where she could not even hear their voices, nor that soft habitual nursery hum which was a necessary accompaniment to her life? She had to sit down in a kind of despair and talk to Mr. Ochterlony, who took a seat beside her, and was very friendly. The summer evening had begun to decline, and it was at this meditative moment that the master of Earlston liked to sit and contemplate his Psyche and his Venus, and call a stranger's attention to their beauties, and tell pleasant anecdotes about how he picked them up. Mrs. Ochterlony sat by her brother-in-law's side, and listened to his talk about Art with her ear strained to the most intense attention, prepared at any moment to hear a shriek from the outraged housekeeper, or a howl of unanimous woe from three culpable and terrified voices. There was something comic in the situation, but Mary's attention was not sufficiently disengaged to be amused.

"I have long wished to have some information about Indian Art," said Mr. Ochterlony. "I should be glad to know what an intelligent observer like yourself, with some practical knowledge, thought of my theory. My idea is—But I am afraid you have a headache? I hope you have all the attention you require, and are comfortable? It would give me great pain to think that you were not perfectly comfortable. You must not feel the least hesitation in telling me—"

"Oh no, we have everything," said Mary. She thought she heard something outside like little steps and distant voices, and her heart began to beat. But as for her companion, he was not thinking about such extraneous things.

"I hope so," said Mr. Ochterlony; and then he looked at his Psyche with the lingering look of a connoisseur, dwelling lovingly upon her marble beauty. "You must have that practical acquaintance which, after all, is the only thing of any use," he continued. "My idea is—"

And it was at this moment that the door was thrown open, and they all rushed in—all, beginning with little Wilfrid, who had just commenced to walk, and who came with a tottering dash, striking against a pedestal in his way, and making its precious burden tremble. Outside at the open door appeared for an instant the ayah as she had set down her charge, and Mrs. Gilsland, gracious but formidable, in her rustling gown, who had headed the procession. Poor woman, she meant no harm, but it was not in the heart of woman to believe that in the genial hour after dinner, when all the inner and the outer man was mollified and comforted, the sight of three such "bonnie boys," all curled, brushed, and shining for the occasion, could disturb Mr. Ochterlony. Baby Wilfrid dashed across the room in a straight line with "flicherin' noise and glee" to get to his mother, and the others followed, not, however, without stoppages on the way. They were bonnie boys—brave, little, erect, clear-eyed creatures, who had never known anything but love in their lives, and feared not the face of man; and to Mary, though she quaked and trembled, their sudden appearance changed the face of everything, and made the Earlston drawing-room glorious. But the effect was different upon Mr. Ochterlony, as might be supposed.

"How do you do, my little man," said the discomfited uncle. "Oh, this is Hugh, is it? I think he is like his father. I suppose you intend to send them to school. Good heavens! my little fellow, take care!" cried Mr. Ochterlony. The cause of this sudden animation was, that Hugh, naturally facing his uncle when he was addressed by him, had leant upon the pillar on which Psyche stood with her immortal lover. He had put his arm round it with a vague sense of admiration, and as he stood was, as Mary thought, a prettier sight than even the group above; but Mr. Ochterlony could not be expected to be of Mary's mind.

"Come here, Hugh," said his mother, anxiously. "You must not touch anything; your uncle will kindly let you look at them, but you must not touch. It was so different, you know, in our Indian house—and then on board ship," said Mary, faltering. Islay, with his big head thrown back a little, and his hands in his little trousers pockets, was roving about all the while in a manly way, inspecting everything, looking, as his mother thought, for the most favourable opening for mischief. What was she to do? They might do more damage in ten minutes than ten years of her little income could set right. As for Mr. Ochterlony, though he groaned in spirit, nothing could overcome his politeness; he turned his back upon little Hugh, so that at least he might not see what was going on, and resumed the conversation with all the composure that he could assume.

"You will send them to school of course," he said; "we must inquire for a good school for them. I don't myself think that children can begin their education too soon. I don't speak of the baby," said Mr. Ochterlony, with a sigh. The baby evidently was inevitable. Mary had set him down at her feet, and he sat there in a peaceable way, making no assault upon anything, which was consolatory at least.

"They are so young," said Mary, tremulously.

"Yes, they are young, and it is all the better," said the uncle. His eye was upon Islay, who had sprung upon a chair, and was riding and spurring it with delightful energy. Naturally, it was a unique rococo chair of the daintiest and most fantastic workmanship, and the unhappy owner expected to see it fall into sudden destruction before his eyes; but he was benumbed by politeness and despair, and took no notice. "There is nothing," said the poor man with distracted attention, his eye upon Islay, his face turned to his sister-in-law, and horror in his heart, "like good training begun early. For my part—"

"Oh, mamma, look here. How funny this is!" cried little Hugh. When Mary turned sharply round in despair, she found her boy standing behind her with a priceless Etruscan vase in his hand. He had just taken it from the top of a low, carved bookcase, where the companion vase still stood, and held it tilted up as he might have held a drinking mug in the nursery. "It's a fight," cried Hugh; "look, mamma, how that fellow is putting his lance into him. Isn't it jolly? Why don't we have some brown sort of jugs with battles on them, like this?"

"What is it? Let me see," cried Islay, and he gave a flying leap, and brought the rococo chair down on its back, where he remounted leisurely after he had cast a glance at the brown sort of jug. "I don't think it's worth looking at," said the four-year-old hero. Mrs. Ochterlony heard her brother-in-law say, "Good heavens!" again, and heard him groan as he turned away his head. He could not forget that they were his guests and his dead brother's children, and he could not turn them out of the room or the house, as he was tempted to do; but at the same time he turned away that at least he might not see the full extent of the ruin. As for Mary, she felt her own hand tremble as she took the vase out of Hugh's careless grasp. She was terrified to touch its brittle beauty, though she was not so enthusiastic about it as, perhaps, she ought to have been. And it was with a sudden impulse of desperation that she caught up her baby, and lifted Islay off the prostrate chair.

"I hope you will excuse them," she said, all flushed and trembling. "They are so little, and they know no better. But they must not stay here," and with that poor Mary swept them out with her, making her way painfully over the dangerous path, where snares and perils lay on every side. She gave the astonished Islay an involuntary "shake" as she dropped him in the sombre corridor outside, and hurried along towards the darkling nursery. The little flock of wicked black sheep trotted by her side full of questions and surprise. "Why are we coming away? What have we done?" said Hugh. "Mamma! mamma! tell me!" and Islay pulled at her dress, and made more demonstratively the same demand. What had they done? If Mr. Ochterlony, left by himself in the drawing-room, could but have answered the question! He was on his knees beside his injured chair, examining its wounds, and as full of tribulation as if those fantastic bits of tortured wood had been flesh and blood. And to tell the truth, the misfortune was greater than if it had been flesh and blood. If Islay Ochterlony's sturdy little legs had been broken, there was a doctor in the parish qualified to a certain extent to mend them. But who was there among the Shap Fells, or within a hundred miles of Earlston, who was qualified to touch the delicate members of a rococo chair? He groaned over it as it lay prostrate, and would not be comforted. Children! imps! come to be the torture of his life, as, no doubt, they had been of poor Hugh's. What could Providence be thinking of to send such reckless, heedless, irresponsible creatures into the world? A vague notion that their mother would whip them all round as soon as she got them into the shelter of the nursery, gave Mr. Ochterlony a certain consolation; but even that judicial act, though a relief to injured feeling, would do nothing for the fractured chair.

Mary, we regret to say, did not whip the boys when she got into her own apartments. They deserved it, no doubt, but she was only a weak woman. Instead of that, she put her arms round the three, who were much excited and full of wonder, and very restless in her clasp, and cried—not much, but suddenly, in an outburst of misery and desolation. After all, what was the vase or the Psyche in comparison with the living creatures thus banished to make place for them? which was a reflection which some people may be far from acquiescing in, but that came natural to her, being their mother, and not in any special way interested in art. She cried, but she only hugged her boys and kissed them, and put them to bed, lingering that she might not have to go downstairs again till the last moment. When she went at last, and made Mr. Ochterlony's tea for him, that magnanimous man did not say a word, and even accepted her apologies with a feeble deprecation. He had put the wounded article away, and made a sublime resolution to take no further notice. "Poor thing, it is not her fault," he said to himself; and, indeed, had begun to be sorry for Mary, and to think what a pity it was that a woman so unobjectionable should have three such imps to keep her in hot water. But he looked sad, as was natural. He swallowed his tea with a sigh, and made mournful cadences to every sentence he uttered. A man does not easily get over such a shock;—it is different with a frivolous and volatile woman, who may forget or may dissimulate, and look as if she does not care; but a man is not so lightly moved or mended. If it had been Islay's legs, as has been said, there was a doctor within reach; but who in the north country could be trusted so much as to look at the delicate limbs of a rococo chair?

CHAPTER XIII

The experience of this evening, though it was only the second of her stay at Earlston, proved to Mary that the visit she was paying to her brother-in-law must be made as short as possible. She could not get up and run away because Hugh had put an Etruscan vase in danger, and Islay had broken his uncle's chair. It was Mr. Ochterlony who was the injured party, and he was magnanimously silent, saying nothing, and even giving no intimation that the presence of these objectionable little visitors was not to be desired in the drawing-room; and Mary had to stay and keep her boys out of sight, and live consciously upon sufferance, in the nursery and her bedroom, until she could feel warranted in taking leave of her brother-in-law, who, without doubt, meant to be kind. It was a strange sort of position, and strangely out of accord with her character and habits. She had never been rich, nor lived in such a great house, but she had always up to this time been her own mistress—mistress of her actions, free to do what she thought best, and to manage her children according to her own wishes. Now she had, to a certain extent, to submit to the housekeeper, who changed their hours, and interfered with their habits at her pleasure. The poor ayah went weeping away, and nobody was to be had to replace her except one of the Earlston maids, who naturally was more under Mrs. Gilsland's authority than Mrs. Ochterlony's; and to this girl Mary had to leave them when she went down to the inevitable dinner which had always to be eaten downstairs. She made several attempts to consult her brother-in-law upon her future, but Mr. Ochterlony, though very polite, was not a sympathetic listener. He had received the few details which she had been moved at first, with restrained tears, to give him about the Major, with a certain restlessness which chilled Mary. He was sorry for his brother; but he was one of those men who do not care to talk about dead people, and who think it best not to revive and recall sorrow—which would be very true and just if true sorrow had any occasion to be revived and recalled; and her own arrangements were all more or less connected with this (as Mr. Ochterlony called it) painful subject. And thus it was that her hesitating efforts to make her position clear to him, and to get any advice which he could give, was generally put aside or swallowed up in some communication from the Numismatic Society, or questions which she could not answer about Indian art.

"We must leave Earlston soon," Mrs. Ochterlony took courage to say one day, when the housekeeper, and the continued exclusion of the children, and her own curious life on sufferance, had been too much for her. "If you are at leisure, would you let me speak to you about it? I have so little experience of anything but India—and I want to do what is best for my boys."

"Oh—ah—yes," said Mr. Ochterlony, "you must send them to school. We must try and hear of some good school for them. It is the only thing you can do—"

"But they are so young," said Mary. "At their age they are surely best with their mother. Hugh is only seven. If you could advise me where it would be best to go—"

"Where it would be best to go!" said Mr. Ochterlony. He was a little surprised, and not quite pleased for the moment. "I hope you do not find yourself uncomfortable here?"

"Oh, no," said Mary, faltering; "but—they are very young and troublesome, and—I am sure they must worry you. Such little children are best by themselves," she said, trying to smile—and thus, by chance, touched a chord of pity in her brother-in law's heart.

"Ah," he said, shaking his head, "I assure you I feel the painfulness of your position. If you had been unencumbered, you might have looked forward to so different a life; but with such a burden as these children, and you so young still—"

"Burden?" said Mary; and it may be supposed how her eyes woke up, and what a colour came to her cheek, and how her heart took to beating under her crape. "You can't really think my children are a burden to me? Ah! you don't know—I would not care to live another day if I had not my boys."

And here, her nerves being weak with all she had come through, she would have liked to cry—but did not, the moment being unsuitable, and only sat facing the virtuoso, all lighted up and glowing, brightened by indignation, and surprise, and sudden excitement, to something more like the former Mary than ever yet had been seen underneath her widow's cap.

"Oh!" said Mr. Ochterlony. He could have understood the excitement had it been about a Roman camp or a newly-discovered statue; but boys did not commend themselves in the same way to his imagination. He liked his sister-in-law, however, in his way. She was a good listener, and pleasant to look at, and even when she was unintelligible was never without grace, or out of drawing, and he felt disposed even to take a little trouble for her. "You must send them to school," he said. "There is nothing else to be done. I will write to a friend of mine who knows about such matters; and I am sure, for my part, I shall be very glad if you can make yourself comfortable at Earlston—you and—and the baby, of course," Mr. Ochterlony said, with a slightly wry face. The innocent man had not an idea of the longing she had for that cottage with the fire in it. It was a notion which never could have been made intelligible to him, even had he been told in words.

"Thank you," said Mary, faltering more and more; indeed she made a dead pause, and he thought she had accepted his decision, and that there was to be no more about it—which was comforting and satisfactory. He had just risen up to leave the room, breakfast being over, when she put out her hand to stop him. "I will not detain you a minute," she said, "it is so desolate to have no one to tell me what to do. Indeed, we cannot stay here—though it is so good of you; they are too young to leave me, and I care for nothing else in life," Mrs. Ochterlony said, yielding for an instant to her emotion; but she soon recovered herself. "There are good schools all over England, I have heard; in places where we could live cheaply. That is what I want to do. Near one of the good grammar schools. I am quite free; it does not matter where I live. If you would give me your advice," she added, timidly. Mr. Ochterlony, for his part, was taken so much by surprise that he stood between the table and the door, with one foot raised to go on, and not believing his ears. He had behaved like an angel, to his own conviction, and had never said a word about the chair, though it had to be sent to town to be repaired. He had continued to afford shelter to the little ruffian who did it, and had carefully abstained from all expression of his feelings. What could the woman want more?—and what should he know about grammar-schools, and places where people could live cheaply? A woman, too, whom he liked, and had explained his theory of ancient art more fully to than he had ever done to any one. And she wanted to leave Earlston and his society, and the Psyches and Venuses, to settle down in some half-pay neighbourhood, where people with large families lived for the sake of education. No wonder Mr. Ochterlony turned round, struck dumb with wonder, and came slowly back before giving his opinion, which, but for an unexpected circumstance, would no doubt have been such an opinion as to overwhelm his companion with confusion, and put an instant stop to her foolish plans.

But circumstances come wildly in the way of the best intentions, and cut off the wisest speech sometimes on a man's very lips. At this moment the door opened softly, and a new interlocutor presented herself. The apparition was one which took not only the words but the very breath from the lips of the master of Earlston. Aunt Agatha was twenty years older than her niece, but so was Francis Ochterlony; and such a thing was once possible as that the soft ancient maiden and the elderly solitary dilettante might have made a cheerful human household at Earlston. They had not met for years, not since the time when Miss Seton was holding on by her lingering youth, and looking forward to the loss of it with an anxious and care-worn countenance. She was twenty times prettier now than she had been in those days—prettier perhaps, if the truth were told, than she ever had been in her life. She was penitent, too, and tearful in her white-haired sweetness, though Mr. Ochterlony did not know why—with a soft colour coming and going on her checks, and a wistful look in her dewy eyes. She had left her home at least two hours before, and came carrying all the freshness and odours of the morning, surrounded with sunshine and sweet air, and everything that seems to belong to the young. Francis Ochterlony was so bewildered by the sight that he stepped back out of her way, and could not have told whether she was eighteen or fifty. Perhaps the sight of him had in some degree the same effect upon Aunt Agatha. She made a little rush at Mary, who had risen to meet her, and threw herself, soft little woman as she was, upon her niece's taller form. "Oh, my dear love, I have been a silly old woman—forgive me!" said Aunt Agatha. She had put up with the estrangement as long as ever it was in human nature to put up with it. She had borne Peggy's sneers, and Winnie's heartless suggestions that it was her own doing. How was Winnie to know what made it so difficult for her to have any communications with Earlston? But finally Aunt Agatha's heart had conquered everything else. She had made such pictures to herself of Mary, solitary and friendless ("for what is a Man? no company when one is unhappy" Miss Seton had said to herself with unconscious eloquence), until instinct and impulse drove her to this decided step. The hall door at Earlston had been standing open, and there was nobody to announce her. And this was how Aunt Agatha arrived just at the critical moment, cutting off Mr. Ochterlony's utterance when he was on the very point of speech.

The poor man, for his part, did not know what to do; after the first moment of amaze he stood dumb and humble, with his hand stretched out, waiting to greet his unexpected visitor. But the truth was, that the two women as they clung together were both so dreadfully disposed to cry that they dared not face Mr. Ochterlony. The sudden touch of love and unlooked-for sympathy had this effect upon Mary, who had been agitated and disturbed before; and as for Aunt Agatha, she was not an old maid by conviction, and perhaps would not have objected to this house or its master, and the revival of these old associations was hard upon her. She clasped Mary tight, as if it was all for Mary's sake; but perhaps there was also a little personal feeling involved. Mr. Ochterlony stood speechless for a moment, and then he heard a faint sob, and fled in consternation. If that was coming, it was high time for him to go. He went away and took refuge in his library, in a confused and uncomfortable state of mind. This was the result of having a woman in the house; a man who had nothing to do in his own person with the opposite half of humanity became subject to the invasion of other women, and still worse, to the invasion of recollections and feelings which he had no wish to have recalled. What did Agatha Seton mean by looking so fresh and fair at her age? and yet she had white hair too, and called herself an old woman. These thoughts came dreadfully in his way when he sat down to work. He was writing a monograph upon Icelandic art, and naturally had been much interested in a subject so characteristic and exciting; but somehow after that glimpse of his old love his mind would not stick to his theme. The two women clinging together, though one of them had a bonnet on, made a pretty "subject." He was not mediæval, to speak of, but rather classical in his tastes; yet it did strike him that a painter might have taken an idea for a Visitation out of that embrace. And so that was how Agatha Seton looked when she was an old woman! This idea fluttered in and out before his mind's eye, and threw such reflections upon his paper as came dreadfully in the way of his monograph. He lost his notes and forgot his researches in the bewilderment produced by it; for, to tell the truth, Agatha Seton was in a very much finer state of preservation, not to say fairer to look upon, than most of the existing monuments of Icelandic art.

"He has gone away," said Aunt Agatha, who was aware of that fact sooner than Mary was, though Mrs. Ochterlony's face was towards her brother-in-law; and she gave Mary a sudden hug and subsided into that good cry, which is such a relief and comfort to the mind; Mary's tears came too, but they were fewer and not by any means so satisfactory as Aunt Agatha's, who was crying for nothing particular. "Oh, my dear love, don't think me a wretch," the old lady said. "I have never been able to get you out of my head, standing there on the platform all by yourself with the dear children; and I, like an old monster, taking offence and going away and leaving you! If it is any comfort to you, Mary, my darling, I have been wretched ever since. I tried to write, but I could not write. So now I've come to ask you to forgive me; and where are my dear, dear, darling boys?"

The poor little boys! Mary's heart gave a little leap to hear some one once more talk of those poor children as if they were not in the way. "Mr. Ochterlony is very kind," she said, not answering directly; "but we must not stay, Aunt Agatha, we cannot stay. He is not used to children, you know, and they worry him. Oh, if I had but any little place of my own!"

"You shall come to me, my darling love," said Aunt Agatha in triumph. "You should have come to me from the first. I am not saying anything against Francis Ochterlony. I never did; people might think he did not quite behave as was expected; but I am sure I never said a word against him. But how can a Man understand? or what can you look for from them? My dearest Mary, you must come to me!"

"Thank you, Aunt Agatha," said Mary, doubtfully. "You are very kind—you are all very kind"—and then she repeated, under her breath, that longing aspiration, "Oh, that I had but any little place of my very own!"

"Yes, my love, that is what we must do," said Aunt Agatha. "I would take you with me if I could, or I would take the dear boys with me. Nobody will be worried by them at the cottage. Oh, Mary, my darling, I never would say anything against poor dear Hugh, or encourage you to keep his relations at a distance; but just at this moment, my dear love, I did think it was most natural that you should go to your own friends."

"I think when one has little children one should be by one's-self," said Mary, "it is more natural. If I could get a little cottage near you, Aunt Agatha—"

"My love, mine is a little cottage," said Miss Seton; "it is not half nor quarter so big as Earlston—have you forgotten? and we are all a set of women together, and the dear boys will rule over us. Ah, Mary, you must come to me!" said the soft old lady. And after that she went up to the dim Earlston nursery, and kissed and hugged the tabooed children, whom it was the object of Mary's life to keep out of the way. But there was a struggle in Aunt Agatha's gentle bosom when she heard of the Etruscan vase and the rococo chair. Her heart yearned a little over the pretty things thus put in peril, for she had a few pretty things herself which were dear to her. Her alarm, however, was swallowed up by a stronger emotion. It was natural for a woman to take thought for such things, but it went to her heart to think of "poor Francis," once her hero, in such a connection. "You see he has nothing else to care for," she said—and the fair old maiden paused and gave a furtive sigh over the poor old bachelor, who might have been so different. "It was his own fault," she added to herself, softly; but still the idea of Francis Ochterlony "wrapped up," as Miss Seton expressed it, in chairs and vases, gave a shock to her gentle spirit. It was righteous retribution, but still Aunt Agatha was a woman, and pitiful. She was still more moved when Mary took her into the drawing-room, where there were so many beautiful things. She looked upon them with silent and reverent admiration, but still not without a personal reference. "So that is all he cares for, now-a-days," she said with a sigh; and it was just at the same moment that Mr. Ochterlony, in his study, disturbed by visions of two women in his peaceable house, gave up his monograph on Icelandic art in despair.

This, it may be said, was how Mrs. Ochterlony's first experiment terminated. She did not leave Earlston at once, but she did so shortly after—without any particular resistance on the part of her brother-in-law. After Aunt Agatha's visit, Mr. Ochterlony's thoughts took a different turn. He was very civil to her before she left, as indeed it was his nature to be to all women, and showed her his collections, and paid her a certain alarmed and respectful deference. But after that he did not do anything to detain Mary in his house. Where one woman was, other women were pretty sure to come, and nobody could tell what unseen visitants might enter along with them, to disturb a man in his occupations, and startle him out of his tranquillity. He never had the heart to resume that monograph on Icelandic art—which was a great loss to the Society of Antiquaries and the æsthetic world in general; and though he had no advice in particular to give to his sister-in-law as to her future movements, he did not say anything further to deter her from leaving Earlston. "I hope you will let me know what your movements are, and where you decide upon settling," he said, as he shook hands with her very gravely at the carriage door, "and if I can be of any use." And this was how the first experiment came to an end.

Then Mrs. Ochterlony kissed her boys when they were fairly out of the grey shadow of their uncle's house, and shed a few tears over them. "Now at least I shall not have to keep my bonnie boys out of the way any more," said Mary. But she caught sight again of the cheery cottage, with the fire burning within, and the hospitable door open, as she drove down to the railway; and her heart longed to alight and take possession, and find herself at home. When should she be at home? or was there no such place in the world? But happily she had no maid, and no time to think or calculate probabilities—and thus she set out upon her second venture, among "her own friends."

CHAPTER XIV

Aunt Agatha's cottage was very different from Earlston. It was a woman's house, and bore that character written all over it. The Psyche and the Venus would have been dreadfully out of place in it, it is true, but yet there was not a spot left vacant where an ornament could be; little fanciful shelves nestled in all the corners—which it was a great comfort to Mary's mind to see were just above her boys' range—bearing little vases, and old teacups and curiosities of all kinds, not valuable like Francis Ochterlony's, nor chosen with such refined taste, but yet dear to Aunt Agatha's heart. Nothing so precious as the ware of Henri II. had ever come in Miss Seton's way; but she had one or two trifling articles that were real Wedgewood, and she had some bits of genuine Sèvres, and a great deal of pretty rubbish, which answered the purpose quite as well as if it had been worth countless sums of money; and then there were flowers, wherever flowers could find a place. The rooms all opened out with liberal windows upon the garden, and the doors stood open, and sun and air, sound and fragrance, went through and through the little house. It was the same house as that in which Mary had felt the English leaves rustling, and the English breezes blowing, as she read Aunt Agatha's letter in India, ages ago, before any of those great events had happened which had thrown such a shadow on her life. The two ladies of the cottage went to the railway to meet their visitors, and it was Peggy, the real head of the establishment, who stood in her best cap, in a flutter of black ribbons and white apron, to receive "Miss Mary." And the glowing colour of the flowers, and the sunshine and the open house, and the flutter of womanish welcome, made the difference still more marked. When Mrs. Ochterlony was placed in the easiest chair in the brightest corner in that atmosphere of sunshine and sweetness, and saw her forlorn little boys take their place in the foreground of the picture, elected autocrats over the household in general, the sense of relief and difference was so sweet to her that she no longer felt that yearning for some place of her own. The greatest infidel, the most hard-hearted cynic could not have felt otherwise than at home under such circumstances. The children were taken out of Mary's hands on the instant, she whose time had been entirely devoted to keeping them invisible and inaudible, and out of the way—and Peggy took possession of the baby, and pretty Winnie flashed away into the garden with the two boys, with floating curls and flying ribbons, and all the gay freedom of a country girl, taking the hearts of her little companions by storm. Her sister, who had not "taken to her" at first, sat in Aunt Agatha's chair, in the first moment of conscious repose she had known in England, and looked out at the fair young figure moving about among the flowers, and began to be in love with Winnie. Here she was safe at last, she and her fatherless children. Life might be over for her in its fullest sense—but still she was here at peace among her own people, and again some meaning seemed to come back to the word home. She was lingering upon this thought in the unusual repose of the moment, and wiping some quiet tears from her cheeks, when Aunt Agatha came and sat down beside her and took Mary's hand. She had been partially incoherent with satisfaction and delight until now, but by this time any little tendency to hysterics which might be in Aunt Agatha's nature, had been calmed down by the awe-inspiring presence of Peggy, and the comfort of perceiving nothing but satisfaction in that difficult woman's countenance. The baby had behaved himself like an angel, and had made no objections whatever to the cap or features of his new guardian; and Peggy, too, was visible from the open windows walking up and down the garden with little Wilfrid in her arms, in all the glory of content. This sight brought Miss Seton's comfort to a climax, as it did Mary's. She came and took her niece's hand, and sat down beside her with a tearful joy.

"Ah, Mary, this is what ought to have been from the very first," she said; "this is different from Francis Ochterlony and his dreary house. The dear children will be happy here."

"Yes, it is very different," said Mary, returning the pressure of the soft little white hand; but her heart was full, and she could not find much more to say.

"And you, too, my dear love," Aunt Agatha went on, who was not a wise woman, looking into the new-comer's face—"you, too Mary, my darling—you will try to be happy in your old home? Well, dear, never mind answering me—I ought to know it is not the same for you as for us. I can't help feeling so happy to have you and the dear children. Look at Winnie, how delighted she is—she is so fond of children, though you would not think so just at first. Doesn't it make you feel the difference, Mary, to think you left her a baby, as one may say, and find her grown up into such a great girl?"

"I have so many things to make me feel the difference," said Mary—for Miss Seton was not one of those people who can do without an answer; and then Aunt Agatha was very sorry, and kissed her, with tears in her eyes.

"Yes, my love—yes, my dear love;" she said, as if she were soothing a child. "It was very foolish of me to use that expression; but you must try not to mind me, Mary. Cry, my dear, or don't answer me, or do just as you please. I never mean to say anything to recall—Look at the dear boys, how delighted they are. I know they will be fond of Winnie—she has such a nice way with children. Don't you think she has a very nice way?"

"She is very handsome," said Mary, looking out wistfully upon the young imperious creature, whose stage of existence seemed the very antipodes of her own.

"My dear love, she is beautiful," said Aunt Agatha. "Sir Edward told me he had never, even at court—and you know he was a great deal about the court in his young days—seen any one that promised to be such a beautiful woman. And to think she should just be our Winnie all the same! And so simple and sweet—such a perfect child with it all! You may wonder how I have kept her so long," continued Winnie's adoring guardian, "when you were married, Mary, before you were her age."

Mrs. Ochterlony tried hard to look up with the look of inquiry and interest which was expected of her in Aunt Agatha's face; but she could not. It was difficult enough to struggle with the recollections that hung about this place, without having them thrust continually in her face in this affectionately heartless way. Thus the wheel turned softly round again, and the reality of the situation crept out in bare outline from under the cloak of flowers and tenderness, as hard and clear as at Earlston. Mary's grief was her own concern, and not of very much consequence to anybody else in the world. She had no right to forget that fact, and yet she did forget it, not being used yet to stand alone. While Aunt Agatha, on her side, could not but think it was rather hard-hearted of Mary to show so little interest in her own sister, and such a sister as Winnie.

"It is not because she is not appreciated," Miss Seton went on, feeling all the more bound to celebrate her favourite's praises, "but I am so anxious she should make a good choice. She is not a girl that could marry anybody, you know. She has her own little ways, and such a great deal of character. I cannot tell you what a comfort it is to me, Mary, my dear love, to think that now we shall have your experience to guide us," Aunt Agatha added, melting into tenderness again.

"I am afraid experience is good for very little in such cases," said Mary, "but I hope there will be no guidance needed—she seems very happy now."

"To tell the truth, there is somebody at the Hall—" said Aunt Agatha, "and I want to have your opinion, my dear. Oh, Mary, you must not talk of no guidance being needed. I have watched over her ever since she was born. The wind has never blown roughly on her; and if my darling was to marry just an ordinary man, and be unhappy, perhaps—or no happier than the rest of us—" said Aunt Agatha, with a sigh. This last touch of nature went to Mary's heart.

"She is rich in having such love, whatever may happen to her," said Mrs. Ochterlony, "and she looks as if, after all, she might yet have the perfect life. She is very, very handsome—and good, I am sure, and sweet—or she would not be your child, Aunt Agatha; but we must not be too ready with our guidance. She would not be happy if her choice did not come spontaneously, and of itself."

"But oh, my dear love, the risk of marrying!" said Miss Seton, with a little sob—and she gave again a nervous pressure to Mary's hand, and did not restrain her tears. They sat thus in the twilight together, looking out upon the young little creatures for whom life was all brightly uncertain—one of them regarding with a pitiful flutter of dread and anxiety the world she had never ventured to enter into for herself. Perhaps a vision of Francis Ochterlony mingled with Miss Seton's thoughts, and a wistful backward glance at the life which might have been, but had not. The other sat very still, holding Aunt

Agatha's soft little fluttering hand in her own, which was steady, and did not tremble, with a strange pang of anguish and pity in her heart. Mary looked at life through no such fanciful mists—she knew, as she thought, its deepest depth and profoundest calamity; but the fountain of her tears was all sealed up and closed, because nobody but herself had any longer anything to do with it. And she, too, yearned over the young creature whose existence was all to come, and felt that it was had to think that she might be "no happier than the rest of us." It was these words which had arrested Mary, who, perhaps, might have otherwise thought that her own unquestionable sorrows demanded more sympathy than Winnie's problematical future. Thus the two elder ladies sat, until Winnie and the children came in, bring life and commotion with them. The blackbird was still singing in the bushes, the soft northern twilight lingering, and the dew falling, and all the sweet evening odours coming in. As for Aunt Agatha, her heart, though it was old, fluttered with all the agitation and disturbance of a girl's—while Mary, in the calm and silence of her loneliness, felt herself put back as it were into history, along with Ruth and Rachel, and her own mother, and all the women whose lives had been and were over. This was how it felt to her in the presence of Aunt Agatha's soft agitation—so that she half smiled at herself sitting there composed and tranquil, and soothing her companion into her usual calm.

"Mary agrees with me that this is better than Earlston, Winnie," said Aunt Agatha, when the children were all disposed of for the night, and the three who were so near to each other in blood, and who were henceforward to be close companions, yet who knew so little of each other in deed and truth, were left alone. The lamp was lighted, but the windows were still open, and the twilight still lingered, and a wistful blue-green sky looked in and put itself in swift comparison with the yellow lamplight. Winnie stood in one of the open windows, half in and half out, looking across the garden, as if expecting some one, and with a little contraction in her forehead that marred her fine profile slightly—giving a kind of careless half-attention to what was said.

"Does she?" she answered, indifferently; "I should have thought Earlston was a much handsomer house."

"It was not of handsome houses we were thinking, my darling," said Aunt Agatha, with soft reproof; "it was of love and welcome like what we are so glad as to give her here."

"Wasn't Mr. Ochterlony kind?" said Winnie, with half contempt. "Perhaps he does not fancy children. I don't wonder so very much at that. If they were not my own nephews, very likely I should think them dreadful little wretches. I suppose Mary won't mind me saying what I think. I always have been brought up to speak out."

"They are dear children," said poor Aunt Agatha, promptly. "I wish you would come in, my love. It is a great deal too late now to go out."

And at that moment Mary, who was the spectator, and could observe what was going on, had her attention attracted by a little jar and rattle of the window at which Winnie was standing. It was the girl's impatient movement which had done it; and whether it was in obedience to Miss Seton's mild command, or something more urgent, Winnie came in instantly with a lowering brow, and shut the window with some noise and sharpness. Probably Aunt Agatha was used to it, for she took no notice; but even her patient spirit seemed moved to astonishment by the sudden clang of the shutters, which the hasty young woman began to close.

"Leave that to Peggy, my darling," she said; "besides, it was nice to have the air, and you know how I like the last of the gloaming. That is the window where one can always see poor Sir Edward's light when he is at home. I suppose they are sure to be at home, since they have not come here to-night."

"Shall I open the window again, and let you look at the light, since you like it so much?" said the undutiful Winnie. "I closed it for that. I don't like to have anybody staring down at us in that superior sort of way—as if we cared; and I am sure nobody here was looking for them to-night."

"No, my dear, of course not," said Miss Seton. "Sir Edward is far too much of a gentleman to think of coming the night that Mary was expected home."

And then Winnie involuntarily turned half-round, and darted upon Mary an inquiring defiant look out of her stormy eyes. The look seemed to say, "So it was you who were the cause of it!" and then she swept past her sister with her streaming ribbons, and pulled out an embroidery frame which stood in a corner, and sat down to it in an irritated restless way. In that pretty room, in the soft evening atmosphere, beside the gentle old aunt, who was folding her soft hands in the sweet leisure that became her age, and the fair, mature, but saddened presence of the elder sister, who was resting in the calm of her exhaustion, a beautiful girl bending over an embroidery frame was just the last touch of perfection needed by the scene; but nobody would have thought so to see how Winnie threw herself down to her work, and dashed at it, all because of the innocent light that had been lighted in Sir Edward's window. Aunt Agatha did her best, by impressive looks and coughs, and little gestures, and transparently significant words, to subdue the spoilt child into good behaviour; and then, in despair, she thought herself called upon to explain.

"Sir Edward very often walks over of an evening," she said, edging herself as it were between Mary and her sister. "We are always glad to see him you know. It is a little change; and then he has some nice young friends who stay with him occasionally," said the deceitful woman. "But to be sure, he has too much feeling to think of making his appearance on the night of your coming home."

"I hope you will make no difference for me," said Mary.

"My love, I hope I know what is proper," said Aunt Agatha, with her little air of decision. And once more Winnie gave her sister a defiant accusing glance. "It is I that will be the sufferer, and it is all on your account," this look said, and the beautiful profile marked itself out upon the wall with that contraction across the forehead which took away half its loveliness. And then an uncomfortable silence ensued. Mrs. Ochterlony could say nothing more in a matter of which she knew so little, and Aunt Agatha, though she was the most yielding of guardians, still came to a point of propriety now and then on which she would not give way. This was how Mary discovered that instead of the Arcadian calm and retirement of which the cottage seemed an ideal resting place, she had come into another little centre of agitated human life, where her presence made a jar and discord without any fault of hers.

But it would have been worse than ungrateful, it would have been heartless and unkind, to have expressed such a feeling. So she, who was the stranger, had to put force on herself, and talk and lead her two companions back, so far as that was possible, from their pre-occupation; but at the best it was an unsatisfactory and forced conversation, and Mrs. Ochterlony was but too glad to own herself tired, and to leave her aunt and sister to themselves. They had given her their best room, with the fresh chintz and the pictures. They had made every arrangement for her comfort that affection and thoughtful care could suggest. What they had not been able to do was to let her come into their life without disturbing it, without introducing forced restrictions and new rules, without, in short, making her, all innocently and unwittingly on both sides, the discord in the house. Thus Mary found that, without changing her position, she had simply changed the scene; and the thought made her heart sick.

When Mrs. Ochterlony had retired, the two ladies of the cottage said nothing to each other for some time. Winnie continued her work in the same restless way as she had begun, and poor Aunt Agatha took up a book, which trembled in her hand. The impetuous girl had thrown open the window when she was reproved for closing it, and the light in Sir Edward's window shone far off on the tree tops, shedding an irritating influence upon Winnie when she looked up; and at the same time she could see the book shaking in Aunt Agatha's hand. Winnie was very fond of the guardian of her youth, and would have indignantly declared herself incapable of doing anything to vex her; but at the same time there could be no doubt that Aunt Agatha's nervousness gave a certain satisfaction to the young tyrant who ruled over her. Winnie saw that she was suffering, and could not help feeling pleased, for had not she too suffered all the evening? And she made no attempt to speak, or to take any initiative, so that it was only after Miss Seton had borne it as long as she was capable of bearing it, that the silence was broken at last.

"Dear Winnie," said Aunt Agatha, with a faltering voice, "I think, when you think of it, that you will not think you have been quite considerate in making poor Mary uncomfortable the first night."

"Mary feel uncomfortable?" cried Winnie. "Good gracious, Aunt Agatha, is one never to hear of anything but Mary? What has anybody done? I have been sitting working all the evening, like—like a dressmaker or poor needlewoman; does she object to that, I wonder?" and the young rebel put her frame back into its corner, and rose to the fray. Sir Edward's window still threw its distant light over the tree tops, and the sight of it made her smouldering passion blaze.

"Oh, my dear, you know that was not what I meant," said the disturbed and agitated aunt.

"I wish then, please, you would say what you mean," said Winnie. "She would not come with us at first, when we were all ready for her, and then she would not stay at Earlston after going there of her own free will. I dare say she made Mr. Ochterlony's life wretched with her trouble and widow's cap. Why didn't she be burnt with her Major, and be done with it?" said Winnie. "I am sure it would be by far the most comfortable way."

"Oh, Winnie, I thought you would have had a little sympathy for your sister," said Aunt Agatha, with tears.

"Everybody has sympathy for my sister," said Winnie, "from Peggy up to Sir Edward. I don't see why she should have it all. Hasn't she had her day? Nobody came in upon her, when she was my age, to put the house in mourning, and banish all one's friends. I hate injustice," cried the young revolutionary. "It is the injustice that makes me angry. I tell you, Aunt Agatha, she has had her day."

"Oh, Winnie," cried Miss Seton, weeping—"Oh, my darling child! don't be so hard upon poor Mary. When she was your age she had not half nor quarter the pleasures you have; and it was I that said she ought to come among her own friends."

"I am sure she would be a great deal better in some place of her own," said Winnie, with a little violence. "I wonder how she can go to other people's houses with all that lot of little children. If I should ever come home a widow from India, or anywhere else—"

"Winnie!" cried Aunt Agatha, with a little scream, "for Heaven's sake, don't say such things. Sorrow comes soon enough, without going to meet it; and if we can give her a little repose, poor dear—And what do a few pleasant evenings signify to you at your time of life?"

"A few pleasant evenings!" said Winnie; and she gave a kind of gasp, and threw herself into a chair, and cried too, for passion, and vexation, and disgust—perhaps, a little, too, out of self-disgust, though she would not acknowledge it. "As if that were all! And nobody thinks how the days are flying, and how it may all come to an end!" cried the passionate girl. After having given vent to such words, shame and remorse seized upon Winnie. Her cheeks blazed so that the scorching heat dried up her tears, and she sprang up again and flew at the shutters, on which her feelings had already expended themselves more than once, and brought down the bar with a clang that startled the whole house. As for Aunt Agatha, she sat aghast, and gazed, and could not believe her eyes or ears. What were the days that were flying, or the things that might come to an end? Could this wild exclamation have anything to do with the fact that Captain Percival was only on a visit at the Hall, and that his days were, so to speak, numbered? Miss Seton was not so old as to have forgotten what it was to be thus on the eve of losing sight of some one who had, as she would herself have said, "interested you." But Aunt Agatha had never in her life been guilty of violence or passion, and the idea of committing such a sin against all propriety and good taste as to have her usual visitors while the family was in affliction, was something which she could not take into her mind. It looked a breach of morals to Miss Seton; and for the moment it actually seemed as if Winnie, for the first time in her life, was not to have her way.

CHAPTER XV

"Everybody has sympathy with my sister," was what Winnie had said; and perhaps that was the hardest thing of all to bear. She was like the respectable son who came in disgusted into the midst of a merry-making all consecrated to the return of his disreputable prodigal brother. What did the fellow mean by coming home? Why did not he stay where he was, and fill his belly with the husks? If Mary had but been left to her young sister's sympathy, Winnie would (or thought she would) have lavished tenderness upon her. But the fact was, that it was very very hard to think how the days were passing by, and how perhaps all the precious evenings which remained might be cut off for ever, and its fairest prospect taken from her life, by Aunt Agatha's complaisance to Mary. It was true that it was Captain Percival's visit that Winnie was thinking of. Perhaps it was a little unmaidenly of her to own as much even to herself. It was a thing which Aunt Agatha would have died sooner than do, and which even Mary could not have been guilty of; but then girls now are brought up so differently. He might find himself shut out from the house, and might think the "family affliction" only a pretence, and might go away and make an end of it for ever—and Winnie was self-willed and passionate, and felt she must move heaven and earth sooner than let this be so. It seemed to her as if the happiness of her life hung upon it, and she could not but think, being young and fond of poetry, of the many instances in books in which the magical moment was thus lost, and two lives made miserable. And how could it harm Mary to see a strange face or two about; she who had had the fortitude to come home all the way from India, and had survived, and was in sufficiently good health after her grief, which of itself was a thing for which the critic of eighteen was disposed to despise a woman?

As she brooded over this at night in her own room with the window open, and her long hair streaming over her shoulders like a romantic heroine, and the young moonlight whitening over the trees, turrets, and windows of the Hall, a wild impatience of all the restrictions which were at that moment pressing upon her came upon Winnie. She had been very bright and pleasant with the little boys in the garden; which was partly because her heart melted towards the helpless children who were her own flesh and blood, and partly because at that time nothing had occurred to thwart or vex her; but from the moment when she had seen Sir Edward's window suddenly gleam into the twilight matters had changed. Then Winnie had perceived that the event which had been the central point of her daily life for some time back, the visit of Sir Edward and his "young friend," was not going to happen. It was the first time it had occurred to her that Mary's arrival was in any way to limit or transform her own existence; and her pride, her independence, her self-love and self-will were all immediately in arms. She, who had a little scorned her sister for the faculty of surviving, and for the steadiness with which she bore her burden, now asked herself indignantly, if Mary wanted to devote herself to her grief why she did not go into some seclusion to do it, instead of imposing penance upon other people? And what harm could it possibly have done Mary to see some one wandering in the garden by Winnie's side whose presence made the world complete, and left no more to be desired in it? or to look at poor Sir Edward talking to Aunt Agatha, who took an innocent pleasure in his talk? what harm could all this do to the ogress in the widow's cap who had come to trample on the happiness of the cottage? What pleasure could it be to her to turn the innocent old man, and the charming young one, away from the little flowery bower which they were so fond of?—for to be sure it did not occur to Winnie that Mrs. Ochterlony had nothing to do with it, and that it was of his own will and pleasure that Sir Edward had stayed away. Such were the thoughts which ran riot in the girl's mind while she stood in the moonlight at the open window. There was no balcony to go forth upon, and these were not sweet musings like Juliet's, but fiery discontented thoughts. Winnie did not mean to let her happiness slip by. She thought it was her happiness, and she was imperious and self-willed, and determined not to let her chance be stolen from her, as so many people do. As for Mary she had had her day. Let her be twenty times a widow, she had once been wooed, and had tasted all the delights of youth, and nobody had interfered with her—and Winnie too had made up her mind to have her day. Such a process of thinking could never, as has been already said, have gone through the minds of either of the other women in the cottage; but Winnie was a girl of the nineteenth century, in which young ladies are brought up differently—and she meant to have her rights, and the day of her delight, and all the privileges of her youth, whatever anybody might say.

As for Aunt Agatha on the other side, she too was making up her mind. She would have cut herself up in little pieces to please her darling, but she could not relinquish those rules of propriety which were dearer than herself—she was making up her mind to the struggle with tears and a kind of despair. It was a heartrending prospect, and she did not know how she could live without the light of her pretty Winnie's countenance, and see her looking sulky and miserable as she had done that night. But still in consideration of what was right, Miss Seton felt that she must and could bear anything. To expect a family in mourning, and who had just received a widow into their house, to see visitors, was an inhuman idea; and Aunt Agatha would have felt herself deeply humiliated could she really have supposed that anybody thought her capable of such a dereliction of duty. But she cried a little as she considered the awful results of her decision. Winnie, disappointed, sullen, and wretched, roused to rebellion, and taking no pleasure in her life, was a terrible picture to contemplate. Aunt Agatha felt that all the pleasure of her own existence was over, and cried a few salt tears over the sacrifice; but she knew her duty, and at least there was, or ought to be, a certain comfort in that.

Sir Edward came next day to pay a solemn visit at the cottage, and it gave her a momentary gleam of comfort to feel that this was the course of conduct which he at least expected of her. He came, and his "young friend" came with him, and for the moment smiles and contentment came back to the household. Sir Edward entered the drawing-room and shook hands tenderly with Mrs. Ochterlony, and sat down beside her, and began to talk as only an old friend could; but the young friend stayed in the garden with Winnie, and the sound of their voices came in now and then along with the songs of the birds and the fragrance of the flowers—all nature conspiring as usual to throw a charm about the young creatures, who apart from this charm did not make the loveliest feature in the social landscape. Sir Edward, on the other hand, sat down as a man sits down in a room where there is a seat which is known as his, and where he is in the way of doing a great deal of pleasant talk most days of his life. This was a special occasion, and he behaved himself accordingly. He patted Mary's hand softly with one of his, and held it in the other, and looked at her with that tender curiosity and inquiry which comes natural after a long absence. "She is changed, but I can see our old Mary still in her face," said the old man, patting her hand; and then he asked about the journey, and if he should see the children; and then the ordinary talk began.

"We did not come last evening, knowing you expected Mary," Sir Edward said, "and a most unpleasant companion I had all the night in consequence. Young people will be young people, you know—indeed, I never can help remembering, that just the other day I was young myself."

"Yes," said Aunt Agatha, faltering; "but you see under the circumstances, Sir Edward, Winnie could not expect that her sister—"

"Dear aunt," said Mary, "I have already begged you to make no difference for me."

"I am sure, my love, you are very kind," said Aunt Agatha; "you always were the most unselfish—But I hope I know my duty, whatever your good heart may induce you to say."

"And I hope, after a while," said Sir Edward, "that Mary too will be pleased to see her friends. We are all friends here, and everybody I know will be glad to welcome her home."

Most likely it was those very words that made Mary feel faint and ill, and unable to reply. But though she did not say anything, she at least made no sort of objection to the hope; and immediately the pleasant little stream of talk gushed up and ran past her as she knew it would. The two old people talked of the two young ones who were so interesting to them, and all that was special in Sir Edward's visit came to a close.

"Young Percival is to leave me next week," Sir Edward said. "I shall miss him sadly, and I am afraid it will cost him a heartache to go."

Aunt Agatha knew so well what her friend meant that she felt herself called upon to look as if she did not know. "Ah," she said, "I don't wonder. It is not often that he will find such a friend as you have been, Sir Edward: and to leave you, who are always such pleasant company—"

"My dear Miss Seton," said Sir Edward, with a gentle laugh, "you don't suppose that I expect him to have a heartache for love of me? He is a nice young fellow, and I am sorry to lose him; but if it were only my pleasant company—"

Then Aunt Agatha blushed as if it had been herself who was young Percival's attraction. "We shall all miss him, I am sure," she said. "He is so delicate and considerate. He has not come in, thinking no doubt that Mary is not equal to seeing strangers; but I am so anxious that Mary should see him—that is, I like her to know our friends," said the imprudent woman, correcting herself, and once more blushing crimson, as if young Percival had been a lover of her very own.

"He is a very nice fellow," said Sir Edward; "most people like him; but I don't know that I should have thought of describing him as considerate or delicate. Mary must not form too high an idea. He is just a young man like other young men," said the impartial baronet, "and likes his own way, and is not without a proper regard for his own interest. He is not in the least a hero of romance."

"I don't think he is at all mercenary, Sir Edward, if that is what you mean," said Aunt Agatha, blushing no longer, but growing seriously red.

"Mercenary!" said Sir Edward. "I don't think I ever dreamt of that. He is like other young men, you know. I don't want Mary to form too high an idea. But one thing I am sure of is that he is very sorry to go away."

And then a little pause happened, which was trying to Aunt Agatha, and in the interval the voices of the two young people in the garden sounded pleasantly from outside. Sitting thus within hearing of them, it was difficult to turn to any other subject; but yet Miss Seton would not confess that she could by any possibility understand what her old neighbour meant; and by way of escaping from that embarrassment plunged without thought into another in which she floundered helplessly after the first dash.

"Mary has just come from Earlston," she said. "It has grown quite a museum, do you know?—every sort of beautiful thing, and all so nicely arranged. Francis—Mr. Ochterlony," said Aunt Agatha, in confusion, "had always a great deal of taste—Perhaps you may remember—"

"Oh, yes, I remember," said Sir Edward—"such things are not easily forgotten—but I hope you don't mean to suppose that Percival—"

"I was thinking nothing about Captain Percival," Miss Seton said, feeling ready to cry—"What I meant was, I thought—I supposed you might have some interest—I thought you might like to know—"

"Oh, if that is all," said Sir Edward, "of course I take a great interest—but I thought you meant something of the same kind might be going on here. You must never think of that. I would never forgive myself if I were twice to be the occasion—"

"I was thinking nothing about Captain Percival," said Aunt Agatha, with tears of vexation in her eyes; "nor—nor anything else—I was talking for the sake of conversation: I was thinking perhaps you might like to hear—"

"May I show you my boys, Sir Edward?" said Mary, ringing the bell—"I should like you to see them; and I am going to ask you, by-and-by, what I must do with them. My brother-in-law is very much a recluse—I should be glad to have the advice of somebody who knows more of the world."

"Ah, yes, let us see the boys," said Sir Edward. "All boys are they?—that's a pity. You shall have the best advice I can give you, my dear Mary—and if you are not satisfied with that, you shall have better advice than mine; there is nothing so important as education; come along, little ones. So these are all?—three—I thought you had more than three. Ah, I beg your pardon. How do you do, my little man? I am your mamma's old friend—I knew her long before you were born—come and tell me your name."

And while Sir Edward got at these particulars, and took the baby on his knee, and made himself agreeable to the two sturdy little heroes who stood by, and stared at him, Aunt Agatha came round behind their backs, and gave Mary a quiet kiss—half by way of consolation, half by way of thanks—for, but for that happy inspiration of sending for the children, there was no telling what bog of unfortunate talk Miss Seton might not have tumbled into. Sir Edward was one of those men who know much, too much, about everybody—everything, he himself thought. He could detect allusions in the most careless conversation, and never forgot anything even when it was expedient and better that it should be forgotten. He was a man who had been unlucky in his youth, and who now, in his old age, though he was as well off as a man living all alone, in forlorn celibacy, could be, was always called poor Sir Edward. The very cottagers called him so, who might well have looked upon his life as a kind of paradise; and being thus recognised as an object of pity, Sir Edward had on the whole a very pleasant life. He knew all about everybody, and was apt at times to confuse his neighbours sadly, as he had just done Aunt Agatha, by a reference to the most private bits of their individual history; but it was never done with ill-nature—and after all there is a charm about a person who knows everything about everybody. He was a man who could have told you all about the Gretna Green marriage, which had cost poor Major Ochterlony so much trouble, as well, or perhaps even better, than if he had been present at it; and he was favourable to marriages in general, though he had never himself made the experience, and rather liked to preside over a budding inclination like that between Winifred Seton and young Percival. He took little Wilfrid on his knee when the children were thus brought upon the scene, in a fatherly, almost grand-fatherly way, and was quite ready to go into Mary's plans about them. He thought it was quite right, and the most suitable thing she could do, to settle somewhere where there was a good grammar-school; and he had already begun to calculate where the best grammar-schools were situated, and which would be the best plan for Mrs. Ochterlony, when the voices in the garden were heard approaching. Aunt Agatha had escaped from her embarrassment by going out to the young people, and was now bringing them in to present the young man for Mary's approval and criticism. Miss Seton came first, and there was anxiety in her face; and after her Winnie stepped in at the window, with a little flush upon her pretty cheek, and an unusual light in her eye; and after her—but at that moment the whole party were startled by a sudden sound of surprise, the momentary falling back of the stranger's foot from the step, and a surprised, half-suppressed exclamation. "Oh!—Mrs. Ochterlony!" exclaimed Sir Edward's young friend. As it happened all the rest were silent at that moment, and his voice was distinctly audible, though perhaps he had not meant it to be so. He himself was half hidden by the roses which clambered all over the cottage, but Mary naturally turned round, and turned her face to the window, when she heard her own name—as indeed they all did—surprised at the exclamation, and still more at the tone. And it was thus under the steady gaze of four pairs of eyes that Captain Percival came into the room. Perhaps but for that exclamation Mary might not have recognised him; but her ear had been trained to quick understanding of that inflection, half of amusement, half of contempt, which she had not heard for so long. To her ears it meant, "Oh, Mrs. Ochterlony!—she who was married over again, as people pretended—she who took in the Kirkmans, and all the people at the station." Captain Percival came in, and he felt his blood run cold as he met all those astonished eyes, and found Mary looking so intently at him. What had he done that they should all stare at him like that? for he was not so well aware of what he had given utterance to, nor of his tone in giving utterance to it, as they were. "Good heavens, what is the matter?" he said; "you all look at me as if I were a monster. Miss Seton, may I ask you to introduce me—"

"We have met before, I think," Mary said, quietly. "When I heard of Captain Percival I did not know it was the same I used to hear so much about in India. I think, when I saw you last, it was at—"

She wanted by sudden instinct to say it out and set herself right for ever and ever, here where everything about her was known; but the words seemed to choke her. In spite of herself she stopped short; how could she refer to that, the only great grievance in her life, her husband's one great wrong against her, now that he was in his grave, and she left in the world the defender and champion of all his acts and ways? She could not do it—she was obliged to stop short in the middle, and swallow the sob that would have choked her with the next word. And they stood all gazing at her, wondering what it was.

"Yes," said the young man, with a confidential air—"I remember it very well indeed—I heard all about it from Askell, you know;—but I never imagined, when I heard you talking of your sister, that it was the same Mrs. Ochterlony," he added, turning to Winnie, who was looking on with great and sudden interest. And then there was a pause—such a pause as occurs sometimes when there is an evident want of explanation somewhere, and all present feel that they are on the borders of a mystery. Somehow it changed the character of the assembled company. A few minutes before it had been the sad stranger, in her widow's cap, who was the centre of all, and to whom the visitors had to be presented in a half apologetic way, as if to a queen. Aunt Agatha, indeed, had been quite anxious on the subject, pondering how she could best bring Sir Edward's young friend, Winnie's admirer, under Mrs. Ochterlony's observation, and have her opinion of him; and now in an instant the situation was reversed, and it was Mary and Captain Percival alone who seemed to know each other, and to have recollections in common! Mary felt her cheeks flush in spite of herself, and Winnie grew pale with incipient jealousy and dismay, and Aunt Agatha fluttered about in a state of the wildest anxiety. At last both she and Sir Edward burst out talking at the same moment, with the same visible impulse. And they brought the children into the foreground, and lured them into the utterance of much baby nonsense, and even went so far as to foster a rising quarrel between Hugh and Islay, all to cover up from each other's eyes and smother in the bud this mystery, if it was a mystery. It was a singular disturbance to bring into such a quiet house; for how could the people who dwelt at home tell what those two strangers might have known about each other in India, how they might have been connected, or what secret might lie between them?—no more than people could tell in a cosy sheltered curtained room what might be going on at sea, or even on the dark road outside. And here there was the same sense of insecurity—the same distrust and fear. Winnie stood a little apart, pale, and with her delicate curved nostril a little dilated. Captain Percival was younger than Mary, and Mary up to this moment had been hedged round with a certain sanctity, even in the eyes of her discontented young sister. But there was some intelligence between them, something known to those two which was known to no one else in the party. This was enough to set off the thoughts of a self-willed girl, upon whose path Mary had thrown the first shadow, wildly into all kinds of suspicions. And to tell the truth, the elder people, who should have known better, were not much wiser than Winnie. Thus, while Hugh and Islay had a momentary struggle in the foreground, which called for their mother's active interference, the one ominous cloud of her existence once more floated up upon the dim firmament over Mary's head; though if she had but finished her sentence it would have been no cloud at all, and might never have come to anything there or thereafter. But this did not occur to Mrs. Ochterlony. What did occur to her in her vexation and pain was that her dead Hugh would be hardly dealt with among her kindred, if the stranger should tell her story. And she was glad, heartily glad, that there was little conversation afterwards, and that very soon the two visitors went away. But it was she who was the last to be aware that a certain doubt, a new and painful element of uncertainty stayed behind them in Aunt Agatha's pretty cottage after they were gone.

CHAPTER XVI

That night was a painful night for Winnie. The girl was self-willed and self-loving, as has been said. But she was not incapable of the more generous emotions, and when she looked at her sister she could no more suspect her of any wrong or treachery than she could suspect the sun shining over their heads. And her interest in the young soldier had gone a great length. She thought he loved her, and it was very hard to think that he was kept apart from her by a reason which was no reason at all. She roved about the garden all the evening in an unsettled way, thinking he would come again—thinking he could not stay away—explaining to herself that he must come to explain. And when she glanced indoors at the lamp which was lighted so much earlier than it needed to be, for the sake of Mary's sewing, and saw Mary seated beside it, in what looked like perfect composure and quietness, Winnie's impatience got the better of her. He was to be banished, or confined to a formal morning call, for Mary's sake, who sat there so calm, a woman for whom the fret and cares of life were over, while for Winnie life was only beginning, and her heart going out eagerly to welcome and lay claim to its troubles. And then the thought that it was the same Mrs. Ochterlony came sharp as a sting to Winnie's heart. What could he have had to do with Mrs. Ochterlony? what did she mean coming home in the character of a sorrowful widow, and shutting out their visitors, and yet awakening something like agitation and unquestionable recognition in the first stranger she saw? Winnie wandered through the garden, asking herself those questions, while the sweet twilight darkened, and the magical hour passed by, which had of late associated itself with so many dreams. And again he did not come. It was impossible to her, when she looked at Mary, to believe that there could be anything inexplicable in the link which connected her lover with her sister—but still he ought to have come to explain. And when Sir Edward's windows were lighted once more, and the certainty that he was not coming penetrated her mind, Winnie clenched her pretty hands, and went crazy for the moment with despite and vexation. Another long dull weary evening, with all the expectation and hope quenched out of it; another lingering night; another day in which there was as much doubt as hope. And next week he was going away! And it was all Mary's fault, however you took it—whether she had known more of him than she would allow in India, or whether it was simply the fault of that widow's cap which scared people away? This was what was going on in Winnie's agitated mind while the evening dews fell upon the banks of Kirtell, and the soft stars came out, and the young moon rose, and everything glistened and shone with the sweetness of a summer night. This fair young creature, who was in herself the most beautiful climax of all the beauty around her, wandered among her flowers with her small hands clenched, and the spirit of a little fury in her heart. She had nothing in the world to trouble her, and yet she was very unhappy, and it was all Mary's fault. Probably if Mary could but have seen into Winnie's heart she would have thought it preferable to stay at Earlston, where the Psyche and the Venus were highly indifferent, and had no hearts, but only arms and noses that could be broken. Winnie was more fragile than the Etruscan vases or the Henri II. porcelain. They had escaped fracture, but she had not; but fortunately this thought did not occur to Mrs. Ochterlony as she sat by the lamp working at Hugh's little blouses in Aunt Agatha's chair.

And Aunt Agatha, more actively jealous than Winnie herself, sat by knitting little socks—an occupation which she had devoted herself to, heart and soul, from the moment when she first knew the little Ochterlonys were coming home. She was knitting with the prettiest yarn and the finest needles, and had a model before her of proportions so shapely as to have filled any woman's soul with delight; but all that was eclipsed for the time by the doubt which hung over Mary, and the evident unhappiness of her favourite. Aunt Agatha was less wise than Winnie, and had not eyes to perceive that people were characteristic even in their wrong-doing, and that Captain Percival of himself could have nothing to do with the shock which Mary had evidently felt at the sight of him. Probably Miss Seton had not been above a little flirtation in her own day, and she did not see how that would come unnatural to a woman of her own flesh and blood. And she sat accordingly on the other side of the lamp and knitted, with a pucker of anxiety upon her fair old brow, casting wistful glances now and then into the garden where Winnie was.

"And I suppose, my dear, you know Captain Percival very well?" said Aunt Agatha, with that anxious look on her face.

"I don't think I ever saw him but once," said Mary, who was a little impatient of the question.

"But once, my dear love! and yet you both were so surprised to meet," said Aunt Agatha, with reasonable surprise.

"There are some moments when to see a man is to remember him ever after," said Mary. "It was at such a time that I saw Sir Edward's friend. It would be best to tell you about it, Aunt Agatha. There was a time when my poor Hugh—"

"Oh, Mary, my darling, you can't think I want to vex you," cried Aunt Agatha, "or make you go back again upon anything that is painful. I am quite satisfied, for my part, when you say so. And so would Winnie be, I am sure."

"Satisfied?" said Mary, wondering, and yet with a smile; and then she forgot the wonder of it in the anxiety. "I should be sorry to think that Winnie cared much for anything that could be said about Captain Percival. I used to hear of him from the Askells who were friends of his. Do not let her have anything to do with him, Aunt Agatha; I am sure he could bring her nothing but disappointment and pain."

"I—Mary?—Oh, my dear love, what can I do?" cried Miss Seton, in sudden confusion; and then she paused and recovered herself. "Of course if he was a wicked young man, I—I would not let Winnie have anything to do with him," she added, faltering; "but—do you think you are sure, Mary? If it should be only that you do not—like him; or that you have not got on—or something—"

"I have told you that I know nothing of him, Aunt," said Mary. "I saw him once at the most painful moment of my life, and spoke half-a-dozen words to him in my own house after that—but it is what I have heard the gentlemen say. I do not like him. I think it was unmannerly and indelicate to come to my house at such a time—"

"My darling!" said Aunt Agatha, soothing her tenderly. Miss Seton was thinking of the major's death, not of any pain that might have gone before; and Mary by this time in the throng of recollections that came upon her had forgotten that everybody did not know.

"But that is not the reason," Mrs. Ochterlony said, composing herself: "the reason is that he could not, unless he is greatly changed, make Winnie otherwise than unhappy. I know the reputation he had. The Heskeths would not let him come to their house after Annie came out; and I have even heard Hugh—"

"My dear love, you are agitating yourself," cried Aunt Agatha. "Oh, Mary, if you only knew how anxious I am to do anything to recall—"

"Thank you," said Mrs. Ochterlony, with a faint smile: "it is not so far off that I should require anything to recall all that has happened to me—but for Winnie's sake—"

And it was just at that moment that the light suddenly appeared in Sir Edward's window, and brought Winnie in, white and passionate, with a thunder-cloud full of tears and lightnings and miserable headache and self-reproach, lowering over her brilliant eyes.

"It is very good of Mary, I am sure, to think of something for my sake," said Winnie. "What is it, Aunt Agatha? Everything is always so unpleasant that is for one's good. I should like to know what it was."

And then there was a dead silence in the pretty room. Mary bent her head over her work, silenced by the question, and Aunt Agatha, in a flutter of uncertainty and tribulation, turned from one to the other, not knowing which side to take nor what to say.

"Mary has come among us a stranger," said Winnie, "and I suppose it is natural that she should think she knows our business better than we do. I suppose that is always how it seems to a stranger; but at the same time it is a mistake, Aunt Agatha, and I wish you would let Mary know that we are disposed to manage for ourselves. If we come to any harm it is we who will have to suffer, and not Mary," the impetuous girl cried, as she drew that unhappy embroidery frame out of its corner.

And then another pause, severe and startling, fell upon the little party. Aunt Agatha fluttered in her chair, looking from one to another, and Winnie dragged a violent needle through her canvas, and a great night moth came in and circled about them, and dashed itself madly against the globe of light on the table. As for Mary, she sat working at Hugh's little blouse, and for a long time did not speak.

"My dear love!" Aunt Agatha said at last, trembling, "you know there is nothing in the world I would not do to please you, Winnie,—nor Mary either. Oh, my dear children, there are only you two in the world. If one says anything, it is for the other's good. And here we are, three women together, and we are all fond of each other, and surely, surely, nothing ever can make any unpleasantness!" cried the poor lady, with tears. She had her heart rent in two, like every mediatrix, and yet the larger half, as was natural, went to her darling's side.

"Winnie is right enough," Mary said, quietly. "I am a stranger, and I have no right to interfere; and very likely, even if I were permitted to interfere, it would do no good. It is a shame to vex you, Aunt Agatha. My sister must submit to hear my opinion one time, but I am not going to disturb the peace of the house, nor yours."

"Oh, Mary, my dear, it is only that she is a little impatient, and has always had her own way," said Aunt Agatha, whispering across the table. And then no more was said. Miss Seton took up her little socks, and Winnie continued to labour hotly at her embroidery, and the sound of her work, and the rustle of Mary's arm at her sewing, and the little click of Aunt Agatha's knitting-needles, and the mad dashes of the moth at the lamp, were all the sounds in the room, except, indeed, the sound of the Kirtell, flowing softly over its pebbles at the foot of the brae, and the sighing of the evening air among the trees, which were sadly contradictory of the spirit of the scene within; and at a distance over the woods, gleamed Sir Edward's window, with the ill-disposed light which was, so to speak, the cause of all. Perhaps, after all, if Mrs. Ochterlony had stayed at Earlston, where the Psyche and the Venus were not sensitive, and there was nothing but marble and china to jar into discord, it might have been better; and what would have been better still, was the grey cottage on the roadside, with fire on the hearth and peace and freedom in the house; and it was to that, with a deep and settled longing, that Mary's heart and thoughts went always back.

When Mrs. Ochterlony had withdrawn, the scene changed much in Aunt Agatha's drawing-room. But it was still a pretty scene. Then Winnie came and poured out her girlish passion in the ears and at the feet of her tender guardian. She sank down upon the carpet, and laid her beautiful head upon Aunt Agatha's knee, and clasped her slender arms around her. "To think she should come and drive every one I care for away from the house, and set even you against me!" cried Winnie, with sobs of vexation and rage.

"Oh, Winnie! not me! Never me, my darling," cried Aunt Agatha; and they made a group which a painter would have loved, and which would have conveyed the most delicate conception of love and grief to an admiring public, had it been painted. Nothing less than a broken heart and a blighted life would have been suggested to an innocent fancy by the abandonment of misery in Winnie's attitude. And to tell the truth, she was very unhappy, furious with Mary, and with herself, and with her lover, and everybody in the wide world. The braids of her beautiful hair got loose, and the net that confined them came off, and the glistening silken flood came tumbling about her shoulders. Miss Seton could not but take great handfuls of it as she tried to soothe her darling; and poor Aunt Agatha's heart was rent in twain as she sat with this lovely burden in her lap, thinking, Oh, if nobody had ever come to distract Winnie's heart with love-making, and bring such disturbance to her life; oh, if Hugh Ochterlony had thought better of it, and had not died! Oh, if Mary had never seen Captain Percival, or seeing him, had approved of him, and thought him of all others the mate she would choose for her sister! The reverse of all these wishes had happened, and Aunt Agatha could not but look at the combination with a certain despair.

"What can I do, my dear love?" she said. "It is my fault that Mary has come here. You know yourself it would have been unnatural if she had gone anywhere else: and how could we go on having people, with her in such deep mourning? And as for Captain Percival, my darling—"

"I was not speaking of Captain Percival," said Winnie, with indignation. "What is he to me?—or any man? But what I will not bear is Mary interfering. She shall not tell us what we are to do. She shan't come in and look as if she understood everything better than we do. And, Aunt Agatha, she shan't—she shall never come, not for a moment, between you and me!"

"My darling child! my dear love!" cried poor Aunt Agatha, "as if that was possible, or as if poor Mary wanted to. Oh, if you would only do her justice, Winnie? She is fond of you; I know she is fond of you. And what she was saying was entirely for your good—"

"She is fond of nobody but her children," said Winnie, rising up, and gathering her bright hair back into the net. "She would not care what happened to us, as long as all was well with her tiresome little boys."

Aunt Agatha wrung her hands, as she looked in despair at the tears on the flushed cheek, and the cloud which still hung upon her child's brow. What could she say? Perhaps there was a little truth in what Winnie said. The little boys, though Miss Seton could not help feeling them to be so unimportant in comparison with Winnie and her beginning of life, were all in all to Mrs. Ochterlony; and when she had murmured again that Mary meant it all for Winnie's good, and again been met by a scornful protestation that anything meant for one's good was highly unpleasant, Aunt Agatha was silenced, and had not another word to say. All that she could do was to pet her wilful darling more than ever, and to promise with tears that Mary should never, never make any difference between them, and that she herself would do anything that Winnie wished or wanted. The interview left her in such a state of agitation that she could not sleep, nor even lie down, till morning was breaking, and the new day had begun—but wandered about in her dressing-gown, thinking she heard Winnie move, and making pilgrimages to her room to find her, notwithstanding all her passion and tears, as fast asleep as one of Mary's boys—which was very, very different from Aunt Agatha's case, or Mary's either, for that matter. As for Mrs. Ochterlony, it is useless to enter into any description of her feelings. She went to bed with a heavy heart, feeling that she had made another failure, and glad, as people are when they have little comfort round them, of the kind night and the possible sleep which, for a few hours at least, would make her free of all this. But she did not sleep as Winnie did, who felt herself so ill-used and injured. Thus, Mrs. Ochterlony's return, a widow, brought more painful agitation to Miss Seton's cottage than had been known under its quiet roof since the time when she went away a bride.

CHAPTER XVII

And after this neither Sir Edward nor his young friend appeared for two whole days. Any girl of Winifred Seton's impetuous character, who has ever been left in such a position on the very eve of the telling of that love-tale, which had been all but told for several weeks past, but now seemed suddenly and artificially arrested just at the moment of utterance—will be able to form some idea of Winnie's feelings during this dreadful interval. She heard the latch of the gate lifted a hundred times in the day, when, alas, there was no one near to lift the latch. She was afraid to go out for an instant, lest in that instant "they" should come; her brain was ringing with supposed sounds of footsteps and echoes of voices, and yet the road lay horribly calm and silent behind the garden hedge, with no passengers upon it. And these two evenings the light came early into Sir Edward's window, and glared cruelly over the trees. And to be turned inward upon the sweet old life from which the charm had fled, and to have to content one's self with flowers and embroidery, and the canary singing, and the piano, and Aunt Agatha! Many another girl has passed through the same interval of torture, and felt the suspense to be killing, and the crisis tragic—but yet to older eyes perhaps even such a dread suspension of all the laws of being has also its comic side. Winnie, however, took care to keep anybody from laughing at it in the cottage. It was life and death to her, or at least so she thought. And her suppressed frenzy of anxiety, and doubt, and fear, were deep earnest to Aunt Agatha, who seemed now to be living her own early disappointments over again, and more bitterly than in the first version of them. She tried hard to remember the doubt thrown upon Captain Percival by Mary, and to persuade herself that this interposition was providential, and meant to save her child from an unhappy marriage. But when Miss Seton saw Winnie's tragic countenance, her belief in Providence was shaken. She could not see the good of anything that made her darling suffer. Mary might be wrong, she might be prejudiced, or have heard a false account, and it might be simply herself who was to blame for shutting her doors, or seeming to shut her doors, against her nearest and oldest neighbours. Could it be supposed that Sir Edward would bring any one to her house who was not a fit associate or a fit suitor, if things should take such a turn, for Winnie? Under the painful light thrown upon the subject by Winnie's looks, Aunt Agatha came altogether to ignore that providential view which had comforted her at first, and was so far driven in the other direction at last as to write Sir Edward a little note, and take the responsibility upon her own shoulders. What Miss Seton wrote was, that though, in consequence of their late affliction, the family were not equal to seeing visitors in a general way, yet that it would be strange indeed if they were to consider Sir Edward a stranger, and that she hoped he would not stay away, as she was sure his company would be more a comfort to Mary than anything else. And she also hoped Captain Percival would not leave the Hall without coming to see them. It was such a note as a maiden lady was fully justified in writing to an old friend—an invitation, but yet given with a full consideration of all the proprieties, and that tender regard for Mary's feelings which Aunt Agatha had shown throughout. It was written and despatched when Winnie had gone out, as she did on the third day, in proud defiance and desperation, so that if Sir

Edward's sense of propriety and respect for Mary's cap should happen to be stronger than Aunt Agatha's, no further vexation might come to the young sufferer from this attempt to set all right.

And Winnie went out without knowing of this effort for her consolation. She went down by the Kirtell, winding down the wooded banks, in the sweet light and shade of the August morning, seeing nothing of the brightness, wrapped up and absorbed in her own sensations. She felt now that the moment of fate had passed,—that moment that made or marred two lives;—and had in her heart, in an embryo unexpressed condition, several of Mr. Browning's minor poems, which were not then written; and felt a general bitterness against the world for the lost climax, the dénouement which had not come. She thought to herself even, that if the tale had been told, the explanation made, and something, however tragical, had happened after, it would not have been so hard to bear. But now it was clear to Winnie that her existence must run on soured and contracted in the shade, and that young Percival must stiffen into a worldly and miserable old bachelor, and that their joint life, the only life worth living, had been stolen from them, and blighted in the bud. And what was it all for?—because Mary, who had had all the good things of this life, who had loved and been married in the most romantic way, and had been adored by her husband, and reigned over him, had come, so far, to an end of her career. Mary was over thirty, an age at which Winnie could not but think it must be comparatively indifferent to a woman what happened—at which the snows of age must have begun to benumb her feelings, under any circumstances, and the loss of a husband or so did not much matter; but at eighteen, and to lose the first love that had ever touched your heart! to lose it without any reason—without the satisfaction of some dreadful obstacle in the way, or misunderstanding still more dreadful; without ever having heard the magical words and tasted that first rapture!—Ah, it was hard, very hard; and no wonder that Winnie was in a turmoil of rage, and bitterness, and despair.

The fact was, that she was so absorbed in her thoughts as not to see him there where he was waiting for her. He had seen her long ago, as she came down the winding road, betraying herself at the turnings by the flutter of her light dress—for Winnie's mourning was slight—and he had waited, as glad as she could be of the opportunity, and the chance of seeing her undisturbed, and free from all critical eyes. There is a kind of popular idea that it is only a good man, or one with a certain "nobility" in his character, who is capable of being in love; but the idea is not so justifiable as it would seem to be. Captain Percival was not a good young man, nor would it be safe for any conscientious historian to claim for him generous or noble qualities to any marked degree; but at the same time I am not disposed to qualify the state of his sentiments by saying, as is generally said of unsatisfactory characters, that he loved Winnie as much as he could love anything. He was in love with her, heart and soul, as much as if he had been a paladin. He would not have stayed at any obstacle, nor regarded either his own comfort or hers, or any other earthly bar between them. When Winnie thought him distant from her, and contemplating his departure, he had been haunting all the old walks which he knew Miss Seton and her niece were in the habit of taking. He was afraid of Mary—that was one thing indisputable—and he thought she would harm him, and bring up his old character against him; and felt instinctively that the harm which he thought he knew of her, could not be used against her here. And it was for this reason that he had not ventured again to present himself at the cottage; but he had been everywhere about, wherever he thought there was any chance of meeting the lady of his thoughts. And if Winnie had not been so anxious not to miss that possible visitor; if she had been coming and going, and doing all she usually did, their meeting must have taken place two days ago, and all the agony and trouble been spared. He watched her now, and held his breath, and traced her at all the turnings of the road, now by a puff of her black and white muslin dress, and then by a long streaming ribbon catching among the branches—for Winnie was fond of long ribbons wherever she could introduce them. And she was so absorbed with her own settled anguish, that she had stepped out upon him from among the trees before she was aware.

"Captain Percival!" said Winnie, with an involuntary cry; and she felt the blood so rush to her cheeks with sudden delight and surprise, that she was in an instant put on her guard, and driven to account for it.—"I did not see there was any one here—what a fright you have given me. And we, who thought you had gone away," added Winnie, looking suddenly at him with blazing defiant eyes.

If he had not been in love, probably he would have known what it all meant—the start, the blush, the cry, and that triumphant, indignant, reproachful, exulting look. But he had enough to do with his own sensations, which makes a wonderful difference in such a case.

"Gone away!" he said, on the spur of the moment—"as if I could go away—as if you did not know better than that."

"I was not aware that there was anything to detain you," said Winnie; and all at once from being so tragical, her natural love of mischief came back, and she felt perfectly disposed to play with her mouse. "Tell me about it. Is it Sir Edward? or perhaps you, too, have had an affliction in your family. I think that is the worst of all," she said, shaking her pretty head mournfully—and thus the two came nearer to each other and laughed together, which was as good a means of rapprochement as anything else.

But the young soldier had waited too long for this moment to let it all go off in laughter. "If you only knew how I have been trying to see you," he said. "I have been at the school and at the mill, and in the woods—in all your pet places. Are you condemned to stay at home because of this affliction? I could not come to the cottage because, though Miss Seton is so kind, I am sure your sister would do me an ill turn if she could."

Winnie was startled, and even a little annoyed by this speech—for it is a fact always to be borne in mind by social critics, that one member of a family may be capable of saying everything that is unpleasant about another, without at the same time being disposed to hear even an echo of his or her own opinion from stranger lips. Winnie was of this way of thinking. She had not taken to her sister, and was quite ready herself to criticise her very severely; but when somebody else did it, the result was very different. "Why should my sister do you an ill turn?" she said.

"Oh!" said young Percival; "it is because you know she knows that I know all about it—"

"All about it!" said Winnie. She was tall already, but she grew two inches taller as she stood and expanded and looked her frightened lover into nothing. "There can be nothing about Mary, Captain Percival, which you and all the world may not know."

And then the young man saw he had made a wrong move. "I have not been haunting the road for hours to talk about Mrs. Ochterlony," he said. "She does not like me, and I am frightened for her. Oh, Winnie, you know very well why. You know I would tremble before anybody who might make you think ill of me. It is cruel to pretend you don't understand."

And then he took her hand and told her everything—all that she looked for, and perhaps more than all—for there are touches of real eloquence about what a man says when he is really in love (even if he should be no great things in his own person) which transcend as much as they fall short of, the suggestions of a woman's curious fancy. She had said it for him two or three times in her own mind, and had done it far more elegantly and neatly. But still there was something about the genuine article which had not been in Winnie's imagination. There were fewer words, but there was a great deal more excitement, though it was much less cleverly expressed. And then, before they knew how, the crisis was over, the dénouement accomplished, and the two sitting side by side as in another world. They were sitting on the trunk of an old beech-tree, with the leaves rustling and the birds twittering over them, and Kirtell running, soft and sweet, hushed in its scanty summer whisper at their feet; all objects familiar, and well-known to them—and yet it was another world. As for Mr. Browning's poems about the unlived life, and the hearts all shrivelled up for want of a word at the right moment, Winnie most probably would have laughed with youthful disdain had they been suggested to her now. This little world, in which the fallen beech-tree was the throne, and the fairest hopes and imaginations possible to man, crowded about the youthful sovereigns, and paid them obsequious court, was so different from the old world, where Sir Edward at the Hall, and Aunt Agatha in the Cottage, were expecting the young people, that these two, as was not unnatural, forgot all about it, and lingered together, no one interfering with them, or even knowing they were there, for long enough to fill Miss Seton's tender bosom with wild anxieties and terrors. Winnie had not reached home at the early dinner-hour—a thing which was to Aunt Agatha as if the sun had declined to rise, or the earth (to speak more correctly) refused to perform her proper revolutions. She became so restless, and anxious, and unhappy, that Mary, too, was roused into uneasiness. "It must be only that she is detained somewhere," said Mrs. Ochterlony. "She never would allow herself to be detained," cried Aunt Agatha, "and oh, Mary, my darling is unhappy. How can I tell what may have happened?" Thus some people made themselves very wretched about her, while Winnie sat in perfect blessedness, uttering and listening to all manner of heavenly nonsense on the trunk of the fallen tree.

Aunt Agatha's wretchedness, however, dispersed into thin air the moment she saw Winnie come in at the garden-gate, with Captain Percival in close attendance. Then Miss Seton, with natural penetration, saw in an instant what had happened; felt that it was all natural, and wondered why she had not foreseen this inevitable occurrence. "I might have known," she said to Mary, who was the only member of the party upon whom this wonderful event had no enlivening effect; and then Aunt Agatha recollected herself, and put on her sad face, and faltered an apology. "Oh, my dear love, I know it must be hard upon you to see it," she said, apologizing as it were to the widow for the presence of joy.

"I would be a poor soul indeed, if it was hard upon me to see it," said Mary. "No, Aunt Agatha, I hope I am not so shabby as that. I have had my day. If I look grave, it is for other reasons. I was not thinking of myself."

"My love! you were always so unselfish," said Miss Seton. "Are you really anxious about him? See how happy he looks—he cannot be so fond of her as that, and so happy, and yet a deceiver. It is not possible, Mary."

This was in the afternoon, when they had come out to the lawn with their work, and the two lovers were still together—not staying in one place, as their elders did, but flitting across the line of vision now and then and, as it were, pervading the atmosphere with a certain flavour of romance and happiness.

"I did not say he was a deceiver—he dared not be a deceiver to Winnie," said Mrs. Ochterlony; "there may be other sins than that."

"Oh, Mary, don't speak as if you thought it would turn out badly," cried Aunt Agatha, clasping her hands; and she looked into Mrs. Ochterlony's face as if somehow she had the power by retracting her opinion to prevent things from turning out badly. Mary was not a stoic, nor above the sway of all the influences around her. She could not resist the soft pleading eyes that looked into her face, nor the fascination of her young sister's happiness. She held her peace, and even did her best to smile upon the spectacle, and to hope in her heart that true love might work magically upon the man who had now, beyond redemption, Winnie's future in his hands. For her own part, she shrank from him with a vague sense of alarm and danger; and had it been possible to do any good by it, would have felt herself capable of any exertion to cast the intruder out. But it was evident that under present circumstances there was no good to be done. She kept her boys out of his way with an instinctive dread which she could not explain to herself, and shuddered when poor Aunt Agatha, hoping to conciliate all parties, set little Wilfrid for a moment on their visitor's knee, and with a wistful wile reminded him of the new family relationships Winnie would bring him. Mary took her child away with a shivering sense of peril which was utterly unreasonable. Why had it been Wilfrid of all others who was brought thus into the foreground? Why should it be he who was selected as a symbol of the links of the future? Wilfrid was but an infant, and derived no further impression from his momentary perch upon Captain Percival's knee, than that of special curiosity touching the beard which was a new kind of ornament to the fatherless baby, and tempting for closer investigation; but his mother took him away, and carried him indoors, and disposed of him carefully in the room which Miss Seton had made into a nursery, with an anxious tremor which was utterly absurd and out of all reason. But though instinct acted upon her to this extent, she made no further attempt to warn Winnie or hinder the course of events which had gone too fast for her. Winnie would not have accepted any warning—she would have scorned the most trustworthy advice, and repulsed even the most just and right interference—and so would Mary have done in Hugh Ochterlony's case, when she was Winnie's age. Thus her mouth was shut, and she could say nothing. She watched the two with a pathetic sense of impotence as they went and came, thinking, oh, if she could but make him what Hugh Ochterlony was; and yet the Major had been far, very far from perfect, as the readers of this history are aware. When Captain Percival went away, the ladies were still in the garden; for it was necessary that the young man should go home to the Hall to join Sir Edward at dinner, and tell his story. Winnie, a changed creature, stood at the garden-gate, leaning upon the low wall, and watched him till he was out of sight; and her aunt and her sister looked at her, each with a certain pathos in her face. They were both women of experience in their different ways, and there could not but be something pathetic to them in the sight of the young creature at the height of her happiness, all-confident and fearing no evil. It came as natural to them to think of the shadows that must, even under the happiest conditions, come over that first incredible brightness, as it was to her to feel that every harm and fear was over, and that now nothing could touch or injure her more. Winnie turned sharp round when her lover disappeared, and caught Mary's eye, and its wistful expression, and blazed up at once into momentary indignation, which, however, was softened by the contempt of youth for all judgment other than its own, and by the kindly influence of her great happiness. She turned round upon her sister, sudden and sharp as some winged creature, and set her all at once on her defence.

"You do not like him," she said, "but you need not say anything, Mary. It does not matter what you say. You had your day, and would not put up with any interference—and I know him a hundred—a thousand times better than you can do; and it is my day now."

"Yes," said Mary. "I did not mean to say anything. I do not like him, and I think I have reason; but Winnie, dear, I would give anything in the world to believe that you know best now."

"Oh, yes, I know best," said Winnie, with a soft laugh; "and you will soon find out what mistakes people make who pretend to know—for I am sure he thinks there could be something said, on the other side, about you."

"About me," said Mary—and though she did not show it, but stood before her sister like a stately tower firm on its foundation, she was aware of a thrill of nervous trembling that ran through her limbs, and took the strength out of them. "What did he say about me?"

"He seemed to think there was something that might be said," said Winnie, lightly. "He was afraid of you. He said you knew that he knew all about you; see what foolish ideas people take up! and I said," Winnie went on, drawing herself up tall and straight by her stately sister's side, with that superb assumption of dignity which is fair to see at her age, "that there never could be anything about you that he and all the world might not know!"

Mary put out her hand, looking stately and firm as she did so—but in truth it was done half groping, out of a sudden mist that had come up about her. "Thank you, Winnie," she said, with a smile that had anguish in it; and Winnie with a sudden tender impulse out of her own happiness, feeling for the first time the contrast, looked at Mary's black dress beside her own light one, and at Mary's hair as bright as her own, which was put away beneath that cap which she had so often mocked at, and threw her arms round her sister with a sudden thrill of compassion and tenderness unlike anything she had ever felt before.

"Oh, Mary, dear!" she cried, "does it seem heartless to be so happy and yet to know that you—"

"No," said Mary, steadily—taking the girl, who was as passionate in her repentance as in her rebellion, to her own bosom. "No, Winnie; no, my darling—I am not such a poor soul as that. I have had my day."

And it was thus that the cloud rolled off, or seemed to roll off, and that even in the midst of that sharp reminder of the pain which life might still have in store for her, the touch of nature came to heal and help. The enemy who knew all about it might have come in bringing with him sickening suggestions of horrible harm and mischief; but anything he could do would be in vain here, where everybody knew more about her still; and to have gained as she thought her little sister's heart, was a wonderful solace and consolation. Thus Mary's faith was revived again at the moment when it was most sorely shaken, and she began to feel, with a grateful sense of peace and security, the comfort of being, as Aunt Agatha said, among her own friends.

CHAPTER XVIII

The announcement of Winnie's engagement made, as was to be looked for, a considerable commotion among all the people connected with her. The very next morning Sir Edward himself came down to the Cottage with a very serious face. He had been disposed to play with the budding affection and to take pleasure in the sight of the two young creatures as they drew towards each other; for Percival, though in love, was not without prudence (his friend thought), and Winnie, though very open to impressions, was capricious and fanciful, and not the kind of girl, Sir Edward imagined, to say Yes to the first man who asked her. Thus the only sensible adviser on the spot had wilfully blinded himself. It had not occurred to him that Winnie might think of Percival, not as the first man who had ever asked her, but as the only man whom she loved; nor that Percival, though prudent enough, liked his own way, and was as liable to be carried away by passion as a better man. These reflections had not come into Sir Edward's head, and consequently he had rather encouraged the growing tenderness, which now all at once had turned into earnest, and had become a matter of responsibility and serious concern. Sir Edward came into Miss Seton's pretty drawing-room with care on his brow. The young people had gone out together to Kirtell-side to visit the spot of their momentous interview, and doubtless to go over it all again, as people do at that foolish moment, and only Aunt Agatha and Mrs. Ochterlony were at home. Sir Edward went in, and sat down between the two ladies, and offered his salutations with a pensive gravity which made Mary smile, but brought a cloud of disquietude over Aunt Agatha's gentle countenance. He sighed as he said it was a fine day. He even looked sympathetically at the roses, as if he knew of some evil that was about to befall them;—and his old neighbour knew his ways and knew that he meant something, and with natural consciousness divined at once what it was.

"You have heard what has happened," said Aunt Agatha, trembling a little, and laying down her work. "It is so kind of you to come over at once; but I do hope that is not why you are looking so grave?"

"Am I looking grave?" said Sir Edward, clearing up in an elaborate way; "I did not mean it, I am sure. I suppose we ought to have seen it coming and been prepared; but these sort of things always take one by surprise. I did not think Winnie was the sort of girl to—to make up her mind all at once, you know—the very first man that asked her. I suppose it was my mistake."

"If you think it was the very first that asked her!" cried Aunt Agatha, who felt this reproach go to her heart, "it is a mistake. She is only eighteen—a mere child—but I was saying to Mary only yesterday, that it was not for want of being admired—"

"Oh, yes," said Sir Edward, with a little wave of his hand, "we all know she has been admired. One's eyes alone would have proved that; and she deserves to be admired; and that is generally a girl's chief stronghold, in my opinion. She knows it, and learns her own value, and does not yield to the first fellow who has the boldness to say right out—"

"I assure you, Sir Edward," said Aunt Agatha, growing red and very erect in her chair, and assuming a steadiness which was unfortunately quite contradicted by the passionate quiver of her lip, "that you do Winnie great injustice—so far as being the first goes—"

"What does it matter if he were the first or the fiftieth, if she likes him?" said Mary, who had begun by being much amused, but who had ended by being a little indignant; for she had herself married at eighteen and never had a lover but Hugh Ochterlony, and felt herself disapproved of along with her sister.

Upon which Sir Edward shook his head.

"Certainly, my dear Mary, if she likes him," said the Baronet; "but the discouraging thing is, that an inexperienced girl—a girl so very well brought up as Winnie has been—should allow herself, as I have said, to like the very first man who presents himself. One would have thought some sort of introduction was necessary before such a thought could have penetrated into her mind. After she had been obliged to receive it in that way—then, indeed—But I am aware that there are people who have not my scruples," said Sir Edward, with a sigh; for he was, as all the neighbourhood was aware, a man of the most delicate mind.

"If you think my dear, pure-minded child is not scrupulous, Sir Edward!" cried poor Aunt Agatha—but her emotion was so great that her voice failed her; and Mary, half amused and half angry, was the only champion left for Winnie's character, thus unexpectedly assailed.

"Poor child, I think she is getting very hard measure," said Mary. "I don't mean to blame you, but I think both of you encouraged her up to the last moment. You let them be always together, and smiled on them; and they are young, and what else could you expect? It is more delicate to love than to flirt," said Mrs. Ochterlony. She had not been nearly so well brought up as her sister, nor with such advanced views, and what she said brought a passing blush upon her matron cheek. Winnie could have discussed all about love without the shadow of a blush, but that was only the result of the chronological difference, and had nothing to do with purity of heart.

"If we have had undue confidence," said Sir Edward, with a sigh, "we will have to pay for it. Mary speaks—as I have heard many women speak—without making any consideration of the shock it must be to a delicate young girl; and I think, after the share which I may say I have myself had in Winnie's education, that I might be permitted to express my surprise; and Percival ought to have shown a greater regard for the sacredness of hospitality. I cannot but say that I was very much vexed and surprised."

It may well be supposed that such an address, after poor Aunt Agatha's delight and exultation in her child's joy, and her willingness to see with Winnie's eyes and accept Winnie's lover on his own authority, was a most confounding utterance. She sat silent, poor lady, with her lips apart and her eyes wide open, and a kind of feeling that it was all over with Winnie in her heart. Aunt Agatha was ready to fight her darling's battles to her last gasp, but she was not prepared to be put down and made an end of in this summary way. She had all sorts of pretty lady-like deprecations about their youth and Winnie's inexperience ready in her mind, and had rather hoped to be assured that to have her favourite thus early settled in life was the very best that anybody would desire for her. Miss Seton had been so glad to think in former days that Sir Edward always understood her, and she had thought Winnie's interests were as dear to him as if she had been a child of his own; and now to think that Sir Edward regarded an event so important for Winnie as an evidence of indelicacy on her part, and of a kind of treachery on her lover's! All that Aunt Agatha could do was to throw an appealing look at Mary, who had hitherto been the only one dissatisfied or disapproving. She knew more about Captain Percival than any one. Would not she say a word for them now?

"He must have thought that was what you meant when you let them be so much together," said Mary. "I think, if you will forgive me, Sir Edward, that it is not their fault."

Sir Edward answered this reproach only by a sigh. He was in a despondent rather than a combative state of mind. "And you see I do not know so much as I should like to know about him," he said, evading the personal question. "He is a very nice fellow; but I told you the other day I did not consider him a paladin; and whether he has enough to live upon, or anything to settle on her—My dear Mary, at least you will agree with me, that considering how short a time they have known each other, things have gone a great deal too far."

"I do not know how long they have known each other," said Mary, who now felt herself called upon absolutely to take Aunt Agatha's part.

"Ah, I know," said Sir Edward, "and so does your aunt; and things did not go at railway speed like this in our days. It is only about six weeks, and they are engaged to be married! I suppose you know as much about him as anybody—or so he gave me to understand at least; and do you think him a good match for your young sister?" added Sir Edward, with a tone of superior virtue which went to Mary's heart.

Mary was too true a woman not to be a partisan, and had the feminine gift of putting her own private sentiments out of the question in comparison with the cause which she had to advocate; but still it was an embarrassing question, especially as Aunt Agatha was looking at her with the most pathetic appeal in her eyes.

"I know very little of Captain Percival," she said; "I saw him once only in India, and it was at a moment very painful to me. But Winnie likes him—and you must have approved of him, Sir Edward, or you would not have brought him here."

Upon which Aunt Agatha rose and kissed Mary, recognising perfectly that she did not commit herself on the merits of the case, but at the same time sustained it by her support. Sir Edward, for his part, turned a deaf ear to the implied reproach, but still kept up his melancholy view of the matter, and shook his head.

"He has good connexions," he said; "his mother was a great friend of mine. In other circumstances, and could we have made up our minds to it at the proper moment, she might have been Lady—. But it is vain to talk of that. I think we might push him a little if he would devote himself steadily to his profession; but what can be expected from a man who wants to marry at five-and-twenty? I myself," said Sir Edward, with dignity, "though the eldest son—"

"Yes," said Aunt Agatha, unable to restrain herself longer, "and see what has come of it. You are all by yourself at the Hall, and not a soul belonging to you; and to see Francis Ochterlony with his statues and nonsense!—Oh, Sir Edward! when you might have had a dozen lovely children growing up round you—"

"Heaven forbid!" said Sir Edward, piously; and then he sighed—perhaps only from the mild melancholy which possessed him at the moment, and was occasioned by Winnie's indelicate haste to fall in love; perhaps, also, from some touch of personal feeling. A dozen lovely children might be rather too heavy an amount of happiness, while yet a modified bliss would have been sweet. He sighed and leant his head upon his hand, and withdrew into himself for the moment in that interesting way which was habitual to him, and had gained him the title of "poor Sir Edward." It might be very foolish for a man (who had his own way to make in the world) to marry at five-and-twenty; but still, perhaps it was rather more foolish when a man did not marry at all, and was left in his old age all alone in a great vacant house. But naturally, it was not this view of the matter which he displayed to his feminine companions, who were both women enough to have triumphed a little over such a confession of failure. He had a fine head, though he was old, and his hand was as delicate and almost as pale as ivory, and he could not but know that he looked interesting in that particular attitude, though, no doubt, it was his solicitude for these two indiscreet young people which chiefly moved him. "I am quite at a loss what to do," he said. "Mrs. Percival is a very fond mother, and she will naturally look to me for an account of all this; and there is your Uncle Penrose, Mary—a man I could never bear, as you all know—he will come in all haste, of course, and insist upon settlements and so forth; and why all this responsibility should come on me, who have no desire in this world but for tranquillity and peace—"

"It need not come on you," said Mrs. Ochterlony; "we are not very great business people, but still, with Aunt Agatha and myself—"

Sir Edward smiled. The idea diverted him so much that he raised his head from his hand. "My dear Mary," he said, "I have the very highest opinion of your capacity; but in a matter of this kind, for instance—And I am not so utterly selfish as to forsake my old neighbour in distress."

Here Aunt Agatha took up her own defence. "I don't consider that I am in distress," she said. "I must say, I did not expect anything like this, Sir Edward, from you. If it had been Mr. Penrose, with his mercenary ideas—I was very fond of Mary's poor dear mamma, and I don't mean any reflection on her, poor darling—but I suppose that is how it always happens with people in trade. Mr. Penrose is always a trial, and Mary knows that; but I hope I am able to bear something for my dear child's sake," Aunt Agatha continued, growing a little excited; "though I never thought that I should have to bear—" and then the poor lady gave a stifled sob, and added in the midst of it, "this from you!"

This was a kind of climax which had arrived before in the familiar friendship so long existing between the Hall and the Cottage. The two principals knew how to make it up better than the spectator did who was looking on with a little alarm and a little amusement. Perhaps it was as well that Mary was called away to her own individual concerns, and had to leave Aunt Agatha and Sir Edward in the height of their misunderstanding. Mary went away to her children, and perhaps it was only in the ordinary course of human nature that when she went into the nursery among those three little human creatures, who were so entirely dependent upon herself, there should be a smile upon her face as she thought of the two old people she had left. It seemed to her, as perhaps it seems to most women in the presence of their own children, at sight of those three boys—who were "mere babies" to Aunt Agatha, but to Mary the most important existences in the world—as if this serio-comic dispute about Winnie's love affairs was the most quaintly-ridiculous exhibition. When she was conscious of this thought in her own mind, she rebuked it, of course; but at the first glance it seemed as if Winnie's falling in love was so trivial a matter—so little to be put in comparison with the grave cares of life. There are moments when the elder women, who have long passed through all that, and have entered upon another stage of existence, cannot but smile at the love-matters, without considering that life itself is often decided by the complexion of the early romance, which seems to belong only to its lighter and less serious side. Sir Edward and Aunt Agatha for their part had never, old as they both were, got beyond the first stage—and it was natural it should bulk larger in their eyes. And this time it was they who were right, and not Mary, whose children were but children, and in no danger of any harm. Whereas, poor Winnie, at the top of happiness—gay, reckless, daring, and assured of her own future felicity—was in reality a creature in deadly peril and wavering on the verge of her fate.

But when the day had come to an end, and Captain Percival had at last retired, and Winnie, a little languid after her lover's departure, sat by the open window watching, no longer with despite or displeasure, the star of light which shone over the tree-tops from the Hall, there occurred a scene of a different description. But for the entire change in Winnie's looks and manner, the absence of the embroidery frame at which she had worked so violently, and the languid softened grace with which she had thrown herself down upon a low chair, too happy and content to feel called upon to do anything, the three ladies were just as they had been a few evenings before; that is to say, that Aunt Agatha and Mary, to neither of whom any change was possible, were just as they had been before, while to the girl at the window, everything in heaven and earth had changed. The two others had had their day and were done with it. Though Miss Seton was still scarcely an old woman, and Mary was in the full vigour and beauty of life, they were both ashore high up upon the beach, beyond the range of the highest tide;

while the other, in her boat of hope, was playing with the rippling incoming waters, and preparing to put to sea. It was not in nature that the two who had been at sea, and knew all the storms and dangers, should not look at her wistfully in her happy ignorance; perhaps even they looked at her with a certain envy too. But Aunt Agatha was not a woman who could let either ill or well alone—and it was she who disturbed the household calm which might have been profound that night, so far as Winnie was concerned.

"My dear love," said Aunt Agatha, with a timidity which implied something to tell, "Sir Edward has been here. Captain Percival had told him, you know—"

"Yes," said Winnie, carelessly, "I know."

"And, my darling," said Miss Seton. "I am sure it is what I never could have expected from him, who was always such a friend; but I sometimes think he gets a little strange—as he gets old, you know—"

This was what the unprincipled woman said, not caring in the least how much she slandered Sir Edward, or anybody else in the world, so long as she gave a little comfort to the child of her heart. And as for Winnie, though she had been brought up at his feet, as it were, and was supposed by himself and others to love him like a child of his own, she took no notice of this unfounded accusation. She was thinking of quite a different person, just as Aunt Agatha was thinking of her, and Mary of her boys. They were women, each preoccupied and absorbed in somebody else, and they did not care about justice. And thus Sir Edward for the moment fared badly among them, though, if any outside assailant had attacked him, they would all have fought for him to the death.

"Well!" said Winnie, still very carelessly, as Miss Seton came to a sudden stop.

"My dear love!" said Aunt Agatha, "he has not a word to say against Captain Percival, that I can see—"

"Against Edward?" cried Winnie, raising herself up. "Good gracious, Aunt Agatha, what are you thinking of? Against Edward! I should like to know what he could say. His own godfather—and his mother was once engaged to him—and he is as good as a relation, and the nearest friend he has. What could he possibly have to say? And besides, it was he who brought him here; and we think he will leave us the most of his money," Winnie said, hastily—and then was very sorry for what she had said, and blushed scarlet and bit her lips, but it was too late to draw back.

"Winnie," said Miss Seton, solemnly, "if he has been calculating upon what people will leave to him when they die, I will think it is all true that Sir Edward said."

"You said Sir Edward did not say anything," cried Winnie. "What is it you have heard? It is of no use trying to deceive me. If there has been anything said against him, it is Mary who has said it. I can see by her face it is Mary. And if she is to be heard against him," cried Winnie, rising up in a blaze of wrath and indignation, "it is only just that he should be heard on the other side. He is too good and too kind to say things about my sister to me; but Mary is only a woman, and of course she does not mind what she says. She can blacken a man behind his back, though he is far too honourable and too—too delicate to say what he knows of her!"

This unlooked-for assault took Mary so entirely by surprise, that she looked up with a certain bewilderment, and could not find a word to say. As for Aunt Agatha, she too rose and took Winnie's hands, and put her arms round her as much as the angry girl would permit.

"It was not Mary," she said. "Oh, Winnie, my darling, if it was for your good, and an ease to my mind, and better for you in life—if it was for your good, my dear love—that is what we are all thinking of—could not you give him up?"

It was, perhaps, the boldest thing Aunt Agatha had ever done in all her gentle life—and even Winnie could not but be influenced by such unusual resolution. She made a wild effort to escape for the first moment, and stood with her hands held fast in Aunt Agatha's hands, averting her angry face, and refusing to answer. But when she felt herself still held fast, and that her fond guardian had the courage to hold to her question, Winnie's anger turned into another kind of passion. The tears came pouring to her eyes in a sudden violent flood, which she neither tried to stop nor to hide. "No!" cried Winnie, with the big thunder-drops falling hot and heavy. "What is my good without him? If it was for my harm I shouldn't care. Don't hold me, don't look at me, Aunt Agatha! I don't care for anything in the world but Edward. I would not give him up—no, not if it was to break everybody's heart. What is it all to me without Edward?" cried the passionate girl. And when Miss Seton let her go, she threw herself on her chair again, with the tears coming in floods, but still facing them both through this storm-shower with crimson cheeks and shining eyes. As for poor Aunt Agatha, she too tottered back to her chair, frightened and abashed, as well as in distress; for young ladies had not been in the habit of talking so freely in her days.

"Oh, Winnie—and we have loved you all your life; and you have only known him a few weeks," she said, faltering, and with a natural groan.

"I cannot help it," said Winnie; "you may think me a wretch, but I like him best. Isn't it natural I should like him best? Mary did, and ran away, and nobody was shocked at her; and even you yourself—"

"I never, never, could have said such a thing all my life!" cried Aunt Agatha, with a maiden blush upon her sweet old cheeks.

"If you had, you would not have been a—as you are now," said the dauntless Winnie; and she recovered in a twinkling of an eye, and wiped away her tears, and was herself again. Possibly what she had said was true and natural, as she asserted; but it is an unquestionable fact, that neither her aunt nor her sister could have said it for their lives. She was a young lady of the nineteenth century, and she acted accordingly; but it is a certain fact, as Aunt Agatha justly observed, whatever people may think now, that girls did not speak like that in our day.

CHAPTER XIX

The few weeks which ensued were the most stormy and troublous period of all Miss Seton's life; and through her there was naturally a considerable disturbance of the peace of the Cottage. Though she lived so quietly, she had what is called in the country "a large circle," and had dwelt among her own people all her life, and was known to everybody about. It was a quiet neighbourhood, but yet there never was a neighbourhood so quiet as not to have correspondents and relations living out in the world, to whom all news went, and from whom all news came. And there were a number of "families" about Kirtell, not great people certainly, but very respectable people, gentry, and well-connected persons, hanging on by various links to the great world. In this way Winnie's engagement, which nobody wanted to conceal, came to be known far and wide, as such facts are so apt to get known. And a great many people out in the world, who had once known Miss Seton, wrote letters to her, in which they suggested that perhaps she had forgotten them, but hoped that she would excuse them, and attribute it to the regard which they had never ceased to feel for her, if they asked, Did she know Captain Percival very well, who was said to be engaged to her pretty niece? Had she heard what happened in the Isle of Man when his regiment was stationed there? and why it was that he did not go out to Gibraltar after he had got that appointment? Other people, who did not know Aunt Agatha, took what was after all the more disagreeable step of writing to their friends in the parish about the young man, whose career had certainly left traces, as it appeared, upon the memory of his generation. To rise every morning with a sense that such an epistle might be awaiting her on the breakfast-table—or to receive a visitor with the horrible conviction that she had come to look into her face, and hold her hand, and be confidential and sympathetic, and deliver a solemn warning—was an ordeal which Aunt Agatha found it hard to bear. She was a woman who never forgot her character as a maiden lady, and liked to be justified by precedents and to be approved of by all the world. And these repeated remonstrances had no doubt a great effect upon her mind. They filled her with terrible misgivings and embittered her life, and drove her now and then into so great a panic that she felt disposed to thrust Captain Percival out of the house and forbid his reappearance there. But then, Winnie. Winnie was not the girl to submit to any such violent remedies. If she could not see her lover there, she would find means to see him somewhere else. If she could not be married to him with stately propriety in her parish church, she would manage to marry him somehow in any irregular way, and she would by no means hesitate to say so or shrink from the responsibility. And if it must be done, would it not be better that it should be done correctly than incorrectly, and with all things decent and in order? Thus poor Aunt Agatha would muse as she gathered up her bundle of letters. It might have been all very well for parents to exercise their authority in the days when their children obeyed them; but what was the use of issuing commands to which nobody would pay any attention? Winnie had very plainly expressed her preference for her own happiness rather than her aunt's peace of mind; and though Miss Seton would never have consented to admit that Winnie was anything less than the most beautiful character, still she was aware that unreasoning obedience was not her faculty. Besides, another sentiment began to mingle with this prudential consideration. Everybody was against the poor young man. The first letters she received about him made her miserable; but after that there was no doubt a revulsion. Everybody was against him, poor fellow!—and he was so young, and could not, after all, have done so much harm in the world. "He has not had the time, Mary," she said, with an appeal to Mrs. Ochterlony for support. "If he had been doing wrong from his very cradle, he could not have had the time." She could not refuse to believe what was told her, and yet notwithstanding her belief she clung to the culprit. If he had found any other advocate it might have been different; but nobody took the other side of the question: nobody wrote a pretty letter to say what a dear fellow he was, and how glad his friends were to think he had found some one worthy of him—not even his mother; and Aunt Agatha's heart accordingly became the avvocato del diavolo. Fair play was due even to Captain Percival. It was impossible to leave him assailed as he was by so many without one friend.

It was a curious sight to see how she at once received and ignored all the information thus conveyed to her. A woman of a harder type would probably, as women do, have imputed motives, and settled the matter with the general conclusion that "an enemy hath done this;" but Aunt Agatha could not help, for the moment at least, believing in everybody. She could not say right out, "It is not true," even to the veriest impostor who deceived and got money from her, and their name was legion. In her own innocent soul she had no belief in lies, and could not understand them; and it was easier for her to give credence to the wildest marvel than to believe that anybody could tell her a deliberate falsehood. She would have kissed the ladies who wrote to her of those stories about Captain Percival, and cried and wrung her hands, and asked, What could she do?—and yet her heart was by no means turned against him, notwithstanding her belief in what everybody said; which is a strange and novel instance, well enough known to social philosophers, but seldom remarked upon, of the small practical influence of belief upon life. "How can it be a lie, my dear child? what motive could they all have to tell lies?" she would say to Winnie, mournfully; and yet ten minutes after, when it was Mrs. Ochterlony she was speaking to, she would make her piteous appeal for him, poor fellow!—"Everybody is against him; and he is so young still; and oh, Mary, how much he must need looking after," Aunt Agatha would say, "if it is all true!"

Perhaps it was stranger still that Mary, who did not like Captain Percival, and was convinced of the truth of all the stories told of him, and knew in her heart that he was her enemy and would not scruple to do her harm if the chance should come in his way—was also a little moved by the same argument. Everybody was against him. It was the Cottage against the world, so far as he was concerned; and even Mrs. Ochterlony, though she ought to have known better, could not help feeling herself one of a "side," and to a certain extent felt her honour pledged to the defence of her sister's lover. Had she, in the very heart of this stronghold which was standing out for him so stoutly, lifted up a testimony against him, she would have felt herself in some respects a domestic traitor. She might be silent on the subject, and avoid all comment, but she could not utter an adverse opinion, or join in with the general voice against which Aunt Agatha and Winnie stood forth so stedfastly. As for Winnie, every word that was said to his detriment made her more determined to stick to him. What did it matter whether he was good or bad, so long as it was indisputably he? There was but one Edward Percival in the world, and he would still be Edward Percival if he had committed a dozen murders, or gambled twenty fortunes away. Such was Winnie's defiant way of treating the matter which concerned her more closely than anybody else. She carried things with a high hand in those days. All the world was against her, and she scorned the world. She attributed motives, though Aunt Agatha did not. She said it was envy and jealousy and all the leading passions. She made wild counter-accusations, in the style of that literature which sets forth the skeleton in every man's closet. Who could tell what little incidents could be found out in the private history of the ladies who had so much to say about Captain Percival? This is so ordinary a mode of defence, that no doubt it is natural, and Winnie went into it with good will. Thus his standard was planted upon the Cottage, and however unkindly people might think of him outside, shelter and support were always to be found within. Even Peggy, though she did not always agree with her mistress, felt, as Mrs. Ochterlony did, that she was one of a side, and became a partisan with an earnestness that was impossible to Mary. Sir Edward shook his head still, but he was disarmed by the close phalanx and the determined aspect of Percival's defenders. "It is true love," he said in his sentimental way; "and love can work miracles when everything else has failed. It may be his salvation." This was what he wrote to Percival's mother, who, up to this moment, had been but doubtful in her approbation, and very anxious, and uncertain, as she said, whether she ought not to tell Miss Seton that Edward had been "foolish." He had been "foolish," even in his mother's opinion; and his other critics were, some of them, so tolerant as to say "gay," and some "wild," while a few used a more solemn style of diction;—but everybody was against him, whatever terms they might employ; everybody except the ladies at the Cottage, who set up his standard, and accepted him with all his iniquities upon his head.

It may be worth while at this point, before Mr. Penrose arrives, who played so important a part in the business, to say a word about the poor young man who was thus universally assailed. He was five-and-twenty, and a young man of expectations. Though he had spent every farthing which came to himself at his majority, and a good deal more than that, still his mother had a nice estate, and Sir Edward was his godfather, and the world was full of obliging tradespeople and other amiable persons. He was a handsome fellow, nearly six feet high, with plenty of hair, and a moustache of the most charming growth. The hair was of dull brown, which was rather a disadvantage to him, but then it went perfectly well with his pale complexion, and suited the cloudy look over the eyes, which was the most characteristic point in his face. The eyes themselves were good, and had, when they chose, a sufficiently frank expression, but there lay about the eyebrows a number of lurking hidden lines which looked like mischief—lines which could be brought into action at any moment, and could scowl, or lower, or brood, according to the fancy of their owner. Some people thought this uncertainty in his face was its greatest charm; you could never tell what a moment might bring forth from that moveable and changing forehead. It was suggestive, as a great many persons thought—suggestive of storm and thunder, and sudden disturbance, or even in some eyes of cruelty and gloom—though he was a fine young man, and gay and fond of his pleasure. Winnie, as may be supposed, was not of this latter opinion. She even loved to bring out those hidden lines, and call the shadows over his face, for the pleasure of seeing how they melted away again, according to the use and wont of young ladies. It was a sort of uncertainty that was permissible to him, who had been a spoiled child, and whom everybody, at the beginning of his career, had petted and taken notice of; but possibly it was a quality which would not have called forth much admiration from a wife.

And with Winnie standing by him as she did—clinging to him closer at every new accusation, and proclaiming, without faltering, her indifference to anything that could be said, and her conviction that the worse he was the more need he had of her—Captain Percival, too, took matters very lightly. The two foolish young creatures even came to laugh, and make fun of it in their way. "Here is Aunt Agatha coming with another letter; I wonder if it is to say that I poisoned my grandmother, this time?" cried the young man; and they both laughed as if it was the best joke in the world. If ever there was a moment in which, when they were alone, Winnie did take a momentary thought of the seriousness of the position, her gravity soon dissipated itself. "I know you have been very naughty," she would say, clasping her pretty hands upon his arm; "but you will never, never do it again," and the lover, thus appealed to, would make the tenderest and most eager assurances. What temptation could he ever have to be "naughty" with such an angel by his side? And Winnie was pleased enough to play the part of the angel—though that was not, perhaps, her most characteristic development—and went home full of happiness and security; despising the world which never had understood Edward, and thinking with triumph of the disappointed women less happy than herself, who, out of revenge, had no doubt got up this outcry against him. "For I don't mean to defend him out and out," she said, her eyes sparkling with malice and exultation; "I don't mean to say that he has not behaved very badly to a great many people;" and there was a certain sweet self-glorification in the thought which intoxicated Winnie. It was wicked, but somehow she liked him better for having behaved badly to a great many people; and naturally any kind of reasoning was entirely ineffectual with a foolish girl who had taken such an idea into her mind.

Thus things went on; and Percival went away and returned again, and paid many flying visits, and, present and absent, absorbed all Winnie's thoughts. It was not only a first love, but it was a first occupation to the young woman, who had never felt, up to this time, that she had a sufficient sphere for her energies. Now she could look forward to being married, to receiving all the presents, and being busy about all the business of that important moment; and beyond lay life—life without any one to restrain her, without even the bondage of habit, and the necessity of taking into consideration what people would think. Winnie said frankly that she would go with him anywhere, that she did not mind if it was India, or even the Cape of Good Hope; and her eyes sparkled to think of the everything new which would replace to her all the old bonds and limits: though, in one point of view, this was a cruel satisfaction, and very wounding and injurious to some of the other people concerned.

"Oh, Winnie, my darling! and what am I to do without you?" Aunt Agatha would cry; and the girl would kiss her in her laughing way. "It must have come, sooner or later," she said; "you always said so yourself. I don't see why you should not get married too, Aunt Agatha; you are perfectly beautiful sometimes, and a great deal younger than—many people; or, at least, you will have Mary to be your husband," Winnie would add, with a laugh, and a touch of affectionate spite: for the two sisters, it must be allowed, were not to say fond of each other. Mary had been brought up differently, and was often annoyed, and sometimes shocked, by Winnie's ways: and Winnie—though at times she seemed disposed to make friends with her sister—could not help thinking of Mary as somehow at the bottom of all that had been said about Edward. This, indeed, was an idea which her lover and she shared: and Mary's life was not made pleasanter to her by the constant implication that he, too, could tell something about her—which she despised too much to take any notice of, but which yet was an offence and an insult. So that on the whole—even before the arrival of Mr. Penrose—the Cottage on Kirtell-side, though as bowery and fair as ever, was, in reality, an agitated and even an uncomfortable home.

CHAPTER XX

Mr. Penrose was the uncle of Mary and Winnie, their mother's only brother. Mrs. Seton had come from Liverpool originally, and though herself very "nice," had not been, according to Aunt Agatha's opinion, "of a nice class." And her brother shared the evil conditions, without sharing the good. He was of his class, soul and body, and it was not a nice class—and, to tell the truth, his nieces had been brought up to ignore rather than to take any pleasure in him. He was not a man out of whom, under the best circumstances, much satisfaction could be got. He was one of the men who always turn up when something about money is going on in the house. He had had to do with all the wills and settlements in the family, though they were of a very limited description; but Mr. Penrose did not despise small things, and was of opinion, that even if you had only a hundred pounds; you ought to know all about it, and how to take care of it. And he had once been very kind to Aunt Agatha, who was always defective in her arithmetic, and who, in earlier days, while she still thought of a possible change in her condition, had gone beyond the just limit of her income, and got into difficulties. Mr. Penrose had interfered at that period, and had been very kind, and set her straight, and had given her a very telling address upon the value of money; and though Miss Seton was not one of the people who take a favour as an injury, still she could have forgiven him a great many ill turns sooner than that good one. He had been very kind to her, and had ruffled all her soft plumes, and rushed up against her at all her tender points; and the very sound of his name was a lively irritant to Aunt Agatha. But he had to be acquainted with Winnie's engagement, and when he received the information, he lost no time in coming to see about it. He was a large, portly, well-to-do man, with one of his hands always in his pocket, and seemed somehow to breathe money, and to have no ideas which did not centre in it; and yet he had a good many ideas, and was a clever man in his way. With him, as with many people in the world, there was one thing needful, and that one thing was money. He thought it was a duty to possess something—a duty which a man owed absolutely to himself, and to all who belonged to him—and if he did not acquit himself well on this point, he was, in Mr. Penrose's opinion, a very indifferent sort of person. There is something immoral to most people in the fact of being poor, but to Mr. Penrose it was a crime. He was very well off himself, but he was not a man to communicate of his goods as he did of his advice; and then he had himself a family, and could not be expected to give anything except advice to his nieces—and as for that one good thing, it was at their command in the most liberal way. He came to the Cottage, which was so especially a lady's house, and pervaded the whole place with his large male person, diffusing through it that moral fragrance which still betrays the Englishman, the man of business, the Liverpool man, wherever he may happen to bless the earth. Perhaps in that sweet-smelling dainty place, the perfume which breathed from Mr. Penrose told more decidedly than in the common air. As soon as you went in at the garden-gate you became sensible that the atmosphere was changed, and that a Man was there. Perhaps it may be thought that the presence of a man in Aunt Agatha's maiden bower was not what might be called strictly proper, and Miss Seton herself had doubts on the subject; but then, Mr. Penrose never asked for any invitation, and it would have been very difficult to turn him out; and Mary was there, who at least was a married lady. He came without any invitation, and asked which was his room as if it had been his own house—and he complained of what he called "the smell" of the roses, and declared he would tear down all the sickly jasmine from the side of the house if it belonged to him. All this Miss Seton endured silently, feeling it her duty, for Winnie's sake, to keep all her connexions in good humour; but the poor lady suffered terribly under the process, as everybody could see.

"I hope it is only a conditional sort of engagement," Mr. Penrose said, after he had made himself comfortable, and had had a good dinner, and came into the drawing-room the first evening. The lovers had seized the opportunity to escape to Kirtell-side, and Mary was with her boys in the garden, and poor Aunt Agatha, a martyr of civility, was seated alone, awaiting the reappearance of her guest, and smiling upon him with anxious politeness. He threw himself into the largest and most solid chair he could find, and spread himself, as it seemed, all over the room—a Man, coarse and undisguised, in that soft feminine paradise. Poor Sir Edward's graceful presence, and the elegant figure of Captain Percival, made no such impression. "I hope you have not settled it all without consulting anybody. To be sure, that don't matter very much; but I know you ladies have a summary way of settling such affairs."

"Indeed, I—I am afraid—I—I hope—it is all settled," said Aunt Agatha, with tremulous dignity. "It is not as if there was a great deal of money to settle. They are not—not rich, you know," she added, nervously. This was the chief thing to tell, and she was anxious to get it over at once.

"Not rich?" said Mr. Penrose. "No, I suppose not. A rich fellow would not have been such a fool as to entangle himself with Winnie, who has only her pretty face; but he has something, of course. The first thing to ascertain is, what they will have to live on, and what he can settle upon her. I suppose you have not let it go so far without having a kind of idea on these points?"

"Oh, yes," said Aunt Agatha, with a very poor pretence at composure; "oh, yes, Mr. Penrose, that is all quite right. He has very nice expectations. I have always heard that Mrs. Percival had a charming little property; and Sir Edward is his godfather, and very fond of him. You will see it will come all right about that."

"Yes," said Mr. Penrose, who was nursing one of his legs—a colossal member, nearly as big as his hostess—in a meditative way, "I hope it will when I come to look into it. But we must have something more than expectations. What has he of his own?—and what do his mother and Sir Edward mean to do for him? We must have it in pounds, shillings, and pence, or he shan't have Winnie. It is best that he should make up his mind about that."

Aunt Agatha drew a frightened, panting breath; but she did not say anything. She had known what she would have to brave, and she was aware that Winnie would not brave it, and that to prevent a breach with her darling's only rich relation, it was necessary and expedient as long as she was alone to have it all out.

"Let me see," said Mr. Penrose, "you told me what he was in your letter—Captain, ain't he? As for his pay, that don't count. Let us go systematically to work if we are to do any good. I know ladies are very vague about business matters, but still you must know something. What sort of a fellow is he, and what has he got of his own?"

"Oh, he is very nice," cried Aunt Agatha, consoled to find a question she could answer; "very, very nice. I do think you will like him very much; such a fine young fellow, and with what you gentlemen call no nonsense about him," said the anxious woman; "and with excellent connexions," she added, faltering again, for her enthusiasm awoke no answer in Mr. Penrose's face.

"My dear Miss Agatha," he said in his offensive way—and he always called her Miss Agatha, which was very trying to her feelings—"you need not take the trouble to assure me that a handsome young fellow who pays her a little attention, is always very nice to a lady. I was not asking whether he was nice; I was asking what were his means—which is a very much more important part of the subject, though you may not think so," Mr. Penrose added. "A charming little house like this, for instance, where you can have everything within yourself, and can live on honey and dew I suppose, may be kept on nothing—though you and I, to be sure, know a little different—"

"Mr. Penrose," said Aunt Agatha, trembling with indignation, "if you mean that the dinner was not particular enough—"

"It was a charming little dinner," said Mr. Penrose, "just what it ought to have been. Nothing could have been nicer than that white soup; and I think I am a judge. I was speaking of something to live on; a pretty house like this, I was saying, is not an analogous case. You have everything within yourself—eggs, and vegetables, and fruit, and your butter and milk so cheap. I wish we could get it like that in Liverpool; and—pardon me—no increase of family likely, you know."

"My niece Mary and her three children have come to the Cottage since you were last here, Mr. Penrose," said Aunt Agatha, with a blush of shame and displeasure. "It was the only house of all her relations that she could come to with any comfort, poor dear—perhaps you don't call that an increase of family; and as for the milk and butter—"

"She must pay you board," said Mr. Penrose, decisively; "there can be no question about that; your little money has not always been enough for yourself, as we both know. But all this is merely an illustration I was giving. It has nothing to do with the main subject. If these young people marry, my dear Miss Agatha, their family may be increased by inmates who will pay no board."

This was what he had the assurance to say to an unmarried lady in her own house—and to laugh and chuckle at it afterwards, as if he thought it a capital joke. Aunt Agatha was struck dumb with horror and indignation. Such eventualities might indeed, perhaps must, be discussed by the lawyers where there are settlements to make; but to talk of them to a maiden lady when alone, was enough to make her drop through the very floor with consternation. She made no attempt to answer, but she did succeed in keeping her seat, and to a certain extent her self-possession, for Winnie's sake.

"It is a different sort of thing altogether," said the family adviser. "Things may be kept square in a quiet lady's house—though even that is not always the case, as we are both aware; but two young married people, who are just as likely as not to be extravagant and all that—If he has not something to settle on her, I don't see how I can have anything to do with it," Mr. Penrose continued; "and you will not answer me as to what he has of his own."

"He has his—his pay," said poor Aunt Agatha. "I am told it is a great deal better than it used to be; and he has, I think, some—some money in the Funds. I am sure he will be glad to settle that on Winnie; and then his mother, and Sir Edward. I have no doubt myself, though really they are too young to marry, that they will do very well on the whole."

"Do you know what living means, Miss Agatha?" asked Mr. Penrose, solemnly, "when you can speak in this loose way? Butchers' bills are not so vague as your statements, I can tell you; and a pretty girl like that ought to do very well, even though she has no money. It is not her fault, poor thing," the rich uncle added, with momentary compassion; and then he asked, abruptly, "What will Sir Edward do for them?" as if he had presented a pistol at his companion's head.

"Oh, Mr. Penrose!" cried Aunt Agatha, forgetting all her policy, and what she had just said. "Surely, surely, you would not like them to calculate upon Sir Edward! He is not even a relation. He is only Edward's godfather. I would not have him applied to, not for the world."

"Then what have you been talking to me all this while about?" cried Mr. Penrose, with a look and sense of outraged virtue. And Aunt Agatha, seeing how she had betrayed her own position, and weary of the contest, and driven to her wits' end, gave way and cried a little—which at that moment, vexed, worried, and mortified as she was, was all she could do.

And then Mr. Penrose got up and walked away, whistling audibly, through the open window, into the garden, leaving the chintz cover on his chair so crumpled up and loosened out of all its corners, that you could have told a mile off that a man had been there. What he left behind him was not that subtle agreeable suggestion of his presence which hung around the footsteps of young Percival, or even of Sir Edward, but something that felt half like an insult to the feminine inhabitants—a disagreeable assertion of another kind of creature who thought himself superior to them—which was an opinion which they did not in the least share, having no illusions so far as he went. Aunt Agatha sank back into her chair with a sense of relief, which she afterwards felt she ought not to have entertained. She had no right to such a feeling, for she had done no good; and instead of diverting the common enemy from an attack upon Winnie or her lover, had actually roused and whetted him, and made him more likely than ever to rush at those young victims, as soon as ever he should have the chance. But notwithstanding, for the moment to be rid of him, and able to draw breath a little, and dry her incipient tears, and put the cover straight upon that ill-used chair, did her good. She drew a long breath, poor soul, and felt the ease and comfort of being left to herself; even though next moment she might have to brace herself up and collect all her faculties, and face the adversary again.

But in the meantime he had gone out to the garden, and was standing by Mary's side, with his hand in his pocket. He was telling Mary that he had come out in despair to her, to see if she knew anything about this sad business—since he found her Aunt Agatha quite as great a fool about business matters as she always was. He wanted to know if she, who knew what was what, could give him any sort of a reasonable idea about this young fellow whom Winnie wanted to marry—which was as difficult a question for Mrs. Ochterlony as it had been for Miss Seton. And then in the midst of the conversation the two culprits themselves appeared, as careless about the inquiring uncle as they were about the subject of his anxiety. Winnie, who was not given to the reticences practised by her aunt and her sister, had taken care to convey a very clear idea of her Uncle Penrose, and her own opinion of him, to the mind of Percival. He was from Liverpool, and not "of a nice class." He was not Winnie's guardian, nor had he any legal control over her; and in these circumstances it did not seem by any means necessary to either of the young people to show any undue attention to his desires, or be disturbed by his interference; for neither of them had been brought up to be dutiful to all the claims of nature, like their seniors. "Go away directly, that he may not have any chance of attacking you," Winnie had said to her lover; for though she was not self-denying or unselfish to speak of, she could be so where Percival was concerned. "We can manage him among us," she added, with a laugh—for she had no doubt of the cooperation of both her aunt and sister, in the case of Uncle Penrose. And in obedience to this arrangement, Captain Percival did nothing but take off his hat in honour of Mary, and say half a dozen words of the most ordinary salutation to the stranger before he went away. And then Winnie came in, and came to her sister's side, and stood facing Mr. Penrose, in all the triumph and glory of her youth. She was beautiful, or would be beautiful, everybody had long allowed; but she had still retained a certain girlish meagreness up to a very recent date. Now all that had changed, like everything else; she had expanded, it appeared, like her heart expanded and was satisfied—everything about her looked rounder, fuller, and more magnificent. She came and stood before the Liverpool uncle, who was a man of business, and thinking of no such vanities, and struck him dumb with her splendour. He could talk as he liked to Aunt Agatha, or even to Mary in her widow's cap, but this radiant creature, all glowing with love and happiness, took away his breath. Perhaps it was then, for the first time in his life, that Mr. Penrose actually realized that there was something in the world for which a man might even get to be indifferent about the balance at his banker's. He gave an involuntary gasp; and though up to this moment he had thought of Winnie only as a child, he now drew back before her, and stopped whistling, and took his hand out of his pocket, which perhaps was as decided an act of homage as it was in him to pay.

But of course such a manifestation could not last. After another moment he gave a "humph" as he looked at her, and then his self-possession came back. "So that was your Captain, I suppose?" he said.

"Yes, uncle, that was my Captain," said the dauntless Winnie, "and I hope you approve of him; though it does not matter if you don't, for you know it is all settled, and nobody except my aunt and his mother has any right to say a word."

"If his mother is as wise a judge as your aunt—" said Mr. Penrose; but yet all the same, Winnie's boldness imposed upon him a little. It was impossible to imagine that a grand creature like this, who was not pale nor sentimental, nor of Agatha Seton's kind, could contemplate with such satisfaction any Captain who had asked her to marry him upon nothing a year.

"That is all very fine," Mr. Penrose added, taking courage; "you can make your choice as you please, but it is my business to look after the money. If you and your children come to me starving, twenty years hence and ask how I could possibly let you marry such a—"

"Do you think you will be living in twenty years, Uncle Penrose?" said Winnie. "I know you are a great deal older than Aunt Agatha;—but if you are, we will not come, I promise you. We shall keep our starvation to ourselves."

"I can't tell how old your Aunt Agatha is," said Mr. Penrose, with natural offence; "and you must know, Miss Winnie, that this is not how you should talk to me."

"Very well, uncle," said the daring girl; "but neither is your way the way to talk to me. You know I have made up my mind, and that everything is settled, and that it does not matter the least to me if Edward was a beggar; and you come here with your money, as if that was the only thing to be thought of. What do I care about money?—and you might try till the end of the world, and you never would break it off," she cried, flashing into a brilliant glow of passion and vehemence such as Mr. Penrose did not understand. He had expected to have a great deal of difficulty, but he had never expected to be defied after this fashion; and the wildness of her womanish folly made the good man sad.

"You silly girl!" he said, with profound pathos, "if you only knew what nonsense you were speaking. There is nobody in this world but cares about money; you can do nothing without it, and marry least of all. And you speak to me with such an example before your eyes; look at your sister Mary, how she has come with all those helpless children to be, most likely, a burden on her friends—"

"Uncle Penrose!" cried Winnie, putting up her two beautiful hands to stop his mouth; but Mr. Penrose was as plain-spoken as Winnie herself was, though in a different way.

"I know perfectly well she can hear me," he said, "and she ought to hear me, and to read you a lesson. If Mary had been a sensible girl, and had married a man who could make proper settlements upon her, and make a provision for his family, do you think she would have required to come here to seek a shelter—do you think—"

"Oh, Mary, he is crazy; don't mind him!" cried Winnie, forgetting for the moment all about her own affairs, and clinging to her sister in real distress.

And then it was Mrs. Ochterlony's turn to speak.

"I did not come to seek a shelter," she said; "though I know they would have given it me all the same. I came to seek love and kindness, uncle, which you cannot buy with money: and if there was nothing more than want of money between Winnie and Captain Percival—"

"Mary!" cried Winnie, impetuously, "go in and don't say any more. You shall not be insulted while I am here; but don't say anything about Edward. Leave me to have it out with Uncle Penrose, and go away."

And somehow Mary obeyed. She would not have done it a month ago; but she was wearied of contention, and broken in spirit, and, instead of standing still and defending herself, she withdrew from the two belligerents, who were both so ready to turn their arms against her, and went away. She went to the nursery, which was deserted; for her boys were still outside in the lingering daylight. None of them were able to advise, or even to sympathize with their mother. They could give her their childish love, but nothing else in the world. The others had all some one to consult, some one to refer to, but Mary was alone. Her heart beat dull and low, with no vehement offence at the bitter words she had just heard, but with a heavy despondency and sense of solitude, which her very attitude showed—for she did not sit down, or lie down, or try to find any fictitious support, but stood up by the vacant fire-place with her eyes fixed upon nothing, holding unconsciously the little chain which secured her watch, and letting its beads drop one by one from her fingers. "Mary has come home to be a burden on her friends," said Uncle Penrose. She did not resent it wildly, as she might have done some time before, but pondered with wondering pain and a dull sense of hopelessness. How did it happen that she, of all women, had come to such a position? what correspondence was there between that and all her past? and what was the future to be? which, even now, she could make no spasmodic changes in, but must accept and endure. This was how Mary's mind was employed, while Winnie, reckless and wilful, defied Uncle Penrose in the garden. For the time, the power of defying any one seemed to have died out of Mary's breast.

CHAPTER XXI

Mr. Penrose, however, was not a man of very lively feelings, and bore no malice against Winnie for her defiance, nor even against Mary, to whom he had been so cruel, which was more difficult. He was up again, cheerful and full of energy in the morning, ready for his mission. If Winnie began the world without something to live upon, or with any prospect of ever being a burden on her friends, at all events it would not be his fault. As it happened, Aunt Agatha received at the breakfast-table the usual invariable letter containing a solemn warning against Captain Percival, and she was affected by it, as she could not help always being affected; and the evident commotion it excited in the party was such that Mr. Penrose could not but notice it. When he insisted upon knowing what it was, he was met by what was, in reality, very skilful fencing on Miss Seton's part, who was not destitute altogether of female skill and art; but Aunt Agatha's defence was made useless by the impetuosity of Winnie, who scorned disguise.

"Oh, let us hear it, please," she said, "let us hear. We know what it is about. It is some new story—some lie, about my poor Edward. They may save themselves the trouble. I would not believe one of them, if it was written on the wall like Belshazzar's feast; and if I did believe them I would not care," said Winnie, vehemently; and she looked across, as she never could help looking, to where her sister sat.

"What is it?" said Mr. Penrose, "something about your Captain? Miss Agatha, considering my interest in the matter, I hope you will let me hear all that is said."

"It is nothing, absolutely nothing," said Aunt Agatha, faltering. "It is only some foolish gossip, you know—garrison stories, and that sort of thing. He was a very young man, and was launched upon life by himself—and—and—I think I may say he must have been imprudent. Winnie, my dear love, my heart bleeds to say it, but he must have been imprudent. He must have entangled himself and—and—And then there are always so many designing people about to lead poor young men astray," said Aunt Agatha, trembling for the result of her explanation; while Winnie divided her attention between Mr. Penrose, before whom this new view of the subject was unfolded for the first time, and Mary, whom she regarded as a natural enemy and the probable origin of it all.

"Wild, I suppose?" said Mr. Penrose, with sublime calm. "They're all alike, for that matter. So long as he doesn't bet or gamble—that's how those confounded young fellows ruin themselves." And then he dismissed the subject with a wave of the hand. "I am going up to the Hall to talk it all over with Sir Edward, and see what can be done. This sort of penniless nonsense makes me sick," the rich man added; "and you women are the most unreasonable creatures—one might as well talk to a stone wall."

Thus it was that for once in their lives the two Miss Setons, Agatha and Winnie, found Uncle Penrose for the moment half divine; they looked at him with wide open eyes, with a wondering veneration. They were only women after all, and had been giving themselves a great deal of trouble about Captain Percival's previous history; but it all sank in mere contemptible gossip under the calm glance of Mr. Penrose. He was not enthusiastic about Edward, and therefore his impartial calm was all the more satisfying. He thought nothing of it at all, though it had been driving them distracted. When he went away on his mission to the Hall, Winnie, in her enthusiasm, ran into Aunt Agatha's arms.

"You see he does not mind," said Winnie,—though an hour before she had been far from thinking Mr. Penrose an authority. "He thinks it is all gossip and spite, as I always said."

And Aunt Agatha for her part was quite overcome by the sudden relief. It felt like a deliverance, though it was only Mr. Penrose's opinion. "My dear love, men know the world," she said; "that is the advantage of having somebody to talk to; and I always said that your uncle, though he is sometimes disagreeable, had a great deal of sense. You see he knows the world."

"Yes, I suppose he must have sense," said Winnie; and in the comfort of her heart she was ready to attribute all good gifts to Mr. Penrose, and could have kissed him as he walked past the window with his hand in his pocket. She would not have forsaken her Edward whatever had been found out about him, but still to see that his wickedness (if he had been wicked) was of no consequence in the eyes of a respectable man like Uncle Penrose, was such a consolation even to Winnie as nothing can express. "We are all a set of women, and we have been making a mountain out of a molehill," she said, and the tears came to her bright eyes; and then, as Mary was not moved into any such demonstrations of delight, Winnie turned her arms upon her sister in pure gaiety of heart.

"Everybody gets talked about," she said. "Edward was telling me about Mary even—that she used to be called Madonna Mary at the station; and that there was some poor gentleman that died. I supposed he thought she ought to be worshipped like Our Lady. Didn't you feel dreadfully guilty and wretched, Mary, when he died?"

"Poor boy," said Mrs. Ochterlony, who had recovered her courage a little with the morning light. "It had nothing to do with Our Lady as you say; it was only because he had been brought up in Italy, poor fellow, and was fond of the old Italian poets, and the soft Italian words."

"Then perhaps it was Madonna Mary he was thinking of," said Winnie, with gay malice, "and you must have felt a dreadful wretch when he died."

"We felt very sad when he died," said Mary,—"he was only twenty, poor boy; but, Winnie dear, Uncle Penrose is not an angel, and I think now I will say my say. Captain Percival is very fond of you, and you are very fond of him, and I think, whatever the past may have been, that there is hope if you will be a little serious. It is of consequence. Don't you think that I wish all that is best in the world for you, my only little sister? And why should you distrust me? You are not silly nor weak, and I think you might do well yet, very well, my dear, if you were really to try."

"I think we shall do very well without trying," said Winnie, partly touched and partly indignant; "but it is something for you to say, Mary, and I am sure I am much obliged to you for your good advice all the same."

"Winnie," said Mrs. Ochterlony, taking her hands, "I know the world better than you do—perhaps even better than Uncle Penrose, so far as a woman is concerned. I don't care if you are rich or poor, but I want you to be happy. It will not do very well without trying. I will not say a word about him, for you have set your heart on him, and that must be enough. And some women can do everything for the people they love. I think, perhaps, you could, if you were to give your heart to it, and try."

It was not the kind of address Winnie had expected, and she struggled against it, trying hard to resist the involuntary softening. But after all nature was yet in her, and she could not but feel that what Mary was saying came from her heart.

"I don't see why you should be so serious," she said; "but I am sure it is kind of you, Mary. I—I don't know if I could do—what you say; but whatever I can do I will for Edward!" she added hastily, with a warmth and eagerness which brought the colour to her cheek and the light to her eye; and then the two sisters kissed each other as they had never done before, and Winnie knelt down by Mary's knee, and the two held each other's hands, and clung together, as it was natural they should, in that confidence of nature which is closer than any other except that between mother and daughter—the fellow-feeling of sisters, destined to the same experience, one of whom has gone far in advance, and turning back can trace, step by step, in her own memory, the path the other has to go.

"Don't mistrust me, Winnie," said Mrs. Ochterlony. "I have had a little to bear, though I have been very happy, and I could tell you many things—though I will not, just now; but, Winnie dear, what I want is, that you should make up your mind to it; not to have everything you like, and live in a fairy tale, but to keep right, and to keep him right. If you will promise to think of this, and to take it bravely upon you, I will still hope that all may be well."

Her look was so serious that for the first time Winnie's heart forgave her. Neither jealousy, nor ill-temper, nor fear of evil report on her own side could have looked out of Mary's eyes at her little sister with such a wistful longing gaze. Winnie was moved in spite of herself, and thrilled by the first pang of uncertainty that had yet touched her. If Mary had no motive but natural affection, was it then really a hideous gulf of horrible destruction, on the verge of which she was herself tripping so lightly? Something indefinable came over Winnie's face as that thought moved her. Should it be so, what then? If it was to save him, if it was to perish with him, what did it matter? the only place in the world for her was by his side. She had made her choice, and there was no other choice for her, no alternative even should see the gulf as Curtius did, and leap conscious into it in the eye of day. All this passed through her mind in a moment, as she knelt by Mary's side holding her hands—and came out so on her face that Mary could read something like it in the sudden changing of the fair features and expansion of the eyes. It was as if the soul had been startled, and sprang up to those fair windows, to look out upon the approaching danger, making the spectator careless of their beauty, out of regard to the nobler thing that used them for the moment. Then Winnie rose up suddenly, and gave her sister a hearty kiss, and threw off her sudden gravity as if it had been a cloud.

"Enough of that," she said; "I will try and be good, and so I think will—we all. And Mary, don't look so serious. I mean to be happy, at least as long as I can," cried Winnie. She was the same Winnie again—gay, bold, and careless, before five minutes had passed; and Mary had said her say, and there was now no more to add. Nothing could change the destiny which the thoughtless young creature had laid out for herself. If she could have foreseen the distinctest wretchedness it would have been all the same. She was ready to take the plunge even into the gulf—and nothing that could be said or done could change it now.

In the meantime, Mr. Penrose had gone up to the Hall to talk it over with Sir Edward, and was explaining his views with a distinctness which was not much more agreeable in the Hall than it had been in the Cottage. "I cannot let it go on unless some provision can be made," he said. "Winnie is very handsome, and you must all see she might have done a great deal better. If I had her over in Liverpool, as I have several times thought of doing, I warrant you the settlements would have been of a different description. She might have married anybody, such a girl as that," continued Mr. Penrose, in a regretful business way. It was so much capital lost that might have brought in a much greater profit; and though he had no personal interest in it, it vexed him to see people throwing their chances away.

"That may be, but it is Edward Percival she chooses to marry, and nobody else," said Sir Edward testily; "and she is not a girl to do as you seem to think, exactly as she is told."

"We should have seen about that," said Mr. Penrose; "but in the meantime, he has his pay and she has a hundred a year. If Mrs. Percival will settle three hundred on him, and you, perhaps, two—"

"I, two!" cried Sir Edward, with sudden terror; "why should I settle two? You might as well tell me to retire from the Hall, and leave them my house. And pray, Mr. Penrose, when you are so liberal for other people, what do you mean to give yourself?"

"I am a family man," said Uncle Penrose, taking his other hand out of his pocket, "and what I can give must be, in justice to my family, very limited. But Mrs. Percival, who has only four sons, and yourself who have none, are in very different circumstances. If he had had a father, the business might have been entered into more satisfactorily—but as you are his godfather, I hear—"

"I never understood before, up to this minute," said Sir Edward, with great courtesy, "that it was the duty of a godfather to endow his charge with two hundred a year."

"I beg your pardon, Sir Edward," said Mr. Penrose; "I am a plain man, and I treat things in a business way. I give my godchildren a silver mug, and feel my conscience clear: but if I had introduced a young man, not otherwise very eligible, to a handsome girl, who might have done a great deal better for herself, that would make a great difference in the responsibility. Winnie Seton is of very good family by her father's side, as you know, I suppose, better than I do; and of very good business connexions by her mother's; and her beauty is first rate—I don't think there can be any doubt about that. If she had been an ordinary pretty girl, I would not have said so much; but with all her advantages, I should say that any fair equivalent in the shape of a husband should be worth at least five thousand a year."

Mr. Penrose spoke with such seriousness that Sir Edward was awed out of his first feeling of amusement. He restrained his smile, and acknowledged the logic. "But I did not introduce him in any special way," he said. "If I can negotiate with Mrs. Percival for a more liberal allowance, I will do it. She has an estate of her own, and she is free to leave it to any of her sons: but Edward, I fear, has been rather unsatisfactory—"

"Ah, wild?" said Mr. Penrose: "all young men are alike for that. I think, on the whole, that it is you who should negotiate with the mother. You know her better than I do, and have known all about it from the beginning, and you could show her the state of the case better. If such a mad thing could be consented to by anybody in their senses, it must at least be apparent that Winnie would bring twice as much as the other into the common stock. If she were with me in Liverpool she would not long be Winnie Seton; and you may trust me she should marry a man who was worthy of her," the rich uncle added, with a confirmatory nod of his head. When he spoke of a man who would be worthy of Winnie, he meant no sentimental fitness such as Aunt Agatha would have meant, had she said these words, nor was it even moral worth he was thinking of. What Mr. Penrose meant, was a man who would bring a fair equivalent in silver and gold to Winnie's beauty and youth, and he meant it most seriously, and could not but groan when he contemplated the possibility of so much valuable capital being thrown away.

And he felt that he had made a good impression when he went back to the Cottage. He seemed to himself to have secured Mrs. Percival's three hundred a-year, and even Sir Edward's more problematical gift to the young people; and he occupied the interval in thinking of a silver tea-service which had rather caught his fancy, in a shop window, and which he thought if his negotiations succeeded, he would give to his niece for a wedding present. If they did not succeed it would be a different question—for a young woman who married upon a captain's pay and a hundred a-year of her own, would have little occasion for a silver tea-service. So Mr. Penrose mused as he returned to the Cottage. Under the best of circumstances it was now evident that there could be nothing to "settle" upon Winnie. The mother and the friends might make up a little income, but as for capital—which after all was what Mr. Penrose prized most—there was none in the whole matter, except that which Winnie had in her face and person, and was going to throw so lamentably away. Mr. Penrose could not but make some reflections on Aunt Agatha's feminine idiocy and the cruel heedlessness of Sir Edward, as he walked along the rural road. A girl who had so many advantages, whose husband, to be worthy of her, should have had five thousand a-year at the least, and something handsome to "settle"—and yet her natural guardians had suffered her to get engaged to a captain in a marching regiment, with only his pay! No wonder that Mr. Penrose was sad. But he went home with a sense that, painful as the position was, he had done his duty, at least.

This was how Winnie's marriage got itself accomplished notwithstanding all opposition. Captain Percival was the second of his mother's four sons, and consequently the natural heir of her personal fortune if he had not been "foolish," as she said; and the thought that it might be the saving of him, which was suggested by Sir Edward, was naturally a very moving argument. A beautiful young wife whom he was very fond of, and who was ready to enter with him into all the risks of life,—if that did not keep him right, what would? And after all he was only five-and-twenty, an age at which reformation was quite possible. So his friends thought, persuading themselves with natural sophistry that the influence of love and a self-willed girl of eighteen would do what all other inducements had failed to do; and as for her friends, they were so elated to see that in the eyes of Uncle Penrose the young man's faults bore only the most ordinary aspect, and counted for next to nothing, that their misgivings all but disappeared, and their acceptance of the risk was almost enthusiastic. Sometimes indeed a momentary shadow would cross the mind of Aunt Agatha—sometimes a doubt would change Sir Edward's countenance—but then these two old people were believers in love, and besides had the faculty of believing what they wished to believe, which was a still more important circumstance. And Mary for her part had said her say. The momentary hope she had felt in Winnie's strength of character, and in her love—a hope which had opened her heart to speak to her sister—found but little to support it after that moment. She could not go on protesting, and making her presence a thorn in the flesh of the excited household; and if she felt throughout all a sense that the gulf was still there, though all these flowers had been strewed over it—a sense of the terrible risk which was so poorly counterbalanced by the vaguest and most doubtful of hopes—still Mary was aware that this might be simply the fault of her position, which led her to look upon everything with a less hopeful eye. She was the spectator, and she saw what was going on as the actors themselves could not be expected to see it. She saw Winnie's delight at the idea of freedom from all restraint—and she saw Percival's suppressed impatience of the anxious counsels addressed to him, and the look which Winnie and he exchanged on such occasions, as if assuring each other that in spite of all this they would take their own way. And then Mrs. Ochterlony's own relations with the bridegroom were not of a comfortable kind. He knew apparently by instinct that she was not his friend, and he approached her with a solemn politeness under which Mary, perhaps over-sensitive on that point, felt that a secret sneer was concealed. And he made references to her Indian experiences, with a certain subtle implication of something in them which he knew and nobody else did—something which would be to Mrs. Ochterlony's injury should it be known—which awoke in Mary an irritation and exasperation which nothing else could have produced. She avoided him as much as it was possible to avoid him during the busy interval before the marriage, and he perceived it and thought it was fear, and the sneer that lay under his courtesy became more and more evident. He took to petting little Wilfrid with an evident consciousness of Mary's vexation and the painful effect it produced upon her; not Hugh nor Islay, who were of an age to be a man's plaything, but the baby, who was too young for any but a woman's interest; and Captain Percival was not the kind of man who is naturally fond of children. When she saw her little boy on her future brother-in-law's knee, Mary felt her heart contract with an involuntary shiver, of which she could have given no clear explanation. She did not know what she was afraid of, but she was afraid.

Perhaps it was a relief to them all when the marriage day arrived—which had to be shortly, for the regiment was ordered to Malta, and Captain Percival had already had all the leave he could ask for. Mr. Penrose's exertions had been crowned with such success that when he came to Winnie's wedding he brought her the silver tea-service which in his heart he had decided conditionally to give her as a marriage gift. Mrs. Percival had decided to settle two hundred and fifty pounds a-year upon her son, which was very near Mr. Penrose's mark; and Sir Edward, after long pondering upon the subject, and a half-amused, half-serious, consideration of Winnie's capital which was being thrown away, had made up his mind to a still greater effort. He gave the young man in present possession what he had left him in his will, which was a sum of five thousand pounds—a little fortune to the young soldier. "You might have been my son, my boy, if your mother and I could have made up our minds," the old baronet said, with a momentary weakness; though if anybody else had suggested such an idea no doubt Sir Edward would have said, "Heaven forbid!" And Mr. Penrose pounced upon it and had it settled upon Winnie, and was happy, though the bridegroom resisted a little. After that there could be no doubt about the tea-service. "If you should ever be placed in Mary's position you will have something to fall back upon," Uncle Penrose said; "or even if you should not get on together, you know." It was not a large sum, but the difficulty there had been about getting it, and the pleasant sense that it was wholly owing to his own exertions, made it sweet to the man of capital, and he gave his niece his blessing and the tea-service with a full heart.

As for Winnie, she was radiant in her glow of beauty and happiness on that momentous day. A thunder-shower of sudden tears when she signed the register, and another when she was taking leave of Aunt Agatha, was all that occurred to overcloud her brightness; and even these did not overcloud her, but were in harmony—hot, violent, and sudden as they were—with the passionate happiness and emancipation of the married girl. She kissed over and over again her tender guardian—who for her part sat speechless and desolate to see her child go away, weeping with a silent anguish which could not find any words—and dropped that sudden shower over Aunt Agatha's gown; but a moment after threw back the veil which had fallen over her face, and looked back from the carriage window upon them in a flush of joy, and pride, and conscious freedom, which, had no other sentiments been called for at the moment, it would have done one's heart good to see. She was so happy that she could not cry, nor be sentimental, nor think of broken links, as she said—and why should she pretend to be sad about parting? Which was very true, no doubt, from Winnie's point of view. And there was not the vestige of a cloud about when she waved her hand to them for the last time as she drove away. She was going away to the world and life, to see everything and enjoy everything, and have her day. Why should she not show her delight? While poor old Aunt Agatha, whose day was so long over, fell back into Mary's arms, who was standing beside her, and felt that now at last and finally, her heart was broken, and the joy of her life gone. Was it not simply the course of nature and the way of the world?

CHAPTER XXII

There followed after this a time of such tranquillity as never yet entered into Mrs. Ochterlony's life. Mary had known joy, and she had known sorrow, as people do to whom life comes with full hands, giving and taking; but it had always been life, busy and personal, which left her little leisure for anything beyond the quickly recurring duties of the hour and the day. She had had no time to watch the current how it flowed, being as it were part of it, and going along with it in its ceaseless course. But now all this was changed. After Winnie's marriage a sudden tranquillity fell upon the ladies in the Cottage. Life had gone on and left them; they were no longer going with the tide, but standing by upon the bank watching it. They were not unhappy, nor was their existence sad,—for the three boys were world enough to satisfy the two women and keep them occupied and cheerful; and when the children were asleep, Aunt Agatha and her niece were, as people say, company for each other, and talked over their work as they sat by the evening lamp, or in the twilight garden, which was always so green and so sweet,—and were content, or more than content; but still sometimes Mrs. Ochterlony would bethink herself, and it would seem as a dream to her that she, too, had once taken her part with the others and gone with the stream, and suffered cruel sufferings and tasted sudden joys, and been Hugh Ochterlony's wife. Was it so? Or had she never been but with Aunt Agatha by the little river that ran steadily one day like another under the self-same trees? This strange sense of unreality in the past turned her giddy by times, and made her head swim and the world to go round and round; but, to be sure, she never spoke of these sensations, and life continued, and the boys grew, and everything went very well at Kirtell-side.

Everything went so well that Aunt Agatha many a day pitied the poor people who were out in the world, or the young men who set out from the parish to begin their career, and would say, "Oh, if they but knew how much better everybody is at home!" Mary was younger, and perhaps she was not quite of the same mind; but still it was peace that had fallen upon her and was wrapping her all round like a garment. There was the same quiet routine every day; the same things to do, the same places to walk to, the same faces to see. Nothing unforeseen ever arrived to break the calm. When Hugh was old enough to begin serious lessons, a curate turned up in the course of nature who took pupils, and to whom Islay, too went by-and-by, and even little Wilfrid, who was always delicate. The boys went to him with shining morning faces, and came back growing louder and stronger, and, as Peggy said, more "stirring" every day. And Sir Edward made his almost daily visit, and let a thin and gentle echo of the out-of-door din into the Cottage quiet. He told them in his mild way what was going on, and talked about the news in the papers, and about the books reviewed, and about the occasional heavenly visitant in the shape of a new publication that found its way to Kirtell-side. There were few magazines then, and no cheap ones, and a single Blackwood did for a good many families. Sir Edward himself, who had been always considered intellectual, took in the Edinburgh all for himself, and lent it to his neighbours; but then it could not be expected that many people in a district could be so magnificent as that. When the Curate, on the other hand, came to tea (he was not the sort of man, as Aunt Agatha said, that one would think of making a dinner for), it was all about the parish that he talked; and as Mrs. Ochterlony was a perverse woman in her way, and had her own ideas about her poor neighbours, such conversation was not so interesting to her as it might have been. But it was in this sort of way that she spent the next ten or twelve years of her life.

As for Winnie, she was having her day, as she had said, and was, it is to be supposed, enjoying it. She wrote letters regularly and diligently, which is one point in which a woman, however little elevated she may be above her masculine companion in other respects, always has the better of him. And she possessed a true feminine gift which ought also to be put in the compensating scale against those female drawbacks which are so often insisted upon. Sometimes she was ill-tempered, sometimes bitter in her letters, for the honeymoon happiness naturally did not last for ever; but, whatever mood Winnie might be in, she always threw an unconscious halo of interest around herself when she wrote. It was, as everybody might see, an instinctive and unpremeditated act, but it was successful to the highest extent. Whether she described her triumphs or her disappointments, her husband's kindness or his carelessness, their extravagant living or their want of money, Winnie herself, in the foreground of the picture, was always charmingly, and sometimes touchingly, posed. A word or two did it, and it was done to perfection; and the course of her history thus traced was followed by Aunt Agatha with unfailing enthusiasm. She herself went through it all in the person of her favourite, and Mary connected herself with a vague but still fairer future in the persons of her boys. And thus the peaceful existence went on day by day, with nothing more serious to trouble it than a transitory childish ailment, or a passing rumour that the Percivals were "going too fast," or did not "get on,"—clouds which only floated mistily and momentarily about the horizon, and never came down to trouble the quiet waters. It was a time which left no record, and which by times felt languid and lingering to the younger woman, who was still too young to be altogether satisfied with so dead a calm in the middle of her existence; but still, perhaps, it was, on the whole, the happiest time of Mary's life.

This halcyon time lasted until the boys were so far grown up as to bring the disturbing plans and speculations of their beginning life into the household calm. It lasted until Islay was sixteen and ready to pass his examination for Woolwich, the long-headed boy having fixed his affections upon scientific soldiership in a way which was slightly disappointing to his mother, who, as was natural, had thought him capable of a more learned profession. It roused the Cottage into something like a new stage of existence to think of and prepare for the entry of its nursling into that great vague unseen sphere which Aunt Agatha called the world. But, after all, it was not Islay who was the troublesome member of the family. He had fixed his thoughts upon his chosen profession almost as soon as he knew what was meant by his father's sword, which had hung in Mrs. Ochterlony's room from his earliest recollection; and though there might be a little anxiety about how he would succeed at his examination, and how he would get on when he left home, still Islay was so steady that no one felt any alarm or absolute disquiet about him.

But it was rather different with Hugh. Hugh was supposed to be his uncle's heir, and received as such wherever he went, with perhaps more enthusiasm than might have fallen to his share merely as Mary's son. He was heir presumptive, recognised to a certain extent at Earlston itself as elsewhere in that capacity; and yet Mr. Ochterlony had not, so far as anybody was aware, made any distinct decision, and might still alter his mind, and, indeed, was not too old to marry and have heirs of his own, which was a view of the subject chiefly taken by Aunt Agatha. And, to aggravate the position, Hugh was far from being a boy of fixed resolutions, like his brother. He was one of the troublesome people, who have no particular bias. He liked everything that was pleasant. He was not idle, nor had he any evil tendencies; he was fond of literature in a way, and at the same time fond of shooting and hunting, and all the occupations and amusements of a country life. Public opinion in the country-side proclaimed him one of the nicest young fellows going; and if he had been Francis Ochterlony's son, and indisputably the heir of Earlston, Hugh would have been as satisfactory a specimen of a budding country gentleman as could have been found. But the crook in his lot was, that he was the heir presumptive, and at the same time was generous and proud and high-spirited, and not the kind of nature which could lie in wait for another man's place, or build his fortunes upon another man's generosity. His own opinion, no doubt, was that he had a right to Earlston; but he was far too great a Quixote, too highly fantastical in youthful pride and independence, to permit any one to say that it was his uncle's duty to provide for him. And withal, he did not himself know what manner of life to take up, or what to do. He would have made a good soldier, or a good farmer, different though the two things are; and would have filled, as well as most people, almost any other practical position which Providence or circumstances had set clearly before him. But no intuitive perception of what he was most fit for was in him to enlighten his way; and at the same time he began to be highly impatient, being eighteen, and a man as he thought, of waiting and doing nothing, and living at home.

"If we could but have sent him to Oxford," Aunt Agatha said; "if I had the means!"—but it is very doubtful whether she ever could have had the means; and of late Aunt Agatha too had been disturbed in her quiet. Her letters to Winnie had begun to convey enclosures of which she did not speak much, even to Mrs. Ochterlony, but which were dead against any such possibility for Hugh.

"If I had been brought up at school where I might have got a scholarship, or something," said Hugh; "but I don't know why I should want to go to Oxford. We must send Will if we can, mother; he has the brains for it. Oxford is too grand an idea for me—"

"Not if you are to have Earlston, Hugh," said his mother.

"I wish Earlston was at the bottom of the sea," cried the poor boy; "but for Earlston, one would have known what one was good for. I wish my uncle would make up his mind and found a hospital with it, or marry, as Aunt Agatha says—"

"He will never marry," said Mary; "he was a great deal older than your father; he is quite an old man."

"Indeed, Mary, he is not old at all, for a man," said Aunt Agatha, with eagerness. "Ladies are so different. He might get a very nice wife yet, and children, for anything any one could tell. Not too young, you know—I think it would be a great pity if he were to marry anybody too young; but a nice person, of perhaps forty or so," said Aunt Agatha; and she rounded off her sentence with a soft little sigh.

"He will never marry, I am sure," said Mary, almost with indignation; for, not to speak of the injustice to Hugh, it sounded like an imputation upon her brother-in-law, who was sober-minded, and not thinking of anything so foolish; not to say that his heart was with his marble Venus, and he was indifferent to any other love.

"Well, if you think so, my dear—" said Miss Seton; and a faint colour rose upon her soft old cheek. She thought Mary's meaning was, that after his behaviour to herself, which was not exactly what people expected, he was not likely to entertain another affection; which was probably as true as any other theory of Mr. Ochterlony's conduct. Aunt Agatha thought this was Mary's meaning, and it pleased her. It was an old story, but still she remembered it so well, that it was pleasant to think he had not forgotten. But this, to be sure, had very little to do with Hugh.

"I wish he would marry," said his heir presumptive, "or put one out of pain one way or another. Things can't go on for ever like this. Islay is only sixteen, and he is starting already; and here am I eighteen past, and good for nothing. You would not like me to be a useless wretch all my life?" said Hugh, severely, turning round upon his mother, who was not prepared for such an address; but Hugh, of all the boys, was the one most like his father, and had the Major's "way."

"No," cried Mary, a little alarmed, "anything but that. I still think you might wait a little, and see what your uncle means. You are not so very old. Well, my dear boy! don't be impatient; tell me what you wish to do."

But this was exactly what Hugh could not tell. "If there had been no Earlston in the question, one would have known," he said. "It is very hard upon a fellow to be another man's nephew. I think the best thing I could do would be to ignore Earlston altogether, and go in for—anything I could make my own living by. There's Islay has had the first chance—"

"My dear, one is surely enough in a family to be a soldier," said Aunt Agatha, "if you would consider your poor mamma's feelings and mine; but I never thought, for my part, that that was the thing for Islay, with his long head. He had always such a very peculiar head. When he was a child, you know, Mary, we never could get a child's hat to fit him. Now, I think, if Hugh had gone into a very nice regiment, and Islay had studied for something—"

"Do you think he will have no study to do, going in for the Engineers?" said Hugh, indignantly. "I am not envious of Islay. I know he is the best fellow among us; but, at the same time—The thing for me would be to go to Australia or New Zealand, where one does not need to be good for anything in particular. That is my case," said the disconsolate youth; and out of the depths, if not of his soul, at least of his capacious chest, there came a profound, almost despairing sigh.

"Oh, Hugh, my darling boy! you cannot mean to break all our hearts," cried Aunt Agatha.

It was just what poor Hugh meant to do, for the moment, at least; and he sat with his head down and despair in his face, with a look which went to Mary's heart, and brought the tears to her eyes, but a smile to her lips. He was so like his father; and Mrs. Ochterlony knew that he would not, in this way, at least, break her heart.

"Would you like to go to Uncle Penrose?" she said; to which Hugh replied with a vehement shake of his head. "Would you like to go into Mr. Allonby's office? You know he spoke of wanting an articled pupil. Would you think of that proposal Mr. Mortare, the architect, made us?—don't shake your head off, Hugh; or ask Sir Edward to let you help old Sanders—or—or—Would you really like to be a soldier, like your brother?" said Mary, at her wits' end; for after this, with their limited opportunities, there seemed no further suggestion to make.

"I must do something, mother," said Hugh, and he rose up with another sigh; "but I don't want to vex you," he added, coming up and putting his arms round her with that admiring fondness which is perhaps sweeter to a woman from her son than even from her lover; and then, his mind being relieved, he had no objection to change the conversation. "I promised to look at the young colts, and tell Sir Edward what I thought of them," he suddenly said, looking up at Mary with a cloudy, doubtful look—afraid of being laughed at, and yet himself ready to laugh—such as is not unusual upon a boy's face. Mrs. Ochterlony did not feel in the least inclined for laughter, though she smiled upon her boy; and when he went away, a look of anxiety came to her face, though it was not anything like the tragical anxiety which contracted Aunt Agatha's gentle countenance. She took up her work again, which was more than Miss Seton could do. The boys were no longer children, and life was coming back to her with their growing years. Life which is not peace, but more like a sword.

"My dear love, something must be done," said Aunt Agatha. "Australia or New Zealand, and for a boy of his expectations! Mary, something must be done."

"Yes," said Mary. "I must go and consult my brother-in-law about it, and see what he thinks best. But as for New Zealand or Australia, Aunt Agatha—"

"Do you think it will be nice, Mary?" said Miss Seton, with a soft blush like a girl's. "It will be like asking him, you know, what he means; it will be like saying he ought to provide—"

"He said Hugh was to be his heir," said Mary, "and I believe he meant what he said; at all events, it would be wrong to do anything without consulting him, for he has always been very kind."

These words threw Aunt Agatha into a flutter which she could not conceal. "It may be very well to consult him," she said; "but rather than let him think we are asking his help—And then, how can you see him, Mary? I am afraid it would be—awkward, to say the least, to ask him here—"

"I will go to Earlston to-morrow," said Mary. "I made up my mind while Hugh was talking. After Islay has gone, it will be worse for poor Hugh. Will is so much younger, poor boy."

"Will," said Aunt Agatha, sighing, "Oh, Mary, if they had only been girls! we could have brought them up without any assistance, and no bother about professions or things. When you have settled Hugh and Islay, there will be Will to open it up again; and they will all leave us, after all. Oh, Mary, my dear love, if they had been but girls!"

"Yes, but they are not girls," said Mrs. Ochterlony, with a half smile; and then she too sighed. She was glad her boys were boys, and had more confidence in them, and Providence and life, than Aunt Agatha had. But she was not glad to think that her boys must leave her, and that she had no daughter to share her household life. The cloud which sat on Aunt Agatha's careful brow came over her, too for the moment, and dimmed her eyes, and made her heart ache. "They came into the world for God's uses and not for ours," she said, recovering herself, "and though they are boys, we must not keep them unhappy. I will go over to Earlston to-morrow by the early train."

"If you think it right," said Miss Seton: but it was not cordially spoken. Aunt Agatha was very proud and sensitive in her way. She was the kind of woman to get into misunderstandings, and shun explanations, as much as if she had been a woman in a novel. She was as ready to take up a mistaken idea, and as determined not to see her mistake, as if she had been a heroine forced thereto by the exigencies of three volumes. Miss Seton had never come to the third volume herself; she thought it more dignified for her own part to remain in the complications and perplexities of the second; and it struck her that it was indelicate of Mary thus to open the subject, and lead Francis Ochterlony on, as it were, to declare his mind.

The question was quite a different one so far as Mary was concerned, to whom Francis Ochterlony had never stood in the position of a lover, nor was the subject of any delicate difficulties. With her it was a straightforward piece of business enough to consult her brother-in-law, who was the natural guardian of her sons, and who had always been well disposed towards them, especially while they kept at a safe distance. Islay was the only one who had done any practical harm at Earlston, and Mr. Ochterlony had forgiven, and, it is to be hoped, forgotten the downfall of the rococo chair. If she had had nothing more important to trouble her than a consultation so innocent! Though, to tell the truth, Mary did not feel that she had a great deal to trouble her, even with the uncertainty of Hugh's future upon her hands. Even if his uncle were to contemplate anything so absurd as marriage or the founding of a hospital, Hugh could still make his own way in the world, as his brothers would have to do, and as his father had done before him. And Mrs. Ochterlony was not even overwhelmed by consideration of the very different characters of the boys, nor of the immense responsibility, nor of any of the awful thoughts with which widow-mothers are supposed to be overwhelmed. They were all well, God bless them; all honest and true, healthful and affectionate. Hugh had his crotchets and fidgety ways, but so had his father, and perhaps Mary loved her boy the better for them; and Wilfrid was a strange boy, but then he had always been strange, and it came natural to him. No doubt there might be undeveloped depths in both, of which their mother as yet knew nothing; but in the meantime Mary, like other mothers, took things as she saw them, and was proud of her sons, and had no disturbing fears. As for Islay, he was steady as a rock, and almost as strong, and did the heart good to behold, and even the weakest woman might have taken heart to trust him, whatever might be the temptations and terrors of "the world." Mary had that composure which belongs to the better side of experience, as much as suspicion and distrust belong to its darker side. The world did not alarm her as it did Aunt Agatha; neither did Mr. Ochterlony alarm her, whose sentiments ought at least to be known by this time, and whose counsel she sought with no artful intention of drawing him out, but with an honest desire to have the matter settled one way or another. This was how the interval of calm passed away, and the new generation brought back a new and fuller life.

It was not all pleasure with which Mary rose next morning to go upon her mission to Earlston; but it was with a feeling of resurrection, a sense that she lay no longer ashore, but that the tide was once more creeping about her stranded boat, and the wind wooing the idle sail. There might be storms awaiting her upon the sea; storm and shipwreck and loss of all things lay in the future; possible for her boys as for others, certain for some; but that pricking, tingling thrill of danger and pain gave a certain vitality to the stir of life renewed. Peace is sweet, and there are times when the soul sighs for it; but life is sweeter. And this is how Mary, in her mother's anxiety,—with all the possibilities of fate to affright her, if they could, yet not without a novel sense of exhilaration, her heart beating more strongly, her pulse fuller, her eye brighter,—went forth to open the door for her boy into his own personal and individual career.

CHAPTER XXIII

It was a cheerful summer morning when Mary set out on her visit to her brother-in-law. She had said nothing to her boys about it, for Hugh was fantastical, like Aunt Agatha, and would have denounced her intention as an expedient to make his uncle provide for him. Hugh had gone out to attend to some of the many little businesses he had in hand for Sir Edward; and Islay was working in his own room preparing for the "coach," to whom he was going in a few days; and Wilfrid, or Will, as everybody called him, was with his curate-tutor. The Cottage held its placid place upon the high bank of Kirtell, shining through its trees in a purple cloud of roses, and listening in the sun to that everlasting quiet voice that sung in its ear, summer and winter, the little river's changeful yet changeless song. It looked like a place to which no changes could ever come; calm people in the stillness of age, souls at rest, little children, were the kind of people to live in it; and the stir and quickening of pleasurable pain which Mary felt in her own veins,—the sense of new life and movement about her,—felt out of place with the quiet house.

Aunt Agatha was out of sight, ordering her household affairs; and the drawing-room was silent and deserted as a fairy palace, full of a thousand signs of a habitation, but without a single tenant audible or visible, except the roses that clambered about the open windows, and the bee that went in and made a confused investigation, and came out again none the wiser. An odd sense of the contrast struck Mrs. Ochterlony; but a little while before, her soul had been in unison with the calm of the place, and she had thought nothing of it; now she had woke up out of that fair chamber turned to the sunrising, the name which is Peace, and had stepped back into life, and felt the tingle and thrill of resurrection. And an unconscious smile came on her face as she looked back. To think that out of that silence and sunshine should pour out such a tide of new strength and vigour—and that henceforth hearts should leap with eagerness and wistfulness under that roof, and perhaps grow wild with joy, or perhaps, God knows, break with anguish, as news came good or evil! She had been but half alive so long, that the sense of living was sweet.

It was a moment to call forth many thoughts and recollections, but the fact was that she did not have time to entertain them. There happened to her one of those curious coincidences which occur so often, and which it is so difficult to account for. Long before she reached the little station, a tall figure broke the long vacant line of the dusty country road, a figure which Mary felt at once to be that of a stranger, and yet one she seemed to recognise. She could not believe her eyes, nor think it was anything but the association of ideas which misled her, and laughed at her own fantastic imagination as she went on. But nevertheless it is true that it was her brother-in-law himself who met her, long before she reached the railway by which she had meant to go to him. Her appearance struck him too, it was evident, with a little surprise; but yet she was at home, and might have been going anywhere; whereas the strange fact of his coming required a more elaborate explanation than he had in his power to give.

"I do not know exactly what put it into my head," said Mr. Ochterlony; "perhaps some old work of mine which turned up the other day, and which I was doing when you were with me. I thought I would come over and have a talk with you about your boy."

"It is very strange," said Mary, "for this very morning I had made up my mind to come to you, and consult you. It must be some kind of magnetism, I suppose."

"Indeed, I can't say; I have never studied the natural sciences," said Mr. Ochterlony, with gravity. "I have had a very distinguished visitor lately: a man whose powers are as much above the common mind as his information is—Dr. Franklin, whose name of course you have heard—a man of European reputation."

"Yes," said Mary, doubtfully, feeling very guilty and ignorant, for to tell the truth she had never heard of Dr. Franklin; but her brother-in-law perceived her ignorance, and explained in a kind of compassionate way:

"He is about the greatest numismatist we have in England," said Mr. Ochterlony, "and somehow my little monograph upon primitive art in Iceland came to be talked of. I have never completed it, though Franklin expressed himself much interested—and I think that's how it was suggested to my mind to come and see you to-day."

"I am very glad," said Mary, "I wanted so much to have your advice. Hugh is almost a man now—"

"A man!" said Mr. Ochterlony, with a smile; "I don't see how that is possible. I hope he is not so unruly as he used to be; but you are as young as ever, and I don't see how your children can be men."

And oddly enough, just at that moment, Hugh himself made his appearance, making his way by a cross road down to the river, with his basket over his shoulder, and his fishing-rod. He was taller than his uncle, though Mr. Ochterlony was tall; and big besides, with large, mighty, not perfectly developed limbs, swinging a little loosely upon their hinges like the limbs of a young Newfoundland or baby lion. His face was still smooth as a girl's, and fair, with downy cheeks and his mother's eyes, and that pucker in his forehead which Francis Ochterlony had known of old in the countenance of another Hugh. Mary did not say anything, but she stopped short before her boy, and put her hand on his shoulder, and looked at his uncle with a smile, appealing to him with her proud eyes and beaming face, if this was not almost a man. As for Mr. Ochterlony, he gave a great start and said, "God bless us!" under his breath, and was otherwise speechless for the moment. He had been thinking of a boy, grown no doubt, but still within the limits of childhood; and lo, it was an unknown human creature that faced him, with a will and thoughts of his own, like its father and mother, and yet like nobody but itself. Hugh, for his part, looked with very curious eyes at the stranger, and dimly recognised him, and grew shamefaced and a little fidgety, as was natural to the boy.

"You see how he has grown," said Mary, who, being the triumphant one among the three, was the first to recover herself. "You do not think him a child now? It is your uncle, Hugh, come to see us. It is very kind of him—but of course you knew who he was."

"I am very glad to see my uncle," said Hugh, with eager shyness. "Yes, I knew. You are like my father's picture, sir;—and your own that we have at the Cottage—and Islay a little. I knew it was you."

And then they all walked on in silence; for Mr. Ochterlony was more moved by this sudden encounter than he cared to acknowledge; and Mary, too, for the moment, being a sympathetic woman, saw her boy with his uncle's eyes, and saw what the recollections were that sprang up at sight of him. She told Hugh to go on and do his duty, and send home some trout for dinner; and, thus dismissing him, guided her unlooked-for visitor to the Cottage. He knew the way as well as she did, which increased the embarrassment of the situation. Mary saw only the stiles and the fields, and the trees that over-topped the hedges, familiar objects that met her eyes every day; but Francis Ochterlony saw many a past day and past imagination of his own life, and seemed to walk over his own ashes as he went on. And that was Hugh!—Hugh, not his brother, but his nephew and heir, the representative of the Ochterlony's, occupying the position which his own son should have occupied. Mr. Ochterlony had not calculated on the progress of time, and he was startled and even touched, and felt wonderingly—what it is so difficult for a man to feel—that his own course was of no importance to anybody, and that here was his successor. The thought made him giddy, just as Mary's wondering sense of the unreality of her own independent life, and everlastingness of her stay at the Cottage, had made her; but yet in a different way. For perhaps Francis Ochterlony had never actually realized before that most things were over for him, and that his heir stood ready and waiting for the end of his life.

There was still something of this sense of giddiness in his mind when he followed Mary through the open window into the silent drawing-room where nobody was. Perhaps he had not behaved just as he ought to have done to Agatha Seton; and the recollection of a great many things that had happened, came back upon him as he wound his way with some confusion through the roses. He was half ashamed to go in, like a familiar friend, through the window. Of all men in the world, he had the least right to such a privilege of intimacy. He ought to have gone to the door in a formal way and sent in his card, and been admitted only if Miss Seton pleased; and yet here he was, in the very sanctuary of her life, invited to sit down as it were by her side, led in by the younger generation, which could not but smile at the thought of any sort of sentiment between the old woman and the old man. For indeed Mary, though she was not young, was smiling softly within herself at the idea. She had no sort of sympathy with Mr. Ochterlony's delicate embarrassment, though she was woman enough to hurry away to seek her aunt and prepare her for the meeting, and shield the ancient maiden in the first flutter of her feelings. Thus the master of Earlston was left alone in the Cottage, with leisure to look round and recognise the identity of the place, and see all its differences, and become aware of its pleasant air of habitation, and all the signs of daily use and wont which had no existence in his own house. All this confused him, and put him at a great disadvantage. The probabilities were that Agatha Seton would not have been a bit the happier had she been mistress of Earlston. Indeed the Cottage had so taken her stamp that it was impossible for anybody, whose acquaintance with her was less than thirty years old, to imagine her with any other surroundings. But Francis Ochterlony had known her for more than thirty years, and naturally he felt that he himself was a possession worth a woman's while, and that he had, so to speak, defrauded her of so important a piece of property; and he was penitent and ashamed of himself. Perhaps too his own heart was moved a little by the sense of something lost. His own house might have borne this sunny air of home; instead of his brother Hugh's son, there might have been a boy of his own to inherit Earlston; and looking back at it quietly in this cottage drawing-room, Francis Ochterlony's life seemed to him something very like a mistake. He was not a hard-hearted man, and the inference he drew from this conclusion was very much in his nephew's favour. Hugh's boy was almost a man, and there was no doubt that he was the natural heir, and that it was to him everything ought to come. Instead of thinking of marrying, as Aunt Agatha imagined, or founding a hospital, or making any other ridiculous use of his money, his mind, in its softened and compunctious state, turned to its natural and obvious duty. "Let there be no mistake, at least, about the boy," he said to himself. "Let him have all that is good for him, and all that best fit him for his position;" for, Heaven be praised, there was at least no doubt about Hugh, or question as to his being the lawful and inevitable heir.

It was this process of reasoning, or rather of feeling, that made Mrs. Ochterlony so entirely satisfied with her brother-in-law when she returned (still alone, for Miss Seton was not equal to the exertion all at once, and naturally there was something extra to be ordered for dinner), and began to talk to their uncle about the children.

"There has been no difficulty about Islay," she said: "he always knew what he wanted, and set his heart at once on his profession; but Hugh had no such decided turn. It was very kind what you said when you wrote—but I—don't think it is good for the boy to be idle. Whatever you might think it right to arrange afterwards, I think he should have something to do—"

"I did not think he had been so old," said Mr. Ochterlony, almost apologetically. "Time does not leave much mark of its progress at Earlston. Something to do? I thought what a young fellow of his age enjoyed most was amusing himself. What would he like to do?"

"He does not know," said Mary, a little abashed; "that is why I wanted so much to consult you. I suppose people have talked to him of—of what you might do for him; but he cannot bear the thought of hanging, as it were, on your charity—"

"Charity!" said Mr. Ochterlony, "it is not charity, it is right and nature. I hope he is not one of those touchy sort of boys that think kindness an injury. My poor brother Hugh was always fidgety—"

"Oh no, it is not that," said the anxious mother, "only he is afraid that you might think he was calculating upon you; as if you were obliged to provide for him—"

"And so I am obliged to provide for him," said Mr. Ochterlony, "as much as I should be obliged to provide for my own son, if I had one. We must find him something to do. Perhaps I ought to have thought of it sooner. What has been done about his education? What school has he been at? Is he fit for the University? Earlston will be a better property in his days than it was when I was young," added the uncle with a natural sigh. If he had but provided himself with an heir of his own, perhaps it would have been less troublesome on the whole. "I would send him to Oxford, which would be the best way of employing him; but is he fit for it? Where has he been to school?"

Upon which Mary, with some confusion, murmured something about the curate, and felt for the first time as if she had been indifferent to the education of her boy.

"The curate!" said Mr. Ochterlony; and he gave a little shrug of his shoulders, as if that was a very poor security for Hugh's scholarship.

"He has done very well with all his pupils," said Mary, "and Mr. Cramer, to whom Islay is going, was very much satisfied—"

"I forgot where Islay was going?" said Mr. Ochterlony, inquiringly.

"Mr. Cramer lives near Kendal," said Mary; "he was very highly recommended; and we thought the boy could come home for Sunday—"

Mr. Ochterlony shook his head, though still in a patronizing and friendly way. "I am not sure that it is good to choose a tutor because the boy can come home on Sunday," he said, "nor send them to the curate that you may keep them with yourself. I know it is the way with ladies; but it would have been better, I think, to have sent them to school."

Mrs. Ochterlony was confounded by this verdict against her. All at once her eyes seemed to be opened, and she saw herself a selfish mother keeping her boys at her own apron-strings. She had not time to think of such poor arguments in her favour as want of means, or her own perfectly good intentions. She was silent, struck dumb by this unthought-of condemnation; but just then a champion she had not thought of appeared in her defence.

"Mr. Small did very well for Hugh," said a voice at the window; "he is a very good tutor so far as he goes. He did very well for Hugh—and Islay too," said the new-comer, who came in at the window as he spoke with a bundle of books under his arm. The interruption was so unexpected that Mr. Ochterlony, being quite unused to the easy entrance of strangers at the window, and into the conversation, started up alarmed and a little angry. But, after all, there was nothing to be angry about.

"It is only Will," said Mary. "Wilfrid, it is your uncle, whom you have not seen for so long. This was my baby," she added, turning to her brother-in-law, with an anxious smile—for Wilfrid was a boy who puzzled strangers, and was not by any means so sure to make a good impression as the others were. Mr. Ochterlony shook hands with the new-comer, but he surveyed him a little doubtfully. He was about thirteen, a long boy, with big wrists and ankles visible, and signs of rapid growth. His face did not speak of country air and fare and outdoor life and healthful occupation like his brother's, but was pale and full of fancies and notions which he did not reveal to everybody. He came in and put down his books and threw himself into a chair with none of his elder brother's shamefacedness. Will, for his part, was not given to blushing. He knew nothing of his uncle's visit, but he took it quietly as a thing of course, and prepared to take part in the conversation, whatever its subject might be.

"Mr. Small has done very well for them all," said Mary, taking heart again; "he has always done very well with his pupils. Mr. Cramer was very much satisfied with the progress Islay had made; and as for Hugh—"

"He is quite clever enough for Hugh," said Will, with the same steady voice.

Mr. Ochterlony, though he was generally so grave, was amused. "My young friend, are you sure you are a judge?" he said. "Perhaps he is not clever enough for Wilfrid—is that what you meant to say?"

"It is not so much the being clever," said the boy. "I think he has taught me as much as he knows, so it is not his fault. I wish we had been sent to school; but Hugh is all right. He knows as much as he wants to know, I suppose; and as for Islay, his is technical," the young critic added with a certain quiet superiority. Will, poor fellow, was the clever one of the family, and somehow he had found it out.

Mr. Ochterlony looked at this new representative of his race with a little alarm. Perhaps he was thinking that, on the whole, it was as well not to have boys; and then, as much from inability to carry on the conversation as from interest in his own particular subject, he returned to Hugh.

"The best plan, perhaps, will be for Hugh to go back with me to Earlston; that is, if it is not disagreeable to you," he said, in his old-fashioned, polite way. "I have been too long thinking about it, and his position must be made distinct. Oxford would be the best; that would be good for him in every way. And I think afterwards he might pay a little attention to the estate. I never could have believed that babies grew into boys, and boys to men, so quickly. Why, it can barely be a few years since—Ah!" Mr. Ochterlony got up very precipitately from his chair. It was Aunt Agatha who had come into the room, with her white hair smoothed under her white cap, and her pretty Shetland shawl over her shoulders. Then he perceived that it was more than a few years since he had last seen her. The difference was more to him than the difference in the boys, who were creatures that sprang up nobody knew how, and were never to be relied upon. That summer morning when she came to Earlston to claim her niece, Miss Seton had been old; but it was a different kind of age from that which sat upon her soft countenance now. Francis Ochterlony had not for many a year asked himself in his seclusion whether he was old or young. His occupations were all tranquil, and he had not felt himself unable for them; but if Agatha Seton was like this, surely then it must indeed be time to think of an heir.

The day passed with a curious speed and yet tardiness, such as is peculiar to days of excitement. When they were not talking of the boys, nobody could tell what to talk about. Once or twice, indeed, Mr. Ochterlony began to speak of the Numismatic Society, or the excavations at Nineveh, or some other cognate subject; but he always came to a standstill when he caught Aunt Agatha's soft eyes wondering over him. They had not talked about excavations, nor numismatics either, the last time he had been here; and there was no human link between that time and this, except the boys, of whom they could all talk; and to this theme accordingly everybody returned. Hugh came in audibly, leaving his basket at the kitchen door as he passed, and Islay, with his long head and his deep eyes, came down from his room where he was working, and Will kept his seat in the big Indian chair in the corner, where he dangled his long legs, and listened. Everybody felt the importance of the moment, and was dreadfully serious, even when lighter conversation was attempted. To show the boys in their best light, each of the three, and not so to show them as if anybody calculated upon, or was eager about the uncle's patronage; to give him an idea of their different characters, without any suspicion of "showing off," which the lads could not have tolerated; all this was very difficult to the two anxious women, and required such an amount of mental effort as made it hard to be anything but serious. Fortunately, the boys themselves were a little excited by the novelty of such a visitor, and curious about their uncle, not knowing what his appearance might mean. Hugh flushed into a singular mixture of exaltation, and suspicion, and surprise, when Mr. Ochterlony invited him to Earlston; and looked at his mother with momentary distrust, to see if by any means she had sought the invitation; and Wilfrid sat and dangled his long legs, and listened, with an odd appreciation of the fact that the visit was to Hugh, and not to himself, or any more important member of the family. As for Islay, he was always a good fellow, and like himself; and his way was clear before him, and admitted of no hopes or fears except as to whether or not he should succeed at his examination, which was a matter about which he had himself no very serious doubts, though he said little about it; and perhaps on the whole it was Islay, who was quite indifferent, whom Mr. Ochterlony would have fixed his choice upon, had he been at liberty to choose.

When the visitor departed, which he did the same evening, the household drew a long breath; everybody was relieved, from Peggy in the kitchen, whose idea was that the man was "looking after our Miss Agatha again," down to Will, who had now leisure and occasion to express his sentiments on the subject. Islay went back to his work, to make up for the lost day, having only a moderate and temporary interest in his uncle. It was the elder and the younger who alone felt themselves concerned. As for Hugh, the world seemed to have altered in these few hours; Mr. Ochterlony had not said a great deal to him; but what he said had been said as a man speaks who means and has the power to carry out his words; and the vague heirship had become all of a sudden the realest fact in existence, and a thing which could not be, and never could have been, otherwise. And he was slightly giddy, and his head swam with the sudden elevation. But as for Wilfrid, what had he to do with it, any more than any other member of the family? though he was always a strange boy, and there never was any reckoning what he might do or say.

CHAPTER XXIV

Will's room was a small room opening from his mother's, which would have been her dressing-room had she wanted such a luxury; and when Mrs. Ochterlony went upstairs late that night, after a long talk with Aunt Agatha, she found the light still burning in the little room, and her boy seated, with his jacket and his shoes off, on the floor, in a brown study. He was sitting with his knees drawn up to his chin in a patch of moonlight that shone in from the window. The moonlight made him look ghastly, and his candle had burnt down, and was flickering unsteadily in the socket, and Mary was alarmed. She did not think of any moral cause for the first moment, but only that something was the matter with him, and went in with a sudden maternal panic to see what it was. Will took no immediate notice of her anxious questions, but he condescended to raise his head and prop up his chin with his hands, and stare up into her face.

"Mother," he said, "you always go on as if a fellow was ill. Can't one be thinking a little without anything being the matter? I should have put out my light had I known you were coming upstairs."

"You know, Will, that I cannot have you sit here and think, as you say. It is not thinking—it is brooding, and does you harm," said Mrs. Ochterlony. "Jump up, and go to bed."

"Presently," said the boy. "Is it true that Hugh will go to Oxford, mamma?"

"Very likely," said Mary, with some pride. "Your uncle will see how he has got on with his studies, and after that I think he will go."

"What for?" said Will. "What is the good? He knows as much as he wants to know, and Mr. Small is quite good enough for him."

"What for?" said Mary, with displeasure. "For his education, like other gentlemen, and that he may take his right position. But you are too young to understand all that. Get up, and go to bed."

"I am not too young to understand," said Wilfrid; "what is the good of throwing money and time away? You may tell my uncle, Hugh will never do any good at Oxford; and I don't see, for my part, why he should be the one to go."

"He is the eldest son, and he is your uncle's heir," said Mary, with a conscious swelling of her motherly heart.

"I don't see what difference being the eldest makes," said Will, embracing his knees. "I have been thinking over it this long time. Why should he be sent to Oxford, and the rest of us stay at home? What does it matter about the eldest? A fellow is not any better than me because he was born before me. You might as well send Peggy to Oxford," said Will, with vehemence, "as send Hugh."

Mrs. Ochterlony, whose mind just then was specially occupied by Hugh, was naturally disturbed by this speech. She put out the flickering candle, and set down her own light, and closed the door. "I cannot let you speak so about your brother, Will," she said. "He may not be so quick as you are for your age, but I wish you were as modest and as kind as Hugh is. Why should you grudge his advancement? I used to think you would get the better of this feeling when you ceased to be a child."

"Of what feeling?" cried Will, lifting his pale face from his knees.

"My dear boy, you ought to know," said Mary; "this grudge that any one should have a pleasure or an advantage which you have not. A child may be excused, but no man who thinks so continually of himself—"

"I was not thinking of myself," said Will, springing up from the floor with a flush on his face. "You will always make a moral affair of it, mother. As if one could not discuss a thing. But I know that Hugh is not clever, though he is the eldest. Let him have Earlston if he likes, but why should he have Oxford? And why should it always be supposed that he is better, and a different kind of clay?"

"I wonder where you learned all that, Will," said Mary, with a smile. "One would think you had picked up some Radical or other. I might be vexed to see Lady Balderston walk out of the room before me, if it was because she pretended to be a better woman; but when it is only because she is Lady Balderston, what does it matter? Hugh can't help being the eldest: if you had been the eldest—"

"Ah!" said Will, with a long breath; "if I had been the eldest—" And then he stopped short.

"What would you have done?" said Mrs. Ochterlony, smiling still.

"I would have done what Hugh will never do," cried the boy. "I would have taken care of everybody. I would have found out what they were fit for, and put them in the right way. The one that had brains should have been cultivated—done something else. There should have been no such mistake as—But that is always how it is in the world—everybody says so," said Wilfrid; "stupid people who know nothing about it are set at the head, and those who could manage—"

"Will," said his mother, "do you know you are very presumptuous, and think a great deal too well of yourself? If you were not such a child, I should be angry. It is very well to be clever at your lessons, but that is no proof that you are able to manage, as you say. Let Hugh and his prospects alone for to-night, and go to bed."

"Yes, I can let him alone," said Will. "I suppose it is not worth one's while to mind—he will do no good at Oxford, you know, that is one thing;—whereas other people—"

"Always yourself, Will," said Mary, with a sigh.

"Myself—or even Islay," said the boy, in the most composed way; "though Islay is very technical. Still, he could do some good. But Hugh is an out-of-door sort of fellow. He would do for a farmer or gamekeeper, or to go to Australia, as he says. A man should always follow his natural bent. If, instead of going by eldest sons and that sort of rubbish, they were to try for the right man in the right place. And then you might be sure to be done the best for, mother, and that he would take care of you."

"Will, you are very conceited and very unjust," said Mary; but she was his mother, and she relented as she looked into his weary young face: "but I hope you have your heart in the right place, for all your talk," she said, kissing him before she went away. She went back to her room disturbed, as she had often been before, but still smiling at Will's "way." It was all boyish folly and talk, and he did not mean it; and as he grew older he would learn better. Mary did not care to speculate upon the volcanic elements which, for anything she could tell, might be lying under her very hand. She could not think of different developments of character, and hostile individualities, as people might to whom the three boys were but boys in the abstract, and not Hugh, Islay, and Will—the one as near and dear to her as the other. Mrs. Ochterlony was not philosophical, neither could she follow out to their natural results the tendencies which she could not but see. She preferred to think of it, as Will himself said, as a moral affair—a fault which would mend; and so laid her head on her pillow with a heart uneasy—but no more uneasy than was consistent with the full awakening of anxious yet hopeful life.

As for Will, he was asleep ten minutes after, and had forgotten all about it. His heart was in its right place, though he was plagued with a very arrogant, troublesome, restless little head, and a greater amount of "notions" than are good for his age. He wanted to be at the helm of affairs, to direct everything—a task for which he felt himself singularly competent; but, after all, it was for the benefit of other people that he wanted to rule. It seemed to him that he could arrange for everybody so much better than they could for themselves; and he would have been liberal to Hugh, though he had a certain contempt for his abilities. He would have given him occupation suited to him, and all the indulgences which he was most fitted to appreciate: and he would have made a kind of beneficent empress of his mother, and put her at the head of all manner of benevolences, as other wise despots have been known to do. But Will was the youngest, and nobody so much as asked his advice, or took him into consideration; and the poor boy was thus thrown back upon his own superiority, and got to brood upon it, and scorn the weaker expedients with which other people sought to fill up the place which he alone was truly qualified to fill. Fortunately, however, he forgot all this as soon as he had fallen asleep.

Hugh had no such legislative views for his part. He was not given to speculation. He meant to do his duty, and be a credit to everybody belonging to him; but he was a great deal "younger" than his boy-brother, and it did not occur to him to separate himself in idea—even to do them good—from his own people. The future danced and glimmered before him, but it was a brightness without any theory in it—a thing full of spontaneous good-fortune and well-doing, with which his own cleverness had nothing to do. Islay, for his part, thought very little about it. He was pleased for Hugh's sake, but as he had always looked upon Hugh's good fortune as a certainty, the fact did not excite him, and he was more interested about a tough problem he was working at, and which his uncle's visit had interrupted. It was a more agitated household than it had been a few months before—ere the doors of the future had opened suddenly upon the lads; but there was still no agitation under the Cottage roof which was inconsistent with sweet rest and quiet sleep.

It made a dreadful difference in the house, as everybody said, when the two boys went away—Islay to Mr. Cramer's, the "coach" who was to prepare him for his examination, and Hugh to Earlston. The Cottage had always been quiet, its inhabitants thought, but now it fell into a dead calm, which was stifling and unearthly. Will, the only representative of youth left among them, was graver than Aunt Agatha, and made no gay din, but only noises of an irritating kind. He kicked his legs and feet about, and the legs of all the chairs, and let his books fall, and knocked over the flower-stands—which were all exasperating sounds; but he did not fill the house with snatches of song, with laughter, and the pleasant evidence that a light heart was there. He used to "read" in his own room, with a diligence which was much stimulated by the conviction that Mr. Small was very little ahead of him, and, to keep up his position of instructor, must work hard, too; and, when this was over, he planted himself in a corner of the drawing-room, in the great Indian chair, with a book, beguiling the two ladies into unconsciousness of his presence, and then interposing in their conversation in the most inconvenient way. This was Will's way of showing his appreciation of his mother's society. He was not her right hand, like Hugh, nor did he watch over her comfort in Islay's steady, noiseless way. But he liked to be in the same room with her, to haunt the places where she was, to interfere in what she was doing, and seize the most unfit moments for the expression of his sentiments. With Aunt Agatha he was abrupt and indifferent, being insensible to all conventional delicacies; and he took pleasure, or seemed to take pleasure, in contradicting Mrs. Ochterlony, and going against all her conclusions and arguments; but he paid her the practical compliment of preferring her society, and keeping by her side.

It was while thus left alone, and with the excitement of this first change fresh upon her, that Mrs. Ochterlony heard another piece of news which moved her greatly. It was that the regiment at Carlisle was about to leave, and that it was Our regiment which was to take its place. She thought she was sorry for the first moment. It was upon one of those quiet afternoons, just after the boys had left the Cottage, when the two ladies were sitting in silence, not talking much, thinking how long it was to post-time, and how strange it was that the welcome steps and voices which used to invade the quiet so abruptly and so sweetly, were now beyond hoping for. And the afternoon seemed to have grown so much longer, now that there was no Hugh to burst in with news from the outer world, no Islay to emerge from his problem. Will sat, as usual, in the great chair, but he was reading, and did not contribute to the cheerfulness of the party. And it was just then that Sir Edward came in, doubly welcome, to talk of the absent lads, and ask for the last intelligence of them, and bring this startling piece of news. Mrs. Ochterlony was aware that the regiment had finished its service in India long ago, and there was, of course, no reason why it should not come to Carlisle, but it was not an idea which had ever occurred to her. She thought she was sorry for the first moment, and the news gave her an unquestionable shock; but, after all, it was not a shock of pain; her heart gave a leap, and kept on beating faster, as with a new stimulus. She could think of nothing else all the evening. Even when the post came, and the letters, and all the wonderful first impressions of the two new beginners in the world, this other thought returned as soon as it was possible for any thought to regain a footing. She began to feel as if the very sight of the uniform would be worth a pilgrimage; and then there would be so many questions to ask, so many curiosities and yearnings to satisfy. She could not keep her mind from going out into endless speculations—how many would remain of her old friends?—how many might have dropped out of the ranks, or exchanged, or retired, or been promoted?—how many new marriages there had been, and how many children?—little Emma Askell, for instance, how many babies she might have now? Mary had kept up a desultory correspondence with some of the ladies for a year or two, and even had continued for a long time to get serious letters from Mrs. Kirkman; but these correspondences had dropped off gradually, as is their nature, and the colonel's wife was not a woman to enlarge on Emma Askell's babies, having matters much more important on hand.

This new opening of interest moved Mrs. Ochterlony in spite of herself. She forgot all the painful associations, and looked forward to the arrival of the regiment as an old sailor might look for the arrival of a squadron on active service. Did the winds blow and the waves rise as they used to do on those high seas from which they came? Though Mary had been so long becalmed, she remembered all about the conflicts and storms of that existence more vividly than she remembered what had passed yesterday, and she had a strange longing to know whether all that had departed from her own life existed still for her old friends. Between the breaks of the tranquil conversation she felt herself continually relapse into the regimental roll, always beginning again and always losing the thread; recalling the names of the men and of their wives whom she had been kind to once, and feeling as if they belonged to her, and as if something must be brought back to her by their return.

There was, however, little said about it all that evening, much as it was in Mrs. Ochterlony's mind. When the letters had been discussed, the conversation languished. Summer had begun to wane, and the roses were over, and it began to be impracticable to keep the windows open all the long evening. There was even a fire for the sake of cheerfulness—a little fire which blazed and crackled and made twice as much display as if it had been a serious winter fire and essential to existence—and all the curtains were drawn except over the one window from which Sir Edward's light was visible. Aunt Agatha had grown more fanciful than ever about that window since Winnie's marriage. Even in winter the shutters were never closed there until Miss Seton herself went upstairs, and all the long night the friendly star of Sir Edward's lamp shone faint but steady in the distance. In this way the hall and the cottage kept each other kindly company, and the thought pleased the old people, who had been friends all their lives. Aunt Agatha sat by her favourite table, with her own lamp burning softly and responding to Sir Edward's far-off light, and she never raised her head without seeing it and thinking thoughts in which Sir Edward had but a small share. It was darker than usual on this special night, and there were neither moon nor stars to diminish the importance of the domestic Pharos. Miss Seton looked up, and her eyes lingered upon the blackness of the window and the distant point of illumination, and she sighed as she often did. It was a long time ago, and the boys had grown up in the meantime, and intruded much upon Aunt Agatha's affections; but still these interlopers had not made her forget the especial child of her love.

"My poor dear Winnie!" said the old lady. "I sometimes almost fancy I can see her coming in by that window. She was fond of seeing Sir Edward's light. Now that the dear boys are gone, and it is so quiet again, does it not make you think sometimes of your darling sister, Mary? If we could only hear as often from her as we hear from Islay and Hugh—"

"But it is not long since you had a letter," said Mary, who, to tell the truth, had not been thinking much of her darling sister, and felt guilty when this appeal was made to her.

"Yes," said Aunt Agatha, with a sigh, "and they are always such nice letters; but I am afraid I am very discontented, my dear love. I always want to have something more. I was thinking some of your friends in the regiment could tell you, perhaps, about Edward. I never would say it to you, for I knew that you had things of your own to think about; but for a long time I have been very uneasy in my mind."

"But Winnie has not complained," said Mary, looking up unconsciously at Sir Edward's window, and feeling as if it shone with a certain weird and unconscious light, like a living creature aware of all that was being said.

"She is not a girl ever to complain," said Aunt Agatha, proudly. "She is more like what I would have been myself, Mary, if I had ever been—in the circumstances, you know. She would break her heart before she would complain. I think there is a good deal of difference, my dear, between your nature and ours; and that was, perhaps, why you never quite understood my sweet Winnie. I am sure you are more reasonable; but you are not—not to call passionate, you know. It is a great deal better," cried Aunt Agatha, anxiously. "You must not think I do not see that; but Winnie and I are a couple of fools that would do anything for love; and, rather than complain, I am sure she would die."

Mary did not say that Winnie had done what was a great deal more than complaining, and had set her husband before them in a very uncomfortable light—and she took the verdict upon herself quietly, as a matter of course. "Mr. Askell used to know him very well," she said; "perhaps he knows something. But Edward Percival never was very popular, and you must not quarrel with me if I bring you back a disagreeable report. I think I will go into Carlisle as soon as they arrive—I should like to see them all again."

"I should like to hear the truth whatever it is," said Aunt Agatha, "but my dear love, seeing them all will be a great trial for you."

Mary was silent, for she was thinking of other things: not merely of her happy days, and the difference which would make such a meeting "a great trial;" but of the one great vexation and mortification of her life, of which the regiment was aware—and whether the painful memory of it would ever return again to vex her. It had faded out of her recollection in the long peacefulness and quiet of her life. Could it ever return again to shame and wound, as it had once done? From where she was sitting with her work, between the cheerful lamp and the bright little blazing fire, Mary went away in an instant to the scene so distant and different, and was kneeling again by her husband's side, a woman humbled, yet never before so indignantly, resentfully proud, in the little chapel of the station. Would it ever come back again, that one blot on her life, with all its false, injurious suggestions? She said to herself "No." No doubt it had died out of other people's minds as out of her own, and on Kirtell-side nobody would have dared to doubt on such a subject; and now that the family affairs were settled, and Hugh was established at Earlston, his uncle's acknowledged heir, this cloud, at least, could never rise on her again to take the comfort out of her life. She dismissed the very thought of it from her mind, and her heart warmed to the recollection of the old faces and the old ways. She had a kind of a longing to see them, as if her life would be completer after. It was not as "a great trial" that Mary thought of it. She was too eager and curious to know how they had all fared; and if, to some of them at least, the old existence, so long broken up for herself, continued and flourished as of old.

CHAPTER XXV

It was accordingly with a little excitement that when the regiment had actually arrived Mrs. Ochterlony set out for the neighbouring town to renew her acquaintance with her old friends. It was winter by that time, and winter is seldom very gentle in Cumberland: but she was too much interested to be detained by the weather. She had said nothing to Wilfrid on the subject, and it startled her a little to find him standing at the door waiting for her, carefully dressed, which was not usually a faculty of his, and evidently prepared to accompany her. When she opened the Cottage door to go out, and saw him, an unaccountable panic seized her. There he stood in the sunshine,—not gay and thoughtless like his brother Hugh, nor preoccupied like Islay,—with his keen eyes and sharp ears, and mind that seemed always to lie in wait for something. The recollection of the one thing which she did not want to be known had come strongly to her mind once more at that particular moment; a little tremor had run through her frame—a sense of half-painful, half-pleasant, excitement. When her eye fell on Wilfrid, she went back a step unconsciously, and her heart for the moment seemed to stop beating. She wanted to bring her friends to Kirtell, to show them her boys and make them acquainted with all her life; and probably, had it been Hugh, he would have accompanied her as a matter of course. But somehow Wilfrid was different. Without knowing what her reason was, she felt reluctant to undergo the first questionings and reminiscences with this keen spectator standing by to hear and see all, and to demand explanation of matters which it might be difficult to explain.

"Did you mean to go with me, Will?" she said. "But you know we cannot leave Aunt Agatha all by herself. I wanted to see you to ask you to be as agreeable as possible while I am gone."

"I am never agreeable to Aunt Agatha," said Will; "she always liked the others best; and besides, she does not want me, and I am going to take care of you."

"Thank you," said Mary, with a smile; "but I don't want you either for to-day. We shall have so many things to talk about—old affairs that you would not understand."

"I like that sort of thing," said Will; "I like listening to women's talk—especially when it is about things I don't understand. It is always something new."

Mary smiled, but there was something in his persistence that frightened her. "My dear Will, I don't want you to-day," she said with a slight shiver, in spite of herself.

"Why, mamma?" said Will, with open eyes.

He was not so well brought up as he ought to have been, as everybody will perceive. He did not accept his mother's decision, and put away his Sunday hat, and say no more about it. On the contrary, he looked with suspicion (as she thought) at her, and kept his position—surprised and remonstrative, and not disposed to give in.

"Will," said Mrs. Ochterlony. "I will not have you with me, and that must be enough. These are all people whom I have not seen since you were a baby. It may be a trial for us all to meet, for I don't know what may have happened to them. I can speak of my affairs before you, for you—know them all," Mary went on with a momentary faltering; "but it is not to be supposed that they could speak of theirs in the presence of a boy they do not know. Go now and amuse yourself, and don't do anything to frighten Aunt Agatha: and you can come and meet me by the evening train."

But she could not get rid of a sense of fear as she left him. He was not like other boys, from whose mind a little contradiction passes away almost as soon as it is spoken. He had that strange faculty of connecting one thing with another, which is sometimes so valuable, and sometimes leads a lively intellect so much astray; and if ever he should come to know that there was anything in his mother's history which she wished to keep concealed from him—It was a foolish thought, but it was not the less painful on that account. Mary had come to the end of her little journey before she got free from its influence. The united household at the cottage was not rich enough to possess anything in the shape of a carriage, but they were near the railway, which served almost the same purpose. It seemed to Mrs. Ochterlony as if the twelve intervening years were but a dream when she found herself in a drawing-room which had already taken Mrs. Kirkman's imprint, and breathed of her in every corner. It was not such a room, it is true, as the hot Indian chamber in which Mary had last seen the colonel's wife. It was one of the most respectable and sombre, as well as one of the best of the houses which let themselves furnished, with an eye to the officers. It had red curtains and red carpets, and blinds drawn more than half way down; and there were two or three boxes, with a significant slit in the lid, distributed about the different tables. In the centre of the round table before the fire there was a little trophy built up of small Indian gods, which were no doubt English manufacture, but which had been for a long time Mrs. Kirkman's text, and quite invaluable to her as a proof of the heathen darkness, which was her favourite subject; and at the foot of this ugly pyramid lay a little heap of pamphlets, reports of all the societies under heaven. Mary recognised, too, as she sat and waited, the large brown-paper cover, in which she knew by experience Mrs. Kirkman's favourite tracts were enclosed; and the little basket which contained a smaller roll, and which had room besides occasionally for a little tea and sugar, when circumstances made them necessary; and the book with limp boards, in which the Colonel's wife kept her list of names, with little biographical comments opposite, which had once amused the subalterns so much when it fell into their hands. She had her sealed book besides, with a Bramah lock, which was far too sacred to be revealed to profane eyes; but yet, perhaps, she liked to tantalize profane eyes with the sight of its undiscoverable riches, for it lay on the table like the rest. This was how Mary saw at a glance that, whatever might have happened to the others, Mrs. Kirkman at least was quite unchanged.

She came gliding into the room a minute after, so like herself that Mrs. Ochterlony felt once more that time was not, and that her life had been a dream. She folded her visitor in a silent embrace, and kissed her with inexpressible meaning, and fanned her cheeks with those two long locks hanging out of curl, which had been her characteristic embellishments since ever any one remembered. The light hair was now a little grey, but that made no difference to speak of either in colour or general aspect; and, so far as any other change went, those intervening years might never have been.

"My dear Mary!" she said at last. "My dear friend! Oh, what a thought that little as we deserve it, we should have been both spared to meet again!"

There was an emphasis on the both which it was very touching to hear; and Mary naturally could not but feel that the wonder and the thankfulness were chiefly on her own account.

"I am very glad to see you again," she said, feeling her heart yearn to her old friend—"and so entirely unchanged."

"Oh, I hope not," said Mrs. Kirkman. "I hope we have both profited by our opportunities, and made some return for so many mercies. One great thing I have looked forward to ever since I knew we were coming here, was the thought of seeing you again. You know I always considered you one of my own little flock, dear Mary! one of those who would be my crown of rejoicing. It is such a pleasure to have you again."

And Mrs. Kirkman gave Mrs. Ochterlony another kiss, and thought of the woman that was a sinner with a gush of sweet feeling in her heart.

As for Mary, she took it very quietly, having no inclination to be affronted or offended—but, on the contrary, a kind of satisfaction in finding all as it used to be; the same thoughts and the same kind of talk, and everything unchanged, while all with herself had changed so much. "Thank you," she said; "and now tell me about yourself and about them all; the Heskeths and the Churchills, and all our old friends. I am thirsting to hear about them, and what changes there may have been, and how many are here."

"Ah, my dear Mary, there have been many changes," said Mrs. Kirkman. "Mrs. Churchill died years ago—did you not hear?—and in a very much more prepared state of mind, I trust and hope; and he has a curacy somewhere, and is bringing up the poor children—in his own pernicious views, I sadly fear."

"Has he pernicious views?" said Mary. "Poor Mrs. Churchill—and yet one could not have looked for anything else."

"Don't say poor," said Mrs. Kirkman. "It is good for her to have been taken away from the evil to come. He is very lax, and always was very lax. You know how little he was to be depended upon at the station, and how much was thrown upon me, unworthy as I am, to do; and it is sad to think of those poor dear children brought up in such opinions. They are very poor, but that is nothing in comparison. Captain Hesketh retired when we came back to England. They went to their own place in the country, and they are very comfortable, I believe—too comfortable, Mary. It makes them forget things that are so much more precious. And I doubt if there is anybody to say a faithful word—"

"She was very kind," said Mary, "and good to everybody. I am very sorry they are gone."

"Yes, she was kind," said Mrs. Kirkman, "that kind of natural amiability which is such a delusion. And everything goes well with them," she added, with a sigh: "there is nothing to rouse them up. Oh, Mary, you remember what I said when your pride was brought low—anything is better than being let alone."

Mrs. Ochterlony began to feel her old opposition stirring in her mind, but she refrained heroically, and went on with her interrogatory. "And the doctor," she said, "and the Askells?—they are still in the regiment. I want you to tell me where I can find Emma, and how things have gone with her—poor child! but she ought not to be such a baby now."

Mrs. Kirkman sighed. "No, she ought not to be a baby," she said. "I never like to judge any one, and I would like you to form your own opinion, Mary. She too has little immortal souls committed to her; and oh! it is sad to see how little people think of such a trust—whereas others who would have given their whole souls to it—But no doubt it is all for the best. I have not asked you yet how are your dear boys? I hope you are endeavouring to make them grow in grace. Oh, Mary, I hope you have thought well over your responsibility. A mother has so much in her hands."

"Yes," said Mrs. Ochterlony, quickly; "but they are very good boys, and I have every reason to be content with them. Hugh is at Earlston, just now, with his uncle. He is to succeed him, you know; and he is going to Oxford directly, I believe. And Islay is going to Woolwich if he can pass his examination. He is just the same long-headed boy he used to be. And Will—my baby; perhaps you remember what a little thing he was?—I think he is going to be the genius of the family." Mary went on with a simple effusiveness unusual to her, betrayed by the delight of talking about her boys to some one who knew and yet did not know them. Perhaps she forgot that her listener's interest could not possibly be so great as her own.

Mrs. Kirkman sat with her hands clasped on her knee, and she looked in Mary's eyes with a glance which was meant to go to her soul—a mournful inquiring glance which, from under the dropped eyelids, seemed to fall as from an altitude of scarcely human compassion and solicitude. "Oh, call them not good," she said. "Tell me what signs of awakening you have seen in their hearts. Dear Mary, do not neglect the one thing needful for your precious boys. Think of their immortal souls. That is what interests me much more than their worldly prospects. Do you think their hearts have been truly touched—"

"I think God has been very kind to us all, and that they are good boys," said Mary; "you know we don't think quite alike on some subjects; or, at least, we don't express ourselves alike. I can see you do as much as ever among the men, and among the poor—"

"Yes," said Mrs. Kirkman, with a sigh; "I feel unworthy of it, and the flesh is weak, and I would fain draw back; but it happens strangely that there is always a very lukewarm ministry wherever we are placed, my dear. I would give anything in the world to be but a hearer of the word like others; but yet woe is unto me if I neglect the work. This is some one coming in now to speak with me on spiritual matters. I am at home to them between two and three; but, my dear Mary, it is not necessary that you, who have been in the position of an inquiring soul yourself, should go away."

"I will come back again," said Mary, rising; "and you will come to see me at Kirtell, will not you? It makes one forget how many years have passed to see you employed exactly as of old."

"Ah, we are all too apt to forget how the years pass," said Mrs. Kirkman. She gave a nod of recognition to some women who came shyly in at the moment, and then she took Mary's hand and drew her a step aside. "And nothing more has happened, Mary?" she said; "nothing has followed, and there is to be no inquiry or anything? I am very thankful, for your sake."

"Inquiry!" said Mary, with momentary amazement. "What kind of inquiry? what could have followed? I do not know what you mean!!"

"I mean about—what gave us all so much pain—your marriage, Mary," said Mrs. Kirkman. "I hope there has been nothing about it again?"

This was a very sharp trial for the superstition of old friendship in Mrs. Ochterlony's heart, especially as the inquiring souls who had come to see Mrs. Kirkman were within hearing, and looked with a certain subdued curiosity upon the visitor and the conversation. Mary's face flushed with a sudden burning, and indignation came to her aid; but even at that moment her strongest feeling was thankfulness that Wilfrid was not there.

"I do not know what could have been about it," she said: "I am among my own people here; my marriage was well known, and everything about it, in my own place."

"You are angry, dear," said Mrs. Kirkman. "Oh, don't encourage angry feelings; you know I never made any difference; I never imagined it was your fault. And I am so glad to hear it has made no unpleasantness with the dear boys."

Perhaps it was not with the same charity as at first that Mrs. Ochterlony felt the long curls again fan her cheek, but still she accepted the farewell kiss. She had expected some ideal difference, some visionary kind of elevation, which would leave the same individual, yet a loftier kind of woman, in the place of her former friend. And what she had found was a person quite unchanged—the same woman, harder in her peculiarities rather than softer, as is unfortunately the most usual case. The Colonel's wife had the best meaning in the world, and she was a good woman in her way; but not a dozen lives, let alone a dozen years, could have given her the finer sense which must come by nature, nor even that tolerance and sweetness of experience, which is a benefit which only a few people in the world draw from the passage of years. Mary was disappointed, but she acknowledged in her heart—having herself acquired that gentleness of experience—that she had no right to be disappointed; and it was with a kind of smile at her own vain expectations that she went in search of Emma Askell, her little friend of old—the impulsive girl, who had amused her, and loved her, and worried her in former times. Young Askell was Captain now, and better off, it was to be hoped: but yet they were not well enough off to be in a handsome house, or have everything proper about them, like the Colonel's wife. It was in the outskirts of the town that Mary had to seek them, in a house with a little bare garden in front, bare in its winter nakedness, with its little grass-plot trodden down by many feet, and showing all those marks of neglect and indifference which betray the stage at which poverty sinks into a muddle of discouragement and carelessness, and forgets appearances. It was a dirty little maid who opened the door, and the house was another very inferior specimen of the furnished house so well known to all unsettled and wandering people. The chances are, that delicate and orderly as Mrs. Ochterlony was by nature, the sombre shabbiness of the place would not have struck her in her younger days, when she, too, had to take her chance of furnished houses, and do her best, as became a soldier's wife. And then poor little Emma had been married too early, and began her struggling, shifty life too soon, to know anything about that delicate domestic order, which is half a religion. Poor little Emma! she was as old now as Mary had been when she came back to Kirtell with her boys, and it was difficult to form any imagination of what time might have done for her. Mrs. Ochterlony went up the narrow stairs with a sense of half-amused curiosity, guided not only by the dirty little maid, but by the sound of a little voice crying in a lamentable, endless sort of way. It was a kind of cry which in itself told the story of the family—not violent, as if the result of a sudden injury or fit of passion, which there was somebody by to console or to punish, but the endless, tedious lamentation, which nobody took any particular notice of, or cared about.

And this was the scene that met Mrs. Ochterlony's eyes when she entered the room. She had sent the maid away and opened the door herself, for her heart was full. It was a shabby little room on the first floor, with cold windows opening down to the floor, and letting in the cold Cumberland winds to chill the feet and aggravate the temper of the inhabitants. In the foreground sat a little girl with a baby sleeping on her knee, one little brother in front of her and another behind her chair, and that pretty air of being herself the domestic centre and chief mover of everything, which it is at once sweet and sad to see in a child. This little woman neither saw nor heard the stranger at the door. She had been hushing and rocking her baby, and, now that it had peaceably sunk to sleep, was about to hear her little brother's lesson, as it appeared; while at the same time addressing a word of remonstrance to the author of the cry, another small creature who sat rubbing her eyes with two fat fists, upon the floor. Of all this group, the only one aware of Mary's appearance was the little fellow behind his sister's chair, who lifted wondering eyes to the door, and stared and said nothing, after the manner of children. The little party was so complete in itself, and seemed to centre so naturally in the elder sister, that the spectator felt no need to seek further. It was all new and unlooked for, yet it was a kind of scene to go to the heart of a woman who had children of her own; and Mary stood and looked at the little ones, and at the child-mother in the midst of them, without even becoming aware of the presence of the actual mother, who had been lying on a sofa, in a detached and separate way, reading a book, which she now thrust under her pillow, as she raised herself on her cushions and gazed with wide-open eyes at her visitor, who did not see her. It was a woman very little like the pretty Emma of old times, with a hectic colour on her cheeks, her hair hanging loosely and disordered by lying down, and the absorbed, half-awakened look, natural to a mind which had been suddenly roused up out of a novel into an actual emergency. The hushing of the baby to sleep, the hearing of the lessons, the tedious crying of the little girl at her feet, had all gone on without disturbing Mrs. Askell. She had been so entirely absorbed in one of Jane Eyre's successors and imitators (for that was the epoch of Jane Eyre in novels), and Nelly was so completely responsible for all that was going on, that the mother had never even roused up to a sense of what was passing round her, until the door opened and the stranger looked in with a face which was not a stranger's face.

"Good gracious!" cried Mrs. Askell, springing up. "Oh, my Madonna, can it be you? Are you sure it is you, you dear, you darling! Don't go looking at the children as if they were the principal, but give me a kiss and say it is you,—say you are sure it is you!"

And the rapture of delight and welcome she went into, though it showed how weak-minded and excitable she was, was in its way not disagreeable to Mary, and touched her heart. She gave the kiss she was asked for, and received a flood in return, and such embraces as nearly took her breath away; and then Nelly was summoned to take "the things" off an easy chair, the only one in the room, which stood near her mother's sofa. Mary was still in Mrs. Askell's embrace when this command was given, but she saw the girl gather up the baby in her arms, and moving softly not to disturb the little sleeper, collect the encumbering articles together and draw the chair forward. No one else moved or took any trouble. The bigger boy stood and watched behind his sister's chair, and the younger one turned round to indulge in the same inspection, and little Emma took her fists out of her eyes. But there was nobody but the little woman with the baby who could get for the guest the only comfortable chair.

"Now sit down and be comfortable, and let me look at you; I could be content just to look at you all day," said Emma. "You are just as you always were, and not a bit changed. It is because you have not had all our cares. I look a perfect fright, and as old as my grandmother, and I am no good for anything; but you are just the same as you used to be. Oh, it is just like the old times, seeing you! I have been in such a state, I did not know what to do with myself since ever I knew we were coming here."

"But I do not think you are looking old, though you look delicate," said Mary. "Let me make acquaintance with the children. Nelly, you used to be in my arms as much as your mamma's when you were a baby. You are just the same age as my Will, and you were the best baby that ever was. Tell me their names and how old they all are. You know they are all strangers to me."

"Yes," said their mother, with a little fretfulness. "It was such a mercy Nelly was the eldest. I never could have kept living if she had been a boy. I have been such a suffering creature, and we have been moved about so much, and oh, we have had so much to do! You can't fancy what a life we have had," cried poor Emma; and the mere thought of it brought tears to her eyes.

"Yes, I know it is a troublesome life," said Mary; "but you are young, and you have your husband, and the children are all so well—"

"Yes, the children are all well," said Emma; "but then every new place they come to, they take measles or something, and I am gone to a shadow before they are right again; and then the doctors' bills—I think Charley and Lucy and Emma have had everything," said the aggrieved mother; "and they always take them so badly; and then Askell takes it into his head it is damp linen or something, and thinks it is my fault. It is bad enough when a woman is having her children," cried poor Emma, "without all their illnesses, you know, and tempers and bills, and everything besides. Oh, Madonna! you are so well off. You live quiet, and you know nothing about all our cares."

"I think I would not mind the cares," said Mary; "if you were quiet like me, you would not like it. You must come out to Kirtell for a little change."

"Oh, yes, with all my heart," said Emma. "I think sometimes it would do me all the good in the world just to be out of the noise for a little, and where there was nothing to be found fault with. I should feel like a girl again, my Madonna, if I could be with you."

"And Nelly must come too," said Mrs. Ochterlony, looking down upon the little bright, anxious, careful face.

Nelly was thirteen—the same age as Wilfrid; but she was little, and laden with the care of which her mother talked. Her eyes were hazel eyes, such as would have run over with gladness had they been left to nature, and her brown hair curled a little on her neck. She was uncared for, badly dressed, and not old enough yet for the instinct that makes the budding woman mindful of herself. But the care that made Emma's cheek hollow and her life a waste, looked sweet out of Nelly's eyes. The mother thought she bore it all, and cried and complained under it, while the child took it on her shoulders unawares and carried it without any complaint. Her soft little face lighted up for a moment as Mary spoke, and then her look turned on the sleeping baby with that air half infantile, half motherly, which makes a child's face like an angel's.

"I do not think I could go," she said; "for the children are not used to the new nurse; and it would make poor papa so uncomfortable; and then it would do mamma so much more good to be quiet for a little without the children—"

Mary rose up softly just then, and, to Nelly's great surprise, bent over her and kissed her. Nobody but such another woman could have told what a sense of envy and yearning was in Mary's heart as she did it. How she would have surrounded with tenderness and love that little daughter who was but a domestic slave to Emma Askell! and yet, if she had been Mary's daughter, and surrounded by love and tenderness, she would not have been such a child. The little thing brightened and blushed, and looked up with a gleam of sweet surprise in her eyes. "Oh, thank you, Mrs. Ochterlony," she said, in that sudden flush of pleasure; and the two recognised each other in that moment, and knitted between them, different as their ages were, that bond of everlasting friendship which is made oftener at sight than in any more cautious way.

"Come and sit by me," said Emma, "or I shall be jealous of my own child. She is a dear little thing, and so good with the others. Come and tell me about your boys. And, oh, please, just one word—we have so often spoken about it, and so often wondered. Tell me, dear Mrs. Ochterlony, did it never do any harm?"

"Did what never do any harm?" asked Mary, with once more a sudden pang of thankfulness that Wilfrid was not there.

Mrs. Askell threw her arms round Mary's neck and kissed her and clasped her close. "There never was any one like you," she said; "you never even would complain."

This second assault made Mary falter and recoil, in spite of herself. They had not forgot, though she might have forgotten. And, what was even worse than words, as Emma spoke, the serious little woman-child, who had won Mrs. Ochterlony's heart, raised her sweet eyes and looked with a mixture of wonder and understanding in Mary's face. The child whom she would have liked to carry away and make her own—did she, too, know and wonder? There was a great deal of conversation after this—a great deal about the Askells themselves, and a great deal about Winnie and her husband, whom Mrs. Askell knew much more about than Mrs. Ochterlony did. But it would be vain to say that anything she heard made as great an impression upon Mary as the personal allusions which sent the blood tingling through her veins. She went home, at last, with that most grateful sense of home which can only be fully realized by those who return from the encounter of an indifferent world, and from friends who, though kind, are naturally disposed to regard everything from their own point of view. It is sweet to have friends, and yet by times it is bitter. Fortunately for Mary, she had the warm circle of her own immediate belongings to return into, and could retire, as it were, into her citadel, and there smile at all the world. Her boys gave her that sweetest youthful adoration which is better than the love of lovers, and no painful ghost lurked in their memory—or so, at least, Mrs. Ochterlony thought.

CHAPTER XXVI

The Cottage changed its aspect greatly after the arrival of the regiment, and it was a change which lasted a long time, for the depôt was established at Carlisle, and Captain Askell got an appointment which smoothed the stony way of life a little for himself and his wife. Kirtell was very accessible and very pretty, and there was always a welcome to be had at the Cottage; and the regiment returned in the twinkling of an eye to its old regard for its Madonna Mary. The officers came about the house continually, to the great enlivenment of the parish in general. And Mrs. Kirkman came, and very soon made out that the vicar and his curate were both very incompetent, and did what she could to form a missionary nucleus, if not under Mrs. Ochterlony's wing, at least protected by her shadow; and the little Askells came and luxuriated in the grass and the flowers; and Miss Sorbette and the doctor, who were still on the strength of the regiment, paid many visits, bringing with them the new people whom Mary did not know. When Hugh and Islay came home at vacation times, they found the house so lively, that it acquired new attractions for them, and Aunt Agatha, who was not so old as to be quite indifferent to society, said to herself with natural sophistry, that it was very good for the boys, and made them happier than two solitary women could have done by themselves, which no doubt was true. As for Mrs. Ochterlony herself, she said frankly that she was glad to see her friends; she liked to receive them in her own house. She had been rather poor in India, and not able to entertain them very splendidly; and though she was poor still, and the Cottage was a very modest little dwelling-place, it could receive the visitors, and give them pleasant welcome, and a pleasant meal, and pleasant faces, and cheerful companionship. Mrs. Ochterlony was not yet old, and she had lived a quiet life of late, so peaceful that the incipient wrinkles which life had outlined in her face, had been filled up and smoothed out by the quietness. She was in perfect health, and her eyes were bright, and her complexion sweet, and her hair still gave by time a golden gleam out of its brown masses.

No wonder then that her old friends saw little or no change in her, and that her new ones admired her as much as she had ever been admired in her best days. Some women are sweet by means of being helpless, and fragile, and tender; and some have a loftier charm by reason of their veiled strength and composure, and calm of self-possession. Mary was one of the last; she was a woman not to lean, but to be leant upon; soft with a touch like velvet, and yet as steady as a rock—a kind of beauty which wears long, and does not spoil even by growing old.

It was a state of affairs very agreeable to everybody in the place, except, perhaps, to Will, who was very jealous of his mother. Hugh and Islay when they came home took it all for granted, in an open-handed boyish way, and were no more afraid of anything Mrs. Ochterlony might do, than for their own existence. But Will was always there. He haunted the drawing-room, whoever might be in it at the moment; yet—though to Aunt Agatha's consciousness, the boy was never absent from the big Indian chair in the corner—he was at the same time always ready to pursue his curate to the very verge of that poor gentleman's knowledge, and give him all the excitement of a hairbreadth 'scape ten times in a morning. Nobody could tell when he learned his lessons, or what time he had for study—for there he was always, taking in everything, and making comments in his own mind, and now and then interposing in the conversation to Aunt Agatha's indignation. Mary would not see it, she said; Mary thought that all her boys did was right—which was, perhaps, to some extent true; and it was said in the neighbourhood, as was natural, that so many gentlemen did not come to the Cottage for nothing; that Mrs. Ochterlony was still a young woman; that she had devoted herself to the boys for a long time, and that if she were to marry again, nobody could have any right to object. Such reports spring up in the country so easily, either with or without foundation; and Wilfrid, who found out everything, heard them, and grew very watchful and jealous, and even doubtful of his mother. Should such an idea have entered into her head, the boy felt that he would despise her; and yet at the same time he was very fond of her and filled with unbounded jealousy. While all the time, Mary herself was very glad to see her friends, and, perhaps, was not entirely unconscious of exciting a certain respectful admiration, but had as little idea of severing herself from her past life, and making a new fictitious beginning, as if she had been eighty; and it never occurred to her to imagine that she was watched or doubted by her boy.

It was a pleasant revival, but it had its drawbacks—for one thing, Aunt Agatha did not, as she said, get on with all Mary's friends. There was between Miss Seton and Mrs. Kirkman an enmity which was to the death. The Colonel's wife, though she might be, as became her position, a good enough conservative in secular politics, was a revolutionary, or more than a revolutionary, an iconoclast, in matters ecclesiastical. She had no respect for anything, Aunt Agatha thought. A woman who works under the proper authorities, and reveres her clergyman, is a woman to be regarded with a certain respect, even if she is sometimes zealous out of season; but when she sets up on her own foundation, and sighs over the shortcomings of the clergy, and believes in neither rector nor curate, then the whole aspect of affairs is changed. "She believes in nobody but herself," Aunt Agatha said; "she has no respect for anything. I wonder how you can put up with such a woman, Mary. She talks to our good vicar as if he were a boy at school—and tells him how to manage the parish. If that is the kind of person you think a good woman, I have no wish to be good, for my part. She is quite insufferable to me."

"She is often disagreeable," said Mary, "but I am sure she is good at the bottom of her heart."

"I don't know anything about the bottom of her heart," said Aunt Agatha; "from all one can see of the surface, it must be a very unpleasant place. And then that useless Mrs. Askell; she is quite strong enough to talk to the gentlemen and amuse them, but as for taking a little pains to do her duty, or look after her children—I must say I am surprised at your friends. A soldier's life is trying, I suppose," Miss Seton added. "I have always heard it was trying; but the gentlemen should be the ones to feel it most, and they are not spoiled. The gentlemen are very nice—most of them," Aunt Agatha added with a little hesitation, for there was one whom she regarded as Wilfrid did with jealous eyes.

"The gentlemen are further off, and we do not see them so clearly," said Mary; "and if you knew what it is to wander about, to have no settled home, and to be ailing and poor—"

"My dear love," said Aunt Agatha, with a little impatience, "you might have been as poor, and you never would have been like that; and as for sick—You know I never thought you had a strong constitution—nor your sister either—my pretty Winnie! Do you think that sickness, or poverty, or anything else, could ever have brought down Winnie to be like that silly little woman?"

"Hush," said Mary, "Nelly is in the garden, and might hear."

"Nelly!" said Aunt Agatha, who felt herself suddenly pulled up short. "I have nothing to say against Nelly, I am sure. I could not help thinking last night, that some of these days she would make a nice wife for one of the boys. She is quite beginning to grow up now, poor dear. When I see her sitting there it makes me think of my Winnie;—not that she will ever be beautiful like Winnie. But Mary, my dear love, I don't think you are kind to me. I am sure you must have heard a great deal about Winnie, especially since she has come back to England, and you never tell me a word."

"My dear aunt," said Mary, with a little embarrassment, "you see all these people as much as I do; and I have heard them telling you what news of her they know."

"Ah, yes," said Aunt Agatha, with a sigh. "They tell me she is here or there, but I know that from her letters; what I want to know is, something about her, how she looks, and if she is happy. She never says she is not happy, you know. Dear, dear! to think she must be past thirty now—two-and-thirty her last birthday—and she was only eighteen when she went away. You were not so long away, Mary—"

"But Winnie has not had my reason for coming back upon your hands, Aunt Agatha," said Mrs. Ochterlony, gravely.

"No," said Aunt Agatha: and again she sighed; and this time the sigh was of a kind which did not sound very complimentary to Captain Percival. It seemed to say "More's the pity!" Winnie had never come back to see the kind aunt who had been a mother to her. She said in her letters how unlucky she was, and that they were to be driven all round the world, she thought, and never to have any rest; but no doubt, if Winnie had been very anxious, she might have found means to come home. And the years were creeping on imperceptibly, and the boys growing up—even Will, who was now almost as tall as his brothers. When such a change had come upon these children, what a change there must be in the wilful, sprightly, beautiful girl whose image reigned supreme in Aunt Agatha's heart. A sudden thought struck the old lady as she sighed. The little Askells were at Kirtell at the moment with the nurse, and Nelly, who was more than ever the mother of the little party. Aunt Agatha sat still for a little with her heart beating, and then she took up her work in a soft stealthy way, and went out into the garden. "No, my dear, oh no, don't disturb yourself," she said, with anxious deprecation to Mary, who would have risen too, "I am only going to look at the lilies," and she was so conscientious that she did go and cast an undiscerning, preoccupied glance upon the lilies, though her real attraction was quite in an opposite quarter. At the other side, audible but not visible, was a little group which was pretty to look at in the afternoon sunshine. It was outside the garden, on the other side of the hedge, in the pretty green field, all white and yellow with buttercups and daisies, which belonged to the Cottage. Miss Seton's mild cow had not been able to crop down all that flowery fragrant growth, and the little Askells were wading in it, up to their knees in the cool sweet grass, and feeding upon it and drawing nourishment out of it almost as much as the cow did. But in the corner close by the garden hedge there was a more advanced development of youthful existence. Nelly was seated on the grass, working with all her might, yet pausing now and then to lift her serious eyes to Will, who leant upon an old stump of oak which projected out of the hedge, and had the conversation all in his own hands. He was doing what a boy under such circumstances loves to do; he was startling, shocking, frightening his companion. He was saying a great deal that he meant and some things that he did not mean, and taking a great secret pleasure in the widening of Nelly's eyes and the consternation of her face. Will had grown into a very long lank boy, with joints which were as awkward as his brother's used to be, yet not in the same way, for the limbs that completed them were thin and meagre, and had not the vigour of Hugh's. His trousers were too short for him, and so were his sleeves. His hair had no curls in it, and fell down over his forehead. He was nearly sixteen, and he was thoroughly discontented—a misanthrope, displeased with everything without knowing why. But time had been kinder to Nelly, who was not long and lean like her companion, but little and round and blooming, with the soft outlines and the fresh bloom of earliest youth just emerging out of childhood. Her eyes were brown, very serious, and sweet—eyes that had "seen trouble," and knew a great many more things in the world than were dreamt of in Will's philosophy: but then she was not so clever as Will, and his talk confused her. She was looking up to him and taking all in with a mixture of willing faith and instinctive scepticism which it was curious to see.

"You two are always together, I think," said Aunt Agatha, putting down a little camp-stool she had in her hand beside Nelly—for she had passed the age when people think of sitting on the grass. "What are you talking about? I suppose he brings all his troubles to you."

"Oh, no," said Nelly, with a blush, which was on Aunt Agatha's account, and not on Will's. He was a little older than herself actually; but Nelly was an experienced woman, and could not but look down amiably on such an unexercised inhabitant of the world as "only a boy."

"Then I suppose, my dear, he must talk to you about Greek and Latin," said Aunt Agatha, "which is a thing young ladies don't much care for: I am very sure old ladies don't. Is that what you talk about?"

"Oh, yes, often," said Nelly, brightening, as she looked at Will. That was not the sort of talk they had been having, but still it was true.

"Well," said Miss Seton, "I am sure he will go on talking as long as you will listen to him. But he must not have you all to himself. Did he tell you Hugh was coming home to see us? We expect him next week."

"Yes," said Nelly, who was not much of a talker. And then, being a little ashamed of her taciturnity, she added, "I am sure Mrs. Ochterlony will be glad."

"We shall all be glad," said Aunt Agatha. "Hugh is very nice. We must have you to see a little more of him this time; I am sure you would like him. Then you will be well acquainted with all our family," the old lady continued, artfully approaching her real object; "for you know my dear Winnie, I think—I ought to say, Mrs. Percival; she is the dearest girl that ever was. You must have met her, my dear—abroad."

Nelly looked up a little surprised. "We knew Mrs. Percival," she said, "but she—was not a girl at all. She was as old—as old as mamma—like all the other ladies," she added, hastily; for the word girl had limited meanings to Nelly, and she would have laughed at its application in such a case, if she had not been a natural gentlewoman with the finest manners in the world.

"Ah, yes," said Aunt Agatha, with a sigh, "I forget how time goes; and she will always be a girl to me: but she was very beautiful, all the same; and she had such a way with children. Were you fond of her, Nelly? Because, if that were so, I should love you more and more."

Nelly looked up with a frightened, puzzled look in Aunt Agatha's eyes. She was very soft-hearted, and had been used to give in to other people all her life; and she almost felt as if, for Aunt Agatha's sake, she could persuade herself that she had been fond of Mrs. Percival; but yet at the same time honesty went above all. "I do not think we knew them very well," she said. "I don't think mamma was very intimate with Mrs. Percival; that is, I don't think papa liked him," added Nelly, with natural art.

Aunt Agatha gave another sigh. "That might be, my dear," she said, with a little sadness; "but even when gentlemen don't take to each other, it is a great pity when it acts upon their families. Some of our friends here even were not fond at first of Captain Percival, but for my darling Winnie's sake—You must have seen her often at least; I wonder I never thought of asking you before. She was so beautiful, with such lovely hair, and the sweetest complexion. Was she looking well—and—and happy?" asked Aunt Agatha, growing anxious as she spoke, and looking into Nelly's face.

It was rather hard upon Nelly, who was one of those true women, young as she was, who can see what other women mean when they put such questions, and hear the heart beat under the words. Nelly had heard a great deal of talk in her day, and knew things about Mrs. Percival that would have made Aunt Agatha's hair stand on end with horror. But her heart understood the other heart, and could not have breathed a whisper that would wound it, for the world.

"I was such a little thing," said Nelly; "and then I always had the little ones to look after—mamma was so delicate. I remember the people's names more than themselves."

"You have always been a very good girl, I am sure," said Aunt Agatha, giving her young companion a sudden kiss, and with perhaps a faint instinctive sense of Nelly's forbearance and womanful skill in avoiding a difficult subject; but she sighed once more as she did it, and wondered to herself whether nobody would ever speak to her freely and fully of her child. And silence ensued, for she had not the heart to ask more questions. Will, who had not found the conversation amusing, had gone in to find his mother, with a feeling that it was not quite safe to leave her alone, which had something to do with his frequent presence in the drawing room; so that the old lady and Nelly were left alone in the corner of the fragrant field. The girl went on with her work, but Aunt Agatha, who was seated on her camp-stool, with her back against the oak stump, let her knitting fall upon her knee, and her eyes wander into vacancy with a wistful look of abstraction that was not natural to them. Nelly, who did not know what to say, and yet would have given a great deal to be able to say something, watched her from under the shadow of her curls, and at last saw Miss Seton's abstract eyes brighten up and wake into attention and life. Nelly looked round, and her impulse was to jump up in alarm when she saw it was her own mother who was approaching—her mother, whom Nelly had a kind of adoration for as a creature of divine helplessness, for whom everything had to be done, but in whose judgment she had an instinctive want of confidence. She jumped up and called to the children on the spur of this sudden impulse: "Oh! here is mamma, we must go in," cried Nelly; and it gave her positive pain to see that Miss Seton's attitude remained unchanged, and that she had no intention of being disturbed by Mrs. Askell's approach.

"Oh how deliciously comfortable you are here," cried Emma, throwing herself down on the grass. "I came out to have a little fresh air and see after those tiresome children. I am sure they have been teasing you all day long; Nelly is not half severe enough, and nurse spoils them; and after a day in the open air like this, they make my head like to split when they come home at night."

"They have not been teasing me," said Aunt Agatha; "they have been very good, and I have been sitting here for a long time talking to Nelly. I wanted her to tell me something about my dear child, Mary's own sister—Mrs. Percival, you know."

"Oh!" said Mrs. Askell, making a troubled pause,—"and I hope to goodness you did not tell Miss Seton anything that was unpleasant," she said sharply, turning to Nelly. "You must not mind anything she said," the foolish little woman added; "she was only a child and she did not know. You should have asked me."

"What could there be that was not pleasant?" cried Aunt Agatha. "If there is anything unpleasant that can be said about my Winnie, that is precisely what I ought to hear."

"Mamma!" cried Nelly, in what was intended to be a whisper of warning, though her anxiety made it shrill and audible. But Emma was not a woman to be kept back.

"Goodness, child, you have pulled my dress out of the gathers," she said. "Do you think I don't know what I am talking about? When I say unpleasant, I am sure I don't mean anything serious; I mean only, you know, that—and then her husband is such a man—I am sure I don't wonder at it, for my part."

"What is it your mamma does not wonder at, Nelly?" said Aunt Agatha, who had turned white and cold, and leaned back all feeble and broken upon the old tree.

"Her husband neglected her shamefully," said Emma; "it was a great sin for her friends to let her marry him; I am sure Mrs. Ochterlony knew what a dreadful character he had. And, poor thing, when she found herself so deserted—Askell would never let me see much of her, and I had always such wretched health; but I always stood up for Mrs. Percival. She was young, and she had nobody to stand by her—"

"Oh, mamma," cried Nelly, "don't you see what you are doing? I think she is going to faint—and it will be all our fault."

"Oh, no; I am not going to faint," said Aunt Agatha, feebly; but when she laid back her head upon Nelly's shoulder, who had come to support her, and closed her eyes, she was like death, so pale did she look and ghastly; and then Mrs. Askell in her turn took fright.

"Goodness gracious! run and get some water, Will," she cried to Wilfrid, who had rejoined them. "I am sure there was nothing in what I said to make anybody faint. She was talked about a little, that was all—there was no harm in it. We have all been talked about, sometime or other. Why, fancy what a talk there was about our Madonna, her very self."

"About my mother?" said Wilfrid, standing bolt upright between Aunt Agatha, in her half swoon, and silly little Emma, who sat, a heap of muslin and ribbons, upon the grass. He had managed to hear more about Mrs. Percival than anybody knew, and was very indifferent on the subject. And he was not alarmed about Aunt Agatha; but he was jealous of his mother, and could not bear even the smallest whisper in which there was any allusion to her.

"Goodness, boy, run and get some water!" cried Mrs. Askell, jumping up from the grass in her fright. "I did not mean anything; there was nothing to be put out about—indeed there was not, Miss Seton. It was only a little silly talk; what happens to us all, you know: not half, nor quarter so bad as—Oh, goodness gracious, Nelly, don't make those ridiculous signs, as if it was you that was my mother, and I did not know what to say."

"Will!" said Nelly. Her voice was perfectly quiet and steady, but it made him start as he stood there jealous, and curious, and careless of everybody else. When he met her eye, he grew red and frowned, and made a momentary stand against her; but the next moment turned resolutely and went away. If it was for water, Aunt Agatha did not need it. She came to herself without any restorative; and she kissed Nelly, who had been whispering in her ear. "Yes, my dear, I know you are right—it could have been nothing," she said faintly, with a wan sort of smile; "but I am not very strong, and the heat, you know—" And when she got up, she took the girl's arm, to steady her. Thus they went back to the house, Mrs. Askell following, holding up her hands in amazement and self-justification. "Could I tell that she was so weak?" Emma said to herself. "Goodness gracious, how could anybody say it was my fault?" As for Nelly, she said nothing; but supported her trembling companion, and held the soft old hand firm on her arm. And when they approached the house, Nelly, carried away by her feelings, did, what in full possession of herself she never would have done. She bent down to Aunt Agatha's ear—for though she was not tall, she was a little taller at that moment than the poor old lady who was bowed down with weakness and the blow she had just received. "Mamma says things without meaning them," said Nelly, with an undutiful frankness, which it is to be hoped was forgiven her. "She does not mean any harm, and sometimes she says whatever comes into her head."

"Yes, my dear, your mamma is a very silly little woman," said Aunt Agatha, with a little of her old spirit; and she gave Nelly, who was naturally much startled by this unexpected vivacity, a kiss as she reached the door of her room and left her. The door closed, and the girl had no pretext nor right to follow. She turned away feeling as if she had received a sudden prick which had stimulated all the blood in her veins, but yet yearning in her good little heart over Aunt Agatha who was alone. Miss Seton's room, to which she had retired, was on the ground floor, as were all the sitting-rooms in the house, and Nelly, as she turned away, suddenly met Wilfrid, and came to a stand-still before him looking him severely in the face.

"I say, Nell!" said Will.

"And I say, Will!" said Nelly. "I will never like you nor care for you any more. You are a shocking, selfish, disagreeable prig. To stand there and never mind when poor Aunt Agatha was fainting—all for the sake of a piece of gossip. I don't want ever to speak to you again."

"It was not a piece of gossip,—it was something about my mother," said Will, in self-defence.

"And what if it were fifty times about your mother?" cried Nelly,—"what right had you to stand and listen when there was something to do? Oh, I am so ashamed! and after talking to you so much and thinking you were not so bad—"

"Nelly," said Wilfrid, "when there is anything said about my mother, I have always a right to listen what it is—"

"Well, then, go and listen," said Nelly, with indignation, "at the keyhole if you like; but don't come afterwards and talk to me. There, good-bye, I am going to the children. Mamma is in the drawing-room, and if you like to go there I dare say you will hear a great many things; I don't care for gossip myself, so I may as well bid you good-bye."

And she went out by the open door with fine youthful majesty, leaving poor Will in a very doubtful state of mind behind her. He knew that in this particular Nelly did not understand him, and perhaps was not capable of sympathizing in the jealous watch he kept over his mother. But still Nelly was pleasant to look at and pleasant to talk to, and he did not want to be cast off by her. He stood and hesitated for a moment—but he could see the sun shining at the open door, and hear the river, and the birds, and the sound of Nelly's step—and the end was that he went after her, there being nothing in the present crisis, as far as he could see, to justify a stern adoption of duty rather than pleasure; and there was nobody in the world but Nelly, as he had often explained to himself, by whom, when he talked, he stood the least chance of being understood.

This was how the new generation settled the matter. As for Aunt Agatha she cried over it in the solitude of her chamber, but by-and-by recovered too, thinking that after all it was only that silly woman. And she wrote an anxious note to Mrs. Percival, begging her now she was in England to come and see them at the Cottage. "I am getting old, my dear love, and I may not be long for this world, and you must let me see you before I die," Aunt Agatha said. She thought she felt weaker than usual after her agitation, and regarded this sentence, which was in a high degree effective and sensational, with some pride. She felt sure that such a thought would go to her Winnie's heart.

And so the Cottage lapsed once more into tranquillity, and into that sense that everything must go well which comes natural to the mind after a long interval of peace.

CHAPTER XXVII

"I like all your people, mamma," said Hugh, "and I like little Nelly best of all. She is a little jewel, and as fresh as a little rose."

"And such a thing might happen as that she might make you a nice little wife one of these days," said Aunt Agatha, who was always a match-maker in her heart.

Upon which Hugh nodded and laughed and grew slightly red, as became his years. "I had always the greatest confidence in your good sense, my dear Aunt," he said in his laughing way, and never so much as thought of Wilfrid in the big Indian chair, who had been Nelly's constant companion for at least one long year.

"I should like to know what business he has with Nelly," said Will between his teeth. "A great hulking fellow, old enough to be her father."

"She would never have you, Will," said Hugh, laughing; "girls always despise a fellow of their own age. So you need not look sulky, old boy. For that matter I doubt very much if she'd have me."

"You are presumptuous boys," said Mrs. Ochterlony, "to think she would have either of you. She has too much to do at home, and too many things to think of. I should like to have her all to myself," said Mary, with a sigh. She sighed, but she smiled; for though her boys could not be with her as Nelly might have been, still all was well with them, and the heart of their mother was content.

"My uncle wants you all to come over to Earlston," said Hugh. "I think the poor old boy is beginning to give in. He looks very shaky in the morning when he comes downstairs. I'd like to know what you think of him, mamma; I don't think his wanting to see you all is a good sign. He's awfully good when you come to know him," said Hugh, clearing his throat.

"Do you mean that Francis Ochterlony is ill?" said Aunt Agatha, with sudden interest. "Your mother must go and see him, but you must not ask me; I am an old woman, and I have old-fashioned notions, you know—but a married lady can go anywhere. Besides he would not care for seeing me," Aunt Agatha added, with a slightly-wistful look, "it is so very—very many years since we used to—"

"I know he wants to see you," said Hugh, who could not help laughing a little; "and with so many people in the house I think you might risk it, Aunt Agatha. He stands awfully in awe of you, I can tell you. And there are to be a lot of people. It's a kind of coming of age affair," said Hugh. "I am to be set up on Psyche's pedestal, and everybody is to look at me and sing out, 'Behold the heir!' That's the sort of thing it's to be. You can bring anybody you like, you two ladies—little Nelly Askell, and all that sort of thing," he added, with a conscious laugh; and grew red again, not at thought of Nelly Askell, but with the thrill which "all that sort of thing" naturally brought into the young man's veins.

The face of Wilfrid grew darker and darker as he sat and listened. It was not a precocious passion for Nelly Askell that moved him. If Nelly had been his sister, his heart might still have swelled with a very similar sentiment. "He'll have her too," was what the boy said to himself. There was no sort of justice or distribution in it; Hugh was the lucky fellow who had everything, while no personal appropriation whatever was to be permitted to Wilfrid. He could not engross his mother as he would have liked to do, for she loved Hugh and Islay just as well as she loved himself, and had friends and acquaintances, and people who came and talked, and occupied her time, and even one who was supposed to have the audacity to admire her. And there was no one else to supply the imperious necessity which existed in Will's mind, to be the chief object of somebody's thoughts. His curate had a certain awe of him, which was satisfactory enough in its way; but nobody watched and worshipped poor Will, or did anything more than love him in a reasonable unadoring way; and he had no sister whom he could make his slave, nor humble friend to whom he could be the centre of interest. Nelly's coming had been a God-send to the boy. She had found out his discontent, and taken to comforting him instinctively, and had been introduced into a world new to her by means of his fancies: and the budding woman had regarded the budding man with that curiosity, and wonder, and respect, and interest, which exists by nature between the two representatives of humanity. And now here was Hugh, who, not content with being an Oxford scholar, and the heir of Earlston, and his mother's eldest son, and Sir Edward's favourite, and the most interesting member of the family to the parish in general, was about to seize on Nelly too. Will, though he was perhaps of a jealous temper, was not mean or envious, nor did he grudge his brother his elevation. But he thought it hard that all should go to one, and that there should be no shares: if he had had the arranging of it, it would have been otherwise arranged; Hugh should still have had Earlston, and any other advantages suited to his capacity—but as for Oxford and Nelly—It was unfair—that was the sting; all to one, and nothing to the other. This sentiment made Wilfrid very unwilling to accompany the rest of the family to Earlston. He did not want to go and survey all the particulars of Hugh's good-fortune, and to make sure once again, as he had already so often decided, that Hugh's capacities were inferior to his luck, and that it was really of little advantage to him to be so well off. But Will's inclinations, as it happened, were not consulted on the subject; the expedition was all settled without any room being left for his protest. Aunt Agatha was to go, though she had very little desire to do so, being coy about Mr. Ochterlony's house, and even not too well pleased to think that coyness was absurd in her case, and that she was old enough to go to anybody's house, and indeed do what she pleased. And Sir Edward was going, who was older than any of them, and was still inclined to believe that Francis Ochterlony and Agatha Seton might make it up; and then, though Mrs. Askell objected greatly, and could not tell what she was to do with the children, and limited the expedition absolutely to two days, Nelly was going too. Thus Will had to give in, and withdraw his opposition. It was, as Hugh said, "a coming of age sort of affair," but it was not precisely a coming of age, for that important event had taken place some time before, when Hugh, whose ambition was literary, had been working like a coal-heaver to take his degree, and had managed to take it and please his uncle. But there was to be a great dinner to introduce the heir of Earlston to his country neighbours, and everything was to be conducted with as much solemnity as if it had been the heir-apparent's birthday. It was so great an occasion, that Mrs. Ochterlony got a new dress, and Aunt Agatha brought forth among the sprigs of lavender her silver-grey which she wore at Winnie's marriage. It was not Hugh's marriage, but it was an event almost as important; and if his own people did not try to do him credit, what was to be expected of the rest of the world?

And for Nelly Askell it was a very important crisis. She was sixteen, but up to this moment she had never had a dress "made long," and the excitement of coming to this grandeur, and of finding Hugh Ochterlony by her side, full of unspeakable politeness, was almost too much for Nelly; the latter complication was something she did not quite understand. Will, for his part, carried things with a high hand, and behaved to her as a brother behaves to the sister whom he tyrannizes over. It is true that she sometimes tyrannized over him in her turn, as has been seen, but they did not think it necessary to be civil, nor did either of them restrain their personal sentiments in case anything occurred they disapproved of. But Hugh was altogether different—Hugh was one of "the gentlemen;" he was grown up, he had been to the University, he rode, and shot, and hunted, and did everything that the gentlemen are expected to do—and he lowered his voice when he spoke to Nelly, and schemed to get near her, and took bouquets from the Cottage garden which were not intended for Mrs. Askell. Altogether, he was like the hero of a story to Nelly, and he made her feel as if she, just that very moment as it were, translated into a long dress, was a young lady in a story too. Will was her friend and companion, but this was something quite different from Will; and to be taken to see his castle, and his guardian, and his future domains, and assist at the recognition of the young prince, was but the natural continuation of the romance. Nelly's new long dresses were only muslin, but they helped out the force of the situation, and intensified that vague thrill of commencing womanhood and power undreamed of, which Hugh's presence had helped to produce. Could it be possible that she could forget the children, and her mamma's head which was always so bad, and go off for two whole days from her duty? Mrs. Askell could scarcely believe it, and Nelly felt guilty when she realized the dreadful thought, but still she wanted to go; and she had no patience with Will's objections, but treated them with summary incivility. "Why shouldn't you like to go?" said Nelly, "you would like it very much if you were your brother. And I would not be jealous like you, not for all the world;" and then Nelly added, "it is not because it is a party that I care for it, but because it is such a pleasure to dear Mrs. Ochterlony, and to—Mr. Hugh—"

"Ah, yes, I knew you would go over to Hugh's side," said Will; "I said so the very day he came here."

"Why should I go over to his side?" cried Nelly, indignantly; "but I am pleased to see people happy; and I am Mr. Hugh's friend, just as I am your friend," added the little woman, with dignity; "it is all for dear Mrs. Ochterlony's sake."

Thus it was that the new generation stepped in and took up all the foreground of the stage, just as Winnie and her love affairs had done, who was of the intermediate generation—thrusting the people whose play was played out, and their personal story over, into the background. Mary, perhaps, had not seen how natural it was, when her sister was the heroine; but when she began to suspect that the everlasting romance might, perhaps, begin again under her very eyes, with her children for the actors, it gave her a sweet shock of surprise and amusement. She had been in the shade for a long time, and yet she had still been the central figure, and had everything in her hands. What if, now, perhaps, Aunt Agatha's prophecy should come true, and Hugh, whose future was now secure, should find the little waif all ready for him at the very outset of his career? Such a possibility gave his mother, who had not yet arrived at the age which can consent to be passive and superannuated, a curious thrill—but still it might be a desirable event. When Mary saw her son hanging over the fair young creature, whom she had coveted to be her daughter, a true perception of what her own future must be came over her. The boys must go away, and would probably marry and set up households, and the mother who had given up the best part of her life to them must remain alone. She was glad, and yet it went with a curious penetrating pang to her heart. Some women might have been jealous of the girl who had first revealed this possibility to them; but Mary, for her part, knew better, and saw that it was Nature and not Nelly that was to blame; and she was not a woman to go in the face of Nature. "Hugh will marry early," she said to Aunt Agatha, with a smile; but her heart gave a little flutter in her breast as she said it, and saw how natural it was. Islay was gone already, and very soon Will would have to go; and there would be no more for their mother to do but to live on, with her occupation over, and her personal history at an end. The best thing to do was to make up her mind to it. There was a little moisture in her eyes as she smiled upon Nelly the night before they set out for Earlston. The girl had to spend the previous night at the Cottage, to be ready for their start next day; and Mrs. Ochterlony smiled upon and kissed her, with a mingled yearning and revulsion. Ah, if she had but been her own—that woman-child! and yet it required a little effort to accept her for her own, at the cost, as it were, of her boy—for women are inconsistent, especially when they are women who have children. But one thing, at least, Mary was sure about, and that was, that her own share of the world would henceforward be very slight. Nothing would ever happen to her individually. Perhaps she regretted the agitations and commotions of life, and felt as if she would prefer still to endure them, and feel herself something in the world; but that was all over; Will must go. Islay was gone. Hugh would marry; and Mary's remaining years would flow on by necessity like the Kirtell, until some day they would come to a noiseless end. She said to herself that she ought to accept, and make up her mind to it; that boys must go out into the world, and quit the parent nest; and that she ought to be very thankful for the calm and secure provision which had been made for the rest of her life.

And next morning they started for Earlston, on the whole a very cheerful party. Nelly was so happy, that it did every one's heart good to see her; and she had given Will what she called "such a talking to," that he was as good as gold, and made no unpleasant remarks. And Sir Edward was very suave and benign, though full of recollections which confused and embarrassed Aunt Agatha. "I remember travelling along this same road when we still thought it could be all arranged," he said; "and thinking what a long way it would be to have to go to Earlston to see you; but there was no railroad then, and everything is very much changed."

"Yes, everything," said Aunt Agatha; and then she talked about the weather in a tremulous way. Sir Edward would not have spoken as he did, if he had not thought that even yet the two old lovers might make it up, which naturally made it very confusing for Aunt Agatha to be the one to go to Earlston, and make, as it were, the first advances. She felt just the same heart thumping a little against her breast, and her white hair and soft faded cheek could not be supposed to be so constantly visible to her as they were to everybody else; and if Francis Ochterlony were to take it into his head to imagine—For Miss Seton, though nothing would have induced her to marry at her age, was not so certainly secure as her niece was that nothing now would ever happen in her individual life.

Nothing did happen, however, when they arrived at Earlston, where the master of the house received them, not with open arms, which was not his nature, but with all the enthusiasm he was capable of. He took them to see all his collections, everything he had that was most costly and rare. To go back to the house in this way, and see the scene of her former tortures; tortures which looked so light to look back upon, and were so amusing to think of, but which had been all but unbearable at the time, was strange to Mary. She told the story of her miseries, and they all laughed; but Mr. Ochterlony was still seen to change colour, when she pointed out the Etruscan vase which Hugh had taken into his hand, and the rococo chair which Islay had mounted. "This is the chair," the master of Earlston said; and he did not laugh so frankly as the rest, but turned aside to show Miss Seton his Henri II. porcelain. "It was nothing to laugh at, at the time," he said, confidentially, in a voice which sank into Aunt Agatha's heart; and, to restore her composure, she paid great attention to the Henri Deux ware. She said she remembered longing very much to have a set like that when she was a girl. "I never knew you were fond of china," said Mr. Ochterlony. "Oh, yes," Aunt Agatha replied; but she did not explain that the china she had longed for was a toy service for her doll's and little companions' tea. Mr. Ochterlony put the costly cups away into a little cabinet, and locked it, after this; and he offered Aunt Agatha his arm, to lead her to the library, to see his collection there. She took it, but she trembled a little, the tender-hearted old woman. They looked such an old couple as they walked out of the room together, and yet there was something virginal and poetic about them, which they owed to their lonely lives. It was as if the roses that Hugh had just gathered for Nelly had been put away for half a century, and brought out again all dried and faded, but still roses, and with a lingering pensive perfume. And Sir Edward sat and smiled in a corner, and whispered to Mary to leave them to themselves a little: such things had been as that they might make it up.

There was a great dinner in the evening, at which Hugh's health was drunk, and everybody hoped to see him for many a happy year at Earlston, yet prayed that it might be many a year before he had to take any other place than the one he now occupied at his uncle's side. There were some county ladies present, who were very gracious to Mary, and anxious to know all about her boys, and whether she, too, was coming to Earlston; but who were disposed to snub Nelly, who was not Mrs. Ochterlony's daughter, nor "any relation," and who was clearly an interloper on such an occasion. Nelly did not care much for being snubbed; but she was very glad to seize the moment to propitiate Wilfrid, who had come into the room looking in what Nelly called "one of his states of mind;" for it must not be forgotten that she was a soldier's daughter, and had been brought up exclusively in the regiment, and used many very colloquial forms of speech. She managed to glide to the other end of the room where Wilfrid was scowling over a collection of cameos without being noticed. To tell the truth, Nelly was easier in her mind when she was at a little distance from the Psyche and the Venus. She had never had any training in art, and she would have preferred to throw a cloak or, at the least, a lace shawl, or something, over those marble beauties. But she was, at least, wise enough to keep her sentiments to herself.

"Why have you come up so early, Will?" she said.

"What need I stay for, I wonder?" said Will; "I don't care for their stupid county talk. It is just as bad as parish talk, and not a bit more rational. I suppose my uncle must have known better one time or other, or he could not have collected all these things here."

"Do you think they are very pretty?" said Nelly, looking back from a safe distance, and thinking that, however pretty they might be, they were not very suitable for a drawing-room, where people in general were in the habit of putting on more decorous garments: by which it will be perceived that she was a very ignorant little girl and knew nothing about it, and had no natural feeling for art.

"Pretty!" said Will, "you have only to look and see what they are—or to hear their names would be enough. And to think of all those asses downstairs turned in among them, that probably would like a few stupid busts much better,—whereas there are plenty of other people that would give their ears—"

"Oh, Will!" cried Nelly, "you are always harping on the old string!"

"I am not harping on any string," said Will. "All I want is, that people should stick to what they understand. Hugh might know how much money it was all worth, but I don't know what else he could know about it. If my uncle was in his senses and left things in shares as they do in France and everywhere where they have any understanding—"

"And then what would become of the house and the family?" cried Nelly,—"if you had six sons and Hugh had six sons—and then your other brother. They would all come down to have cottages and be a sort of clan—instead of going and making a fortune like a man, and leaving Earlston to be the head—" Probably Nelly had somewhere heard the argument which she stated in this bewildering way, or picked it out of a novel, which was the only kind of literature she knew much about—for it would be vain to assert that the principles of primogeniture had ever been profoundly considered in her own thoughts—"and if you were the eldest," she added, forsaking her argumentation, "I don't think you would care so much for everybody going shares."

"If I were the eldest it would be quite different," said Will. And then he devoted himself to the cameos, and would enter into no further explanation. Nelly sat down beside him in a resigned way, and looked at the cameos too, without feeling very much interest in them, and wondered what the children were doing, and whether mamma's head was bad; and her own astonishing selfishness in leaving mamma's headache and the children to take care of themselves, struck her vividly as she sat there in the twilight and saw the Psyche and Venus, whom she did not approve of, gleaming white in the grey gloaming, and heard the loud voices of the ladies at the other end of the room. Then it began to come into her head how vain pleasures are, and how to do one's duty is all one ought to care for in the world. Mrs. Ochterlony was at the other end of the drawing-room, talking to the other ladies, and "Mr. Hugh" was downstairs with a quantity of stupid men, and Will was in one of his "states of mind." And the chances were that something had gone wrong at home; that Charley had fallen downstairs, or baby's bath had been too hot for her, or something—a judgment upon Nelly for going away. At one moment she got so anxious thinking of it all, that she felt disposed to get up and run home all the way, to make sure that nothing had happened. Only that just then Aunt Agatha came to join them in looking over the cameos, and began to tell Nelly, as she often did, little stories about Mrs. Percival, and to call her "my dear love," and to tell her her dress looked very nice, and that nothing was so pretty as a sweet natural rose in a girl's hair. "I don't care for artificial flowers at your age, my dear," Aunt Agatha was saying, when the gentlemen came in and Hugh made his appearance; and gradually the children's possible mischances and her mamma's headache faded out of Nelly's thoughts.

It was the pleasantest two days that had been spent at Earlston in the memory of man. Mrs. Ochterlony went over all the house with very different feelings from those she had felt when she was an inmate of the place, and smiled at her own troubles and found her misery very comical; and little Nelly, who never in all her life before had known what it was to have two days to herself, was so happy that she was perfectly wretched about it when she went to bed. For it had never yet occurred to Nelly, as it does to so many young ladies, that she had a right to everything that was delightful and pleasant, and that the people who kept her out of her rights were ogres and tyrants. She was frightened and rather ashamed of herself for being so happy; and then she made it up by resolving to be doubly good and make twice as much a slave of herself as ever as soon as she got home. This curious and unusual development of feeling probably arose from the fact that Nelly had never been brought up at all, so to speak, but had simply grown; and had too much to do to have any time for thinking of herself—which is the best of all possible bringings up for some natures. As for Aunt Agatha, she went and came about this house, which could never be otherwise than interesting to her, with a wistful look and a flickering unsteady colour that would not have shamed even Nelly's sixteen-year old cheek. Miss Seton saw ghosts of what might have been in every corner; she saw the unborn faces shine beside the never-lighted fire. She saw herself as she might have been, rising up to receive her guests, sitting at the head of the long, full, cheerful table. It was a curious sensation, and made her stop to think now and then which was the reality and which the shadow; and yet there could be no doubt that there was in it a certain charm.

And there could be no doubt, either, that a certain sadness fell upon Mr. Ochterlony when they were all gone. He had a fire lighted in his study that night, though it was warm, "to make it look a little more cheerful," he said; and made Hugh sit with him long after the usual time. He sat buried in his great chair, with his thin, long limbs looking longer and thinner than ever, and his head a little sunk upon his breast. And then he began to moralize and give his nephew good advice.

"I hope you'll marry, Hugh," he said. "I don't think it's good to shut one's self out from the society of women; they're very unscientific, but still—And it makes a great difference in a house. When I was a young fellow like you—But, indeed, it is not necessary to go back so far. A man has it in his power to amuse himself for a long time, but it doesn't last for ever—And there are always things that might have been better otherwise—" Here Mr. Ochterlony made a long pause and stared into the fire, and after a while resumed without any preface: "When I'm gone, Hugh, you'll pack up all that Henri Deux ware and send it over to—to your Aunt Agatha. I never thought she cared for china. John will pack it for you—he is a very careful fellow for that sort of thing. I put it all into the Louis Quinze cabinet; now mind you don't forget."

"Time enough for that, sir," said Hugh, cheerfully, and not without a suppressed laugh; for the loves of Aunt Agatha and Francis Ochterlony were slightly comical to Hugh.

"That is all you know about it," said his uncle. "But I shall expect you altogether to be of more use in the world than I have been, Hugh; and you'll have more to do. Your father, you know, married when he was a boy, and went out of my reach; but you'll have all your people to look after. Don't play the generous prince and spoil the boys—mind you don't take any stupid notions into your head of being a sort of

Providence to them. It's a great deal better for them to make their own way; but you'll be always here, and you'll lend a helping hand. Stand by them—that's the great thing; and as for your mother, I needn't recommend her to your kindest care. She has done a great deal for you."

"Uncle, I wish you would not talk like this," said Hugh; "there's nothing the matter with you? What's the good of making a fellow uneasy and sending him uncomfortable to bed? Leave those sort of things till you're old and ill, and then I'll attend to what you say."

Mr. Ochterlony softly shook his head. "You won't forget about the Henri Deux," he said; and then he paused again and laughed as it were under his breath, with a kind of laugh that was pathetic and full of quaint tenderness. "If it had ever come to that, I don't think you would have been any the worse," he added; "we were not the sort of people to have heirs," and the laugh faded into a lingering, wistful smile, half sad, half amused, with which on his face, he sat for a long time and gazed into the fading fire. It was, perhaps, simply that the presence of such visitors had stirred up the old recollections in his heart—perhaps that it felt strange to him to look back on his own past life in the light thrown upon it by the presence of his heir, and to feel that it was ending, while yet, in one sense, it had never begun. As for Hugh, to tell the truth, he was chiefly amused by his uncle's reflective mood. He thought, which no doubt was to some extent true, that the old man was thinking of an old story which had come to nothing, and of which old Aunt Agatha was the heroine. There was something touching in it he could not but allow, but still he gave a laugh within himself at the superannuated romance. And all that immediately came of it, was the injunction not to forget about the Henri Deux.

CHAPTER XXVIII

Of the visit to Earlston, this was all that came immediately; but yet, if anybody had been there with clear-sighted eyes, there might have been other results perceptible and other symptoms of a great change at hand. Such little shadows of an event might have been traced from day to day if that once possible lady of the house, whose ghost Aunt Agatha had met with in all the rooms, had been there to watch over its master. There being nobody but Hugh, everything was supposed to go on in its usual way. Hugh had come to be fond of his uncle, and to look up to him in many ways; but he was young, and nothing had ever occurred to him to put insight into his eyes. He thought Mr. Ochterlony was just as usual—and so he was; and yet there were some things that were not as usual, and which might have aroused an experienced observer. And in the meantime something happened at the Cottage, where things did not happen often, which absorbed everybody's thoughts for the moment, and threw Earlston and Mr. Ochterlony entirely into the shade.

It happened on the very evening after their return home. Aunt Agatha had been troubled with a headache on the previous night—she said, from the fatigue of the journey, though possibly the emotions excited at Earlston had something to do with it—and had been keeping very quiet all day; Nelly Askell had gone home, eager to get back to her little flock, and to her mother, who was the greatest baby of all; Mary had gone out upon some village business; and Aunt Agatha sat alone, slightly drowsy and gently thoughtful, in the summer afternoon. She was thinking, with a soft sigh, that perhaps everything was for the best. There are a great many cases in which it is very difficult to say so—especially when it seems the mistake or blindness of man, instead of the direct act of God, that has brought the result about. Miss Seton had a meek and quiet spirit; and yet it seemed strange to her to make out how it could be for the best that her own life and her old lover's should thus end, as it were, unfulfilled, and all through his foolishness. Looking at it in an abstract point of view, she almost felt as if she could have told him of it, had he been near enough to hear. Such a different life it might have been to both; and now the moment for doing anything had long past, and the two barren existences were alike coming to an end. This was what Miss Seton could not help thinking; and feeling as she did that it was from beginning to end a kind of flying in the face of Providence, it was difficult to see how it could be for the best. If it had been her own fault, no doubt she would have felt as Mr. Ochterlony did, a kind of tender and not unpleasant remorse; but one is naturally less tolerant and more impatient when one feels that it is not one's own, but another's fault. The subject so occupied her mind, and her activity was so lulled to rest by the soft fatigue and languor consequent upon the ending of the excitement, that she did not take particular notice how the afternoon glided away. Mary was out, and Will was out, and no visitor came to disturb the calm. Miss Seton had cares of more immediate force even at that moment—anxieties and apprehensions about Winnie, which had brought of late many a sickening thrill to her heart; but these had all died away for the time before the force of recollections and the interest of her own personal story thus revived without any will of her own; and the soft afternoon atmosphere, and the murmuring of the bees, and the roses at the open windows, and the Kirtell flowing audible but unseen, lulled Aunt Agatha, and made her forget the passage of time. Then all at once she roused herself with a start. Perhaps—though she did not like to entertain such an idea—she had been asleep, and heard it in a dream; or perhaps it was Mary, whose voice had a family resemblance. Miss Seton sat upright in her chair after that first start and listened very intently, and said to herself that of course it must be Mary. It was she who was a fantastical old woman to think she heard voices which in the course of nature could not be within hearing. Then she observed how late it was, and that the sunshine slanted in at the west window and lay along the lawn outside almost in a level line. Mary was late, later than usual; and Aunt Agatha blushed to confess, even to herself, that she must have, as she expressed it, "just closed her eyes," and had a little dream in her solitude. She got up now briskly to throw this drowsiness off, and went out to look if Mary was coming, or Will in sight, and to tell Peggy about the tea—for nothing so much revives one as a cup of tea when one is drowsy in the afternoon. Miss Seton went across the little lawn, and the sun shone so strongly in her eyes as she reached the gate that she had to put up her hand to shade them, and for the moment could see nothing. Was that Mary so near the gate? The figure was dark against the sunshine, which shone right into Aunt Agatha's eyes, and made everything black between her and the light. It came drifting as it were between her and the sun, like the phantom ship in the mariner's vision. She gazed and did not see, and felt as if a kind of insanity was taking possession of her. "Is it Mary?" she said, in a trembling voice, and at the same moment felt by something in the air that it was not Mary. And then Aunt Agatha gave such a cry as brought Peggy, and indeed all the household, in alarm to the door.

It was a woman who looked as old as Mary, and did not seem ever to have been half so fair. She had a shawl drawn tightly round her shoulders, as if she were cold, and a veil over her face. She was of a very thin meagre form, with a kind of forlorn grace about her, as if she might have been splendid under better conditions. Her eyes were hollow and large, her cheek-bones prominent, her face worn out of all freshness, and possessing only what looked like a scornful recollection of beauty. The noble form had missed its development, the fine capabilities had been checked or turned in a false direction. When Aunt Agatha uttered that great cry which brought Peggy from the utmost depths of the house, the new-comer showed no corresponding emotion. She said, "No; it is I," with a kind of bitter rather than affectionate meaning, and stood stock-still before the gate, and not even made a movement to lift her veil. Miss Seton made a tremulous rush forward to her, but she did not advance to meet it; and when Aunt Agatha faltered and was likely to fall, it was not the stranger's arm that interposed to save her. She stood still, neither advancing nor going back. She read the shock, the painful recognition, the reluctant certainty in Miss Seton's eye. She was like the returning prodigal so far, but she was not content with his position. It was no happiness for her to go home, and yet it ought to have been; and she could not forgive her aunt for feeling the shock of recognition. When she roused herself, after a moment, it was not because she was pleased to come home, but because it occurred to her that it was absurd to stand still and be stared at, and make a scene.

And when Peggy caught her mistress in her arms, to keep her from falling, the stranger made a step forward and gave a hurried kiss, and said, "It is I, Aunt Agatha. I thought you would have known me better. I will follow you directly;" and then turned to take out her purse, and give a shilling to the porter, who had carried her bag from the station—which was a proceeding which they all watched in consternation, as if it had been something remarkable. Winnie was still Winnie, though it was difficult to realize that Mrs. Percival was she. She was coming back wounded, resentful, remorseful to her old home; and she did not mean to give in, nor show the feelings of a prodigal, nor gush forth into affectionateness. To see her give the man the shilling brought Aunt Agatha to herself. She raised her head upon Peggy's shoulder, and stood upright, trembling, but self-restrained. "I am a silly old woman to be so surprised," she said; "but you did not write to say what day we were to expect you, my dear love."

"I did not write anything about it," said Winnie, "for I did not know. But let me go in, please; don't let us stay here."

"Come in, my darling," said Aunt Agatha. "Oh, how glad, how thankful, how happy I am, Winnie, my dear love, to see you again!"

"I think you are more shocked than glad," said Winnie; and that was all she said, until they had entered the room where Miss Seton had just left her maiden dreams. Then the wanderer, instead of throwing herself into Aunt Agatha's kind longing arms, looked all round her with a strange passionate mournfulness and spitefulness. "I don't wonder you were shocked," she said, going up to the glass, and looking at herself in it. "You, all just the same as ever, and such a change in me!"

"Oh, Winnie, my darling!" cried Aunt Agatha, throwing herself upon her child with a yearning which was no longer to be restrained; "do you think there can ever be any change in you to me? Oh, Winnie, my dear love! come and let me look at you; let me feel I have you in my arms at last, and that you have really come home."

"Yes, I have come home," said Winnie, suffering herself to be kissed. "I am sure I am very glad that you are pleased. Of course Mary is still here, and her children? Is she going to marry again? Are her boys as tiresome as ever? Yes, thank you, I will take my things off—and I should like something to eat. But you must not make too much of me, Aunt Agatha, for I have not come only for a day."

"Winnie, dear, don't you know if it was for your good I would like to have you for ever?" cried poor Aunt Agatha, trembling so that she could scarcely form the words.

And then for a moment, the strange woman, who was Winnie, looked as if she too was moved. Something like a tear came into the corner of her eye. Her breast heaved with one profound, unnatural, convulsive swell. "Ah, you don't know me now," she said, with a certain sharpness of anguish and rage in her voice. Aunt Agatha did not understand it, and trembled all the more; but her good genius led her, instead of asking questions as she was burning to do, to take off Winnie's bonnet and her shawl, moving softly about her with her soft old hands, which shook yet did their office. Aunt Agatha did not understand it, but yet it was not so very difficult to understand. Winnie was abashed and dismayed to find herself there among all the innocent recollections of her youth—and she was full of rage and misery at the remembrance of all her injuries, and to think of the explanation which she would have to give. She was even angry with Aunt Agatha because she did not know what manner of woman her Winnie had grown—but beneath all this impatience and irritation was such a gulf of wretchedness and wrong that even the unreasonableness took a kind of miserable reason. She did well to be angry with herself, and all the world. Her friends ought to understand the difference, and see what a changed creature she was, without exacting the humiliation of an explanation; and yet at the same time the poor soul in her misery was angry to perceive that Aunt Agatha did see a difference. She suffered her bonnet and shawl to be taken off, but started when she felt Miss Seton's soft caressing hand upon her hair. She started partly because it was a caress she was unused to, and partly that her hair had grown thin and even had some grey threads in it, and she did not like that change to be observed; for she had been proud of her pretty hair, and taken pleasure in it as so many women do. She rose up as she felt that touch, and took the shawl which had been laid upon a chair.

"I suppose I can have my old room," she said. "Never mind coming with me as if I was a visitor. I should like to go upstairs, and I ought to know the way, and be at home here."

"It is not for that, my darling," said Aunt Agatha, with hesitation; "but you must have the best room, Winnie. Not that I mean to make a stranger of you. But the truth is one of the boys—and then it is too small for what you ought to have now."

"One of the boys—which of the boys?" said Winnie. "I thought you would have kept my old room—I did not think you would have let your house be overrun with boys. I don't mind where it is, but let me go and put my things somewhere and make myself respectable. Is it Hugh that has my room?"

"No,—Will," said Aunt Agatha, faltering; "I could change him, if you like, but the best room is far the best. My dear love, it is just as it was when you went away. Will! Here is Will. This is the little one that was the baby—I don't think that you can say he is not changed."

"Not so much as I am," said Mrs. Percival, under her breath, as turning round she saw the long-limbed, curious boy, with his pale face and inquiring eyes, standing in the open window. Will was not excited, but he was curious; and as he looked at the stranger, though he had never seen her before, his quick mind set to work on the subject, and he put two and two together and divined who it was. He was not like her in external appearance—at least he had never been a handsome boy, and Winnie had still her remains of wasted beauty—but yet perhaps they were like each other in a more subtle, invisible way. Winnie looked at him, and she gave her shoulders a shrug and turned impatiently away. "It must be a dreadful nuisance to be interrupted like that, whatever you may be talking about," she said. "It does not matter what room I am to have, but I suppose I may go upstairs?"

"My dear love, I am waiting for you," said poor Aunt Agatha, anxiously. "Run, Will, and tell your mother that my dear Winnie has come home. Run as fast as ever you can, and tell her to make haste. Winnie, my darling, let me carry your shawl. You will feel more like yourself when you have had a good rest; and Mary will be back directly, and I know how glad she will be."

"Will she?" said Winnie; and she looked at the boy and heard him receive his instructions, and felt his quick eyes go through and through her. "He will go and tell his mother the wreck I am," she said to herself, with bitterness; and felt as if she hated Wilfrid. She had no children to defend and surround her, or even to take messages. No one could say, referring to her, "Go and tell your mother." It was Mary that was well off, always the fortunate one, and for the moment poor Winnie felt as if she hated the keen-eyed boy.

Will, for his part, went off to seek his mother, leaving Aunt Agatha to conduct her dear and welcome, but embarrassing and difficult, guest upstairs. He did not run, nor show any symptoms of unnecessary haste, but went along at a very steady, leisurely way. He was so far like Winnie that he did not see any occasion for disturbing himself much on account of other people. He went to seek Mrs. Ochterlony with his hands in his pockets, and his mind working steadily on the new position of affairs. Why this new-comer should have arrived so unexpectedly? why Aunt Agatha should look so anxious, and helpless, and confused, as if, notwithstanding her love, she did not know what to do with her visitor? were questions which exercised all Will's faculties. He walked up to his mother, who was coming quietly along the road from the village, and joined her without disturbing himself. "Aunt Agatha sent me to look for you," he said, and turned with her towards the Cottage in the calmest way.

"I am afraid she thought I was late," said Mary.

"It was not that," said Will. "Mrs. Percival has just come, so far as I could understand, and she sent me to tell you."

"Mrs. Percival?" cried Mary, stopping short. "Whom do you mean? Not Winnie? Not my sister? You must have made some mistake."

"I think it was. It looked like her," said Will, in his calm way.

Mary stood still, and her breath seemed to fail her for the moment; she had what the French call a serrement du coeur. It felt as if some invisible hand had seized upon her heart and compressed it tightly; and her breathing failed, and a chill went through her veins. The next moment her face flushed with shame and self-reproach. Could she be thinking of herself and any possible consequences, and grudging her sister the only natural refuge which remained to her? She was incapable for the moment of asking any further questions, but went on with a sudden hasty impulse, feeling her head swim, and her whole intelligence confused. It seemed to Mary, for the moment, though she could not have told how, as if there was an end of her peaceful life, of her comfort, and all the good things that remained to her; a chill presentiment, confounding and inexplicable, went to her heart; and at the same time she felt utterly ashamed and horrified to be thinking of herself at all, and not of poor Winnie, the returned wanderer. Her thoughts were so busy and full of occupation that she had gone a long way before it occurred to her to say anything to her boy.

"You say it looked like her, Will," she began at last, taking up the conversation where she had left off; "tell me, what did she look like?"

"She looked just like other women," said Will; "I didn't remark any difference. As tall as you, and a sort of a long nose. Why I thought it looked like her, was because Aunt Agatha was in an awful way."

"What sort of a way?" cried Mary.

"Oh, well, I don't know. Like a hen, or something—walking round her, and looking at her, and cluck-clucking; and yet all the same as if she'd like to cry."

"And Winnie," said Mrs. Ochterlony, "how did she look?—that is what I want most to know."

"Awfully bored," said Will. He was so sometimes himself, when Aunt Agatha paid any special attentions to him, and he said it with feeling. This was almost all the conversation that passed between them as Mrs. Ochterlony hurried home. Poor Winnie! Mary knew better than Miss Seton did what a dimness had fallen upon her sister's bright prospects—how the lustre of her innocent name had been tarnished, and all the freshness and beauty gone out of her life; and Mrs. Ochterlony's heart smote her for the momentary reference to herself, which she had made without meaning it, when she heard of Winnie's return. Poor Winnie! if the home of her youth was not open to her, where could she find refuge? if her aunt and her sister did not stand by her, who would? and yet—The sensation was altogether involuntary, and Mary resisted it with all her might; but she could not help a sort of instinctive sense that her peace was over, and that the storms and darkness of life were about to begin again.

When she went in hurriedly to the drawing-room, not expecting to see anybody, she found, to her surprise, that Winnie was there, reclining in an easy chair, with Aunt Agatha in wistful and anxious attendance upon her. The poor old lady was hovering about her guest, full of wonder, and pain, and anxious curiosity. Winnie as yet had given no explanation of her sudden appearance. She had given no satisfaction to her perplexed and fond companion. When she found that Aunt Agatha did not leave her, she had come downstairs again, and dropped listlessly into the easy chair. She wanted to have been left alone for a little, to have realized all that had befallen her, and to feel that she was not dreaming, but was actually in her own home. But Miss Seton would have thought it the greatest unkindness, the most signal want of love and sympathy, and all that a wounded heart required, to leave Winnie alone. And she was glad when Mary came to help her to rejoice over, and overwhelm with kindness, her child who had been lost and was found.

"It is your dear sister, thank God!" she cried, with tears. "Oh, Mary! to think we should have her again; to think she should be here after so many changes! And our own Winnie through it all. She did not write to tell us, for she did not quite know the day—"

"I did not know things would go further than I could bear," said Winnie, hurriedly. "Now Mary is here, I know you must have some explanation. I have not come to see you; I have come to escape, and hide myself. Now, if you have any kindness, you won't ask me any more just now. I came off last night because he went too far. There! that is why I did not write. I thought you would take me in, whatever my circumstances might be."

"Oh, Winnie, my darling! then you have not been happy?" said Aunt Agatha, tearfully clasping Winnie's hands in her own, and gazing wistfully into her face.

"Happy!" she said, with something like a laugh, and then drew her hand away. "Please, let us have tea or something, and don't question me any more."

It was then only that Mary interposed. Her love for her sister was not the absorbing love of Aunt Agatha; but it was a wiser affection. And she managed to draw the old lady away, and leave the new-comer to herself for the moment. "I must not leave Winnie," Aunt Agatha said; "I cannot go away from my poor child; don't you see how unhappy and suffering she is? You can see after everything yourself, Mary, there is nothing to do; and tell Peggy—"

"But I have something to say to you," said Mary, drawing her reluctant companion away, to Aunt Agatha's great impatience and distress. As for Winnie, she was grateful for the moment's quiet, and yet she was not grateful to her sister. She wanted to be alone and undisturbed, and yet she rather wanted Aunt Agatha's suffering looks and tearful eyes to be in the same room with her. She wanted to resume the sovereignty, and be queen and potentate the moment after her return; and it did not please her to see another authority, which prevailed over the fascination of her presence. But yet she was glad to be alone. When they left her, she lay back in her chair, in a settled calm of passion which was at once twenty times more calm than their peacefulness, and twenty times more passionate than their excitement. She knew whence she came, and why she came, which they did not. She knew the last step which had been too far, and was still tingling with the sense of outrage. She had in her mind the very different scene she had left, and which stood out in flaming outlines against the dim background of this place, which seemed to have stopped still just where she left it, and in all these years to have grown no older; and her head began to steady a little out of the whirl. If he ventured to seek her here, she would turn to bay and defy him. She was too much absorbed by active enmity, and rage, and indignation, to be moved by the recollections of her youth, the romance that had been enacted within these walls. On the contrary, the last exasperation which had filled her cup to overflowing was so much more real than anything that followed, that Aunt Agatha was but a pale ghost to Winnie, flitting dimly across the fiery surface of her own thoughts; and this calm scene in which she found herself, almost without knowing how, felt somehow like a pasteboard cottage in a theatre, suddenly let down upon her for the moment. She had come to escape and hide herself, she said, and that was in reality what she intended to do; but at the same time the thought of living there, and making the change real, had never occurred to her. It was a sudden expedient, adopted in the heat of battle; it was not a flight for her life.

"She has come back to take refuge with us, the poor darling," said Aunt Agatha. "Oh, Mary, my dear love, don't let us be hard upon her! She has not been happy, you heard her say so, and she has come home; let me go back to Winnie, my dear. She will think that we are not glad to see her, that we don't sympathize—And oh, Mary, her poor dear wounded heart! when she looks upon all the things that surrounded her, when she was so happy!—"

And Mary could not succeed in keeping the tender old lady away, nor stilling the thousand questions that bubbled from her kind lips. All she could do was to provide for Winnie's comfort, and in her own person to leave her undisturbed. And the night fell over a strangely disquieted household. Aunt Agatha could not tell whether to cry for joy or distress, whether to be most glad that Winnie had come home, or most concerned and anxious how to account for her sudden arrival, and keep up appearances, and prevent the parish from thinking that anything unpleasant had happened. In Winnie's room there was such a silent tumult of fury, and injury, and active conflict, as had never existed before near Kirtell-side. Winnie was not thinking, nor caring where she was; she was going over the last battle from which she had fled, and anticipating the next, and instead of making herself wretched by the contrast of her former happiness, felt herself only, as it were, in a painted retirement, no more real than a dream. What was real was her own feelings, and nothing else on earth. As for Mary, she too was strangely, and she thought ridiculously affected by her sister's return. She tried to explain to herself that except for her natural sympathy for Winnie, it affected her in no other way, and was indignant, with herself for dwelling upon a possible derangement of domestic peace, as if that could not be guarded against, or even endured if it came about. But nature was too strong for her. It was not any fear for the domestic peace that moved her; it was an indescribable conviction that this unlooked-for return was the onslaught signal for a something lying in wait—that it was the touch of revolution, the opening of the flood-gates—and that henceforward her life of tranquil confidence was over, and that some mysterious trouble which she could not at present identify, had been let loose upon her, let it come sooner or later, from that day.

CHAPTER XXIX

After that first bewildered night, and when the morning came, the recollection that Winnie was in the house had a curious effect upon the thoughts of the entire household. Even Aunt Agatha's uneasy joy was mingled with many feelings that were not joyful. She had never had anything to do before with wives who "were not happy." Any such cases which might have come to her knowledge among her acquaintance she had been in the way of avoiding and tacitly condemning. "A man may be bad," she had been in the habit of saying, "but still if his wife had right feelings"—and she was in the way of thinking that it was to a woman's credit to endure all things, and to make no sign. Such had been the pride and the principles of Aunt Agatha's generation. But now, as in so many cases, principle and theory came right in the face of fact, and gave way. Winnie must be right at whatever cost. Poor Winnie! to think what she had been, to remember her as she left Kirtell splendid in her bridal beauty, and to look at her now! Such arguments made an end of all Aunt Agatha's old maiden sentiments about a wife's duty; but nevertheless her heart still ached. She knew how she would herself have looked upon a runaway wife, and she could not endure to think that other people would so look upon Winnie; and she dried an indignant tear, and made a vow to herself to carry matters with a high hand, and to maintain her child's discretion, and wisdom, and perfect propriety of action, in the face of all comers. "My dear child has come to pay me a visit, the very first chance she has had," she said to herself, rehearsing her part; "I have been begging and begging her to come, and at last she has found an opportunity. And to give me a delightful surprise, she never named the day. It was so like Winnie." This was what, omitting all notice of the feelings which made the surprise far from delightful, Aunt Agatha made up her mind to say.

As for Winnie, when she woke up in the sunshine and stillness, and heard nothing but the birds singing, and Kirtell in the distance murmuring below her window, her heart stood still for a moment and wondered; and then a few hot salt tears came scalding to her eyes; and then she began over again in her own mind the recapitulation of her wrongs. She thought very little indeed of Aunt Agatha, or of her present surroundings. What she thought of was the late scenes of exciting strife she had gone through, and future scenes which might still be before her, and what he would say to her, and what she would say to him; for matters had gone so far between them that the constantly progressing duel was as absorbing as the first dream of love, and swallowed up every thought. It cost her an effort to be patient with all the morning greetings, with Aunt Agatha's anxious talk at the breakfast-table, and discussion of the old neighbours, whom, doubtless, Winnie, she thought, would like to hear of. Winnie did not care a great deal for the old neighbours, nor did she take much interest in hearing of the boys. Indeed she did not know the boys. They had been but babies when she went away, and she had no acquaintance with the new creatures who bore their names. It gave her a little pang when she looked at Mary and saw the results of peace and tranquillity in her face, which seemed to have grown little older—but that was almost the sole thing that drew Winnie from her own thoughts. There was a subtle sort of connection between it and the wrongs which were rankling at her heart.

"There used to be twelve years between us," she said, abruptly. "I was eighteen when Mary was thirty. I think anybody that saw us would ask which was the eldest now."

"My darling, you are thin," said poor Aunt Agatha, anxiously; "but a few weeks of quiet and your native air will soon round out your dear cheeks—"

"Well," said Winnie, paying no attention, "I suppose it's because I have been living all the time, and Mary hasn't. It is I that have the wrinkles—but then I have not been like the Sleeping Beauty. I have been working hard at life all this time."

"Yes," said Mary, with a smile, "it makes a difference:—and of the two I think I would rather live. It is harder work, but there is more satisfaction in it."

"Satisfaction!" Winnie said, bitterly. There had been no satisfaction in it to her, and she felt fierce and angry at the word—and then her eye fell upon Will, who had been listening as usual. "I wonder you keep that great boy there," she said; "why isn't he doing something? You ought to send him to the army, or put him to go through some examinations. What does he want at his mother's lap? You should mind you don't spoil them, Mary. Home is the ruin of boys. I have always heard so wherever I have been."

"My dear love," cried Aunt Agatha, fearful that Mary might be moved to reply, "it is very interesting to hear you; but I want you to tell me a little about yourself. Tell me about yourself, my darling—if you are fixed there now, you know; and all where you have been."

"Before that boy?" said Winnie, with a kind of smile, looking Wilfrid in the face with her great sunken eyes.

"Now, Will, be quiet, and don't say anything impertinent," cried Aunt Agatha. "Oh, my darling, never mind him. He is strange, but he is a good boy at the bottom. I should like to hear about all my dearest child has been doing. Letters never tell all. Oh, Winnie, what a pleasure it is, my love, to see your dear face again."

"I am glad you think so, aunt—nobody else does, that I know of; and you are likely to have enough of it," said Winnie, with a certain look of defiance at her sister and her sister's son.

"Thank you, my dear love," said Aunt Agatha, trembling; for the maid was in the room, and Miss Seton's heart quailed with fear lest the sharp eyes of such a domestic critic should be opened to something strange in the conversation. "I am so glad to hear you are going to pay me a long visit; I did not like to ask you just the first morning, and I was dreadfully frightened you might soon be going again; you owe me something, Winnie, for staying away all these long years."

Aunt Agatha in her fright and agitation continued this speech until she had talked the maid safely out of the room, and then, being excited, she fell, without knowing it, into tears.

Winnie leant back in her chair and folded a light shawl she wore round her, and looked at Miss Seton. In her heart she was wondering what Aunt Agatha could possibly have to cry about; what could ever happen to her, that made it worth her while to cry? But she did not put this sentiment into words.

"You will be tired of me before I go," she said, and that was all; not a word, as Aunt Agatha afterwards explained to Mary, about her husband, or about how she had been living, or anything about herself. And to take her by the throat, as it were, and demand that she should account for herself, was not to be thought of. The end was that they all dispersed to their various occupations, and that the day went on almost as if Winnie was not there. But yet the fact that Winnie was there tinged every one's thoughts, and made a difference in every corner of the house. They had all their occupations to betake themselves to, but she had nothing to do, and unconsciously every individual in the place took to observing the new-comer, with that curious kind of feminine observation which goes so little way, and yet goes so far. She had brought only a portmanteau with her, a gentleman's box, not a lady's, and yet she made no move towards unpacking, but let her things remain in it, notwithstanding that the wardrobe was empty and open, and her dresses, if she had brought any, must have been crushed up like rags in that tight enclosure. And she sat in the drawing-room with the open windows, through which every one in the house now and then got a glimpse of her, doing nothing, not even reading; she had her thin shawl round her shoulders, though it was so warm, and she sat there with nothing to occupy her, like a figure carved out of stone. Such an attitude, in a woman's eyes, is the embodiment of everything that is saddest, and most listless, and forlorn. Doing nothing, not trying to take an interest in anything, careless about the books, indifferent to the garden, with no curiosity about anybody or anything. The sight of her listless figure filled Aunt Agatha with despair.

And then, to make things worse, Sir Edward made his appearance the very next day to inquire into it all. It was hard to make out how he knew, but he did know, and no doubt all the parish knew, and were aware that there was something strange about it. Sir Edward was an old man, about eighty now, feeble but irreproachable, and lean limbs that now and then were slightly unsteady, but a toilette which was always everything it ought to be. He came in, cool and fresh in his summer morning dress, but his brow was puckered with anxiety, and there was about him that indescribable air of coming to see about it, which has so painful an effect in general upon the nerves of the persons whose affairs are to be put under investigation. When Sir Edward made his appearance at the open window, Aunt Agatha instinctively rose up and put herself before Winnie, who, however, did not show any signs of disturbance in her own person, but only wound herself up more closely in her shawl.

"So Winnie has come to see us at last," said Sir Edward, and he came up to her and took both her hands, and kissed her forehead in a fatherly way. He did so almost without looking at her, and then he gave an unaffected start; but he had too much delicacy to utter the words that came to his lips. He did not say how much changed she was, but he gave Aunt Agatha a pitiful look of dismay and astonishment as he sat down, and this Winnie did not fail to see.

"Yes, at last," cried Aunt Agatha, eagerly. "I have begged and begged of her to come, and was wondering what answer I should get, when she was all the while planning me such a delightful surprise; but how did you know?"

"News travels fast," said Sir Edward, and then he turned to the stranger. "You will find us much changed, Winnie. We are getting old people now, and the boys whom you left babies—you must see a great deal of difference."

"Not so much difference," said Winnie, "as you see in me."

"It was to be expected there should be a difference," said Sir Edward. "You were but a girl when you went away. I hope you are going to make a good long stay. You will find us just as quiet as ever, and as humdrum, but very delighted to see you."

To this Winnie made no reply. She neither answered his question, nor gave any response to his expression of kindness, and the old man sat and looked at her with a deeper wrinkle than ever across his brow.

"She must pay me a long visit," said poor Aunt Agatha, "since she has been so long of coming. Now that I have her she shall not go away."

"And Percival?" said Sir Edward. He had cast about in his own mind for the best means of approaching this difficult subject, but had ended by feeling there was nothing for it but plain speaking. And then, though there were reports that they did not "get on," still there was nothing as yet to justify suspicions of a final rupture. "I hope you left him quite well; I hope we are to see him, too."

"He was very well when I left him, thank you," said Winnie, with steady formality; and then the conversation once more came to a dead stop.

Sir Edward was disconcerted. He had come to examine, to reprove, and to exhort, but he was not prepared to be met with this steady front of unconsciousness. He thought the wanderer had most likely come home full of complaints and outcries, and that it might be in his power to set her right. He hemmed and cleared his throat a little, and cast about what he should say, but he had no better inspiration than to turn to Aunt Agatha and disturb her gentle mind with another topic, and for this moment let the original subject rest.

"Ah—have you heard lately from Earlston?" he said, turning to Miss Seton. "I have just been hearing a report about Francis Ochterlony. I hope it is not true."

"What kind of report?" said Aunt Agatha, breathlessly. A few minutes before she could not have believed that any consideration whatever would have disturbed her from the one subject which was for the moment dearest to her heart—but Sir Edward with his usual felicity had found out another chord which vibrated almost as painfully. Her old delusion recurred to Aunt Agatha with the swiftness of lightning. He might be going to marry, and divert the inheritance from Hugh, and she did her best to persuade her lips to a kind of smile.

"They say he is ill," said Sir Edward; "but of course if you have not heard—I thought he did not look like himself when we were there. Very poorly I heard—not anything violent you know, but a sort of breaking up. Perhaps it is not true."

Aunt Agatha's heart had been getting hard usage for some time back. It had jumped to her mouth, and sunk into depths as deep as heart can sink to, time after time in these eventful days. Now she only felt it contract as it were, as if somebody had seized it violently, and she gave a little cry, for it hurt her.

"Oh, Sir Edward, it cannot be true," she said. "We had a letter from Hugh on Monday, and he does not say a word. It cannot be true."

"Hugh is very young," said Sir Edward, who did not like to be supposed wrong in a point of fact. "A boy with no experience might see a man all but dying, and as long as he did not complain would never know."

"But he looked very well when we were there," said Aunt Agatha, faltering. If she had been alone she would have shed silent tears, and her thoughts would have been both sad and bitter; but this was not a moment to think of her own feelings—nor above all to cry.

Sir Edward shook his head. "I always mistrust those sort of looks for my part," he said. "A big man has always an appearance of strength, and that carries it off."

"Is it Mr. Ochterlony?" said Winnie, interposing for the first time. "What luck Mary has and her boys! And so Hugh will come into the property without any waiting. It may be very sad of course, Aunt Agatha, but it is great luck for him at his age."

"Oh, Winnie, my dear love!" cried Aunt Agatha, feebly. It was a speech that went to her heart, but she was dumb between the two people who did not care for Francis Ochterlony, and could find nothing to say.

"I hope that is not the way in which any of us look at it," said Sir Edward with gentle severity; and then he added, "I always thought if you had been left a little more to yourselves when we were at Earlston that still you might have made it up."

"Oh no, no!" said Aunt Agatha, "now that we are both old people—and he was always far too sensible. But it was not anything of that sort. Francis Ochterlony and I were—were always dear friends."

"Well, you must let me know next time when Hugh writes," said Sir Edward, "and I hope we shall have better news." When he said this he turned again quite abruptly to Winnie, who had dropped once more into her own thoughts, and expected no new assault.

"Percival is coming to fetch you, I suppose?" he said. "I think I can offer him some good shooting in a month or two. This may overcloud us all a little if—if anything should happen to Francis Ochterlony. But after what your Aunt Agatha says, I feel disposed to hope the best."

"Yes, I hope so," said Winnie; which was a very unsatisfactory reply.

"Of course you are citizens of the world, and we are very quiet people," said Sir Edward. "I suppose promotion comes slow in these times of peace. I should have thought he was entitled to another step by this time; but we civilians know so little about military affairs."

"I thought everybody knew that steps were bought," said Winnie; and once more the conversation broke off dead.

It was a relief to them all when Mary came into the room, and had to be told about Mr. Ochterlony's supposed illness, and to take a reasonable place between Aunt Agatha's panic-stricken assurance that it was not true, and Sir Edward's calmly indifferent belief that it was. Mary for the first time suggested that a man might be ill, and yet not at the point of death, which was a conclusion to which the others had leapt. And then they all made a little effort at ordinary talk.

"You will have everybody coming to call," said Sir Edward, "now that Winnie is known to have come home; and I daresay Percival will find Mary's military friends a great resource when he comes. Love-making being over, he will want some substitute—"

"Who are Mary's military friends?" said Winnie, suddenly breaking in.

"Only some people in our old regiment," said Mary. "It is stationed at Carlisle, strangely enough. You know the Askells, I think, and—"

"The Askells!" said Winnie, and her face grew dark. "Are they here, all that wretched set of people?—Mary's friends. Ah, I might have known—"

"My dear love, she is a very silly little woman; but Nelly is delightful, and he is very nice, poor man," cried Aunt Agatha, eager to interfere.

"Yes, poor man, he is very nice," said Winnie, with contempt; "his wife is an idiot, and he doesn't beat her; I am sure I should, if I were he. Who's Nelly? and that horrid Methodist of a woman, and the old maid that reads novels? Why didn't you tell me of them? If I had known, I should never have come here."

"Oh, Winnie, my darling!" cried Aunt Agatha; "but I did mention them; and so did Mary, I feel sure."

"They are Mary's friends," said Winnie, with bitterness, and then she stopped herself abruptly. The others were like an army of observation round a beleaguered city, which was not guided by the most perfect wisdom, but lost its temper now and then, and made injudicious sallies. Now Winnie shut up her gates, and drew in her garrison once more; and her companions looked at each other doubtfully, seeing a world of sore and wounded feeling, distrust, and resistance, and mystery to which they had no clue. She had gone away a girl, full of youthful bravado, and fearing nothing. She had come back a stranger, with a long history unknown to them, and with no inclination to make it clear. Her aunt and sister were anxious and uneasy, and did not venture on direct assault; but Sir Edward, who was a man of resolution, sat down before the fortress, and was determined to fight it out.

"You should have sent us word you were coming," he said; "and your husband should have been with you, Winnie. It was he who took you away, and he ought to have come back to give an account of his stewardship. I shall tell him so when he comes."

Again Winnie made no answer; her face contracted slightly; but soon settled back again into its blank look of self-concentration, and no response came.

"He has no appointment, I suppose; no adjutantship, or anything to keep him from getting away?"

"No," said Winnie.

"Perhaps he has gone to see his mother?" said Sir Edward, brightening up. "She is getting quite an old woman, and longs to see him; and you, my pretty Winnie, too. I suppose you will pay her your long-deferred visit, now you have returned to this country? Percival is there?"

"No—I think not," said Winnie, winding herself up in her shawl, as she had done before.

"Then you have left him at—, where he is stationed now," said Sir Edward, becoming more and more point-blank in his attack.

"Look here, Sir Edward," said Winnie; "we are citizens of the world, as you say, and we have not lived such a tranquil life as you have. I did not come here to give an account of my husband; he can take care of himself. I came to have a little quiet and rest, and not to be asked questions. If one could be let alone anywhere, it surely should be in one's own home."

"No, indeed," said Sir Edward, who was embarrassed, and yet more arbitrary than ever; "for in your own home people have a right to know all about you. Though I am not exactly a relative, I have known you all your life; I may say I brought you up, like a child of my own; and to see you come home like this, all alone, without baggage or attendant, as if you had dropped from the skies, and nobody knowing where you come from, or anything about it,—I think, Winnie, my dear, when you consider of it, you will see it is precisely your own friends who ought to know."

Then Aunt Agatha rushed into the mêlée, feeling in her own person a little irritated by her old friend's lecture and inquisition.

"Sir Edward is making a mistake, my dear love," she said; "he does not know. Dear Winnie has been telling me everything. It is so nice to know all about her. Those little details that can never go into letters; and when—when Major Percival comes—"

"It is very good of you, Aunt Agatha," said Winnie, with a certain quiet disdain; "but I did not mean to deceive anybody—Major Percival is not coming that I know of. I am old enough to manage for myself: Mary came home from India when she was not quite my age."

"Oh, my dear love, poor Mary was a widow," cried Aunt Agatha; "you must not speak of that."

"Yes, I know Mary has always had the best of it," said Winnie, under her breath; "you never made a set against her as you do against me. If there is an inquisition at Kirtell, I will go somewhere else. I came to have a little quiet; that is all I want in this world."

It was well for Winnie that she turned away abruptly at that moment, and did not see Sir Edward's look, which he turned first upon Mary and then on Aunt Agatha. She did not see it, and it was well for her. When he went away soon after, Miss Seton went out into the garden with him, in obedience to his signals, and then he unburdened his mind.

"It seems to me that she must have run away from him," said Sir Edward. "It is very well she has come here; but still it is unpleasant, to make the best of it. I am sure he has behaved very badly; but I must say I am a little disappointed in Winnie. I was, as you may remember, at the very first when she made up her mind so soon."

"There is no reason for thinking she has run away," said Aunt Agatha. "Why should she have run away? I hope a lady may come to her aunt and her sister without compromising herself in any way."

Sir Edward shook his head. "A married woman's place is with her husband," he said, sententiously. He was old, and he was more moral, and perhaps less sentimental, in his remarks than formerly. "And how she is changed! There must have been a great deal of excitement and late hours, and bills and all that sort of thing, before she came to look like that."

"You are very hard upon my poor Winnie," said Aunt Agatha, with a long-restrained sob.

"I am not hard upon her. On the contrary, I would save her if I could," said Sir Edward, solemnly. "My dear Agatha, I am sorry for you. What with poor Francis Ochterlony's illness, and this heavy burden—"

Miss Seton was seized with one of those passions of impatience and indignation to which a man's heavy way of blundering over sore subjects sometimes moves a woman. "It was all Francis Ochterlony's fault," she said, lifting her little tremulous white hands. "It was his fault, and not mine. He might have had some one that could have taken care of him all these years, and he chose his marble images instead—and I will not take the blame; it was no fault of mine. And then my poor darling child—"

But here Miss Seton's strength, being the strength of excitement solely, gave way, and her voice broke, and she had to take both her hands to dry her fast-coming tears.

"Well, well, well!" said Sir Edward. "Dear me, I never meant to excite you so. What I was saying was with the kindest intention. Let us hope Ochterlony is better, and that all will turn out pleasantly for Winnie. If you find yourself unequal to the emergency, you know—and want a man's assistance—"

"Thank you," said Aunt Agatha, with dignity; "but I do not think so much of a man's assistance as I used to do. Mary is so very sensible, and if one does the very best one can—"

"Oh, of course I am not a person to interfere," said Sir Edward; and he walked away with an air still more dignified than that which Aunt Agatha had put on, but very shaky, poor old gentleman, about his knees, which slightly diminished the effect. As for Aunt Agatha, she turned her back upon him steadily, and walked back to the Cottage with all the stateliness of a woman aggrieved. But nevertheless the pins and needles were in her heart, and her mind was full of anxiety and distress. She had felt very strongly the great mistake made by Francis Ochterlony, and how he had spoiled both their lives—but that was not to say that she could hear of his illness with philosophy. And then Winnie, who was not ill, but whose reputation and position might be in deadly danger for anything Miss Seton knew. Aunt Agatha knew nothing better to do than to call Mary privately out of the room and pour forth her troubles. It did no good, but it relieved her mind. Why was Sir Edward so suspicious and disagreeable—why had he ceased "to understand people;"—and why was Hugh so young and inexperienced, and incapable of judging whether his uncle was or was not seriously ill;—and why did not "they" write? Aunt Agatha did not know whom she meant by "they," nor why she blamed poor Hugh. But it relieved her mind. And when she had pushed her burden off on to Mary's shoulders, the weight was naturally much lightened on her own.

CHAPTER XXX

Hugh, however, it is quite true, was very inexperienced. He did not even notice that his uncle was very ill. He sat with him at dinner and saw that he did not eat anything, and yet never saw it; and he went with him sometimes when he tottered about the garden in the morning, and never found out that he tottered; and sat with him at night, and was very kind and attentive, and was very fond of his uncle, and never remarked anything the matter with his breathing. He was very young, and he knew no better, and it never seemed to him that short breathing and unequal steps and a small appetite were anything remarkable at Mr. Ochterlony's age. If there had been a lady in the house it might have made a wonderful difference; but to be sure it was Francis Ochterlony's own doing that there was not a lady in the house. And he was not himself so shortsighted as Hugh. His own growing weakness was something of which he was perfectly well aware, and he knew, too, how his breath caught of nights, and looking forward into the future saw the shadow drawing nearer to his door, and was not afraid of it. Probably the first thought went chill to his heart, the thought that he was mortal like other people, and might have to die. But his life had been such a life as to make him very much composed about it, and not disinclined to think that a change might be for the better. He was not very clear about the unseen world—for one thing, he had nobody there in particular belonging to him except the father and mother who were gone ages ago; and it did not seem very important to himself personally whether he was going to a long sleep, or going to another probation, or into pure blessedness, which of all the three was, possibly, the hypothesis which he understood least. Perhaps, on the whole, if he had been to come to an end altogether he would not have much minded; but his state of feeling was, that God certainly knew all about it, and that He would arrange it all right. It was a kind of pagan state of mind; and yet there was in it something of the faith of the little child which was once set up as the highest model of faith by the highest authority. No doubt Mr. Ochterlony had a great many thoughts on the subject, as he sat buried in the deep chair in his study, and gazed into the little red spark of fire which was lighted for him all that summer through, though the weather was so genial. His were not bright thoughts, but very calm ones; and perhaps his perfect composure about it all was one reason why Hugh took it as a matter of course, and went on quite cheerily and lightly, and never found out there was anything the matter with him until the very last.

It was one morning when Mr. Ochterlony had been later than usual of coming downstairs. When he did make his appearance it was nearly noon, and he was in his dressing-gown, which was an unheard-of thing for him. Instead of going out to the garden, he called Hugh, and asked him to give him his arm while he made a little tour of the house. They went from the library to the dining-room, and then upstairs to the great drawing-room where the Venus and the Psyche were. When they had got that length Mr. Ochterlony dropped into a chair, and gasped for breath, and looked round upon his treasures. And then Hugh, who was looking on, began to feel very uneasy and anxious for the first time.

"One can't take them with one," said Mr. Ochterlony, with a sigh and a smile; "and you will not care for them much, Hugh. I don't mean to put any burden upon you: they are worth a good deal of money; but I'd rather you did not sell them, if you could make up your mind to the sacrifice."

"If they were mine I certainly should not sell them," said Hugh; "but as they are yours, uncle, I don't see that it matters what I would do."

Mr. Ochterlony smiled, and looked kindly at him, but he did not give him any direct answer. "If they were yours," he said—"suppose the case—then what would you do with them?"

"I would collect them in a museum somewhere, and call them by your name," said Hugh, on the spur of the moment. "You almost ought to do that yourself, uncle, there are so few people to see them here."

Mr. Ochterlony's languid eyes brightened a little. "They are worth a good deal of money," he said.

"If they were worth a mint of money, I don't see what that matters," said Hugh, with youthful extravagance.

His uncle looked at him again, and once more the languid eye lighted up, and a tinge of colour came to the grey cheek.

"I think you mean it, Hugh," he said, "and it is pleasant to think you do mean it now, even if—I have been an economical man, in every way but this, and I think you would not miss it. But I won't put any bondage upon you. By the way, they would belong to the personalty. Perhaps there's a will wanted for that. It was stupid of me not to think of it before. I ought to see about it this very day."

"Uncle," said Hugh, who had been sitting on the arm of a chair looking at him, and seeing, as by a sudden revelation, all the gradual changes which he had not noticed when they began: the shortened breath, the emaciated form, and the deep large circle round the eyes,—"Uncle, will you tell me seriously what you mean when you speak to me like this?"

"On second thoughts, it will be best to do it at once," said Mr. Ochterlony. "Hugh, ring the bell—What do I speak like this, for, my boy? For a very plain reason; because my course is going to end, and yours is only going to begin."

"But, uncle!" cried Hugh.

"Hush—the one ought to be a kind of continuation of the other," said Mr. Ochterlony, "since you will take up where I leave off; but I hope you will do better than that. If you should feel yourself justified in thinking of the museum afterward—But I would not like to leave any burden upon you. John, let some one ride into Dalken directly, and ask Mr. Preston, the attorney, to come to me—or his son will do. I should like to see him to-day—And stop," said Mr. Ochterlony, reluctantly, "he may fetch the doctor, too."

"Uncle, do you feel ill?" said Hugh. He had come up to his uncle's side, and he had taken fright, and was looking at him wistfully as a woman might have done—for his very inexperience which had prevented him from observing gave him a tender anguish now, and filled him full of awe and compunction, and made him in his wistfulness almost like a woman.

"No," said Mr. Ochterlony, holding out his hand. "Not ill, my boy, only dying—that's all. Nothing to make a fuss about—but sit down and compose yourself, for I have a good deal to say."

"Do you mean it, uncle?" asked Hugh, searching into the grey countenance before him with his suddenly awakened eyes.

Mr. Ochterlony gave a warm grasp to the young hand which held his closely yet trembling. "Sit down," he said. "I'm glad you are sorry. A few years ago there would have been nobody to mind—except the servants, perhaps. I never took the steps I might have done, you know," he added, with a certain sadness, and yet a sense of humour which was curious to see, "to have an heir of my own—And speaking of that, you will be sure to remember what I said to you about the Henri Deux. I put it away in the cabinet yonder, the very last day they were here."

Then Mr. Ochterlony talked a great deal, and about many things. About there being no particular occasion for making a will—since Earlston was settled by his father's will upon his own heirs male, or those of his brother—how he had bethought himself all at once, though he did not know exactly how the law stood, that there was some difference between real and personal property, and how, on the whole, perhaps, it was better to send for Preston. "As for the doctor, I daren't take it upon me to die without him, I suppose," Mr. Ochterlony said. He had never been so playful before, as long as Hugh had known him. He had been reserved—a little shy, even with his nephew. Now his own sense of failure seemed to have disappeared. He was going to make a change, to get rid of all his old disabilities, and incumbrances, and antecedents, and no doubt it would be a change for the better. This was about the substance of Mr. Ochterlony's thoughts.

"But one can't take Psyche, you know," he said. "One must go alone to look into the face of the Immortals. And I don't think your mother, perhaps, would care to have her here—so if you should feel yourself justified in thinking of the museum—But you will have a great deal to do. In the first place your mother—I doubt if she'll be so happy at the Cottage, now Mrs. Percival has come back. I think you ought to ask her to come here. And I shouldn't wonder if Will gave you some trouble. He's an odd boy. I would not say he had not a sense of honour, but—And he has a jealous, dissatisfied temper. As for Islay, he's all safe, I suppose. Always be kind to them, Hugh, and give Will his education. I think he has abilities; but don't be too liberal. Don't take them upon your shoulders. You have your own life to think of first of all."

All this Mr. Ochterlony uttered, with many little breaks and pauses, but with very little aid from his companion, who was too much moved to do more than listen. He was not suffering in any acute way, and yet, somehow, the sense of his approaching end seemed to have loosened his tongue, which had been to some extent bound all his life.

"For you must marry, you know," he said. "I consider that a bargain between us. Don't trust to your younger brother, as I did—not but what it was the best thing for you. Some little bright thing like that—that was with your mother. You may laugh, but I can remember when Agatha Seton was as pretty a creature—"

"I think she is pretty now," said Hugh, half because he did think so, and half because he was anxious to find something he could say.

Then Mr. Ochterlony brightened up in the strangest pathetic way, laughing a little, with a kind of tender consciousness that he was laughing at himself. He was so nearly separated from himself now that he was tender as if it was the weakness of a dear old familiar friend at which he was laughing. "She is very pretty," he said. "I am glad you have the sense to see it,—and good; and she'll go now and make a slave of herself to that girl. I suppose that is my fault, too. But be sure you don't forget about the Henri Deux."

And then all of a sudden, while his nephew was sitting watching him, Mr. Ochterlony fell asleep. When he was sleeping he looked so grey, and worn, and emaciated, that Hugh's heart smote him. He could not explain to himself why it was that he had never noticed it before; and he was very doubtful and uncertain what he ought to do. If he sent for his mother, which seemed the most natural idea, Mr. Ochterlony might not like it, and he had himself already sent for the doctor. Hugh had the good sense finally to conclude upon doing the one thing that was most difficult—to do nothing. But it was not an enlivening occupation. He went off and got some wraps and cushions, and propped his uncle up in the deep chair he was reclining in, and then he sat down and watched him, feeling a thrill run through him every time there was a little drag in the breathing or change in his patient's face. He might die like that, with the Psyche and the Venus gleaming whitely over him, and nobody by who understood what to do. It was the most serious moment that had ever occurred in Hugh's life; and it seemed to him that days, and not minutes, were passing. When the doctor arrived, it was a very great relief. And then Mr. Ochterlony was taken to bed and made comfortable, as they said; and a consciousness crept through the house, no one could tell how, that the old life and the old times were coming to a conclusion—that sad change and revolution hung over the house, and that Earlston would soon be no more as it had been.

On the second day Hugh wrote to his mother, but that letter had not been received at the time of Sir Edward's visit. And he made a very faithful devoted nurse, and tended his uncle like a son. Mr. Ochterlony did not die all at once, as probably he had himself expected and intended—he had his spell of illness to go through like other people, and he bore it very cheerfully, as he was not suffering much. He was indeed a great deal more playful and at his ease than either the doctor or the attorney, or Mrs. Gilsland, the housekeeper, thought quite right.

The lawyer did not come until the following day; and then it was young Mr. Preston who came, his father being occupied, and Mr. Ochterlony had a distaste somehow to young Mr. Preston. He was weak, too, and not able to go into details. All that he would say was, that Islay and Wilfrid were to have the same younger brother's portion as their father had, and that everything else was to go to Hugh. He would not suffer himself to be tempted to say anything about the museum, though the suggestion had gone to his heart—and to make a will with so little in it struck the lawyer almost as an injury to himself.

"No legacies?" he said—"excuse me, Mr. Ochterlony—nothing about your beautiful collection? There ought to be some stipulation about that."

"My nephew knows all my wishes," Mr. Ochterlony said, briefly, "and I have no time now for details. Is it ready to be signed? Everything else of which I die possessed to my brother, Hugh Ochterlony's eldest son. That is what I want. The property is his already, by his grandfather's will. Everything of which I die possessed, to dispose of according as his direction and circumstances may permit."

"But there are other friends—and servants," pleaded Mr. Preston; "and then your wonderful collection—"

"My nephew knows all my wishes," said Mr. Ochterlony; and his weakness was so great that he sank back on his pillows. He took his own way in this, while poor Hugh hung about the room wistfully looking on. It was to Hugh's great advantage, but he was not thinking of that. He was asking himself could he have done anything to stop the malady if he had noticed it in time? And he was thinking how to arrange the Ochterlony Museum. If it could only have been done in his lifetime, so that its founder could see. When the doctor and the attorney were both gone, Hugh sat down by his uncle's bedside, and, half afraid whether he was doing right, began to talk of it. He was too young and too honest to pretend to disbelieve what Mr. Ochterlony himself and the doctor had assured him of. The room was dimly lighted, the lamp put away on a table in a corner with a shade over it, and the sick room "made comfortable," and everything arranged for the night. And then the two had an hour of very affectionate, confidential, almost tender talk. Mr. Ochterlony was almost excited about the museum. It was not to be bestowed on his college, as Hugh at first thought, but to be established at Dalken, the pretty town of which everybody in the Fells was proud. And then the conversation glided off to more familiar subjects, and the old man who was dying gave a great deal of very sound advice to the young man who was about to begin to live.

"Islay will be all right," said Mr. Ochterlony; "he will have what your father had, and you will always make him at home in Earlston. It is Will I am thinking about. I am not fond of Will. Don't be too generous to him, or he will think it is his right. I know no harm of the boy, but I would not put all my affairs into his hands as I put them into yours."

"It will not be my fault if I don't justify your confidence, uncle," said Hugh, with something swelling in his throat.

"If I had not known that, I would not have trusted you, Hugh," said Mr. Ochterlony. "Take your mother's advice—always be sure to take your mother's advice. There are some of us that never understand women; but after all it stands to reason that the one-half of mankind should not separate itself from the other. We think we are the wisest; but I am not so sure—"

Mr. Ochterlony stopped short and turned his eyes, which were rather languid, to the distant lamp, the one centre of light in the room. He looked at it for a long time in a dreamy way. "I might have had a woman taking care of me like the rest," he said. "I might have had the feeling that there was somebody in the house; but you see I did not give my mind to it, Hugh. Your father left a widow, and that's natural—I am leaving only a collection. But it's better for you, my boy. If you should ever speak to Agatha Seton about it, you can tell her that—"

Then there was a pause, which poor young Hugh, nervous, and excited, and inexperienced, did not know how to break, and Mr. Ochterlony continued to look at the lamp. It was very dim and shaded, but still a pale ray shone sideways between the curtains upon the old man who lay a-dying, and cast an enlarged shadow of Hugh's head upon the wall. When Mr. Ochterlony turned round a little, his eye caught that, and a tender smile came over his face.

"It looks like your father," he said to Hugh, who was startled, and did not know what he meant. "It is more like him than you are. He was a good fellow at the bottom—fidgety, but a very good fellow—as your mother will tell you. I am glad it is you who are the eldest, and not one of the others. They are fine boys, but I am glad it is you."

"Oh, uncle," said Hugh, with tears in his eyes, "you are awfully good to me. I don't deserve it. Islay is a far better fellow than I am. If you would but get well again, and never mind who was the eldest—"

Mr. Ochterlony smiled and shook his head. "I have lived my day," he said, "and now it is your turn; and I hope you'll make Earlston better than ever it was. Now go to bed, my boy; we've talked long enough. I think if I were quiet I could sleep."

"And you'll call me, uncle, if you want me? I shall be in the dressing-room," said Hugh, whose heart was very full.

"There is no need," said Mr. Ochterlony, smiling again. "But I suppose it pleases you. You'll sleep as sound as a top wherever you are—that's the privilege of your age; but John will be somewhere about, and nothing is going to happen before morning. Good night."

But he called Hugh back before he reached the door. "You'll be sure to remember about the Henri Deux?" he said, softly. That was all. And the young man went to the dressing-room, and John, who had just stolen in, lay down on a sofa in the shadow, and sleep and quiet took possession of the room. If Mr. Ochterlony slept, or if he still lay looking at the lamp, seeing his life flit past him like a shadow, giving a sigh to what might have been, and thinking with perhaps a little awakening thrill of expectation of what was so soon to be, nobody could tell. He was as silent as if he slept—almost as silent as if he had been dead.

But Aunt Agatha was not asleep. She was in her room all alone, praying for him, stopping by times to think how different it might have been. She might have been with him then, taking care of him, instead of being so far away; and when she thought of that, the tears stood in her eyes. But it was not her fault. She had nothing to upbraid herself with. She was well aware whose doing it was—poor man, and it was he who was the sufferer now; but she said her prayers for him all the same.

When a few days had passed, the event occurred of which there had never been any doubt. Francis Ochterlony died very peaceably and quietly, leaving not only all of which he died possessed, but his blessing and thanks to the boy who had stood in the place of a son to him. He took no unnecessary time about his dying, and yet he did not do anything hastily to shock people. It was known he was ill, and everybody had the satisfaction of sending to inquire for him, and testifying their respect before he died. Such a thing was indeed seen on one day as seven servants, all men on horseback, sent with messages of inquiry, which was a great gratification to Mrs. Gilsland, and the rest of the servants. "He went off like a lamb at the last," they all said; and though he was not much like a lamb, there might have been employed a less appropriate image. He made a little sketch with his own hands as to how the Museum was to be arranged, and told Hugh what provision to make for the old servants; and gave him a great many advices, such as he never had taken himself; and was so pleasant and cheery about it, that they scarcely knew the moment when the soft twilight sank into absolute night. He died an old man, full of many an unexpressed philosophy, and yet, somehow, with the sentiment of a young one: like a tree ripe and full of fruit, yet with blossoms still lingering on the topmost branches, as you see on orange-trees—sage and experienced, and yet with something of the virginal and primal state. Perhaps it was not a light price to give for this crowning touch of delicacy and purity—the happiness (so to speak) of his own life and of Aunt Agatha's. And yet the link between the old lovers, thus fancifully revived, was very sweet and real. And they had not been at all unhappy apart, on the whole, either of them. And it is something to preserve this quintessence of maidenhood and primal freshness to the end of a long life, and leave the visionary perfume of it among a community much given to marrying and giving in marriage. It was thus that Francis Ochterlony died.

Earlston, of course, was all shut up immediately, blinds drawn and shutters closed, and what was more unusual, true tears shed, and a true weight, so long as it lasted, upon the hearts of all the people about. The servants, perhaps, were not quite uninfluenced by the thought that all their legacies, &c., were left in the hands of their new master, who was little more than a boy. And the Cottage, too, was closed, and the inmates went about in a shadowed atmosphere, and were very sorry, and thought a little of Mr. Ochterlony—not all as Aunt Agatha did, who kept her room, and shed many tears; but still he was thought of in the house. It is true that Mary could not help remembering that now her Hugh was no longer a boy, dependent upon anybody's pleasure, but the master of the house of his fathers—the house his own father was born in; and an important personage. She could not help thinking of this, nor, in spite of herself, feeling her heart swell, and asking herself if it was indeed her Hugh who had come to this promotion. And yet she was very sorry for Mr. Ochterlony's death. He had been good to her children, always courteous and deferential to herself; and she was sorry for him as a woman is sorry for a man who has nobody belonging to him—sorrier far, in most cases, than the man is for himself. He was dead in his loneliness, and the thought of it brought a quiet moisture to Mary's eyes; but Hugh was living, and it was he who was the master of all; and it was not in human nature that his mother's grief should be bitter or profound.

"Hugh is a lucky boy," said Mrs. Percival; "I think you are all lucky, Mary, you and your children. To come into Earlston with so little waiting, and have everything left in his own hands."

"I don't think he will be thinking of that," said Mary. "He was fond of his uncle; I am sure he will feel his loss."

"Oh, yes, no doubt; I ought not to have said anything so improper," said Winnie, with that restrained smile and uncomfortable inference which comes so naturally to some people. She knew nothing and cared nothing about Francis Ochterlony; and she was impatient of what she called Aunt Agatha's nonsense; and she could not but feel it at once unreasonable and monstrous that anything but the painful state of her own affairs should occupy people in the house she was living in. Yet the fact was that this event had to a certain extent eclipsed Winnie. The anxiety with which everybody looked for a message or letter about Mr. Ochterlony's state blinded them a little to her worn looks and listless wretchedness. They did not neglect her, nor were they indifferent to her; for, indeed, it would be difficult to be indifferent to a figure which held so prominent a place in the foreground of everything; but still when they were in such a state of suspense about what was happening at Earlston, no doubt Winnie's affairs were to a certain extent overlooked. It is natural for an old man to die: but it is not natural for a young woman—a woman in the bloom and fulness of life—one who has been, and ought still to be, a great beauty—to be driven by her wrongs out of all that makes life endurable. This was how Winnie reasoned; and she was jealous of the attention given to Mr. Ochterlony as he accomplished the natural act of dying. What was that in comparison with the terrible struggles of life?

But naturally it made a great difference when it was all over, and when Hugh, subdued and very serious, but still another man from the Hugh who the other day was but a boy, came to the Cottage "for a little change," and to give his mother all the particulars. He came all tender in his natural grief, with eyes ready to glisten, and a voice that sometimes faltered; but, nevertheless, there was something about him which showed that it was he who was Mr. Ochterlony of Earlston now.

CHAPTER XXXI

This was the kind of crisis in the family history at which Uncle Penrose was sure to make his appearance. He was the only man among them, he sometimes said—or, at least, the only man who knew anything about money; and he came into the midst of the Ochterlonys in their mourning, as large and important as he had been when Winnie was married, looking as if he had never taken his left hand out of his pocket all the time. He had not been asked to the funeral, and he marked his consciousness of that fact by making his appearance in buff waistcoats and apparel which altogether displayed light-heartedness if not levity—and which was very wounding to Aunt Agatha's feelings. Time, somehow, did not seem to have touched him. If he was not so offensively and demonstratively a Man, in the sweet-scented feminine house, as he used to be, it was no reticence of his, but because the boys were men, or nearly so, and the character of the household changed. And Hugh was Mr. Ochterlony of Earlston; which, perhaps, was the fact that made the greatest difference of all.

He came the day after Hugh's return, and in the evening there had been a very affecting scene in the Cottage. In faithful discharge of his promise, Hugh had carried the Henri Deux, carefully packed, as became its value and fragile character, to Aunt Agatha; and she had received it from him with a throbbing heart and many tears. "It was almost the last thing he said to me," Hugh had said. "He put it all aside with his own hand, the day you admired it so much; and he told me over and over again, to be sure not to forget." Aunt Agatha had been sitting with her hands clasped upon the arm of his chair, and her eyes fixed upon him, not to lose a word; but when he said this, she covered her face with those soft old hands, and was silent and did not even weep. It was the truest grief that was in her heart, and yet with that, there was an exquisite pang of delight, such as goes through and through a girl when first she perceives that she is loved, and sees her power! She was as a widow, and yet she was an innocent maiden, full of experience and inexperience, feeling the heaviness of the evening shadows, and yet still in the age of splendour in the grass and glory in the flower. The sense of that last tenderness went through her with a thrill of joy and grief beyond description. It gave him back to her for ever and ever, but not with that sober appropriation which might have seemed natural to her age. She could no more look them in the face while it was being told, than had he been a living lover and she a girl. It was a supreme conjunction and blending of the two extremes of life, a fusion of youth and of age.

"I never thought he noticed what I said," she answered at last with a soft sob—and uncovered the eyes that were full of tears, and yet dazzled as with a sudden light; and she would let no one touch the precious legacy, but unpacked it herself, shedding tears that were bitter and yet sweet, over its many wrappings. Though he was a man, and vaguely buoyed up, without knowing it, by the strange new sense of his own importance, Hugh could have found it in his heart to shed tears, too, over the precious bits of porcelain, that had now acquired an interest so much more near and touching than anything connected with Henri Deux; and so could his mother. But there were two who looked on with dry eyes: the one was Winnie, who would have liked to break it all into bits, as she swept past it with her long dress, and could not put up with Aunt Agatha's nonsense; the other was Will, who watched the exhibition curiously with close observation, wondering how it was that people were such fools, and feeling the shadow of his brother weigh upon him with a crushing weight. But these two malcontents were not in sympathy with each other, and never dreamt of making common cause.

And it was when the house was in this condition, that Uncle Penrose arrived. He arrived, as usual, just in time to make a fuss necessary about a late dinner, and to put Peggy out of temper, which was a fact that soon made itself felt through the house; and he began immediately to speak to Hugh about Earlston, and about "your late uncle," without the smallest regard for Aunt Agatha's feelings. "I know there was something between him and Miss Agatha once," he said, with a kind of smile at her, "but of course that was all over long ago." And this was said when poor Miss Seton, who felt that the bond had never before been so sweet and so close, was seated at the head of her own table, and had to bear it and make no sign.

"Probably there will be a great deal to be done on the estate," Mr. Penrose said; "these studious men always let things go to ruin out of doors; but there's a collection of curiosities or antiquities, or something. If that's good, it will bring in money. When a man is known, such things sell."

"But it is not to be sold," said Hugh quickly. "I have settled all about that."

"Not to be sold?—nonsense!" said Mr. Penrose; "you don't mean to say you are a collector—at your age? No, no, my boy; they're no good to him where he is now; he could not take them into his vault with him. Feelings are all very well, but you can't be allowed to lose a lot of money for a prejudice. What kind of things are they—pictures and that sort? or—"

"I have made all the necessary arrangements," said Hugh with youthful dignity. "I want you to go with me to Dalken, mother, to see some rooms the mayor has offered for them—nice rooms belonging to the Town Hall. They could have 'Ochterlony Museum' put up over the doors, and do better than a separate building, besides saving the expense."

Mr. Penrose gave a long whistle, which under any circumstances would have been very indecorous at a lady's table. "So that is how it's to be!" he said; "but we'll talk that over first, with your permission, Mr. Ochterlony of Earlston. You are too young to know what you're doing. I suppose the ladies are at the bottom of it; they never know the value of money. And yet we know what it costs to get it when it is wanted, Miss Agatha," said the insolent man of money, who never would forget that Miss Seton herself had once been in difficulties. She looked at him with a kind of smile, as politeness ordained, but tears of pain stood in Aunt Agatha's eyes. If ever she hated anybody in her gentle life, it was Mr. Penrose; and somehow he made himself hateful in her presence to everybody concerned.

"It costs more to get it than it is ever worth," said Winnie, indignant, and moved for the first time, to make a diversion, and come to Aunt Agatha's aid.

"Ah, I have no doubt you know all about it," said Mr. Penrose, turning his arms upon her. "You should have taken my advice. If you had come to Liverpool, as I wanted you, and married some steady-going fellow with plenty of money, and gone at a more reasonable pace, you would not have changed so much at your age. Look at Mary, how well preserved she is: I don't know what you can have been doing with yourself to look so changed."

"I am sorry you think me a fright," said Winnie, with an angry sparkle in her eye.

"You are not a fright," said Uncle Penrose; "one can see that you've been a very handsome woman, but you are not what you were when I saw you last, Winnie. The fault of your family is that you are extravagant,—I am sure you did not get it from your mother's side;—extravagant of your money and your hospitality, and your looks and everything. I am sure Mary has nothing to spare, and yet I've found people living here for weeks together. I can't afford visitors like that—I have my family to consider, and people that have real claims upon me—no more than I could afford to set up a museum. If I had a lot of curiosities thrown on my hands, I should make them into money. It is not everybody that can appreciate pictures, but everybody understands five per cent. And then he might have done something worth while for his brothers: not that I approve of a man impoverishing himself for the sake of his friends, but still two thousand pounds isn't much. And he might have done something for his mother, or looked after Will's education. It's family pride, I suppose; but I'd rather give my mother a house of her own than set up an Ochterlony Museum. Tastes differ, you know."

"His mother agrees with him entirely in everything he is doing," said Mary, with natural resentment. "I wish all mothers had sons as good as mine."

"Hush," said Hugh, who was crimson with indignation and anger: "I decline to discuss these matters with Uncle Penrose. Because he is your uncle, mother, he shall inquire into the estates as much as he likes; but I am the head of the house, and I am responsible only to God and to those who are dead—and, mother, to you," said Hugh, with his eyes glistening and his face glowing.

Uncle Penrose gave another contemptuous prolonged whistle at this speech, but the others looked at the young man with admiration and love; even Winnie, whose heart could still be touched, regarded the young paladin with a kind of tender envy and admiration. She was too young to be his mother, but she did not feel herself young; and her heart yearned to have some one who would stand by her and defend her as such a youth could. A world of softer possibilities than anything she would permit herself to think of now, came into her mind, and she looked at him. If she too had but been the mother of children like her sister! but it appeared that Mary was to have the best of it, always and in every way.

As for Will, he looked at the eldest son with very different feelings. Hugh was not particularly clever, and his brother had long entertained a certain contempt for him. He thought what he would have done had he been the head of the house. He was disposed to sneer, like Mr. Penrose, at the Ochterlony Museum. Was it not a confession of a mean mind, an acknowledgment of weakness, to consent to send away all the lovely things that made Will's vision of Earlston like a vision of heaven? If it had been Will he would not have thought of five per cent., but neither would he have thought of making a collection of them at Dalken, where the country bumpkins might come and stare. He would have kept them all to himself, and they would have made his life beautiful. And he scorned Hugh for dispossessing himself of them, and reducing the Earlston rooms into rooms of ordinary habitation. Had they but been his—had he but been the eldest, the head of the house—then the world and the family and Uncle Penrose would have seen very different things.

But yet Hugh had character enough to stand firm. He made his mother get her bonnet and go out with him after dinner; and everybody in the house looked after the two as they went away—the mother and her firstborn—he, with his young head towering above her, though Mary was tall, and she putting her arm within his so proudly—not without a tender elation in his new importance, a sense of his superior place and independent rank, which was strangely sweet. Winnie looked after them, envying her sister, and yet with an envy which was not bitter; and Will stood and looked fiercely on this brother who, by no virtue of his own, had been born before him. As for Aunt Agatha, who was fond of them all, she went to her own room to heal her wounds; and Mr. Penrose, who was fond of none of them, went up to the Hall to talk things over with Sir Edward, whom he had once talked over to such purpose. And the only two who could stray down to the soft-flowing Kirtell, and listen to the melody of the woods and waters, and talk in concert of what they had wished and planned, were Mary and Hugh.

"The great thing to be settled is about Will," the head of the house was saying. "You shall see, mother, when he is in the world and knows better, all that will blow away. His two thousand pounds is not much, as Uncle Penrose says; but it was all my father had: and when he wants it, and when Islay wants it, there can always be something added. It is my business to see to that."

"It was all your father had," said Mary, "and all your uncle intended; and I see no reason why you should add to it, Hugh. There will be a little more when I am gone; and in the meantime, if we only knew what Will would like to do—"

"Why, they'll make him a fellow of his college," said Hugh. "He'll go in for all sorts of honours. He's awfully clever, mother; there's no fear of Will. The best thing I can see is to send him to read with somebody—somebody with no end of a reputation, that he would have a sort of an awe for—and then the University. It would be no use doing it if he was just like other people; but there's everything to be made of Will."

"I hope so," said Mary, with a little sigh. And then she added, "So I shall be left quite alone?"

"No; you are coming to Earlston with me," said Hugh; "that is quite understood. There will be a great deal to do; and I don't think things are quite comfortable at the Cottage, with Mrs. Percival here."

"Poor Winnie!" said Mrs. Ochterlony. "I don't think I ought to leave Aunt Agatha—at least, while she is so much in the dark about my sister. And then you told me you had promised to marry, Hugh?"

"Yes," said the young man; and straightway the colour came to his cheek, and dimples to the corners of his mouth; "but she is too y—I mean, there is plenty of time to think of that."

"She is too young?" said Mary, startled. "Do I know her, I wonder? I did not imagine you had settled on the person as well as the fact. Well; and then, you know, I should have to come back again. I will come to visit you at Earlston: but I must keep my head-quarters here."

"I don't see why you should have to come back again," said Hugh, somewhat affronted. "Earlston is big enough, and you would be sure to be fond of her. No, I don't know that the person is settled upon. Perhaps she wouldn't have me; perhaps—But, anyhow, you are coming to Earlston, mother dear. And, after a while, we could have some visitor perhaps—your friends: you know I am very fond of your friends, mamma."

"All my friends, Hugh?" said his mother, with a smile.

This was the kind of talk they were having while Mr. Penrose was laying the details of Hugh's extravagance before Sir Edward, and doing all he could to incite him to a solemn cross-examination of Winnie. Whether she had run away from her husband, or if not exactly that, what were the circumstances under which she had left him; and whether a reconciliation could be brought about;—all this was as interesting to Sir Edward as it was to Uncle Penrose; but what the latter gentleman was particularly anxious about was, what they had done with their money, and if the unlucky couple were very deeply in debt. "I suspect that is at the bottom of it," he said. And they were both concerned about Winnie, in their way—anxious to keep her from being talked about, and to preserve to her a place of repentance. Mrs. Percival, however, was not so simple as to subject herself to this ordeal. When Sir Edward called in an accidental way next morning, and Uncle Penrose drew a solemn chair to her side, Winnie sprang up and went away. She went off, and shut herself up in her own room, and declined to go back, or give any further account of herself. "If they want to drive me away, I will go away," she said to Aunt Agatha, who came up tremulously to her door, and begged her to go downstairs.

"My darling, they can't drive you away; you have come to see me," said Aunt Agatha. "It would be strange if any one wanted to drive you from my house."

Winnie was excited, and driven out of her usual self-restraint. Perhaps she had begun to soften a little. She gave way to momentary tears, and kissed Aunt Agatha, whose heart in a moment forsook all other pre-occupations, and returned for ever and ever to her child.

"Yes, I have come to see you," she cried; "and don't let them come and hunt me to death. I have done nothing to them. I have injured nobody; and I will not be put upon my trial for anybody in the wide world."

"My dear love! my poor darling child!" was all that Aunt Agatha said.

And then Winnie dried her eyes. "I may as well say it now," she said. "I will give an account of myself to nobody but you; and if he should come after me here—"

"Yes, Winnie darling?" said Aunt Agatha, in great suspense, as Mrs. Percival stopped to take breath.

"Nothing in the world will make me see him—nothing in the world!" cried Winnie. "It is best you should know. It is no good asking me—nothing in the world!"

"Oh, Winnie, my dear child!" cried Aunt Agatha in anxious remonstrance, but she was not permitted to say any more. Winnie kissed her again in a peremptory way, and led her to the door, and closed it softly upon her. She had given forth her ultimatum, and now it was for her defender to carry on the fight.

But within a few days another crisis arose of a less manageable kind. Uncle Penrose made everybody highly uncomfortable, and left stings in each individual mind, but fortunately business called him back after two days to his natural sphere. And Sir Edward was affronted, and did not return to the charge; and Mrs. Percival, with a natural yearning, had begun to make friends with her nephew, and draw him to her side to support her if need should be. And Mary was preparing to go with her boy after a while to Earlston; and Hugh himself found frequent business at Carlisle, and went and came continually; when it happened one day that her friends came to pay Mrs. Ochterlony a visit, to offer their condolences and congratulations upon Hugh's succession and his uncle's death.

They came into the drawing-room before any one was aware; and Winnie was there, with her shawl round her as usual. All the ladies of the Cottage were there: Aunt Agatha seated within sight of her legacy, the precious Henri Deux, which was all arranged in a tiny little cupboard, shut in with glass, which Hugh had found for her; and Mary working as usual for her boys. Winnie was the one who never had anything to do; instead of doing anything, poor soul, she wound her arms closer and closer into her shawl. It was not a common visit that was about to be paid. There was Mrs. Kirkman, and Mrs. Askell, and the doctor's sister, and the wife of a new Captain, who had come with them; and they all swept in and kissed Mary, and took possession of the place. They kissed Mary, and shook hands with Aunt Agatha; and then Mrs. Kirkman stopped short, and looked at Winnie, and made her a most stately curtsey. The others would have done the same, had their courage been as good; but both Mrs. Askell and Miss Sorbette were doubtful how Mary would take it, and compromised, and made some sign of recognition in a distant way. Then they all subsided into chairs, and did their best to talk.

"It is a coincidence that brings us all here together to-day," said Mrs. Kirkman; "I hope it is not too much for you, my dear Mary. How affecting was poor Mr. Ochterlony's death! I hope you have that evidence of his spiritual state which is the only consolation in such a case."

"He was a good man," said Mary; "very kind, and generous, and just. Hugh, who knew him best, was very fond of him—"

"Ah, fond of him; We are all fond of our friends," said Mrs. Kirkman; "but the only real comfort is to know what was their spiritual state. Do you know I am very anxious about your parish here. If you would but take up the work, it would be a great thing. And I would like to have a talk with Hugh: he is in an important position now; he may influence for good so many people. Dear Miss Seton, I am sure you will help me all you can to lead him in the right way."

"He is such a dear!" said Emma Askell. "He has been to see us four or five times: it was so good of him. I didn't know Mr. Ochterlony, Madonna dear; so you need not be vexed if I say right out that I am so glad. Hugh will make a perfect Squire; and he is such a dear. Oh, Miss Seton, I know you will agree with me—isn't he a dear?"

"He's a very fine young fellow," said Miss Sorbette. "I remember him when he was only that height, so I think I may speak. It seems like yesterday when he was at that queer marriage, you know—such a funny, wistful little soul. I daresay you recollect, Mary, for it was rather hard upon you."

"We all recollect," said Mrs. Kirkman; "don't speak of it. Thank Heaven, it has done those dear children no harm."

There was something ringing in Mary's ears, but she could not say a word. Her voice seemed to die on her lips, and her heart in her breast. If her boys were to hear, and demand an explanation! Something almost as bad happened. Winnie, who was looking on, whom nobody had spoken to, now took it upon herself to interpose.

"What marriage?" she said. "It must have been something of consequence, and I should like to know."

This question fluttered the visitors in the strangest way; none of them looked at Winnie, but they looked at each other, with a sudden movement of skirts and consultation of glances. Mrs. Kirkman put her bonnet-strings straight, slowly, and sighed; and Miss Sorbette bent down her head with great concern, and exclaimed that she had lost the button of her glove; and Emma Askell shrank behind backs, and made a great rustling with her dress. "Oh, it was nothing at all," she said; being by nature the least hard-hearted of the three. That was all the answer they gave to Winnie, who was the woman who had been talked about. And the next moment all three rushed at Mary, and spoke to her in the same breath, in their agitation; for at least they were agitated by the bold coup they had made. It was a stroke which Winnie felt. She turned very red and then very pale, but she did not flinch: she sat there in the foreground, close to them all, till they had said everything they had to say; and held her head high, ready to meet the eye of anybody who dared to look at her. As for the other members of the party, Mary had been driven hors du combat, and for the first moment was too much occupied with her own feelings to perceive the insult that had been directed at her sister; and Aunt Agatha was too much amazed to take any part. Thus they sat, the visitors in a rustle of talk and silk and agitation and uneasiness, frightened at the step they had taken, with Winnie immovable and unflinching in the midst of them, until the other ladies of the house recovered their self-possession. Then an unquestionable chill fell upon the party. When such visitors came to Kirtell on ordinary occasions, they were received with pleasant hospitality. It was not a ceremonious call, it was a frank familiar visit, prolonged for an hour or two; and though five o'clock tea had not then been invented, it was extemporized for the occasion, and fruit was gathered, and flowers, and all the pleasant country details that please visitors from a town. And when it was time to go, everybody knew how many minutes were necessary for the walk to the station, and the Cottage people escorted their visitors, and waved their hands to them as the train started. Such had been the usual routine of a visit to Kirtell. But matters were changed now. After that uneasy rustle and flutter, a silence equally uneasy fell upon the assembly. The new Captain's wife, who had never been there before, could not make it out. Mrs. Percival sat silent, the centre of the group, and nobody addressed a word to her; and Aunt Agatha leaned back in her chair and never opened her lips; and even Mary gave the coldest, briefest answers to the talk which everybody poured upon her at once. It was all quite mysterious and unexplicable to the Captain's wife.

"I am afraid we must not stay," Mrs. Kirkman said at last, who was the superior officer. "I hope we have not been too much for you, my dear Mary. I want so much to have a long talk with you about the parish and the work that is to be done in it. If I could only see you take it up! But I see you are not able for it now."

"I am not the clergyman," said Mary, whose temper was slightly touched. "You know that never was my rôle."

"Ah, my dear friend!" said Mrs. Kirkman, and she bent her head forward pathetically to Mrs. Ochterlony's, and shook it in her face, and kissed her, "if one could always feel ones' self justified in leaving it in the hands of the clergyman! But you are suffering, and I will say no more to-day."

And Miss Sorbette, too, made a pretence of having something very absorbing to say to Mrs. Ochterlony; and the exit of the visitors was made in a kind of scuffle very different from their dignified entrance. They had to walk back to the station in the heat of the afternoon, and to sit there in the dusty waiting-room an hour and a half waiting for the train. Seldom is justice so promptly or poetically executed. And they took to upbraiding each other, as was natural, and Emma Askell cried, and said it was not her fault. And the new Captain's wife asked audibly, if that was the Madonna Mary the gentlemen talked about, and the house that was so pleasant? Perhaps the three ladies in the Cottage did not feel much happier; Aunt Agatha rose up tremblingly when they were gone, and went to Winnie and kissed her. "Oh, what does it all mean?" Miss Seton cried. It was the first time she had seen any one belonging to her pointed at by the finger of scorn.

"It means that Mary's friends don't approve of me," said Winnie; but her lip quivered as she spoke. She did not care! But yet she was a woman, and she did care, whatever she might say.

And then Mary, too, came and kissed her sister. "My poor Winnie!" she said, tenderly. She could not be her sister's partizan out and out, like Aunt Agatha. Her heart was sore for what she knew, and for what she did not know; but she could not forsake her own flesh and blood. The inquisition of Uncle Penrose and Sir Edward was a very small matter indeed in comparison with this woman's insult, but yet it drew Winnie imperceptibly closer to her only remaining friends.

CHAPTER XXXII

It was not likely that Will, who had speculated so much on the family history, should remain unmoved by all these changes. His intellect was very lively, and well developed, and his conscience was to a great extent dormant. If he had been in the way of seeing, or being tempted into actual vices, no doubt the lad's education would have served him in better stead, and his moral sense would have been awakened. But he had been injured in his finer moral perceptions by a very common and very unsuspected agency. He had been in the way of hearing very small offences indeed made into sins. Aunt Agatha had been almost as hard upon him forgetting a text as if he had told a lie—and his tutor, the curate, had treated a false quantity, or a failure of memory, as a moral offence. That was in days long past, and it was Wilfrid now who found out his curate in false quantities, and scorned him accordingly; and who had discovered that Aunt Agatha herself, if she remembered the text, knew very little about it. This system of making sins out of trifles had passed quite harmlessly over Hugh and Islay; but Wilfrid's was the exceptional mind to which it did serious harm. And the more he discovered that the sins of his childhood were not sins, the more confused did his mind become, and the more dull his conscience, as to those sins of thought and feeling, which were the only ones at present into which he was tempted. What had any one to do with the complexion of his thoughts? If he felt one way or another, what matter was it to any one but himself? Other people might dissemble and take credit for the emotions approved of by public opinion, but he would be true and genuine. And accordingly he did not see why he should pretend to be pleased at Hugh's advancement. He was not pleased. He said to himself that it went against all the rules of natural justice. Hugh was no better than he; on the contrary, he was less clever, less capable of mental exertion, which, so far as Will knew, was the only standard of superiority; and yet he was Mr. Ochterlony of Earlston, with a house and estate, with affairs to manage, and tenants to influence, and the Psyche and the Venus to do what he liked with: whereas Will was nobody, and was to have two thousand pounds for all his inheritance. He had been talking, too, a great deal to Mr. Penrose, and that had not done him any good; for Uncle Penrose's view was that nothing should stand in the way of acquiring money or other wealth—nothing but the actual law. To do anything dishonest, that could be punished, was of course pure insanity—not to say crime; but to let any sort of false honour, or pride, or delicacy stand between you and the acquisition of money was almost as great insanity, according to his ideas. "Go into business and keep at it, and you may buy him up—him and his beggarly estate"—had been Uncle Penrose's generous suggestion; and it was a good deal in Wilfrid's mind. To be sure it was quite opposed to the intellectual tendency which led him to quite a different class of pursuits. But what was chiefly before him in the meantime was Hugh, preferred to so much distinction, and honour, and glory; and yet if the truth were known, a very stupid fellow in comparison with himself—Will. And it was not only that he was Mr. Ochterlony of Earlston. He was first with everybody. Sir Edward, who took but little notice of Will, actually consulted Hugh, and he was the first to be thought of in any question that occurred in the Cottage; and, what went deepest of all, Nelly—Nelly Askell whom Will had appropriated, not as his love, for his mind had not as yet opened to that idea, but as his sympathizer-in-chief—the listener to all his complaints and speculations—his audience whom nobody had any right to take from him—Nelly had gone over to his brother's side. And the idea of going into business, even at the cost of abandoning all his favourite studies, and sticking close to it, and buying him up—him and his beggarly estate—was a good deal at this moment in Wilfrid's thoughts. Even the new-comer, Winnie, who might if she pleased have won him to herself, had preferred Hugh. So that he was alone on his side, and everybody was on his brother's—a position which often confuses right and wrong, even to minds least set upon their own will and way.

He was sauntering on Kirtell banks a few days after the visit above recorded, in an unusually uncomfortable state of mind. Mrs. Askell had felt great compunction about her share in that event, and she had sent Nelly, who was known to be a favourite at the cottage, with a very anxious letter, assuring her dear Madonna that it was not her fault. Mary had not received the letter with much favour, but she had welcomed Nelly warmly; and Hugh had found means to occupy her attention; and Will, who saw no place for him, had wandered out, slightly sulky, to Kirtell-side. He was free to come and go as he liked. Nobody there had any particular need of him; and a solitary walk is not a particularly enlivening performance when one has left an entire household occupied and animated behind. As he wound his way down the bank he saw another passenger on the road before him, who was not of a description of man much known on Kirtell-side. It seemed to Will that he had seen this figure somewhere before. It must be one of the regiment, one of the gentlemen of whom the Cottage was a little jealous, and who were thought to seek occasions of visiting Kirtell oftener than politeness required. As Will went on, however, he saw that the stranger was somebody whom he had never seen before, and curiosity was a lively faculty in him, and readily awakened. Neither was the unknown indifferent to Will's appearance or approach; on the contrary, he turned round at the sound of the youth's step and scrutinized him closely, and lingered that he might be overtaken. He was tall, and a handsome man, still young, and with an air which only much traffic with the world confers. No man could have got that look and aspect who had lived all his life on Kirtell; and even Will, inexperienced as he was, could recognise this. It did not occur to him, quick as his intellect was at putting things together, who it was; but a little expectation awoke in his mind as he quickened his steps to overtake the stranger, who was clearly waiting to be overtaken.

"I beg your pardon," he said, as soon as Wilfrid had come up to him; "are you young Ochterlony? I mean, one of the young Ochterlonys?"

"No," said Will, "and yet yes; I am not young Ochterlony, but I am one of the young Ochterlonys, as you say."

Upon this his new companion gave a keen look at him, as if discerning some meaning under the words.

"I thought so," he said; "and I am Major Percival, whom you may have heard of. It is a queer question, but I suppose there is no doubt that my wife is up there?"

He gave a little jerk with his hand as he spoke in the direction of the Cottage. He was standing on the very same spot where he had seen Winnie coming to him the day they first pledged their troth; and though he was far from being a good man, he remembered it, having still a certain love for his wife, and the thought gave bitterness to his tone.

"Yes, she is there," said Will.

"Then I will thank you to come back with me," said Percival. "I don't want to go and send in my name, like a stranger. Take me in by the garden, where you enter by the window. I suppose nobody can have any objection to my seeing my wife: your aunt, perhaps, or your mother?"

"Perhaps she does not wish to see you," said Will.

The stranger laughed.

"It is a pleasant suggestion," he said; "but at least you cannot object to admit me, and let me try."

Wilfrid might have hesitated if he had been more fully contented with everybody belonging to him; but, to tell the truth, he knew no reason why Winnie's husband should not see her. He had not been sufficiently interested to wish to fathom the secret, and he had accepted, not caring much about it, Aunt Agatha's oft-repeated declaration, that their visitor had arrived so suddenly to give her "a delightful surprise." Wilfrid did not care much about the matter, and he made no inquiries into it. He turned accordingly with the new-comer, not displeased to be the first of the house to make acquaintance with him. Percival had all a man's advantage over his wife in respect to wear and tear. She had lost her youth, her freshness, and all that gave its chief charm to her beauty, but he had lost very little in outward appearance. Poor Winnie's dissipations were the mildest pleasures in comparison with his, and yet he had kept even his youth, while hers was gone for ever. And he had not the air of a bad man—perhaps he was not actually a bad man. He did whatever he liked without acknowledging any particular restraint of duty, or truth, or even honour, except the limited standard of honour current among men of his class—but he had no distinct intention of being wicked; and he was, beyond dispute, a little touched by seeing, as he had just done, the scene of that meeting which had decided Winnie's fate. He went up the bank considerably softened, and disposed to be very kind. It was he who had been in the wrong in their last desperate struggle, and he found it easy to forgive himself; and Aunt Agatha's garden, and the paths, and flower-pots he remembered so well, softened him more and more. If he had gone straight in, and nothing had happened, he would have kissed his wife in the most amiable way, and forgiven her, and been in perfect amity with everybody—but this was not how it was to be.

Winnie was sitting as usual, unoccupied, indoors. As she was not doing anything her eyes were free to wander further than if they had been more particularly engaged, and at that moment, as it happened, they were turned in the direction of the window from which she had so often watched Sir Edward's light. All at once she started to her feet. It was what she had looked for from the first; what, perhaps, in the stagnation of the household quiet here she had longed for. High among the roses and waving honeysuckles she caught a momentary glimpse of a head which she could have recognised at any distance. At that sight all the excitement of the interrupted struggle rushed back into her heart. A pang of fierce joy, and hatred, and opposition moved her. There he stood who had done her so much wrong; who had trampled on all her feelings and insulted her, and yet pretended to love her, and dared to seek her. Winnie did not say anything to her companions; indeed she was too much engrossed at the moment to remember that she had any companions. She turned and fled without a word, disappearing swiftly, noiselessly, in an instant, as people have a gift of doing when much excited. She was shut up in her room, with her door locked, before any one knew she had stirred. It is true he was not likely to come upstairs and assail her by force; but she did not think of that. She locked her door and sat down, with her heart beating, and her breath coming quick, expecting, hoping—she would herself have said fearing—an attack.

Winnie thought it was a long time before Aunt Agatha came, softly, tremulously, to her door, but in reality it was but a few minutes. He had come in, and had taken matters with a high hand, and had demanded to see his wife. "He will think it is we who are keeping you away from him. He will not believe you do not want to come," said poor Aunt Agatha, at the door.

"Nothing shall induce me to see him," said Winnie, admitting her. "I told you so: nothing in the world—not if he were to go down on his knees—not if he were—"

"My dear love, I don't think he means to go down on his knees," said Aunt Agatha, anxiously. "He does not think he is in the wrong. Oh, Winnie, my darling!—if it was only for the sake of other people—to keep them from talking, you know—"

"Aunt Agatha, you are mistaken if you think I care," said Winnie. "As for Mary's friends, they are old-fashioned idiots. They think a woman should shut herself up like an Eastern slave when her husband is not there. I have done nothing to be ashamed of. And he—Oh, if you knew how he had insulted me!—Oh, if you only knew! I tell you I will not consent to see him, for nothing in this world."

Winnie was a different woman as she spoke. She was no longer the worn and faded creature she had been. Her eyes were sparkling, her cheeks glowing. It was a clouded and worn magnificence, but still it was a return to her old splendour.

"Oh, Winnie, my dear love, you are fond of him in spite of all," said Aunt Agatha. "It will all come right, my darling, yet. You are fond of each other in spite of all."

"You don't know what you say," said Winnie, in a blaze of indignation.—"Fond of him!—if you could but know! Tell him to think of how we parted. Tell him I will never more trust myself near him again."

It was with this decision, immovable and often repeated, that Miss Seton at last returned to her undesired guest. But she sent for Mary to come and speak to her before she went into the drawing-room. Aunt Agatha was full of schemes and anxious desires. She could not make people do what was right, but if she could so plot and manage appearances as that they should seem to do what was right, surely that was better than nothing. She sent for Mrs. Ochterlony into the dining-room, and she began to take out the best silver, and arrange the green finger-glasses, to lose no time.

"What is the use of telling all the world of our domestic troubles?" said Aunt Agatha. "My dear, though Winnie will not see him, would it not be better to keep him to dinner, and show that we are friendly with him all the same? So long as he is with us, nobody is to know that Winnie keeps in her own room. After the way these people behaved to the poor dear child—"

"They were very foolish and ill-bred," said Mary; "but it was because she had herself been foolish, not because she was away from her husband: and I don't like him to be with my boys."

"But for your dear sister's sake! Oh, Mary, my love, for Winnie's sake!" said Aunt Agatha; and Mary yielded, though she saw no benefit in it. It was her part to go back into the drawing-room, and make the best of Winnie's resistance, and convey the invitation to this unlooked-for guest, while Aunt Agatha looked after the dinner, and impressed upon Peggy that perhaps Major Percival might not be able to stay long; and was it not sad that the very day her husband came to see her, Mrs. Percival should have such a very bad headache? "She is lying down, poor dear, in hopes of being able to sit up a little in the evening," said the anxious but innocent deceiver—doubly innocent since she deceived nobody, not even the housemaid, far less Peggy. As for Major Percival, he was angry and excited, as Winnie was, but not to an equal extent. He did not believe in his wife's resistance. He sat down in the familiar room, and expected every moment to see Winnie rush down in her impulsive way, and throw herself into his arms. Their struggles had not terminated in this satisfactory way of late, but still she had gone very far in leaving him, and he had gone very far in condescending to come to seek her; and there seemed no reason why the monster quarrel should not end in a monster reconciliation, and all go on as before.

But it was bad policy to leave him with Mary. The old instinctive dislike that had existed between them from the first woke up again unawares. Mrs. Ochterlony could not conceal the fact that she took no pleasure in his society, and had no faith in him. She stayed in the room because she could not help it, but she did not pretend to be cordial. When he addressed himself to Will, and took the boy into his confidence, and spoke to him as to another man of the world, he could see, and was pleased to see, the contraction in Mary's forehead. In this one point she was afraid of him, or at least he thought so. Winnie stayed upstairs with the door locked, watching to see him go away; and Hugh, to whom Winnie had been perhaps more confidential than to any one else in the house, went out and in, in displeasure ill-concealed, avoiding all intercourse with the stranger. And Mary sat on thorns, bearing him unwilling company, and Nelly watched and marvelled. Poor Aunt Agatha all the time arranged her best silver, and filled the old-fashioned épergne with flowers, thinking she was doing the very best for her child, saving her reputation, and leaving the way open for a reconciliation between her and her husband, and utterly unconscious of any other harm that could befall.

When the dinner-hour arrived, however (which was five o'clock, an hour which Aunt Agatha thought a good medium between the early and the late), Major Percival's brow was very cloudy. He had waited and listened, and Winnie had not come, and now, when they sat down at table, she was still invisible. "Does not my wife mean to favour us with her company?" he asked, insolently, incredulous after all that she could persevere so long, and expecting to hear that she was only "late as usual;" upon which Aunt Agatha looked at Mary with anxious beseeching eyes.

"My sister is not coming down to-day," said Mary, with hesitation, "at least I believe—"

"Oh, my dear love, you know it is only because she has one of her bad headaches!" Aunt Agatha added, precipitately, with tears of entreaty in her eyes.

Percival looked at them both, and he thought he understood it all. It was Mary who was abetting her sister in her rebellion, encouraging her to defy him. It was she who was resisting Miss Seton's well-meant efforts to bring them together. He saw it all as plain, or thought he saw it, as if he had heard her tactics determined upon. He had let her alone, and restrained his natural impulse to injure the woman he disliked, but now she had set herself in his way, and let her look to it. This dinner, which poor Aunt Agatha had brought about against everybody's will, was as uncomfortable a meal as could be imagined. She was miserable herself, dreading every moment that he might burst out into a torrent of rage against Winnie before "the servants," or that Winnie's bell would ring violently and she would send a message—so rash and inconsiderate as she was—to know when Major Percival was going away. And nobody did anything to help her out of it. Mary sat at the foot of the table as stately as a queen, showing the guest only such attentions as were absolutely necessary. Hugh, except when he talked to Nelly, who sat beside him, was as disagreeable as a young man who particularly desires to be disagreeable and feels that his wishes have not been consulted, can be. And as for the guest himself, his countenance was black as night. It was a heavy price to pay for the gratification of saying to everybody that Winnie's husband had come to see her, and had spent the day at the Cottage. But then Aunt Agatha had not the remotest idea that beyond the annoyance of the moment it possibly could do any harm.

It was dreadful to leave him with the boys after dinner, who probably—or at least Hugh—might not be so civil as was to be wished; but still more dreadful ten minutes after to hear Hugh's voice with Nelly in the garden. Why had he left his guest?

"He left me," said Hugh. "He went out under the verandah to smoke his cigar. I don't deny I was very glad to get away."

"But I am sure, Hugh, you are very fond of smoking cigars," said Aunt Agatha, in her anxiety and fright.

"Not always," Hugh answered, "nor under all circumstances." And he laughed and coloured a little, and looked at Nelly by his side, who blushed too.

"So there is nobody with him but Will?" said Aunt Agatha with dismay, as she went in to where Mary was sitting; and the news was still more painful to Mary. Will was the only member of the family who was really civil to the stranger, except Aunt Agatha, whose anxiety was plainly written in her countenance. He was sitting now under the verandah which shaded the dining-room windows, quite at the other side of the house, smoking his cigar, and Will sat dutifully and not unwillingly by, listening to his talk. It was a new kind of talk to Will—the talk of a man blasé yet incapable of existing out of the world of which he was sick—a man who did not pretend to be a good man, nor even possessed of principles. Perhaps the parish of Kirtell in general would not have thought it very edifying talk.

"It is he who has come into the property, I suppose," said Percival, pointing lazily with his cigar towards the other end of the garden, where Hugh was visible far off with Nelly. "Get on well with him, eh? I should say not if the question was asked of me?"

"Oh yes, well enough," said Will, in momentary confusion, and with a clouding of his brows. "There is nothing wrong with him. It's the system of the eldest sons that is wrong. I have nothing to say against Hugh."

"By Jove," said Percival, "the difficulty is to find out which is anybody's eldest son. I never find fault with systems, for my part."

"Oh, about that there can't be any doubt," said Will; "he is six years older than I am. I am only the youngest; though I don't see what it matters to a man, for my part, being born in '32 or '38."

"Sometimes it makes a great deal of difference," said Percival; and then he paused: for a man, even when he is pushed on by malice and hate and all uncharitableness, may hesitate before he throws a firebrand into an innocent peaceful house. However, after his pause he resumed, making a new start as it were, and doing it deliberately, "sometimes it may make a difference to a man whether he was born in '37 or '38. You were born in '38 were you? Ah! I ought to recollect."

"Why ought you to recollect?" asked Will, startled by the meaning of his companion's face.

"I was present at a ceremony that took place about then," said Percival; "a curious sort of story. I'll tell it you some time. How is the property left, do you know? Is it to him in particular as being the favourite, and that sort of thing?—or is it simply to the eldest son?"

"Simply to the eldest son," said Will, more and more surprised.

Percival gave such a whistle as Uncle Penrose had given when he heard of the museum, and nodded his head repeatedly. "It would be good fun to turn the tables," he said, as if he were making a remark to himself.

"How could you turn the tables? What do you mean? What do you know about it?" cried Will, who by this time was getting excited. Hugh came within his line of vision now and then, with Nelly—always with Nelly. It was only the younger brother, the inferior member of the household, who was left with the unwelcome guest. If any one could turn the tables! And again he said, almost fiercely, "What do you mean?"

"It is very easy to tell you what I mean; and I wonder what your opinion will be of systems then?" said Percival. "By Jove! it's an odd position, and I don't envy you. You think you're the youngest, and you were born as you say in '38."

"Good heavens! what is that to do with it?" cried Wilfrid. "Of course I was born in '38. Tell me what you mean."

"Well, then, I'll tell you what I mean," said Percival, tossing away the end of his cigar, "and plainly too. That fellow there, who gives himself such airs, is no more the eldest son than I am. The property belongs to you."

CHAPTER XXXIII

Wilfrid was so stunned by the information thus suddenly given him, that he had but a confused consciousness of the explanations which followed. He was aware that it was all made clear to him, and that he uttered the usual words of assent and conviction; but in his mind he was too profoundly moved, too completely shaken and unsettled, to be aware of anything but the fact thus strangely communicated. It did not occur to him for a moment that it was not a fact. He saw no improbability, nothing unnatural in it. He was too young to think that anything was unlikely because it was extraordinary, or to doubt what was affirmed with so much confidence. But, in the meantime, the news was so startling, that it upset his mental balance, and made him incapable of understanding the details. Hugh was not the eldest son. It was he who was the eldest son. This at the moment was all that his mind was capable of taking in. He stayed by Percival as long as he remained, and had the air of devouring everything the other said; and he went with him to the railway station when he went away. Percival, for his part, having once made the plunge, showed no disinclination to explain everything, but for his own credit told his story most fully, and many particulars undreamt of when the incident took place. But he might have spared his pains so far as Will was concerned. He was aware of the one great fact stated to him to begin with, but of nothing more.

The last words which Percival said as he took leave of his young companion at the railway were, however, caught by Wilfrid's half-stupefied ears. They were these: "I will stay in Carlisle for some days. You can hear where I am from Askell, and perhaps we may be of use to each other." This, beyond the startling and extraordinary piece of news which had shaken him like a sudden earthquake, was all Percival had said, so far as Will was aware. "That fellow is no more the eldest son than I am—the property is yours;" and "I will stay in Carlisle for some days—perhaps we may be of use to each other." The one expression caught on the other in his mind, which was utterly confused and stunned for the first time in his life. He turned them over and over as he walked home alone, or rather, they turned over and over in his memory, as if possessed of a distinct life; and so it happened that he had got home again and opened the gate and stumbled into the garden before he knew what the terrific change was which had come over everything, or had time to realize his own sensations. It was such a moment as is very sweet in a cottage-garden. They had all been watering the flowers in the moment of relief after Percival's departure, and the fragrance of the grateful soil was mounting up among the other perfumes of the hour. Hugh and Nelly were still sprinkling a last shower upon the roses, and in the distance in the field upon which the garden opened were to be seen two figures wandering slowly over the grass—Winnie, whom Aunt Agatha had coaxed out to breathe the fresh air after her self-imprisonment, and Miss Seton herself, with a shawl over her head. And the twilight was growing insensibly dimmer and dimmer, and the dew falling, and the young moon sailing aloft. When Mary came across the lawn, her long dress sweeping with a soft rustle over the grass, a sudden horror seized Wilfrid. It took him all his force of mind and will to keep his face to her and await her coming. His face was not the treacherous kind of face which betrays everything; but still there was in it a look of preoccupation which Mary could not fail to see.

"Is he gone?" she said, as she came up. "You are sure he has gone, Will? It was kind of you to be civil to him; but I am almost afraid you are interested in him too."

"Would it be wrong to be interested in him?" said Will.

"I don't like him," said Mary, simply; and then she added, after a pause, "I have no confidence in him. I should be very sorry to see any of my boys attracted by the society of such a man."

And it was at this moment that his new knowledge rushed upon Wilfrid's mind and embittered it; any of her boys, of whom he was the youngest and least important; and yet she must know what his real position was, and that he ought to be the chief of all.

"I don't care a straw for him," said Will, hastily; "but he knows a great many things, and I was interested in his talk."

"What was he saying to you?" said Mrs. Ochterlony.

He looked into her face, and he saw that there was uneasiness in it, just as she, looking at him, saw signs of a change which he was himself unaware of; and in his impetuosity he was very near saying it all out and betraying himself. But then his uncertainty of all the details stood him in good stead.

"He was saying lots of things," said Will. "I am sure I can't tell you all that he was saying. If I were Hugh I would not let Nelly make a mess of herself with those roses. I am going in-doors."

"A lovely evening like this is better than the best book in the world," said Mary. "Stay with me, and talk to me, Will. You see I am the only one who is left alone."

"I don't care about lovely evenings," said Will; "I think you should all come in. It is getting dreadfully cold. And as for being alone, I don't see how that can be, when they are all there. Good night, mother. I think I shall go to bed."

"Why should you go to bed so early?" said Mary; but he was already gone, and did not hear her. And as he went, he turned right round and looked at Hugh and Nelly, who were still together. When Mrs. Ochterlony remarked that look, she was at once troubled and comforted. She thought her boy was jealous of the way in which his brother engrossed the young visitor, and she was sorry, but yet knew that it was not very serious—while, at the same time, it was a comfort to her to attribute his pre-occupation to anything but Percival's conversation. So she lingered about the lawn a little, and looked wistfully at the soft twilight country, and the wistful moon. She was the only one who was alone. The two young creatures were together, and they were happy; and poor Winnie, though she was far from happy, was buoyed up by the absorbing passion and hostility which had to-day reached one of its climaxes, and had Aunt Agatha for her slave, ready to receive all the burning outburst of grievance and misery. This fiery passion which absorbed her whole being was almost as good as being happy, and gave her mind full occupation. But as for Mary, she was by herself, and all was twilight with her; and the desertion of her boy gave her a little chill at her heart. So she, too, went in presently, and had the lamp lighted, and sat alone in the room, which was bright and yet dim—with a clear circle of light round the table, yet shadowy as all the corners are of a summer evening, when there is no fire to aid the lamp. But she did not find her son there. His discontent had gone further than to be content with a book, as she had expected; and he had really disappeared for the night.

"I can't have you take possession of Nelly like this," she said to Hugh, when, after a long interval, they came in. "We all want a share of her. Poor Will has gone to bed quite discontented. You must not keep her all to yourself."

"Oh! is he jealous?" said Hugh, laughing; and there was no more said about it; for Will's jealousy in this respect was not a thing to alarm anybody much.

But Will had not gone to bed. He was seated in his room at the table, leaning his head upon both his hands, and staring into the flame of his candle. He was trying to put what he had heard into some sort of shape. That Hugh, who was downstairs so triumphant and successful, was, after all, a mere impostor; that it was he himself, whom nobody paid any particular attention to, who was the real heir; that his instinct had not deceived him, but from his birth he had been ill-used and oppressed: these thoughts went all circling through his mind as the moths circled round his light, taking now a larger, and now a shorter flight. This strange sense that he had been right all along was, for the moment, the first feeling in his mind. He had been disinherited and thrust aside, but still he had felt all along that it was he who was the natural heir; and there was a satisfaction in having it thus proved and established. This was the first distinct reflection he was conscious of amid the whirl of thoughts; and then came the intoxicating sense that he could now enter upon his true position, and be able to arrange everybody's future wisely and generously, without any regard for mere proprieties, or for the younger brother's two thousand pounds. Strange to say, in the midst of this whirlwind of egotistical feeling, Will rushed all at once into imaginations that were not selfish, glorious schemes of what he would do for everybody. He was not ungenerous, nor unkind, but only it was a necessity with him that generosity and kindness should come from and not to himself.

All this passed through the boy's mind before it ever occurred to him what might be the consequences to others of his extraordinary discovery, or what effect it must have upon his mother, and the character of the family. He was self-absorbed, and it did not occur to him in that light. Even when he did come to think of it, he did it in the calmest way. No doubt his mother would be annoyed; but she deserved to be annoyed—she who had so long kept him out of his rights; and, after all, it would still be one of her sons who would have Earlston. And as for Hugh, Wilfrid had the most generous intentions towards him. There was, indeed, nothing that he was not ready to do for his brothers. As soon as he believed that all was to be his, he felt himself the steward of the family. And then his mind glanced back upon the Psyche and the Venus, and upon Earlston, which might be made into a fitter shrine for these fair creations. These ideas filled him like wine, and went to his head, and made him dizzy; and all the time he was as unconscious of the moral harm, and domestic treachery, as if he had been one of the lower animals; and no scruple of any description, and no doubt of what it was right and necessary to do, had so much as entered into his primitive and savage mind.

We call his mind savage and primitive because it was at this moment entirely free from those complications of feeling and dreadful conflict of what is desirable, and what is right, which belong to the civilized and cultivated mind. Perhaps Will's affections were not naturally strong; but, at all events, he gave in to this temptation as a man might have given in to it in the depths of Africa, where the "good old rule" and "simple plan" still exist and reign; and where everybody takes what he has strength to take, and he keeps who can. This was the real state of the case in Wilfrid's mind. It had been supposed to be Hugh's right, and he had been obliged to give in; now it was his right, and Hugh would have to make up his mind to it. What else was there to say? So far as Will could see, the revolution would be alike certain and instantaneous. It no more occurred to him to doubt the immediate effect of the new fact than to doubt its truth. Perhaps it was his very egotism, as well as his youth and inexperience, which made him so credulous. It had been wonder enough to him how anybody could leave him in an inferior position, even while he was only the youngest; to think of anybody resisting his rights, now that he had rights, was incredible.

Yet when the morning came, and the sober daylight brightened upon his dreams, Will, notwithstanding all his confidence, began to see the complication of circumstances. How was he to announce his discovery to his mother? How was he to acquaint Hugh with the change in their mutual destinies? What seemed so easy and simple to him the night before, became difficult and complicated now. He began to have a vague sense that they would insist, that Mrs. Ochterlony would fight for her honour, and Hugh for his inheritance, and that in claiming his own rights, he would have to rob his mother of her good name, and put a stigma ineffaceable upon his brother. This idea startled him, and took away his breath; but it did not make him falter; Uncle Penrose's suggestion about buying up him and his beggarly estate, and Major Percival's evident entire indifference to the question whether anything it suited him to do was right or wrong, had had their due effect on Will. He did not see what call he had to sacrifice himself for others. No doubt, he would be sorry for the others, but after all it was his own life he had to take care of, and his own rights that he had to assert. But he mused and knitted his brows over it as he had never done before in his life. Throughout it will be seen that he regarded the business in a very sober, matter-of-fact way—not in the imaginative way which leads you to enter into other people's position, and analyse their possible feelings. As for himself, he who had been so jealous of his mother's visitors, and watched over her so keenly, did not feel somehow that horror which might have been expected at the revelation that she was not the spotless woman he thought her. Perhaps it was the importance of the revelation to himself—perhaps it was a secret disbelief in any guilt of hers—perhaps it was only the stunned condition in which the announcement left him. At all events, he was neither horrified at the thought, nor profoundly impressed by the consciousness that to prove his own rights, would be to take away everything from her, and to shut her up from all intercourse with the honourable and pure. When the morning roused him to a sense of the difficulties as well as the advantages of his discovery, the only thing he could think of was to seek advice and direction from Percival, who was so experienced a man of the world. But it was not so easy to do this without betraying his motive. The only practical expedient was that of escorting Nelly home; which was not a privilege he was anxious for of itself; for though he was jealous that she had been taken away from him, he shrank instinctively from her company in his present state of mind. Yet it was the only thing that could be done.

When the party met at the breakfast-table, there were three of them who were ill at ease. Winnie made her appearance in a state of headache, pale and haggard as on the day of her arrival; and Aunt Agatha was pale too, and could not keep her eyes from dwelling with a too tender affectionateness upon her suffering child. And as for Will, the colour of his young face was indescribable, for youth and health still contended in it with those emotions which contract the skin and empty the veins. But on the other hand, there were Hugh and Nelly handsome and happy, with hearts full of charity to everybody, and confidence in the brightness of their own dawning lot. Mary sat at the head of the table, with the urn before her, superintending all. The uneasiness of last night had passed from her mind; her cheek was almost as round and fair as that of the girl by her side—fairer perhaps in its way; her eyes were as bright as they had ever been; her dress, it is true, was still black, but it had not the shadowy denseness of her widow's garb of old. It was silk, that shone and gave back subdued reflections to the light, and in her hair there were still golden gleams, though mixed with here and there a thread of silver. Her mourning, which prevented any confusion of colours, but left her a sweet-complexioned woman, rich in the subdued tints of nature, in the soft austerity of black and white, did all for her that toilette could do. This was the figure which her son Wilfrid saw at the head of a pretty country breakfast-table, between the flowers and the sunshine—an unblemished matron and a beloved mother. He knew, and it came into his mind as he looked at her, that in the parish, or even in the country, there was nobody more honoured; and yet—He kept staring at her so, and had so scared a look in his eyes, that Mrs. Ochterlony herself perceived it at last.

"What is the matter, Will?" she said. "I could think there was a ghost standing behind you, from your eyes. Why do you look so startled?"

"Nothing," said Will, hastily; "I didn't know I looked startled. A fellow can't help how he looks. Look here, Nelly, if you're going home to-day, I'll go with you, and see you safe there."

"You'll go with her?" said Hugh, with a kind of good-natured elder-brotherly contempt. "Not quite so fast, Will. We can't trust young ladies in your care. I am going with Nelly myself."

"Oh! I am sure Will is very kind," said Nelly; and then she stopped short, and looked first at Mrs. Ochterlony and then at Hugh. Poor Nelly had heard of brothers being jealous of each other, and had read of it in books, and was half afraid that such a case was about to come under her own observation. She was much frightened, and her impulse was to accept Will's guardianship, that no harm might come of it, though the sacrifice to herself would be considerable; but then, what if Hugh should be jealous too?

"I see no reason why you should not both go," said Mrs. Ochterlony: "one of you shall take care of Nelly, and one shall do my commissions; I think that had better be Will—for I put no confidence, just now, in Hugh."

"Of course it must be Will," said Hugh. "A squire of dames requires age and solidity. It is not an office for a younger brother. Your time will come, old fellow; it is mine now."

"Yes, I suppose it is yours now," said Will.

He did not mean to put any extraordinary significance in his tone, but yet he was in such a condition of mind that his very voice betrayed him against his will. Even Winnie, preoccupied as she was, intermitted her own thoughts a moment to look at him, and Hugh reddened, though he could not have told why. There was a certain menace, a certain implication of something behind, which the inexperienced boy had no intention of betraying, but which made themselves apparent in spite of him. And Hugh too grew crimson in spite of himself. He said "By Jove!" and then he laughed, and cleared his mind of it, feeling it absurd to be made angry by the petulance of his boy-brother. Then he turned to Nelly, who had drawn closer to him, fearing that the quarrel was about to take place as it takes place in novels, trembling a little, and yet by the aid of her own good sense, feeling that it could not be so serious after all.

"If we are going to the Lady's Well we must go early," he said; and his face changed when he turned to her. She was growing prettier every day,—every day at least she spent in Hugh's society,—opening and unfolding as to the sun. Her precocious womanliness, if it had been precocious, melted under the new influence, and all the natural developments were quickened. She was more timid, more caressing, less self-reliant, and yet she was still as much as ever head of the house at home.

"But not if it will vex Will," she said, almost in a whisper, in his ear; and the close approach which this whisper made necessary, effaced in an instant all unbrotherly feelings towards Wilfrid from Hugh's mind. They both looked at Will, instinctively, as they spoke, the girl with a little wistful solicitude in case he might be disturbed by the sight of their confidential talk. But Will was quite unmoved. He saw the two draw closer together, and perceived the confidential communication that passed between them, but his countenance did not change in the slightest degree. By this time he was far beyond that.

"You see he does not mind," said Hugh, carrying on the half-articulate colloquy, of which one half was done by thoughts instead of words; and Nelly, with the colour a little deepened on her cheek, looked up at him with a look which Hugh could not half interpret. He saw the soft brightness, the sweet satisfaction in it tinged by a certain gleam of fun, but he did not see that Nelly was for a moment ashamed of herself, and was asking herself how she ever could, for a moment, have supposed Will was jealous. It was a relief to her mind to see his indifference, and yet it filled her with shame.

When the meal was over, and they all dispersed with their different interests, it was Mary who sought to soften what she considered the disappointment of her boy. She came to him as he stood at the window under the verandah, where the day before Percival had given him his fatal illumination, and put her arm within his, and did her best to draw his secret from his clouded and musing eyes.

"My dear boy, let us give in to Hugh," said Mary; "he is only a guest now, you know, and you are at home." She was smiling when she said this, and yet it made her sigh. "And then I think he is getting fond of Nelly, and you are far too young for anything of that sort," Mrs. Ochterlony said, with anxiety and a little doubt, looking him in the face all the time.

"There are some things I am not too young for," said Will. "Mamma, if I were Hugh I would be at home nowhere unless you were at home there as well."

"My dear Will, that is my own doing," said Mary. "Don't blame your brother. I have refused to go to Earlston. It will always be best for me, for all your sakes, to have a house of my own."

"If Earlston had been mine, I should not have minded your refusal," said Will. Perhaps it was as a kind of secret atonement to her and to his own heart that he said so, and yet it was done instinctively, and was the utterance of a genuine feeling. He was meditating in his heart her disgrace and downfall, and yet the first effects of it, if he could succeed, would be to lay everything that he had won by shaming her, at her feet. He would do her the uttermost cruelty and injury without flinching, and then he would overwhelm her with every honour and grandeur that his ill-got wealth could supply. And he did not see how inconsistent those two things were.

"But my boys must mind when I make such a decision," said Mary; and yet she was not displeased with the sentiment. "You shall go to Carlisle for me," she added. "I want some little things, and Hugh very likely would be otherwise occupied. If you would like to have a little change, and go early, do not wait for them, Will. There is a train in half an hour."

"Yes, I would like a little change," he answered vaguely—feeling somehow, for that moment solely, a little prick of conscience. And so it was by his mother's desire to restore his good-humour and cheerfulness, that he was sent upon his mission of harm and treachery.

CHAPTER XXXIV

While Hugh showed Nelly the way to the Lady's Well with that mixture of brotherly tenderness and a dawning emotion of a much warmer kind, which is the privileged entrance of their age into real love and passion; and while Will made his with silent vehemence and ardour to Carlisle, Winnie was left very miserable in the Cottage. It was a moment of reaction after the furious excitement of the previous day. She had held him at bay, she had shown him her contempt and scorn, she had proved to him that their parting was final, and that she would never either see or listen to him again; and the excitement of doing this had so supported her that the day which Aunt Agatha thought a day of such horrible trial to her poor Winnie, was, in short, the only day in which she had snatched a certain stormy enjoyment since she returned to the Cottage. But the day after was different. He was gone; he had assented to her desire, and accepted her decision to all appearance, and poor Winnie was very miserable. For the moment all seemed to her to be over. She had felt sure he would come, and the sense of the continued conflict had buoyed her up; but she did not feel so sure that he would come again, and the long struggle which had occupied her life and thoughts for so many years seemed to have come to an abrupt end, and she had nothing more to look forward to. When she realized this fact, Winnie stood aghast. It is hard when love goes out of a life; but sometimes, when it is only strife and opposition which go out of it, it is almost as hard to bear. She thought she had sighed for peace for many a long day. She had said so times without number, and written it down, and persuaded herself that was what she wanted; but now that she had got it she found out that it was not that she wanted. The Cottage was the very home of peace, and had been so for many years. Even the growth of young life within it, the active minds and varied temperaments of the three boys, and Will's cloudy and uncomfortable disposition, had not hitherto interfered with its character. But so far from being content, Winnie's heart sank within her when she realized the fact, that War had marched off in the person of her husband, and that she was to be "left in peace"—horrible words that paralysed her very soul.

This event, however, if it had done nothing else, had opened her mouth. Her history, which she had kept to herself, began to be revealed. She told her aunt and her sister of his misdeeds, till the energy of her narrative brought something like renewed life to her. She described how she had herself endured, how she had been left to all the dangers that attend a beautiful young woman whose husband has found superior attractions elsewhere; and she gave such sketches of the women whom she imagined to have attracted him, as only an injured wife in a chronic state of wrath and suffering could give. She was so very miserable on that morning that she had no alternative but to speak or die; and as she could not die, she gave her miseries utterance. "And if he can do you any harm—if he can strike me through my friends," said Winnie, "if you know of any point on which he could assail you, you had better keep close guard."

"Oh, my dear love!" said Aunt Agatha, with a troubled smile, "what harm could he do us? He could hurt us only in wounding you; and now we have you safe, my darling, and can defend you, so he never can harm us."

"Of course I never meant you," said Winnie. "But he might perhaps harm Mary. Mary is not like you; she has had to make her way in the world, and no doubt there may be things in her life, as in other people's, that she would not care to have known."

Mary was startled by this speech, which was made half in kindness, half in anger; for the necessity of having somebody to quarrel with had been too great for Winnie. Mrs. Ochterlony was startled, but she could not help feeling sure that her secret was no secret for her sister, and she had no mind for a quarrel, though Winnie wished it.

"There is but one thing in my life that I don't wish to have known," she said, "and Major Percival knows it, and probably so do you, Winnie. But I am here among my own people, and everybody knows all about me. I don't think it would be possible to do me harm here."

"It is because you don't know him," said Winnie. "He would do the Queen harm in her own palace. You don't know what poison he can put on his arrows, and how he shoots them. I believe he will strike me through my friends."

All this time Aunt Agatha looked at the two with her lips apart, as if about to speak; but in reality it was horror and amazement that moved her. To hear them talking calmly of something that must be concealed! of something, at least, that it was better should not be known!—and that in a house which had always been so spotless, so respectable, and did not know what mystery meant!

Mary shook her head, and smiled. She had felt a little anxious the night before about what Percival might be saying to Wilfrid; but, somehow, all that had blown away. Even Will's discontent with his brother had taken the form of jealous tenderness for herself, which, in her thinking, was quite incompatible with any revelation which could have lowered her in his eyes; and it seemed to her as if the old sting, which had so often come back to her, which had put it in the power of her friends in "the regiment" to give her now and then a prick to the heart, had lost its venom. Hugh was peacefully settled in his rights, and Will, if he had heard anything, must have nobly closed his ears to it. Sometimes this strange feeling of assurance and confidence comes on the very brink of the deadliest danger, and it was so with Mary at the present moment that she had no fear.

As for Winnie, she too was thinking principally of her own affairs, and of her sister's only as subsidiary to them. She would have rather believed in the most diabolical rage and assault than in her husband's indifference and the utter termination of hostilities between them. "He will strike me through my friends," she repeated; and perhaps in her heart she was rather glad that there still remained this oblique way of reaching her, and expressed a hope rather than a fear. This conversation was interrupted by Sir Edward, who came in more cheerfully and alertly than usual, taking off his hat as soon as he became visible through the open window. He had heard what he thought was good news, and there was satisfaction in his face.

"So Percival is here," he said. "I can't tell you how pleased I was. Come, we'll have some pleasant days yet in our old age. Why hasn't he come up to the Hall?"

There was an embarrassed pause—embarrassed at least on the part of Miss Seton and Mrs. Ochterlony; while Winnie fixed her eyes, which looked so large and wild in their sunken sockets, steadily upon him, without attempting to make any reply.

"Yes, Major Percival was here yesterday," said Aunt Agatha with hesitation; "he spent the whole day with us—I was very glad to have him, and I am sure he would have gone up to the Hall if he had had time—But he was obliged to go away."

How difficult it was to say all this under the gaze of Winnie's eyes, and with the possibility of being contradicted flatly at any moment, may be imagined. And while Aunt Agatha made her faltering statement, her own look and voice contradicted her; and then there was a still more embarrassed pause, and Sir Edward looked from one to another with amazed and unquiet eyes.

"He came and spent the day with you," said their anxious neighbour, "and he was obliged to go away! I confess I think I merited different treatment. I wish I could make out what you all mean—"

"The fact is, Sir Edward," said Winnie, "that Major Percival was sent away.... He is a very important person, no doubt; but he can't do just as he pleases. My aunt is so good that she tries to keep up a little fiction, but he and I have done with each other," said Winnie in her excitement, notwithstanding that she had been up to this moment so reticent and self-contained.

"Who sent him away?" asked Sir Edward, with a pitiful, confidential look to Aunt Agatha, and a slight shake of his head over the very bad business—a little pantomime which moved Winnie to deeper wrath and discontent.

"I sent him away," said Mrs. Percival, with as much dignity as this ebullition of passion would permit her to assume.

"My dear Winnie," said Sir Edward, "I am very, very sorry to hear this. Think a little of what is before you. You are a young woman still; you are both young people. Do you mean to live here all the rest of your life, and let him go where he pleases—to destruction, I suppose, if he likes? Is that what you mean? And yet we all remember when you would not hear a word even of advice—would not listen to anybody about him. He had not been quite sans reproche when you married him, my dear; and you took him with a knowledge of it. If that had not been the case, there might have been some excuse. But what I want you to do is to look it in the face, and consider a little. It is not only for to-day, or to-morrow—it is for your life."

Winnie gave a momentary shudder, as if of cold, and drew her shawl closer around her. "I had rather not discuss our private affairs," she replied: "they are between ourselves."

"But the fact is, they are not between yourselves," said Sir Edward, who was inspired by the great conviction of doing his duty. "You have taken the public into your confidence by coming here. I am a very old friend, both of yours and his, and I might do some good, if you let me try. I dare say he is not very far from here; and if I might mediate between you—"

A sudden gleam shot out from Winnie's eyes—perhaps it was a sudden wild hope—perhaps it was merely the flash of indignation; but still the proposal moved her. "Mediate!" she said, with an air which was intended for scorn; but her lips quivered as she repeated the word.

"Yes," said Sir Edward, "I might, if you would have confidence in me. No doubt there are wrongs on both sides. He has been impatient, and you have been exacting, and—Where are you going?"

"It is no use continuing this conversation," said Winnie. "I am going to my room. If I were to have more confidence in you than I ever had in any one, it would still be useless. I have not been exacting. I have been—But it is no matter. I trust, Aunt Agatha, that you will forgive me for going to my own room."

Sir Edward shook his head, and looked after her as she withdrew. He looked as if he had said, "I knew how it would be;" and yet he was concerned and sorry. "I have seen such cases before," he said, when Winnie had left the room, turning to Aunt Agatha and Mary, and once more shaking his head: "neither will give in an inch. They know that they are in a miserable condition, but it is neither his fault nor hers. That is how it always is. And only the bystanders can see what faults there are on both sides."

"But I don't think Winnie is so exacting," said Aunt Agatha, with natural partisanship. "I think it is worse than that. She has been telling me two or three things—"

"Oh, yes," said Sir Edward, with mild despair, "they can tell you dozens of things. No doubt he could, on his side. It is always like that; and to think that nothing would have any effect on her!—she would hear no sort of reason—though you know very well you were warned that he was not immaculate before she married him: nothing would have any effect."

"Oh, Sir Edward!" cried Aunt Agatha, with tears in her eyes: "it is surely not the moment to remind us of that."

"For my part, I think it is just the moment," said Sir Edward; and he shook his head, and made a melancholy pause. Then, with an obvious effort to change the subject, he looked round the room, as if that personage might, perhaps, be hidden in some corner, and asked where was Hugh?

"He has gone to show Nelly Askell the way to the Lady's Well," said Mary, who could not repress a smile.

"Ah! he seems disposed to show Nelly Askell the way to a great many things," said Sir Edward. "There it is again you see! Not that I have a word to say against that little thing. She is very nice, and pretty enough; though no more to be compared to what Winnie was at her age—But you'll see Hugh will have engaged himself and forestalled his life before we know where we are."

"It would have been better had they been a little older," said Mary; "but otherwise everything is very suitable; and Nelly is very good, and very sweet—"

Again Sir Edward sighed. "You must know that Hugh might have done a very great deal better," he said. "I don't say that I have any particular objections, but only it is an instance of your insanity in the way of marriage—all you Setons. You go and plunge into it head foremost, without a moment's reflection; and then, of course, when leisure comes—I don't mean you, Mary. What I was saying had no reference to you. So far as I am aware, you were always very happy, and gave your friends no trouble. Though in one way, of course, it ought to be considered that you did the worst of all."

"Captain Askell's family is very good," said Mary, by the way of turning off too close an inquiry into her own affairs; "and he is just in the same position as Hugh's father was; and I love Nelly like a child of my own. I feel as if she ought to have been a child of my own. She and Will used to lie in the same cradle—"

"Ah, by the way," said Sir Edward, looking round once more into the corners, "where is Will?"

And then it had to be explained where Will had gone, which the old man thought very curious. "To Carlisle? What did he want to go to Carlisle for? If he had been out with his fishing rod, or out with the keepers, looking after the young pheasants—But what could he want going into Carlisle? Is Percival there?"

"I hope not," said Mary, with sudden anxiety. It was an idea which had not entered into her mind before.

"Why should you hope not? If he really wants to make peace with Winnie, I should think it very natural," said Sir Edward; "and Will is a curious sort of boy. He might be a very good sort of auxiliary in any negotiation. Depend upon it that's why he is gone."

"I think not. I think he would have told me," said Mary, feeling her heart sink with sudden dread.

"I don't see why he should have told you," said Sir Edward, who was in one of his troublesome moods, and disposed to put everybody at sixes and sevens. "He is old enough to act a little for himself. I hope you are not one of the foolish women, Mary, that like to keep their boys always at their apron-strings?"

With this reproach Sir Edward took his leave, and made his way placidly homeward, with the tranquillity of a man who has done his duty. He felt that he had discharged the great vocation of man, at least for the past hour. Winnie had heard the truth, whether she liked it or not, and so had the other members of the family, over whom he shook his head kindly but sadly as he went home. Their impetuosity, their aptitude to rush into any scrape that presented itself—and especially their madness in respect to marriage, filled him with pity. There was Charlie Seton, for example, the father of these girls, who had married that man Penrose's sister. Sir Edward's memory was so long, that it did not seem to him a very great stretch to go back to that. Not that the young woman was amiss in herself, but the man who, with his eyes open, burdened his unborn descendants with such an uncle, was worse then lunatic—he was criminal. This was what Sir Edward thought as he went quietly home, with a rather comfortable dreary sense of satisfaction in his heart in the thought that his own behaviour had been marked by no such aberrations; and, in the meantime, Winnie was fanning the embers of her own wrath, and Mary had sickened somehow with a sense of insecurity and unexplainable apprehension. On the other hand, the two young creatures were very happy on the road to the Lady's Well, and Will addressed himself to his strange business with resolution: and, painful as its character was, was not pained to speak of, but only excited. So ran the course of the world upon that ordinary summer day.

CHAPTER XXXV

Of the strangest kind were Wilfrid's sensations when he found himself in the streets of Carlisle on his extraordinary mission. It was the first time he had ever taken any step absolutely by himself. To be sure, he had been brought up in full possession of the freedom of an English boy, in whose honour everybody has confidence—but never before had he been moved by an individual impulse to independent action, nor had he known what it was to have a secret in his mind, and an enterprise which had to be conducted wholly according to his own judgment, and in respect to which he could ask for no advice. When he emerged out of the railway station, and found himself actually in the streets, a thrill of excitement, sudden and strange, came over him. He had known very well all along what he was coming to do, and yet he seemed only to become aware of it at that moment, when he put his foot upon the pavement, and was appealed to by cab-drivers, eager to take him somewhere. Here there was no time or opportunity for lingering; he had to go somewhere, and that instantly, were it only to the shops to execute his mother's innocent commissions. It might be possible to loiter and meditate on the calm country roads about Kirtell, but the town and the streets have other associations. He was there to do something, to go somewhere, and it had to be begun at once. He was not imaginative, but yet he felt a kind of palpable tearing asunder as he took his first step onward. He had hesitated, and his old life seemed to hold out its arms to him. It was not an unhappy life; he had his own way in most things, he had his future before him unfettered, and he knew that his wishes would be furthered, and everything possible done to help and encourage him. All this passed through his mind like a flash of lightning. He would be helped and cared for and made much of, but yet he would only be Will, the youngest, of whom nobody took particular notice, and who sat in the lowest room; whereas, by natural law and justice, he was the heir. After he had made that momentary comparison, he stepped on with a firm foot, and then it was that he felt like the tearing asunder of something that had bound him. He had thrown the old bonds, the old pleasant ties, to the wind; and now all that he had to do was to push on by himself and gain his rights. This sensation made his head swim as he walked on. He had put out to sea, as it were, and the new movement made him giddy—and yet it was not pain; love was not life to him, but he had never known what it was to live without it. There seemed no reason why he should not do perfectly well for himself; Hugh would be affronted, of course—but it could make no difference to Islay, for example, nor much to his mother, for it would still be one of her sons. These were the thoughts that went through Wilfrid's mind as he walked along; from which it will be apparent that the wickedness he was about to do was not nearly so great in intention as it was in reality; and that his youth, and inexperience, and want of imagination, his incapacity to put himself into the position of another, or realize anything but his own wants and sentiments, pushed him unawares, while he contemplated only an act of selfishness, into a social crime.

But yet the sense of doing this thing entirely alone, of doing it in secret, which was contrary to all his habitudes of mind, filled him with a strange inquietude. It hurt his conscience more to be making such a wonderful move for himself, out of the knowledge of his mother and everybody belonging to him, than to be trying to disgrace his mother and overthrow her good name and honour; of the latter, he was only dimly conscious, but the former he saw clearly. A strange paradox, apparently, but yet not without many parallels. There are poor creatures who do not hesitate at drowning themselves, and yet shrink from the chill of the "black flowing river" in which it is to be accomplished. As for Will, he did not hesitate to throw dark anguish and misery into the peaceful household he had been bred in—he did not shrink from an act which would embitter the lives of all who loved him, and change their position, and disgrace their name—but the thought of taking his first great step in life out of anybody's knowledge, made his head swim, and the light fail in his eyes—and filled him with a giddy mingling of excitement and shame. He did not realize the greater issue, except as it affected him solely—but he did the other in its fullest sense. Thus he went on through the common-place streets, with his heart throbbing in his ears, and the blood rushing to his head; and yet he was not remorseful, nor conscience-stricken, nor sorry, but only strongly excited, and moved by a certain nervous shyness and shame.

Notwithstanding this, a certain practical faculty in Wilfrid led him, before seeking out his tempter and first informant, to seek independent testimony. It would be difficult to say what it was that turned his thoughts towards Mrs. Kirkman; but it was to her he went. The colonel's wife received him with a sweet smile, but she was busy with much more important concerns; and when she had placed him at a table covered with tracts and magazines, she took no further notice of Will. She was a woman, as has been before mentioned, who laboured under a chronic dissatisfaction with the clergy, whether as represented in the person of a regimental chaplain, or of a Dean and Chapter; and she was not content to suffer quietly, as so many people do. Her discontent was active, and expressed itself not only in lamentation and complaint, but in very active measures. She could not reappoint to the offices in the Cathedral, but she could do what was in her power, by Scripture-readers, and societies for private instruction, to make up the deficiency; and she was very busy with one of her agents when Will entered, who certainly had not come about any evangelical business. As time passed, however, and it became apparent to him that Mrs. Kirkman was much more occupied with her other visitor than with any curiosity about his own boyish errand, whatever it might be, Will began to lose patience. When he made a little attempt to gain a hearing in his turn, he was silenced by the same sweet smile, and a clasp of the hand. "My dear boy, just a moment; what we are talking of is of the greatest importance," said Mrs. Kirkman. "There are so few real means of grace in this benighted town, and to think that souls are being lost daily, hourly—and yet such a show of services and prayers—it is terrible to think of it. In a few minutes, my dear boy."

"What I want is of the greatest importance, too," said Wilfrid, turning doggedly away from the table and the magazines.

Mrs. Kirkman looked at him, and thought she saw spiritual trouble in his eye. She was flattered that he should have thought of her under such interesting circumstances. It was a tardy but sweet compensation for all she had done, as she said to herself, for his mother; and going on this mistaken idea she dismissed the Scripture-reader, having first filled him with an adequate sense of the insufficiency of the regular clergy. It was, as so often happens, a faithful remnant, which was contending alone for religion against all the powers of this world. They were sure of one thing at least, and that was that everybody else was wrong. This was the idea with which her humble agent left Mrs. Kirkman; and the same feeling, sad but sweet, was in her own mind as she drew a chair to the table and sat down beside her dear young friend.

"And so you have come all the way from Kirtell to see me, my dear boy?" she said. "How happy I shall be if I can be of some use to you. I am afraid you won't find very much sympathy there."

"No," said Wilfrid, vaguely, not knowing in the least what she meant. "I am sorry I did not bring you some flowers, but I was in a hurry when I came away."

"Don't think of anything of the kind," said the colonel's wife, pressing his hand. "What are flowers in comparison with the one great object of our existence? Tell me about it, my dear Will; you know I have known you from a child."

"You knew I was coming then," said Will, a little surprised, "though I thought nobody knew? Yes, I suppose you have known us all our lives. What I want is to find out about my mother's marriage. I heard you knew all about it. Of course you must have known all about it. That is what I want to understand."

"Your mother's marriage!" cried Mrs. Kirkman; and to do her justice she looked aghast. The question horrified her, and at the same time it disappointed her. "I am sure that is not what you came to talk to me about," she said coaxingly, and with a certain charitable wile. "My dear, dear boy, don't let shyness lead you away from the greatest of all subjects. I know you came to talk to me about your soul."

"I came to ask you about my mother's marriage," said Will. His giddiness had passed by this time, and he looked her steadily in the face. It was impossible to mistake him now, or think it a matter of unimportance or mere curiosity. Mrs. Kirkman had her faults, but she was a good woman at the bottom. She did not object to make an allusion now and then which vexed Mary, and made her aware, as it were, of the precipice by which she was always standing. It was what Mrs. Kirkman thought a good moral discipline for her friend, besides giving herself a pleasant consciousness of power and superiority; but when Mary's son sat down in front of her, and looked with cold but eager eyes in his face, and demanded this frightful information, her heart sank within her. It made her forget for the moment all about the clergy and the defective means of grace; and brought her down to the common standing of a natural Christian woman, anxious and terror-stricken for her friend.

"What have you to do with your mother's marriage?" she said, trembling a little. "Do you know what a very strange question you are asking? Who has told you anything about that? O me! you frighten me so, I don't know what I am saying. Did Mary send you? Have you just come from your mother? If you want to know about her marriage, it is of her that you should ask information. Of course she can tell you all about it—she and your Aunt Agatha. What a very strange question to ask of me!"

Wilfrid looked steadily into Mrs. Kirkman's agitated face, and saw it was all true he had heard. "If you do not know anything about it," he said, with pitiless logic, "you would say so. Why should you look so put out if there was nothing to tell?"

"I am not put out," said Mrs. Kirkman, still more disturbed. "Oh, Will, you are a dreadful boy. What is it you want to know? What is it for? Did you tell your mother you were coming here?"

"I don't see what it matters whether I told my mother, or what it is for," said Will. "I came to you because you were good, and would not tell a lie. I can depend on what you say to me. I have heard all about it already, but I am not so sure as I should be if I had it from you."

This compliment touched the colonel's wife on a susceptible point. She calmed a little out of her fright. A boy with so just an appreciation of other people's virtues could not be meditating anything unkind or unnatural to his mother. Perhaps it would be better for Mary that he should know the rights of it; perhaps it was providential that he should have come to her, who could give him all the details.

"I don't suppose you can mean any harm," she said. "Oh, Will, our hearts are all desperately wicked. The best of us is little able to resist temptation. You are right in thinking I will tell you the truth if I tell you anything; but oh, my dear boy, if it should be to lead you to evil and not good—"

"Never mind about the evil and the good," said Will impatiently. "What I want is to know what is false and what is true."

Mrs. Kirkman hesitated still; but she began to persuade herself that he might have heard something worse than the truth. She was in a great perplexity; impelled to speak, and yet frightened to death at the consequences. It was a new situation for her altogether, and she did not know how to manage it. She clasped her hands helplessly together, and the very movement suggested an idea which she grasped at, partly because she was really a sincere, good woman who believed in the efficacy of prayer, and partly, poor soul, to gain a little time, for she was at her wits' end.

"I will," she said. "I will, my dear boy; I will tell you everything; but oh, let us kneel down and have a word of prayer first, that we may not make a bad use of—of what we hear."

If she had ever been in earnest in her life it was at that moment; the tears were in her eyes, and all her little affectations of solemnity had disappeared. She could not have told anybody what it was she feared; and yet the more she looked at the boy beside her, the more she felt their positions change, and feared and stood in awe, feeling that she was for the moment his slave, and must do anything he might command.

"Mrs. Kirkman," said Will, "I don't understand that sort of thing. I don't know what bad use you can think I am going to make of it;—at all events it won't be your fault. I shall not detain you five minutes if you will only tell me what I want to know."

And she did tell him accordingly, not knowing how to resist, and warmed in the telling in spite of herself, and could not but let him know that she thought it was for Mary's good, and to bring her to a sense of the vanity of all earthly things. She gave him scrupulously all the details. The story flowed out upon Will's hungry ears with scarcely a pause. She told him all about the marriage, where it had happened, and who had performed it, and who had been present. Little Hugh had been present. She had no doubt he would remember, if it was recalled to his memory. Mrs. Kirkman recollected perfectly the look that Mary had thrown at her husband when she saw the child there. Poor Mary! she had thought so much of reputation and a good name. She had been so much thought of in the regiment. They all called her by that ridiculous name, Madonna Mary—and made so much of her, before—

"And did they not make much of her after?" said Will, quickly.

"It is a different thing," said Mrs. Kirkman, softly shaking her long curls and returning to herself. "A poor sinner returning to the right way ought to be more warmly welcomed than even the best, if we can call any human creature good; but—"

"Is it my mother you call a poor sinner?" asked Will.

Then there was a pause. Mrs. Kirkman shook her head once more, and shook the long curls that hung over her cheeks; but it was difficult to answer. "We are all poor sinners," she said. "Oh, my dear boy, if I could only persuade you how much more important it is to think of your own soul. If your poor dear mamma has done wrong, it is God who is her judge. I never judged her for my part, I never made any difference. I hope I know my own shortcomings too well for that."

"I thought I heard you say something odd to her once," said Will. "I should just like to see any one uncivil to my mother. But that's not the question. I want that Mr. Churchill's address, please."

"I can truly say I never made any difference," said Mrs. Kirkman; "some people might have blamed me—but I always thought of the Mary that loved much—Oh, Will, what comforting words! I hope your dear mother has long, long ago repented of her error. Perhaps your father deceived her, as she was so young; perhaps it was all true the strange story he told about the register being burnt, and all that. We all thought it was best not to inquire into it. We know what we saw; but remember, you pledged your word not to make any dispeace with what I have told you. You are not to make a disturbance in the family about it. It is all over and past, and everybody has agreed to forget it. You are not going to make any dispeace—"

"I never thought of making any dispeace," said Will; but that was all he said. He was brief, as he always was, and uncommunicative, and inclined, now he had got all he wanted, to get up abruptly and go away.

"And now, my dear young friend, you must do something for me," said Mrs. Kirkman, "in repayment for what I have done for you. You must read these, and you must not only read them, but think over them, and seek light where it is to be found. Oh, my dear boy, how anxious we are to search into any little mystery in connection with ourselves, and how little we think of the mysteries of eternity! You must promise to give a little attention to this great theme before this day has come to an end."

"Oh, yes, I'll read them," said Will, and he thrust into his pocket a roll of tracts she gave him without any further thought what they were. The truth was, that he did not pay much attention to what she was saying; his head had begun to throb and feel giddy again, and he had a rushing in his ears. He had it all in his hands now, and the sense of his power overwhelmed him. He had never had such an instrument in his hands before, he had never known what it was to be capable of moving anybody, except to momentary displeasure or anxiety; and he felt as a man might feel in whose hand there had suddenly been placed the most powerful of weapons, with unlimited license to use it as he would—to break down castles with it or crowns, or slay armies at a blow—and only his own absolute pleasure to decide when or where it should fall. Something of intoxication and yet of alarm was in that first sense of power. He was rapt into a kind of ecstacy, and yet he was alarmed and afraid. He thrust the tracts into his pocket, and he received, cavalierly enough, Mrs. Kirkman's parting salutations. He had got all he wanted from her, and Will's was not a nature to be very expansive in the way of gratitude. Perhaps even, any sort of dim moral sense he might have on the subject, made him feel that in the news he had just heard there was not much room for gratitude. Anyhow he made very little pretence at those hollow forms of courtesy which are current in the elder world. He went away having got what he wanted, and left the colonel's wife in a state of strange excitement and growing compunction. Oddly enough, Will's scanty courtesy roused more compunctions in her mind than anything else had done. She had put Mary's fate, as it were, into the hands of a boy who had so little sense of what was right as to withdraw in the most summary and abrupt way the moment his curiosity was satisfied; who had not even grace enough, or self-control enough, to go through the ordinary decorums, or pay common attention to what she said to him; and now this inexperienced undisciplined lad had an incalculable power in his hands—power to crush and ruin his own family, to dispossess his brother and disgrace his mother: and nothing but his own forbearance or good pleasure to limit him. What had she done?

Will walked about the streets for a full hour after, dizzy with the same extraordinary, intoxicating, alarming sense of power. Before, it had all been vague, now it was distinct and clear; and even beyond his desire to "right" himself, came the inclination to set this strange machine in motion, and try his new strength. He was still so much a boy, that he was curious to see the effect it would produce, eager to ascertain how it would work, and what it could do. He was like a child in possession of an infernal machine, longing to try it, and yet not unconscious of the probable mischief. The sense of his power went to his head, and intoxicated him like wine. Here it was all ready in his hands, an instrument which could take away more than life, and he was afraid of it, and of the strength of the recoil: and yet was full of eagerness to see it go off, and see what results it would actually bring forth. He walked about the town, not knowing where he was going, forgetting all about his mother's commissions, and all about Percival, which was more extraordinary—solely occupied with the sensation that the power was in his hands. He went into the cathedral, and walked all round it, and never knew he had been there; and when at last he found himself at the railway station again, he woke up again abruptly, as if he had been in a dream. Then making an effort he set his wits to work about Percival, and asked himself what he was to do. Percival was nothing to Will: he was his Aunt Winnie's husband, and perhaps had not used her well, and he could furnish no information half so clear or distinct as that which Mrs. Kirkman had given. Will did not see any reason in particular why he should go out of his way to seek such a man out. He had been no doubt his first informant, but in his present position of power and superiority, he did not feel that he had any need of Percival. And why should he seek him out? When he had sufficiently recovered his senses to go through this reasoning, Will went deliberately back to town again, and executed his mother's commissions. He went to several shops, and gave orders which she had charged him with, and even took the trouble to choose the things she wanted, in the most painstaking way, and was as concerned that they should be right as if he had been the most dutiful and tender of sons; and all the while he was thinking to ruin her, and disgrace her, and put the last stigma upon her name, and render her an outcast from the peaceful world. Such was the strange contradiction that existed within him; he went back without speaking to any one, without seeing anybody, knitting his brows and thinking all the way. The train that carried him home, with his weapon in his hands, passed with a rush and shriek the train which was conveying Nelly, with a great basket of flowers in her lap, and a vague gleam of infinite content in her eyes, back to her nursery and her duties, with Hugh by her side, who was taking care of her, and losing himself, if there had been any harm in it. That sweet loss and gain was going on imperceptibly in the carriage where the one brother sat happy as a young prince, when the other brother shot past as it were on wings of flame like a destroying angel. Neither thought of the other as they thus crossed, the one being busy with the pre-occupation of young love, the other lost in a passion, which was not hate, nor even enmity, which was not inconsistent with a kind of natural affection, and yet involved destruction and injury of the darkest and most overwhelming kind. Contrasts so sharply and clearly pointed occur but seldom in a world so full of modifications and complicated interests; yet they do occur sometimes. And this was how it was with Mary's boys.

CHAPTER XXXVI

When Wilfrid reached home, he found his mother by herself in the drawing-room. Winnie had a headache, or some other of those aches which depend upon temper and the state of the mind, and Aunt Agatha was sitting by her, in the darkened room, with bottles of eau de Cologne, and sal volatile, and smelling salts, and all the paraphernalia of this kind of indisposition. Aunt Agatha had been apt to take headaches herself in her younger days when she happened to be crossed, and she was not without an idea that it was a very orthodox resource for a woman when she could not have her own way. And thus they were shut up, exchanging confidences. It did poor Winnie good, and it did not do Miss Seton any harm. And Mary was alone downstairs. She was not looking so bright as when Wilfrid went away. The idea which Sir Edward had suggested to her, even if it had taken no hold of her mind, had breathed on her a possible cloud; and she looked up wistfully at her boy as he came in. Wilfrid, too, bore upon his face, to some extent, the marks of what he had been doing; but then his mother did not know what he had been doing, and could not guess what the dimness meant which was over his countenance. It was not a bright face at any time, but was often lost in mists, and its meaning veiled from his mother's eyes; and she could not follow him, this time any more than other times, into the uncertain depths. All she could do was to look at him wistfully, and long to see a little clearer, and wonder, as she had so often wondered, how it was that his thoughts and ways were so often out of her ken—how it was that children could go so far away, and be so wholly sundered, even while at the very side of those who had nursed them on their knees, and trained them to think and feel. A standing wonder, and yet the commonest thing in nature. Mary felt it over again with double force to-day, as he came and brought her her wool and bits of ribbon, and she looked into his face and did not know what its meaning was.

As for Will, it was a curious sensation for him, too, on his part. It was such an opportunity as he could scarcely have looked for, for opening to his mother the great discovery he had made, and the great changes that might follow. He could have had it all out with her and put his power into operation, and seen what its effects were, without fear of being disturbed. But he shrank from it, he could not tell why. He was not a boy of very fastidious feelings, but still to sit there facing her and look into her face, and tell her that he had been inquiring into her past life, and had found out her secret, was more than Will was capable of. To meditate doing it, and to think over what he would say, and to arrange the words in which he would tell her that it was still one of her sons who would have Earlston—was a very different thing from fairly looking her in the face and doing it. He stared at her for a moment in a way which startled Mary; and then the impossibility became evident to him, and he turned his eyes away from her and sat down.

"You look a little strange, Will," said Mary. "Are you tired, or has anything happened? You startled me just now, you looked so pale."

"No, I am not tired," said Will, in his curt way. "I don't know anything about being pale."

"Well, you never were very rosy," said Mrs. Ochterlony. "I did not expect you so soon. I thought you would have gone to the Askells', and come home with Hugh."

"I never thought of that. I thought you wanted your wool and things," said Will.

It was very slight, ordinary talk, and yet it was quivering with meaning on both sides, though neither knew what the other's meaning was. Will, for his part, was answering his mother's questions with something like the suppressed mania of homicide within him, not quite knowing whether at any moment the subdued purpose might not break out, and kill, and reveal itself; whereas his mother, totally unsuspecting how far things had gone, was longing to discover whether Percival had gained any power over him, and what that adversary's tactics were.

"Have you seen anybody?" she said. "By the way, Sir Edward was talking of Major Percival—he seemed to think that he might still be in Carlisle. Did you by any chance see anything of him there?"

She fixed her eyes full upon him as she spoke, but Will did not in any way shrink from her eyes.

"No," he said carelessly. "I did not see him. He told me he was going to stay a day or two in Carlisle, but I did not look out for him, particularly. He gets to be a bore after the first."

When Mary heard this, her face cleared up like the sky after a storm. It had been all folly, and once more she had made herself unhappy about nothing. How absurd it was! Percival was wicked, but still he had no cause to fix any quarrel upon her, or poison the mind of her son. It was on Winnie's account he came, and on Winnie's account, no doubt, he was staying; and in all likelihood Mrs. Ochterlony and her boys were as utterly unimportant to him, as in ordinary circumstances he was to them. Mary made thus the mistake by which a tolerant and open mind, not too much occupied about itself, sometimes goes astray. People go wrong much more frequently from thinking too much of themselves, and seeing their own shadow across everybody's way; but yet there may be danger even in the lack of egotism: and thus it was that Mary's face cleared up, and her doubts dispersed, just at the moment when she had most to dread.

Then there was a pause, and the homicidal impulse, so to speak, took possession of Will. He was playing with the things he had bought, putting them into symmetrical and unsymmetrical shapes on the table, and when he suddenly said "Mother," Mrs. Ochterlony turned to him with a smile. He said "Mother," and then he stopped short, and picked to pieces the construction he was making, but at the same time he never raised his eyes.

"Well, Will?" said Mary.

And then there was a brief, but sharp, momentary struggle in his mind. He meant to speak, and wanted to speak, but could not. His throat seemed to close with a jerk when he tried; the words would not come from his lips. It was not that he was ashamed of what he was going to do, or that any sudden compunction for his mother seized him. It was a kind of spasm of impossibility, as much physical as mental. He could no more do it, then he could lift the Cottage from its solid foundations. He went on arranging the little parcels on the table into shapes, square, oblong, and triangular, his fingers busy, but his mind much more busy, his eyes looking at nothing, and his lips unable to articulate a single word.

"Well, Will, what were you going to say?" said Mary, again.

"Nothing," said Will; and he got up and went away with an abruptness which made his mother wonder and smile. It was only Willy's way; but it was an exaggerated specimen of Will's way. She thought to herself when he was gone, with regret, that it was a great pity he was so abrupt. It did not matter at home, where everybody knew him; but among strangers, where people did not know him, it might do him so much injury. Poor Will! but he knew nothing about Percival, and cared nothing, and Mary was ashamed of her momentary fear.

As for the boy himself, he went out, and took himself to task, and felt all over him a novel kind of tremor, a sense of strange excitement, the feeling of one who had escaped a great danger. But that was not all the feeling which ought to have been in his mind. He had neglected and lost a great opportunity, and though it was not difficult to make opportunities, Will felt by instinct that his mother's mere presence had defeated him. He could not tell her of the discovery he had made. He might write her a letter about it, or send the news to her at secondhand; but to look in her face and tell her, was impossible. To sit down there by her side, and meet her eyes, and tell her that he had been making inquiries into her character, and that she was not the woman she was supposed to be, nor was the position of her children such as the world imagined, was an enterprise which Wilfrid had once and for ever proved impossible. He stood blank before this difficulty which lay at the very beginning of his undertaking; he had not only failed, but he saw that he must for ever fail. It amazed him, but he felt it was final. His mouth was closed, and he could not speak.

And then he thought he would wait until Hugh came home. Hugh was not his mother, nor a woman. He was no more than Will's equal at the best, and perhaps even his inferior; and to him, surely, it could be said. He waited for a long time, and kept lingering about the roads, wondering what train his brother would come by, and feeling somehow reluctant to go in again, so long as his mother was alone. For in Mrs. Ochterlony's presence Will could not forget that he had a secret—that he had done something out of her knowledge, and had something of the most momentous character to tell her, and yet could not tell it to her. It would be different with Hugh. He waited loitering about upon the dusty summer roads, biting his nails to the quick, and labouring hard through a sea of thought. This telling was disagreeable, even it was only Hugh that had to be told—more disagreeable than anything else about the business, far more disagreeable, certainly, than he had anticipated it would be; and Wilfrid did not quite make out how it was that a simple fact should be so difficult to communicate. It enlarged his views so far, and gave him a glimpse into the complications of maturer life, but it did not in any way divert him from his purpose, or change his ideas about his rights. At length the train appeared by which it was certain Hugh must come home. Wilfrid sauntered along the road within sight of the little station to meet his brother, and yet when he saw Hugh actually approaching, his heart gave a jump in his breast. The moment had come, and he must do it, which was a very different thing from thinking it over, and planning what he was to say.

"You here, Will!" said Hugh. "I looked for you in Carlisle. Why didn't you go to Mrs. Askell's and wait for me?"

"I had other things to do," said Will, briefly.

Hugh laughed. "Very important things, I have no doubt," he said; "but still you might have waited for me, all the same. How is Aunt Winnie? I saw that fellow,—that husband of hers,—at the station. I should like to know what he wants hanging about here."

"He wants her, perhaps," said Will, though with another jump of his heart.

"He had better not come and bother her," said Hugh. "She may not be perfect herself, but I won't stand it. She is my mother's sister, after all, and she is a woman. I hope you won't encourage him to hang about here."

"I!" cried Will, with amazement and indignation.

"Yes," said Hugh, with elder-brotherly severity. "Not that I think you would mean any harm by it, Will; it is not a sort of thing you can be expected to understand. A fellow like that should be kept at a distance. When a man behaves badly to a woman—to his wife—to such a beautiful creature as she has been—"

"I don't see anything very beautiful about her," said Will.

"That doesn't matter," said Hugh, who was hot and excited, having been taken into Winnie's confidence. "She has been beautiful, and that's enough. Indeed, she ought to be beautiful now, if that fellow hadn't been a brute. And if he means to come back here—"

"Perhaps it is not her he wants," said Will, whose profound self-consciousness made him play quite a new part in the dialogue.

"What could he want else?" said Hugh, with scorn. "You may be sure it is no affection for any of us that brings him here."

Here was the opportunity, if Will could but have taken it. Now was the moment to tell him that something other than Winnie might be in Percival's mind—that it was his own fortune, and not hers, that hung in the balance. But Will was dumb; his lips were sealed; his tongue clove to the roof of his mouth. It was not his will that was in fault. It was a rebellion of all his physical powers, a rising up of nature against his purpose. He was silent in spite of himself; he said not another word as they walked on together. He suffered Hugh to stray into talk about the Askells, about the Museum, about anything or nothing. Once or twice he interrupted the conversation abruptly with some half-dozen words, which brought it to a sudden stop, and gave him the opportunity of broaching his own subject. But when he came to that point he was struck dumb. Hugh, all innocent and unconscious, in serene elderly-brotherly superiority, good humoured and condescending, and carelessly affectionate, was as difficult to deal with as Mary herself. Without withdrawing from his undertaking, or giving up his "rights," Wilfrid felt himself helpless; he could not say it out. It seemed to him now that so far from giving in to it, as he once imagined, without controversy, Hugh equally without controversy would set it aside as something monstrous, and that his new hope would be extinguished and come to an end if his elder brother had the opportunity of thus putting it down at once. When they reached home, Will withdrew to his own room, with a sense of being baffled and defeated—defeated before he had struck a blow. He did not come downstairs again, as they remembered afterwards—he did not want any tea. He had not a headache, as Aunt Agatha, now relieved from attendance upon Winnie, immediately suggested. All he wanted was to be left alone, for he had something to do. This was the message that came downstairs. "He is working a great deal too much," said Aunt Agatha, "you will see he will hurt his brain or something;" while Hugh, too, whispered to his mother, "You shall see; I never did much, but Will will go in for all sorts of honours," the generous fellow whispered in his mother's ear; and Mary smiled, in her heart thinking so too. If they had seen Will at the moment sitting with his face supported by both his hands, biting his nails and knitting his brows, and pondering more intently than any man ever pondered over classic puzzle or scientific problem, they might have been startled out of those pleasant thoughts.

And yet the problem he was considering was one that racked his brain, and made his head ache, had he been sufficiently at leisure to feel it. The more impossible he felt it to explain himself and make his claim, the more obstinately determined was he to make it, and have what belonged to him. His discouragement and sense of defeat did but intensify his resolution. He had failed to speak, notwithstanding his opportunities; but he could write, or he could employ another voice as his interpreter. With all his egotism and determination, Wilfrid was young, nothing but a boy, and inexperienced, and at a loss what to do. Everything seemed easy to him until he tried to do it; and when he tried, everything seemed impossible. He had thought it the most ordinary affair in the world to tell his discovery to his mother and brother, until the moment came which in both cases proved the communication to be beyond his powers. And now he thought he could write. After long pondering, he got up and opened the little desk upon which he had for years written his verses and exercises, troubled by nothing worse than a doubtful quantity, and made an endeavour to carry out his last idea. Will's style was not a bad style. It was brief and terse, and to the point,—a remarkable kind of diction for a boy,—but he did not find that it suited his present purpose. He put himself to torture over his letters. He tried it first in one way, and then in another; but however he put it, he felt within himself that it would not do. He had no sort of harsh or unnatural meaning in his mind. They were still his mother and brother to whom he wanted to write, and he had no inclination to wound their feelings, or to be disrespectful or unkind. In short, it only required this change, and his establishment in what he supposed his just position, to make him the kindest and best of sons and brothers. He toiled over his letters as he had never toiled over anything in his life. He could not tell how to express himself, nor even what to say. He addressed his mother first, and then Hugh, and then his mother again; but the more he laboured the more impossible he found his task. When Mrs. Ochterlony came upstairs and opened his door to see what her boy was about, Wilfrid stumbled up from his seat red and heated, and shut up his desk, and faced her with an air of confusion and trouble which she could not understand. It was not too late even then to bring her in and tell her all; and this possibility bewildered Will, and filled him with agitation and excitement, to which naturally his mother had no clue.

"What is the matter?" she said, anxiously; "are you ill, Will? Have you a headache? I thought you were in bed."

"No, I am all right," said Will, facing her with a look, which in its confusion seemed sullen. "I am busy. It is too soon to go to bed."

"Tell me what is wrong," said Mary, coming a step further into the room. "Will, my dear boy, I am sure you are not well. You have not been quarrelling with any one—with Hugh—?"

"With Hugh!" said Will, with a little scorn; "why should I quarrel with Hugh?"

"Why, indeed!" said Mrs. Ochterlony, smiling faintly; "but you do not look like yourself. Tell me what you have been doing, at least."

Will's heart thumped against his breast. He might put her into the chair by which she was standing, and tell her everything and have it over. This possibility still remained to him. He stood for a second and looked at her, and grew breathless with excitement, but then somehow his voice seemed to die away in his throat.

"If I were to tell you what I was doing, you would not understand it," he said, repeating mechanically words which he had used in good faith, with innocent schoolboy arrogance, many a time before. As for Mary, she looked at him wistfully, seeing something in his eyes which she could not interpret. They had never been candid, frank eyes like Hugh's. Often enough before, they had been impatient of her scrutiny, and had veiled their meaning with an apparent blank; but yet there had never been any actual harm hid by the artifice. Mary sighed; but she did not insist, knowing how useless it was. If it was anything, perhaps it was some boyish jealousy about Nelly,—an imaginary feeling which would pass away, and leave no trace behind. But, whatever it was, it was vain to think of finding it out by questions; and she gave him her good-night kiss and left him, comforting herself with the thought that most likely it was only one of Will's uncomfortable moments, and would be over by to-morrow. But when his mother went away, Will for his part sank down, with the strangest tremor, in his chair. Never before in his life had this sick and breathless excitement, this impulse of the mind and resistance of the flesh, been known to him, and he could not bear it. It seemed to him he never could stand in her presence, never feel his mother's eyes upon him, without feeling that now was the moment that he must and ought to tell her, and yet could not tell her, no more than if he were speechless. He had never felt very deeply all his life before, and the sense of this struggle took all his strength from him. It made his heart beat, so that the room and the house and the very solid earth on which he stood seemed to throb and tingle round him; it was like standing for ever on the edge of a precipice over which the slightest movement would throw him, and the very air seemed to rush against his ears as it would do if he were falling. He sank down into his chair, and his heart beat, and the pulses throbbed in his temples. What was he to do?—he could not speak, he could not write, and yet it must be told, and his rights gained, and the one change made that should convert him into the tenderest son, the most helpful brother, that ever man or woman had. At last in his despair and pertinacity, there came into his mind that grand expedient which occurs naturally to everything that is young and unreasonable under the pressure of unusual trials. He would go away; he could not go on seeing them continually, with this communication always ready to break from the lips which would not utter it,—nor could he write to them while he was still with them, and when any letter must be followed by an immediate explanation. But he could fly; and when he was at a safe distance, then he could tell them. No doubt it was cowardice to a certain extent; but there were other things as well. Partly it was impatience, and partly the absoluteness and imperious temper of youth, and that intolerance of everything painful that comes natural to it. He sat in his chair, noiseless and thinking, in the stillness of night, a poor young soul, tempted and yielding to temptation, sinful, yet scarcely conscious how sinful he was, and yet at the same time forlorn with that profound forlornness of egotism and ill-doing which is almost pathetic in the young. He could consult nobody, take no one into his confidence. The only counsellors he had known in all his small experience were precisely those upon whom he was about to turn. He was alone, and had everything to plan, everything to do for himself.

And yet was there nobody whom he could take into his confidence? Suddenly, in the stillness of the night a certain prosperous, comfortable figure came into the boy's mind—one who thought it was well to get money and wealth and power, anyhow except dishonestly, which of course was an impracticable and impolitic way. When that idea came to him like an inspiration, Will gave a little start, and looked up, and saw the blue dawn making all the bars of his window visible against the white blind that covered it. Night was gone with its dark counsels, and the day had come. What he did after that was to take out his boy's purse, and count over carefully all the money it contained. It was not much, but yet it was enough. Then he took his first great final step in life, with a heart that beat in his ears, but not loud enough to betray him. He went downstairs softly as the dawn brightened, and all the dim staircase and closed doors grew visible, revealed by the silent growth of the early light. Nobody heard him, nobody dreamed that any secret step could ever glide down those stairs or out of the innocent honest house. He was the youngest in it, and should have been the most innocent; and he thought he meant no evil. Was it not his right he was going to claim? He went softly out, going through the drawing-room window, which it was safer to leave open than the door, and across the lawn, which made no sound beneath his foot. The air of the summer morning was like balm, and soothed him, and the blueness brightened and grew rosy as he went his way among the early dews. The only spot on which, like Gideon's fleece, no dew had fallen, was poor Will's beating heart, as he went away in silence and secrecy from his mother's door.

CHAPTER XXXVII

The breakfast-table in the Cottage was as cheerful as usual next morning, and showed no premonitory shadow. Winnie did not come downstairs early; and perhaps it was all the more cheerful for her absence. And there were flowers on the table, and everything looked bright. Will was absent, it is true, but nobody took much notice of that as yet. He might be late, or he might have gone out; and he was not a boy to be long negligent of the necessities of nature. Aunt Agatha even thought it necessary to order something additional to be kept hot for him. "He has gone out, I suppose," Miss Seton said; "and it is rather cold this morning, and a long walk in this air will make the boy as hungry as a hunter. Tell Peggy not to cook that trout till she hears him come in."

The maid looked perturbed and breathless; but she said, "Yes, ma'am," humbly—as if it was she who was in the wrong; and the conversation and the meal were resumed. A minute or two after, however, she appeared once more: "If you please, there's somebody asking for Mr. Hugh," said the frightened girl, standing, nervous and panting, with her hand upon the door.

"Somebody for me?" said Hugh. "The gamekeeper, I suppose; he need not have been in such a hurry. Let him come in and wait a little. I'll be ready presently."

"But, my dear boy," said Aunt Agatha, "you must not waste the man's time. It is Sir Edward's time, you know; and he may have quantities of things to do. Go and see what he wants: and your mother will not fill out your coffee till you come back."

And Hugh went out, half laughing, half grumbling—but he laughed no more, when he saw Peggy standing severe and pale at the kitchen door, waiting for him. "Mr. Hugh," said Peggy, with the aspect of a chief justice, "tell me this moment, on your conscience, is there any quarrel or disagreement between your brother and you?"

"My brother and me? Do you mean Will?" said Hugh, in amazement. "Not the slightest. What do you mean? We were never better friends in our life."

"God be thanked!" said Peggy; and then she took him by the arm, and led the astonished young man upstairs to Will's room. "He's never sleepit in that bed this night. His little bag's gone, with a change in't. He's putten on another pair of boots. Where is the laddie gone? And me that'll have to face his mother, and tell her she's lost her bairn!"

"Lost her bairn! Nonsense," cried Hugh, aghast; "he's only gone out for a walk."

"When a boy like that goes out for a walk, he does not take a change with him," said Peggy. "He may be lying in Kirtell deeps for anything we can tell. And me that will have to break it to his mother—"

Hugh stood still in consternation for a moment, and then he burst into an agitated laugh. "He would not have taken a change with him, as you say, into Kirtell deeps," he said. "Nonsense, Peggy! Are you sure he has not been in bed? Don't you go and frighten my mother. And, indeed, I daresay he does not always go to bed. I see his light burning all the night through, sometimes. Peggy, don't go and put such ridiculous ideas into people's heads. Will has gone out to walk, as usual. There he is, downstairs. I hear him coming in: make haste, and cook his trout."

Hugh, however, was so frightened himself by all the terrors of inexperience, that he precipitated himself downstairs, to see if it was really Will who had entered. It was not Will, however, but a boy from the railway, with a note, in Will's handwriting, addressed to his mother, which took all the colour out of Hugh's cheeks—for he was still a boy, and new to life, and did not think of any such easy demonstration of discontent as that of going to visit Uncle Penrose. He went into the breakfast-room with so pale a face, that both the ladies got up in dismay, and made a rush at him to know what it was.

"It is nothing," said Hugh, breathless, waving them off, "nothing—only a note—I have not read it yet—wait a little. Mother, don't be afraid."

"What is there to be afraid of?" asked Mary, in amazement and dismay.

And then Hugh again burst into an unsteady and tremulous laugh. He had read the note, and threw it at his mother with an immense load lifted off his heart, and feeling wildly gay in the revulsion. "There's nothing to be frightened about," said Hugh. "By Jove! to think the fellow has no more taste—gone off to see Uncle Penrose. I wish them joy!"

"Who is it that has gone to visit Mr. Penrose?" said Aunt Agatha; and Hugh burst into an explanation, while Mary, not by any means so much relieved, read her boy's letter.

"I confess I got a fright," said Hugh. "Peggy dragged me upstairs to show me that he had not slept in his bed, and said his carpet-bag was gone, and insinuated—I don't know what—that we had quarrelled, and all sorts of horrors. But he's gone to see Uncle Penrose. It's all right, mother; I always thought it was all right."

"And had you quarrelled?" asked Aunt Agatha, in consternation.

"I am not sure it is all right," said Mary; "why has he gone to see Uncle Penrose? and what has he heard? and without saying a word to me."

Mary was angry with her boy, and it made her heart sore—it was the first time any of them had taken a sudden step out of her knowledge—and then what had he heard? Something worse than any simple offence or discontent might be lurking behind.

But Hugh, of course, knew nothing at all about that. He sat down again to his interrupted breakfast, and laughed and talked, and made merry. "I wonder what Uncle Penrose will say to him?" said Hugh. "I suppose he has gone and spent all his money getting to Liverpool; and what could his motive be, odd fellow as he is? The girls are all married—"

"My dear boy, Will is not thinking of girls as you are," said Mary, beguiled into a smile.

Hugh laughed and grew red, and shook his abundant youthful locks. "We are not talking of what I think," he said; "and I suppose a man may do worse than think about girls—a little: but the question is, what was Will thinking about? Uncle Penrose cannot have ensnared him with his odious talk about money? By-the-way, I must send him some. We can't let an Ochterlony be worried about a few miserable shillings there."

"I don't think we can let an Ochterlony, at least so young a one as Will, stay uninvited," said Mary. "I feel much disposed to go after him and bring him home, or at least find out what he means."

"No, you shall do nothing of the kind," said Hugh, hastily. "I suppose our mother can trust her sons out of her sight. Nobody must go after him. Why, he is seventeen—almost grown up. He must not feel any want of confidence—"

"Want of confidence!" said Aunt Agatha. "Hugh, you are only a boy yourself. What do you know about it? I think Mary would be very wrong if she let Will throw himself into temptation; and one knows there is every kind of temptation in those large, wicked towns," said Miss Seton, shuddering. It was she who knew nothing about it, no more than a baby, and still less did she know or guess the kind of temptation that was acting upon the truant's mind.

"If that were all," said Mary, slowly, and then she sighed. She was not afraid of the temptations of a great town. She did not even know what she feared. She wanted to bring back her boy, to hear from his own lips what his motive was. It did not seem possible that there could be any harm meant by his boyish secrecy. It was even hard for his mother to persuade herself that Will could think of any harm; but still it was strange. When she thought of Percival's visit and Will's expedition to Carlisle, her heart fluttered within her, though she scarcely knew why. Will was not like other boys of his age; and then it was "something he had heard." "I think," she said, with hesitation, "that one of us should go—either you or I—"

"No," said Hugh. "No, mother, no; don't think of it; as if he were a girl or a Frenchman! Why it's Will! What harm can he do? If he likes to visit Uncle Penrose, let him; it will not be such a wonderful delight. I'll send him some money to-day."

This, of course, was how it was settled; for Mary's terrors were not strong enough to contend with her natural English prejudices against surveillance and restraint, backed by Hugh's energetic remonstrances. When Winnie heard of it, she dashed immediately at the idea that her husband's influence had something to do with Will's strange flight, and was rather pleased and flattered by the thought. "I said he would strike me through my friends," she said to Aunt Agatha, who was bewildered, and did not know what this could mean.

"My dear love, what good could it do him to interfere with Will?" said Miss Seton. "A mere boy, and who has not a penny. If he had wanted to injure us, it would have been Hugh that he would have tried to lead away."

"To lead away?" said Winnie scornfully. "What does he care for leading away? He wants to do harm, real harm. He thinks he can strike me through my friends."

When Aunt Agatha heard this she turned round to Mary, who had just come into the room, and gave a little deprecating shake of her head, and a pathetic look. Poor Winnie! She could think of nothing but her husband and his intentions; and how could he do this quiet household real harm? Mary said nothing, but her uneasiness increased more and more. She could not sit down to her work, or take up any of her ordinary occupations. She went to Will's room and examined it throughout, and looked through his wardrobe to see what he had taken with him, and searched vainly for any evidence of his meaning; and then she wrote him a long letter of questions and appeals, which would have been full of pathetic eloquence to anybody who knew what was in her mind, but would have appeared simply amazing and unintelligible to anybody ignorant of her history, as she herself perceived, and burnt it, and wrote a second, in which there was still a certain mystery. She reminded him that he might have gone away comfortably with everybody's knowledge, instead of making the household uneasy about him; and she could not but let a little wonder creep through, that of all people in the world it was Uncle Penrose whom he had elected to visit; and then she made an appeal to him: "What have I done to forfeit my boy's confidence? what can you have heard, oh Will, my dear boy, that you could not tell to your mother?" Her mind was relieved by writing, but still she was uneasy and disquieted. If he had been severely kept in, or had any reason to fear a refusal;—but to steal away when he might have full leave and every facility; this was one of the things which appeared the most strange.

The servants, for their part, set it down to a quarrel with his brother, and jealousy about Nelly, and took Hugh's part, who was always the favourite. And as for Hugh himself, he sent his brother a cheque (his privilege of drawing cheques being still new, and very agreeable), and asked why he was such an ass as to run away, and bade him enjoy himself. The house was startled—but after all, it was no such great matter; and nobody except Mary wasted much consideration upon Will's escapade after that first morning. He was but a boy; and it was natural, everybody thought, that boys should do something foolish now and then.

CHAPTER XXXVIII

In a curious state of mind, Will was flying along towards Liverpool, while this commotion arose in the Cottage. Not even now had the matter taken any moral aspect to him. He did not feel that he had gone skulking off to deliver a cowardly blow. All that he was conscious of was the fact, that having something to tell which he could not somehow persuade himself to tell, he was going to make the communication from a distance under Uncle Penrose's advice. And yet the boy was not comfortable. It had become apparent to him vaguely, that after this communication was made, the relations existing between himself and his family must be changed. That his mother might be "angry," which was his boyish term for any or every displeasure that might cloud Mrs. Ochterlony's mind; that Hugh might take it badly—and that after all it was a troublesome business, and he would be pleased to get it over. He was travelling in the cheapest way, for his money was scanty; but he was not the kind of boy to be beguiled from his own thoughts by the curious third-class society into which he was thus brought, or even by the country, which gradually widened and expanded under his eyes from the few beaten paths he knew so well, into that wide unknown stretch of hill and plain which was the world. A vague excitement, it is true, came into his mind as he felt himself to have passed out of the reach of everything he knew, and to have entered upon the undiscovered; but this excitement did not draw him out of his own thoughts. It did but mingle with them, and put a quickening thrill of life into the strange maze. The confused country people at the stations, who did not know which carriage to take, and wandered, hurried and disconsolate, on the platforms, looking into all—the long swift moment of passage over the silent country, in which the train, enveloped in its own noise, made for itself a distinct atmosphere—and then again a shriek, a pause, and another procession of faces looking in at the window—this was Will's idea of the long journey. He was not imaginative; but still everybody appeared to him hurried, and downcast, and pre-occupied. Even the harmless country folks had the air of having something on their minds. And through all he kept on pondering what his mother and what Hugh would say. Poor boy! his discovery had given him no advantage as yet; but it had put a cross upon his shoulders—it had bound him so hard and fast that he could not escape from it. It had brought, if not guilt, yet the punishment of guilt into all his thoughts.

Mr. Penrose had a handsome house at some distance from Liverpool, as was usual. And Will found it a very tedious and troublesome business to get there, not to speak of the calls for sixpences from omnibuses and porters, and everybody (he thought) who looked at him, which was very severe on his slender purse. And when he arrived, his uncle's servants looked upon him with manifest suspicion; he had never been there before, and Mr. Penrose was now living alone, his wife being dead, and all his children married, so that there was nobody in the house who could identify the unknown nephew. The Cottage was not much bigger than Mr. Penrose's porter's lodge, and yet that small tenement had looked down upon the great mansion all its life, and been partly ashamed of it, which sentiment gave Will an unconscious sense that he was doing Uncle Penrose an honour in going to visit him. But when he was met at the door by the semi-polite suspicion of the butler, who proposed that he should call again, with an evident reference in his mind to the spoons, it gave the boy the forlornest feeling that can be conceived. He was alone, and they thought him an impostor, and nobody here knew or cared whether he was shut out from the house or not. His heart went back to his home with that revulsion which everybody knows. There, everybody would have rushed to open the door to him, and welcome him back; and though his errand here was simply to do that home as much injury as possible, his heart swelled at the contrast. While he stood, however, insisting upon admittance in his dogged way, without showing any feelings, it happened that Mr. Penrose drove up to the door, and hailed his nephew with much surprise. "You here, Will?" Mr. Penrose said. "I hope nothing has gone wrong at the Cottage?" and his man's hand instantly, and as by magic, relaxed from the door.

"There is nothing wrong, sir," said Will, "but I wanted to speak to you;" and he entered triumphantly, not without a sense of victory, as the subdued servant took his bag out of his hand. Mr. Penrose was, as we have said, alone. He had shed, as it were, all incumbrances, and was ready, unfettered by any ties or prejudices, to grow richer and wiser and more enlightened every day. His children were all married, and his wife having fulfilled all natural offices of this life, and married all her daughters, had quietly taken her dismissal when her duties were over, and had a very handsome tombstone, which he looked at on Sunday. It occurred to very few people, however, to lament over Mr. Penrose's loneliness. He seemed to have been freed from all impediments, and left at liberty to grow rich, to get fat, and to believe in his own greatness and wisdom. Nor did it occur to himself to feel his great house lonely. He liked eating a luxurious dinner by himself, and knowing how much it had cost, all for his single lordly appetite—the total would have been less grand if wife and children had shared it. And then he had other things to think of—substantial things, about interest and investments, and not mere visionary reflections about the absence of other chairs or other faces at his table. But he had a natural interest in Wilfrid, as in a youth who had evidently come to ask his advice, which was an article he was not disinclined to give away. And then "the Setons," as he called his sister's family and descendants, had generally shut their ears to his advice, and shown an active absence of all political qualities, so that Will's visit was a compliment of the highest character, something like an unexpected act of homage from Mordecai in the gate.

But even Mr. Penrose was struck dumb by Will's communication. He put up his hand to his cravat and gasped, and thumped himself on the breast, staring at the boy with round, scared, apoplectic eyes—like the eyes of a boiled fish. He stared at Will,—who told the story calmly enough, with a matter-of-fact conciseness—and looked as if he was disposed to ring the bell and send for a doctor, and get out of the difficulty by concluding his nephew to be mad. But there was no withstanding the evidence of plain good faith and sincerity in Will's narration. Mr. Penrose remained silent longer than anybody had ever known him to remain silent before, and he was not even very coherent when he had regained the faculty of speech.

"That woman was present, was she?" he said, "and Winnie's husband—good Lord! And so you mean to tell me Mary has been all this time—When I asked her to my house, and my wife intended to make a party for her, and all that—and when she preferred to visit at Earlston, and that old fool, Sir Edward, who never had a penny—except what he settled on Winnie—and all that time, you know, Mary was—good Lord!"

"I don't see what difference it makes to my mother," said Will. "She is just what she always was—the difference it makes is to me—and of course to Hugh."

But this was not a view that Mr. Penrose could take, who knew more about the world than Will could be supposed to know—though his thoughts were usually so preoccupied by what he called the practical aspect of everything. Yet he was disturbed in this case by reflections which were almost imaginative, and which utterly amazed Will. He got up, though he was still in the middle of dessert, and walking about the room, making exclamations. "That's what she has been, you know, all this time—Mary, of all people in the world! Good Lord! That's what she was, when we asked her here." These were the exclamations that kept bursting from Uncle Penrose's amazed lips—and Will at last grew angry and impatient, and hurried into the practical matter on his own initiative.

"When you have made up your mind about it, Uncle, I should be glad to know what you think best to be done," said Will, in his steady way, and he looked at his adviser with those sceptical, clear-sighted eyes, which, more than anything else, make a practical man ashamed of having indulged in any momentary aberration.

Mr. Penrose came back to his chair and sat down, and looked with respect, and something that was almost awe, in Will's face. Then the boy continued, seeing his advantage: "You must see what an important thing it is between Hugh and me," he said. "It is a matter of business, of course, and it would be far better to settle it at once. If I am the right heir, you know, Earlston ought to be mine. I have heard you say, feelings had nothing to do with the right and wrong."

"No," said Mr. Penrose, with a slight gasp; "that is quite true; but it is all so sudden, you know—and Mary—I don't know what you want me to do—"

"I want you to write and tell them about it," said Will.

Mr. Penrose put his lips into the shape they would naturally have taken had he been whistling as usual; but he was not capable of a whistle. "It is all very easy to talk," he said, "and naturally business is business, and I am not a man to think too much about feelings. But Mary—the fact is, it must be a matter of arrangement, Will. There can't be any trial, you know, or publicity to expose her—"

"I don't see that it would matter much to her," said Will. "She would not mind; it would only be one of her sons instead of the other, and I suppose she likes me the same as Hugh."

"I was not thinking of Hugh, or you either. I was thinking of your mother," said Mr. Penrose, thrusting his hands into the depths of his pockets, and staring with vacant eyes into the air before him. He was matter-of-fact himself, but he could not comprehend the obtuseness of ignorance and self-occupation and youth.

"Well?" said Will.

"Well," cried the uncle, turning upon him, "are you blind, or stupid, or what? Don't you see it never can come to publicity, or she will be disgraced? I don't say you are to give up your rights, if they are your rights, for that. I daresay you'll take a deal better care of everything than that fellow Hugh, and won't be so confounded saucy. But if you go and make a row about it in public, she can never hold up her head again, you know. I don't mind talk myself in a general way; but talk about a woman's marriage,—good Lord! There must be no public row, whatever you do."

"I don't see why there should be any public row," said Will; "all that has to be done is to let them know."

"I suppose you think Hugh will take it quite comfortable," said Mr. Penrose, "and lay down everything like a lamb. He's not a business man, nor good for much; but he will never be such an idiot as that; and then you would need to have your witnesses very distinct, if it was to come to anything. He has possession in his favour, and that is a good deal, and it is you who would have to prove everything. Are you quite sure that your witnesses would be forthcoming, and that you could make the case clear?"

"I don't know about making the case clear," said Will, who began to get confused; "all I know is what I have told you. Percival was there, and Mrs. Kirkman—they saw it, you know—and she says Hugh himself was there. Of course he was only a child. But she said no doubt he would remember, if it was brought to his mind."

"Hugh himself!" said Mr. Penrose—again a little startled, though he was not a person of fine feelings. The idea of appealing to the recollections of the child for evidence against the man's rights, struck him as curious at least. He was staggered, though he felt that he ought to have been above that. Of course it was all perfectly just and correct, and nobody could have been more clear than he, that any sort of fantastic delicacy coming between a man and his rights would be too absurd to be thought of. And yet it cannot be denied that he was staggered in spite of himself.

"I think if you told him distinctly, and recalled it to his recollection, and he knew everything that was involved," said Will, with calm distinctness, "that Hugh would give in. It is the only thing he could do; and I should not say anything to him about a younger brother's portion, or two thousand pounds," the lad added, kindling up. "He should have everything that the money or the estate could do for him—whatever was best for him, if it cost half or double what Earlston was worth."

"Then why on earth don't you leave him Earlston, if you are so generous?" said Mr. Penrose. "If you are to spend it all upon him, what good would it do you having the dreary old place?"

"I should have my rights," said Will with solemnity. It was as if he had been a disinherited prince whom some usurper had deprived of his kingdom; and this strange assumption was so honest in its way, and had such an appearance of sincerity, that Mr. Penrose was struck dumb, and gazed at the boy with a consternation which he could not express. His rights! Mary's youngest son, whom everybody, up to this moment, had thought of only as a clever, not very amiable boy, of no particular account anywhere. The merchant began to wake up to the consciousness that he had a phenomenon before him—a new development of man. As he recovered from his surprise, he began to appreciate Will—to do justice to the straightforward ardour of his determination that business was business, and that feelings had nothing to do with it; and to admire his calm impassibility to every other view of the case but that which concerned himself. Mr. Penrose thought it was the result of a great preconcerted plan, and began to awake into admiration and respect. He thought the solemnity, and the calm, and that beautiful confidence in his rights, were features of a subtle and precocious scheme which Will had made for himself; and his thoughts, which had been dwelling for the moment on Mary, with a kind of unreflective sympathy, turned towards the nobler object thus presented before him. Here was a true apotheosis of interest over nature. Here was such a man of business, heaven-born, as had never been seen before. Mr. Penrose warmed and kindled into admiration, and he made a secret vow that such a genius should not be lost.

As for Will, he never dreamt of speculating as to what were his uncle's thoughts. He was quite content that he had told his own tale, and so got over the first preliminary difficulty of getting it told to those whom it most concerned; and he was very sleepy—dreadfully tired, and more anxious to curl up his poor, young, weary head under his wing, and get to bed, than for anything else in the world. Yet, notwithstanding, when he lay down, and had put out his light, and had begun to doze, the thought came over him that he saw the glow of his mother's candle shining in under his door, and heard her step on the stairs, which had been such a comfort to him many a night when he was a child, and woke up in the dark and heard her pass, and knew her to be awake and watching, and was not even without a hope that she might come in and stand for a moment, driving away all ghosts and terrors of the night, by his bed. He thought he saw the light under his door, and heard the foot coming up the stairs. And so probably he did: but the poor boy woke right up under this fancy, and remembered with a compunction that he was far away from his mother, and that probably she was "angry," and perhaps anxious about his sudden departure; and he was very sorry in his heart to have come away so, and never to have told her. But he was not sorry nor much troubled anyhow about the much more important thing he was about to do.

And Uncle Penrose, under the strange stimulus of his visitor's earnestness, addressed himself to the task required of him, and wrote to Hugh. He, too, thought first of writing to Mrs. Ochterlony; but, excellent business man as he was, he could not do it; it went against his heart, if he had a heart,—or, if not his heart, against some digestive organ which served him instead of that useful but not indispensable part of the human frame. But he did write to Hugh—that was easier; and then Hugh had been "confounded saucy," and had rejected his advice, not about the Museum only, but in other respects. Mr. Penrose wrote the letter that very night while Will was dreaming about his mother's light; and so the great wheel was set a-going, which none of them could then stop for ever.

CHAPTER XXXIX

Hugh had left the Cottage the day after Will's departure. He had gone to Earlston, where a good deal of business about the Museum and the estate awaited him; and he had gone off without any particular burden on his mind. As for Will's flight from home, it was odd, no doubt; but then Will himself was odd, and out-of-the-way acts were to be expected from him. When Hugh, with careless liberality, had sent him the cheque, he dismissed the subject from his mind—at least, he thought of his younger brother only with amusement, wondering what he could find to attract him in Uncle Penrose's prosaic house,—trying to form an imagination of Will wandering about the great Liverpool docks, looking at the big ships, and all the noisy traffic; and Hugh laughed within himself to think how very much all that was out of Will's way. No doubt he would come home in a day or two bored to death, and would loathe the very name of Liverpool all his life thereafter. As for Mr. Ochterlony of Earlston himself, he had a great deal to do. The mayor and corporation of Dalken had come to a final decision about the Museum, and all that had to be done was to prepare the rooms which were to receive Mr. Francis Ochterlony's treasures, and to transfer with due tenderness and solemnity the Venus and the Psyche, and all the delicate wealth which had been so dear to the heart of "the old Squire." The young Squire went round and looked at them all, with a great tenderness in his own, remembering his uncle's last progress among them, and where he sat down to rest, and the wistful looks he gave to those marble white creations which stood to him in the place of wife and children; and the pathetic humour with which he had said, "It is all the better for you." It was the better for Hugh; but still the young man in the fulness of his hopes had a tender compunction for the old man who had died without getting the good of his life, and with no treasures but marble and bronze and gold and silver to leave behind him. "My poor uncle!" Hugh said; and yet the chances were that Francis Ochterlony was not, either in living or dying, sorry for himself. Hugh had a kind of reluctance to change the aspect of everything, and make the house his own house, and not Francis Ochterlony's. It seemed almost impious to take from it the character it had borne so long, and at the same time it was his uncle's wish. These were Hugh's thoughts at night, but in the fresh light of the morning it would be wrong to deny that another set of ideas took possession of his mind. Then he began to think of the new aspect, and the changes he could make. It was not bright enough for a home for—well, for any lady that might happen to come on a visit or otherwise; and, to be sure, Hugh had no intention of accepting as final his mother's determination not to leave the Cottage. He made up his mind that she would come, and that people—various people, ladies and others—would come to visit her; that there should be flowers and music and smiles about the place, and perhaps some one as fair and as sweet as Psyche to change the marble moonlight into sacred living sunshine. Now the fact was, that Nelly was not by any means so fair as Psyche—that she was not indeed what you would call a regular beauty at all, but only a fresh, faulty, sweet little human creature, with warm blood in her veins, and a great many thoughts in her little head. And when Hugh thought of some fair presence coming into these rooms and making a Paradise of them, either it was not Nelly Askell he was thinking of, or else he was thinking like a poet—though he was not poetical, to speak of. However, he did not himself give any name to his imaginations—he could afford to be vague. He went all over the house in the morning, not with the regretful, affectionate eye with which he made the same survey the night before, but in a practical spirit. At his age, and in his position, the practical was only a pleasanter variation of the romantic aspect of affairs. As he thought of new furniture, scores of little pictures flashed into his mind—though in ordinary cases he was not distinguished by a powerful imagination. He had no sooner devised the kind of chair that should stand in a particular corner, than straightway a little figure jumped into it, a whisper of talk came out of it, with a host of imaginary circumstances which had nothing to do with upholstery. Even the famous rococo chair which Islay had broken was taken possession of by that vague, sweet phantom. And he went about the rooms with an unconscious smile on his face, devising and planning. He did not know he was smiling; it was not at anything or about anything. It was but the natural expression of the fresh morning fancies and sweet stir of everything hopeful, and bright, and uncertain, which was in his heart.

And when he went out of doors he still smiled. Earlston was a grey limestone house, as has been described in the earlier part of this history. A house which chilled Mrs. Ochterlony to the heart when she first went there with her little children in the first forlornness of her widowhood. What Hugh had to do now was to plan a flower-garden for—his mother; yes, it was truly for his mother. He meant that she should come all the same. Nothing could make any difference so far as she was concerned. But at the same time, to be sure, he did not mean that his house should make the same impression on any other stranger as that house had made upon Mary. He planned how the great hedges should be cut down, and the trees thinned, and the little moorland burn should be taken in within the enclosure, and followed to its very edge by the gay lawn with its flower-beds. He planned a different approach—where there might be openings in the dark shrubberies, and views over the hills. All this he did in the morning, with a smile on his face, though the tears had been in his eyes at the thought of any change only the previous night. If Francis Ochterlony had been by, as perhaps he was, no doubt he would have smiled at that tender inconsistency—and there would not have been any bitterness in the smile.

And then Hugh went in to breakfast. He had already some new leases to sign and other business matters to do, and he was quite pleased to do it—as pleased as he had been to draw his first cheques. He sat down at his breakfast-table, before the little pile of letters that awaited him, and felt the importance of his new position. Even his loneliness made him feel its importance the more. Here were questions of all sorts submitted to him, and it was he who had to answer, without reference to anybody—he whose advice a little while ago nobody would have taken the trouble to ask. It was not that he cared to exercise his privilege—for Hugh, on the whole, had an inclination to be advised—but still the sense of his independence was sweet. He meant to ask Mr. Preston, the attorney, about various things, and he meant to consult his mother, and to lay some special affairs before Sir Edward—but still, at the time, it was he who had everything to do, and Mr. Ochterlony of Earlston sat down before his letters with a sense of satisfaction which does not always attend the mature mind in that moment of trial. One of the uppermost was from Uncle Penrose, redirected from the Cottage, but it did not cause any thrill of interest to Hugh's mind, who put it aside calmly, knowing of no thunderbolts that might be in it. No doubt it was some nonsense about the Museum, he thought, as if he himself was not a much better judge about the Museum than a stranger and business-man could be. There was, however, a letter from Mary, which directed her son's attention to this epistle. "I send you a letter directed in Uncle Penrose's hand," wrote Mrs. Ochterlony, "which I have had the greatest inclination to open, to see what he says about Will. I daresay you would not have minded; but I conclude, on the whole, that Mr. Ochterlony of Earlston should have his letters to himself; so I send it on to you uninvaded. Let me know what he says about your brother." Hugh could not but laugh when he read this, half with pleasure, half with amusement. His mother's estimate of his importance entertained him greatly, and the idea of anything private being in Uncle Penrose's letter tickled him still more. Then he drew it towards him lightly, and began to read it with eyes running over with laughter. He was all alone, and there was nobody to see any change of sentiment in his face.

He was all alone—but yet presently Hugh raised his eyes from the letter which he had taken up so gaily, and cast a scared look round him, as if to make sure that nobody was there. The smile had gone off his face, and the laughter out of his eyes,—and not only that, but every particle of colour had left his face. And yet he did not see the meaning of what he had read. "Will!" he said to himself. "Will!" He was horror-stricken and bewildered, but that was the sole idea it conveyed to him—a sense of treachery—the awful feeling of unreality and darkness round about, with which the young soul for the first time sees itself injured and betrayed. He laid down the letter half read, and paused, and put up his hands to his head as if to convince himself that he was not dreaming. Will! Good God! Will! Was it possible? Hugh had to make a convulsive effort to grasp this unnatural horror. Will, one of themselves, to have gone off, and put himself into the hands of Uncle Penrose, and set himself against his mother and her sons! The ground seemed to fail under his feet, the solid world to fall off round him into bewildering mystery. Will! And yet he did not apprehend what it was. His mind could not take in more than one discovery at a time. A minute before, and he was ready to have risked everything on the good faith of any and every human creature he knew. Now, was there anybody to be trusted? His brother had stolen from his side, and was striking at him by another and an unfriendly hand. Will! Good heavens, Will!

It would be difficult to tell how long it was before the full meaning of the letter he had thus received entered into Hugh's mind. He sat with the breakfast things still on the table so long, that the housekeeper herself came at last with natural inquisitiveness to see if anything was the matter, and found Hugh with a face as grey and colourless as that of the old Squire, sitting over his untasted coffee, unaware, apparently, what he was about. He started when she came in, and bundled up his letters into his pocket, and gave an odd laugh, and said he had been busy, and had forgotten. And then he sprang up and left the room, paying no attention to her outcry that he had eaten nothing. Hugh was not aware he had eaten nothing, or probably in the first horror of his discovery of the treachery in the world, he too would have taken to false pretences and saved appearances, and made believe to have breakfasted. But the poor boy was unaware, and rushed off to the library, where nobody could have any pretext for disturbing him, and shut himself up with this first secret—the new, horrible discovery which had changed the face of the world. This was the letter which he had crushed up in his hand as he might have crushed a snake or deadly reptile, but which nothing could crush out of his heart, where the sting had entered and gone deep:—

"MY DEAR NEPHEW,—It is with pain that I write to you, though it is my clear duty to do so in the interests of your brother, who has just put his case into my hands—and I don't doubt that the intelligence I am about to convey will be a great blow, not only to your future prospects but to your pride and sense of importance, which so fine a position at your age had naturally elevated considerably higher than a plain man like myself could approve of. Your brother arrived here to-day, and has lost no time in informing me of the singular circumstances under which he left home, and of which, so far as I understand him, you and your mother are still in ignorance. Wilfrid's perception of the fact that feelings, however creditable to him as an individual, ought not to stand in the way of what is, strictly speaking, a matter of business, is very clear and uncompromising; but still he does not deny that he felt it difficult to make this communication either to you or his mother. Accident, the nature of which I do not at present, before knowing your probable course of action, feel myself at liberty to indicate more plainly, has put him in possession of certain facts, which would change altogether the relations between him and yourself, as well as your (apparent) position as head of the family. These facts, which, for your mother's sake, I should be deeply grieved to make known out of the family, are as follows: your father, Major Ochterlony, and my niece, instead of being married privately in Scotland, as we all believed, in the year 1830, or thereabouts—I forget the exact date—were in reality only married in India in the year 1837, by the chaplain, the Rev.—Churchill, then officiating at the station where your father's regiment was. This, as you are aware, was shortly before Wilfrid's birth, and not long before Major Ochterlony died. It is subject of thankfulness that your father did my niece this tardy justice before he was cut off, as may be said, in the flower of his days, but you will see at a glance that it entirely reverses your respective positions—and that in fact Wilfrid is Major Ochterlony's only lawful son.

"I am as anxious as you can be that this should be made a matter of family arrangement, and should never come to the public ears. To satisfy your own mind, however, of the perfect truth of the assertion I have made, I beg to refer you to the Rev. Mr. Churchill, who performed the ceremony, and whose present address, which Wilfrid had the good sense to secure, you will find below—and to Mrs. Kirkman, who was present. Indeed, I am informed that you yourself were present—though probably too young to understand what it meant. It is possible that on examining your memory you may find some trace of the occurrence, which though not dependable upon by itself, will help to confirm the intelligence to your mind. We are in no hurry, and will leave you the fullest time to satisfy yourself, as well as second you in every effort to prevent any painful consequence from falling upon your mother, who has (though falsely) enjoyed the confidence and esteem of her friends so long.

"For yourself you may reckon upon Wilfrid's anxious endeavours to further your prospects by every means in his power. Of course I do not expect you to take a fact involving so much, either upon his word or mine. Examine it fully for yourself, and the more entirely the matter is cleared up, the more will it be for our satisfaction, as well as your own. The only thing I have to desire for my own part is that you will spare your mother—as your brother is most anxious to do. Hoping for an early reply, I am, your affectionate uncle and sincere friend,—J. P. PENROSE."

Hugh sat in Francis Ochterlony's chair, at his table, with his head supported on his hands, looking straight before him, seeing nothing, not even thinking, feeling only this letter spread out upon the table, and the intelligence conveyed in it, and holding his head, which ached and throbbed with the blow, in his hands. He was still, and his head throbbed and his heart and soul ached, tingling through him to every joint and every vein. He could not even wonder, nor doubt, nor question in any way, for the first terrible interval. All he could do was to look at the fact and take it fully into his mind, and turn it over and over, seeing it all round on every side, looking at it this way and that way, and feeling as if somehow heaven and earth were filled with it, though he had never dreamt of such a ghost until that hour. Not his, after all—nor Earlston, nor his name, nor the position he had been so proud of; nothing his—alas, not even his mother, his spotless mother, the woman whom it had been an honour and glory to come from and belong to. When a groan came from the poor boy's white lips it was that he was thinking of. Madonna Mary! that was the name they had called her by—and this was how it really was. He groaned aloud, and made an unconscious outcry of his pain when it came to that. "Oh, my God, if it had only been ruin, loss of everything—anything in the world but that!" This was the first stage of stupefaction and yet of vivid consciousness, before the indignation came. He sat and looked at it, and realized it, and took it into his mind, staring at it until every drop of blood ebbed away from his face. This was how it was before the anger came. After a while his countenance and his mood changed—the colour and heat came rushing back to his cheeks and lips, and a flood of rage and resentment swept over him like a sudden storm. Will! could it be Will? Liar! coward! traitor! to call her mother, and to tax her with shame even had it been true—to frame such a lying, cursed, devilish accusation against her! Then it was that Hugh flashed into a fiery, burning shame to think that he had given credence to it for one sole moment. He turned his eyes upon her, as it were, and looked into her face and glowed with a bitter indignation and fury. His mother's face! only to think of it and dare to fancy that shame could ever have been there. And then the boy wept, in spite of his manhood—wept a few, hot, stinging tears, that dried up the moment they fell, half for rage, half for tenderness.—And, oh, my God, was it Will? Then as his mind roused more and more to the dread emergency, Hugh got up and went to the window and gazed out, as if that would help him; and his eye lighted on the tangled thicket which he had meant to make into his mother's flower-garden, and upon the sweep of trees through which he had planned his new approach, and once more he groaned aloud. Only this morning so sure about it all, so confidently and carelessly happy—now with not one clear step before him to take, with no future, no past that he could dare look back upon—no name, nor rights of any kind—if this were true. And could it be otherwise than true? Could any imagination frame so monstrous and inconceivable a falsehood?—such a horrible impossibility might be fact, but it was beyond all the bounds of fancy;—and then the blackness of darkness descended again upon Hugh's soul. Poor Mary, poor mother! It came into the young man's mind to go to her and take her in his arms, and carry her away somewhere out of sight of men and sound of their voices—and again there came to his eyes those stinging tears. Fault of hers it could not be; she might have been deceived; and then poor Hugh's lips, unaccustomed to curses, quivered and stopped short as they were about to curse the father whom he never knew. Here was the point at which the tide turned again. Could it be Hugh Ochterlony who had deceived his wife? he whose sword hung in Mary's room, whose very name made a certain music in her voice when she pronounced it, and whom she had trained her children to reverence with that surpassing honour which belongs to the dead alone. Again a storm of rage and bitter indignation swept in his despair and bewilderment over the young man's mind; an accursed scheme, a devilish, hateful lie—that was how it was: and oh, horror! that it should be Will.

Through all these changes it was one confused tempest of misery and dismay that was in Hugh's mind. Now and then there would be wild breaks in the clouds—now they would be whirled over the sky in gusts—now settled down into a blackness beyond all reckoning. Lives change from joy to misery often enough in this world; but seldom thus in a moment, in the twinkling of an eye. His careless boat had been taking its sweet course over waters rippled with a favourable breeze, and without a moment's interval he was among the breakers; and he knew so little how to manage it, he was so inexperienced to cope with wind and waves. And he had nobody to ask counsel from. He was, as Will had been, separated from his natural adviser, the one friend to whom hitherto he had confided all his difficulties. But Hugh was older than Will, and his mind had come to a higher development, though perhaps he was not so clever as his brother. He had no Uncle Penrose to go to; no living soul would hear from him this terrible tale; he could consult nobody. Not for a hundred Earlstons, not for all the world, would he have discussed with any man in existence his mother's good name.

Yet with that, too, there came another complication into Hugh's mind. Even while he actually thought in his despair of going to his mother, and telling her any tender lie that might occur to him, and carrying her away to Australia, or any end of the world where he could work for her, and remove her for ever from shame and pain, a sense of outraged justice and rights assailed was in his mind. He was not one of those who can throw down their arms. Earlston was his, and he could not relinquish it and his position as head of the house without a struggle. And the thought of Mr. Penrose stung him. He even tried to heal one of his deeper wounds by persuading himself that Uncle Penrose was at the bottom of it, and that poor Will was but his tool. Poor Will! Poor miserable boy! And if he ever woke and came to himself, and knew what he had been doing, how terrible would his position be! Thus Hugh tried to think till, wearied out with thinking, he said to himself that he would put it aside and think no more of it, and attend to his business; which vain imagination the poor boy tried to carry out with hands that shook and brain that refused to obey his guidance. And all this change was made in one little moment. His life came to a climax, and passed through a secret revolution in that one day; and yet he had begun it as if it had been an ordinary day—a calm summer morning in the summer of his days.

This was what Hugh said to his mother of Mr. Penrose's letter:—"The letter you forwarded to me from Uncle Penrose was in his usual business strain—good advice, and that sort of thing. He does not say much about Will; but he has arrived all safe, and I suppose is enjoying himself—as well as he can, there."

And when he had written and despatched that note he sat down to think again. He decided at last that he would not go on with the flower-garden and the other works—till he saw; but that he would settle about the Museum without delay. "If it came to the worst they would not recall the gift," he said to himself, brushing his hand across his eyes. It was his uncle's wish; and it was he, Hugh, and not any other, whom Francis Ochterlony wished for his heir. Hugh's hand was wet when he took it from his eyes, and his heart was full, and he could have wept like a child. But he was a man, and weeping could do no good; and he had nobody in the world to take his trouble to—nobody in the world. Love and pride made a fence round him, and isolated him. He had to make his way out of it as best he could, and alone. He made a great cry to God in his trouble; but from nobody in the world could he have either help or hope. And he read the letter over and over, and tried to recollect and to go back into his dim baby-memory of India, and gather out of the thick mists that scene which they said he had been present at. Was there really some kind of vague image of it, all broken and indistinct and effaced, on his mind?

CHAPTER XL

While all this was going on at Earlston, there were other people in whose minds, though the matter was not of importance so overwhelming, pain and excitement and a trembling dread of the consequences had been awakened. Mary, to whom it would be even more momentous than to Hugh, knew nothing of it as yet. She had taken Mr. Penrose's letter into her hand and looked at it, and hesitated, and then had smiled at her boy's new position in the world, and redirected it to him, passing on as it were a living shell just ready to explode without so much as scorching her own delicate fingers. But Mrs. Kirkman felt herself in the position of a woman who had seen the shell fired and had even touched the fatal trigger, and did not know where it had fallen, nor what death and destruction it might have scattered around. She was not like herself for these two or three days. She gave a divided attention to her evangelical efforts, and her mind wandered from the reports of her Bible readers. She seemed to see the great mass of fire and flame striking the ground, and the dead and wounded lying around it in all directions; and it might be that she too was to blame. She bore it as long as she could, trying to persuade herself that she, like Providence, had done it "for the best," and that it might be for Mary's good or Hugh's good, even if it should happen to kill them. This was how she attempted to support and fortify herself; but while she was doing so Wilfrid's steady, matter of fact countenance would come before her, and she would perceive by the instinct of guilt, that he would neither hesitate nor spare, but was clothed in the double armour of egotism and ignorance; that he did not know what horrible harm he could do, and yet that he was sensible of his power and would certainly exercise it. She was like the other people involved—afraid to ask any one's advice, or betray the share she had taken in the business; even her husband, had she spoken to him about it, would probably have asked, what the deuce she had to do interfering? For Colonel Kirkman though a man of very orthodox views, still was liable in a moment of excitement to forget himself, and give force to his sentiments by a mild oath. Mrs. Kirkman could not bear thus to descend in the opinion of any one, and yet she could not satisfy her conscience about it, nor be content with what she had done. She stood out bravely for a few days, telling herself she had only done her duty; but the composure she attained by this means was forced and unnatural. And at last she could bear it no longer; she seemed to have heard the dreadful report, and then to have seen everything relapse into the most deadly silence; no cry coming out of the distance, nor indications if everybody was perishing, or any one had escaped. If she had but heard one outcry—if Hugh, poor fellow, had come storming to her to know the truth of it, or Mary had come with her fresh wounds, crying out against her, Mrs. Kirkman could have borne it; but the silence was more than she could bear. Something within compelled her to get up out of her quiet and go forth and ask who had been killed, even though she might bring herself within the circle of responsibility thereby.

This was why, after she had put up with her anxiety as long as she could, she went out at last by herself in a very disturbed and uneasy state to the Cottage, where all was still peaceful, and no storm had yet darkened the skies. Mary had received Hugh's letter that morning, which he had written in the midst of his first misery, and it had never occurred to her to think anything more about Uncle Penrose after the calm mention her boy made of his letter. She had not heard from Will, it is true, and was vexed by his silence; but yet it was a light vexation. Mrs. Ochterlony, however, was not at home when Mrs. Kirkman arrived; and, if anything could have increased her uneasiness and embarrassment it would have been to be ushered into the drawing-room, and to find Winnie seated there all by herself. Mrs. Percival rose in resentful grandeur when she saw who the visitor was. Now was Winnie's chance to repay that little demonstration of disapproval which the Colonel's wife had made on her last visit to the Cottage. The two ladies made very stately salutations to each other, and the stranger sat down, and then there was a dead pause. "Let Mrs. Ochterlony know when she comes in," Winnie had said to the maid; and that was all she thought necessary to say. Even Aunt Agatha was not near to break the violence of the encounter. Mrs. Kirkman sat down in a very uncomfortable condition, full of genuine anxiety; but it was not to be expected that her natural impulses should entirely yield even to compunction and fright, and a sense of guilt. When a few minutes of silence had elapsed, and Mary did not appear, and Winnie sat opposite to her, wrapt up and gloomy, in her shawl, and her haughtiest air of preoccupation, Mrs. Kirkman began to come to herself. Here was a perishing sinner before her, to whom advice, and reproof, and admonition, might be all important, and such a favourable moment might never come again. The very sense of being rather faulty in her own person gave her a certain stimulus to warn the culpable creature, whose errors were so different, and so much more flagrant than hers. And if in doing her duty, she had perhaps done something that might harm one of the family, was it not all the more desirable to do good to another? Mrs. Kirkman cleared her throat, and looked at the culprit. And as she perceived Winnie's look of defiance, and absorbed self-occupation, and determined opposition to anything that might be advanced, a soft sense of superiority and pity stole into her mind. Poor thing, that did not know the things that belonged to her peace!—was it not a Christian act to bring them before her ere they might be for ever hid from her eyes?

Once more Mrs. Kirkman cleared her throat. She did it with an intention; and Winnie heard, and was roused, and fixed on her one corner of her eye. But she only made a very mild commencement—employing in so important a matter the wisdom of the serpent, conjoined, as it always ought to be, with the sweetness of the dove.

"Mrs. Ochterlony is probably visiting among the poor," said Mrs. Kirkman, but with a sceptical tone in her voice, as if that, at least, was what Mary ought to be doing, though it was doubtful whether she was so well employed.

"Probably," said Winnie, curtly; and then there was a pause.

"To one who occupies herself so much as she does with her family, there must be much to do for three boys," continued Mrs. Kirkman, still with a certain pathos in her voice. "Ah, if we did but give ourselves as much trouble about our spiritual state!"

She waited for a reply, but Winnie gave no reply. She even gave a slight, scarcely perceptible, shrug of her shoulders, and turned a little aside.

"Which is, after all, the only thing that is of any importance," said Mrs. Kirkman. "My dear Mrs. Percival, I do trust that you agree with me?"

"I don't see why I should be your dear Mrs. Percival," said Winnie. "I was not aware that we knew each other. I think you must be making a mistake."

"All my fellow-creatures are dear to me," said Mrs. Kirkman, "especially when I can hope that their hearts are open to grace. I can be making no mistake so long as I am addressing a fellow-sinner. We have all so much reason to abase ourselves, and repent in dust and ashes! Even when we have been preserved more than others from active sin, we must know that the root of all evil is in our hearts."

Winnie gave another very slight shrug of her shoulders, and turned away, as far as a mingled impulse of defiance and politeness would let her. She would neither be rude nor would she permit her assailant to think that she was running away.

"If I venture to seize this moment, and speak to you more plainly than I would speak to all, oh, my dear Mrs. Percival," cried Mrs. Kirkman, "my dear fellow sinner! don't think it is because I am insensible to the existence of the same evil tendency in my own heart."

"What do you mean by talking to me of evil tendencies?" cried Winnie, flushing high. "I don't want to hear you speak. You may be a sinner if you like, but I don't think there is any particular fellowship between you and me."

"There is the fellowship of corrupt hearts," said Mrs. Kirkman. "I hope, for your own sake, you will not refuse to listen for a moment. I may never have been tempted in the same way, but I know too well the deceitfulness of the natural heart to take any credit to myself. You have been exposed to many temptations—"

"You know nothing about me, that I am aware," cried Winnie, with restrained fury. "I do not know how you can venture to take such liberty with me."

"Ah, my dear Mrs. Percival, I know a great deal about you," said Mrs. Kirkman. "There is nothing I would not do to make a favourable impression on your mind. If you would but treat me as a friend, and let me be of some use to you: I know you must have had many temptations; but we know also that it is never too late to turn away from evil, and that with true repentance—"

"I suppose what you want is to drive me out of the room," said Winnie, looking at her fiercely, with crimson cheeks. "What right have you to lecture me? My sister's friends have a right to visit her, of course, but not to make themselves disagreeable—and I don't mean my private affairs to be discussed by Mary's friends. You have nothing to do with me."

"I was not speaking as Mary's friend," said Mrs. Kirkman, with a passing twinge of conscience. "I was speaking only as a fellow-sinner. Dear Mrs. Percival, surely you recollect who it was that objected to be his brother's keeper. It was Cain; it was not a loving Christian heart. Oh, don't sin against opportunity, and refuse to hear me. The message I have is one of mercy and love. Even if it were too late to redeem character with the world, it is never too late to come to—"

Winnie started to her feet, goaded beyond bearing.

"How dare you! how dare you!" she said, clenching her hands,—but Mrs. Kirkman's benevolent purpose was far too lofty and earnest to be put down by any such demonstration of womanish fury.

"If it were to win you to think in time, to withdraw from the evil and seek good, to come while it is called to-day," said the Evangelist, with much stedfastness, "I would not mind even making you angry. I can dare anything in my Master's service—oh, do not refuse the gracious message! Oh, do not turn a deaf ear. You may have forfeited this world, but, oh think of the next; as a Christian and a fellow-sinner—"

"Aunt Agatha!" cried Winnie, breathless with rage and shame, "do you mean to let me be insulted in your house?"

Poor Aunt Agatha had just come in, and knew nothing about Mrs. Kirkman and her visit. She stood at the door surprised, looking at Winnie's excited face, and at the stranger's authoritative calm. She had been out in the village, with a little basket in her hand, which never went empty, and she also had been dropping words of admonition out of her soft and tender lips.

"Insulted! My dear love, it must be some mistake," said Aunt Agatha. "We are always very glad to see Mrs. Kirkman, as Mary's friend; but the house is Mrs. Percival's house, being mine," Miss Seton added, with a little dignified curtsey, thinking the visitor had been uncivil, as on a former occasion. And then there was a pause, and Winnie sat down, fortifying herself by the presence of the mild little woman who was her protector. It was a strange reversal of positions, but yet that was how it was. The passionate creature had now no other protector but Aunt Agatha, and even while she felt herself assured and strengthened by her presence, it gave her a pang to think it was so. Nobody but Aunt Agatha to stand between her and impertinent intrusion—nobody to take her part before the world. That was the moment when Winnie's heart melted, if it ever did melt, for one pulsation and no more, towards her enemy, her antagonist, her husband, who was not there to take advantage of the momentary thaw.

"I am Mary's friend," said Mrs. Kirkman, sweetly; "and I am all your friends. It was not only as Mary's friend I was speaking—it was out of love for souls. Oh, my dear Miss Seton, I hope you are one of those who think seriously of life. Help me to talk to your dear niece; help me to tell her that there is still time. She has gone astray; perhaps she never can retrieve herself for this world,—but this world is not all,—and she is still in the land of the living, and in the place of hope. Oh, if she would but give up her evil ways and flee! Oh, if she would but remember that there is mercy for the vilest!"

Speaker and hearers were by this time wound up to such a pitch of excitement, that it was impossible to go on. Mrs. Kirkman had tears in her eyes—tears of real feeling; for she thought she was doing what she ought to do; while Winnie blazed upon her with rage and defiance, and poor Aunt Agatha stood up in horror and consternation between them, horrified by the entire breach of all ordinary rules, and yet driven to bay and roused to that natural defence of her own which makes the weakest creature brave.

"My dear love, be composed," she said, trembling a little. "Mrs. Kirkman, perhaps you don't know that you are speaking in a very extraordinary way. We are all great sinners; but as for my dear niece, Winnie—My darling, perhaps if you were to go upstairs to your own room, that would be best—"

"I have no intention of going to my own room," said Winnie. "The question is, whether you will suffer me to be insulted here?"

"Oh, that there should be any thought of insult!" said Mrs. Kirkman, shaking her head, and waving her long curls solemnly. "If anyone is to leave the room, perhaps it should be me. If my warning is rejected, I will shake off the dust of my feet, and go away, as commanded. But I did hope better things. What motive have I but love of her poor soul? Oh, if she would think while it is called to-day—while there is still a place of repentance—"

"Winnie, my dear love," said Aunt Agatha, trembling more and more, "go to your own room."

But Winnie did not move. It was not in her to run away. Now that she had an audience to fortify her, she could sit and face her assailant, and defy all attacks;—though at the same time her eyes and cheeks blazed, and the thought that it was only Aunt Agatha whom she had to stand up for her, filled her with furious contempt and bitterness. At length it was Mrs. Kirkman who rose up with sad solemnity, and drew her silk robe about her, and shook the dust, if there was any dust, not from her feet, but from the fringes of her handsome shawl.

"I will ask the maid to show me up to Mary's room," she said, with pathetic resignation. "I suppose I may wait for her there; and I hope it may never be recorded against you that you have rejected a word of Christian warning. Good-by, Miss Seton; I hope you will be faithful to your poor dear niece yourself, though you will not permit me."

"We know our own affairs best," said Aunt Agatha, whose nerves were so affected that she could scarcely keep up to what she considered a correct standard of polite calm.

"Alas, I hope it may not prove to be just our own best interests that we are most ignorant of," said Mrs. Kirkman, with a heavy sigh—and she swept out of the room following the maid, who looked amazed and aghast at the strange request. "Show me to Mrs. Ochterlony's room, and kindly let her know when she comes in that I am there."

As for Winnie, she burst into an abrupt laugh when her monitress was gone—a laugh which wounded Aunt Agatha, and jarred upon her excited nerves. But there was little mirth in it. It was, in its way, a cry of pain, and it was followed by a tempest of hot tears, which Miss Seton took for hysterics. Poor Winnie! she was not penitent, nor moved by anything that had been said to her, except to rage and a sharper sense of pain. But yet, such an attack made her feel her position, as she did not do when left to herself. She had no protector but Aunt Agatha. She was open to all the assaults of well-meaning friends, and social critics of every description. She was not placed above comment as a woman is who keeps her troubles to herself—for she had taken the world in general into her confidence, as it were, and opened their mouths, and subjected herself voluntarily to their criticism. Winnie's heart seemed to close up as she pondered this—and her life rose up before her, wilful and warlike—and all at once it came into her head what her sister had said to her long ago, and her own decision: were it for misery, were it for ruin, rather to choose ruin and misery with him, than peace without him? How strange it was to think of the change that time had made in everything. She had been fighting him, and making him her chief antagonist, almost ever since. And yet, down in the depths of her heart poor Winnie remembered Mary's words, and felt with a curious pang, made up of misery and sweetness, that even yet, even yet, under some impossible combination of circumstances—this was what made her laugh, and made her cry so bitterly—but Aunt Agatha, poor soul, could not enter into her heart and see what she meant.

They were in this state of agitation when Mary came in, all unconscious of any disturbance. And a further change arose in Winnie at sight of her sister. Her tears dried up, but her eyes continued to blaze.

"It is your friend, Mrs. Kirkman, who has been paying us a visit," she said, in answer to Mary's question; and it seemed to Mrs. Ochterlony that the blame was transferred to her own shoulders, and that it was she who had been doing something, and showing herself the general enemy.

"She is a horrid woman," said Aunt Agatha, hotly. "Mary, I wish you would explain to her, that after what has happened it cannot give me any pleasure to see her here. This is twice that she has insulted us. You will mention that we are not—not used to it. It may do for the soldiers' wives, poor things! but she has no right to come here."

"She must mean to call Mary to repentance, too," said Winnie. She had been thinking, with a certain melting of heart, of what Mary had once said to her; yet she could not refrain from flinging a dart at her sister ere she returned to think about herself.

At this time, Mrs. Kirkman was seated in Mary's room, waiting. Her little encounter had restored her to herself. She had come back to her lofty position of superiority and goodness. She would have said herself that she had carried the Gospel message to that poor sinner, and that it had been rejected; and there was a certain satisfaction of woe in her heart. It was necessary that she should do her duty to Mary also, about whom, when she started, she had been rather compunctious. There is nothing more strange than the processes of thought by which a limited understanding comes to grow into content with itself, and approval of its own actions. It seemed to this good woman's straitened soul that she had been right, almost more than right, in seizing upon the opportunity presented to her, and making an appeal to a sinner's perverse heart. And she thought it would be right to point out to Mary, how any trouble that might be about to overwhelm her was for her good, and that she herself had, like Providence, acted for the best. She looked about the room with actual curiosity, and shook her head at the sight of the Major's sword, hanging over the mantel-piece, and the portraits of the three boys underneath. She shook her head, and thought of creature-worship, and how some stroke was needed to wean Mrs. Ochterlony's heart from its inordinate affections. "It will keep her from trusting to a creature," she said to herself, and by degrees came to look complacently on her own position, and to settle how she should tell the tale to be also for the best. It never occurred to her to think what poor hands hers were to meddle with the threads of fate, or to decide which or what calamity was "for the best." Nor did any consideration of the mystery of pain disturb her mind. She saw no complications in it. Your dearest ties—your highest assurances of good—were but "blessings lent us for a day," and it seemed only natural to Mrs. Kirkman that such blessings should be yielded up in a reasonable way. She herself had neither had nor relinquished any particular blessings. Colonel Kirkman was very good in a general way, and very correct in his theological sentiments; but he was a very steady and substantial possession, and did not suggest any idea of being lent for a day—and his wife felt that she herself was fortunately beyond that necessity, but that it would be for Mary's good if she had another lesson on the vanity of earthly endowments. And thus she sat, feeling rather comfortable about it, and too sadly superior to be offended by her agitation downstairs, in Mrs. Ochterlony's room.

Mary went in with her face brightened by her walk, a little soft anxiety (perhaps) in her eyes, or at least curiosity,—a little indignation, and yet the faintest touch of amusement about her mouth. She went in and shut the door, leaving her sister Aunt Agatha below, moved by what they supposed to be a much deeper emotion. Nobody in the house so much as dreamt that anything of any importance was going on there. There was not a sound as of a raised voice or agitated utterance as there had been when Mrs. Kirkman made her appeal to Winnie. But when the door of Mrs. Ochterlony's room opened again, and Mary appeared, showing her visitor out, her countenance was changed, as if by half-a-dozen years. She followed her visitor downstairs, and opened the door for her, and looked after her as she went away, but not the ghost of a smile came upon Mary's face. She did not offer her hand, nor say a word at parting that any one could hear. Her lips were compressed, without smile or syllable to move them, and closed as if they never would open again, and every drop of blood seemed to be gone from her face. When Mrs. Kirkman went away from the door, Mary closed it, and went back again to her own room. She did not say a word, nor look as if she had anything to say. She went to her wardrobe and took out a bag, and put some things into it, and then she tied on her bonnet, everything being done as if she had planned it all for years. When she was quite ready, she went downstairs and went to the drawing-room, where Winnie, agitated and disturbed, sat talking, saying a hundred wild things, of which Aunt Agatha knew but half the meaning. When Mary looked in at the door, the two who were there, started, and stared at her with amazed eyes. "What has happened, Mary?" cried Aunt Agatha; and though she was beginning to resume her lost tranquillity, she was so scared by Mrs. Ochterlony's face that she had a palpitation which took away her breath, and made her sink down panting and lay her hands upon her heart. Mary, for her part, was perfectly composed and in possession of her senses. She made no fuss at all, nor complaint,—but nothing could conceal the change, nor alter the wonderful look in her eyes.

"I am going to Liverpool," she said, "I must see Will immediately, and I want to go by the next train. There is nothing the matter with him. It is only something I have just heard, and I must see him without loss of time."

"What is it, Mary?" gasped Aunt Agatha. "You have heard something dreadful. Are any of the boys mixed up in it? Oh, say something, and don't look in that dreadful fixed way."

"Am I looking in a dreadful fixed way?" said Mary, with a faint smile. "I did not mean it. No there is nothing the matter with any of the boys. But I have heard something that has disturbed me, and I must see Will. If Hugh should come while I am away—"

But here her strength broke down. A choking sob came from her breast. She seemed on the point of breaking out into some wild cry for help or comfort; but it was only a spasm, and it passed. Then she came to Aunt Agatha and kissed her. "Good-bye; if either of the boys come, keep them till I come back," she said. She had looked so fair and so strong in the composure of her middle age when she stood there only an hour before, that the strange despair which seemed to have taken possession of her, had all the more wonderful effect. It woke even Winnie from her preoccupation, and they both came round her, wondering and disquieted, to know what was the matter. "Something must have happened to Will," said Aunt Agatha.

"It is that woman who has brought her bad news," cried Winnie; and then both together they cried out, "What is it, Mary? have you bad news?"

"Nothing that I have not known for years," said Mrs. Ochterlony, and she kissed them both, as if she was kissing them for the last time, and disengaged herself, and turned away. "I cannot wait to tell you any more," they heard her say as she went to the door; and there they stood, looking at each other, conscious more by some change in the atmosphere than by mere eyesight, that she was gone. She had no time to speak or to look behind her; and when Aunt Agatha rushed to the window, she saw Mary far off on the road, going steady and swift with her bag in her hand. In the midst of her anxiety and suspicion, Miss Seton even felt a pang at the sight of the bag in Mary's hand. "As if there was no one to carry it for her!" The two who were left behind could but look at each other, feeling somehow a sense of shame, and instinctive consciousness that this new change, whatever it was, involved trouble far more profound than the miseries over which they had been brooding. Something that she had known for years! What was there in these quiet words which made Winnie's veins tingle, and the blood rush to her face? All these quiet years was it possible that a cloud had ever been hovering which Mary knew of, and yet held her way so steadily? As for Aunt Agatha, she was only perplexed and agitated, and full of wonder, making every kind of suggestion. Will might have broken his leg—he might have got into trouble with his uncle. It might be something about Islay. Oh! Winnie, my darling, what do you think it can be? Something that she had known for years!

This was what it really was. It seemed to Mary as if for years and years she had known all about it; how it would get to be told to her poor boy; how it would act upon his strange half-developed nature; how Mrs. Kirkman would tell her of it, and the things she would put into her travelling bag, and the very hour the train would leave. It was a miserably slow train, stopping everywhere, waiting at a dreary junction for several trains in the first chill of night. But she seemed to have known it all, and to have felt the same dreary wind blow, and the cold creeping to the heart, and to be used and deadened to it. Why is it that one feels so cold when one's heart is bleeding and wounded? It seemed to go in through the physical covering, which shrinks at such moments from the sharp and sensitive soul, and to thrill her with a shiver as of ice and snow. She passed Mrs. Kirkman on the way, but could not take any notice of her, and she put down her veil and drew her shawl closely about her, and sat in a corner that she might escape recognition. But it was hard upon her that the train should be so slow, though that too she seemed to have known for years.

Thus the cross of which she had partially and by moments tasted the bitterness for so long, was laid at last full upon Mary's shoulders. She went carrying it, marking her way, as it were, by blood-drops which answered for tears, to do what might be done, that nobody but herself might suffer. For one thing, she did not lose a moment. If Will had been ill, or if he had been in any danger, she would have done the same. She was a woman who had no need to wait to make up her mind. And perhaps she might not be too late, perhaps her boy meant no evil. He was her boy, and it was hard to associate evil or unkindness with him. Poor Will! perhaps he had but gone away because he could not bear to see his mother fallen from her high estate. Then it was that a flush of fiery colour came to Mary's face, but it was only for a moment; things had gone too far for that. She sat at the junction waiting, and the cold wind blew in upon her, and pierced to her heart—and it was nothing that she had not known for years.

CHAPTER XLI

When Mary went away, she left the two ladies at the Cottage in a singular state of excitement and perplexity. They were tingling with the blows which they had themselves received, and yet at the same time they were hushed and put to shame, as it were, for any secondary pang they might be feeling, by the look in Mrs. Ochterlony's face, and by her sudden departure. Aunt Agatha, who knew of few mysteries in life, and thought that where neither sickness nor death was, nor any despairs of blighted love or disappointed hope, there could not be anything very serious to suffer, would have got over it, and set it down as one of Mary's ways, had she been by herself. But Winnie was not so easily satisfied; her mind was possessed by the thought, in which no doubt there was a considerable mingling of vanity, that her husband would strike her through her friends. It seemed as if he had done so now; Winnie did not know precisely what it was that Percival knew about her sister, but only that it was something discreditable, something that would bring Mary down from her pinnacle of honour and purity. And now he had done it, and driven Mrs. Ochterlony to despair; but what was it about Will? Or was Will a mere pretence on the part of the outraged and terrified woman to get away? Something she had known for years! This was the thought which had chiefly moved Winnie, going to her heart. She herself had lived a stormy life; she had done a great many things which she ought not to have done; she had never been absolutely wicked or false, nor forfeited her reputation; but she knew in her heart that her life had not been a fair and spotless life; and when she thought of its strivings, and impatience, and self-will, and bitter discontent, and of the serene course of existence which her sister had led in the quietness, her heart smote her. Perhaps it was for her sake that this blow, which Mary had known of for years, had at last descended upon her head. All the years of her own stormy career, her sister had been living at Kirtell, doing no harm, doing good, serving God, bringing up her children, covering her sins, if she had sinned, with repentance and good deeds; and yet for Winnie's sake, for her petulance, and fury, and hotheadness, the angel (or was it the demon?) had lifted his fiery sword and driven Mary out of Paradise. All this moved Winnie strangely; and along with these were other thoughts—thoughts of her own strange miserable unprotectedness, with only Aunt Agatha to stand between her and the world, while she still had a husband in the world, between whom and herself there stood no deadly shame nor fatal obstacle, and whose presence would shield her from all such intrusions as that she had just suffered from. He had sinned against her, but that a woman can forgive—and she had not sinned against him, not to such an extent as is unpardonable in a woman. Perhaps there might even be something in the fact that Winnie had found Kirtell and quiet not the medicine suited to her mind, and that even Mary's flight into the world had brought a tingling into her wings, a longing to mount into freer air, and rush back to her fate. Thus a host of contradictory feelings joined in one great flame of excitement, which rose higher and higher all through the night. To fly forth upon him, and controvert his wicked plans, and save the sister who was being sacrificed for her sake; and yet to take possession of him back again, and set him up before her, her shield and buckler against the world; and at the same time to get out and break loose from this flowery cage, and rush back into the big world, where there would be air and space to move in—such were Winnie's thoughts. In the morning, when she came downstairs, which was an hour earlier than usual, to Aunt Agatha's great amazement, she wore her travelling dress, and had an air of life and movement in her, which startled Miss Seton, and which, since her return to Kirtell, had never been seen in Winnie's looks before.

"It is very kind of you to come down, Winnie, my darling, when you knew I was alone," said Aunt Agatha, giving her a tender embrace.

"I don't think it is kind in me," said Winnie; and then she sat down, and took her sister's office upon her, to Miss Seton's still greater bewilderment, and make the tea, without quite knowing what she was doing. "I suppose Mary has been travelling all night," she said; "I am going into Carlisle, Aunt Agatha, to that woman, to know what it is all about."

"Oh, my darling, you were always so generous," cried Aunt Agatha, in amaze; "but you must not do it. She might say things to you, or you might meet people—"

"If I did meet people, I know how to take care of myself," said Winnie; and that flush came to her face, and that light to her eye, like the neigh of the war-horse when he hears the sound of battle.

Aunt Agatha was struck dumb. Terror seized her, as she looked at the kindling cheeks and rapid gesture, and saw the Winnie of old, all impatient and triumphant, dawning out from under the cloud.

"Oh, Winnie, you are not going away," she cried, with a thrill of presentiment. "Mary has gone, and they have all gone. You are not going to leave me all by myself here?"

"I?" said Winnie. There was scorn in the tone, and yet what was chiefly in it was a bitter affectation of humility. "It will be time enough to fear my going, when any one wants me to go."

Miss Seton was a simple woman, and yet she saw that there lay more meaning under these words than the plain meaning they bore. She clasped her hands, and lifted her appealing eyes to Winnie's face—and she was about to speak, to question, to remonstrate, to importune, when her companion suddenly seized her hands tight, and silenced her by the sight of an emotion more earnest and violent than anything Aunt Agatha knew.

"Don't speak to me," she said, with her eyes blazing, and clasped the soft old hands in hers till she hurt them. "Don't speak to me; I don't know what I am going to do—but don't talk to me, Aunt Agatha. Perhaps my life—and Mary's—may be fixed to-day."

"Oh, Winnie, I don't understand you," cried Aunt Agatha, trembling, and freeing her poor little soft crushed hands.

"And I don't understand myself," said Winnie. "Don't let us say a word more."

What did it mean, that flush in her face, that thrill of purpose and meaning in her words, and her step, and her whole figure?—and what had Mary to do with it?—and how could their fate be fixed one way or other?—Aunt Agatha asked herself these questions vainly, and could make nothing of them. But after breakfast she went to her room and said her prayers—which was the best thing to do; and in that moment Winnie, whose prayers were few though her wants were countless, took a rose from the trellis, and pinned it in with her brooch, and went softly away. I don't know what connection there was between the rose and Aunt Agatha's prayers, but somehow the faint perfume softened the wild, agitated, stormy heart, and suggested to it that sacrifice was being made and supplications offered somewhere for its sins and struggles. Thus, when his sons and daughters went out to their toils and pleasures, Job drew near the altar lest some of them might curse God in their hearts.

It was strange to see her sallying forth by herself, she who had been shielded from every stranger's eye;—and yet there was a sense of freedom in it—freedom, and danger, and exhilaration, which was sweet to Winnie. She went rushing in to Carlisle in the express train, flying as it were on the wings of the wind. But Mrs. Kirkman was not at home. She was either working in her district, or she was teaching the infant school, or giving out work to the poor women, or perhaps at the mothers' meeting, which she always said was the most precious opportunity of all; or possibly she might be making calls—which, however, was an hypothesis which her maid rejected as unworthy of her. Mrs. Percival found herself brought to a sudden standstill when she heard this. The sole audible motive which she had proposed to herself for her expedition was to see Mrs. Kirkman, and for the moment she did not know what to do. After a while, however, she turned and went slowly and yet eagerly in another direction. She concluded she would go to the Askells, who might know something about it. They were Percival's friends; they might be in the secret of his plans—they might convey to him the echo of her indignation and disdain; possibly even he might himself—But Winnie would not let herself consider that thought. Captain Askell's house was not the same cold and neglected place where Mary had seen Emma after their return. They had a little more money—and that was something; and Nelly was older—which was a great deal more; but even Nelly could not altogether abrogate the character which her mother gave to her house. The maid who opened the door had bright ribbons in her cap, but yet was a sloven, half-suppressed; and the carpets on the stairs were badly fitted, and threatened here and there to entangle the unwary foot. And there was a bewildering multiplicity of sounds in the house. You could hear the maids in the kitchen, and the children in the nursery—and even as Winnie approached the drawing-room she could hear voices thrilling with an excitement which did not become that calm retreat. There was a sound as of a sob, and there was a broken voice a little loud in its accents. Winnie went on with a quicker throb of her heart—perhaps he himself—But when the door opened, it was upon a scene she had not thought of. Mrs. Kirkman was there, seated high as on a throne, looking with a sad but touching resignation upon the disturbed household. And it was Emma who was sobbing—sobbing and crying out, and launching a furious little soft incapable clenched hand into the air—while Nelly, all glowing red, eyes lit up with indignation, soft lips quivering with distress, stood by, with a gaze of horror and fury and disgust fixed on the visitor's face. Winnie went in, and they all stopped short and stared at her, as if she had dropped from the skies. Her appearance startled and dismayed them, and yet it was evidently in perfect accordance with the spirit of the scene. She could see that at the first glance. She saw they were already discussing this event, whatever it might be. Therefore Winnie did not hesitate. She offered no ordinary civilities herself, nor required any. She went straight up to where Mrs. Kirkman sat, not looking at others. "I have come to ask you what it means," she said; and Winnie felt that they all stopped and gave way to her as to one who had a right to know.

"That is what I am asking," cried Emma, "what does it mean? We have all known it for ages, and none of us said a word. And she that sets up for being a Christian! As if there was no honour left in the regiment, and as if we were to talk of everything that happens! Ask her, Mrs. Percival. I don't believe half nor a quarter what they say of any one. When they dare to raise up a scandal about Madonna Mary, none of us are safe. And a thing that we have all known for a hundred years!"

"Oh, mamma!" said Nelly, softly, under her breath. The child knew everything about everybody, as was to have been expected; every sort of tale had been told in her presence. But what moved her to shame was her mother's share. It was a murmured compunction, a vicarious acknowledgment of sin. "Oh, mamma!"

"It is not I that am saying it," cried Emma, again resuming her sob. "I would have been torn to pieces first. Me to harm her that was always a jewel! Oh, ask her, ask her! What is going to come of it, and what does it mean?"

"My dear, perhaps Nelly had better retire before we speak of it any more," said Mrs. Kirkman, meekly. "I am not one that thinks it right to encourage delusions in the youthful mind, but still, if there is much more to be said—"

And then it was Nelly's turn to speak. "You have talked about everything in the world without sending me away," cried the girl, "till I wondered and wondered you did not die of shame. But I'll stay now. One is safe," said Nelly, with a little cry of indignation and youthful rage, "when you so much as name Mrs. Ochterlony's name."

All this time Winnie was standing upright and eager before Mrs. Kirkman's chair. It was not from incivility that they offered her no place among them. No one thought of it, and neither did she. The conflict around her had sobered Winnie's thoughts. There was no trace of her husband in it, nor of that striking her through her friends which had excited and exhilarated her mind; but the family instinct of mutual defence awoke in her. "My sister has heard something which has—which has had a singular effect upon her," said Winnie, pausing instinctively, as if she had been about to betray something. "And it is you who have done it; I want to know what it means."

"Oh, she must be ill!" wailed poor Emma; "I knew she would be ill. If she dies it will be your fault. Oh, let me go up and see. I knew she must be ill."

As for Mrs. Kirkman, she shook her head and her long curls, and looked compassionately upon her agitated audience. And then Winnie heard all the long-hoarded well-remembered tale. The only difference made in it was that by this time all confidence in the Gretna Green marriage, which had once been allowed, at least as a matter of courtesy, had faded out of the story. Even Mrs. Askell no longer thought of that. When the charm of something to tell began to work, the Captain's wife chimed in with the narrative of her superior officer. All the circumstances of that long-past event were revealed to the wonder-stricken hearers. Mary's distress, and Major Ochterlony's anxiety, and the consultations he had with everybody, and the wonderful indulgence and goodness of the ladies at the station, who never made any difference, and all their benevolent hopes that so uncomfortable an incident was buried in the past, and could now have no painful results;—all this was told to Winnie in detail; and in the confidential committee thus formed, her own possible deficiencies and shortcomings were all passed over. "Nothing would have induced me to say a syllable on the subject if you had not been dear Mary's sister," Mrs. Kirkman said; and then she relieved her mind and told it all.

Winnie, for her part, sat dumb and listened. She was more than struck dumb—she was stupified by the news. She had thought that Mary might have been "foolish," as she herself had been "foolish;" even that Mary might have gone further, and compromised herself; but of a dishonour which involved such consequences she had never dreamed. She sat and heard it all in a bewildered horror, with the faces of Hugh and Will floating like spectres before her eyes. A woman gone astray from her duty as a wife was not, Heaven help her! so extraordinary an object in poor Winnie's eyes—but, good heavens! Mary's marriage, Mary's boys, the very foundation and beginning of her life! The room went round and round with her as she sat and listened. A public trial, a great talk in the papers, one brother against another, and Mary, Mary, the chief figure in all! Winnie put her hands up to her ears, not to shut out the sound of this incredible story, but to deaden the noises in her head, the throbbing of all her pulses, and stringing of all her nerves. She was so stupified that she could make no sort of stand against it, no opposition to the evidence, which, indeed, was crushing, and left no opening for unbelief. She accepted it all, or rather, was carried away by the bewildering, overwhelming tide. And even Emma Askell got excited, and woke up out of her crying, and added her contribution of details. Poor little Nelly, who had heard it all before, had retired to a corner and taken up her work, and might be seen in the distance working furiously, with a hot flush on her cheek, and now and then wiping a furtive tear from her eye. Nelly did not know what to say, nor how to meet it—but there was in her little woman's soul a conviction that something unknown must lie behind, and that the inference at least was not true.

"And you told Will?" said Winnie, rousing up at last. "You knew all the horrible harm it might do, and you told Will."

"It was not I who told him," said Mrs. Kirkman; and then there was a pause, and the two ladies looked at each other, and a soft, almost imperceptible flutter, visible only to a female eye, revealed that there might be something else to say.

"Who told him?" said Winnie, perceiving the indications, and feeling her heart thrill and beat high once more.

"I am very sorry to say anything, I am sure, to make it worse," said Mrs. Kirkman. "It was not I who told him. I suppose you are aware that—that Major Percival is here? He was present at the marriage as well as I. I wonder he never told you. It was he who told Will. He only came to get the explanations from me."

They thought she would very probably faint, or make some demonstration of distress, not knowing that this was what poor Winnie had been waiting, almost hoping for; and on the contrary, it seemed to put new force into her, and a kind of beauty, at which her companions stood aghast. The blood rushed into her faded cheek, and light came to her eyes. She could not speak at first, so overwhelming was the tide of energy and new life that seemed to pour into her veins. After all, she had been a true prophet. It was all for her sake. He had struck at her through her friends, and she could not be angry with him. It was a way like another of showing love, a way hard upon other people, no doubt, but carrying a certain poignant sweetness to her for whose sake the blow had fallen. But Winnie knew she was in the presence of keen observers, and put restraint upon herself.

"Where is Major Percival to be found?" she said, with a measured voice, which she thought concealed her excitement, but which was overdone, and made it visible. They thought she was meditating something desperate when she spoke in that unnatural voice, and drew her shawl round her in that rigid way. She might have been going to stab him, the bystanders thought, or do him some grievous harm.

"You would not go to him for that?" said Emma, with a little anxiety, stopping short at once in her tears and in her talk. "They never will let you talk to them about what they have done; and then they always say you take part with your own friends."

Mrs. Kirkman, too, showed a sudden change of interest, and turned to the new subject with zeal and zest: "If you are really seeking a reconciliation with your husband—" she began; but this was more than Winnie could bear.

"I asked where Major Percival was to be found," she said; "I was not discussing my own affairs: but Nelly will tell me. If that is all about Mary, I will go away."

"I will go with you," cried Emma: "only wait till I get my things. I knew she would be ill; and she must not think that we are going to forsake her now. As if it could make any difference to us that have known it for ever so long! Only wait till I get my things."

"Poor Mary! she is not in a state of mind to be benefited by any visit," said Mrs. Kirkman, solemnly. "If it were not for that, I would go."

As for Winnie, she was trembling with impatience, eager to be free and to be gone, and yet not content to go until she had left a sting behind her, like a true woman. "How you all talk!" she cried; "as if your making any difference would matter. You can set it going, but all you can do will never stop it. Mary has gone to Will, whom you have made her enemy. Perhaps she has gone to ask her boy to save her honour; and you think she will mind about your making a difference, or about your visits—when it is a thing of life or death!"

And she went to the door all trembling, scarcely able to support herself, shivering with excitement and wild anticipation. Now she must see him—now it was her duty to go to him and ask him why—She rushed away, forgetting even that she had not obtained the information she came to seek. She had been speaking of Mary, but it was not of Mary she was thinking. Mary went totally out of her mind as she hurried down the stairs. Now there was no longer any choice; she must go to him, must see him, must renew the interrupted but never-ended struggle. It filled her with an excitement which she could not subdue nor resist. Her heart beat so loud that she did not hear the sound of her own step on the stairs, but seemed somehow to be carried down by the air, which encircled her like a soft whirlwind; and she did not hear Nelly behind her calling her, to tell her where he lived. She had no recollection of that. She did not wait for any one to open the door for her, but rushed out, moved by her own purpose as by a supernatural influence; and but for the violent start he gave, it would have been into his arms she rushed as she stepped out from the Askells' door.

This was how their meeting happened. Percival had been going there to ask some questions about the Cottage and its inmates, when his wife, with that look he knew so well, with all the coming storm in her eyes, and the breath of excitement quick on her parted lips—stepped out almost into his arms. He was fond of her, notwithstanding all their mutual sins; and their spirits rushed together, though in a different way from that rush which accompanies the meeting of the lips. They rushed together with a certain clang and spark; and the two stood facing each other in the street, defying, hating, struggling, feeling that they belonged to each other once more.

"I must speak with you," said Winnie, in her haste; "take me somewhere that I may speak. Is this your revenge? I know what you have done. When everything is ended that you can do to me, you strike me through my friends."

"If you choose to think so—" said Percival.

"If I choose to think so? What else can I think?" said the hot combatant; and she went on by his side with hasty steps and a passion and force which she had not felt in her since the day when she fled from him. She felt the new tide in her veins, the new strength in her heart. It was not the calm of union, it was the heat of conflict; but still, such as it was, it was her life. She went on with him, never looking or thinking where they were going, till they reached the rooms where he was living, and then, all by themselves, the husband and wife looked each other in the face.

"Why did you leave me, Winnie?" he said. "I might be wrong, but what does it matter? I may be wrong again, but I have got what I wanted. I would not have minded much killing the boy for the sake of seeing you and having it out. Let them manage it their own way; it is none of our business. Come back to me, and let them settle it their own way."

"Never!" cried Winnie, though there was a struggle in her heart. "After doing all the harm you could do to me, do you think you can recall me by ruining my sister? How dare you venture to look me in the face?"

"And I tell you I did not mind what I did to get to see you and have it out with you," said Percival; "and if that is why you are here, I am glad I did it. What is Mary to me? She must look after herself. But I cannot exist without my wife."

"It was like that, your conduct drove me away," said Winnie, with a quiver on her lips.

"It was like it," said he, "only that you never did me justice. My wife is not like other men's wives. I might drive you away, for you were always impatient; but you need not think I would stick at anything that had to be done to get you back."

"You will never get me back," said Winnie, with flashing eyes. All her beauty had come back to her in that moment. It was the warfare that did it, and at the same time it was the homage and flattery which were sweet to her, and which she could see in everything he said. He would have stuck at nothing to get her back. For that object he would have ruined, killed, or done anything wicked. What did it matter about the other people? There was a sort of magnificence in it that took her captive; for neither of the two had pure motives or a high standard of action, or enough even of conventional goodness to make them hypocrites. They both acknowledged, in a way, that themselves, the two of them, were the chief objects in the universe, and everything else in the world faded into natural insignificance when they stood face to face, and their great perennial conflict was renewed.

"I do not believe it," said Percival. "I have told you I will stick at nothing. Let other people take care of their own affairs. What have you to do in that weedy den with that old woman? You are not good enough, and you never were meant for that. I knew you would come to me at the last."

"But you are mistaken," said Winnie, still breathing fire and flame. "The old woman, as you call her, is good to me, good as nobody ever was. She loves me, though you may think it strange. And if I have come to you it is not for you; it is to ask what you have done, what your horrible motive could be, and why, now you have done every injury to me a man could do, you should try to strike me through my friends."

"I do not care that for your friends," said Percival. "It was to force you to see me, and have it out. Let them take care of themselves. Neither man nor woman has any right to interfere in my affairs."

"Nobody was interfering in your affairs," cried Winnie; "do you think they had anything to do with it?—could they have kept me if I wanted to go? It is me you are fighting against. Leave Mary alone, and put out your strength on me. I harmed you, perhaps, when I gave in to you and let you marry me. But she never did you any harm. Leave Mary, at least, alone."

Percival turned away with a disdainful shrug of his shoulders. He was familiar enough with the taunt. "If you harmed me by that act, I harmed you still more, I suppose," he said. "We have gone over that ground often enough. Let us have it out now. Are you coming back to your duty and to me."

"I came to speak of Mary," said Winnie, facing him as he turned. "Set those right first who have never done you any harm, and then we can think of the others. The innocent come first. Strike at me like a man, but not through my friends."

She sat down as she spoke, without quite knowing what she did. She sat down, because, though the spirit was moved to passionate energy, the flesh was weak. Perhaps something in the movement touched the man who hated and loved her, as she loved and hated him. A sudden pause came to the conflict, such as does occur capriciously in such struggles; in the midst of their fury a sudden touch of softness came over them. They were alone—nothing but mists of passion were between them, and though they were fighting like foes, their perverse souls were one. He came up to her suddenly and seized her hands, not tenderly, but rudely, as was natural to his state of mind.

"Winnie," he said, "this will not do; come away with me. You may struggle as you please, but you are mine. Don't let us make a laughing-stock of ourselves! What are a set of old women and children between you and me? Let them fight it out; it will all come right. What is anything in the world between you and me? Come! I am not going to be turned off or put away as if you did not mind. I know you better than that. Come! I tell you, nothing can stand between you and me."

"Never!" said Winnie, blazing with passion; but even while she spoke the course of the torrent changed. It leaped the feeble boundaries, and went into the other channel—the channel of love which runs side by side with that of hate. "You leave me to be insulted by everybody who has a mind—and if I were to go with you, it is you who would insult me!" cried Winnie. And the tears came pouring to her eyes suddenly like a thunder-storm. It was all over in a moment, and that was all that was said. What were other people that either he or she should postpone their own affairs to any secondary consideration? Their spirits rushed together with a flash of fire, and roll of thunder. The suddenness of it was the thing that made it effectual. Something "smote the chord of self, that trembling" burst into a tumult of feeling and took to itself the semblance of love; no matter how it had been brought about. Was not anything good that set them face to face, and showed the two that life could not continue for them apart? Neither the tears, nor the reproaches, nor the passion were over, but it changed all at once into such a quarrel as had happened often enough before then. As soon as Winnie came back to her warfare, she had gone back, so to speak, to her duties according to her conception of them. Thus the conflict swelled, and rose, and fluctuated, and softened, like many another; but no more thoughts of the Cottage, or of Aunt Agatha, or of Mary's sudden calamity drew Winnie from her own subject. After all, it was, as she had felt, a pasteboard cottage let down upon her for the convenience of the moment—a thing to disappear by pulleys when the moment of necessity was over. And when they had had it out, she went off with her husband the same evening, sending a rapid note of explanation to Aunt Agatha—and not with any intention of unkindness, but only with that superior sense of the importance of her own concerns which was natural to her. She hoped Mary would come back soon, and that all would be comfortably settled, she said. "And Mary is more of a companion to you than I ever could be," Winnie added in her letter, with a touch of that strange jealousy which was always latent in her. She was glad that Mary should be Miss Seton's companion, and yet was vexed that anybody should take her place with her aunt, to whom she herself had been all in all. Thus Winnie, who had gone into Carlisle that morning tragically bent upon the confounding of her husband's plans, and the formation of one eternal wall of separation between them, eloped with him in the evening as if he had been her lover. And there was a certain thrill of pride and tenderness in her bosom to think that to win her back he would stick at nothing, and did not hesitate to strike her through her friends.

CHAPTER XLII

There is something wonderful in the ease with which the secondary actors in a great crisis can shake themselves free of the event, and return to their own affairs, however exciting the moment may be at which it suits them to strike off. The bystanders turn away from the most horrible calamity, and sit down by their own tables and talk about their own trivial business before the sound of the guns has ceased to vibrate on the air, or the smoke of the battle has dispersed which has brought ruin and misery to their dearest friends. The principle of human nature, that every man should bear his own burden, lies deeper than all philosophy. Winnie, though she had been excited about her sister's mysterious misfortune and roused by it, and was ready, to her own inconvenience, to make a great effort on Mary's behalf, yet could turn off on her way without any struggle, with that comfortable feeling that all must come right in the end which is so easy for the lookers-on. But the real sufferers could not entertain so charming a confidence. That same day rose heavily over poor Hugh, who, all alone in Earlston, still debated with himself. He had written to his uncle to express his amazement and dismay, and to ask for time to give full consideration to the terrible news he had heard. "You need not fear that I will do anything to wound my mother," the poor boy had written, with a terrible pang in his heart. But after that he had sunk into a maze of questions and discussions with himself, and of miserable uncertainty as to what he ought to do. The idea of asking anybody for information about it seemed almost as bad to him as owning the fact at once; asking about his mother—about facts in her life which she had never herself disclosed—inquiring if, perhaps, she was a woman dishonoured and unworthy of her children's confidence! It seemed to Hugh as if it would be far easier to give up Earlston, and let Will or any one else who pleased have it. He had tried more than once to write to Mr. Churchill, the chaplain, of whom he had heard his mother speak, and of whom he had even a faint traditional sort of recollection; but the effort always sickened him, and made him rush away in disgust to the open air, and the soothing sounds of nature. He was quite alone during those few days. His neighbours did not know of his return, for he had been so speedily overtaken by this news as to have had no heart to go anywhere or show himself among them. Thus he was left to his own thoughts, and they were bitter. In the very height of his youthful hopes and satisfaction, just at the moment when he was most full of plans, and taking the most perfect pleasure in his life, this bewildering cloud had come on him. He did not even go on with his preparations for the transfer of the Museum, in the sickness of his heart, notwithstanding the eagerness he felt whenever he thought of it to complete that arrangement at least, and secure his uncle's will to that extent, if no more. But it did not seem possible to exert himself about one thing without exerting himself about all, and he who had been so fresh and full of energy, fell supine into a kind of utter wretchedness. The course of his life was stopped when it had been in full career. He was suddenly thrown out of all he had been doing, all he had been planning. The scheme of his existence seemed all at once turned into folly and made a lie of. What could he do? His lawyer wrote to say that he meant to come to Earlston on some business connected with the estate, but Hugh put him off, and deferred everything. How could he discuss affairs which possibly were not his affairs, but his brother's? How could he enter into any arrangements, or think of anything, however reasonable or necessary, with this sword hanging over his head? He got up early in the morning, and startled the servants before they were up, by opening the doors and shutters in his restlessness; and he sat up at night thinking it all over, for ever thinking of it and never coming to any result. How could he inquire, how could he prove or disprove the horrible assertion? Even to think of it seemed a tacit injury to his mother. The only way to do his duty by her seemed to be to give up all and go away to the end of the world. And yet he was a man, and right and justice were dear to him, and he revolted against doing that. It was as if he had been caught by some gigantic iron hand of fate in the sweetness of his fearless life. He had never heard nor read of, he thought, anything so cruel. By times bitter tears came into his eyes, wrung from him by the intolerable pressure. He could not give up his own cause and his mother's cause without a struggle. He could not relinquish his life and rights to another; and yet how could he defend himself by means that would bring one question to careless lips, one light laugh to the curious world, over his mother's name? Such an idea had never so much as entered into his head. It made his life miserable.

He read over Mr. Penrose's letter a dozen times in the day, and he sat at night with his eyes fixed on the flame of his lamp, calling back his childhood and its events. It was as vague as a dream, and he could not identify his broken recollections. If he could have gone to Mrs. Ochterlony and talked it over with her, Hugh might have remembered many things, but wanting that thread of guidance he lost himself in the misty maze. By dint of thinking it over and over, and representing the scene to his mind in every possible way, it came to him finally to believe that some faint impression of the event which he was asked to remember did linger in his memory, and that thought, which he could not put away, stung him like a serpent. Was it really true that he remembered it? Then the accusation must be true, and he nameless and without rights, and Mary—. Not much wonder that the poor boy, sick to the heart, turned his face from the light and hid himself, and felt that he would be glad if he could only die. Yet dying would be of no use, for there was Islay who would come next to him, who never would have dreamt of dispossessing him, but who, if this was true, would need to stand aside in his turn and make room for Will. Will!—It was hard for Hugh not to feel a thrill of rage and scorn and amaze mixing with his misery when he thought of the younger brother to whom he had been so continually indulgent and affectionate. He who had been always the youngest, the most guarded and tender, whom Hugh could remember in his mother's arms, on her knee, a part of her as it were; he to turn upon them all, and stain her fame, and ruin the family honour for his own base advantage! These thoughts came surging up one after another, and tore Hugh's mind to pieces and made him as helpless as a child, now with one suggestion, now with another. What could he do? And accordingly he did nothing but fall into a lethargy and maze of despair, did not sleep, did not eat, filled the servants' minds with the wildest surmises, and shut himself up, as if that could have deferred the course of events, or shut out the coming fate.

This had lasted only a day or two, it is true, but it might have been for a century, to judge by Hugh's feelings. He felt indeed as if he had never been otherwise, never been light-hearted or happy, or free to take pleasure in his life; as if he had always been an impostor expecting to be found out. Nature itself might have awakened him from his stupor had he been left to himself; but, as it happened, there came a sweeter touch. He had become feverishly anxious about his letters ever since the arrival of that one which had struck him so unlooked-for a blow; and he started when something was brought to him in the evening at an hour when letters did not arrive, and a little note with a little red seal, very carefully folded that no curious eye might be able to penetrate. Poor Hugh felt a certain thrill of fright at the innocent-seeming thing, coming insidiously at this moment when he thought himself safe, and bringing, for anything he could tell, the last touch to his misery. He held it in his hand while it was explained to him that one of the servants had been to Carlisle with an order given before the world had changed—an order made altogether antiquated and out of course by having been issued three days before; and that he had brought back this note. Only when the door closed upon the man and his explanation did Hugh break the tiny seal. It was not a letter to be alarmed at. It was written as it were with tears, sweet tears of sympathy and help and tender succour. This was what Nelly's little letter said:—

"DEAR MR. HUGH,—I want to let you know of something that has happened to-day, and at which you may perhaps be surprised. Mrs. Percival met Major Percival here, and I think they have made friends; and she has gone away with him. I think you ought to know, because she told us dear Mrs. Ochterlony had gone to Liverpool; and Miss Seton will be left alone. I should have asked mamma to let me go and stay with her, but I am going into Scotland to an old friend of papa's, who is living at Gretna. I remember hearing long ago that it was at Gretna dear Mrs. Ochterlony was married—and perhaps there is somebody there who remembers her. If you see Aunt Agatha, would you please ask her when it happened? I should so like to see the place, and ask the people if they remember her. I think she must have been so beautiful then; she is beautiful now—I never loved anybody so much in my life. And I am afraid she is anxious about Will. I should not like to trouble you, for I am sure you must have a great deal to occupy your mind, but I should so like to know how dear Mrs. Ochterlony is, and if there is anything the matter with Will. He always was very funny, you know, and then he is only a boy, and does not know what he means. Mamma sends her kind regards, and I am, dear Mr. Hugh, very sincerely yours,—NELLY."

This was the letter. Hugh read it slowly over, every word—and then he read it again; and two great globes of dew got into his eyes, and Nelly's sweet name grew big as he read through them, and wavered over all the page; and when he had come to that signature the second time he put it down on the table, and leant his face on it, and cried. Yes, cried, though he was a man—wept hot tears over it, few but great, that felt to him like the opening of a spring in his soul, and drew the heat and the horror out of his brain. His young breast shook with a few great sobs—the passion climbing in his throat burst forth, and had utterance; and then he rose up and stretched his young arms, and drew himself up to the fulness of his height. What did it matter, after all? What was money, and lands, and every good on earth, compared to the comfort of living in the same world with a creature such as this, who was as sweet as the flowers, and as true as the sky? She had done it by instinct, not knowing, as she herself said, what she meant, or knowing only that her little heart swelled with kind impulses, tender pity, and indignation, and yet pity over all; pity for Will, too, who, perhaps, was going to make them all miserable. But Nelly could not have understood the effect her little letter had upon Hugh. He shook himself free after it, as if from chains that had been upon him. He gave a groan, poor boy, at the calamity which was not to be ignored, and then he said to himself, "After all!" After all, and in spite of all, while there was Nelly living, it was not unmingled ill to live. And when he looked at it again, a more reasonable kind of comfort seemed to come to him out of the girl's letter; his eye was caught by the word struck out, which yet was not too carefully struck out, "where dear Mrs. Ochterlony was first married." He gave a cry when this new light entered into his mind. He roused himself up from his gloom and stupor, and thought and thought until his very brain ached as with labour, and his limbs began to thrill as with new vigour coming back. And a glimmering of the real truth suddenly rushed, all vague and dazzling, upon Hugh's darkness. There had been no hint in Mr. Penrose's letter of any such interpretation of the mystery. Mr. Penrose himself had received no such hint, and even Will, poor boy, had heard of it only as a fable, to which he gave no attention. They two, and Hugh himself in his utter misery, had accepted as a probable fact the calumny of which Nelly's pure mind instinctively demanded an explanation. They had not known it to be impossible that Mary should be guilty of such sin; but Nelly had known it, and recognised the incredible mystery, and demanded the reason for it, which everybody else had ignored or forgotten. He seemed to see it for a moment, as the watchers on a sinking ship might see the gleam of a lighthouse;—and then it disappeared from him in the wild waste of ignorance and wonder, and then gleamed out again, as if in Nelly's eyes. That was why she was going, bless her! She who never went upon visits, who knew better, and had insight in her eyes, and saw it could not be. These thoughts passed through Hugh's mind in a flood, and changed heaven and earth round about him, and set him on solid ground, as it were, instead of chaos. He was not wise enough, good enough, pure enough, to know the truth of himself—but Nelly could see it, as with angel eyes. He was young, and he loved Nelly, and that was how it appeared to him. Shame that had been brooding over him in the darkness, fled away. He rose up and felt as if he were yet a man, and had still his life before him, whatever might happen; and that he was there not only to comfort and protect his mother, but to defend and vindicate her; not to run away and keep silent like the guilty, but to face the pain of it, and the shame of it, if such bitter need was, and establish the truth. All this came to Hugh's mind from the simple little letter, which Nelly, crying and burning with indignation and pity, and an intolerable sense of wrong, had written without knowing what she meant. For anything Hugh could tell, his mother's innocence and honour, even if intact, might never be proved,—might do no more for him than had it been guilt and shame. The difference was that he had seen this accusation, glancing through Nelly's eyes, to be impossible; that he had found out that there was an interpretation somewhere, and the load was taken off his soul.

The change was so great, and his relief so immense, that he felt as if even that night he must act upon it. He could not go away, as he longed to do, for all modes of communication with the world until the morning were by that time impracticable. But he did what eased his mind at least. He wrote to Mr. Penrose a very grave, almost solemn letter, with neither horror nor even anger in it. "I do not know what the circumstances are, nor what the facts may be," he wrote, "but whatever they are, I do not doubt that my mother will explain—and I shall come to you immediately, that the truth may be made clearly apparent." And he wrote to Mr. Churchill, as he had never yet had the courage to do, asking to be told how it was. When he had done this, he rose up, feeling himself still more his own master. Hugh did not deceive himself; he did not think, because Nelly had communicated to his eyes her own divine simplicity of sight, that therefore it was certain that everything would be made clear and manifest to the law or the world. It might be otherwise; Mrs. Ochterlony might never be able to establish her own spotless fame, and her elder children's rights. It might be, by some horrible conspiracy of circumstances, that his name and position should be taken from him, and his honour stained beyond remedy. Such a thing was still possible. But Hugh felt that even then all would not be lost, that God would still be in heaven, and justice and mercy to some certain extent on the earth, and duty still before him. The situation was not changed, but only the key-note of his thoughts was changed, and his mind had come back to itself. He rose up, though it was getting late, and rang the bell for Francis Ochterlony's favourite servant, and began to arrange about the removal of the Museum. He might not be master long—in law; but he was master by right of nature and his uncle's will, and he would at least do his duty as long as he remained there.

Mrs. Gilsland, the housekeeper, was in the hall as he went out, and she curtseyed and stood before him, rustling in her black silk gown, and eyeing him doubtfully. She was afraid to disturb the Squire, as she said, but there was a poor soul there, if so be as he would speak a word to her. It annoyed Hugh to be drawn away from his occupations just as he was roused to return to them; but Nelly's letter and the influence of profound emotion had given a certain softness to his soul. He asked what it was, and heard it was a poor woman who had come with a petition. She had come a long way, and had a child with her, but nobody had liked to disturb the young Squire: and now it was providential, Mrs. Gilsland thought, that he should have passed just at that moment. "She has been gone half her lifetime, Mr. Hugh—I mean Sir," said the housekeeper, "though she was born and bred here; and her poor man is that bad with the paralytics that she has to do everything, which she thought if perhaps you would give her the new lodge—"

"The new lodge is not built yet," said Hugh, with a pang in his heart, feeling, notwithstanding his new courage, that it was hard to remember all his plans and the thousand changes it might never be in his power to make; "and it ought to be some one who has a claim on the family," he added, with a half-conscious sigh.

"And that's what poor Susan has," said Mrs. Gilsland. "Master would never have said no if it had been in his time; for he knew as he had been unjust to them poor folks; and a good claim on you, Mr. Hugh. She is old Sommerville's daughter, as you may have heard talk on, and as decent a woman—"

"Who was old Sommerville?" said Hugh.

"He was one as was a faithful servant to your poor papa," said the housekeeper. "I've heard as he lost his place all for the Captain's sake, as was Captain Ochterlony then, and as taking a young gentleman as ever was. If your mother was to hear of it, Mr. Hugh, she is not the lady to forget. A poor servant may be most a friend to his master—I've heard many and many a one say so that was real quality—and your mamma being a true lady—"

"Yes," said Hugh, "a good servant is a friend; and if she had any claims upon my father, I will certainly see her; but I am busy now. I have not been—well. I have been neglecting a great many things, and now that I feel a little better, I have a great deal to do."

"Oh, sir, it isn't lost time as makes a poor creature's heart to sing for joy!" said Mrs. Gilsland. She was a formidable housekeeper, but she was a kind woman; and somehow a subtle perception that their young master had been in trouble had crept into the mind of the household. "Which it's grieved as we've all been to see as you was not—well," she added with a curtsey; "it's been the watching and the anxiety; and so good as you was, sir, to the Squire. But poor Susan has five mile to go, and a child in arms, as is a load to carry; and her poor sick husband at home. And it was borne in upon them as perhaps for old Sommerville's sake—"

"Well, who was he?" said Hugh, with languid interest, a little fretted by the interruption, yet turning his steps towards the housekeeper's room, from which a gleam of firelight shone, at the end of a long corridor. He did not know anything about old Sommerville; the name awakened no associations in his mind, and even the housekeeper's long narrative as she followed him caught his attention only by intervals. She was so anxious to produce an effect for her PROTÉGÉE'S sake that she began with an elaborate description of old Sommerville's place and privileges, which whizzed past Hugh's ear without ever touching his mind. But he was too good-hearted to resist the picture of the poor woman who had five miles to go, and a baby and a sick husband. She was sitting basking before the fire in Mrs. Gilsland's room, poor soul, thinking as little about old Sommerville as the young Squire was; her heart beating high with anxiety about the new lodge—beating as high as if it was a kingdom she had hopes of conquering; with excitement as profound as that which moved Hugh himself when he thought of his fortune hanging in the balance, and of the name and place and condition of which perhaps he was but a usurper. It was as much to poor Susan to have the lodge as it was to him to have Earlston, or rather a great deal more. And he went in, putting a stop to Mrs. Gilsland's narrative, and began to talk to the poor suitor; and the firelight played pleasantly on the young man's handsome face, as he stood full in its ruddy illumination to hear her story, with his own anxiety lying at his heart like a stone. To look at this scene, it looked the least interesting of all that was going on at that moment in the history of the Ochterlony family—less important than what was taking place in Liverpool, where Mary was—or even than poor Aunt Agatha's solitary tears over Winnie's letter, which had just been taken in to her, and which went to her heart. The new lodge might never be built, and Hugh Ochterlony might never have it in his power to do anything for poor Susan, who was old Sommerville's daughter. But at least he was not hard-hearted, and it was a kind of natural grace and duty to hear what the poor soul had to say.

CHAPTER XLIII

It was morning when Mary arrived in Liverpool, early morning, chilly and grey. She had been detained on the road by the troublesome delays of a cross route, and the fresh breath of the autumnal morning chilled her to the heart. And she had not come with any distinct plan. She did not know what she was going to do. It had seemed to her as if the mere sight of her would set her boy right, had there been evil in his mind; and she did not know that there was any evil in his mind. She knew nothing of what was in Mr. Penrose's letter, which had driven Hugh to such despair. She did not even know whether Will had so much as mentioned his discovery to Uncle Penrose, or whether he might not have fled there, simply to get away from the terrible thought of his mother's disgrace. If it were so, she had but to take her boy in her arms, to veil her face with shame, yet raise it with conscious honour, and tell him how it all was. This, perhaps, was what she most thought of doing—to show him the rights of the story, of which he had only heard the evil-seeming side, and to reconcile him to herself and the world, and his life, on all of which a shadow must rest, as Mary thought, if any shadow rested on his mother. By times she was grieved with Will—"angry," as he would have said—to think he had gone away in secret without unfolding his troubles to the only creature who could clear them up; but by times it seemed to her as though it was only his tenderness of her, his delicacy for her, that had driven him away. That he could not endure the appearance of a stain upon her, that he was unable to let her know the possibility of any suspicion—this was chiefly what Mrs. Ochterlony thought. And it made her heart yearn towards the boy. Anything about Earlston, or Hugh, or the property, or Will's rights, had not crossed her mind; even Mrs. Kirkman's hints had proved useless, so far as that was concerned. Such a thing seemed to her as impossible as to steal or to murder. When they were babies, a certain thrill of apprehension had moved her whenever she saw any antagonism between the brothers; but when the moment of realizing it came, she was unable to conceive of such a horror. To think of Will harming Hugh! It was impossible—more than impossible; and thus as she drove through the unknown streets in the early bustle of the morning, towards the distant suburb in which Mr. Penrose lived, her thoughts rejected all tragical suppositions. The interview would be painful enough in any case, for it was hard for a mother to have to defend herself, and vindicate her good fame, to her boy; but still it could have been nothing but Will's horror at such a revelation—his alarm at the mere idea of such a suspicion ever becoming known to his mother—his sense of disenchantment in the entire world following his discovery, that made him go away: and this she had it in her power to dissipate for ever. This was how she was thinking as she approached Mr. Penrose's great mansion, looking out eagerly to see if any one might be visible at the windows. She saw no one, and her heart beat high as she looked up at the blank big house, and thought of the young heart that would flutter and perhaps sicken at the sight of her, and then expand into an infinite content. For by this time she had so reasoned herself into reassurance, and the light and breath of the morning had so invigorated her mind, that she had no more doubt that her explanations would content him, and clear away every cloud from his thoughts, than she had of his being her son, and loyal as no son of hers could fail to be.

The servants did not make objections to her as they had done to Will. They admitted her to the cold uninhabited drawing-room, and informed her that Mr. Penrose was out, but that young Mr. Ochterlony was certainly to be found. "Tell him it is his mother," said Mary, with her heart yearning over him: and then she sat down to wait. There was nothing after all in the emergency to tremble at. She smiled at herself when she thought of her own horrible apprehensions, and of the feelings with which she had hurried from the Cottage. It would be hard to speak of the suspicion to which she was subjected, but then she could set it to rest for ever: and what did the pang matter? Thus she sat with a wistful smile on her face, and waited. The moments passed, and she heard sounds of steps outside, and something that sounded like the hurried shutting of the great door; but no eager foot coming to meet her—no rapid entrance like that she had looked for. She sat still until the smile became rigid on her lip, and a wonderful depression came to her soul. Was he not coming? Could it be that he judged her without hearing her, and would not see his mother? Then her heart woke up again when she heard some one approaching, but it was only the servant who had opened the door.

"I beg your pardon, ma'am," said the man, with hesitation, "but it appears I made a mistake. Young Mr. Ochterlony was not—I mean he has gone out. Perhaps, if it was anything of importance, you could wait."

"He has gone out? so early?—surely not after he knew I was here?" said Mary, wildly; and then she restrained herself with an effort. "It is something of importance," she said, giving a groan in her heart, which was not audible. "I am his mother, and it is necessary I should see him. Yes, I will wait; and if you could send some one to tell him, if you know where he is—"

"I should think, ma'am, he is sure to be home to luncheon," said the servant, evading this demand. To luncheon—and it was only about ten o'clock in the morning now. Mary clasped her hands together to keep herself from crying out. Could he have been out before she arrived—could he have fled to avoid her? She asked herself the question in a kind of agony; but Mr. Penrose's man stood blank and respectful at the door, and offered no point of appeal. She could not take him into her counsel, or consult him as to what it all meant; and yet she was so anxious, so miserable, so heart-struck by this suspense, that she could not let him go without an effort to find something out.

"Has he gone with his uncle?" she said. "Perhaps I might find it at Mr. Penrose's office. No? Or perhaps you can tell me if there is any place he is in the habit of going to, or if he always goes out so early. I want very much to see him; I have been travelling all night; it is very important," Mary added, wistfully looking in the attendant's face.

Mr. Penrose's butler was very solemn and precise, but yet there was something in the sight of her restrained distress which moved him. "I don't know as I have remarked what time the young gentleman goes out," he said. "He's early this morning—mostly he varies a bit—but I don't make no doubt as he'll be in to luncheon." When he had said this the man did not go away, but stood with a mixture of curiosity and sympathy, sorry for the new-comer, and wondering what it all meant. If Mary herself could but have made out what it all meant! She turned away, with the blood, as she thought, all going back upon her heart, and the currents of life flowing backward to their source. Had he fled from her? What did it mean?

In this state of suspense Mrs. Ochterlony passed the morning. She had a maid sent to her, and was shown, though with a little wonder and hesitation, into a sleeping room, where she mechanically took off her travelling wraps and assumed her indoor appearance so far as that was possible. It was a great, still, empty, resounding house; the rooms were large, coldly furnished, still looking new for want of use, and vacant of any kind of occupation or interest. Mary came downstairs again, and placed herself at one of the great windows in the drawing-room. She would not go out, even to seek Will, lest she might miss him by the way. She went and sat down by the window, and gazed out upon the strip of suburban road which was visible through the shrubberies, feeling her heart beat when any figure, however unlike her boy, appeared upon it. It might be he, undiscernible in the distance, or it might be some one from him, some messenger or ambassador. It was what might be called a handsome room, but it was vacant, destitute of everything which could give it interest, with some trifling picture-books on the table and meaningless knick-nacks. When Mrs. Ochterlony was sick of sitting watching at the window she would get up and walk round it, and look at the well-bound volumes on the table, and feel herself grow wild in the excess of her energy and vehemence, by contrast with the deadly calm of her surroundings. What was it to this house, or its master, or the other human creatures in it, that she was beating her wings thus, in the silence, against the cage? Thus she sat, or walked about, the whole long morning, counting the minutes on the time-piece or on her watch, and feeling every minute an hour. Where had he gone? had he fled to escape? or was his absence natural and accidental? These questions went through her head, one upon another, with increasing commotion and passion, until she found herself unable to rest, and felt her veins tingling, and her pulses throbbing in a wild harmony. It seemed years since she had arrived when one o'clock struck, and a few minutes later the sound of a gong thrilled through the silence. This was for luncheon. It was not a bell, which might be heard outside and quickened the steps of any one who might be coming. Mary stood still and watched at her window, but nobody came. And then the butler, whose curiosity was more and more roused, came upstairs with steady step, and shoes that creaked in a deprecating, apologetic way, to ask if she would go down to luncheon, and to regret respectfully that the young gentleman had not yet come in. "No doubt, ma'am, if he had known you were coming, he'd have been here," the man said, not without an inquiring look at her, which Mrs. Ochterlony was vaguely conscious of. She went downstairs with a kind of mechanical obedience, feeling it an ease to go into another room, and find another window at which she could look out. She could see another bit of road further off, and it served to fill her for the moment with renewed hope. There, at least, she must surely see him coming. But the moments still kept going on, gliding off the steady hand of the time-piece like so many months or years. And still Will did not come.

It was all the more dreadful to her, because she had been totally unprepared for any such trial. It had never occurred to her that her boy, though he had run away, would avoid her now. By this time even the idea that he could be avoiding her went out of her mind, and she began to think some accident had happened to him. He was young and careless, a country boy—and there was no telling what terrible thing might have happened on those thronged streets, which had felt like Pandemonium to Mary's unused faculties. And she did not know where to go to look for him, or what to do. In her terror she began to question the man, who kept coming and going into the room, sometimes venturing to invite her attention to the dishes, which were growing cold, sometimes merely looking at her, as he went and came. She asked about her boy, what he had been doing since he came—if he were not in the habit of going to his uncle's office—if he had made any acquaintances—if there was anything that could account for his absence? "Perhaps he went out sight-seeing," said Mary; "perhaps he is with his uncle at the office. He was always very fond of shipping." But she got very doubtful and hesitating replies—replies which were so uncertain that fear blazed up within her; and the slippery docks and dangerous water, the great carts in the streets and the string of carriages, came up before her eyes again.

Thus the time passed till it was evening. Mary could not, or rather would not, believe her own senses, and yet it was true. Shadows stole into the corners, and a star, which it made her heart sick to see, peeped out in the green-blue sky—and she went from one room to another, watching the two bits of road. First the one opening, which was fainter and farther off than the other, which was overshadowed by the trees, yet visible and near. Every time she changed the point of watching, she felt sure that he must be coming. But yet the stars peeped out, and the lamps were lighted on the road, and her boy did not appear. She was a woman used to self-restraint, and but for her flitting up and downstairs, and the persistent way she kept by the window, the servants might not have noticed anything remarkable about her; but they had all possession of one fact which quickened their curiosity—and the respectable butler prowled about watching her, in a way which would have irritated Mrs. Ochterlony, had she been at sufficient leisure in her mind to remark him. When the time came that the lamp must be lighted and the windows closed, it went to her heart like a blow. She had to reason to herself that her watch could make no difference—could not bring him a moment sooner or later—and yet to be shut out from that one point of interest was hard. They told her Mr. Penrose was expected immediately, and that no doubt the young gentleman would be with him. To see Will only in his uncle's presence was not what Mary had been thinking of—but yet it was better than this suspense; and now that her eyes could serve her no longer, she sat listening, feeling every sound echo in her brain, and herself surrounded, as it were, by a rustle of passing feet and a roll of carriages that came and passed and brought nothing to her. And the house was so still and vacant, and resounded with every movement—even with her own foot, as she changed her seat, though her foot had always been so light. That day's watching had made a change upon her, which a year under other circumstances would not have made. Her brow was contracted with lines unknown to its broad serenity; her eyes looked out eagerly from the lids which had grown curved and triangular with anxiety; her mouth was drawn together and colourless. The long, speechless, vacant day, with no occupation in it but that of watching and listening, with its sense of time lost and opportunity deferred, with its dreadful suggestion of other things and thoughts which might be making progress and nourishing harm, while she sat here impeded and helpless, and unable to prevent it, was perhaps the severest ordeal Mary could have passed through. It was the same day on which Winnie went to Carlisle—it was the same evening on which Hugh received Nelly's letter, which found his mother motionless in Mr. Penrose's drawing-room, waiting. This was the hardest of all, and yet not so hard as it might have been. For she did not know, what all the servants in the house knew, that Will had seen her arrive—that he had rushed out of the house, begging the man to deceive her—that he had kept away all day, not of necessity, but because he did not dare to face her. Mary knew nothing of this; but it was hard enough to contend with the thousand spectres that surrounded her, the fears of accident, the miserable suspense, the dreary doubt and darkness that seemed to hang over everything, as she waited ever vainly in the silence for her boy's return.

When some one arrived at the door, her heart leaped so into her throat that she felt herself suffocated; she had to put her hands to her side and clasp them there to support herself as footsteps came up the stair. She grew sick, and a mist came over her eyes; and then all at once she saw clearly, and fell back, fainting in the body, horribly conscious and alive in the mind, when she saw it was Mr. Penrose who came in alone.

CHAPTER XLIV

Will had seen his mother arrive. He was coming downstairs at the moment, and he heard her voice, and could hear her say, "Tell him it is his mother," and fright had seized him. If only three days could have been abrogated, and he could have gone to her in his old careless way, to demand an account of why she had come!—but there stood up before him a ghost of what he had been doing—a ghost of uncomprehended harm and mischief, which now for the first time showed to him, not in its real light, but still with an importance it had never taken before. If it had been hard to tell her of the discovery he had made before he left the Cottage, it was twenty times harder now, when he had discussed it with other people, and taken practical steps about it. He went out hurriedly, and with a sense of stealth and panic. And the panic and the stealth were signs to him of something wrong. He had not seen it, and did not see it yet, as regarded the original question. He knew in his heart that there was no favouritism in Mrs. Ochterlony's mind, and that he was just the same to her as Hugh—and what could it matter which of her sons had Earlston?—But still, nature was stronger in him than reason, and he was ashamed and afraid to meet her, though he did not know why. He hurried out, and said to himself that she was "angry," and that he could not stay in all day long to be scolded. He would go back to luncheon, and that would be time enough. And then he began to imagine what she would say to him. But that was not so easy. What could she say? After all, he had done no harm. He had but intimated to Hugh, in the quietest way, that he had no right to the position he was occupying. He had made no disturbance about it, nor upbraided his brother for what was not his brother's fault. And so far from blaming his mother, it had not occurred to him to consider her in the matter, except in the most secondary way. What could it matter to her? If Will had it, or if Hugh had it, it was still in the family. And the simple transfer was nothing to make any fuss about. This was how he reasoned; but Nature held a different opinion upon the subject. She had not a word to say, nor any distinct suggestion even, of guiltiness or wrong-doing to present to his mind. She only carried him away out of the house, made him shrink aside till Mary had passed, and made him walk at the top of his speed out of the very district in which Mr. Penrose's house was situated. Because his mother would be "angry"—because she might find fault with him for going away or insist upon his return, or infringe his liberty. Was that why he fled from her?—But Will could not tell—he fled because he was driven by an internal consciousness which could not find expression so much as in thought. He went away and wandered about the streets, thinking that now he was almost a man, and ought to be left to direct his own actions; that to come after him like this was an injury to him which he had a right to resent. It was treating him as Hugh and Islay had never been treated. When he laid himself out for these ideas they came to him one by one, and at last he succeeded in feeling himself a little ill-used; but in his heart he knew that he did not mean that, and that Mrs. Ochterlony did not mean it, and that there was something else which stood between them, though he could not tell what it was.

All this time he contemplated going in facing his mother, and being surprised to see her, and putting up with her anger as he best could. But when midday came, he felt less willing than ever. His reluctance grew upon him. If it had all come simply, if he had rushed into her presence unawares, then he could have borne it; but to go back on purpose, to be ushered in to her solemnly, and to meet her when her wrath had accumulated and she had prepared what to say—this was an ordeal which Will felt he could not bear. She had grown terrible to him, appalling, like the angel with the flaming sword. His conscience arrayed her in such effulgence of wrath and scorn, that his very soul shrank. She would be angry beyond measure. It was impossible to fancy what she might say or do; and he could not go in and face her in cold blood. Therefore, instead of going home, Will went down hastily to his uncle's office, and explained to him the position of affairs. "You go and speak to her," said Will, with a feeling that it was his accomplice he was addressing, and yet a pang to think that he had himself gone over to the enemy, and was not on his natural side; "I am not up to seeing her to-night."

"Poor Mary," said Uncle Penrose, "I should not be surprised to find her in a sad way; but you ought to mind your own business, and it is not I who am to be blamed, but you."

"She will not blame you," said Will; "she will be civil to you. She will not look at you as she would look at me. When she is vexed she gives a fellow such a look. And I'm tired, and I can't face her to-day."

"It is mail-day, and I shall be late, and she will have a nice time of it all by herself," said Mr. Penrose; but he consented at the end. And as for Will, he wandered down to the quays, and got into a steam-boat, and went off in the midst of a holiday party up the busy river. He used to remember the airs that were played on the occasion by the blind fiddler in the boat, and could never listen to them afterwards without the strangest sensations. He felt somehow as if he were in hiding, and the people were pointing him out to each other, and had a sort of vague wonder in his mind as to what they could think he had done—robbed or killed, or something—when the fact was he was only killing the time, and keeping out of the way because his mother was angry, and he did not feel able to face her and return home. And very forlorn the poor boy was; he had not eaten anything, and he did not know what to get for himself to eat, and the host of holiday people filled up all the vacant spaces in the inn they were all bound for, where there were pretty gardens looking on the river. Will was young and alone, and not much in the way of thrusting himself forward, and it was hard to get any one to attend to him, or a seat to sit upon, or anything to eat; and his forlorn sense of discomfort and solitude pressed as hard upon him as remorse could have done. And he knew that he must manage to make the time pass on somehow, and that he could not return until he could feel himself justified in hoping that his mother, tired with her journey, had gone to rest. Not till he felt confident of getting in unobserved, could he venture to go home.

This was how it happened that Mr. Penrose went in alone, and that all the mists suddenly cleared up for Mary, and she saw that she had harder work before her than anything that had yet entered into her mind. He drew a chair beside her, and shook hands, and said he was very glad to see her, and then a pause ensued so serious and significant, that Mary felt herself judged and condemned; and felt, in spite of herself, that the hot blood was rushing to her face. It seemed to her as she sat there, as if all the solid ground had suddenly been cut away from under her, that her plea was utterly ignored and the whole affair decided upon; and only to see Uncle Penrose's meekly averted face made her head swim and her heart beat with a kind of half-delirious rage and resentment. He believed it then—knew all about it, and believed it, and recognised that it was a fallen woman by whose side he sat. All this Mrs. Ochterlony perceived in an instant by the downcast, conscious glance of Mr. Penrose's eye.

"Will has been out all day, has he?" he said. "Gone sight-seeing, I suppose. He ought to be in to dinner. I hope you had a comfortable luncheon, and have been taken care of. It is mail-day, that is why I am so late."

"But I am anxious, very anxious, about Will," said Mary. "I thought you would know where he was. He is only a country boy, and something may happen to him in these dreadful streets."

"Oh no, nothing has happened to him," said Uncle Penrose, "you shall see him later. I am very glad you have come, for I wanted to have a little talk with you. You will always be quite welcome here, whatever may happen. If the girls had been at home, indeed, it might have been different—but whenever you like to come you know—I am very glad that we can talk it all over. It is so much the most satisfactory way."

"Talk what over?" said Mary. "Thank you, uncle, but it was Will I was anxious to see."

"Yes, to be sure—naturally," said Mr. Penrose; "but don't let us go into anything exciting before dinner. The gong will sound in ten minutes, and I must put myself in order. We can talk in the evening, and that will be much the best."

With this he went and left her, to make the very small amount of toilette he considered necessary. And then came the dinner, during which Mr. Penrose was very particular, as he said, to omit all allusion to disagreeable subjects. Mary had to take her place at table, and to look across at the vacant chair that had been placed for Will, and to feel the whole weight of her uncle's changed opinion, without any opportunity of rising up against it. She could not say a word in self-defence, for she was in no way assailed; but she never raised her eyes to him, nor listened to half-a-dozen words, without feeling that Mr. Penrose had in his own consciousness found her out. He was not going to shut his doors against her, or to recommend any cruel step. But her character was changed in his eyes. A sense that he was no longer particular as to what he said or did before her, no longer influenced by her presence, or elevated ever so little by her companionship as he had always been of old, came with terrible effect upon Mary's mind. He was careless of what he said, and of her feelings, and of his own manners. She was a woman who had compromised herself, who had no longer much claim to respect, in Uncle Penrose's opinion. This feeling, which was, as it were, in the air, affected Mary in the strangest way. It made her feel nearly mad in her extreme suppression and quietness. She could not stand on her own defence, for she was not assailed. And Will who should have stood by her, had gone over to the enemy's side, and deserted her, and kept away. Where was he? where could he have gone? Her boy—her baby—the last one, who had always been the most tenderly tended; and he was avoiding—avoiding his mother. Mary realized all this as she sat at the table; and at the same time she had to respect the presence of the butler and Mr. Penrose's servants, and make no sign. When she did not eat Mr. Penrose took particular notice of it, and hoped that she was not allowing herself to be upset; and he talked, in an elaborate way, of subjects that could interest nobody, keeping with too evident caution from the one subject which was in his mind all the while.

This lasted until the servants had gone away, and Mr. Penrose had poured out his first glass of port, for he was an old-fashioned man. He sat and sipped his wine with the quietness of preparation, and Mary, too, buckled on her armour, and made a rapid inspection of all its joints and fastenings. She was sitting at the table which had been so luxuriously served, and where the purple fruit and wine were making a picture still; but she was as truly at the bar as ever culprit was. There was an interval of silence, which was very dreadful to her, and then, being unable to bear it any longer, it was Mary herself who spoke.

"I perceive that something has been passing here in which we are all interested," she said. "My poor boy has told you something he had heard—and I don't know, except in the most general way, what he has heard. Can you tell, uncle? It is necessary I should know."

"My dear Mary, these are very unpleasant affairs to talk about," said Mr. Penrose. "You should have had a female friend to support you—though, indeed, I don't know how you may feel about that. Will has told me all. There was nobody he could ask advice from under the circumstances, and I think it was very sensible of him to come to me."

"I want to know what he wanted advice for," said Mary, "and what it is you call all; and why Will has avoided me? I cannot think it is chance that has kept him out so long. Whatever he has heard, he must have known that it would be best to talk it over with me."

"He thought you would be angry," said Mr. Penrose, between the sips of his wine.

"Angry!" said Mary, and then her heart melted at the childish fear. "Oh, uncle, you should have advised him better," she said, "he is only a boy; and you know that whatever happened, he had better have consulted his own mother first. How should I be angry? This is not like a childish freak, that one could be angry about."

"No," said Mr. Penrose; "it is not like a childish freak; but still I think it was the wisest thing he could do to come to me. It is impossible you could be his best counsellor where you are yourself so much concerned, and where such important interests are at stake."

"Let me know at once what you mean," said Mary faintly. "What important interests are at stake?"

She made a rapid calculation in her mind at the moment, and her heart grew sicker and sicker. Will had been, when she came to think of it, more than a week away from home, and many things might have happened in that time—things which she could not realize nor put in any shape, but which made her spirit faint out of her and all her strength ooze away.

"My dear Mary," said Mr. Penrose, mildly, "why should you keep any pretence with me? Will has told me all. You cannot expect that a young man like him, at the beginning of his life, would relinquish his rights and give up such a fine succession merely out of consideration to your feelings. I am very sorry for you, and he is very sorry. Nothing shall be done on our part to compromise you beyond what is absolutely necessary; but your unfortunate circumstances are not his fault, and it is only reasonable that he should claim his rights."

"What are his rights?" said Mary; "what do you suppose my unfortunate circumstances to be? Speak plainly—or, stop; I will tell you what he has heard. He has heard that my husband and I were married in India before he was born. That is quite true; and I suppose he and you think—" said Mary, coming to a sudden gasp for breath, and making a pause against her will. "Then I will tell you the facts," she said, with a labouring, long-drawn breath, when she was able to resume. "We were married in Scotland, as you and everybody know; it was not a thing done in secret. Everybody about Kirtell—everybody in the county knew of it. We went to Earlston afterwards, where Hugh's mother was, and to Aunt Agatha. There was no shame or concealment anywhere, and you know that. We went out to India after, but not till we had gone to see all our friends; and everybody knew—"

"My wife even asked you here," said Mr. Penrose, reflectively. "It is very extraordinary; I mentioned all that to Will: but, my dear Mary, what is the use of going over it in this way, when there is this fact, which you don't deny, which proves that Hugh Ochterlony thought it necessary to do you justice at the last?"

Mary was too much excited to feel either anger or shame. The colour scarcely deepened on her cheek. "I will tell you about that," she said. "I resisted it as long as it was possible to resist. The man at Gretna died, and his house and all his records were burnt, and the people were all dead who had been present, and I had lost the lines. I did not think them of any consequence. And then my poor Hugh was seized with a panic—you remember him, uncle," said Mary, in her excitement, with the tears coming to her eyes. "My poor Hugh! how much he felt everything, how hard it was for him to be calm and reasonable when he thought our interests concerned. I have thought since, he had some presentiment of what was going to happen. He begged me for his sake to consent that he might be sure there would be no difficulty about the pension or anything. It was like dragging my heart out of my breast," said Mary, with the tears dropping on her hands, "but I yielded to please him."

And then there was a pause, inevitable on her part, for her heart was full, and she had lost the faculty of speech. As for Mr. Penrose, he gave quiet attention to all she was saying, and made mental notes of it while he filled himself another glass of wine. He was not an impartial listener, for he had taken his side, and had the conducting of the other case in his hands. When Mary came to herself, and could see and hear again—when her heart was not beating so wildly in her ears, and her wet eyes had shed their moisture, she gave a look at him with a kind of wonder, marvelling that he said nothing. The idea of not being believed when she spoke was one which had never entered into her mind.

"You expect me to say something," said Mr. Penrose, when he caught her eye. "But I don't see what I can say. All that you have told me just amounts to this, that your first marriage rests upon your simple assertion; you have no documentary or any other kind of evidence. My dear Mary, I don't want to hurt your feelings, but if you consider how strong is your interest in it, what a powerful motive you have to keep up that story, and that you confess it rests on your word alone, you will see that, as Wilfrid's adviser, I am not justified in departing from the course we have taken. It is too important to be decided by mere feeling. I am very sorry for you, but I have Wilfrid's interests to think of," said Mr. Penrose, slowly swallowing his glass of wine.

Mary looked at him aghast; she did not understand him. It seemed to her as if some delusion had taken possession of her mind, and that the words conveyed a meaning which no human words could bear. "I do not understand you," she said; "I suppose there is some mistake. What course is it you have taken? I want to know what you mean."

"It is not a matter to be discussed with you," said Mr. Penrose. "Whatever happens I would not be forgetful of a lady's feelings. From the first I have said that it must be a matter of private arrangement; and I have no doubt Hugh will see it in the same light. I have written to him, but I have not yet received a satisfactory answer. Under all the circumstances I feel we are justified in asserting Wilfrid to be Major Ochterlony's only lawful son—"

An involuntary cry came out of Mary's breast. She pushed her chair away from the table, and sat bending forward, looking at him. The pang was partly physical, as if some one had thrust a spear into her heart; and beyond that convulsive motion she could neither move nor speak.

"—and of course he must be served heir to his uncle," said Mr. Penrose. "Where things so important are concerned, you cannot expect that feeling can be allowed to bear undue sway. It is in this light that Wilfrid sees it. He is ready to do anything for you, anything for his brother; but he cannot be expected to sacrifice his legal rights. I hope Hugh will see how reasonable this is, and I think for your own sake you should use your influence with him. If he makes a stand, you know it will ruin your character, and make everybody aware of the unhappy position of affairs; and it cannot do any good to him."

Mary heard all this and a great deal more, and sat stupified with a dull look of wonder on her face, making no reply. She thought she had formed some conception of what was coming to her, but in reality she had no conception of it; and she sat listening, coming to an understanding, taking it painfully into her mind, learning to see that it had passed out of the region of what might be—that the one great, fanciful, possible danger of her life had developed into a real danger, more dreadful, more appalling than anything she had ever conceived of. She sat thus, with her chair thrust back, looking in Mr. Penrose's face, following with her eyes all his unconcerned movements, feeling his words beat upon her ears like a stinging rain. And this was all true; love, honour, pride, or faith had nothing to do with it. Whether she was a wretched woman, devising a lie to cover her shame, or a pure wife telling her tale with lofty truth and indignation, mattered nothing. It was in this merciless man's hand, and nothing but merciless evidence and proof would be of any use. She sat and listened to him, hearing the same words over and over; that her feelings were to be considered; that nothing was to be done to expose her; that Will had consented to that, and was anxious for that; that it must be matter of private arrangement, and that her character must be spared. It was this iteration that roused Mary, and brought her back, as it were, out of her stupefaction into life.

"I do not understand all you are saying," she said, at last; "it sounds like a horrible dream; I feel as if you could not mean it: but one thing—do you mean that Hugh is to be made to give up his rights, by way of sparing me?"

"By way of sparing a public trial and exposure—which is what it must come to otherwise," said Mr. Penrose. "I don't know, poor boy, how you can talk about his rights."

"Then listen to me," said Mary, rising up, and holding by her chair to support herself; "I may be weak, but I am not like that. My boy shall not give up his rights. I know what I am saying; if there should be twenty trials, I am ready to bear them. It shall be proved whether in England a true woman cannot tell her true story, and be believed. Neither lie nor shame has ever attached to me. If I have to see my own child brought against me—God forgive you!—I will try to bear it. My poor Will! my poor Will!—but Hugh's boy shall not be sacrificed. What! my husband, my son, my own honour—a woman's honour involves all belonging to her—Do you think I, for the sake of pain or exposure, would give them all up? It must be that you have gone out of your senses, and don't know what to say. I, to save myself at my son's expense!"

"But Wilfrid is your son too," said Mr. Penrose, shrinking somewhat into himself.

"Oh, my poor Will! my poor Will!" said Mary, moaning in her heart; and after that she went away, and left the supporter of Will's cause startled, but not moved from his intention, by himself. As for Mrs.

Ochterlony, she went up into her room, and sank down into the first chair that offered, and clasped her hands over her heart lest it should break forth from the aching flesh. She thought no more of seeing Will, or of telling him her story, or delivering him from his delusion. What she thought of was, to take him into her arms in an infinite pity, when the poor boy, who did not know what he was doing, should come to himself. And Hugh—Hugh her husband, who was thought capable of such wrong and baseness—Hugh her boy, whose name and fame were to be taken from him,—and they thought she would yield to it, to save herself a pang! When she came to remember that the night was passing, and to feel the chill that had crept over her, and to recall to herself that she must not exhaust her strength, Mary paused in her thoughts, and fell upon her knees instead. Even that was not enough; she fell prostrate, as one who would have fallen upon the Deliverer's feet; but she could say no prayer. Her heart itself seemed at last to break forth, and soar up out of her, in a speechless supplication—"Let this cup pass!" Did He not say it once Who had a heavier burden to bear?

CHAPTER XLV

So very late it was when Will came in, that he crept up to his room with a silent stealth which felt more like ill-doing to him than any other sin he had been guilty of. He crept to his room, though he would have been glad to have lingered, and warmed himself and been revived with food. But, at the end of this long, wretched day, he was more than ever unfit to face his mother, who he felt sure must be watching for him, watchful and unwearied as she always had been. It did not occur to him that Mrs. Ochterlony, insensible for the moment to all sounds, was lying enveloped in darkness, with her eyes open, and all her faculties at work, and nothing but pain, pain, ever, for ever, in her mind. That she could be wound up to a pitch of emotion so great that she would not have heard whatever noise he might have made, that she would not have heeded him, that he was safe to go and come as he liked, so far as Mary was concerned, was an idea that never entered Will's mind. He stole in, and went softly up the stairs, and swallowed the glass of wine the butler compassionately brought him, without even saying a word of thanks. He was chilled to his bones, and his head ached, and a sense of confused misery was in all his frame. He crept into his bed like a savage, in the dark, seeking warmth, seeking forgetfulness, and hiding; so long as he could be hid, it did not matter. His mother could not come in with the light in her hand to stand by his bedside, and drive all ghosts and terrors away, for he had locked the door in his panic. No deliverance could come to him, as it seemed, any way. If she was "angry" before, what must she be now when he had fled and avoided her? and poor Will lay breathing hard in the dark, wondering within himself why it was he dared not face his mother. What had he done? Instead of having spent the day in his usual fashion, why was he weary, and footsore, and exhausted, and sick in body and in mind? He had meant her no harm, he had done no wrong he knew of. It was only a confused, unintelligible weight on his conscience, or rather on his consciousness, that bowed him down, and made him do things which he did not understand. He went to sleep at last, for he was young and weary, and nothing could have kept him from sleeping; but he had a bad night. He dreamed dreadful dreams, and in the midst of them all saw Mary, always Mary, threatening him, turning away from him, leaving him to fall over precipices and into perils. He started up a dozen times in the course of that troubled night, waking to a confused sense of solitude, and pain, and abandonment, which in the dark and the silence were very terrible to bear. He was still only a boy, and he had done wrong, dreadful wrong, and he did not know what it was.

In the morning when Will woke things were not much better. He was utterly unrefreshed by his night's rest—if the partial unconsciousness of his sleep could be called rest; and the thought he woke to was, that however she might receive him, to-day he must see his mother. She might be, probably was, "angry," beyond anything he could conceive; but however that might be, he must see her and meet her wrath. It was not until he had fully realized that thought, that a letter was brought to Will, which increased his excitement. It was a very unusual thing for him to get letters, and he was startled accordingly. He turned it over and over before he opened it, and thought it must be from Hugh. Hugh, too, must have adopted the plan of pouring out his wrath against his brother for want of any better defence to make. But then he perceived that the writing was not Hugh's. When he opened it Will grew pale, and then he grew red. It was a letter which Nelly Askell had written before she wrote the one to Hugh, which had roused him out of his despondency. Something had inspired the little girl that day. She had written this too, like the other, without very much minding what she meant. This is what Will read upon the morning of the day which he already felt to be in every description a day of fate:—

"WILL!—I don't think I can ever call you dear Will again, or think of you as I used to do—oh, Will, what are you doing? If I had been you I would have been tied to the stake, torn with wild horses, done anything that used to be done to people, rather than turn against my mother. I would have done that for my mother, and if I had had yours! Oh, Will, say you don't mean it? I think sometimes you can't mean it, but have got deluded somehow, for you know you have a bad temper. How could you ever believe it; She is not my mother, but I know she never did any wrong. She may have sinned perhaps, as people say everybody sins, but she never could have done any wrong; look in her face, and just try whether you can believe it. It is one comfort to me that if you mean to be so wicked (which I cannot believe of you), and were to win (which is not possible), you would never more have a day's happiness again. I hope you would never have a day's happiness. You would break her heart, for she is a woman, and though you would not break his heart, you would put his life all wrong, and it would haunt you, and you would pray to be poor, or a beggar, or anything rather than in a place that does not belong to you. You may think I don't know, but I do know. I am a woman, and understand things better than a boy like you. Oh, Will! we used to be put in the same cradle, and dear Mrs. Ochterlony used to nurse us both when we were babies. Sometimes I think I should have been your sister. If you will come back and put away all this which is so dreadful to think of, I will never more bring it up against you. I for one will forget it, as if it had never been. Nobody shall put it into your mind again. We will forgive you, and love you the same as ever; and when you are a man, and understand and see what it is you have been saved from, you will go down on your knees and thank God.

"If I had been old enough to travel by myself, or to be allowed to do what I like, I should have gone to Liverpool too, to have given you no excuse. It is not so easy to write; but oh, Will, you know what I mean. Come back, and let us forget that you were ever so foolish and so wicked. I could cry when I think of you all by yourself, and nobody to tell you what is right. Come back, and nobody shall ever bring it up against you. Dear Will! don't you love us all too well to make us unhappy?—Still your affectionate NELLY."

This letter startled the poor boy, and affected him in a strange way. It brought the tears to his eyes. It touched him somehow, not by its reproaches, but by the thought that Nelly cared. She had gone over to Hugh's side like all the rest—and yet she cared and took upon her that right of reproach and accusation which is more tender than praise. And it made Will's heart ache in a dull way to see that they all thought him wicked. What had he done that was wicked? He ached, poor boy, not only in his heart but in his head, and all over him. He did not get up even to read his letter, but lay in a kind of sad stupor all the morning, wondering if his mother was still in the house—wondering if she would come to him—wondering if she was so angry that she no longer desired to see him. The house was more quiet than usual, he thought—there was no stir in it of voices or footsteps. Perhaps Mrs. Ochterlony had gone away again—perhaps he was to be left here, having got Uncle Penrose on his side, to his sole company—excommunicated and cast off by his own. Wilfrid lay pondering all these thoughts till he could bear it no longer; instead of his pain and shrinking a kind of dogged resistance came into his mind; at least he would go and face it, and see what was to happen to him. He would go downstairs and find out, to begin with, what this silence meant.

Perhaps it was just because it was so much later than usual that he felt as if he had been ill when he got up—felt his limbs trembling under him, and shivered, and grew hot and cold—or perhaps it was the fatigue and mental commotion of yesterday. By this time he felt sure that his mother must be gone. Had she been in the house she would have come to see him. She would have seized the opportunity when he could not escape from her. No doubt she was gone, after waiting all yesterday for him,—gone either hating him or scorning him, casting him off from her; and he felt that he had not deserved that. Perhaps he might have deserved that Hugh should turn his enemy—notwithstanding that, even for Hugh he felt himself ready to do anything—but to his mother he had done no harm. He had meditated nothing but good to her. He would not have thought of marrying, or giving to any one but her the supreme place in his house. He would never have asked her or made any doubt about it, but taken her at once to Earlston, and showed her everything there arranged according to her liking. This was what Will had always intended and settled upon. And his mother, for whom he would have done all this, had gone away again, offended and angry, abandoning him to his own devices. Bitterness took possession of his soul as he thought of it. He meant it only for their good—for justice and right, and to have his own; and this was the cruel way in which they received it, as if he had done it out of unkind feelings—even Nelly! A sense that he was wronged came into Wilfrid's mind as he dressed himself, and looked at his pale face in the glass, and smoothed his long brown hair. And yet he stepped out of his room with the feelings of one who ventures upon an undiscovered country, a new region, in which he does not know whether he is to meet with good or evil. He had to support himself by the rail as he went downstairs. He hesitated and trembled at the drawing-room door, which was a room Mr. Penrose never occupied. Breakfast must be over long ago. If there was any lady in the house, no doubt she would be found there.

He put his hand on the door, but it was a minute or more before he could open it, and he heard no sound within. No doubt she had gone away. He had walked miles yesterday to avoid her, but yet his heart was sore and bled, and he felt deserted and miserable to think that she was gone. But when Will had opened the door, the sight he saw was more wonderful to him than if she had been gone. Mary was seated at the table writing: she was pale, but there was something in her face which told of unusual energy and resolution, a kind of inspiration which gave character to every movement she made. And she was so much preoccupied, that she showed no special excitement at sight of her boy; she stopped and put away her pen, and rose up looking at him with pitiful eyes. "My poor boy!" she said, and kissed him in her tender way. And then she sat down at the table, and went back to her letters again.

It was not simple consternation which struck Will; it was a mingled pang of wonder and humiliation and sharp disappointment. Only her poor boy!—only the youngest, the child as he had always been, not the young revolutionary to whom Nelly had written that letter, whom Mrs. Ochterlony had come anxious and in haste to seek. She was more anxious now about her letters apparently than about him, and there was nothing but tenderness and sorrow in her eyes; and when she did raise her head again, it was to remark his paleness and ask if he was tired. "Go and get some breakfast, Will," she said; but he did not care for breakfast. He had not the heart to move—he sat in the depths of boyish mortification and looked at her writing her letters. Was that all that it mattered? or was she only making a pretence at indifference? But Mary was too much occupied evidently for any pretence. Her whole figure and attitude were full of resolution. Notwithstanding the pity of her voice as she addressed him, and the longing look in her eyes, there was something in her which Wilfrid had never seen before, which revealed to him in a kind of dull way that his mother was wound up to some great emergency, that she had taken a great resolution, and was occupied by matters of life and death.

"You are very busy, it seems," he said, peevishly, when he had sat for some time watching her, wondering when she would speak to him. To find that she was not angry, that she had something else to think about, was not half so great a relief as it appeared.

"Yes, I am busy," said Mary. "I am writing to your brother, Will, and to some people who know all about me, and I have no time to lose. Your Uncle Penrose is a hard man, and I am afraid he will be hard on Hugh."

"No, mother," said Will, feeling his heart beat quick; "he shall not be hard upon Hugh. I want to tell you that. I want to have justice; but for anything else—Hugh shall have whatever he wishes; and as for you—"

"Oh, Will," said Mrs. Ochterlony; and somehow it seemed to poor Will's disordered imagination that she and his letter were speaking together—"I had almost forgotten that you had anything to do with it. If you had but come first and spoken to me—"

"Why should I have come and spoken to you?" said Will, growing into gradual excitement; "it will not do you any harm. I am your son as well as Hugh—if it is his or if it is mine, what does it matter? I knew you would be angry if I stood up for myself; but a man must stand up for himself when he knows what are his rights."

"Will, you must listen to me," said Mary, putting away her papers, and turning round to him. "It is Mr. Penrose who has put all this in your head: it could not be my boy that had such thoughts. Oh, Will! my poor child! And now we are in his pitiless hands," said Mary, with a kind of cry, "and it matters nothing what you say or what I say. You have put yourself in his hands."

"Stop, mother," said Will; "don't make such a disturbance about it. Uncle Penrose has nothing to do with it. It is my doing. I will do anything in the world for you, whatever you like to tell me; but I won't let a fellow be there who has no right to be there. I am the heir, and I will have my rights."

"You are not the heir," said Mrs. Ochterlony, frightened for the moment by the tone and his vehemence, and his strange looks.

"I heard it from two people that were both there," said Will, with a gloomy composure. "It was not without asking about it. I am not blaming you, mother—you might have some reason;—but it was I that was born after that thing that happened in India. What is the use of struggling against it? And if it is I that am the heir, why should you try to keep me out of my rights?"

"Will," said Mary, suddenly driven back into regions of personal emotion, which she thought she had escaped from, and falling by instinct into those wild weaknesses of personal argument to which women resort when they are thus suddenly stung. "Will, look me in the face and tell me. Can you believe your dear father, who was true as—as heaven itself; can you believe me, who never told you a lie, to have been such wretched deceivers? Can you think we were so wicked? Will, look me in the face!"

"Mother," said Will, whose mind was too little imaginative to be moved by this kind of argument, except to a kind of impatience. "What does it matter my looking you in the face? what does it matter about my father being true? You might have some reason for it. I am not blaming you; but so long as it was a fact what does that matter? I don't want to injure any one—I only want my rights."

It was Mary's turn now to be struck dumb. She had thought he was afraid of her, and had fled from her out of shame for what he had done; but he looked in her face as she told him with unhesitating frankness, and even that touch of impatience as of one whose common sense was proof to all such appeals. For her own part, when she was brought back to it, she felt the effect of the dreadful shock she had received; and she could not discuss this matter reasonably with her boy. Her mind fell off into a mingled anguish and horror and agonized sense of his sin and pity for him. "Oh, Will, your rights," she cried; "your rights! Your rights are to be forgiven and taken back, and loved and pitied, though you do not understand what love is. These are all the rights you have. You are young, and you do not know what you are doing. You have still a right to be forgiven."

"I was not asking to be forgiven," said Will, doggedly. "I have done no harm. I never said a word against you. I will give Hugh whatever he likes to get himself comfortably out in the world. I don't want to make any fuss or hurry. It can be quietly managed, if he will; but it's me that Earlston ought to come to; and I am not going to be driven out of it by talk. I should just like to know what Hugh would do if he was in my place."

"Hugh could never have been in your place," cried Mary, in her anguish and indignation. "I ought to have seen this is what it would come to. I ought to have known when I saw your jealous temper, even when you were a baby. Oh, my little Will! How will you ever bear it when you come to your senses, and know what it is you have been doing? Slandering your dear father's name and mine, though all the world knows different—and trying to supplant your brother, your elder brother, who has always been good to you. God forgive them that have brought my boy to this," said Mary, with tears. She kept gazing at him, even with her eyes full. It did not seem possible that he could be insensible to her look, even if he was insensible to her words.

Wilfrid, for his part, got up and began to walk about the room. It was hard, very hard to meet his mother's eyes. "When she is vexed, she gives a fellow such a look." He remembered those words which he had said to Uncle Penrose only yesterday with a vague sort of recollection. But when he got up his own bodily sensations somehow gave him enough to do. He half forgot about his mother in the strange feeling he had in his physical frame, as if his limbs did not belong to him, nor his head either for that part, which seemed to be floating about in the air, without any particular connexion with the rest of him. It must be that he was so very tired, for when he sat down and clutched at the arms of his chair, he seemed to come out of his confusion and see Mrs. Ochterlony again, and know what she had been talking about. He said, with something that looked like sullenness: "Nobody brought me to this—I brought myself," in answer to what she had said, and fell, as it were, into a moody reverie, leaning upon the arms of his chair. Mary saw it, and thought it was that attitude of obstinate and immovable resolve into which she had before seen him fall; and she dried her eyes with a little flash of indignation, and turned again to the half-finished letter which trembled in her hands, and which she could not force her mind back to. She said to herself in a kind of despair, that the bitter cup must be drunk—that there was nothing for it but to do battle for her son's rights, and lose no time in vain outcries, but forgive the unhappy boy when he came to his right mind and returned to her again. She turned away, with her heart throbbing and bleeding, and made an effort to recover her composure and finish her letter. It was a very important letter, and required all her thoughts. But if it had been hard to do it before, it was twenty times harder now.

Just at that moment there was a commotion at the door, and a sound of some one entering below. It might be only Mr. Penrose coming back, as he sometimes did, to luncheon. But every sound tingled through Mrs. Ochterlony in the excitement of her nerves. Then there came something that made her spring to her feet—a single tone of a voice struck on her ear, which she thought could only be her own fancy. But it was not her fancy. Some one came rushing up the stairs, and dashed into the room. Mary gave a great cry, and ran into his arms, and Will, startled and roused up from a sudden oblivion which he did not understand, drew his hand across his heavy eyes, and looked up doubting, and saw Hugh—Hugh standing in the middle of the room holding his mother, glowing with fresh air, and health, and gladness.—Hugh! How did he come there? Poor Will tried to rise from his chair, but with a feeling that he was fixed in it for ever, like the lady in the fable. Had he been asleep? and where was he? Had it been but a bad dream, and was this the Cottage, and Hugh come home to see them all? These were the questions that rose in Will's darkened mind, as he woke up and drew his hand across his heavy eyes, and sat as if glued in Mr. Penrose's chair.

CHAPTER XLVI

Mrs. Ochterlony was almost as much confused and as uncertain of her own feelings as Will was. Her heart gave a leap towards her son; but yet there was that between them which put pain into even a meeting with Hugh. When she had seen him last, she had been all that a spotless mother is to a youth—his highest standard, his most perfect type of woman. Now, though he would believe no harm of her, yet there had been a breath across her perfection; there was something to explain; and Mary in her heart felt a pang of momentary anguish as acute as if the accusation had been true. To have to defend herself; to clear up her character to her boy! She took him into her arms almost that she might not have to look him in the face, and held to him, feeling giddy and faint. Will was younger, and he himself had gone wrong, but Hugh was old enough to understand it all, and had no consciousness on his own side to blunt his perceptions; and to have to tell him how it all was, and explain to him that she was not guilty was almost as hard as if she had been obliged to confess that she was guilty. She could not encounter him face to face, nor meet frankly the wonder and dismay which were no doubt in his honest eyes. Mary thought that to look into them and see that wondering troubled question in them, "Is it so—have you done me this wrong?" would be worse than being killed once for all by a straightforward blow.

But there was no such thought in Hugh's mind. He came up to his mother open-hearted, with no hesitation in his looks. He saw Will was there, but he did not even look at him; he took her into his arms, holding her fast with perhaps a sense that she clung to him, and held on by him as by a support. "Mother, don't be distressed," he said, all at once, "I have found a way to clear it all up." He spoke out loud, with his cheery voice which it was exhilarating to hear, and as if he meant it, and felt the full significance of what he said. He had to put his mother down very gently on the sofa after, and to make her lie back and prop her up with cushions; her high-strung nerves for an instant gave way. It was if her natural protector had come back, whose coming would clear away the mists. Her own fears melted away from her when she felt the warm clasp of Hugh's arms, and the confident tone of his voice, not asking any questions, but giving her assurance, a pledge of sudden safety as it were. It was this that made Mary drop back, faint though not fainting, upon the friendly pillows, and made the room and everything swim in her eyes.

"What is it, Hugh?" she said faintly, as soon as she could speak.

"It is all right, mother," said Hugh; "take my word, and don't bother yourself any more about it. I came on at once to see Uncle Penrose, and get him out of this mess he has let himself into. I could be angry, but it is no good being angry. On the whole, perhaps showing him his folly and making a decided end to it, is the best."

"Oh, Hugh, never mind Uncle Penrose. Will, my poor Will! look, your brother is there," said Mary, rousing up. As for Hugh, he took no notice; he did not turn round, though his mother put her hand on his arm; perhaps because his mind was full of other things.

"We must have it settled at once," he said. "I hope you will not object, mother; it can be done very quietly. I found them last night, without the least preparation or even knowing they were in existence. It was like a dream to me. Don't perplex yourself about it, mother dear. It's all right—trust to me."

"Whom, did you find?" said Mary eagerly; "or was it the lines—my lines?"

"It was old Sommerville's daughter," said Hugh with an unsteady laugh, "who was there. I don't believe you know who old Sommerville or his daughter are. Never mind; I know all about it. I am not so simple as you were when you were eighteen and ran away and thought of nobody. And she says I am like my father," said Hugh, "the Captain, they called him—but not such a bonnie lad; and that there was nobody to be seen like him for happiness and brightness on his wedding-day. You see I know it all, mother—every word; and I am like him, but not such a bonnie lad."

"No," said Mary, with a sob. Her resolution had gone from her with her misery. She had suddenly grown weak and happy, and ready to weep like a child, "No," she said, with the tears dropping out of her eyes, "you are not such a bonnie lad; you are none of you so handsome as your father. Oh, Hugh, my dear, I don't know what you mean—I don't understand what you say."

And she did not understand it, but that did not matter—she could not have understood it at that moment, though he had given her the clearest explanation. She knew nothing, but that there must be deliverance somehow, somewhere, in the air, and that her firstborn was standing by her with light and comfort in his eyes, and that behind, out of her sight, his brother taking no notice of him, was her other boy.

"Will is there," she said, hurriedly. "You have not spoken to him—tell me about this after. Oh, Hugh, Will is there!"

She put her hand on his arm and tried to turn him round; but Hugh's countenance darkened, and became as his mother had never seen it before. He took no notice of what she said, he only bent over her, and began to arrange the cushions, of which Mary now seemed to feel no more need.

"I do not like to see you here," he said; "you must come out of this house. I came that it might be all settled out of hand, for it is too serious to leave in vain suspense. But after this, mother, neither you nor I, with my will, shall cross this threshold more."

"But oh, Hugh! Will!—speak to Will. Do not leave him unnoticed;" said Mary, in a passionate whisper, grasping his hand and reaching up to his ear.

Hugh's look did not relent. His face darkened while she looked at him.

"He is a traitor!" he said, from out his closed lips. And he turned his back upon his brother, who sat at the other side of the room, straining all his faculties to keep awake, and to keep the room steady, which was going round and round him, and to know something of what it all meant.

"He is your brother," said Mary; and then she rose, though she was still weak. "I must go to my poor boy, if you will not," she said. "Will!"

When Will heard the sound of her voice, which came strange to him, as if it came from another world, he too stumbled up on his feet, though in the effort ceiling and floor and walls got all confused to him and floated about, coming down on his brain as if to crush him.

"Yes, mamma," he said; and came straight forward, dimly guiding himself, as it were, towards her. He came against the furniture without knowing it, and struck himself sharply against the great round table, which he walked straight to as if he could have passed through it. The blow made him pause and open his heavy eyes, and then he sank into the nearest chair, with a weary sigh; and at that crisis of fate—at that moment when vengeance was overtaking him—when his cruel hopes had come to nothing, and his punishment was beginning—dropped asleep before their eyes. Even Hugh turned to look at the strange spectacle. Will was ghastly pale. His long brown hair hung disordered about his face; his hands clung in a desolate way to the arms of the chair he had got into; and he had dropped asleep.

At this moment Mrs. Ochterlony forgot her eldest son, upon whom till now her thoughts had been centred. She went to her boy who needed her most, and who lay there in his forlorn youth helpless and half unconscious, deserted as it were by all consolation. She went to him and put her hand on his hot forehead, and called him by his name. Once more Will half opened his eyelids; he said "yes, mamma," drearily, with a confused attempt to look up; and then he slept again. He slept, and yet he did not sleep; her voice went into his mind as in the midst of a dream—something weighed upon his nerves and his soul. He heard the cry she gave, even vaguely felt her opening his collar, putting back his hair, putting water to his lips—but he had not fainted, which was what she thought in her panic. He was only asleep.

"He is ill," said Hugh, who, notwithstanding his just indignation, was moved by the pitiful sight; "I will go for the doctor. Mother, don't be alarmed, he is only asleep."

"Oh, my poor boy!" cried Mary, "he was wandering about all yesterday, not to see me, and I was hard upon him. Oh, Hugh, my poor boy! And in this house."

This was the scene upon which Mr. Penrose came in to luncheon with his usual cheerful composure. He met Hugh at the door going for a doctor, and stopped him; "You here, Hugh," he said, "this is very singular. I am glad you are showing so much good sense; now we can come to some satisfactory arrangement. I hardly hoped so soon to assemble all the parties here."

"Good morning, I will see you later," said Hugh, passing him quickly and hurrying out. Then it struck Mr. Penrose that all was not well. "Mary, what is the matter?" he said; "is it possible that you are so weak as to encourage your son in standing out?"

Mary had no leisure, no intelligence for what he said. She looked at him for a moment vaguely, and then turned her eyes once more upon her boy. She had drawn his head on to her shoulder, and stood supporting him, holding his hands, gazing down in anxiety beyond all words upon the colourless face, with its heavy eyelids closed, and lips a little apart, and quick irregular breath. She was speaking to him softly without knowing it, saying, "Will, my darling—Will, my poor boy—Oh, Will, speak to me;" while he lay back unconscious now, no longer able to struggle against the weight that oppressed him, sleeping heavily on her breast. Mr. Penrose drew near and looked wonderingly, with his hand in his pocket and a sense that it was time for luncheon, upon this unexpected scene.

"What is the matter?" he said, "is he asleep? What are you making a fuss about, Mary? You women always like a fuss; he is tired, I daresay, after yesterday; let him sleep and he'll be all right. But don't stand there and tire yourself. Hallo, Will, wake up and lie down on the sofa. There goes the gong."

"Let us alone, uncle," said Mary piteously; "never mind us. Go and get your luncheon. My poor boy is going to be ill; but Hugh is coming back, and we will have him removed before he gets worse."

"Nonsense!" said Mr. Penrose; but still he looked curiously at the pale sleeping face, and drew a step further off—"not cholera, do you think?" he asked with a little anxiety—"collapse, eh?—it can't be that?"

"Oh, uncle, go away and get your luncheon, and leave us alone," said Mary, whose heart fainted within her at the question, even though she was aware of its absurdity. "Do not be afraid, for we will take him away."

Mr. Penrose gave a "humph," partly indignant, partly satisfied, and walked about the room for a minute, making it shake with his portly form. And then he gave a low, short, whistle, and went downstairs, as he was told. Quite a different train of speculation had entered into his mind when he uttered that sound. If Wilfrid should die, the chances were that some distant set of Ochterlonys, altogether unconnected with himself, would come in for the estate, supposing Will's claim in the meantime to be substantiated. Perhaps even yet it could be hushed up; for to see a good thing go out of the family was more than he could bear. This was what Mr. Penrose was thinking of as he went downstairs.

It seemed to Mary a long time before Hugh came back with the doctor, but yet it was not long: and Will still lay asleep, with his head upon her shoulder, but moving uneasily at times, and opening his eyes now and then. There could be no doubt that he was going to be ill, but what the illness was to be, whether serious and malignant, or the mere result of over-fatigue, over-tension and agitation of mind, even the doctor could not tell. But at least it was possible to remove him, which was a relief to all. Mary did not know how the afternoon passed. She saw Hugh coming and going as she sat by her sick boy, whom they had laid upon the sofa, and heard him downstairs talking to uncle Penrose, and then she was aware by the sound of carriage-wheels at the door that he had come to fetch them; but all her faculties were hushed and quieted as by the influence of poor Will's sleep. She did not feel as if she had interest enough left in the great question that had occupied her so profoundly on the previous night as to ask what new light it was which Hugh had seemed to her for one moment to throw on it. A momentary wonder thrilled through her mind once or twice while she sat and waited; but then Will would stir, or his heavy eyelids would lift unconsciously and she would be recalled to the present calamity, which seemed nearer and more appalling than any other. She sat in the quiet, which, for Will's sake, had to be unbroken, and in her anxiety and worn-out condition, herself by times slept "for sorrow," like those disciples among the olive-trees. And all other affairs fell back in her mind, as into a kind of twilight—a secondary place. It did not seem to matter what happened, or how things came to be decided. She had had no serious illness to deal with for many, many years—almost never before in her life since those days when she lost her baby in India; and her startled mind leapt forward to all tragic possibilities—to calamity and death. It was a dull day, which, no doubt, deepened every shadow. The grey twilight seemed to close in over her before the day was half spent, and the blinds were drawn down over the great staring windows, as it was best they should be for Will, though the sight of them gave Mary a pang. All these conjoined circumstances drove every feeling out of her mind but anxiety for her boy's life, and hushed her faculties, and made her life beat low, and stilled all other interests and emotions in her breast.

Then there came the bustle in the house which was attendant upon Will's removal. Mr. Penrose stood by, and made no objection to it. He was satisfied, on the whole, that whatever it might be—fever, cholera, or decline, or any thing fatal, it should not be in his house; and his thoughts were full of that speculation about the results if Will should die. He shook hands with Mary when she followed her boy into the carriage, and said a word to comfort her:

"Don't worry yourself about what we were talking of," he said; "perhaps, after all, in case anything were to happen, it might still be hushed up."

"What were we talking of?" asked Mary, vaguely, not knowing whether it was the old subject or the new one which he meant; and she made him no further answer, and went away to the lodging Hugh had found for her, to nurse her son. Uncle Penrose went back discomfited into his commodious house. It appeared, on the whole, that it did not matter much to them, though they had made so great a fuss about it. Hugh was the eldest son, even though, perhaps, he might not be the heir; and Will, poor boy, was the youngest, the one to be guarded and taken care of; and whatever the truth might be about Mary's marriage, she was their mother; and even at this very moment, when they might have been thought to be torn asunder, and separated from each other, nature had stepped in and they were all one. It was strange, but so it was. Mr. Penrose had even spoken to Hugh, but had drawn nothing from him but anxiety about the sick boy, to find the best doctor, and the best possible place to remove him to; not a word about the private arrangement he had, no doubt, come to make, or the transfer of Earlston; and if Will should die, perhaps, it could yet be hushed up. This was the last idea in Mr. Penrose's mind, as he went in and shut behind him the resounding door.

CHAPTER XLVII

The illness of Will took a bad turn. Instead of being a mere accumulation of cold and fatigue, it developed into fever, and of the most dangerous kind. Perhaps he had been bringing it on for a long time by his careless ways, by his long vigils and over thought; and that day of wretched wandering, and all the confused agitation of his mind had brought it to a climax. This at least was all that could be said. He was very ill; he lay for six weeks between life and death; and Mrs. Ochterlony, in his sick-room, had no mind nor understanding for anything but the care of him. Aunt Agatha would have come to help her, but she wanted no help. She lived as women do live at such times, without knowing how—without sleep, without food, without air, without rest to her mind or comfort to her heart. Except, indeed, in Hugh's face, which was as anxious as her own, but looked in upon her watching, from time to time like a face out of heaven. She had been made to understand all about it—how her prayer had been granted, and the cup had passed from her, and her honour and her children's had been vindicated for ever. She had been made to understand this, and had given God thanks, and felt one weight the less upon her soul; but yet she did not understand it any more than Will did, who in his wanderings talked without cease of the looks his mother gave him; and what had been done? He would murmur by the hour such broken unreason as he had talked to Mary the morning before he was taken ill—that he meant to injure nobody—that all he wanted was his rights—that he would do anything for Hugh or for his mother—only he must have his rights; and why did they all look at him so, and what did Nelly mean, and what had been done? Mrs. Ochterlony sitting by the bedside with tears on her pale cheeks came to a knowledge of his mind which she had never possessed before—as clear a knowledge as was possible to a creature of so different a nature. And she gave God thanks in her heart that the danger had been averted, and remembered, in a confused way, the name of old Sommerville, which had been engraved on her memory years before, when her husband forced her into the act which had cost her so much misery. Mary could not have explained to any one how it was that old Sommerville's name came back with the sense of deliverance. For the moment she would scarcely have been surprised to know that he had come to life again to remedy the wrongs his death had brought about. All that she knew was that his name was involved in it, and that Hugh was satisfied, and the danger over. She said it to herself sometimes in an apologetic way as if to account to herself for the suddenness with which all interest on the subject had passed out of her thoughts. The danger was over. Two dangers so appalling could not exist together. The chances are that Will's immediate and present peril would have engrossed her all the same, even had all not been well for Hugh.

When he had placed his mother and brother in the rooms he had taken for them, and had seen poor Will laid down on the bed he was not to quit for long, Hugh went back to see Mr. Penrose. He was agitated and excited, and much melted in his heart by his brother's illness; but still, though he might forgive Will, he had no thought of forgiving the elder man, who ought to have given the boy better counsel: but he was very cool and collected, keeping his indignation to himself, and going very fully into detail. Old Sommerville's daughter had been married, and lived with her husband at the border village where Mary's marriage had taken place. It was she who had waited on the bride, with all the natural excitement and interest belonging to the occasion; and her husband and she, young themselves, and full of sympathy with the handsome young couple, had stolen in after them into the homely room where the marriage ceremony, such as it was, was performed. The woman who told Hugh this story had not the faintest idea that suspicion of any kind rested upon the facts she was narrating, neither did her hearer tell her of it. He had listened with what eagerness, with what wonder and delight may be imagined, while she went into all the details. "She mayn't mind me, but I mind her," the anxious historian had said, her thoughts dwelling not on the runaway marriage she was talking of, as if that could be of importance, but on the unbuilt lodge, and the chances of getting it if she could but awake the interest of the young squire. "She had on but a cotton gown, as was not for the likes of her on her wedding-day, and a bit of a straw-bonnet; and it was me as took off her shawl, her hands being trembly a bit, as was to be expected; I took her shawl off afore she came into the room, and I slipped in after her, and made Rob come, though he was shy. Bless your heart, sir, the Captain and the young lady never noticed him nor me."

Hugh had received all these details into his mind with a distinctness which only the emergency could have made possible. It seemed to himself that he saw the scene—more clearly, far more clearly, than that dim vision of the other scene in India, which now he ventured in his heart to believe that he recollected too. He told everything to Mr. Penrose, who sat with glum countenance, and listened. "And now, uncle," he said, "I will tell you what my mother is ready to do. I don't think she understands what I have told her about my evidence; but I found this letter she had been writing when Will was taken ill."

You can read it if you please. It will show you at least how wrong you were in thinking she would ever desert and abandon me."

"I never thought she would desert and abandon you," said Mr. Penrose; "of course every one must see that so long as you had the property it was her interest to stick to you—as well as for her own sake. I don't see why I should read the letter; I daresay it is some bombastical appeal to somebody—she appealed to me last night—to believe her; as if personal credibility was to be built upon in the absence of all proofs."

"But read it all the same," said Hugh, whose face was flushed with excitement.

Mr. Penrose put on his spectacles, and took the half-finished letter reluctantly into his hand. He turned it round and all over to see who it was addressed to; but there was no address; and when he began to read it, he saw it was a letter to a lawyer, stating her case distinctly, and asking for advice. Was there not a way of getting it tried and settled, Mary had written; was there not some court that could be appealed to at once, to examine all the evidence, and make a decision that would be good and stand, and could not be re-opened? "I am ready to appear and be examined, to do anything or everything that is necessary," were the last words Mrs. Ochterlony had written; and then she had forgotten her letter, forgotten her resolution and her fear, and everything else in the world but her boy who was ill. Her other boy, after he had set her heart free to devote itself to the one who now wanted her most, had found the letter; and he, too, had been set free in his turn. Up to that very last moment he had feared and doubted what Mr. Penrose called the "exposure" for his mother; he had been afraid of wounding her, afraid of making any suggestion that could imply publicity. And upon the letter which Mr. Penrose turned thus about in his hand was at least one large round blister of a tear—a big drop of compunction, and admiration, and love, which had dropped upon it out of Hugh's proud and joyful eyes.

"Ah," said Uncle Penrose, who was evidently staggered: and he took off his spectacles and put them back in their case. "If she were to make up her mind to that," he continued slowly, "I would not say that you might not have a chance. It would have the look of being confident in her case. I'll tell you what, Hugh," he went on, changing his tone. "Does the doctor give much hope of Will?"

"Much hope!" cried Hugh, faltering. "Good heavens! uncle, what do you mean? Has he told you anything? Why, there is every chance—every hope."

"Don't get excited," said Mr. Penrose. "I hope so I am sure. But what I have to say is this: if anything were to happen to Will, it would be some distant Ochterlonys, I suppose, that would come in after him—supposing you were put aside, you know. I don't mind working for Will, but I'd have nothing to do with that. I could not be the means of sending the property out of the family. And I don't see now, in the turn things have taken, that there would be any particular difficulty between ourselves in hushing it all up."

"In hushing it up?" said Hugh, with an astonished look.

"Yes, if we hold our tongues. I daresay that is all that would be necessary," said Mr. Penrose. "If you only would have the good sense all of you to hold your tongues and keep your counsel, it might be easily hushed up."

But Uncle Penrose was not prepared for the shower of indignation that fell upon him. Hugh got up and made him an oration, which the young man poured forth out of the fulness of his heart; and said, God forgive him for the harm he had done to one of them, for the harm he had tried to do to all—in a tone very little in harmony with the prayer; and shook off, as it were, the dust off his feet against him, and rushed from the house, carrying, folded up carefully in his pocket-book, his mother's letter. It was she who had found out what to do—she whose reluctance, whose hesitation, or shame, was the only thing that Hugh would have feared. And it was not only that he was touched to the heart by his mother's readiness to do all and everything for him; he was proud, too, with that sweetest of exultation which recognises the absolute best in its best beloved. So he went through the suburban streets carrying his head high, with moisture in his eyes, but the smile of hope and a satisfied heart upon his lips. Hush it up! when it was all to her glory from the first to the last of it. Rather write it up in letters of gold, that all the world might see it. This was how Hugh, being still so young, in the pride and emotion of the moment, thought in his heart.

And Mrs. Ochterlony, by her boy's sick-bed, knew nothing of it all. She remembered to ask for her blotting-book with the letters in it which she had been writing, but was satisfied when she heard Hugh had it; and she accepted the intervention of old Sommerville, dead or living, without demanding too many explanations. She had now something else more absorbing, more engrossing, to occupy her, and two supreme emotions cannot hold place in the mind at the same time. Will required constant care, an attention that never slumbered, and she would not have any one to share her watch with her. She found time to write to Aunt Agatha, who wanted to come, giving the cheerfullest view of matters that was possible, and declaring that she was quite able for what she had to do. And Mary had another offer of assistance which touched her, and yet brought a smile to her face. It was from Mrs. Kirkman, offering to come to her assistance at once, to leave all her responsibilities for the satisfaction of being with her friend and sustaining her strength and being "useful" to the poor sufferer. It was a most anxious letter, full of the warmest entreaties to be allowed to come, and Mary was moved by it, though she gave it to Hugh to read with a faint smile on her lip.

"I always told you she was a good woman," said Mrs. Ochterlony. "If I were to let her come, I know she would make a slave of herself to serve us both."

"But you will not let her come," said Hugh, with a little alarm; "I don't know about your good woman. She would do it, and then tell everybody how glad she was that she had been of so much use."

"But she is a good woman in spite of her talk," said Mary; and she wrote to Mrs. Kirkman a letter which filled the soul of the colonel's wife with many thoughts. Mrs. Ochterlony wrote to her that it would be vain for her to have any help, for she could not leave her boy—could not be apart from him while he was so ill, was what Mary said—but that her friend knew how strong she was, and that it would not hurt her, if God would but spare her boy. "Oh, my poor Will! don't forget to think of him," Mary said, and the heart which was in Mrs. Kirkman's wordy bosom knew what was meant. And then partly, perhaps, it was her fault; she might have been wise, she might have held her peace when Will came to ask that fatal information. And yet, perhaps, it might be for his good, or perhaps—perhaps, God help him, he might die. And then Mrs. Kirkman's heart sank within her, and she was softer to all the people in her district, and did not feel so sure of taking upon her the part of Providence. She could not but remember how she had prayed that Mary should not be let alone, and how Major Ochterlony had died after it, and she felt that that was not what she meant, and that God, so to speak, had gone too far. If the same thing were to happen again! She was humbled and softened to all her people that day, and she spent hours of it upon her knees, praying with tears streaming down her cheeks for Will. And it was not till full twenty-four hours after that she could take any real comfort from the thought that it must be for all their good; which shows that Mrs. Ochterlony's idea of her after all was right.

These were but momentary breaks in the long stretch of pain, and terror, and lingering and sickening hope. Day after day went and came, and Mary took no note of them, and knew nothing more of them than as they grew light and dark upon the pale face of her boy. Hugh had to leave her by times, but there was no break to her in the long-continued vigil. His affairs had to go on, his work to be resumed, and his life to proceed again as if it had never come to that full stop. But as for Mary, it began to appear to her as if she had lived all her life in that sick-room. Then Islay came, always steady and trustworthy. This was towards the end, when it was certain that the crisis must be approaching for good or for evil. And poor Aunt Agatha in her anxiety and her loneliness had fallen ill too, and wrote plaintive, suffering letters, which moved Mary's heart even in the great stupor of her own anxiety. It was then that Hugh went, much against his will, to the Cottage, at his mother's entreaty, to carry comfort to the poor old lady. He had to go to Earlston to see after his own business, and from thence to Aunt Agatha, whose anxiety was no less great at a distance than theirs was at hand; and Hugh was to be telegraphed for at once if there was "any change." Any change!—that was the way they had got to speak, saying it in a whisper, as if afraid to trust the very air with words which implied so much. Hugh stole into the sick room before he went away, and saw poor Will, or at least a long white outline of a face, with two big startling eyes, black and shining, which must be Will's, lying back on the pillows; and he heard a babble of weary words about his mother and Nelly, and what had he done? and withdrew as noiselessly as he entered, with the tears in his eyes, and that poignant and intolerable anguish in his heart with which the young receive the first intimation that one near to them must go away. It seemed an offence to Hugh, as he left the house to see so many lads in the streets, who were of Will's age, and so many children encumbering the place everywhere, unthought of, uncared for, unloved, to whom almost it would be a benefit to die. But it was not one of them who was to be taken, but Will, poor Will, the youngest, who had been led astray, and had still upon his mind a sense of guilt. Hugh was glad to go to work at Earlston to get the thought out of his mind, glad to occupy himself about the museum, and to try to forget that his brother was slowly approaching the crisis, after which perhaps there might be no hope; and his heart beat loud in his ears every time he heard a sound, dreading that it might be the promised summons, and that "some change"—dreadful intimation—had occurred; and it was in the same state of mind that he went on to the Cottage, looking into the railway people's faces at every station to see if, perhaps, they had heard something. He was not much like carrying comfort to anybody. He had never been within reach of the shadow of death before, except in the case of his uncle; and his uncle was old, and it was natural he should die—but Will! Whenever he said, or heard, or even thought the name his heart seemed to swell, and grow "grit," as the Cumberland folks said, and climb into his throat.

But yet there was consolation to Hugh even at such a moment. When he arrived at the Cottage he found Nelly there in attendance upon Aunt Agatha; and Nelly was full of wistful anxiety, and had a world of silent questions in her eyes. He had not written to her in answer to her letter, though it had done so much for him. Nobody had written to the girl, who was obliged to stay quiet at home, and ask no questions, and occupy herself about other matters. And no doubt Nelly had suffered and might have made herself very unhappy, and felt herself deeply neglected and injured, had she been of that manner of nature. She had heard only the evident facts which everybody knew of—that Will had been taken ill, and that Hugh was in Liverpool, and even Islay had been sent for; but whether Will's illness was anything more than ordinary disease, or how the family affairs, which lay underneath, were being settled, Nelly could not tell. Nobody knew; not Aunt Agatha, nor Mrs. Kirkman, though it was her hand which had helped to set everything in motion. Sometimes it occurred to Nelly that Mr. Hugh might have written to her; sometimes she was disposed to fear that he might be angry—might think she had no right to interfere. Men did not like people to interfere with their affairs, she said to herself sometimes, even when they meant—oh! the very kindest; and Nelly dried her eyes and would acknowledge to herself that it was just. But when Hugh came, and was in the same room with her, and sat by her side, and was just the same—nay, perhaps, if that could be, more than just the same—then it was more than Nelly's strength of mind could do to keep from questioning him with her eyes. She gave little glances at him which asked—"Is all well?"—in language plainer than words; and Hugh's eyes, overcast as they were by that shadow of death which was upon them, could not answer promptly—"All is well." And Aunt Agatha knew nothing of this secret which lay between them; so far as Miss Seton had been informed as yet, Will's running away was but a boyish freak, and his illness an ordinary fever. And yet somehow it made Hugh take a brighter view of everything—made him think less drearily of Will's danger, and be less alarmed about the possible arrival of a telegram, when he read the question in Nelly Askell's eyes.

But it was the morning after his arrival before he could make any response. Aunt Agatha, who was an invalid, did not come downstairs early, and the two young creatures were left to each other's company. Then there ensued a little interval of repose to Hugh's mind, which had been so much disturbed of late, which he did not feel willing to break even by entering upon matters which might produce a still greater confidence and rapprochement. All that had been passing lately had given a severe shock to his careless youth, which, before that, had never thought deeply of anything. And to feel himself thus separated as it were from the world of anxiety and care he had been living in, and floated in to this quiet nook, and seated here all tranquil in a nameless exquisite happiness, with Nelly by him, and nobody to interfere with him, did him good, poor fellow. He did not care to break the spell even to satisfy her, nor perhaps to produce a more exquisite delight for himself. The rest, and the sweet unexpressed sympathy, and the soft atmosphere that was about him, gave Hugh all the consolation of which at this moment he was capable; and he was only a man—and he was content to be thus consoled without inquiring much whether it was as satisfactory for her. It was only when the ordinary routine of the day began, and disturbed the tête-à-tête, that he bethought him of how much remained to be explained to Nelly; and then he asked her to go out with him to the garden. "Come and show me the roses we used to water," said Hugh; "you remember?" And so they went out together, with perhaps, if that were possible, a more entire possession of each other's society—a more complete separation from everybody else in the world.

They went to see the roses, and though they were fading and shabby, with the last flowers overblown and disconsolate, and the leaves dropping off the branches, that melancholy sight made little impression on Nelly and Hugh. The two indulged in certain reminiscences of what had been, "you remember?"—comings back of the sweet recent untroubled past, such as give to the pleasant present and fair future their greatest charm. And then all at once Hugh stopped short, and looked in his companion's face. He said it without the least word of introduction, leaping at once into the heart of the subject, in a way which gave poor Nelly no warning, no time to prepare.

"Nelly," he said all at once, "I never thanked you for your letter."

"Oh, Mr. Hugh!" cried Nelly, and her heart gave a sudden thump, and the water sprang to her eyes. She was so much startled that she put her hand to her side to relieve the sudden panting of her breath. "I was going to ask you if you had been angry?" she added, after a pause.

"Angry! How could I be angry?" said Hugh.

"You might have thought it very impertinent of me talking of things I had no business with," said Nelly, with downcast eyes.

"Impertinent! Perhaps you suppose I would think an angel impertinent if it came down from heaven for a moment, and showed a little interest in my concerns?" said Hugh. "And do you really think you have no business with me, Nelly? I did not think you were so indifferent to your friends."

"To be sure we are very old friends," said Nelly, with a blush and a smile; but she saw by instinct that such talk was dangerous. And then she put on her steady little face and looked up at him to put an end to all this nonsense.—"I want so much to hear about dear Mrs. Ochterlony," she said.

"And I have never told you that it had come all right," said Hugh. "I was so busy at first I had no time for writing letters; and last night there was Aunt Agatha, who knows nothing about it; and this morning—well this morning you know, I was thinking of nothing but you—"

"Oh, thank you," said Nelly, with a little confusion, "but tell me more, please. You said it was all right—"

"Yes," said Hugh, "but I don't know if it ever would have come right but for your letter; I was down as low as ever a man could be; I had no heart for anything; I did not know what to think even about my—about anything. And then your dear little letter came. It was that that made me something of a man again. And I made up my mind to face it and not to give in. And then all at once the proof came—some people who lived at Gretna and had seen the marriage. Did you go there?"

"No," said Nelly, with a tremulous voice; and now whatever might come of it, it would have been quite impossible for her to raise her eyes.

"Ah, I see," said Hugh, "it was only to show me what to do—but all the same it was your doing. If you had not written to me like that, I was more likely to have gone and hanged myself, than to have minded my business and seen the people. Nelly, I will always say it was you."

"No—no," said Nelly, withdrawing, not without some difficulty, her hand out of his. "Never mind me; I am so glad—I am so very glad; but then I don't know about dear Mrs. Ochterlony—and oh, poor Will!"

His brother's name made Hugh fall back a little. He had very nearly forgotten everything just then except Nelly herself. But when he remembered that his brother, perhaps, might be dying—

"You know how ill he is," he said, with a little shudder. "It must be selfish to be happy. I had almost forgotten about poor Will."

"Oh, no, no," cried Nelly; "we must not forget about him; he could never mean it—he would have come to himself one day. Oh, Mr. Hugh—"

"Don't call me that," cried the young man; "you say Will—why should I be different. Nelly? If I thought you cared for him more than for me—"

"Oh, hush!" said Nelly, "how can you think of such things when he is so ill, and Mrs. Ochterlony in such trouble. And besides, you are different," she added hastily; and Hugh saw the quick crimson going up to her hair, over her white brow and her pretty neck, and again forgot Will, and everything else in the world.

"Nelly," he said, "you must care for me most. I don't mind about anything without that. I had rather be in poor Will's place if you think of somebody else just the same as of me. Nelly, look here—there is nobody on earth that I can ever feel for as I feel for you."

"Oh, Mr. Hugh!" cried Nelly. She had only one hand to do anything with, for he held the other fast, and she put that up to her eyes, to which the tears had come, though she did not very well know why.

"It is quite true," cried the eager young man. "You may think I should not say it now; but Nelly, if there are ill news shall I not want you to comfort me? and if there are good news you will be as glad as I am. Oh, Nelly, don't keep silent like that, and turn your head away—you know there is nobody in the world that loves you like me."

"Oh, please don't say any more just now," said Nelly, through her tears. "When I think of poor Will who is perhaps—And he and I were babies together; it is not right to be so happy when poor Will—Yes, oh yes—another time I will not mind."

And even then poor Nelly did not mind. They were both so young, and the sick boy was far away from them, not under their eyes as it were; and even whatever might happen, it could not be utter despair for Hugh and Nelly. They were selfish so far as they could not help being selfish—they had their moment of delight standing there under the faded roses, with the dead leaves dropping at their feet. Neither autumn nor any other chill—neither anxiety nor suspense, nor even the shadow of death could keep them asunder. Had not they the more need of each other if trouble was coming? That was Hugh's philosophy, and Nelly's heart could not say him nay.

But when that moment was over Aunt Agatha's voice was heard calling from an upper window. "Hugh, Hugh!" the old lady called. "I see a man leaving the station with a letter in his hand—It is the man who brings the telegraph—Oh, Hugh, my dear boy!"

Hugh did not stop to hear any more. He woke up in a moment out of himself, and rushed forth upon the road to meet the messenger, leaving Nelly and his joy behind him. He felt as if he had been guilty then, but as he flew along the road he had no time to think. As for poor Nelly, she took to walking up and down the lawn, keeping him in sight, with limbs that trembled under her, and eyes half blind with tears and terror. Nelly had suffered to some extent from the influence of Mrs. Kirkman's training. She could not feel sure that to be very happy, nay blessed, to feel one's self full of joy and unmingled content, was not something of an offence to God. Perhaps it was selfish and wicked at that moment, and now the punishment might be coming. If it should be so, would it not be her fault. She who had let herself be persuaded, who ought to have known better. Aunt Agatha sat at her window, sobbing, and saying little prayers aloud without knowing it. "God help my Mary! Oh God, help my poor Mary: give her strength to bear it!" was what Aunt Agatha said. And poor Nelly for her part put up another prayer, speechless, in an agony—"God forgive us," she said, in her innocent heart.

But all at once both of them stopped praying, stopped weeping, and gave one simultaneous cry, that thrilled through the whole grey landscape. And this was why it was;—Hugh, a distant figure on the road, had met the messenger, had torn open the precious despatch. It was too far off to tell them in words, or make any other intelligible sign. What he did was to fling his hat into the air and give a wild shout, which they saw rather than heard. Was it all well? Nelly went to the gate to meet him, and held by it, and Aunt Agatha came tottering downstairs. And what he did next was to tear down the road like a racehorse, the few country folks about it staring at him as if he were mad,—and to seize Nelly in his arms in open day, on the open road, and kiss her publicly before Aunt Agatha, and Peggy, and all the world. "She said she would not mind," cried Hugh, breathlessly, coming headlong into the garden, "as soon as we heard that Will was going to get well; and there's the despatch, Aunt Agatha, and Nelly is to be my wife."

This was how two joyful events in the Ochterlony family intimated themselves at the same moment to Bliss Seton and her astonished house.

CHAPTER XLVIII

And this was how it all ended, so far as any end can be said to have come to any episode in human history. While Will was still only recovering—putting his recollections slowly together—and not very certain about them, what they were, Hugh and his mother went through the preliminaries necessary to have Mrs. Ochterlony's early marriage proved before the proper court—a proceeding which Mary did not shrink from when the time came that she could look calmly over the whole matter, and decide upon the best course. She was surprised to see her own unfinished letter preserved so carefully in Hugh's pocket-book. "Put it in the fire," she said to him, "it will only put us in mind of painful things if you keep it;" and it did not occur to Mary why it was that her son smiled and put it back in its place, and kissed her hand, which had grown thin and white in her long seclusion. And then he told her of Nelly, and Mrs. Ochterlony was glad—glad to the bottom of her heart, and yet touched with a momentary pang for which she was angry with herself. He had stood by her so in all this time of trial, and now he was about to remove himself a little, ever so little further off from her, though he was her first-born and her pride; but then she despised herself, who could grudge, even for half a moment, his reward to Hugh, and made haste to make amends for it, even though he was unconscious of the offence.

"I always thought she should have been my child," Mary said, "the very first time I saw her. I had once one like her; and I hungered and thirsted for Nelly when I saw her first. I did not think of getting her like this. I will love her as if she were my own, Hugh."

"And so she will be your own," said Hugh, not knowing the difference. And he was so happy that the sight of him made his mother happy, though she had care enough in the meantime for her individual share.

For it may be supposed that Will, such a youth as he was, did not come out of his fever changed and like a child. Such changes are few in this world, and a great sickness is not of necessity a moral agent. When the first languor and comfort of his convalescence was over, his mind began to revive and to join things together, as was natural—and he did not know where or how he had broken off in the confused and darkling story that returned to his brain as he pondered. He had forgotten, or never understood about all that happened on the day he was taken ill, but yet a dreamy impression that some break had come to his plans, that there was some obstacle, something that made an end of his rights, as he still called them in his mind, hovered about his recollections. He was as frank and open as it was natural to his character to be, for the first few days after he began to recover, before he had made much progress with his recollections; and then he became moody and thoughtful and perplexed, not knowing how to piece the story out. This was perhaps, next to death itself, the thing which Mary had most dreaded, and she saw that though his sickness had been all but death, it had not changed the character or identity of the pale boy absorbed in his own thoughts, uncommunicating and unyielding, whose weakness compelled him to obey her like an infant in everything external, yet whose heart gave her no such obedience. It was as unlike Hugh's frank exuberance of mind, and Islay's steady but open soul, as could be conceived. But yet he was her boy as much as either; as dear, perhaps even more bound to her by the evil he had tried to do, and by the suffering he himself had borne. And now she had to think not only how to remedy the wrong he had attempted, and to put such harm out of his and everybody's power, but to set the discord in himself at rest, and to reconcile the jangled chords. It was this that gave her a preoccupied look even while Hugh spoke to her of all his plans. It was more difficult than appearing before the court, harder work perhaps than anything she had yet had in her hands to do—and hard as it was, it was she who had to seek the occasion and begin.

She had been sitting with her boy, one winterly afternoon, when all was quiet in the house—they were still in the lodging in Liverpool, not far from Mr. Penrose's, to which Will had been removed when his illness began; he was not well enough yet to be removed, and the doctors were afraid of cold, and very reluctant to send him, in this weak state, still further to the north. She had been reading to him, but he was evidently paying no attention to the reading, and she had left off and began to talk, but he had been impatient of the talk. He lay on the sofa by the fire, with his pale head against the pillow, looking thin, spectral, and shadowy, and yet with a weight of weary thought upon his overhanging brow, and in his close compressed lips, which grieved his mother's heart.

"Will," she said suddenly, "I should like to speak to you frankly about what you have on your mind. You are thinking of what happened before you were taken ill?"

"Yes," he said, turning quickly upon her his great hollow eyes, shining with interest and surprise; and then he stopped short, and compressed his upper lip again, and looked at her with a watchful eye, conscious of the imperfection of his own memory, and unwilling to commit himself.

"I will go over it all, that we may understand each other," said Mary, though the effort made her own cheek pale. "You were told that I had been married in India just before you were born, and you were led to believe that your brothers were—were—illegitimate, and that you were your father's heir. I don't know if they ever told you, my poor boy, that I had been married in Scotland long before; at all events, they made you believe—"

"Made me believe!" said Will, with feverish haste; "do people generally marry each other more than once? I don't see how you can say 'made me believe.'"

"Well, Will, perhaps it seemed very clear as it was told to you," said Mary, with a sigh; "and you have even so much warrant for your mistake, that your father too took fright, and thought because everybody was dead that saw us married that we ought to be married again; and I yielded to his wish, though I knew it was wrong. But it appears everybody was not dead; two people who were present have come to light very unexpectedly, and we have applied to that Court—that new Court, you know, where they treat such things—to have my marriage proved, and Hugh's legitimacy declared. It will cost some money, and it will not be pleasant to me; but better that than such a mistake should ever be possible again."

Will looked in his mother's face, and knew and saw beyond all question that she told him was absolute fact; not even truth, but fact; the sort of thing that can be proved by witnesses and established in law.

His mouth which had been compressed so close, relaxed; his underlip drooped, his eyes hid themselves, as it were, under their lids. A sudden blank of mortification and humbled pride came over his soul. A mistake, simply a mistake, such a blunder as any fool might make, an error about simple facts which he might have set right if he had tried. And now for ever and ever he was nothing but the youngest son; doubly indebted to everybody belonging to him; indebted to them for forgiveness, forbearance, tenderness, and services of every kind. He saw it all, and his heart rose up against it; he had tried to wrong them, and it was his punishment that they forgave him. It all seemed so hopeless and useless to struggle against, that he turned his face from the light, and felt as if it would be a relief if he could be able to be ill again, or if he had wounds that he could have secretly unbound; so that he might get to die, and be covered over and abandoned, and have no more to bear. Such thoughts were about as foreign to Mrs. Ochterlony's mind as any human cogitations could be, and yet she divined them, as it were, in the greatness of her pity and love.

"Will," she said, speaking softly in the silence which had been unbroken for long, "I want you to think if this had been otherwise, what it would have been for me. I would have been a woman shut out from all good women. I would have been only all the more wicked and wretched that I had succeeded in concealing my sin. You would have blushed for your mother whenever you had to name her name. You could not have kept me near you, because my presence would have shut against you every honest house. You would have been obliged to conceal me and my shame in the darkness—to cover me over in some grave with no name on it—to banish me to the ends of the earth—"

"Mother!" said Will, rising up in his gaunt length and paleness on the sofa. He did not understand it. He saw her figure expanding, as it were, her eyes shining in the twilight like two great mournful stars, the hot colour rising to her face, her voice labouring with an excitement which had been long pent up and found no channel; and the thrill and jar in it of suppressed passion, made a thrill in his heart.

"And your father!" she went on, always with growing emotion, "whom you are all proud of, who died for his duty and left his name without a blot;—he would have been an impostor like me, a man who had taken base advantage of a woman, and deceived all his friends, and done the last wrong to his children,—we two that never wronged man nor woman, that would have given our lives any day for any one of you,—that is what you would have made us out."

"Mother!" said Will. He could not bear it any longer. His heart was up at last, and spoke. He came to her, crept to her in his weakness, and laid his long feeble arms round her as she sat hiding her face. "Mother! don't say that. I must have been mad. Not what I would have made you out—"

"Oh, my poor Will, my boy, my darling!" said Mary, "not you—I never meant you!"

And she clasped her boy close, and held him to her, not knowing what she meant. And then she roused herself to sudden recollection of his feebleness, and took him back to his sofa, and brooded over him like a bird over her nest. And after awhile Islay came in, bringing fresh air and news, and a breath from the outer world. And poor Will's heart being still so young, and having at last touched the depths, took a rebound and came up, not like, and yet not unlike the heart of a little child. From that time his moodiness, his heavy brow, his compressed lip, grew less apparent, and out of his long ponderings with himself there came sweeter fruits. He had been on the edge of a precipice, and he had not known it: and now that after the danger was over he had discovered that danger, such a thrill came over him as comes sometimes upon those who are the most foolhardy in the moment of peril. He had not seen the blackness of the pit nor the terror of it until he had escaped.

But probably it was a relief to all, as it was a great relief to poor Will, when his doctor proposed a complete change for him, and a winter in the South. Mary had moved about very little since she brought her children home from India, and her spirit sank before the thought of travel in foreign parts, and among unknown tongues. But she was content when she saw the light come back to her boy's eye. And when he was well enough to move, they went away[A] together, Will and his mother, Mary and her boy. He was the one who needed her most.

[A] They went to San Remo, if any one would like to know, for no particular reason that I can tell, except that the beloved physician, Dr. Antonio, has thrown the shield of his protection over that picturesque little place, with its golden orange groves and its delicious sea.

And when Hugh and Nelly were married, the Percivals sent the little bride a present, very pretty, and of some value, which the Ochterlonys in general accepted as a peace-offering. Winnie's letter which accompanied it was not, however, very peaceful in its tone. "I daresay you think yourself very happy, my dear," Winnie wrote, "but I would not advise you to calculate upon too much happiness. I don't know if we were ever meant for that. Mary, who is the best woman among us, has had a terrible deal of trouble; and I, whom perhaps you will think one of the worst, have not been let off any more than Mary. I wonder often, for my part, if there is any meaning at all in it. I am not sure that I think there is. And you may tell Mrs. Kirkman so if you like. My love to Aunt Agatha, and if you like you can kiss Hugh for me. He always was my favourite among all the boys."

Poor Aunt Agatha heard this letter with a sigh. She said, "My dear love, it is only Winnie's way. She always liked to say strange things, but she does not think like that." And perhaps on the whole it was Aunt Agatha that was worst off in the end. She was left alone when the young creatures paired, as was natural, in the spring; and when the mother Mary went away with her boy. Aunt Agatha had no child left to devote herself to; and it was very silent in the Cottage, where she sat for hours with nothing more companionable than the Henri Deux ware, Francis Ochterlony's gift, before her eyes. And Sir Edward was very infirm that year. But yet Miss Seton found a consolation that few people would have thought of in the Henri Deux, and before the next winter Mary was to come home. And she had always her poor people and her letters, and the Kirtell singing softly under its dewy braes.

Margaret Oliphant – A Short Biography

Margaret Oliphant Wilson was born on April 4th, 1828 to Francis W. Wilson, a clerk, and Margaret Oliphant, at Wallyford, near Musselburgh, East Lothian.

She spent her childhood at Lasswade, near Dalkeith, Glasgow before moving to Liverpool.

Her youth was spent in establishing a writing style so much so that, in 1849, she had her first novel published: Passages in the Life of Mrs. Margaret Maitland based on the Scottish Free Church movement. It met with some success and was a good start to her career.

Two years later, in 1851, her third book Caleb Field was published. It was also now that she met the publisher William Blackwood in Edinburgh and was asked to contribute to his well-received Blackwood's

Magazine. It was to be a lifetimes endeavor. Over the course of the relationship she would have well over 100 articles published.

In May 1852, Margaret married her cousin, Frank Wilson Oliphant, at Birkenhead, and they settled at Harrington Square, Camden, London. He was an artist working primarily in stained glass. With the marriage she became Margaret Oliphant Wilson Oliphant.

Their marriage produced six children but three tragically died in infancy.

When her husband developed signs of the dreaded consumption (tuberculosis) they moved, on the advice of doctors, to warmer climes. In January 1859 it was to Florence, and then to Rome where, sadly, he died.

Margaret was naturally devastated but was also now left without support and only her income from her writing. She returned to England and took up the task of supporting her three remaining children by her literary activity.

By now she was being published both as an established novelist and regularly in Blackwood's Magazine, amongst others. Her incredible and prolific work rate increased both her commercial reputation and the size of her reading audience.

Against this her domestic life continued to be tragic, full of sorrow and disappointment.

In January 1864 her only remaining daughter Maggie died and was buried in her father's grave in Rome. Her brother, who had emigrated to Canada, was shortly afterwards involved in financial ruin. Margaret generously offered a home to him and his children, adding another demand to her already heavy responsibilities.

In 1866 she settled at Windsor to be closer to her sons, who were being educated at near-by Eton School. That year, her second cousin, Annie Louisa Walker, came to live with her as a companion-housekeeper. Windsor was now to be her home for the rest of her life.

Her literary career for three decades was one of constant delivery and success. Whether she wrote historical works or across several genres in fiction: domestic realism, historical, romance or supernatural she was successful.

For more than thirty years she pursued a varied literary career but family life continued to bring problems.

The literary ambitions she wished for her sons were unfulfilled. Cyril Francis, the eldest, died in 1890, leaving a Life of Alfred de Musset, incorporated in his mother's Foreign Classics for English Readers. The younger, Francis, who she nicknamed 'Cecco', collaborated with her in the Victorian Age of English Literature and won a position at the British Museum, but was rejected by Sir Andrew Clark, a famous physician. Cecco died in 1894.

With the last of her children now lost to her, she had but little further interest in life. Her health steadily and inexorably declined.

Margaret Oliphant Wilson Oliphant died at the age of 69 in Wimbledon on 20th June 1897. She is buried in Eton beside her sons.

At her death, Margaret was still working on Annals of a Publishing House, a record of Blackwood's Magazine with which she had enjoyed such a successful relationship.

Her Autobiography and Letters, which present a thoughtful picture of her domestic anxieties, was published in 1899. Only parts were written with a wider audience in mind: she had originally intended the Autobiography for her son, but he died before she could finish it.

Opinions on Oliphant's work are split, with some critics seeing her as a 'domestic novelist', while others recognize her work as influential and important to the Victorian literature canon. Critical reception from her contemporaries is also divided. John Skelton took the view that Oliphant wrote too much and too quickly. Writing a Blackwood's article called 'A Little Chat About Mrs. Oliphant', he asked, "Had Mrs. Oliphant concentrated her powers, what might she not have done? We might have had another Charlotte Brontë or another George Eliot." However not all of the contemporary reception was negative. The esteemed M. R. James admired Oliphant's supernatural fiction, concluding that "the religious ghost story, as it may be called, was never done better than by Mrs. Oliphant in 'The Open Door' and 'A Beleaguered City'. Mary Butts lavished praise on Oliphant's ghost story 'The Library Window', describing it as "one masterpiece of sober loveliness".

More modern critics of Oliphant's work include Virginia Woolf, who asked in Three Guineas whether Oliphant's autobiography does not lead the reader "to deplore the fact that Mrs. Oliphant sold her brain, her very admirable brain, prostituted her culture and enslaved her intellectual liberty in order that she might earn her living and educate her children."

Whatever the merits of their cases Margaret Oliphant has been shamefully neglected in modern years. She is now becoming more widely recognised as a leading writer of her day.

Margaret Oliphant – A Concise Bibliography

A canon of more than 120 works, including novels, travel books, histories, and volumes of literary criticism.

Novels

Margaret Maitland (1849)
Merkland (1850)
Caleb Field (1851)
John Drayton (1851)
Adam Graeme (1852)
The Melvilles (1852)
Katie Stewart (1852)
Harry Muir (1853)
Ailieford (1853)
The Quiet Heart (1854)

Magdalen Hepburn (1854)
Zaidee (1855)
Lilliesleaf (1855)
Christian Melville (1855)
The Athelings (1857)
The Days of My Life (1857)
Orphans (1858)
The Laird of Norlaw (1858)
Agnes Hopetoun's Schools and Holidays (1859)
Lucy Crofton (1860)
The House on the Moor (1861)
The Last of the Mortimers (1862)
Heart and Cross (1863)
Salem Chapel (1863)
The Rector (1863)
Doctor's Family (1863)
The Perpetual Curate (1864)
Miss Marjoribanks (1866)
Phoebe Junior (1876)
A Son of the Soil (1865)
Agnes (1866)
Madonna Mary (1867)
Brownlows (1868)
The Minister's Wife (1869)
The Three Brothers (1870)
John: A Love Story (1870)
Squire Arden (1871)
At his Gates (1872)
Ombra (1872
May (1873)
Innocent (1873)
The Story of Valentine and his Brother (1875)
A Rose in June (1874)
For Love and Life (1874)
Whiteladies (1875)
An Odd Couple (1875)
The Curate in Charge (1876)
Carità (1877)
Young Musgrave (1877)
Mrs. Arthur (1877)
The Primrose Path (1878)
Within the Precincts (1879)
The Fugitives (1879)
A Beleaguered City (1879)
The Greatest Heiress in England (1880)
He That Will Not When He May (1880)
In Trust (1881)
Harry Joscelyn (1881)

Lady Jane (1882)
A Little Pilgrim in the Unseen (1882)
The Lady Lindores (1883)
Sir Tom (1883)
Hester (1883)
It Was a Lover and his Lass (1883)
The Lady's Walk (1883)
The Wizard's Son (1884)
Madam (1884)
The Prodigals and their Inheritance (1885)
Oliver's Bride (1885)
A Country Gentleman and his Family (1886)
A House Divided Against Itself (1886)
Effie Ogilvie (1886)
A Poor Gentleman (1886)
The Son of his Father (1886)
Joyce (1888)
Cousin Mary (1888)
The Land of Darkness (1888)
Lady Car (1889)
Kirsteen (1890)
The Mystery of Mrs. Biencarrow (1890)
Sons and Daughters (1890)
The Railway Man and his Children (1891)
The Heir Presumptive and the Heir Apparent (1891)
The Marriage of Elinor (1891)
Janet (1891)
The Cuckoo in the Nest (1892)
Diana Trelawny (1892)
The Sorceress (1893)
A House in Bloomsbury (1894)
Sir Robert's Fortune (1894)
Who Was Lost and is Found (1894)
Lady William (1894)
Two Strangers (1895)
Old Mr. Tredgold (1895)
The Unjust Steward (1896)
The Ways of Life (1897)

Short stories
Neighbours on the Green (1889)
A Widow's Tale and Other Stories (1898)
That Little Cutty (1898)
The Open Door (1918)

Selected Articles

Mary Russel Mitford (Blackwood's Magazine, Vol. 75, 1854)
Evelin and Pepys (Blackwood's Magazine, Vol. 76, 1854)
The Holy Land (Blackwood's Magazine, Vol. 76, 1854)
Mr. Thackeray and his Novels (Blackwood's Magazine, Vol. 77, 1855)
Bulwer (Blackwood's Magazine, Vol. 77, 1855)
Charles Dickens (Blackwood's Magazine, Vol. 77, 1855)
Modern Novelists—Great and Small (Blackwood's Magazine, Vol. 77, 1855)
Modern Light Literature: Poetry (Blackwood's Magazine, Vol. 79, 1856)
Religion in Common Life (Blackwood's Magazine, Vol. 79, 1856)
Sydney Smith (Blackwood's Magazine, Vol. 79, 1856)
The Laws Concerning Women (Blackwood's Magazine, Vol. 79, 1856)
The Art of Caviling (Blackwood's Magazine, Vol. 80, 1856)
Béranger (Blackwood's Magazine, Vol. 83, 1858)
The Condition of Women (Blackwood's Magazine, Vol. 83, 1858)
The Missionary Explorer (Blackwood's Magazine, Vol. 83, 1858)
Religious Memoirs (Blackwood's Magazine, Vol. 83, 1858)
Social Science (Blackwood's Magazine, Vol. 88, 1860)
Scotland and her Accusers (Blackwood's Magazine, Vol. 90, 1861)
The Chronicles of Carlingford (Blackwood's Magazine 1862–1865)
Girolamo Savonarola (Blackwood's Magazine, Vol. 93, 1863)
The Life of Jesus (Blackwood's Magazine, Vol. 96, 1864)
Giacomo Leopardi (Blackwood's Magazine, Vol. 98, 1865)
The Great Unrepresented (Blackwood's Magazine, Vol. 100, 1866)
Mill on the Subjection of Women (The Edinburgh Review, Vol. 130, 1869)
The Opium-Eater (Blackwood's Magazine, Vol. 122, 1877)
Russian and Nihilism in the Novels of I. Tourgeniéf (Blackwood's Magazine, Vol. 127, 1880)
School and College (Blackwood's Magazine, Vol. 128, 1880)
The Grievances of Women (Fraser's Magazine, New Series, Vol. 21, 1880)
Mrs. Carlyle (The Contemporary Review, Vol. 43, May 1883)
The Ethics of Biography (The Contemporary Review, July 1883)
Victor Hugo (The Contemporary Review, Vol. 48, July/December 1885)
A Venetian Dynasty (The Contemporary Review, Vol. 50, August 1886)
Laurence Oliphant (Blackwood's Magazine, Vol. 145, 1889)
Tennyson (Blackwood's Magazine, Vol. 152, 1892)
Addison, the Humorist (Century Magazine, Vol. 48, 1894)
The Anti-Marriage League (Blackwood's Magazine, Vol. 159, 1896)

Biographies

Edward Irving (1862)
Francis of Assisi (1871)
Count de Montalembert (1872)
Dante (1877)
Cervantes (1880)
Life of Sheridan in the English Men of Letters series (1883)
John Tulloch (1888)

Laurence Oliphant (1892)

Historical & Critical Works

Historical Sketches of the Reign of George II (1869)
The Makers of Florence (1876)
A Literary History of England from 1760 to 1825 (1882)
The Makers of Venice (1887)
Royal Edinburgh (1890)
Jerusalem (1891)
The Makers of Modern Rome (1895)
William Blackwood and his Sons (1897)
The Sisters Brontë. In: Women Novelists of Queen Victoria's Reign (1897)